CONTENT WARNING

Heads Up, Darling Readers!

Alright, let's have a little real talk before you dive into the delicious mayhem I've cooked up. I'm about to serve you a literary feast that's spicy, intense, and sometimes rough around the edges—just like your favorite wing sauce. Consider this your fancy, cloth napkin warning—you might need it to dab at delicate sensibilities.

Sexually Explicit Scenes: Buckle up, buttercup. We're going full steam ahead into unabashed territory with scenes that'll make a nun blush and a pirate cheer. We're talking about the hot, heavy, and sometimes complicated tango of bodies—because, let's face it, sometimes Cupid's arrow looks more like a harpoon. But hey, if explicit romps in the hay—or elsewhere—are not your jam, you might want to bow out of this dance gracefully.

This book includes the following but is not limited to— MM/MMF/*spanking/breath play/edging/degradation/period play/dominating/explicit sex/voyeurism/anal play/bondage/sex toys.*

Violence: This ain't no stroll through the petting zoo, so expect more lions than lambs. If you've got a delicate constitution, beware. There's blood, mutilation, torture, interrogation, brawls, and enough bruises to make a peach wince. My characters don't always play nice, and neither do their enemies. Sharp objects, sharper wit—it's all there, in technicolor detail.

Sensitive Topics: Life's a tangled web, and my characters are dancing in it—sometimes on a tightrope. We're talking about mental minefields, traumatic tangoes, and emotional earthquakes. It's raw, it's real, and it's unapologetically human. But if these thorny issues poke a little too close to home, I've got your back—no judgy eyes here if you need to tag out.

So, here's the deal: your comfort is key. If things get a bit too heavy, put the book down, have a cookie, call your buddy, or chat with that lovely therapist. You come first, capisce? Feel free to skip, skimp, or skim—it's your mental margarita, and you're allowed to leave out the tequila.

Now, if you're still with me, let's put on our grown-up pants (or take 'em off, no judgment) and jump in! It's gonna be a wild ride.

Cheers and Happy Reading (or not, you do you),

Your Pal, The Author with the Most(est)
A.L. Hampton

DARK FATE

THE CROWN OF THE
SEVEN REALMS SERIES

BOOK II

WhisperVale
Light Lands
SunCity
Sun Court
Luminara

Shadow Court
Whispering Woods
Spectre Vales
Crystal Peaks
Crystal Citadel
Frostweaver Hallow
Hidden Valley

LUMINARA

DANICA

1

Panic claws at my throat as I sink into the churning abyss. The current drags me under before I can draw a breath, my limbs flailing uselessly in the suffocating darkness. Shadows swirl around me as I tumble deeper, and no light penetrates these depths. The water is ice-cold, numbing my skin within seconds, stealing the breath from my lungs even before I've fully submerged.

A heavyweight settles in my chest.

This is a pretty shitty way to go. Drowning in some godforsaken, shadow-infested hell-hole? Definitely not the blaze of glory I'd imagined for myself. My thrashing accomplishes nothing—I'm just a puppet with cut strings, spiraling into oblivion with no control over my descent. The cherry on top of this sundae of suck? The darkness. Complete and suffocating. I can't even see my own hand in front of my face, let alone figure out which way is up or down anymore. The disorientation is almost worse than the drowning itself, this sense of being utterly lost in an endless void.

My lungs begin to burn as they demand oxygen, the pressure building behind my ribs like a time bomb counting down. The realization hits me with brutal clarity: this is it. Game over. I'm going to drown in this miserable pit, trapped in shadow-infested waters with no one knowing where I am, and there's not a damn thing I can do about it. No one's coming to save me. No cavalry. No miracle. Just me and the darkness and the cold creeping into my bones.

Then something latches onto my arm with an iron grip that feels like it might break the bone. The sudden jerk stops my downward spiral, and pain shoots through my shoulder like lightning. But I don't care about the pain—I gasp anyway, choking on the foul water flooding my mouth, water that tastes of minerals and decay and things I don't want to identify. A glimmer of pale light appears above me, impossibly far away, and I'm being dragged upward with a force that's almost violent.

The surface seems impossibly distant, like it's receding even as I'm pulled toward it. My vision tunnels, blackness closing in from the edges like a hungry void swallowing everything. Spots dance across my failing vision. My lungs feel like they're going to explode. Just when I'm certain I'm about to slip into oblivion—when the darkness feels inevitable and permanent—I break through into open air.

I retch and cough violently, my body convulsing as strong arms wrap around me and hold me against something solid. Water pours from my mouth and nose. I can't breathe. I can't think. Everything is chaos and pain and the desperate need for oxygen.

"Easy now," a deep voice rumbles against my ear, steady and calm in a way that makes no sense given what's happening.

I squint up through wet lashes at a face that swims into focus. Stunning doesn't even begin to cover it—angular features that look carved from marble, framed by drenched brown hair that clings to sharp cheekbones. Pointed ears peek through the wet strands, and I realize with a jolt what he is.

Fae.

My lungs burn as I cling to the muscular frame that saved me. His powerful arms keep me afloat as he swims, propelling us through the rapids. The shore gradually looms closer, and he guides us into the shallows with final, sure strokes. His feet find the rocky bottom, and he stands, lifting me effortlessly.

Wading onto dry land, he lowers me gently, and I collapse onto my hands and knees, coughing violently as my body expels the poison I inhaled. He crouches beside me, his hand tracing soothing circles on my back.

"Easy now," he murmurs, his deep voice steady and calm, as though he does this every day. "You're safe. Just let it out."

I'm trembling uncontrollably, my entire body wracked with violent spasms that I can't seem to stop. The coughing won't relent—each fit threatens to split me apart from the inside out. My chest feels shredded, raw like I've been scraped from the inside, and every breath is like swallowing broken glass. He's there, his hand steady on my back, a solid anchor in the chaos. His warmth bleeds through my soaked clothes, grounding me as he pulls me closer, holding me against him.

When the spasms finally ease, I lift my head slowly. His face comes into focus—angular features carved from marble, emerald eyes that glow from within, lined with silver and blue. They're full of questions yet ancient with wisdom.

"Thank you," I rasp, my throat shredded from coughing up half the damn lake.

He shushes me gently, his hand moving in soothing circles across my back. "Don't talk," he says firmly, not unkind.

He shifts closer, adjusting his grip. A scent hits me—something sweet and wild, like pine needles and summer rain. I try to pull away, but my limbs feel like lead.

"You can trust me," he says softly.

My mind spins. I don't know him. I don't know anything about him. "I... can't..." I manage between coughing fits, bitter water still trickling from my lips.

"There's no need for alarm," he says gently. "I won't hurt you."

"I don't... know you," I gasp, the words barely a whisper as my body rebels with more coughs. Trust isn't something I hand out freely—not after everything.

I search those endless emerald eyes for any hint of deception but find nothing. Still, I stay guarded. "Where am I?"

His expression darkens. "The Shadow Court. You've stumbled into Dark Fae territory and their king's domain."

Dark Fae? Fantastic. Just what I needed. I scramble away from him like he's made of nettles, my pulse hammering.

The Shadow Court sounds like a bad horror flick, and it's the last place I want to be. Dread settles in my chest like a stone.

He raises his hands in surrender. "Be calm. I promise you're safe. Trust me, please."

Sure, he played lifeguard. Round of applause. A wry smile pulls at my lips. "Yeah, 'cause I've got 'gullible' written all over my face." The edges of my power spark at my fingertips—a silent reminder that I'm not entirely defenseless. Amusement flickers in his green eyes, but he keeps his distance, hands still raised.

My suspicion spikes anyway. Is this some kind of game? A trap? I can't afford to let my guard down, not until I find Rhyland and figure out what the hell is going on. Every stranger is a question mark, a potential threat wearing a beautiful face.

"You're quite the puzzle," he muses, curiosity etched into every line of his features. "A human, yet your aura hums with hidden magic. Not something I encounter every day."

I raise an eyebrow, not thrilled with how he's studying me like I'm some riddle to solve. There's no way I'm handing over my cards to this guy. "Oh, please. I'm nobody special," I shoot back, sarcasm dripping thick.

His brow arches in skepticism. "Just a regular human who survives deadly rapids?"

Silence. I'm not giving him anything. The fact that I survived at all gnaws at me—how the hell did I make it out?

"And you are...?" he asks gently, giving me space but not giving up.

I reluctantly offer it up, because what else can I do? "Dani."

"Dani," he says with a reverence that makes my skin prickle. "I'm Faderyn." He studies me with an intensity that sets my teeth on edge. "Your arrival isn't chance. What brings a human to the Fae Realm, especially one shrouded in mystery?"

DANICA

2

I hesitate, weighing my options. On one hand, spilling my guts to a complete stranger—even a ridiculously attractive one—goes against every survival instinct I've got. But on the other hand, I'm lost, alone, and desperately need answers. And right now, Faderyn is the only lifeline I've got.

I wrestle with my hair, which has apparently declared war on my head and turned into a tangled mess of knots that would make a sailor weep.

"I'm looking for someone," I admit, my voice barely above a whisper. "Someone really important to me."

Faderyn's expression softens, understanding flickering in those ancient emerald eyes. "I see. And you believe this person may be here, within the Shadow Court's domain?"

I wiggle nervously. "It's complicated," I sidestep the full truth.

Faderyn's anticipation doesn't falter, and eventually, I relent, dishing out the Reader's Digest version of Azrael's assault, the unexpected portal, and my plummet into this mess.

His brows furrow, etching lines of worry. "Portals? That's ancient history, practically myths now. We thought those pathways extinct, forgotten by all."

I can sense the empathy radiating off Faderyn like a warm breeze, but I'm no wide-eyed ingénue ready to swoon at the first sign of kindness. I've been around the block a few times, and I know better than to let my guard down just because he's flashing me a sympathetic smile and a set of killer cheekbones.

It's obvious that Faderyn is flying blind when it comes to the true extent of my abilities and the role I play in this whole cosmic cluster-fuck. He may think he's dealing with just another damsel in distress, but little does he know, I've got a few tricks up my sleeve that would make even the jaded Fae double-take.

But I'm not about to lay *all* my cards on the table—yet. I'll play along with his little sympathy parade, but I'm keeping one eye open and my bullshit detector set to maximum sensitivity. If he thinks he can lead me down the primrose path with a few well-placed platitudes and a dazzling smile, he's got another thing coming.

"That old portal?" I say with a casual shrug, masking the lie with breezy nonchalance. "Just my ridiculous luck, I guess. Wrong place, wrong time."

I maintain a façade of indifference, my fib game strong and practiced. It's not my first rodeo with hiding the truth.

But it seems he's got a nose for authenticity. His emerald eyes are fixed on mine, disconcerting intent within their depths. "Portals don't just pop up uninvited, especially for humans. What potent forces could've torn through realities?"

Damn. He's sharp. I squirm, panic rising like the tide—if the word spreads about my power-up...

"I wish I knew," I say, playing the card of genuine confusion. And honestly? That's not even a stretch. I don't know half of what's happening to me anyway.

He watches me carefully, an expression I can't quite read settling over his beautiful features. "Mysteries seem to gravitate toward you," he muses, his tone thoughtful.

A thud of adrenaline hits. I need to tread carefully; this Fae's academic curiosity could swerve into dangerous territory faster than a rollercoaster off its rails.

Faintly nodding, he gives me space—well, sort of. His eagle eyes still pin me, clearly earmarking our chat for further scrutiny.

I'm mentally flipping through conversations with Adrian—his Fae for Dummies crash course didn't exactly cover shadow kings or moonlit courts. "So, the whole Fae thing is just, what, the Fab Five?" I venture, arching an eyebrow to prompt an explanation.

He takes a measured breath before responding. "There used to be many courts," he explains carefully, "but conflict has a way of rewriting history. Only the strongest remain—the Sun and Shadow courts hold power now."

That catches me off guard. Adrian's whole spiel was about various fae sects, but he conveniently left out the part about dark fey kingdoms. "I was told," I say, irritation creeping into my voice, "about five courts, each supposedly perfect in their own way. Nothing about Shadow Courts or dark royalty."

His features darken. "Stories morph over time. The tale of five courts is just a distant echo of the truth, barely capturing their essence before their end."

I go statue-still. So we've been spoon-fed a sparkling version of the Fae, omitting a significant chunk of their reality.

"You look haunted," he notes, misinterpreting my indignation.

Internally, I'm boiling over. Adrian and his 'guidance' feel like an endless reel of betrayal—the buddy system turned traitor. Here I was, doling out trust like he was part of the fam. For what? His cloak-and-dagger games?

The gap between what Adrian taught me and what I'm experiencing firsthand is getting bigger by the second. I need to separate fact from fiction. "Can you tell me about the courts?" I ask.

He lays it out—the Sun Court's glittering beauty on one end, the Shadow Court shrouded in mystery on the other. Complete opposites in every way.

"So, what you're saying is—one's Heaven, the other's Hades," I reason out loud.

He nods in agreement. "Exactly."

It's like getting a single flashlight in a pitch-black cave. If I'm going to survive this Fae maze, I need to collect every piece of information I can.

Suddenly, my mouth's on autopilot, and I'm spitting out questions like seeds from a watermelon. "Which court sways you?" flies out of my lips before my brain can tell it to keep quiet.

Surprise flickers across his face. "I pledge allegiance to neither. Some of us choose a solitary path, free from courtly obligations."

My eyes widen. "Fae without a court?"

"Indeed," he confirms. "Some of us eschew the courtly life, seeking solitude over subjugation."

That raises more questions than answers, and I can't help myself. "So you're just... free agents?"

"Mostly," he nods. "Though we aren't immune to the entanglements of the courts."

His words paint a picture of complicated politics and hidden layers. The Fae world is way more complex than I thought, and he's standing right in the middle of it all—some kind of anomaly.

Despite everything that's happened today, I find myself being genuine. "Regardless, you saved my life. I owe you for that."

Faderyn meets my gaze steadily, something unspoken passing between us. "I offer my aid within reason," he says seriously. "But be warned, Dani. The Fae realm trades in illusion."

The absence of Rhyland and the others gnaws at me like a constant ache. I reach for our bond, searching for that connection, but find nothing but empty silence.

Faderyn notices the shift in me immediately, concern etching his features.

"My friends," I say, urgency bleeding into my voice. "Any sign of them near the river?"

He shakes his head grimly. "You were alone. I heard screams and found only you."

Panic floods through me—what the hell happened to them?

"The Shadow Court's domain shows no mercy," he says, and I can tell he genuinely wants to help. But that doesn't stop the alarm bells ringing in my head.

Is this legit, or am I walking into something worse?

Despite every instinct screaming 'trap,' a Fae willing to help is my best shot at finding my people in this dark playground. I push my doubts aside and nod curtly. "Okay. Thank you."

He gives me a look I can't quite read before rising fluidly to his feet. He takes my hand and pulls me up effortlessly. My legs nearly give out as pain shoots through my knee—I must have wrenched it getting tossed around by the river.

"Can you walk?" His voice is laced with concern.

I test my leg carefully and wince. "Barely."

Before I can protest, I'm shrieking, and my arms lock around his neck as he scoops me up like I weigh nothing.

"Faster travel," he spits out like we're discussing the weather, not him going full superhero. I want to argue because of pride, but the guy's got a point.

I huff out a sigh and lean into it, sinking against his solid frame.

As we walk, the river water chills my bones, and it's like my clothes morphed into a wetsuit without consulting me. The breeze? More like an icy brush-off, and I'm convulsing in a not-so-hot shiver marathon.

Faderyn catches on to my shivering act without missing a beat, pulling me closer with his arms, which feel chiseled from stone. Wrapped up in his heat, I've got to admit it's a solid move—not that I'm about to say it out loud.

Here I am, trying to stay focused on anything but the concrete wall of his chest and the steel of his abs pressing against me. Every molecule in the air around him is practically flexing in my direction. It smells like a forest after a storm, rugged and raw.

Keep your head in the game; I silently reprimand myself as I feel the heat rise in my cheeks, which is ridiculous given everything happening, but I blame the wind, not the proximity to Mr. Fantasy Fae.

His hair whips around his sharp ears, and yeah, okay, he could cut glass with that jawline. Those eyes? They're like staring straight into a fairytale—too perfect to be real. And now he's caught me staring, which is fantastic for my dignity.

Face burning, I launch a question at him like a life raft. "How long have you lived out here?" I ask because conversation is a great human tradition for 'please forget I was just gaping at you.'

I catch the hint of a smirk tugging at his mouth—stupid, gorgeous Fae.

"Centuries," he responds, his expression growing heavier. "Fae exist differently through time. But the winds are shifting, carrying whispers of something darker approaching."

That feeling is like stepping into a freezer—his warning sends shivers down my toes. Could he be hinting at Moretemis's grand entrance? But now's not the time to dig into it. I'll save that conversation for later.

I crane my neck to soak in the fantasy extravaganza around us. The Fae terrain unfolds as a painter's wild dream splashed across an endless canvas. Trees that hit every imaginable green and then some, blues that might've been plucked from the midsummer sky, purples deep enough to get lost in—all of them reach for the sky, their leafy hands clasping each other in an arboreal high five. Rock spires sparkle like the world's most go-getting crystals, and islands hover in the air as if they've forgotten gravity's a thing, sending water tumbling down into the great unknown.

Between limping and Faderyn carrying me for hours, we finally zero in on this rugged balcony of rock tucked away like a secret in the middle of tree mageddon.

He guides me through trees that can't keep a secret, rustling about every which way. "You require rest," he insists, his tone gentle and commanding.

Before us, a secret panel reveals a tunnel carved straight into storybooks, lit by crystals that twinkle like they're up to something. I pause; the cave mouth gapes a big ol' 'Enter if you dare,' and I'm not exactly doing cartwheels to get in there.

Fadeyrn catches the look, probably a mix of 'Help!' and 'Nope!', and pins me with a look, all earnest and vowing protection. "Your safety's on my honor," he declares, and something in the solemn way he says it has me believing him. I scope out his face, expecting to find some sly twist, but apparently, Fae Boy Scouts do exist.

My brain is all 'Red alert! Bad idea!'— Hit the 'Find My Viking' app, but what can you do when your energy bar blinks red? Apparently, you can nod and follow.

"We'll search at first light," he says gently. "You need rest first."

So I follow him down into his cave dwelling, which is way more cozy than I expected—soft rugs, wooden furniture that smells like a forest, a fire crackling in the hearth.

I collapse into a cushioned seat, and the warmth starts chasing the chill from my bones.

A woman appears wordlessly, bringing food and supplies with practiced efficiency. Once she's gone, I dig into the meal—fresh bread still warm from the oven, soft cheese, sliced fruit that bursts with sweetness, and a rich broth that tastes like home. Each bite wakes up senses I didn't realize had shut down, my body greedily absorbing the nourishment.

Faderyn kneels before me, his emerald eyes fixed on my swollen knee. He retrieves a small glass jar from the supplies, filled with a shimmering, iridescent salve that smells like honeysuckle and mint. With careful, practiced movements, he applies it gently to my injured knee, his touch warm and soothing. The moment the balm makes contact with my skin, a cooling sensation spreads through the joint, easing the sharp ache. He works methodically, massaging the salve in slow circles, and I watch as the swelling gradually recedes, the bruising fading to a pale shadow of what it was.

"This should help," he murmurs, his voice soft. "Give it time to work fully, but the worst of the pain should be gone by morning."

"Thank you."

I flex my knee experimentally, and while it's still a bit tender, the relief is undeniable. His presence is oddly soothing, and as he helps me to my feet, exhaustion starts pulling at me harder, my body finally allowing itself to relax now that I'm healing.

He guides me to a chamber down a candlelit hallway, the soft glow of crystal fixtures dancing across the stone walls. The bed is luxurious—piled high with furs and silk pillows—and it's like a dream after everything I've been through. I sink into it gratefully, the mattress cradling me like a cloud.

"Sleep," he whispers, his silhouette framed in the doorway before it disappears as the door closes softly behind him.

Alone, I reach for Rhyland through our bond. The silence that greets me is terrifying—cold and empty.

Then, faintly, I feel something. Pain. Confusion. Panic. It hits me like a gut punch, and then it's gone, leaving me with nothing but static.

The rush of emotion is overwhelming. It's like trying to hear a song buried under static—our connection is frayed and broken, giving me nothing about where he is or how he's doing. The urgency gnaws at me, a constant reminder that time might be slipping away.

The cruel irony? My body's completely shutting down while my mind's firing on all cylinders.

My muscles won't listen, no matter how hard I mentally push them. I'm fading fast while everything inside me wants to jump up and run.

Sleep pulls me under like a riptide, and Rhyland's face burns bright behind my eyelids. It's a silent promise—*Hang on. I'm coming.*

As consciousness slips away, one thought grips me tight—I'm running out of time. They need me, my blood.

Failure isn't an option.

DANICA

3

The morning light filters through the cave entrance with the soft touch of dawn, pulling me out of sleep. I could pretend yesterday was some twisted nightmare, but reality's grip is too tight, too real.

I jolt upright with an urgency that doesn't make sense, gasping like I've been sprinting through my dreams. My chest heaves, and I can't catch my breath. This isn't the time for a meltdown, though—Rhyland and his brothers are still out there, and their absence feels like a weight crushing down on me.

I push the panic down. Losing it won't help anyone. It's go time.

I'm out of the chamber and scanning the main cavern for Faderyn.

He's already there, where breakfast is laid out with an unsettling sense of normalcy. His emerald eyes catch mine as I rush in. "Eat. You will require sustenance," he says with that calm Fae confidence that's somehow both reassuring and irritating.

I stare at the food, my stomach doing backflips. I force myself to eat anyway, but it tastes like cardboard mixed with my own anxiety. The knot in my chest just keeps getting tighter.

Our bond remains silent. The absence is deafening, like there's some cosmic "Out of Order" sign hanging over our connection.

"He's out there, Faderyn," I say, my voice sharp with worry. "We need to search. Like, immediately. Not tomorrow. Today."

He studies me thoughtfully, his brow furrowed like he's solving some complicated riddle. "We shall track along the river," he decides, his tone suggesting he's already figured out the ending.

But my mind won't stop spiraling. How bad is the situation? Are we pulling off some fairytale rescue, or is this heading straight for the tragic ending? I'm not some damsel waiting in a tower, but right now I feel about two seconds away from completely losing it.

My bread sits untouched, and Faderyn's watching me with that intense gaze that makes me feel like he's trying to read my diary.

"You carry yourself with the bearing of a sovereign, yet you are not Fae," he observes.

The crown. I'd finally wrestled it out of my hair this morning. Now my face is probably as red as a traffic light. My lap suddenly feels like the most fascinating thing in existence.

Smooth move, Dani.

His eyes are waiting for an answer, and I can practically feel the weight of his attention.

"So then, what brings you here?" he asks, his tone shifting to something more probing. "What destiny calls a human to the Fae Realm wearing the trappings of royalty?"

I'm caught in the headlights now, and there's no way out of this one.

I'm mentally pacing before I launch the truth at him like a grenade. What choice do I have? I'm completely in the dark here.

"Okay, full transparency," I say, going all-in with the prophecy, the cosmic storm that's apparently my problem, and that shiny Faerite stone that's supposed to unlock my inner superpowers.

Trusting Faderyn feels like walking a tightrope blindfolded, but desperation makes you do stupid things. *Here we go,* I think, steeling myself.

His jaw literally drops. I've apparently just announced I'm Atlantis royalty or something equally insane.

"You claim to be the one foretold, the savior inscribed in the ancient texts?" His voice wavers like he's asking and stating at the same time.

I nod, fully aware of how batshit this sounds. "Yeah, it's wild. But I'm not making this up." His skepticism is written all over his face, and I can practically hear the doubt gears grinding. "You think I'm just screwing with you for fun? Trust me, I've got way better party tricks," I say, half-joking, half-desperate for him to actually believe me.

"I'm the universe's pick and don't exactly have documentation. But this..." I let a ball of light bloom above my palm, shimmering softly, "...is my resume."

His breath hitches, and I can't help but smirk. "Oh, and I didn't just wander into Wonderland. I made my own road."

I snuff out the light and cross my arms with exaggerated casualness. "As for this stone? Think of it as my battery upgrade."

Faderyn's still wrapping his head around it, his expression cycling through shock to confusion. Then he stammers, looking distinctly un-mystical. "You... you wield light magic? How is this possible?"

I lift my chin, radiating confidence like I've just won the lottery. "Elysium? Ring any bells? That's my old man. Literal god of light. So yeah, divine blood, cosmic powers, the whole package—basically unstoppable."

His eyes go wide when I mention Elysium's name. "The Light God's progeny? Extra ordinary... the prophecy makes no mention of such origins."

Faderyn leans forward, his intensity cranked up a notch. "The Faerite stone you speak of? It vanished into legend centuries ago." His ancient eyes gleam with something like hunger. "You believe it remains here?"

I nod decisively. "It's here. And I'm finding it. With the Faerite, I can take down Azrael and stop Moretemis from destroying everything."

His face goes serious. "Moretemis and his servants bring only devastation. But the Faerite's whereabouts have been lost to time itself, even among the eldest of our kind. The search will prove arduous."

My head's spinning with questions—what's Azrael actually planning? How much time do I actually have left? How many frequent-flyer miles does portal jumping get you, and do they expire?

I shove the food away, my voice cutting through the silence. "Faderyn, I can't just sit around playing charades in a cave. Rhyland, Lucian, Erik—they're trapped somewhere, and knowing that is eating me alive."

I stand up, laser-focused. "I've got a list of enemies longer than my arm, and every second we waste is a second they're in danger. We need to move. Now."

He studies me with that penetrating gaze. "These companions—what significance do they hold?"

"Rhyland is my mate. Lucian and Erik are his brothers—my family. Yeah, they're vampires, but they're *my* vampires, and I'd burn the world down before I let anything happen to them."

The desperation in my voice is sharp and real.

But dread slams into me hard, a sucker punch to my senses. They're exposed to the sunlight, and time's a ticking bomb.

His face goes pale. "Vampires? This is... this is dire." Faderyn takes my hand, his grip surprisingly steadying. "We will locate them, Dani."

"They need me—my blood is the liquid lifeline for vampires. Consider it an SPF upgrade for the sun-challenged."

Fadeyrn does a double-take, "SPF?"

I keep forgetting I'm in the land of doublets and codpieces. "My blood protects them. From the sun. It's... complicated, but they can't survive out there without me."

The urgency of it all hits him, and he moves faster.

Next thing I know, I'm climbing onto a horse, and we're tearing through the forest at a speed that would make a race car jealous. Everything blurs.

"Hold tight!" Faderyn shouts over the thundering of hooves and wind that tears at my hair, my clothes, everything.

I press my face against his back, my arms tightening around him as the landscape whips by in streaks of emerald green and golden light—beautiful in an abstract way, but I can barely process it. All I can feel is the desperate pull in my chest, that invisible cord connecting me to Rhyland, tightening with every passing second.

Please be alive. Please still be alive.

The words become a prayer, a mantra I repeat over and over in my head.

My thighs burn from gripping the horse's flanks. My lower back screams in protest with every jolting stride. My butt is absolutely filing a formal complaint—seriously, this is going to bruise—but I don't care. Pain is nothing compared to the terror clawing at my throat.

What if we're too late? What if Rhyland is already—

No. I can't think like that. He's alive. He has to be alive.

The terrain begins to shift beneath us. The vibrant greens fade to muted tones. The sky, which had been a brilliant blue, starts to darken at the edges like someone's dimming the lights. The temperature drops so gradually I almost don't notice it at first, but then the chill seeps into my bones, stealing the warmth from the air itself.

We're moving from the bright, living lands into something else entirely.

Shadow territory.

Faderyn doesn't slow down, if anything he pushes the horse harder. I can feel the change in him—the set of his shoulders, the tension radiating through his body. He's bracing for something, preparing for what we're about to face.

I close my eyes and rest my forehead against his shoulder blade, reaching for that invisible thread connecting me to Rhyland, the one that's been pulling at me since we left the cave. It's not physical—I know that much. It's deeper than flesh and bone, woven into something fundamental about who I am. A beacon. A compass pointing true north. *He's close. He's so close.*

The horse's hooves transition from soft earth to something harder, more treacherous. Volcanic glass. Black and jagged, it cuts through the darkness like shattered mirrors. One wrong step and we'd go tumbling. The forest ahead is no longer a forest at all—it's a void, pure shadow that seems to greedily swallow every photon of light that dares to venture into it. The trees are skeletal and twisted, their branches reaching toward us like clawed hands.

It's a stark, horrifying contrast to the shimmering beauty we left behind in Faderyn's valley.

A chill races up my spine—the kind that's pure instinct, the part of my brain screaming *danger, danger, DANGER.*

But I push past it. I have to push past it.

"We enter the Shadow Court's domain now," Faderyn says grimly. "The ancient lands of the Dark Fae."

The shiver isn't fake. Dread wraps around my throat, but I forge it into steel and purpose. Rhyland's here, trapped in this dark nightmare, and I'll burn it all down to get him out. "There." I point to some black, creepy eyesore.

Faderyn's expression darkens with dread. "The royal palace? If the Shadow Court holds your mate captive..." He doesn't finish, but he doesn't need to.

Fear claws at my heart. Flashes of Rhyland suffering slam through my mind—brutal and vivid. My heartbeat thunders in my ears, deafening in the silence of my determination.

"Get us there. Now." The words tear out of me, every syllable sharp with desperation.

Faderyn doesn't hesitate. He urges the horse into a full gallop. The world lurches as we barrel through the dark forest. My fingers dig into his shoulders, gripping for stability.

Then we stop abruptly. "This is as far as we can go," Faderyn says.

I unstick myself from Fadeyrn, clumsily rolling off the horse, my legs shaky with adrenaline as I confront the monolith.

About fifty yards away sits Rhyland's prison—a nightmare carved from darkness itself. The gates are massive and forbidding, designed to crush anyone stupid enough to try entering. The stench of malevolence hangs so thick I can taste it.

But the fear twists into something sharper: pure determination. This is where Rhyland is. This is where I have to go. There's no room for hesitation here.

Faderyn's body is taut with tension. "This place crawls with Dark Fae," he murmurs grimly. "You must exercise extreme caution, Dani."

I'm frozen by the weight of the evil radiating from this place, but I force myself to move past it. Getting Rhyland out of this hellhole will take everything I've got. Failure isn't an option—not when his life depends on me.

"Who rules this creepy Dr. Suess castle?" I ask quietly, almost afraid of the answer.

Faderyn's jaw tightens. "King Alinar and Queen Amara. They are formidable rulers."

The venom in his voice speaks volumes, but it does nothing to stop my heart from racing. I'm standing at the edge of something huge, completely exposed and terrified.

But I can't afford to be scared. Not now.

RHYLAND

4

These goddamn silver chains, covered in some fairy-tale bullshit scribbles, cut off my vampire strength, leaving me weak as a kitten. A matching collar wraps around my neck, giving this psycho bitch, Queen Amara, the control she craves.

Lucian and I are her playthings, dressed up and paraded out to stroke her sick ego in front of her twisted court. Don't be fooled, though—a golden cage is still a cage, no matter how you dress it up.

Her goons, eyes glued to Queen Crazy, keep us under constant surveillance. Any sign of rebellion gets crushed in a heartbeat, and there's zero chance of breaking free.

We're stuck playing our parts in this twisted, never-ending circus of hers, drowning in the endless horseshit that bleeds into her court's daily life. Lucian with his smart-ass comments, and me, the brooding, defiant captive—we're her twisted entertainment of the day.

When night falls, this hellhole shows its true colors—dark, depraved, and twisted. These chains might loosen up, but they're always there, a heavy reminder of the so-called freedom we'd be fools to chase.

Amara showers my brother with every excess imaginable, trying to chain him to her side with her sick games and pleasure dens. She's desperate to turn him into one of her devoted dogs, addicted to her favors and lies.

She keeps throwing herself at me, thinking I'll take the bait. But I shut the vain bitch down every time. My gut twists thinking about Danica. Our shattered bond tears at me every waking second.

Is my fierce girl lost to me forever?

For a moment, I swear I felt Dani's touch—like she was reaching out through the wreckage of what we had. But it's probably just my mind playing tricks. She's out of reach, our bond destroyed by fae magic. And yet, some stubborn, pathetic part of me won't let go of that sliver of hope.

"My pet, you are so very tense," Amara purrs, her possessive hand trailing down my chest. "Come, allow me to soothe your burdens."

I wrench away, barely keeping my disgust in check. "I require no soothing, *My Queen*."

She is anything but my queen. The title rings hollow, an empty gesture to feed her arrogance. In truth, she wields no legitimate claim over me.

But for now, I have to swallow her delusions of grandeur, stroke her ego with some respect, and pretend devotion.

It grates on me, having to play the groveling bootlicker before her. Bending the knee like some servant isn't my style. I have to bite my tongue, keep my head down, and play this twisted game to stay one step ahead and keep breathing.

"On the contrary, I sense your thoughts are plagued by distractions," she retorts coyly. "Allow me to refocus your attention."

Before I can react, she grasps the collar's engraved ring, using it to pull me close. "There are far better uses for that scowl than glowering into shadows."

It all happened so fast after the raging river tore us apart.

Eighteen hours ago...

The Shadow Court patrol descended swiftly, our powers rendered useless as they bound us in engraved silver chains. We tried explaining our presence, but they hauled us to the throne room like wayward dogs.

Queen Amara lounged on her obsidian throne, lethal beauty and power radiating from her slender frame. Arctic amusement glinted in her crystalline eyes as the guards forced us to kneel before her.

"Trespassers," she mused, her voice a melodic chill. "And vampires to boot. What dark whims bring you before my presence?"

I locked eyes with her, that predatory part of me that thrived in the darkness, acknowledging her dominion. "We got swept into your realm by accident. We're not looking for trouble with you. We just need to find our people and get the hell out of here," I said plainly, refusing to bow despite the chains.

Her interest was piqued with macabre curiosity. "Companions? You're telling me more bloodsuckers are crawling around my domain?"

I opened my mouth to deny it, but Lucian, ever the smart ass, jumped in. "Just one damsel. Beautiful, probably crying her eyes out. Your realm's dark vibe probably has her completely mesmerized."

I silently cursed, every muscle rigid with suppressed rage. His bullshit jesting only tightened our chains.

Amara's eyes narrowed, probing the veiled truths behind our facade. "And this damsel," she inquired like a cat playing with a cornered mouse, "what brought her stumbling into my court's web?"

Lucian, undaunted by danger—hell, maybe even off on the rush—replied with a casual shrug. "Magic screw-up. She's into that supernatural stuff. You know how women are."

His sarcastic tone did us no favors. I glared at him—his mouth was going to get us killed.

Her despotic smile never wavered as she considered his words. "A curious tale," she concluded. "Yet such tales often mask darker intentions. The hunger of your kind is no secret."

Asserting my stance, knowing this was a battle of brains and wills, not fangs and fury, I said, "Look, our history isn't your problem. Just let us go, and you'll never see us again. That's a promise."

So here we are.

Gilded halls fill with writhing figures, and the air pulses with carnal hunger. Scantily clad Fae nobility indulge every lustful desire, passions amplified—orgies and bodies intertwining indiscriminately in ecstasy. Rapturous screams and cries of pleasure echo all around.

Amara trails covetous fingers up my thigh. "Mmm, yes, listen to them enjoy each other so thoroughly. Does it not tempt you?"

I grasp her wrist tightly, every muscle taut with revulsion. "I've got no interest in that kind of depravity."

Amara's eyes flash dangerously. Before I can react, her palm cracks against my cheek, claws raking blood. "You dare reject your queen?"

Cheek burning, I stare her down defiantly. "My interests lie elsewhere."

With a snarl, Amara backhands me again. "Arrogant fool. You will submit or suffer the consequences." I taste the blood and swallow.

I grin mirthlessly through the crimson. "I suppose we'll find out, won't we?"

With a snap of the queen's jeweled fingers, two intertwined Fae males detach from their passionate lovemaking. Backs arched in ecstasy one moment, they straighten obediently under her commanding gaze the next. Sweat still glistens on their skin as they disengage and pad over to kneel reverently before her.

It hits me that everyone here is dancing to her tune, jumping at her every command despite the clear reluctance in their eyes. Yet for some reason, her orders bounce off Lucian and me like water off glass. It has to be some kind of compulsion power at work—and considering Lucian and I are basically walking corpses, that mind-bending trick doesn't take hold on us.

Eyes downcast, the taller one speaks. "How may we serve your pleasure, My Queen?"

His voice strains with unsatisfied need. The queen's ruby lips curl into a cruel smile. Then I see it—the room's thick with her power, black smoky shadows coiling around her as she commandeers their will completely.

With a painted nail, she points to me. "You will rut for my *guest*. Put on a stimulating show so he knows precisely what awaits those who refuse to submit to my will."

She's wielding some twisted, dark power shit. It's uncannily like Azrael's, complete with those same black, smoky-ass shadows.

Her words drip with mocking promise. I resist the urge to puke as the Fae males rise and move like puppets to position themselves before me. This perverse game revolts me, but I keep my expression blank.

At the fuckin' queen's *command*, the smaller Fae turns his back, gets on his knees, and spreads his ass cheeks. His taller partner wastes no time, eager as fuck to ride him, their last session leaving 'em both hard and throbbing.

As the tip of the dominant male pushes past the tight ring of muscle, the receiver lets out a moan of pure ecstasy. With agonizing slowness, the bigger male thrusts himself deep, burying himself balls-deep. Their obscene rhythm builds, the sound of slick flesh slapping together mixed with their desperate cries of pleasure. All for that twisted bitch's sick amusement.

I squeeze my eyes shut, desperate to block out the sight. But her sharp command lashes out, thick black smoke curling around her. "Watch! Or I will gouge out those pretty blue eyes that dare defy me."

Her guards wrench my face forward. Bile rises in my throat again as I'm forced to observe the two Fae males rutting madly, consumed by arousal. The smaller one's back arches with each deep thrust, his moans growing louder as sweat drips down his spine. The taller male's muscles flex and strain, his hips snapping relentlessly as he chases his own release. Their bodies move in perfect sync, a symphony of desperation and need.

The queen urges them on with graphic demands. "Harder! I want to hear the slap of your balls against his ass. Make him scream for me."

They go at it like animals, whipped into a frenzy by her voice alone. Her cold, sick cackling slices through me worse than any blade could. She gets off on the degradation, the power—flexing her muscles by breaking everyone else down.

I've gotta lock this shit out, throw up walls in my head so I don't drown in her filth.

It's Dani's laugh that keeps me from cracking. As long as Dani's out there, breathing and fighting, I can stick it out in this hellhole.

But then Amara's nasty claws clamp down on my face, yanking my gaze back to her twisted circus. "Keep watching," she hisses, each word a threat that makes it clear she's not playing around.

A shudder runs through me as my eyes lock on the writhing bodies before me. They move, bucking and moaning, lost in ecstasy—the dominant male's face buried in the other's neck as he drives deeper. The receiver's body trembles with each thrust, his legs shaking as pleasure consumes him completely.

The queen's voice cuts through my horrified fascination. "See how they give themselves over to pleasure? This could be you, bound in chains before my court, writhing and panting as our most skilled lovers fill you."

The thought of being violated in such a way makes my stomach churn. I keep my expression blank, refusing to give her the satisfaction of seeing my disgust.

She continues taunting me, her voice dripping with scorn. "Perhaps you prefer the company of men? It makes no difference to me." I wrench my face from her grasp, unable to stomach more. "Is this where your appetites lie?"

Jaw tight, I rasp, "No. I desire only *one* woman."

Amara gestures to the entwined forms, both now shuddering in the throes of orgasm.

"One woman?" she laughs. "As if that's possible with you bloodsuckers. Their performance is just one of many that await you when you submit. Or you may continue to resist and endure whatever tortures I deem fit."

My skin crawls at the thought of being subjected to Amara's perverse whims. But I remain silent, unwilling to give her the satisfaction of seeing me flinch.

Her lips curve into a cruel smile. "You will break eventually. There is no escape for you here." She growls. "I may not be able to command you like these fools, but I will break you."

The guards release my head, allowing it to droop forward, but their hands remain on my shoulders, holding me in place.

Amara's voice rings out, commanding my attention. "What say you, Rhyland? Will you bend your will to your queen or endure more torment?"

I raise my head, meeting her gaze defiantly. "I will never submit."

Fury smolders in her violet eyes at my defiance. She means to break me entirely to her will. But my mind and heart remain beyond her reach.

The receiver's peak hits first, his seed spilling onto the polished stone floors in thick spurts. The giver follows moments later, teeth bared in raw ecstasy as he spills himself deep inside. They disengage, completely spent and trembling.

She shrugs, an elegant gesture of indifference. "Very well. You have made your choice," she huffs, eyeing the scene before us. "I am so eager and willing to break you."

Lucian interjects casually, "Hey, I'm down for anything—dudes plowing each other? Kinda hot, honestly." He punctuates this with an exaggerated leer and eyebrow wiggle.

The queen titters are temporarily distracted. But her scrutiny swiftly returns to me. "You will learn to appreciate the pleasures I bestow, pet. In time."

Her smug certainty fuels my rage. But outwardly, I school my features into cool impassivity once more. "As you say...*My Queen*," I say through gritted teeth. I can feel my jaw crack from the pressure. The appellation tastes like ash on my tongue.

Another sharp slap cracks across my cheek for the rudeness in my tone. But even as scarlet welts form, I do not waver. The pain only hardens my resolve.

Her annoyance is palpable when she doesn't get a rise out of me. Her twisted entertainment can't shake me—not the way she wants. I keep my cool by hanging onto that inner sanctuary—I hold sacred space for my mate.

As Amara gets caught up, snickering and gossiping with Lucian, I've gotta admit—I owe him one. Lucian's got his game face on—charming the queen without throwing a punch. His sharp mind and silver tongue may be his secret weapons in this viper's nest.

He catches my glance, giving me that cheeky wink of his. I give him a tight nod; it's the closest thing I can muster to thanks. Crisis dodged—for the moment. But we've gotta stay sharp, not let anything about Danica slip, or we're screwed. Bullshitting's our best bet in this hellhole. Stay the course and wait for our shot.

Amara adjusts her gown. Holding a small blade, she approaches me. She traces a long nail down my cheek, across my jaw, and trails her finger down my neck. "I think it's your turn, pet."

The nauseating scent of her perfume mixed with the reek of sweat and cum. Bile surges in my throat, but I remain composed. My eyes bore coldly into hers, lips thinning in defiance. "No."

Her blade digs into my flesh, drawing blood. She grips my crotch, rubbing cruelly against my dick. "You will obey your queen."

I remain defiant, unflinching as the blade slices deeper into my flesh. Amara issues a frustrated hiss. "Never," I spit in her face.

Amara viciously stabs the blade deep into my thigh. Burning pain spreads through my abdomen. I bellow, thrashing against the guards' hold.

She stares at me, dispassionate, watching me bleed. "So be it."

Her threat hangs there, thick as fog. She's got it in her head to break me, make me her pet. But I'm nobody's bitch.

The way she grins at me, all smug—it's like an icy grip around my spine.

Then the oak doors slam open, and in walks the King himself, Alinar. He's staring daggers. To him, it's just another twisted Tuesday in the cesspool; her sick sexcapades aren't even worth batting an eye.

He struts over to where she's perched, leans close, and whatever he whispers ticks her off something fierce.

She's on her feet quicker than lightning, all fuming and ready to blow. "Out! Leave us, now!" she shrieks.

Thank fuck, I think as I scramble to my feet, making for the doors. I can't get out of this den of filth fast enough.

But before I get two steps, the guards are on me. Hissing in pain at the deep puncture wound in my thigh, watching as my dark vampiric blood slowly trickles from the gash.

The bitch got me good. Thankfully, no major arteries were severed; otherwise, this could have been problematic, even with my supernatural healing. Still, it's a troublesome injury that weakens me. Once I'm free of this place, this sadistic bitch and I are going to have a very unpleasant reckoning for every unjust torment I've suffered.

"Stay put, slave!" One viciously twists my arms back and claps iron around my wrists. The metal bites deep, but not as deeply as my urge to smash their ugly fucking faces. Lucian gets the same treatment as they shove us from the room.

"Move, scum!" A guard clubs me hard across the shoulders.

As they frog march us down the endless hallway, I fantasize about all the ways I'll make these bastards suffer when I'm free. My fury's a caged beast straining at its leash.

We get to our rooms. The guard pushes the door open and tosses me in like I'm a damn sack of potatoes, the impact nearly shattering my side.

Next door, I catch the sound of Lucian getting the same warm 'fuck-you' as the locks snap closed, locking us in.

All alone, I'm struggling to shed this cursed collar like hell—the damn thing's stuck tight. Swearing, I punch the wall so hard it crumbles under my fist.

"Cool it with the temper tantrum, brother," Lucian's voice breaks through the wall.

"I am no one's goddamn lapdog!" I spit through clenched teeth.

He's right, the bastard. Mindless fury isn't going to get me anywhere. They play with control like it's their favorite toy; it's time I show them I'm not playing their game. I force myself to sit, hands shaking with the effort.

Lucian's voice comes again, calmer this time, filtering through the walls. "Alright, listen up, my fellow prisoner of this fetid shithole masquerading as a palace. I know things look bleaker than a goth kid's diary right now, but we can't let these crown-wearing asshats break us."

There's a shuffling sound like he's shifting closer to the wall. "I mean, come on. We've got more brains between us than the entire royal family has in their inbred little pinky fingers. It's time we put those glorious gray matters to work and figure out a way to bust out of this dank hellhole."

Despite the direness of our situation, I can't help but snort out a laugh. Trust Lucian to find a way to make even the most hopeless circumstances seem like just another adventure.

The perfect chance to escape will come. For now, patience and unity must suffice. But soon, this gilded prison will fucking shatter. I'll see it happen or die trying.

I've got a destiny waiting beyond these walls: beautiful caramel-gold eyes, a sweet, sensual woman. Nothing keeps a determined beast caged forever. And once we're free, there'll be hell to pay. I'll rain holy fire down on these shit-licking maggots.

That solemn promise keeps my fury chained—but just barely. Soon, it will be unleashed.

DANICA

5

I dig deep into the bond connecting Rhyland and me, stretching that ethereal thread until it feels like it might snap. My silent calls keep getting more frantic.

"Rhyland, give me something. Anything," I whisper into the emptiness, searching for that familiar warmth.

But the silence that comes back is suffocating—like staring into the void of space. Cold. Empty. Where his presence should be, there's nothing but static.

Panic claws at my chest, threatening to drag me under. An invisible storm of dread is battering my resolve, and I can feel myself starting to crack. Rhyland and his brothers are trapped in this nightmare, and I'm the only one who can get them out.

The castle looms ahead like a monument to everything twisted. I plunge back into our bond, throwing every ounce of desperation into a silent scream.

Suddenly, Faderyn's hand on my shoulder halts my headlong rush into danger. "We can't just walk in," he cautions gravely. "We will be considered enemies—magic will fail us here—drain you."

I look back, defiance sparking in my eyes. "Watch me." With that, I start toward the dark structure. Faderyn doesn't argue, just falls into step behind me like we're marching into battle together.

"Remain vigilant," Faderyn whispers as we creep closer. "Sentries guard these grounds relentlessly. We must avoid detection." The tension in the air is thick enough to strangle on, pressing down on us with every step.

I feel it: that heavy, ominous quiet before everything goes to hell.

Then it happens. A crack splits the air like lightning, and we both freeze. Every predatory instinct kicks into overdrive. My breath catches. My pulse hammers. The world goes into slow motion, and even the forest seems to hold its breath.

Something's coming. Or someone.

Each sound through the underbrush sends a spike of adrenaline through me. I drop low to the ground, pressing myself flat.

The shape emerges from the shadows, all darkness and whispers until—

Silver hair catches the light, and my chest nearly explodes with recognition. Those eyes—silver like the moon and familiar.

"Erik!" The word rips out of me before I can stop it. Joy and disbelief crash together in a tidal wave, and I'm already moving, caution completely abandoned.

Faderyn hisses a warning, but I'm not hearing it. I'm sprinting toward Erik like he's oxygen and I've been drowning.

Erik's exhausted face breaks into a fierce grin the second he sees me rushing toward him. I slam into him with a hug tight enough to crack ribs, needing the solid proof of his existence to stop my spiraling. For one blessed moment, hope cuts through the suffocating darkness.

Faderyn's still on high alert. His jaw is locked, and those piercing green eyes are cataloging Erik's battle-worn appearance like he's reading a threat assessment.

I step into mediator mode because we don't have time for a standoff. "Faderyn, this is Erik—Rhyland's brother and one of the guys we're here to rescue," I say, making sure Erik sounds like the ally he is. Turning to Erik, "And Erik, meet Faderyn. He's basically the only reason I'm not fish food right now."

Faderyn and Erik shake hands like they're both measuring the other's power level. The tension is thick enough to cut.

I mentally shelve Faderyn's distrust because we've got bigger problems. "Erik, talk to me. What the hell happened?"

Pain flashes across his stoic features. "We got ambushed by Fae guards—there was this woman, some kind of demoness leading them. They slapped us in magical chains on the queen's orders. We didn't stand a chance." His voice gets tight. "Rhyland fought like hell to get me out, told me to find you, and then they dragged him away. Lucian..." He swallows hard. "Lucian walked straight into captivity to stay with him."

Rage ignites inside me like a blowtorch. No one—and I mean no one—gets to treat my guys like game pieces.

Erik's stoic exterior hides the pain in his eyes. "I sense their presence here. It led me to investigate," he sighs. "I apologize for not finding you sooner. I didn't know where to start."

I'm trying to keep my temper in check, but my magic is starting to buzz under my skin like angry bees. "It's cool. You're here now, that's what—"

My hands suddenly ignite with flames, and both Faderyn and Erik actually step back. The fire is burning hot and wild, completely out of my control for a few seconds before it fizzles out, leaving me drenched in sweat.

"What in the vales was that?" Faderyn asks.

I take a shaky breath, trying to get my head back in the game. I fix Erik with a stare, taking in the battle damage still fresh on him. "Alright, Her Royal Wickedness made her move," I say, smooth as ice but twice as cold. "She's about to get schooled in the art of repercussions—mess with my boys, prepare for a backlash."

But Faderyn cuts in, his tone grim. "If your adversary is Queen Amara, we walk a precarious line, Dani."

The thought of Rhyland and Lucian playing puppets to Cruella de Mean makes my stomach flip. I steady myself and look at Faderyn like it's time to get serious. "So, what's the game plan? What's the 411 on Wicked Witch of the Worst?"

Faderyn hangs his head, defeat weighing down his shoulders. "Against the Queen in her domain... I fear there may be nothing we can do."

I cross my arms defiantly. "The hell there isn't. No magical queen gets to take my man without a fight."

Underneath this calm exterior, there's a hurricane waiting to break loose. My magic is losing its mind, pounding against every wall inside me, screaming to get out.

Faderyn watches me carefully before speaking. "Dani, I understand your fire burns bright as any warrior's, but we cannot let rage consume us. The Queen's power here is absolute. A direct assault would destroy us. Most magic is suppressed in her domain—neutralized."

His words hit with the sobering slap of reality. My heart's itching to go all 'smash and grab,' but that's page one of the 'How to Die Young and Stupidly' handbook. Rhyland and Lucian deserve more than me flying off the handle.

I breathe, taming the storm inside, my resolve hardening. "Okay. We're not storming the castle gates. So lay it on me, Gandalf. What's your wizard-level stratagem?"

Faderyn hesitates before continuing. "Queen Amara is cruel, but she respects courtly protocol. A formal request for an audience might be our best option. Approaching with respect and acknowledging her station could work in our favor. But you'll need proper attire and training first—court etiquette is everything." His gaze turns serious. "Axilya can prepare you. She can make sure you don't accidentally insult the queen or worse."

"Who's Axilya? And should I trust her?" I ask, my mind already running calculations.

Faderyn nods firmly. "Axilya has rejected the corruption of the courts. She gives sanctuary to those fleeing their politics—she's reliable. More than reliable."

I lean in, meeting his gaze head-on. "Okay, if you're putting your chips on this, Axilya, I'll entertain a chat," I agree. "But the minute things smell fishy, we abort mission 'Kumbaya' and switch to operation 'Disco Inferno,'" I assert. "So let's hope your Fae friend is the real deal because I've got a light show ready."

Faderyn bows his head. "Your caution is wise. We will proceed with care. But this may be our best hope of sparing bloodshed."

I'm crossing my fingers that his faith in Axilya is justified. Too many lives are on the line.

Faderyn turns to Erik with that serious look. "It is best you do not accompany us to meet Axilya. The Fae harbor... complicated feelings about vampires after historical conflicts."

Erik's expression tightens, but he nods like he expected this.

Faderyn continues carefully. "Vampires have not walked these lands in centuries. Your presence will resurrect painful memories—memories best left dormant until Danica can reframe your intentions."

I shift gears, addressing the gap in his knowledge. "Things are different now," I say, keeping my tone measured. "We've moved past the whole 'pitchforks and torches' era. Yeah, vampires and humans had our conflicts, but that's ancient history. We've evolved."

Faderyn looks thoughtful. "Your realm has been fractured for ages," he muses. "We have little knowledge of current relations." His eyes brighten slightly. "Perhaps unity can take root here as well, in time."

Encouraged by his openness, I keep pushing. "Erik and his brothers are good men—honorable. Things aren't like they used to be. Just give them a shot."

Faderyn bows his head respectfully. "You present a compelling argument, Dani. I shall reflect on your words seriously. Understanding might bridge the divisions history created." He turns to Erik, his tone measured. "You may shelter at my dwelling if you wish. Few venture that far. You would find safety there."

As he outlines the path to his secluded abode, I catch myself about to argue against Erik trekking alone to an unknown haven. Faderyn shoots me a look that screams, 'I've been doing this for centuries, trust me.' So I swallow my protest and keep quiet.

"Dani, if you are truly who you claim to be, your safety cannot be compromised. We must depart swiftly." His tone doesn't invite debate.

"I'll catch up with you later," Erik says, his eyes meeting mine with reassurance. He looks at Faderyn hard. "Get her out of here. Keep her safe."

Faderyn sweeps me up in his arms—all pine scent and solid muscle. I'll never admit out loud how much I appreciate being carried like this, or how it actually makes me feel secure.

As we take off through the dark forest, I can feel Erik's protective presence behind us.

"You think Axilya can actually convince Queen Mean Girl to let my guys go?" I ask Faderyn skeptically.

His voice is steady and calm. "If anyone can assist us, it is Axilya. Trust the process."

I crane my neck, scanning the trees behind us. Each time I spot Erik's silver hair moving between the shadows, relief washes through me.

Faderyn says nothing more as we gallop on horseback, his jaw set with grim purpose. I know pushing back would be pointless. All I can do is hope Axilya is as solid as Faderyn believes.

I don't have a backup plan yet—no hidden card up my sleeve. But life's taught me that improvisation is basically my superpower. And if I have to pull a solution out of my ass?

Well, consider that my special talent.

DANICA

6

Time smears into one big, indistinct blur as we journey toward our destination. My poor backside calls for periodic breaks—I mean, mercy, please—even though we're trekking through drop-dead gorgeous landscapes, the beauty doesn't cushion the ride. This realm might be eye candy deluxe, but it's not butt-friendly.

Finally, when we're close enough to see our destination, the sight takes my breath away. It's straight out of a fantasy novel—lodges nestled into the landscape with clusters of tents scattered around like they're having a cozy hangout. The whole setup screams fae hospitality.

I slide off Faderyn's horse like my legs are made of wet noodles, absolutely numb from the thighs down. The air buzzes with energy—that distinctive hum of the fae being completely alive. It's this organic, unfiltered vibe that settles into your bones, pure and real.

Fae kids with pointed ears are running around in adorable chaos, doing whatever fearless immortals do for fun, while adults go about their day like this is just... normal life. Because it is. The fantasy wrapping doesn't change the fact that it's still just people living their lives.

"Dani," Faderyn says, gesturing across the vista with obvious pride. "Welcome to Whispervale."

The place is stunning—like whispers transformed into a physical space. I can't help but stare. "This is like... a hidden slice of paradise," I say, genuinely awed.

He guides me through the village, his pride evident with every step. "Whispervale represents sanctuary and freedom. No rulers casting shadows here. We celebrate autonomy, peace, and the right to be yourself."

I take in the organized chaos around us, the genuine happiness radiating from the people.

"It feels so... connected. Like roots and wings at the same time."

"With Axilya at the helm, we've managed to maintain a haven of solitude among the gales of change. Here, you'll find artists, healers, rebels, and refugees—each contributing to the pulse of this community—each free to live as they choose without the weight of courtly expectations."

A group of fae passes by, nodding respectfully to Faderyn before flashing me warm, curious smiles. It's weird how this place feels both extraordinary and completely normal at the same time.

"You've built something solid here," I say, and I actually mean it. "This is special."

He smiles and gestures deeper into the village. "Come. There's plenty to explore, and the center of Whispervale is just as beautiful as everything else."

Up close, details leap out—the exotic garb of leather, fur, and iridescent silk, the hypnotic glow of the Fae's jewel-bright eyes. Intoxicating scents hang thickly—earthy cooked meats, fragrant oils, crushed herbs, wet stone.

Weaving through the crowds, I'm struck by the incredible diversity—some fae are Faderyn's height with these massive, incredible antlers, while others are barely waist-high with delicate, pointed ears. Their skin colors span literally every shade imaginable—pale white, Faderyn's warm brown, vibrant blue, deep emerald. It's like someone threw a paint palette at the population and called it good.

My eyes catch on a section with creatures I've definitely never seen before—massive felines with dark fur that looks like liquid shadow moving across their bodies.

Faderyn catches me staring and explains, "Those are Night Sabers. They dwell only in our lands."

As we walk through the bustling camp, seeing those beasts sparks something in my brain."The Court of Mystical Beasts... What became of those creatures and fae folk?" My curiosity piques, imagining a lineup of creatures that Disney would kill for.

Fadeyrn gives a nod heavy with meaning. "Much has faded, but remnants linger if one knows where to seek them."

His tone has the gravity of a eulogy, a bit of a buzzkill.

When he drops the 'U' bomb, I literally almost trip. "Wait, unicorns are actually real?!" The words spill out before my brain can filter them. It's part disbelief, part vindication.

"They are indeed," he confirms with the smallest smile. "Though sightings are rare. They trust no outsiders and refuse all contact."

Talk about an exclusive VIP club.

A fae kid sideswipes Fadeyrn, jolting me back to the present and sparking a flicker of recollection. "Is it true unicorns will bond with certain individuals they deem worthy?" I ask, half-expecting him to unfurl a 'So You Want to Be a Unicorn's Bestie?' pamphlet.

"It was so long ago," Fadeyrn confirms. "But they severed ties even with the Fae. No mortal or immortal has earned their trust in centuries."

The information hits me like a brick. Adrian's books made it sound like unicorns were just hanging around waiting to buddy up with the virtuous, but the reality? It's more like they ghosted everyone and blocked their numbers.

Fadeyrn elaborates, "Transformative magic once flowed between unicorns and their riders. But as realms fractured, suspicion poisoned all bonds. Now they keep to their own, heeding no call."

He's definitely stuck in the glory days—full-on nostalgic about it.

His sad tone is kind of contagious, but the science nerd in me is perking up. If these creatures are still out there, maybe trust isn't completely dead. Maybe they're just making us work for it.

Sounds about right.

We pass a fae woman grilling meat, and the smell hits me like a wall. My stomach growls loud enough that Faderyn probably hears it.

"Their mythology stretches back to ancient times," Faderyn continues. "There are different varieties, each possessing distinct abilities tied to their coloring."

Excitement bubbles within me, my mind racing. "Tell me more. How can we find them?"

"The unicorns have cloaked themselves in secrecy." Fadeyrn's voice carries respect for their cunning. "They've vanished into a place untouched by time and strife. Some say they dwell in the Hidden Valley beyond the Crystal Peaks, where none but the purest hearts can tread."

"A hidden valley? Is it possible to find it?"

He looks at me like I've just announced I'm scaling Mount Everest in flip-flops. "Perhaps. But such a journey is perilous, not to be undertaken lightly. The path is obscured by land and magic. Unicorns chose their sanctum amongst the most forbidding reaches for good reason. Only those they wish to be found by will see the valley's truths. To seek them is to embark on a tale even skilled bards deem too fanciful," Faderyn says solemnly. "Their bond, once freely given, was the making of legends, which now endures beyond the passing of ages."

I lean in closer, the lore sparking my curiosity. "But say we tried to find this Hidden Valley, how would we start? Is there a map or guide?"

Faderyn gives me that knowing smile mixed with a serious warning. "No map or guidebook. To attempt this, one would require a compass of the soul and purity of intention. Remember, the unicorns are celestial beings, discerning of whom they reveal themselves to."

"So, it's about being worthy in their eyes?"

"Exactly," he nods. "To traverse the Crystal Peaks is a pilgrimage, a trial testing one's spirit. Many have sought the unicorns, lured by promise and power. Few have returned, and none with proof."

His words send this electric mix of excitement and dread racing down my spine. Unicorns aren't just some biological oddity—they're wrapped in cosmic mystery. Something clicks when he says 'celestial.'

He glances back at the market, and I follow his gaze. The whispers of ancient legend are woven right through this living, breathing community—a reminder that even in a place like Whispervale, mysteries exist that defy imagination.

I dream these beasts might bond willingly, sharing their gifts freely. Looks like my to-do list just got epic. Time to show this realm what an 'Angel on a mission' looks like.

But first things first—I need to get Rhyland back.

Faderyn guides me into an enormous lodge. Guards in full armor bow as we pass through the grand doors.

The interior is massive and bathed in warm lantern light. Tapestries hang everywhere—depicting magical beasts, enchanted forests, and epic battles. Faderyn leads me toward a raised platform holding an ornate throne.

Sitting on it is a fae so elegant she makes everyone else look ordinary. She's draped in robes that blend emerald and silver like they were woven from twilight itself.

Her skin is this stunning lavender shade, her silver hair crowned with a circlet made of thorns and delicate flowers. Everything about her is sharp angles and refined lines—beautiful but with this clear "don't test me" energy. But her eyes? They're this shade of green that literally takes your breath away—like watching leaves unfurl.

Faderyn bows deeply. "Lady Axilya, allow me to present Dani from the mortal realm. She seeks your counsel on a matter of great urgency."

Axilya's eyebrows shoot up. "You are mortal? How did you manage to reach our realm?"

There's no hostility in her voice, so I just dive in and spill everything.

Axilya's completely engaged, leaning forward when I mention the Faerite. She's hanging on every word as I explain—mixing what Adrian taught me with my own experiences—until the whole story's laid out between us.

When I finish, there's this heavy silence. Axilya's expression belongs on the front page of 'The Daily Gobsmacked.'

"The prophecy of the savior was dismissed as legend. And the Faerite vanished ages ago." She's clearly torn between awe and doubt. "You truly believe it exists here?"

"It absolutely does," I say with conviction. "And with it, I can finish what I'm supposed to do."

Axilya takes her time processing. "Your quest carries weight and truth. Darkness is rising, yes, but unity has always escaped our grasp." Hope flickers in her ancient eyes. "Perhaps that is changing. These times demand courage and action. You will have my assistance, provided your intentions are genuine."

Now that Axilya's on board with the whole "save the realms" plan, I hit her with the next problem—Rhyland and his involuntary vacation courtesy of the Shadow Queen. Basically, my mate got kidnapped by the gothic edition of royalty, and I need to fix it.

Her face changes as I talk. The weight of it settles over her features like storm clouds moving in. I can see it click for her—this isn't just my battle or Rhyland's. This darkness is everyone's problem.

Fadeyrn steps forward urgently. "My lady, will you aid Dani in gaining an audience with the queen? For her mate's sake?"

Axilya considers deeply before responding. "An audience may be secured, but the Shadow Court harbors dangers. You must approach with great care, Dani."

She meets my gaze. "We shall send an envoy announcing you, so they cannot dismiss you. I will outfit you in our garb to present properly."

Rising from her throne, she grasps my hands. "The queen is ruthless but adheres to honor. Proper conduct may win your mate's release if her rule is acknowledged." Axilya smiles gently. "There is hope, even in darkness. Go rest; we shall make preparations."

I'm gripping her hands like they're a lifeline, and relief floods through me. "Thank you so much! I seriously want to hug you right now!"

Axilya's lips quirk with amusement at my enthusiasm. "Your appreciation is noted. The road ahead will test you, but we shall provide guidance through the shadows," she says with quiet dignity.

Faderyn clears his throat pointedly. "We are grateful for your wisdom and guidance, my lady."

He gives me a look loaded with meaning.

Right, tone it down, Dani.

Axilya's laugh fills the space. "Your passion is refreshing, a vibrant flame in shadowed times. Let that fervor be your shield and spear, and victory shall not elude you."

Axilya's hand moves toward my crown, and I can practically feel her sensing the ancient magic radiating from it. Her eyes go wide.

"The Crown of Blessings," I say, trying to balance the importance with a light touch.

Her voice is full of reverence and awe. "The fabled diadem," she whispers, reverence painting her tone.

My fingers gesture to the empty sockets, explaining the need to locate the missing counterparts, starting with the elusive Faerite. It's a strategic map laid out, with my role at the forefront.

Axilya stares at the crown, and I can see her trying to keep her composure, but barely. "After generations void of hope... could we witness the prophecy's fate?"

DANICA

7

Faderyn leads me into another tent that's basically the fae version of glamping—if they even had a word for it.

The leather flaps close behind us with this satisfying soft thud. The moment I step inside, the magic hits—these glowing fae lights flicker overhead, bathing everything in this warm, gorgeous glow that makes the whole space feel impossibly fancy.

The air is thick with cedar from the fire crackling in the corner—seriously cozy cabin energy happening right now.

My stomach rumbles at the smell of roasting meat and fresh-baked bread wafting through the tent. Yeah, I'm definitely on board with fae hospitality.

I can't help but run my fingers over these intricate carvings covering the wooden furniture—they're scenes from the forest, from legends, carved so skillfully they almost look alive.

In the corner, there's this bed that's basically a mountain of comfort—piled with quilts embroidered more than a royal wedding dress and furs so soft they'd make a polar bear jealous.

And then there's the table. It's literally loaded with food—fruits that look like they came straight from some magical orchard, cheeses aged enough to be museum pieces, and wine that definitely didn't come from a grocery store.

This is basically the fae equivalent of a five-star resort, and I'm not complaining.

Faderyn gestures around with obvious pride. "Please, make yourself at ease. This will serve as your quarters during your time here." He's clearly pleased with how everything turned out.

Looking around at all this luxury, curiosity gets the better of me. "This is incredible. But where are you staying?"

He glances toward the darkening violet sky outside. "I must return home briefly to attend to matters—particularly after your friend's unexpected arrival." There's a hint of amusement in his smile. "I wish to confirm my attendant hasn't fled in panic."

I can't help but smirk, imagining someone's reaction to a vampire just showing up. "You'll come back, though, right? I'd rather not be alone here for too long."

Faderyn squeezes my hand gently, his emerald eyes warm and reassuring. "I will. It's merely a quick trip to handle things at home. I'll return within a couple of hours."

He smiles encouragingly. "Rest now. You've been through hell. You're safe here. We'll tackle what comes next together."

I turn to him, my detective brain already spinning. "So what's Axilya's actual plan for dealing with the Shadow Court?"

My stomach's doing backflips, and this nervous energy is practically vibrating through me.

Faderyn takes his time before responding. "She will compose a formal letter requesting an audience on your behalf—presenting you as an honored guest. Standard protocol."

I can feel my patience wearing thin like old fabric. "A letter? That's the plan?"

I take a breath, trying to wrap my head around the fact that this ancient realm is literally centuries behind. No texts, no emails, no phones. It's like being stuck in a time machine that decided to park itself in the 1800s—absolutely maddening.

"Yes, regrettably. The raven will carry it. Once it arrives, we await the queen's response. These matters typically require about a week," he says apologetically.

"A week?" I practically shriek, panic flooding through me.

I start pacing across the fur rugs, my agitation matching the chaos in my head. A week is way too long. Anything could happen to Rhyland while I'm stuck here doing absolutely nothing.

The thought of him in that palace, possibly suffering, while I'm just... waiting? No. I can't even let myself go down that road. Every second that ticks by is another second he's in danger, and I'm powerless to stop it. It's like watching him drown from behind glass.

Faderyn notices my panic spiraling and gently takes my hands. "Breathe, Dani. Panic will not aid him."

I try to calm down, but it's impossible. "There has to be a faster way. There just has to be."

Faderyn pushes back his hair, sympathy clear in his eyes. "I understand your urgency. But our customs are deeply rooted. We cannot simply bypass these protocols."

His reasonable tone just makes me angrier. A week of sitting around could be a death sentence for Rhyland. I won't—I can't—accept that.

Faderyn watches me carefully. "The queen must receive proper courtesy..."

"Proper courtesy?" I snap, my voice sharp enough to cut. "She's holding people prisoner. I don't care about etiquette or customs or whatever fae rules exist. That's insane."

"Dani, you must remain calm..." Faderyn reaches for me, but I pull away hard.

"Don't tell me to calm down," I shout, and sparks actually start dancing across my fingertips. "What if she just says no? What if she refuses to even see me? Is that possible?"

Faderyn hesitates, and that hesitation is all the answer I need. "It is... possible, yes."

The admission cracks something open inside me. Power surges through my veins like lava. My vision goes red. My hands ignite with flames—real, burning flames. Fear and rage are feeding it, making it stronger.

Faderyn sees the dangerous energy spiraling out of control and grabs my shoulders. "Dani, you must restrain yourself! This power—I have never witnessed anything like it. It is..."

I slam my eyes shut, forcing air into my lungs in these deep, shaky breaths. My teeth are clenched so hard my jaw aches as I try to lock down the inferno raging inside me. This isn't just anger—it's a full-blown firestorm trying to break free, and I'm barely hanging on by my fingernails.

After what feels like forever—though it's probably only a few minutes—I finally open my eyes. The angry red haze is gone, and I'm shaking like I've been electrocuted. Faderyn's standing there looking genuinely concerned, like he's calculating whether he needs to call in reinforcements.

"It's this place," I blurt out, needing to explain it somehow. "My power here... It's like someone cranked it up to eleven. I went from controlled to absolute chaos." I meet his gaze, trying to explain this fear I can barely name. "If I lose control completely, what happens then?"

The thought sends another wave of terror through me—like standing on the edge of a cliff with no idea if I'm about to soar or crash.

Faderyn takes this seriously. "Magic here is alive. You must learn to work with it, not against it. Flow with it, not force it."

I run my shaking fingers through my hair. "You're not getting this. I'm barely holding it together right now. What happens if it snaps?"

"Then we help you contain it," Faderyn says, squeezing my shoulder. "I haven't encountered magic like yours in centuries. But I know you can master this, Dani. Your will controls the magic, not the other way around."

"Faderyn, you're missing the point," I say, my voice dropping to almost a whisper. "A week is too long. Rhyland could be... I can't even think about it. Our bond, our connection—time matters. This is life or death." I'm practically begging now. "Please. There has to be another way."

He holds my gaze, and I can literally see him wrestling with it—the conflict playing out across his face. Finally, he pulls me into a hug that feels like the safest place in the world. "Hold on, Dani. We'll trust Axilya's plan for now. But if she drags her feet... we won't just sit around. We'll forge our own way," he says quietly, stroking my hair with this unexpected gentleness that somehow eases the panic clawing at my chest.

His words anchor me. I'm not in this alone.

That fierce, stubborn love for Rhyland hardens into pure resolve. I make a silent promise to myself—witnessed by the universe or whatever's listening—nothing will stop me from getting back to him.

Faderyn holds me a bit longer than feels normal, and when I finally look up, there's something in his expression that catches me off guard. Something that looks almost like... longing?

I clear my throat awkwardly and step back, creating some distance.

"I... my apologies," Faderyn stammers, letting his hands drop.

Before I can say anything, he turns and practically bolts out of the tent.

Alone again, the anxiety comes roaring back. I start pacing the plush rugs, my mind spinning with all the variables and unknowns. So much can still go wrong.

I can't figure out what that moment was with Faderyn. Did I imagine that look? We literally just met, and he's been nothing but helpful the entire time.

I force myself to refocus on what actually matters. Rhyland's trapped, my powers are unpredictable, and I need answers. Faderyn might be able to help with both issues, but nothing's guaranteed. Danger is definitely coming.

But staying still is driving me insane. I need to be ready to move the second an opportunity shows up. Too much is on the line—the realms, Rhyland's life, everything. I can't afford to fail.

Faderyn returns to my tent hours later, and Erik's with him—clearly not thrilled about it. Night's completely taken over outside by now. I practically launch myself at Erik, crushing him in a hug like we haven't seen each other in years instead of hours.

"Finally! Where the hell have you guys been?" I demand, planting my hands on my hips as I look between them both.

Faderyn lets out this heavy sigh. "My attendant apparently decided your... acquaintance was too much to handle." He gestures vaguely at Erik. "I was forced to escort him here on foot."

"Fine, lay the fault at my feet for your underling's distress," Erik mutters, shedding his equipment and easing onto a chaise beside the hearth. "Being hauled through the woods on a shared horse was never my plan."

The image of Erik—big, brooding, all serious warrior energy—squeezed onto a horse with lanky Faderyn? That's hilarious. And the several glasses of this honey-sweet wine I've been enjoying are definitely making everything funnier. My cheeks feel warm, and my head has this pleasant, fuzzy quality.

Faderyn catches my glassy expression and asks carefully, "Are you currently... intoxicated?"

"Pfft, no!" I scoff way too loudly, stumbling over to flop next to Erik in the least graceful way possible. "I'm just...relaxed. Wine here is strong stuff—phew!"

I'm absolutely hammered. I dramatically wave my hand in front of my face like I'm fanning myself and stretch toward the fire.

Faderyn looks genuinely concerned about my very unladylike sprawl but recovers quickly. "Yes, our vineyards are quite...potent by mortal standards. Perhaps pace yourself moving forward."

"Relax," I say, dismissing him with a wave. "What else am I supposed to do while we're stuck waiting in a holding pattern, waiting for *Cruella?*" I pin him with a meaningful look, one that he conveniently pretends not to notice.

Erik turns to me, his expression serious in a way that cuts through my buzz. "Any change with the bond? Can you feel him?"

The question sobers me up fast. I shake my head, and the sadness hits hard. "Nothing. It's like we're completely disconnected." My voice gets quieter. "I felt him for just a second earlier, but now... just this empty space where he should be."

Erik's jaw tightens, but he just nods. We both know what that means, and neither of us wants to say it out loud.

Faderyn clears his throat carefully. "Perhaps we could begin your magical training tomorrow, Dani? Only if you feel up to it, naturally."

I squint at him, letting the words process through my wine-soaked brain. "Huh? Yeah, okay," I say brightly. "Fair warning, though—I've never had an actual teacher before, so I might be a disaster. But I'm game if you are, Sensei."

Faderyn's emerald eyes practically light up. "It would be my privilege to instruct you, Dani. The magic here follows its own patterns. Learning to move with it—rather than against it—may help you regain your control."

I wobble to my feet. "I'm totally ready to commune with nature tomorrow," I announce, nearly toppling over before catching myself. I attempt some kind of bow, barely managing not to dissolve into giggles. "But my poor mortal body desperately needs sleep. Shall we continue our mystical adventure in the morning?"

Faderyn clearly has no idea when I'm messing with him. My jokes sail right over his head like he's got some kind of humor-deflecting shield.

Erik actually snorts, trying not to laugh as I stumble around the tent like a newborn foal. I can feel him watching my drunk disaster unfold with barely concealed amusement.

Faderyn smiles politely. "I shall inform Lady Axilya about your... guest," he says, gesturing toward Erik. "Rest well. We shall speak tomorrow." He heads for the exit.

I plop down next to Erik, the room doing slow circles around me. "You need blood before you waste away," I say bluntly, my words getting a little slurry at the edges.

It's been two days. He's not going to last much longer without feeding, especially with the relentless sunlight out there.

I'm desperately hoping Rhyland and Lucian are locked inside somewhere safe.

Erik gives me this flat stare. "I'm not drinking from my brother's drunk mate. That's crossing a line." He shakes his head like I'm being ridiculous. "Besides, your blood right now would just get me buzzed, not fed."

Heat floods my cheeks at how right he is. "Fiiiiine," I drag out dramatically. "Tomorrow, when I'm sober, I'll figure out how to get you some blood. But you're feeding, Erik. I'm not watching you fade away on my watch!"

I try to stand to make my point sound more serious, but the room tilts dangerously. Erik catches me instantly, his hands steady as concern flickers across his usually stoic face. Before I can protest, he's lifting me effortlessly into his arms. I let out a surprised squeal as the tent does a slow spin around me.

"Alright, tough girl, bedtime," he says, carrying me the short distance to the ridiculously comfortable bed. He sets me down gently on top of the furs. I grab a pillow and press it to my face, breathing in the lavender scent.

Erik tucks the blankets around me with surprising gentleness—all big brother energy. "Sleep. We'll sort everything out tomorrow." His silver eyes check me over one more time before he settles onto a thick quilt near the fire.

"Night, Erik," I mumble, my eyes already closing. Between the wine and everything that happened today, exhaustion is dragging me under hard.

"Goodnight, Dani," he says quietly.

The fire crackles softly, Erik's steady breathing filling the silence, and it's weirdly soothing. I'm drifting, drifting... and then I'm out completely.

RHYLAND

8

The servant girl slips in, quiet as a mouse, hauling a silver tray with a crystal decanter and a goblet brimming with blood. The scent, thick with iron, slams into me, sparking a fierce need. Yet I pause, suspicion nipping at me. I'm not taking anything these captors offer without questioning it first.

The girl seems to read my hesitation. "It's not poisoned," she whispers softly.

I'm stunned by her ability to perceive my thoughts and speak to me directly. I stare at her with guarded indifference.

Sensing my distrust, the girl meets my gaze. "The queen wishes to keep you alive—for now. Refusing will only weaken you."

I mull it over as the thirst rages. She's not wrong—I need my strength to get the hell out of this hellhole.

Lucian, channeling his inner smart ass, throws out, "Hey, try not to waste away to nothing on us, brother. Your stubborn willpower isn't exactly going to fill your tank, you know."

His words serve as a reminder that I can't let my guard slip.

She edges closer, the goblet in her hands, and there's a look on her face—almost like she actually cares. I let out a resigned snarl, snatch the cup, and down the blood.

Any second thoughts disappear when the blood hits my taste buds—pure and potent. The goblet's empty before I know it, power pumping back into my starved system. "Thank you," I mumble.

She cracks a small smile, and for a minute, the world doesn't seem like complete garbage.

I knock back two more goblets, chasing away the hunger. The blood's a welcome relief from the energy these cursed chains keep draining from me.

While I'm drinking, my eyes are on the servant girl. She's a slip of a thing—chestnut hair and doe eyes. I brace for the usual—fear, maybe disgust—but her face is all soft lines and gentleness, watching me with actual kindness. It throws me off, the way she radiates concern. Most around here see us as monsters or toys, but not her.

After putting the last cup down, she inches closer, throwing nervous looks at the door.

With a soothing tone, she whispers, "I am so sorry for what's been done to you. The queen's cruelty is not right.

Her words have me staring, dumbfounded. It's rare to find this kind of heart in the queen's ranks. She catches my gaze and looks away. "Some here still honor justice. I wish to help free you if I can."

Before any words can roll off my tongue, the staccato rhythm of boots comes from the hallway. She switches gears like she's done this dance before—going quiet, slipping into that role of 'obedient servant.'

Scooping up the empty vessels, she's the picture of servitude as the door bursts open.

A guard fills the doorway, scanning the scene. His eyes land on me and flick to her. "You're needed back in the kitchens," he barks.

She keeps her head low, makes a quiet sound of agreement, and moves to leave. But as she flits by, she's close enough to drop a bomb in a hushed rush, "The library, east wing. Your answers are there." And then she scurries away.

I'm left standing there, her secret words echoing in my skull.

Is she for real? Could this be a setup, some devious bullshit the queen cooked up?

There's no way to know without playing the hand she dealt. Still, I gotta tread lightly—this could blow up in our faces. But if she's throwing us a lifeline, it's a game-changer.

The guard, oblivious to the exchange, departs after delivering terse warnings.

Once the room is empty, Lucian lets his sardonic amusement ripple through the air. "Whoa—what's this? Holding auditions for a fan club? And look at her go, she's got nerve. Not every day you see someone give the queen the finger—takes guts or a death wish."

I pace, thoughts spinning as I analyze the servant's cryptic hints. What answers does she believe are in the library? Lore that could help remove these collars? It seems too much to hope for, yet hope refuses to die. Not when freedom feels this close.

I reply to Lucian absently, "What the hell are we supposed to find? If that wasn't vague as shit, I don't know what is."

"Let's wager it's a damn book, genius," Lucian's voice rolls out, laced with irritable wit. "I'm so tired of this godforsaken pit and her twisted little torture games."

I scowl toward the wall separating us. "No shit, it's probably a book. But which book, smartass? That's the question. Now shut the fuck up and let me think."

Lucian lets out a chuckle tinged with mock reverence. "Oh, forgive me, oh enlightened one. Go ahead, find your Zen or whatever. I'll just be here, holding my fucking breath for that pearl of wisdom to drop." The sarcasm in his voice is thick enough to cut with a knife.

"Keep it up, and I'll beat that breath out of you once we're free," I shoot back, making him laugh even harder.

"The service here is absolutely shit," he continues loudly. "Free room and board, but they stick us in stinking rooms and serve us cold blood. And the entertainment—being forced to watch Fae getting it on is not my idea of a good time!"

I can picture his exaggerated eye roll and dramatic hand gestures. Leave it to Lucian to find dark humor even in a nightmare like this.

Lucian's voice crackles with sarcasm, "Seriously, I'm writing a scathing Yelp review. 'To whom it may concern: Rooms are disgusting, staff is sadistic, and the food tastes like ass. Barely deserves a star—would rather stake myself than recommend.'"

Even when everything's gone south, Lucian's got a way of running his mouth with those smartass comments that can't help but drag a laugh out of me. His wisecracking is like a life preserver in an ocean of garbage—keeping my head from going completely under.

The door crashes open, and the guard lumbers in. "Turn around, hands behind your back," he barks. "The queen demands your presence."

Of course she does. I figured maybe her Twisted Majesty might leave me alone for a bit. Stupid of me to hope.

With that cold steel collar around my neck, I don't exactly have options. I do the only thing I can: turn around and clasp my hands behind my back.

The second those silver manacles click shut, I can feel them draining the life out of me. Every muscle itches to smash my head into the guard's face, but I grit my teeth and lock it down tight.

Now's not the time. Gotta play the long game.

Lucian calls out sarcastically, "Do I get an invitation to this party, too?"

"Shut your mouth, slave scum," the guard bellows.

"Well, now, I'm almost convinced you actually like me. And here I thought we were getting somewhere." Lucian fires back with attitude.

His fearlessness in mouthing off to our jailers never ceases to get my attention—whether it's guts or stupidity, I haven't figured out yet.

The glowering guard shoves me toward the open door. "Get moving, bloodsucker."

I fantasize about all the ways I'm going to make this asshole pay once I'm free of these chains. The vivid revenge fantasies bring a grim smile as I march forward.

Standing before the massive doors to her chambers, the guard knocks, announcing my arrival. The King's deep voice grumbles out an "Enter."

I hesitate, caught off guard. What the hell's got the King in her chambers when he usually can't stand being near her? Their Cold War is legendary. His showing up could mean opportunity or disaster—I can't tell which yet.

The doors swing open, and I stride in. This place is drowning in luxury, all meant to show off royal excess. Black silks and tapestries hang everywhere. Glowing crystals and fae lights make everything glow—the furniture's carved from woods I can't even name. The floor is this intricate artwork of river stones, and expensive rugs break up the ostentatious display. Windows curve around the entire room, offering views of the eerie forests and jagged peaks outside.

But nothing prepared me for the cozy scene before me—Alinar and his lady lounging like they're on a damn honeymoon, him feeding her grapes, both sipping wine. They're acting like they just made up after some huge fight—a bad feeling knots tight in my gut.

The queen's hungry gaze settles on me, appraising. "Uncuff him," she demands. "Do come in, pet. I've missed your company terribly."

Her fake affection makes my skin crawl. I rub my wrists and move carefully closer, raising my head defiantly. "What do you want?"

Amara lounges upon her chaise, watching me with violet eyes that hold zero warmth. Her night-black hair cascades over her pale skin, contrasting sharply with her blood-red gown. Pointed ears mark her fae heritage.

She pats the empty place beside her. "First, by keeping your queen entertained," she purrs, flashing those white teeth in an unsettling smile.

"I am not your fool to dance for laughs," I bite back.

"I wish to know the purpose of your presence here. Were you sent as an emissary of those self-proclaimed deities, the Sun Court?" Her words reek of disdain as she demands an explanation.

The name blindsides me, and for a moment, I'm drowning in confusion. "The Sun Court?" I parrot back; my brow furrowed as I try to wrap my head around this new piece of the puzzle.

"Yes, those wicked bastards who deign to play gods, considering themselves superior beings," she sneers.

I continue to stare at her, my eyes wide and mind reeling. Confusion doesn't begin to cover it—I'm lost, adrift in a sea of questions.

Her voice drips with venom. "Those wretched, light-wielding fiends of the Sun Court—a perpetual blight upon this realm for centuries. Deluding themselves into believing the foul breath of the gods graces their twisted notions of beauty and nobility." A sneer of revulsion twists her features. "Their arrogance is off the charts, their vanity matched only by their sick depravity. A more vile, self-important group of assholes would be impossible to find."

It doesn't take a genius to read between the lines—there's a shitstorm brewing between these two fae courts, and it sounds like neither one is worth a damn. "No," I reply flatly.

She hums like she's thinking, her response frustratingly vague. It's like she gets off on watching me struggle to understand her bullshit.

Frustration boils over, and the words tumble out before I can stop them. "I'm not from any other court. I've already told you how I got here. Now, if you'd stop being a goddamn bitch and actually listen—"

"Watch that tongue around me." Her eyes spark with fury, her claws slice down my chest like she owns me.

I snatch her wrist, my whole body coiled tight. "Touch me again, and I'll *permanently* remove your hand."

The guards rush me, and Amara raises her other hand to stop them. She looks thrilled by my defiance. She has no idea that each insolent word I speak pushes me closer to full-on rebellion.

She slithers closer, pressing against me like a snake. "Such fire. It will be delicious breaking you."

I meet her gaze coldly. "I'm not some pet for you to break. Don't even try."

Amara's smile widens even more at my pushback. "A challenge—how thrilling. I do love taming willful beasts..."

I clench my jaw with disgust. "Your games don't touch me. Go find some other toy to mess with."

The queen stares at me with frustration, yanking her hand away. "Bullshit doesn't suit you, pet. You will obey me."

Meanwhile, Alinar continues feeding his suddenly devoted wife, acting like he's completely unaware. But his sharp glance in my direction tells me he's paying attention. I'm reminded of a viper just waiting for the right moment to strike.

I let out a harsh laugh, sneering, "I don't bow to anyone, you twisted hag." Fighting off the urge to lose it, I stay standing next to her, every muscle tensed and ready for whatever she throws at me.

Those smoky shadows return, engulfing her completely. "My pet refuses to please me, husband," Amara sulks.

Alinar fixes me with an icy stare. He's tall and pale, with pointed ears and black hair like a raven's wing. But he's thin—almost skeletal—clearly not the type to get his hands dirty. He's probably never faced a real fight in his pampered life. If it wasn't for this magic-infused collar and these runes keeping me locked down, I'd end him right here, right now.

"Why do you deny my wife?" Alinar questions smoothly.

"Her power doesn't work on me." I stare at her pointedly. "I don't want that viper you call a wife," I state boldly, meeting his gaze head-on. "She's got all the appeal of a rotting corpse."

The King's eyes flare, but amusement glints behind them. "Watch yourself, slave. Explain why you reject her."

Crossing my arms, I let the defiance flow. "Her what? You mean that disgusting display she puts on? I'd rather drink piss than look at her. My loyalty? It's already spoken for—it belongs to someone far away from this shithole."

Alinar studies me curiously. "You find my wife unappealing? Or perhaps your tastes run... elsewhere?" His lip curls in disgust.

Amara scoffs bitterly. "As if a soulless monster like you understands anything about loyalty or devotion. You vampires screw like animals, loyal only to yourselves."

I spin on her, my control shattering. "What the hell would some spoiled palace queen like you know about my people? You're completely clueless, drowning in nothing but your own excess."

Her slap cracks across my face hard, and my head snaps back. But when I lock eyes with her again, pure contempt blazes in my gaze—no pain, just pure disdain.

I don't hit women—but this bitch is pushing me to my limit.

Alinar looks more intrigued than offended by my balls. "Still a defiant bastard. But we'll fix that eventually."

"Do your worst," I dare recklessly, "but I'll never grovel or play the obedient pet for your entertainment."

I grit my teeth and force myself to stay calm; it's all about timing, not losing my shit. I repeat this mantra in my head like a prayer, keeping myself together.

I can see Alinar's expression shift to pissed-off surprise mixed with a smirk. Maybe they've finally found their match—a guy who won't bow down or back off, no matter what sick games they throw at me. Let's see who breaks first—it sure as hell won't be me.

Finally, Alinar waves a dismissive hand. "Throw him back in his cell. A few more days of starving on his pride ought to change his mind."

I start to leave, taking slow breaths.

"Wait!" Amara demands, stopping me cold. "I want to know who this person is that's got your head so twisted up." She pauses, staring me down, black shadows creeping toward me. "I can't compel you, which is infuriating, but I have other ways to get what I want."

I halt, fighting back a growl. This bitch thinks she can demand my secrets like they belong to her?

"None of your fucking business," I snap coldly. I step closer, glaring down at her.

Alinar looks mildly amused by my audacity. "Come now. No need to be rude. Surely you can tell my generous wife what she wants to know?"

I bare my lengthening fangs at his mocking tone. "Your 'generous' wife can go fuck herself. I answer to no one here."

Amara gasps in outrage. Alinar chuckles. "Seems the dog still has some bite. He might actually prove entertaining."

I crack a cold grin at the steaming queen. I'm coiled like a spring, desperate for a fight. But I keep my cool, eyes hard as ice. Amara's shaking with rage, her eyes shooting daggers like she's picturing my death.

But I don't give a shit about this second-rate royal's tantrum.

"You'll regret talking to me like that," she seethes.

"The only thing I regret is wasting my time in the presence of your disgusting face."

"Get this cur out of my sight!" Amara shrieks at her guards.

As they grab my arms, I wrench free without effort. My patience is hanging by a thread—violence is right there at the surface, ready to explode at the smallest spark.

I glare at Alinar, acting like his enraged wife doesn't even exist. "I'm done with these games. Either kill me or let me and my brother walk out of here. Stop wasting my time with this bullshit."

Amara moves to hit me again, too furious to think straight. But Alinar stops her without a word. Interest and amusement dance in his crystalline eyes. Maybe I've found the smarter of the two monarchs—someone I can actually work with.

"You're testing me, vampire," the King warns smoothly. But beneath the threat, curiosity simmers.

I offer a mocking bow. "Then we're even, *Your Highness.*"

Alinar's lips crack into a grin, barely holding back a laugh. When the King spots a real contender, he knows it. That's when the first real possibility of an alliance starts to take shape.

Alinar snorts, turning to his wife. "Why do you care? It's not like this female or his mate is wandering around our realm. We'd know by now."

Amara keeps staring at me sharply. "Yes, perhaps you're right," she mutters, though doubt still lingers in her eyes.

The thought of Erik's face hits me hard, and a chill runs through me. I pray he got smart and got the hell out with Dani instead of trying some stupid rescue mission. But Erik, that stubborn bastard, doesn't always think things through.

The possibility of him trying to break us out... no way. He wouldn't drag Dani into danger like that—not intentionally. But the doubt is eating at me raw. Erik swore to protect Dani, but his need to watch my back might override his common sense. The fear of that happening is like a shadow I can't shake.

Not noticing my spiral of anxiety, Amara breaks the tense silence. Turning back to me, she adds with acid in her voice, "I'll be calling for you later, pet. We have plenty to... discuss."

DANICA

9

I wake up with a jackhammer going off behind my eyes—thanks a lot, fancy fae wine. I groan and drag myself upright, pressing my palms to my temples like that's somehow going to fix this headache. Mental note: their alcohol is basically liquid dynamite.

I stumble out of bed and freeze. There's an outfit laid out on the trunk—all leather and straps like someone dressed me for a dominatrix convention instead of a diplomatic mission to save my mate.

We're talking skin-tight leather pants, a leather top that's more straps than actual fabric with my entire midriff exposed, and thigh-high boots that scream "don't mess with me." Subtle, Axilya. Real subtle.

Whoever put this together clearly believes in the "shock and awe" approach to fashion. Or maybe just awe. Preferably of my cleavage.

I groan again and drag myself through the necessities—taking care of my most urgent basic need—before reluctantly squeezing into these leather death traps. The pants feel like they're painted on, and the top is basically a series of strategic straps that barely qualify as support. I feel like a sausage in casing.

I catch my reflection and wince. This is about as far from my normal lab coat look as you can get.

I push through the curtain into the main tent space. Erik's huddled in the corner, staying away from any stray sunlight streaming through gaps. It's been two days since he fed. As much as this sucks, we need each other right now, and I'm not letting him waste away on my watch.

I march over and thrust my wrist at him. "Okay, drink. Now. Before you get any weaker."

Erik literally turns his head away, his lips pressed into this stubborn line. "I will not feed from my brother's mate. It violates sacred law."

"Stop being a dramatic idiot," I say, exasperation bleeding through. "You need blood."

Erik keeps refusing even though it's been literal days. My frustration is climbing fast. I put my hands on my hips. "What, you want me to slice my wrist open and pour it into a fancy goblet for you? Is that less offensive to your vampire honor code?"

One silver eyebrow shoots up at my sarcasm, but he's clearly not budging, no matter how much his stomach probably hurts.

I actually admire his principles most of the time. Right now? I want to strangle him. "Erik, think about this logically. You're useless to me—to both of us—if you're too weak to function," I say urgently. "Just one feeding. Get your strength back. We'll figure out a different solution after that." I extend my wrist again, this time with a more teasing tone. "Come on, you know you're dying for it."

Erik's eyes lock onto my wrist like a predator spotting prey, and I catch a flash of his fangs. But then he forces himself to look away, his voice coming out harsh. "Do not make light of this. You tempt the beast within."

I sigh so hard my shoulders sag. "I'm not trying to be seductive or whatever. You literally need to eat, Erik. I know you've got control." I hold his uncomfortable gaze, putting everything I've got into my next words. "I trust you. Completely." I need him to get that. "We're a team now—we're in this together. So please stop starving yourself because of some honor code. It's not helping either of us, and it's going to get us killed."

"Your faith means more than you know, Little One. But I cannot take from my brother's mate in this way. Accept my stubbornness in this regard." A small smile appears. "Besides, I've weathered far worse than a little hunger."

No matter what I throw at him, Erik's stubbornness is basically immovable. I've been going in circles with this guy for what feels like forever, and I'm getting nowhere. Eventually, I just... give up. I'm frustrated, but honestly? There's a part of me that respects the hell out of his conviction. So here we are—him being all noble and refusing food, me wrestling with magic that doesn't cooperate, and both of us being absolutely ridiculous about it.

I'm literally about to just slice my own wrist open when Faderyn strides in with this big bag slung over his shoulder. His normally bright eyes look worried as he takes in how bad Erik looks—pale, drawn, tense. He turns to me, and his voice goes all gentle, like he's offering a life raft. "May I propose an alternative?" When I nod eagerly, he pulls out what's basically a syringe. "If you allow me to extract your blood into this container, Erik could feed without compromising his principles."

Oh, thank God, exactly what I was about to MacGyver myself. I nod immediately.

Erik considers my compromise with grudging acceptance. "You allowed this once before, you stubborn ass. Don't hesitate now."

Erik scoffs. "That was only because your mate was present and permitted me to drink of you."

I think about that for a minute, and I'm surprised. "Wait, so you have to have Rhyland's permission to drink my blood?"

Erik nods. "Among vampires, a mate's consent must be given before taking blood from their chosen."

"Huh. You guys have some weird customs," I say dryly. "It's my blood. I should have the final say on who drinks it."

Erik shakes his head. "You know little of our ways yet, Little One, but you will learn in time."

I sigh, accepting that arguing vampire politics is a waste of time right now. "Fine, just stop being so damn stubborn about this. Rhyland trusted you to watch my back. So take what you need to stay functional and call it even."

I stare at the equipment Faderyn's laid out on the table. There's a needle and plastic tubing that looks straight out of a horror film, plus some glass vials. This is definitely not the sterile medical setup I'm used to. "Okay, you have got to be joking," I say flatly.

Faderyn catches my expression and smiles reassuringly. "I assure you, this causes no harm. But the decision rests with you."

I let out this long, suffering sigh. "Yeah, I'm not exactly thrilled about this setup. This looks like something straight out of a mad scientist's basement." I pick up the needle carefully, examining the sharp point and what looks like rust spots on the metal. Just looking at it makes my stomach turn. "Any chance we could modernize this and use an actual medical syringe?" I ask dryly. When Faderyn just looks confused, I shake my head. "Never mind. Let's just do this before I chicken out."

I reluctantly stretch my arm across the stone table, making a point not to look at the needle.

I don't love this situation, but I trust Faderyn enough to get through it. If this gets Erik fed, I can survive a little medieval bloodletting. That doesn't mean I have to enjoy getting stabbed with ancient equipment. "Just make it fast," I mutter through clenched teeth. Fingers crossed I don't get some weird infection from this...

Faderyn's touch is surprisingly gentle as he slides the needle into my vein, and I watch the red fluid flow through the tube into the glass. It barely stings—the guy definitely knows what he's doing. He pulls the needle out and presses a cloth to the puncture. "Done," he says respectfully, offering the now-full glass to Erik with a small bow. "Please, regain your strength, friend."

Erik's pale eyes widen slightly at being called "friend." But hunger wins out pretty fast. He takes the glass with quiet gratitude. "You honor me, Dani. I won't forget this sacrifice."

He drinks it down, and color starts flooding back into his face almost immediately. Watching him go from pale and exhausted to looking halfway human again? It's like someone just lifted a weight off my chest.

I turn to Faderyn and squeeze his arm. "Seriously, thank you. For understanding what Erik needs and for actually helping instead of being weird about it. You're good people." I throw in a playful wink.

His response is completely sincere. "You will never face your battles alone, Dani. Now, shall we begin your training?"

I glance over at Erik, and relief floods through me, seeing the color actually back in his cheeks. The guy looks human again instead of like a ghost. It's crazy how fast a single transfusion worked.

He's standing in the sunlight streaming through the tent opening—absolutely glowing in the natural light, which completely contradicts everything the legends say about vampires and sunlight.

I can't help but smile at him warmly. "You look a million times better. How are you feeling?"

His pale eyes meet mine with genuine gratitude. "Much improved, Little One. I owe you my thanks."

I can't resist giving his arm a playful nudge. "Hey, anytime you need more, just say the word. I'm apparently premium vintage."

Erik actually laughs—this deep, rumbling sound that's weirdly comforting. "Rhyland's going to lose his mind over this," he says, almost embarrassed. "I'm going to catch hell for it."

I turn to face him fully, my voice steady and firm. "I've got this. Consider it handled."

Erik's uncertainty flickers across his face, but he eventually nods, though it's clearly not confident.

"And if Rhyland even *thinks* about giving you shit over this," I continue, my voice sharp as a blade, "he's going to have to deal with me. You followed protocol perfectly and showed incredible restraint. If he tries to make you feel guilty about some ancient vampire rule, we're going to have words."

A half-smile plays at Erik's mouth. "You're either very brave or very foolish to confront your mate's temper that way. Let's hope it doesn't come to that."

I straighten up stubbornly. "It won't. Rhyland will understand you did what I basically forced you to do out of necessity."

I notice Faderyn watching Erik with this curious expression. "So it's actually true? You can stand in direct sunlight without being affected?" He sounds impressed but confused. "How is that even possible?"

I shrug. "Being made of pure light apparently comes with some perks."

Faderyn's emerald eyes go wide. "That's... remarkable," he says quietly. "Your abilities are far deeper than I comprehended, Dani."

I smile, knowing that this power feels like a burden most of the time, but if it protects my guys, that's worth something.

Faderyn smoothly shifts gears. "Shall we go?"

He gestures toward the forest with an encouraging smile and leads the way.

RHYLAND

10

I'm burning off nervous energy, pacing this gilded prison, searching every inch for some way out—any weakness I can exploit.

The room is drowning in excess, packed with exotic furnishings that scream money and power. Plush rugs and intricate tapestries cover every surface, designed to impress but leaving a sour taste in my mouth. In the far corner sits a bed massive enough to sleep a damn army, draped in silk sheets that reek of depravity. The lighting is some twisted fae magic, casting an eerie glow that makes my skin crawl. I hate everything about this place, and the second I'm free, I'm burning it all to ash.

This goddamn collar locked around my neck is a constant reminder of how trapped I am. No magic, no way out. I'm stuck playing by the queen's sick rules.

A soft knock at the door, and I'm instantly on edge. The door cracks open, and in slips that small Fae girl—the same one from before.

She sets down the decanter of blood on a table without making a sound, gives me a quick curtsy, her eyes locked on the floor. But then she steps closer, her voice barely above a whisper, "Good day, My Lord. I'm Meadow."

I acknowledge her with a nod, keeping my arms crossed. "Yeah, okay. So you're here to help me get out of this hellhole, right?"

She raises a finger to her lips, a sharp "Shhh," her big brown doe eyes full of anxiety.

From the next room over, Lucian quips, "Hey, brother, try not to lose your mind in there. We don't need your excitement bleeding through the walls, you know?"

I ignore him and focus on Meadow. "Stop hesitating and talk. What's your plan?" My voice barely rises above a whisper.

Meadow lifts her gaze, determination flashing in her eyes. "In the eastern library, there's a book that can break the queen's spell on you. Sneak in there when the castle's asleep tonight, and I'll have the spells decoded to free you."

I let out a harsh laugh, but beneath the scorn, a spark of hope ignites. "I'm locked in this room, remember? The queen will have my head if she catches me wandering around."

I throw the words out quietly, heavy with doubt.

Lucian calls out from the next room, "What, did your balls get put in storage? Come on, fortune favors the bold—and she's definitely worth the risk!"

I throw a murderous glare at the wall—might as well be screaming at stone for all the good it does—then turn back to Meadow. "And why the hell can't you grab the damn book yourself? You clearly know this place inside and out."

Meadow smirks. "Trust me, I have my ways. A special potion will keep the guards knocked out cold until sunrise. But grabbing the book itself? That's on you. It's sitting on a shelf too high for me to reach."

We keep our voices down, barely audible. I study her, noting how small she is.

Letting out a long breath, I level a hard look at her. "I'm not convinced yet. Your story's pushing my patience to the limit. But pull this off tonight, show me you're not full of shit, and maybe this insane plan might actually work."

Meadow lifts her chin. "I just want to fix the wrongs plaguing this realm."

My doubts are still there, but they're starting to crack. Meadow's got guts—she might be exactly what I need to get the hell out of here.

A mix of desperation and the thrill of screwing with the queen stirs inside me. "Alright. We'll try your plan tonight. But listen—if this is a trap, you're going to regret ever meeting me." The threat comes out in a low growl, sharp as broken glass.

Victory flashes in Meadow's eyes, and her voice drops to an excited whisper. "When night falls, you'll be free from these chains."

Staring down at Meadow, I can't help asking out loud. "What's in it for you? Why risk your neck for me?"

Meadow holds my gaze steady. "I have my reasons. Your freedom means more than just you getting out—it's hope for everyone the queen has crushed."

I search her face for any sign of deception, but all I see is genuine conviction and real courage. She knows the risks, but she's willing to take them for something bigger than both of us. That kind of sacrifice gets through my defenses.

"People don't usually throw themselves into the fire for someone they don't even know—especially not for a vampire," I say slowly. "You're either incredibly brave, completely insane, or dead set on taking down the queen."

Meadow straightens up. "I follow my instincts and accept whatever comes."

My guard drops slightly, doubt fading. But trust? That's a different animal, and I'm not there yet.

She takes a deep breath, opens her mouth, then closes it like she's wrestling with her words. I shift impatiently, arms crossed over my chest. "My family was taken from me, and because... I have visions," she hesitates. "I've seen you in them, freeing this realm from darkness."

I keep my expression neutral, trying to dig deeper. "You see anything else when these visions happen?"

"Just one thing—light," Meadow says back.

Her words send off alarm bells in my head. Could her sight be connected to the mission Dani and I are on? Is there a link to the prophecy we're hunting for?

I let out the breath I didn't know I was holding, relieved Meadow seems clueless about Dani's significance.

She's not acting; she's the real deal. I straighten up, her talk of visions catching my attention. "Does the queen know about your... abilities?" I ask quietly.

Meadow shakes her head. "She thinks I'm just a rebellious servant. My visions are something I keep locked down tight."

If Meadow's been using her visions without the queen knowing, that takes serious guts. It tells me she's truly invested in this. And if the queen's in the dark, we've got a secret advantage.

My usual suspicion eases—breaking out isn't just personal anymore; it's crucial to the bigger picture.

Meadow's proving herself worth having as an ally. "Those visions might be exactly what we need to turn this around," I tell her. I lean down, my stare locked on hers. "Okay, Mouse. We'll do this your way. But let's be clear—it better work. I'm done sitting in this hellhole playing the captive in this twisted nightmare."

Her grin flashes bright as she nods with confidence. "You have my word. When night falls, you'll be free."

She gives a quick curtsy, then slips out, probably getting ready for tonight. If this blows up in our faces, we're both screwed, but I'm willing to bet everything on this shot.

Lucian murmurs with dry humor, "Can I get a fucking amen? It's seriously time we get the hell out of this cesspool."

I continue pacing, feeling restless. "Assuming Meadow's plan isn't a trap by the queen," I mutter darkly.

With a sneer, Lucian retorts, "Shocker, Mr. Sunshine is all clouds today. What'd you do, pawn your sense of adventure? I don't see anyone else willing to help us out of this fae *pornucopia*."

Despite myself, a smile quirks up. "I'll leave the boldness to your reckless ass. I prefer keeping my head firmly attached."

Lucian scoffs, "Oh, that's rich, brother. The gratitude is just overwhelming here. Let's not forget who's pulled your ass out of the fire a time or two."

His jab hits a nerve, triggering a flashback—Lucian, charging into that bunker, facing off with the Shadow Brotherhood to drag Erik and me out. He didn't bat an eye at the danger. A flicker of thanks warms me, but I crush it. Lucian's ego doesn't need more fuel. We're bound by blood, but we knock heads just as often as we have each other's backs—his wiseass mouth never fails to light my fuse.

I let out a snort, covering up the churn inside. "Sure, sure. Just remember, if this goes sideways, we're up to our necks in it together."

The image of Dani flickers in my head, and I reach for her—through our connection. But I hit a wall—nothing. A string of curses flies from my lips. It's been days since I felt her pulse in my veins, and it's screwing with my head. This connection—it's like a fuse burning down, and with each moment we're separated, I'm edging closer to losing it.

My control is fraying, and my temper flares like wildfire. I need Dani's calming touch. I'm teetering on the edge; if I drop, it'll be straight into fury and chaos.

She's got to be feeling this, too, right? Is she out there, fighting her own demons? What if this distance is gnawing away at what keeps us grounded?

"Get your shit together, Rhy," Lucian snarls from the other room. "You're losing it, and I don't know shit about this mate crap. But if what they say is true, buckle up, or I'll kick your ass to next Tuesday."

This isolation's eating at me, but I can't let it twist my head. I can't drown in rage and panic—not if I plan to hold Dani again. I've got to play smart, keep my cool. It's wits over brawn.

And when I do reach her—when we're finally side by side—come hell or high water, no force in this world or the next will have the balls to split us up again.

DANICA

11

We weave through the bustling encampment as everyone's going about their morning routines. Faderyn stops at a stall where a woman is selling fresh-baked goods, and my stomach immediately betrays me with this loud, obnoxious growl. The smell hits me like a wall—yeast, sugar, honey—and my mouth starts watering like I'm Pavlov's dog.

Between the wine last night and basically starving myself through the blood donation this morning, I'm absolutely ravenous. My stomach growls again, loud enough that I'm pretty sure the entire encampment heard it, and Faderyn gives me this amused look.

Faderyn pays the vendor and hands me this warm bun covered in cinnamon and drizzled with honey. "Eat. You're going to need the energy for today," he says encouragingly.

I attack that bun like it personally wronged me, making this embarrassing sound of pure bliss. The dough basically dissolves on my tongue, and the honey is just... *chef's kiss*.

Erik watches my completely unsubtle enjoyment with this smirk like he's found the whole thing hilarious. Faderyn grabs himself some kind of fruit pastry and keeps us moving.

Once I'm licking the last of the honey off my fingers, I ask hopefully, "Have we heard anything from Axilya yet?"

Faderyn shakes his head, taking a bite of his breakfast. "Patience is necessary. She will honor her commitment, but these things take time through proper channels."

I sigh and accept it. He's not wrong—stressing about it won't speed things up. But the impatience is definitely still there, gnawing at me.

Faderyn notices me stressing and adds gently, "Let's redirect that nervous energy into your training. Your magic is still volatile, but if you can learn to control it, you'll have real power."

He's right. Ever since I got here, my abilities have been turned up to maximum. Right now, they're like this live wire under my skin—chaotic, demanding, completely unpredictable in a way that's brand new. This realm amplifies everything, or maybe the gaping hole Rhyland's absence left has screwed with my balance. Either way, the result is the same: I need to get control of this wild energy before it controls me.

Faderyn leads us into this quiet grove surrounded by these massive, ancient trees. Sunlight filters through the leaves in these dappled patterns, creating this peaceful, calm atmosphere—basically the perfect place to focus.

"Magic in this realm flows directly from nature itself," Faderyn explains as we stop. "Living energy from the world around us feeds and stabilizes power. This place is saturated with ancient protective magic—the earth itself heals here. That's why we train among the trees and soil. They'll anchor you."

I press my palm against this ancient oak tree, feeling every groove and ridge in the bark like I'm reading braille. Under my hand, I can sense the tree's heartbeat—this steady, patient rhythm that's been going on for centuries. Faderyn's totally right. Just touching this tree calms the chaos inside me.

I close my eyes and let myself sink into the forest symphony—leaves rustling, wind whispering secrets, the earthy smell of the forest floor wrapping around me. For just a moment, all my stress and anxiety melt away. I'm completely present, completely grounded.

When I open my eyes, Faderyn's smiling at me. "There—you felt it. That connection, that shared life force. Magic here isn't a weapon, it's a collaboration," he says seriously. "I believe in you, Dani. Remember this: power flows easily when you let it, not when you force it."

His confidence gives me this surge of energy. I take a deep breath and pull my scattered thoughts together. Yeah, okay. I can do this. I nod at him decisively. If Faderyn thinks I can actually control this mess, then I'm game. Master this magic, and I'm not just a liability to my team—I become their secret weapon.

Let's go. Time to level up and become the powerhouse I'm supposed to be.

Two hours pass, and I'm still basically fighting myself. When I need to go big—boom, instant fireworks. But try to use some actual finesse? That's a hard no. I'm a walking hazard, and the local trees can testify to that. They've got the scorch marks to prove it.

And then there's the time I almost turned Faderyn into toast with an accidental light grenade. He managed to dodge, but barely.

The weird thing about this forest is that it heals itself instantly. Trees, plants, everything just bounces back as if nothing happened—ancient magic protecting the place. Which is great for the environment, terrible for my ego since the evidence of my destruction keeps disappearing.

At least Faderyn's staying chill about all this. But I need to get my act together fast. If I keep throwing around uncontrolled blasts, I'm basically committing environmental terrorism.

"Let it flow naturally from deep inside you, like you're just exhaling," Faderyn instructs. "Feel it wake up, then release it gently."

Okay, deep breaths. *Focus.* Feel that warmth building. Be the light. Oh my God, did I seriously just think that? So cringe.

I take this centering breath and hold my palm out toward the target—this simple bullseye painted on a boulder. I picture the light gathering in my core, then gently flowing outward. A soft shimmer starts forming in my hand. I coax it carefully, feeling it grow... building... building... It's actually working!

Then the boulder explodes.

Fuck. This is going to take literally forever. I'm basically a walking nuclear weapon.

Discouragement crashes over me. Erik's standing close by, keeping watch. He's giving me space to concentrate, but his presence is solid, reassuring. He's leaning casually against a tree, but his eyes never stop scanning the woods. The guy's always on alert.

"You're getting closer—I felt it shift that time," Faderyn says, squeezing my shoulder. "Magic fights back when you try to force it. You have to convince it, not command it."

I swallow down my frustration and push myself to try again. Maybe I'm thinking about this wrong. I'm trying to use power like a weapon, but actual control is about working together, not dominating.

"These abilities aren't meant for destruction—they're about protection and preservation," he explains gently.

Okay, so I seriously need to figure out how to control this explosive light before I accidentally torch the entire realm or permanently blind someone. No big deal! Deep breaths... feel the glow... guide it... and oh look, tree number four is on fire.

Nailed it. Ugh, this is gonna take some work.

"This is useless," I admit, defeated.

"No, it's not. Again," Faderyn insists.

I close my eyes and sink into this meditative state, then carefully wake up the light inside me. Heat builds, but I let it rise slowly, imagining it flowing smoothly from my center outward. The warmth grows, then suddenly flows out in this controlled glow that hits the target dead-on. I hold it for just a second before pulling it back.

"Perfect," Faderyn says, clearly excited.

I feel this rush of accomplishment—I actually did it! But then exhaustion hits like a truck. My legs feel weak, and I gratefully take the waterskin Faderyn hands me. Erik's got this proud smile on his face, giving me this approving nod that means way more than it should.

"Good work, Little One," he says seriously.

But I'm frustrated despite the win. One successful attempt and I'm already wiped out. Faderyn notices and squeezes my shoulder. "Today was huge. Control is the hardest part to master. We're talking years of practice. But you've started the journey."

"Why am I so exhausted from using my powers? Back home, I never got drained like this," I say, frustration creeping back in.

Faderyn takes a moment to think. "The raw magic in this realm amplifies your abilities, but it also demands more energy to channel properly. It's like running a super-powerful electrical current through a device designed for regular voltage. Your human body wasn't built to handle this intensity of magic."

Erik jumps in with his own take. "I think it's also because you need that Faerite stone to properly channel magic here. The crown—" He points at my head. "—remember what Seraphina told you about the stones? They're supposed to help you tap into the realm's power without burning yourself out. Without one, you're basically a live wire trying to handle way too much current." He pauses, his expression getting serious. "And the broken mate bond is making it worse. It's like an open wound draining your reserves. Rhyland's supposed to stabilize you, help regulate your power. Without him, everything just bleeds out faster."

He's right. Seraphina warned me about this—Rhyland acts like some kind of anchor for my abilities. Alone, they're chaos, burning through me like wildfire.

Faderyn nods in agreement. "Precisely. Your mortal form is struggling to adapt to unfiltered magic. But with practice and training, you can build your stamina." He gives me an encouraging smile.

My brain is literally having a full meltdown. My powers are acting up, Rhyland's missing, and I'm on this insane treasure hunt for magical stones—it's a complete disaster with no clear way out. And I hate feeling powerless. It's like running in place on a treadmill while wearing stilettos—totally useless.

I'm a scientist! I need data, a solid hypothesis, something I can actually analyze and reason through. But instead, I'm stuck on this emotional roller coaster with zero control and nowhere to direct all this built-up energy. My abilities are having a tantrum, I'm having a tantrum—it's just tantrums all the way down.

I'm basically a pressure cooker about to explode. I'm pacing back and forth like a caged animal, my mind spinning uselessly, running on the hamster wheel but not getting anywhere. This whole "just wait and see" thing? Not my style. I'm built to solve problems, not sit around like some damsel in a gothic novel, drowning in my own chaos. I need control. I need answers. Instead, I'm chewing on questions like they're stress toys.

Faderyn sees me spiraling and grabs my shoulder. "Patience, Dani. Axilya will deliver. We need to give her plan time to work."

Erik watches me carefully, his expression shifting to concern. "Your emotions are getting out of hand, Little One," he says quietly. "This separation from your mate is hitting harder than you're admitting. You need to get a grip before this blows up in your face."

His calm, steady voice actually helps. I take a breath and nod, trying to pull myself back together. "I know. I feel like I'm on this crazy emotional ride and I'm not even holding the wheel."

Erik grunts in agreement. "You might also be picking up on Rhyland's emotional state through the bond."

"Hang in there, Rhyland," I try sending down the bond, but I just hit nothing but silence and darkness.

DANICA

12

After obliterating yet another tree, I'm ready to just lie down and quit. Sweat's pouring down my back, and I'm glaring daggers at Erik.

"Again," he says flatly, completely unmoved by the death stare I'm throwing his way.

"Give me a break!" I snap, wiping the gross, sweaty strands of hair off my face. "We've been doing this literally all day. I'm completely wiped, Erik. At this point, we might as well just torch the whole forest," I mutter, staring at the smoking remains of yet another tree. That's four in under three hours. I'm sweating, exhausted, and fucking sick of blowing up trees.

"You need to control your magic before it controls you," Erik says like I haven't figured that out on my own. I shoot him and Faderyn both a look that could kill before turning back to the tree.

"Focus, Dani," Faderyn says calmly.

Yeah, thanks, Yoda. Super helpful.

I focus, feeling the magic surge through me, then let loose with a single blast. The tree explodes into splinters, wood flying everywhere, and Erik just sighs quietly.

"Again," he demands. I growl and turn to snap at him, but he's just watching the destroyed tree as a new one grows back in its place.

"Maybe *she* needs an actual break?" I suggest, hopefully, crossing my fingers that he'll actually agree.

Faderyn smirks, and Erik just shakes his head. His eyes soften a little, like he actually gets how tired I am, but his jaw stays set with determination. "You push forward until you master control. Otherwise, your power will own you."

I kick at a charred piece of wood angrily. He's not wrong, and I hate it. One slip-up, one moment of lost control, and someone innocent could get hurt or worse.

I swallow my pride and walk over to the next tree. Faderyn gives me this sympathetic smile and hands me the waterskin. The cool water feels like heaven on my raw throat.

"Perhaps a brief rest would help," Faderyn suggests gently, giving Erik this meaningful look.

Erik's lips press into this thin line before he finally nods. "Thirty minutes maximum. We cannot afford weakness."

I stare at the smoking cedar in absolute misery—my clumsy magic just destroyed it into pieces again.

But before I can spiral into despair, Erik steps forward. "Magic flows from internal willpower and physical strength," he says thoughtfully. "Trying to force it through pure mental effort only weakens your foundation." He gestures at all the destroyed trees around us. "Clearly, we need a different strategy. I suggest we focus on building physical discipline and strength instead."

I look at him skeptically, still dripping sweat. "What, you saying I should hit the gym or something?"

Amusement flickers in Erik's silver eyes. "Not exactly. I'll teach you to access the strength you already possess—speed, reflexes, pure instinct." He circles behind me and grabs my shoulders. "Magic isn't your only weapon in a fight. And you, Little One, have solid instincts buried under years of being civilized."

I tense up, my heart rate jumping as his words hit me. "Wait—you want to train me to fight? Like, kick and punch and stuff?"

Erik smiles, showing just a hint of fang. "Indeed. We shall transform fear into ferocity, chaos into control." His voice drops and gets way too intimate. "Let the warrior awaken..."

A shiver runs through me that has absolutely nothing to do with combat training.

Okay, Dani, get it together. This is Rhyland's brother.

I clear my throat awkwardly and nod. "Right, sign me up for Fight Club 101. Maybe cool it on the whole 'tapping into my wild side' dirty talk there."

Erik looks genuinely confused by my flustered reaction, completely missing the innuendo. Faderyn suddenly becomes very interested in the tree branches above us.

"Very well. Lesson one—evasion," Erik says matter-of-factly.

Without warning, his arm swings toward my head. I jerk back on instinct, my heart nearly jumping out of my chest. His hand stops inches from my face, hovering like a threat. Message received loud and clear.

I laugh nervously, trying to cover my panic with attitude. "Wow, no dinner first? Chivalry really is dead. What's next, you just punch me?"

Erik doesn't react to my jokes at all, just circles me like a predator. "A real fight doesn't wait for politeness. Now, evade me."

He lunges without warning. I jump left, totally caught off guard. His fist grazes my shoulder on the second swing, and I hiss. Maybe taunting a centuries-old vampire warrior isn't my smartest move.

"Faster, Dani!" he orders, not giving me a second to breathe between attacks. I'm running on pure adrenaline now, dodging and weaving around each punch.

Oh shit, he is fast.

"Remember, you're smaller and quicker," Erik says, completely unaffected by our intense sparring. "Use speed and strategy to beat raw power."

As his palm nearly clips my ear, I'm torn between panic and determination. Adrenaline surges as I dodge another strike. Then something shifts—Erik's movements suddenly slow down, like he's moving through molten honey. There's this humming sound from the crown on my head. Without thinking about it, I slide right and watch Erik's reactions lag behind.

What the actual hell?

Time is stretching like taffy, and Erik's basically in slow-motion. I can see every opening before he even moves, my reflexes firing at light speed. It's like someone hit fast-forward on my entire nervous system. I'm moving like a cheetah!

The tingling keeps going at the top of my head, and I glance over to catch Faderyn literally staring at me with his jaw hanging open. Yeah, apparently I'm not your average sparring partner anymore.

Definitely filing that away later...

The world stays slowed, but I'm moving at normal speed—or faster, actually. I'm landing three hits for every one Erik throws. Then all these combat techniques just start flooding into my brain like someone's downloading them straight into my consciousness. It's like my brain became a sponge for fighting moves, soaking up every punch, kick, and block in rapid-fire waves of warrior instinct. I throw an experimental punch that sends Erik sprawling backward.

When he gets up, I can't help myself. "What's wrong, old man? Did Napoleon wear you out back in your day?"

Erik bares his fangs in this feral grin. "The cub has claws! Now the real lesson starts."

He moves forward like a silver blur. I pivot right but totally misjudge his reach. His leg tangles with mine and yanks hard. I hit the ground so fast the air explodes out of my lungs.

I'm gasping like a fish on dry land, glaring up at the smug vampire above me. "That was...a cheap...move...jerkface," I wheeze.

He just crosses his arms, completely unapologetic. "And do you think your enemies will fight fair?"

I grimace as I drag myself up. He's got a point—nobody is going to play nice just because I'm a girl. Real enemies don't follow rules. I set my feet again and motion him forward. "Alright, let's go again."

Erik's grin widens, and he moves in as a silver blur...

He comes at me hard and fast this time, no more holding back now that he knows I'm faster than a normal human. I duck and spin like crazy to avoid the barrage.

I spot an opening and aim a roundhouse kick at his ribs. Erik catches my leg like it's nothing and uses it to flip me onto my back again. All my air escapes for the second time.

"Predictable," he says flatly. "Change your tactics."

I explode backward in a reverse somersault, pushing off with my hands and launching myself upright with my fists ready. "How's this for unpredictable?"

I charge straight at him. Erik braces for impact, but then I just launch into a handspring over his head, my foot lashing out and catching him square in the back as I flip over.

I land perfectly and turn to see Erik stagger for a second. He twists to face me, actually chuckling. "Not bad. You're a quick learner."

We close the distance again, trading a rapid-fire exchange of hits and blocks. Erik's keeping up with my enhanced speed, his preternatural reflexes matching my challenge. I'm throwing everything I've got, but he keeps defending. Only a few of my hits actually get through his guard.

Faderyn watches our intense fight from the sidelines, wincing when Erik dodges my crescent kick and responds with a sweeping move that drops me hard on my back for the third time.

"She perseveres despite lacking a warrior's honed skill," he remarks. "Her spirit shows great promise with training."

I scramble back to my feet, sweat dripping into my eyes. My arms are absolutely burning as I raise them again. Erik just gestures me forward, barely even breathing hard.

"Again, Little Warrior. Your enemies won't give you breaks."

I clench my jaw, nod, and get back into it, ignoring how much my entire body is screaming at me. We keep going as the sun starts getting lower.

The training finally ends only when I literally collapse—too beat up and exhausted to keep standing.

Erik nods with approval despite how pathetic I look. "Well fought. You'll make a true warrior eventually."

I stare at him in disbelief. "How...what...are you seeing the same fight here?" I gesture at myself, covered in dirt and bruises. "I just got my ass completely handed to me like six times!"

Erik shakes his head, smiling slightly. "For one utterly unfamiliar with combat, you moved extraordinarily well. Your reflexes adapt at an unnatural pace. I speak truthfully—few could match your raw potential after just one brief session."

I run a shaky hand through my sweaty hair, my brain trying to process what just happened. "So that whole thing where I turned into a speed demon with ninja moves and time got weird... do you have any theories on what that was?"

Erik thinks for a moment. "I believe it's ancestral power activating. Your dormant magic awakening abilities you didn't know you had."

"Huh..." I reply. "Here I thought poppin' fairy dust and glowing like Vegas was the extent of my weirdness. But I guess Chosen One DNA also chose to toss in Matrix-style bullet-dodging."

I quickly tell them both about the strange time-dilation thing I experienced. Erik rubs his chin, looking intrigued.

"Your celestial bloodline is possibly mixing with vampire traits from bonding with Rhyland. You might be completely unprecedented," he says with a shrug.

I throw my hands up. "Great, so not only am I supercharged with power, but apparently the vampire connection is like fertilizer?"

Erik blinks at my weird metaphors. Faderyn's mouth twitches like he's trying not to laugh.

"Your crude comparison may have some merit," Erik says diplomatically.

I snort and let my aching body collapse on the soft moss. "It's like someone installed a cheat code in me. Next thing I know, I'll sprout adamantium claws or throw lightning bolts..."

Erik tilts his head, frowning. "Claws would offer little tactical advantage for one of your stature... however, daggers would be promising."

I burst into slightly hysterical laughter at Erik completely missing the pop culture reference and being so literal about everything. Training with him is definitely going to be entertaining!

As I'm laughing despite my aching sides, the rush from the fight starts wearing off, leaving me shocked and thoughtful. How did my untrained body just move like some badass assassin? I look down at my shaking hands, and instead of seeing failure, I see potential. It's coursing through me like electricity, looking for somewhere to land.

Yeah, today was basically just a taste—a preview of this dormant powerhouse I've been carrying around without knowing it. But give me time to figure out how to control it, and I'll be unleashing seriously impressive magic and combat skills.

Exhaustion hits hard and fast now that the adrenaline's wearing off. I'm starving and completely wiped out. I gather my stuff, ready to head back to camp.

Faderyn notices how tired I am and steadies me with a hand under my elbow. "You need to eat and rest well once we return. Even the strongest warrior has limits."

I lean into his support gratefully, my legs still shaky. "Does the mess hall have anything decent on the menu tonight?" I ask, hoping. My stomach gives an audible growl at the thought of food. "Maybe mystery meat stew or stale biscuits—either works right now!"

"We shall see the Huntress fed and tended properly," Erik says firmly. "After today's effort, you need proper rest and nutrition."

First priority—ditch this grime-covered couture and peel off these sweat-sodden threads.

I glance back at Erik as we slowly hike toward the camp. "Thanks for actually pushing me hard today," I tell him sincerely. "If you'd gone easy on me during magic training, I'd probably be a pile of ash by now."

Erik gives me a small smile. "You have a warrior's heart, Little One. You needed a chance to discover that."

I pause and look at both of them, feeling genuinely grateful. "Seriously, you guys—thanks for the combat crash course, the encouragement, and putting up with me for hours."

Erik squeezes my shoulder, his silver eyes warm. "I swore an oath to Rhyland to guard you as my own blood. You are a sister to me now, Dani."

My vision goes misty as Erik calls me sister. *Family*—something lost yet somehow found again in this strange realm when I needed it most.

But at the word 'sister,' my heart squeezes with thoughts of my brother in my old world—Damon. Does he know I'm gone? Is he worried? Or does he think I'm dead? And Emily—God, I miss her sarcastic ass so much.

Noticing my mood shift, Erik asks gently, "Something's bothering you, Little Huntress?"

I shake myself out of it and offer him a small smile. "I'm just thinking about my brother Damon. I wonder if I'll ever get to see him again."

Erik squeezes my shoulder again in support. "You will."

RHYLAND

13

This room still stinks like absolute garbage, no matter how much fancy shit they throw at it. The queen can take her silk sheets and cram them straight up her royal ass.

My boots pound heavily on the pristine rugs covering the cold stone. Velvet drapes hang dead over arched windows, blocking out the moonlight. The four-poster bed creaks with every step I take, its silk canopy drooping.

I slam my fist against the stone wall until my knuckles bleed. The pain's nothing compared to being cut off from Dani. Every time I try to reach out through our bond, I hit nothing but silence.

Is she even still alive on the other end?

My mind spins, trying to wrap around this whole mate thing. It's still a complete mystery to me—like I'm wandering around blind, grasping at nothing. I can't shake the question: if something happened to Dani, would I feel it? Wouldn't there be some crushing, devastating sensation that would tell me my other half was in danger?

Being separated from her is worse torture than anything these faerie bastards could throw at me. It's enough to drive a man insane.

The door suddenly shakes hard under the impact of heavy bodies, yanking me out of my head. I freeze, every muscle tense—the queen's guards collapsing.

Lucian's muffled laugh echoes from the next room, his twisted sense of humor getting off on the violence.

About damn time that servant girl's potion plan kicked in! This is our opening to get the hell out of here and find Dani.

The door creaks open, keys jingling, and Meadow rushes inside. "Come on, My Lord! We have to go!"

I pin the faerie with a hard stare. "You're sure those idiots won't wake up?"

Meadow flashes a wicked grin. "But of course! Those dullards are out colder than winter's grasp after the sleeping draught I brewed." She preens proudly. "Why, they'll not wake if the whole west tower came crashing down!"

I grunt, not particularly impressed by her bragging. But she wasn't lying about putting the guards down. This is our shot to escape this hellhole. Once I'm free of this damn collar, I'm going to tear this court apart. And when my rage is unleashed, when it hits like a fucking hurricane, we'll see who's left standing.

I barrel past her, nearly knocking the small girl over in my rush. She yelps, jumping out of the way. Fumbling with her stolen keys, Meadow unlocks Lucian's door next. He explodes out in a blur, stopping inches from her shocked face.

"Boo!" He laughs at her startled shriek. "Easy there, Tinkerbell. No need to wet the fairy dust on my account."

Meadow's expression tightens slightly, though she keeps herself together. "Why do you seem so... different?" she asks, her voice steady but curious, trying to figure out the mystery in front of her.

Lucian bursts out laughing, his eyes sparkling with amusement. "Different? Me? What the hell are you talking about, little fairy?"

I shut him down with a vicious glare. Meadow quickly looks away.

"The library, Mouse," I say sharply. "And move your ass. Dawn's coming, and I've rotted in this shithole long enough."

We slip through the twisted guts of this rotting castle like ghosts. The air is thick and suffocating, reeking of decay hidden beneath all the fancy decorations. No amount of plush rugs or shiny gold can cover up the festering rot at the core of this place.

Ahead, Meadow moves quickly and quietly through the torchlight, slipping between shadows like she's done it a thousand times. When you're enslaved to tyrants, staying invisible becomes second nature.

Lucian trails behind her, chuckling under his breath. He's clearly already imagining the chaos that's about to go down. Violence and destruction always get him going.

Meadow stops at the bottom of a narrow spiral staircase, disappearing into complete darkness above.

"My Lord, the eastern library is up there. The book you need is supposed to be on the top shelf, way in the back—some ancient relic with yellowed pages, wrapped in dragon skin, and held together with tarnished silver clasps."

I hold back a snort. Perfect. Just my rotten fucking luck that some dusty old book too precious to destroy but too dangerous to keep accessible is what's going to save my ass from Amara's grip. Given how my luck's been running, the damn thing will probably fall apart the second I touch it.

Lucian laughs wickedly, thrilled by how absurd this all is. "Well, shit. This just got seriously intense. Our little pixie friend's got a real talent for making things dramatic, doesn't she?"

He grins down at Meadow, waiting for her to bite back. But the small faerie ignores Lucian completely, doesn't even bother glaring at him. Tough little thing—I'll give her that much credit.

Of course, if this entire shit show blows up and lands us chained back in Amara's torture chamber as traitors, I won't hesitate to hand Meadow over to the queen's hellhounds piece by piece. Cold comfort, maybe, but damn satisfying if things go sideways.

"We need to move, My Lord." Meadow's ready to go.

I square my shoulders, forcing myself forward, and start climbing the cramped spiral stairs toward the dusty library above—and hopefully freedom. We reach the top of the twisting stairwell and step into a shadow-filled hallway. My eyes adjust quickly to the darkness. The only sound is our footsteps echoing off the stone. The stench up here is suffocating—like breathing in decades of dust and death.

Moments later, my hand lands on the library's weathered oak door. I push hard on the heavy doors, and the smell of books hits me—old paper, ink, and centuries of history all mixed together. My boots scrape against the marble floor as I stride into the massive library. I see a staircase to my left leading up.

We climb the stairs, and a question finally forces its way out. I shoot Meadow a hard look that nearly makes her stumble. "You said you've seen me in your visions. So lay it out—what exactly did you see?"

Meadow glances away uncomfortably before answering. "Forgive me, but I have seen you many nights in my prophetic dreams... a great warrior surrounded by otherworldly fire, destroying endless darkness." She nervously fidgets with her torn hem. "There's always a presence behind you—blinding with light. I don't know what it means, only that you stand at the center of The Light, My Lord."

Even though she's clearly hinting at Dani's celestial powers, I keep my expression locked down. Better if this girl stays clueless about my mate's importance.

Lucian's mocking snort comes from behind. "Well, well, the brooding warrior with a spotlight. Gotta suck trying to find a dark corner to perfect that whole moody thing, huh?"

I throw Lucian a brutal glare and keep climbing, his laughter echoing behind me.

She hesitates before continuing shakily. "The visions... I have seen lightning rip across the sky above you, My Lord. Thunder crashes through the heavens... a powerful hammer."

I stop dead, pinning the faerie with a stare sharp enough to cut. She shrinks back under my gaze. She's got serious balls bringing up my ancestors—legends that have been dust in people's minds for centuries. Her words send ice down my spine.

How the hell does this tiny thing know to drop references to ancient Norse thunder gods? Is it just a coincidence that she's pulling these old myths out of nowhere, or is there something real to these "visions"?

Or maybe the little seer's got her signals mixed up—confusing who I am with Dani's divine power. "What's this? Are you just making up old stories in your sleep, Mouse? Since when did you become an expert on Thunder Gods?"

Meadow squirms as we stop on the landing, her fingers tangled in her braid, showing exactly how stressed she is. "I'm sorry, My Lord. It's just... these visions are broken pieces—like a puzzle I can't put together," she stammers out. She falters under my hard stare. "It's just... there's so much godly power and chaos around you... lightning and fury."

I stop dead, my glare crushing down on her small frame. "Sounds like your visions are getting their wires crossed, Mouse. You're rambling about my Norse ancestry, and that's it. Nothing more." Meadow opens her mouth to argue, but I cut her off. We don't have time to waste on pointless debates about her fairy-tale nonsense.

I lock eyes with her, dead serious. "Listen, where I come from, we've got legends about badass gods—you ever hear of Thor? God of Thunder and all that crap. But let's be clear—I'm not him. I'm not some godly being," I say, my voice hard as stone.

Meadow pulls at her braid, twisting it anxiously. "But My Lord, the visions—"

"Done. Keep your eyes on the prize, Mouse," I bark, cutting through her words like a knife. My patience is wearing thin. We need to grab that cursed book and get the hell out of this shithole, not stand around chasing her delusions.

Meadow drops her head, properly shut down, and leads us deeper into the library's maze toward what we came for. But inside my head, everything's spinning—thoughts crashing around like a storm.

Lucian, being his usual charming pain in the ass, pipes up, "Oh damn, somebody got a godly promotion to Thunder God! This is hilarious. So do you get the hammer and cape with the job, or what?"

His comment gets cut short by my icy glare. Meadow's eyes flick nervously between us as I force urgency into my voice. "Cut the bullshit." Then my eyes dart to Meadow. "Where's the damn book that's supposed to get us out of this hag's claws?"

We stop in front of a massive shelf, and my stomach drops. Even with vampire strength, climbing this thing won't be easy. It towers up at least fifteen feet, deliberately designed to keep things out of reach. And the grimoire sits inside a locked glass case on top of everything else. Because grabbing an unguarded book would be too fucking simple.

I can't use my telekinesis—it's locked down tight behind this cursed collar's magic. So here I am, stuck doing manual labor like some regular human without any powers at all.

I curse under my breath at this particular brand of hell, then take a few steps back, tensing my muscles. I've got no choice but to do this the hard way. I break into a sprint, launching myself with every ounce of strength I've got, climbing with brutal force and deadly precision.

As I climb, the temperature drops, and each push upward fights against the cold. When my hand finally smashes through the glass barrier that never had a chance, and I grab the grimoire's silver and leather binding, a savage grin spreads across my face. No time to celebrate—I hurl the book down. "Heads up!" The word's barely out before the grimoire's falling toward the hands below.

Meadow yelps, scrambling to catch the falling book. But Lucian, that attention-seeking bastard—always needing to be the center of attention—he's there in a flash, snatching the book with a smug grin, already flipping through the pages like he's the one who climbed that damn shelf.

"Oh, we got ourselves a couple of badasses! Stealing forbidden loot and redecorating the palace? James Dean would be so proud of you, little rebels!"

I barely hold back a growl as I slide down the massive bookshelf. "Shut your mouth before I rearrange your face."

Freedom is right there in those crumbling pages... just as soon as my legs remember how to work.

I hit the ground, teeth bared in a feral grin of triumph. The spellbook we've been hunting is finally in our hands—my ticket out of this enchanted collar.

I lock eyes with Meadow. "Find the countercurse, Mouse," I command, nodding toward the grimoire trembling in her grasp. She's staring at that worn cover like she's in some kind of trance, completely fixated.

"I-I've waited so long just to glimpse this forbidden knowledge! Never did I dare dream I would one day unlock such vast power!" Meadow whispers reverently, stroking the tome.

Lucian inspects his nails with an exaggerated eye roll and lets out a dramatic sigh. "Bra-vo. Now work that magical shit fast, yeah? Unless you want to go back to wearing those stylish iron bracelets."

Meadow nods sharply, flipping through the yellowed pages with careful urgency. The musty parchment crackles loudly in the quiet library. "One moment."

The seconds crawl by like hours. "Take your time. I'll just wander around, maybe check out the naughty section while I'm waiting. I'm sure nobody will mind if I borrow a few more forbidden books—OOF!"

Lucian's smart-ass mouth gets shut down fast by my elbow driving hard into his ribs. Trying not to smile, Meadow shakes her head and goes back to decoding the ancient text, silent as death.

"This inscription—" She points to a spell in the book. "I think this is the runic spell that binds both your collars!" Meadow says excitedly.

My heart suddenly starts racing as I lean over her shoulder.

About fucking time!

"You positive you can reverse the binding magic, Mouse?" I demand harshly.

She meets my stare without flinching this time. "The counter-ritual is complicated, but yes... if I study it carefully, I can break your collars."

Meadow's promise to free us ignites hot hope... then doubt crashes right back down.

"Study it carefully? What the hell does that mean, Mouse? We don't have time for you to sit here like you're cramming for an exam."

Panic spreads across Meadow's pale face. She opens her mouth, but only a shaky sound comes out.

Lucian drags both hands down his face dramatically. "Well, isn't this just fucky luck? Little Miss Brainiac needs a study break before unscrambling fae witchcraft shit..." He rounds on Meadow, eyes a storm. "Here's some math for you, flower—we've got about twenty damn minutes before Mistress Crowned Sadist starts wondering why her boy toys haven't come crawling back to heel yet."

Amara loves her late-night entertainment, and Lucian's nailing it. She'll come looking for us soon.

I fix Meadow with a hard stare, barely keeping it together, and let out a low snarl. "Timeline, Mouse. No bullshit—how long until you break this spell?"

Her throat bobs. "A-at least an hour... maybe longer... I'm sorry!"

I explode, spinning around and driving my fist through the old shelf behind Meadow, destroying it into splinters. A taste of what I'm capable of when I lose it.

Meadow lets out a high-pitched squeak and scrambles backward like a startled mouse, clutching that book like it's her lifeline.

The distance between me and Dani is crushing me—every second feels like a lifetime, and that bond where she used to burn so bright is just dead air now, empty and pulling at my mind like I'm drowning. Without her, I'm just a lost son of a bitch, completely adrift, sinking into darkness with nothing to pull me back.

"For fuck's sake, Rhy, get yourself together!" Lucian snarls, his voice sharp as a blade. "Destroying bookshelves doesn't help us." He grabs my shoulder with brutal strength I barely feel. "We need Pixie Brain working, yeah? So lock down that temper!"

I clench my jaw, fighting the urge to let the rage loose, the beast clawing to break free. Lucian's right—losing it will only make things worse. So I force it back down, muscles tight, shoving the monster back in its cage.

Then the damn shouting shatters the silence in the library, booming through the corridors. The queen's hellhounds are losing their minds below, snarling and snapping, mixed with the heavy clang of guards locking everything down. Lucian and I lock eyes, and it's like we're staring into the same black pit. My stomach drops like it just sprouted wings.

I grab Meadow's thin wrist in a crushing grip, yanking her hard as we sprint through the library's upper levels—my mind racing through escape options.

Hide? Useless—those dogs will hunt us down.

Fight? No way with these magic collars still around our necks.

My eyes snap to the answer—a stunning stained glass window, moonlight turning it into a kaleidoscope of color. It's a desperate move, loaded with risk, but with capture bearing down on us and nowhere else to go, it's our only shot.

I don't waste a second. I sprint straight for that window, our rainbow-colored escape route. Next to me, Meadow's panic spikes, her desperate pleas getting louder as she tries to pull back against my momentum.

"We're seven stories up, My Lord," she gasps. "I won't survive the fall!" Her voice rises in pure terror.

I'm not in the mood for reassurance. In one quick move, I scoop the tiny fae up, tucking her under my arm like dead weight. Her fingers are clamped white-knuckled around that grimoire, fear making her grip brutal, the book pressed hard against her chest.

"Trust me, I'm your best bet. Now hold on." I growl, hearing the urgency in my own voice.

Meadow stares at me, her eyes two terrified pools mirroring the lightning-quick decision in my head. Then we're crashing through the stained glass, an explosion of color shattering all around us.

For one second, we're hanging in freefall, the night air cool against my skin... then gravity hits hard with reality crashing back.

Then Lucian, a shadow against the moon, his howl of pure excitement piercing the night right behind us.

DANICA

14

My entire body feels like one giant bruise as I slowly peel off these sweat-soaked training clothes and collapse onto my bed. I'm pretty sure even my hair is sore at this point. Every single muscle is screaming.

Who knew that learning to kick ass would hurt this much?

I wince and roll onto my side, and my muscles literally protest the movement. Mental note: I need to invent Fantasy World ibuprofen. Or maybe just beg Faderyn for access to some kind of magical hot tub situation.

Not that I'm complaining too hard. Once my heart stopped trying to escape my chest from Erik's surprise attacks, I actually started enjoying myself. Getting to actually trade blows with a centuries-old vampire warrior? That was kind of incredible. And somehow, I didn't get demolished in the first ten seconds.

At least not until he hit me with that dirty sweep kick. My back met dirt hard enough to knock the wind out of me three separate times. But still—I was *moving*, landing actual hits! Once I got over the shock, anger, and stubbornness kicked in, and I kept getting back up.

This speed and reflexes thing that just showed up? It's absolutely insane. Like my cosmic DNA decided today was the perfect day to unlock my warrior mode upgrade.

Is this another part of my whole "prophesied savior" weirdness?

I've never been particularly athletic before. But something just switched on inside me, and suddenly I was operating at some supernatural level.

Maybe crossing into this realm activated dormant abilities?

Maybe it's the Terraglide Stone kicking in.

It's like my body keeps discovering new power-ups from my supposedly special blood-line. Cool when it helps me survive, but also genuinely terrifying.

Like, what else could randomly activate? Wings? Laser vision?

I groan and drag myself up to change before dinner. I'm covered in so much dirt that even my hunger can't override it anymore.

I dig through my trunk for clean clothes and pull out another set of buttery-soft black leather that makes me actually freeze. What is Axilya doing to me? This is basically a battle bikini!

I wash off as much grime as possible in the stone basin.

Now I'm trying to squeeze myself into this leather combat outfit—which absolutely does nothing to hide my chest, by the way—without looking like I'm auditioning for some low-budget fantasy flick. The thing laces up the sides, which somehow makes the whole bondage vibe even stronger, and it has these tiny scraps of fabric pretending to be a skirt. It's like someone took a biker aesthetic, mixed it with burlesque dancer energy, and threw in some post-apocalyptic survival wear for good measure.

I mean, I'm definitely about embracing my badass side. But there's a huge difference between "fierce warrior" and "budget cosplay reject," and I'm genuinely not sure which category I'm falling into here.

That said, my clothing options are basically nonexistent, so I can't really be picky. It's either this or my destroyed cargo pants and T-shirt, which look more like a Mad Max costume every single day.

I sigh and squeeze myself into these leather pants that fit like a second skin. The silver belt and leather gloves add at least some warrior credibility to the whole thing.

I can't help the outraged squeak when I see my reflection. Imagine Kate Beckinsale from "Underworld" but with extra curves, and my boobs are literally about to escape the top.

I'm absolutely mortified. I tug at the leather top, desperately trying to get more cover-age.

Still nothing. It's basically painted on. Please tell me there's a long tunic or cloak that goes with this, because walking around camp looking like I'm offering myself up is not the vibe I'm going for.

I'm genuinely baffled about why Axilya picked this as my "battle outfit." I throw on the boots and try some damage control, using my hair to cover as much as possible. If I can just keep people's eyes north of my neck and make a quick escape to the dining area, maybe nobody will comment on my extremely suggestive leather ensemble.

My face is absolutely on fire as I slip out of my tent, only to nearly crash straight into Erik and Faderyn standing right there. Both of them do a double-take, their eyes going wide with very obvious male appreciation before they both quickly look away and try to act casual.

Erik clears his throat awkwardly. "That's... quite the outfit."

I really want to cross my arms over my chest, but I resist. "Yeah, I have zero clue what Axilya was going for with these," I mutter, turning even redder under their carefully polite gazes.

I can't handle the awkwardness anymore, so I basically speed-walk toward the campfire and food. Maybe if my mouth is busy eating, I won't die from embarrassment over this ridiculously sexy leather get-up.

Erik and Faderyn follow at a respectful distance as I do my mortified power-walk through the entire camp.

I plop down on an empty bench at a long wooden table, grateful for the shadows. Faderyn sets down a steaming wooden bowl filled with rich sauce and tender chunks of meat. My stomach growls loudly at the smell.

I basically demolish the first bites, the flavors hitting my tongue—savory, woodsy, delicious. Some kind of fae game animal, probably. And honestly, I'm not going to ask too many questions about it. I scrape up every last drop of gravy and use the brown bread to get anything I missed.

As I'm still eating, Erik carefully clears his throat. "Your performance today was genuinely impressive, Little Huntress. With proper training, you could become a serious warrior."

I make a sarcastic noise while I'm chewing, but give him a thumbs-up. Coming from Mr. Combat Perfectionist himself, that's basically a standing ovation. It actually makes me feel better about the battles ahead—maybe I'm not completely out of my depth on this whole prophecy thing after all.

I wipe my mouth clean and turn to Faderyn. "Do you think I could request an audience with Lady Axilya? Hopefully, there will be updates on the diplomatic rescue mission for my man from Queen Viper."

Faderyn inclines his head. "I believe that could be arranged without issue. I'll see if she's available—I shall send word tonight."

I breathe a little easier—finally feeling proactive about helping Rhyland.

"Anything from the bond yet?" Erik asks gently, his silver eyes full of concern.

My mood crashes. I shake my head, and fresh worry about Rhyland starts creeping in, threatening to ruin my satisfied stomach.

"Still absolutely nothing. Just darkness. Something's definitely blocking us," I say, trying not to spiral into worst-case scenarios.

Erik notices my distress and reaches over to squeeze my hand. "Trust me, Dani. If anyone can escape and get back to you, it's my stubborn-as-hell brother." His steady confidence actually helps push back some of the anxiety I'm drowning in. "I'm glad to see you actually taking care of yourself, Little Huntress. Today's sparring pushed even me."

I give Erik a grateful smile. The soreness is already fading thanks to good food, apparently having celestial DNA, and looking absolutely ridiculous in this leather outfit. If that's the price for getting stronger, I'll take it.

My worry starts to fade a bit, but then I reach up to run my fingers through my hair and smack right into the crown. I keep forgetting this fancy thing is on my head. My fingers trace the delicate metalwork while my brain circles back to my quest for that mythical fae stone.

Faderyn notices me zoning out and gestures toward the crown. "Tell me more about this relic—the stone and its connection to your arrival here."

I take a sip of honey wine to settle my nerves. Getting drunk two nights in a row probably isn't my smartest move, but here we are.

"The Faerite stone is supposed to turn me into Doctor Dolittle meets Mother Nature. Gives me an edge with critters and greenery."

Faderyn leans forward, genuinely interested. "Do you sense its presence now, even faintly?"

I shake my head in frustration. "Nope, nothing. I felt it for like a second when we first got here—pulling me toward this white tower. But, the feeling shut off quickly as soon as Satan Jr. started his rampage."

His eyes widen with understanding. "The Ivory Tower is what remains of the Sun Court's palace."

I practically spit out my wine. "That's the Sun Court?"

"It was. Most of it's been abandoned now. The Light King and his Radiant Queen only use the central palace these days—the Sun Palace."

My heart starts racing as pieces click together in my head. Erik says what I'm already thinking. "What if the Faerite's been sitting in their stronghold this whole time? And your powers sensed it nearby?"

I turn the idea over in my head. "So you think it's there? Can we go check it out?"

Faderyn clears his throat, basically pouring cold water on my excitement. "Keep in mind that relations between the Sun throne and smaller settlements like ours are... strained. Breaking into their old palace uninvited would have serious consequences."

My enthusiasm completely deflates. I slump back against the bench. "Perfect. Just my luck," I mutter. "The world's literally falling apart, and I'm supposed to do formal introductions with royalty."

I drag my hands through my hair and think about where this stone could possibly be hiding—like some cosmic paperweight in the fae version of a fancy palace.

I give Faderyn a challenging look. "Okay, Mr. All-Knowing, start talking. If we're heading to Queen Snooty's fancy mansion, there has to be a way in. A window we can sneak through? Servant's entrance? Secret passages?"

Faderyn's mouth twitches with amusement. "Your phrasing is certainly unique, My Lady. As for potential vulnerabilities..." He pauses thoughtfully. "While I admire your boldness, perhaps the wiser course would be to approach the Sun Court as formal guests. That's more likely to succeed."

I want to argue, but I force myself to back down. Faderyn knows what he's doing here. Erik's clearly itching for action, but he nods in agreement anyway. We're basically amateurs in this whole fae politics game.

I take a breath, push my stress to the side, and dial back my troublemaker instincts. "Alright, fine. I'll behave and do the whole formal tea thing."

Erik actually chuckles, and it's the kind of laugh that screams he's got mischief on the brain. "Agreed. We'll keep the sneaky option as backup," he says, his mouth quirking with barely suppressed excitement.

Oh, he's absolutely hoping our polite approach fails. That old vampire warrior is definitely itching for a fight way more than he's interested in schmoozing with fancy fae at some stuffy court dinner.

Faderyn nods in relief, happy to avoid my chaotic plans. "We'll pursue this lead after we handle the Shadow Court situation."

Needing a topic change, I look at Faderyn. "So what's the deal with Axilya?" The question comes out interrogating. She's mysterious and weird in ways I can't quite figure out, and I'm dying to know more. Something tells me there's a whole lot more to Madam WhisperVale than meets the eye.

"It's... complicated," Faderyn says, taking his time. "Some stories aren't mine to tell. Let's just say things aren't always what they appear to be."

More cryptic nonsense, but I drop it.

I finish my wine, set the glass down, and point a determined finger at Faderyn. "Tomorrow morning, I'm waking Axilya up to get updates on rescuing Rhyland from Shadow Queen's dungeon. And you—" I wag my finger at him, "—you're going to explain why she's got me dressed like I'm Xena's kinky leather-wearing cousin."

I gather my dishes, catching Erik and Faderyn both trying really hard not to stare at my outfit.

Erik actually looks embarrassed. "You look quite striking in that dark leather, Little Huntress..."

As I walk past, I can't resist flicking him playfully on the ear. His shocked expression almost makes me laugh out loud.

Their warm chuckles follow me back to my tent—cozy and comforting after a weird and exhausting day.

DANICA

15

I stand absolutely frozen, horror choking off any sound. Right before my eyes, shadows wrap around Rhyland in these grasping tendrils until all I can see are those ice-blue eyes peeking through the writhing darkness...

Then those beloved eyes go completely black. His panicked thoughts come screaming through our broken bond—chaos, hunger, insanity—like knives shredding my mind as the darkness completely swallows the man I love.

Rhyland's last bit of light just disappears, and then cruel laughter echoes through everything.

Azrael.

The sound hits my skull like spikes driving in. Behind Rhyland's motionless body, this massive shadow figure emerges—hunger and evil given form. It's waiting for my vampire to finally surrender, to finally break...

Rhyland slowly turns to look at me, and there's nothing there. No recognition, no humanity—just a void. Darkness has completely claimed him. Azrael's whisper cuts through everything like a blade...

"Now he's mine forever—eternal. He'll never see light again..."

I'm screaming, but no sound comes out as Moretemis reaches for him with his smoking claw...

"NO!"

I jolt awake, gasping, my heart pounding so hard I think it might break through my ribs. Cold sweat is plastered all over me as panic slowly releases its grip. I collapse back onto the furs, trying to remember where I am. Canvas walls. Dim fire. Okay. Just a nightmare.

Except it's the third one this week. And Seraphina's warning keeps echoing in my head. *"True darkness dwells not in Rhyland's spirit. But still...he is tempted to darkness and can easily be swayed."*

How much longer can Rhyland fight the darkness without me there to remind him what light feels like?

Our broken bond is too weak for me to reach through, to actually know what he's suffering through alone...

Is he still holding onto his strength against that bitch queen? Or has my nightmare become real? Has Rhyland already fallen into that darkness without my light to hold onto?

Ice-cold fear crashes through me. I have to get to Rhyland before these nightmares come true. We're running out of time...

After more than a week of Erik and Faderyn putting me through this insane training that's left me basically black and blue, I slowly drag myself out of bed.

The silence from the Shadow Court is deafening—there have been no whispers from the Shadow Snatch yet.

To keep myself from going insane waiting around, I've thrown myself into warrior training, which—let me tell you—is brutal when you're basically a regular human who sits at a desk for a living. I'm groaning like I've been shot, desperately fantasizing about a hot bath and someone who knows how to give a serious massage so I can actually walk properly again.

But honestly? Yesterday, when I caught Erik totally off guard with that leg sweep and sent two hundred-plus pounds of cocky vampire flying into the dirt? Absolutely priceless. Sure, he made me pay for it ten times over, but seeing Mr. Broods-a-Lot's shocked face eating soil was worth every bruise.

Even my extraordinary spidey sense warns no quick heal exists against Erik's special brand of cheerful sadism—"Builds grit and reflexes!"

My muscular ass!

But Erik actually made me something awesome—these incredible daggers. He and Faderyn worked together on them, and they're these gorgeous fae silver blades with runes running along them that are genuinely beautiful. Elektra would be jealous.

He grins when he hands them to me. "They're small, dangerous, and quick—just like you, Little Huntress."

There's some hocus pocus on them that makes them mine, all mine. Anyone tries to use them—Poof, right back to me. It's basically the coolest magic trick ever.

Those same runes have another nifty feature—they let me play teleport tag with my new pointy friends. I've been practicing all week, and combined with my new speed, my weapon skills have gotten insanely better. I'm basically twirling these things like I was born doing it, slicing and dicing with actual technique now.

Erik's been incredible. He's clearly trying to keep me occupied and distracted from falling apart while Rhyland's gone. It's working... sort of. But the longer Rhyland's away, the deeper this hollow feeling gets inside me. The pain of being separated from him just keeps growing, like this tide that won't stop rising.

I've been crying myself to sleep every night, and there's this constant nausea sitting in my stomach. It's like I'm stuck replaying those horrible days when the Shadow Brother-hood—or whatever—had him locked up. And through all of it, Erik's been solid—sup-porting me, staying strong, never giving up on me.

I'm also painfully aware that my mood is all over the place. I'm basically a walking PMS commercial—one second I'm fine, the next I'm ready to lose it. Everything annoys me, and my patience is paper-thin. My temper's getting shorter every day, Rhyland isn't here. It's this constant battle between the aching emptiness and this rage that wants to consume everything.

I wince as I drag myself upright, lurching toward my boots with intense effort. I'm so focused on how much everything hurts that I basically walk right into Erik's solid chest as he appears in the tent opening.

"Morning, Little Huntress..." His grey eyes crease with concern as he takes in how much of a mess I look—barely standing, barely functional. "I'm guessing sleep didn't happen?"

I let out this sound that's half exhausted laugh, half whimper. "Welcome to another thrilling episode of 'Dani's Nightmare Boot Camp'... I desperately need coffee. Like, right now."

Erik leads me over to some cushions by the fire, and there's already a steaming mug waiting for me. Actual coffee. Blessed caffeine.

"How did you... Where did you...? Thank you!" I practically run toward the pot sitting in the glowing embers. "Seriously, where did you find this?" The smell alone is making me emotional—that bitter, beautiful caffeine aroma.

I inhale that first scalding sip and basically burn my mouth drinking it before I remember I need to breathe.

"Faderyn got it. A supply wagon came through this morning," Erik explains.

Oh my God, it's been *days* since I've had actual coffee. I clutch the battered metal mug like it's a lifeline, completely ignoring the fact that my tongue is literally burned.

Erik quietly passes me the honey without a word.

I take a more careful sip the second time, and the honey cuts through the bitterness perfectly. "This is amazing," I sigh into the steam, not even caring that I'm basically chugging liquid energy despite barely sleeping.

I end up telling Erik about the nightmares—about Rhyland being consumed by shadow, about Azrael and Moretemis, about that void where his eyes used to be. Erik's quiet as he listens, which somehow feels worse than if he'd said something. The weight of my dream hangs between us, heavy and threatening...

Erik fidgets with an arrowhead from the table, giving me time with my coffee and my spiraling thoughts before he finally speaks carefully. "These nightmares troubling you suggest something serious, Little Huntress," he says awkwardly.

He's clearly uncomfortable talking about emotions—this isn't his strong suit. But he pushes through anyway, visibly struggling.

I feel you, big guy.

I don't want to talk about the dream details. They're too vivid, too terrifying—those shadows wrapping around Rhyland, pulling him away from himself, consuming him completely. I wave Erik off, trying to dismiss it.

But Erik keeps going despite my stricken expression. "If Rhyland stays severed from you—from your light—much longer, the darkness inside him will take over. It'll consume him completely."

His words hit like ice water. Panic spikes through me. I set down my half-finished coffee with a shaking hand, my stomach churning. "How long?" My voice cracks desperately. "How long until he... until he..." I can't even say it out loud.

Erik's broad shoulders sag like he's carrying something heavy. He rubs the back of his neck awkwardly. "Honestly, nobody really understands how bonded pairs work, not even us vampires. Every pair is different." He takes a long drink from a leather flask, his silver eyes going distant. "It's more than just blood or convenience. When two souls connect that deeply across centuries..." He shrugs. "Let's just say the gods and prophecy probably played a role in putting you and my brooding brother together, Little One." A hint of dry humor crosses his face before it fades.

My patience for all this mystical nonsense is basically gone. Rhyland is real, tangible, concrete—I don't need flowery words and poetry.

I huff and stab my spoon into the honey pot way harder than necessary, watching it plop into my almost-empty coffee. "Drop the soulmate crap," I mutter irritably. "You said time's running out for him, so just tell me straight—how long before Rhyland goes full dark side?"

Erik blinks at my reference but gets what I'm asking. "It's impossible to predict exactly. It depends on how strong your bond is and how much willpower he has."

I clench my teeth, trying to hold back the anger and that power bubbling under my skin. "Fantastic, thanks, King of Unhelpful Answers—this is super useful while Rhyland's over there literally on a countdown timer. Give me something concrete," I snap, my frustration exploding. "Explain it in terms I actually understand. What does 'bond strength' even mean? Our connection's been nothing but noise and interference lately, and it's driving me insane."

Erik runs a hand through his silver hair thoughtfully. "Communication is just one part of it. I'm talking about your souls—how deeply you anchor each other's core selves." His intense gaze locks onto mine. "Tell me honestly, Little Huntress—right now, even with everything between you, is part of you still holding onto my brother? Can you still feel him?"

I freeze as something clicks into place. There *is* a connection, this thin thread reaching toward Rhyland that's been holding steady through all the chaos... but I can feel it now, stretched too thin, fraying at the edges from constant stress and erosion. The real concern in Erik's question mirrors the fear I've been trying to ignore.

What if he's right? What if our connection snaps completely if we don't do something soon?

My fingers clamp down on the cold metal mug like it's the only solid thing left in the world. When I finally speak, my voice comes out rough and raw. "It's like... when everything else goes quiet, this thread still connects me to him. But lately it feels less like a strong rope and more like a raw nerve, you know?" My voice drops to barely a whisper.

Tears start spilling despite my best efforts to stop them. I wipe them away aggressively, furious at showing this vulnerability. "It's like something vital is being destroyed piece by piece the longer we're apart. It's torture—the worst pain I've ever felt..."

I'm struggling to breathe, grief and desperation crashing over me. Erik carefully places a hand on my shoulder. "That's exactly it. You're feeling what Rhyland feels, and that connection—that core recognition—is what gets bonded pairs through the worst circumstances."

I force myself to take a deep breath. But then Erik's expression darkens. "However, even that connection can't survive neglect forever. Left alone in the dark too long, even the strongest mate can lose their sanity."

Panic floods through me, completely erasing any calm the coffee gave me. My hands clench into fists, and I press them against my eyes as fresh tears spill. This desperate need to save him, to pull him back from the edge before his light goes out completely, takes over everything.

My voice shakes with desperation. "What keeps this bond intact? How do I fix it when he's unreachable? There has to be some magical solution, right? Something that works?"

Erik takes his time answering, clearly drawing on centuries of lonely vampire existence. He knows solitude and its dangers better than most. "You need to be together. Physically. Soon. Your bond gets stronger over time when you're close. But right now, fighting darkness in any form—that reinforces why you two were meant to be together. The mate bond recognizes actions and loyalty, too."

"So why aren't you falling apart?" I ask, locking eyes with him. His forehead wrinkles in confusion. "Rhyland has our bond tying him to me, but he's closer to breaking than any of you who are alone, unattached."

Erik considers carefully before responding. "Vampires have a certain... resilience. An unbound vampire stays disciplined and stable in solitude until they find a mate. It's grounding. But eventually, over time, without that mate, the constant fight against the darkness wears them down. They slip deeper and deeper until, without an anchor, they're gone completely."

He focuses more intently on me. "Rhyland's situation is different. Your bond is constantly pulling at him—this constant internal war that, if left unresolved, could destroy him from the inside. It's like walking a tightrope between two forces. Meanwhile, those of us without mates don't face that immediate conflict. We survive, we keep fighting, accepting our solitude until either a bond forms or the darkness wins."

Before I can push for more answers, Faderyn appears at the tent opening with a bundle of clean clothes, toiletries, and fabric. Despite the heavy mood, I feel a spark of hope at the sight of it. A bath. Hot food. An escape from this funk and my own sweat.

"I thought you might appreciate a bath and some proper food. Afterward..." He holds up the bundle of scented soaps and fresh clothes. "Lady Axilya has agreed to meet with you privately this afternoon, if you're willing."

I practically jump to my feet, fresh hope blazing through me and burning away some of the dread. It's about damn time. I've asked to speak with her *days* ago. "Does she have updates on getting Rhyland out?"

Faderyn smiles gently, adjusting the bundle in his arms. "The Lady sends merely her assurance that she will discuss matters concerning your quest's progress so far. But optimism never goes amiss."

DANICA

16

The excitement is practically crackling through my veins. We're heading through these mysterious woods with Faderyn leading us toward some hidden spring, and I literally cannot stay still. Above us, birds are singing this beautiful chorus that somehow feels wrong against my mix of anxiety and hope.

Then this secluded pool appears—almost like something out of a dream. Steamy water surrounded by lush ferns and ancient rocks covered in thick moss. The air smells incredible—herbal and warm, like a promise that everything's about to feel better. I have no idea why Faderyn's showing me this now. Maybe his kind doesn't need regular baths like us humans do.

Faderyn and Erik are perfect gentlemen about it—they both look away to give me privacy. Stripping, I waste no time slipping into the welcoming waters with a contented groan, feeling the tension melt from my muscles, dissolving in the heat like sugar in tea.

The air is laced with the comforting aroma of lavender, a touch of cedar, and something richly organic—a bouquet of serenity.

Curiosity piqued, I wander to the edge and uncover jars ensconced in the mossy embankment, their contents a mystery begging to be unveiled. Tentative sniffs uncover a symphony of fragrances—floral entwined with understated hints of fruit and herbs—a veritable cornucopia of faerie cosmetics at my disposal.

I'm digging through all this fae skincare stuff when I find what looks like a tiny blade. I'm skeptical, but I test it on my leg and literally gasp. It removes every bit of stubble perfectly.

Oh my God—a magical razor? This is incredible. Whoever invented this magical hair-removal genius deserves a medal. It's time to say goodbye to Wookie legs, for I have been anointed with the sorcery of hassle-free hair removal!

After dealing with all the stubble on my legs and basically everywhere else, I start working this pearly liquid through my tangled, disgusting hair. My fingers immediately hit knots so bad that I'm cursing the entire time I try to comb through them. The problem is this stupid crown won't come off, so I can't actually wash my hair properly. It's basically impossible.

Honestly, I'd give up my left butt cheek just to get this thing off my head for five minutes.

I'm muttering complaints to literally nobody as I fight with this stubborn crown. "If this irritating tiara doesn't start helping me wash my hair right now, I'm going to look like I lost a fight with a pack of gremlins..."

I've barely finished complaining when this weird buzzing sensation starts tingling against my skull. I yelp and grab at my hair, and suddenly the crown just... vanishes.

"What the actual hell?" I hiss, my heart basically jumping out of my chest. My pulse is racing. Faerie Hijinks, better not steal my one shot at Unity Magic. "Come back! Did you seriously just—?"

Like it's mocking me, the crown decides to reappear. I feel a faint hum at my hairline, and then—boom! That cool metal band settles back on my head like it was never gone.

"Okay, so it teleports," I say shakily to the trees around me. "Great. Creepy magical crown behavior. Wonderful. Just perfect."

But honestly, after dealing with so much weird supernatural stuff, today's brand of strangeness is just another thing in a long list of bizarre occurrences. I shrug it off because there's no point obsessing over every strange thing in this fae-filled circus.

I take a deep breath and focus, treating my willpower like some new muscle I'm learning to flex. I imagine the command like I'm mentally nudging something into action. "Okay, magic crown, you've got my attention. How about you disappear again?" I say, my voice turning playful. "Bibbity Bobbity—be gone."

The crown buzzes like it's excited to comply, and suddenly it's gone. The weight just lifts right off my head and vanishes.

I let out this slightly hysterical laugh—because seriously, what's one more weird thing at this point?—and immediately dump some herbal stuff into my hair, scrubbing like my life depends on it. Who knows when the Turbo Crown 3000 will make a comeback.

I step out of the spring and wrap myself in this linen towel that feels like it's literally holding sunlight. Every part of it smells like herbs and reminds me of lazy summer days in fields of wildflowers—like someone bottled up the feeling of being young and carefree.

I find a bunch of supplies stashed nearby, and my fingers land on this smooth antler comb. I test it on my wet hair, and it's absolutely incredible—it just glides through the tangles like magic. Literally magic, probably.

These fae tools are insane compared to regular combs. This thing does in seconds what my regular brushes back home could only do by painfully ripping through my hair for like an hour. It's unreal.

When I get to where my clothes are folded so neatly, I literally freeze in shock and fury.

There's that same black leather outfit. The one that basically screams "fantasy dungeon fantasy" instead of "practical combat gear."

"You have to be fucking kidding me," I say out loud, my jaw basically hitting the ground. At this point, a scratchy burlap sack would probably be more comfortable.

Right on cue, Erik and Faderyn start laughing from somewhere behind the trees. Their laughter is the complete opposite of my mood. I can't help but roll my eyes. "Oh, yeah, knee-slapper, guys! Yuck it up!" I yell back sarcastically, throwing what's probably the most undignified gesture I can manage in their direction.

Their amusement just gets worse. They're full-on laughing now while I'm standing here soaking wet, trying to decide between looking ridiculous in this leather or just staying here forever.

"Lady Axilya insisted those leathers complement your appearance and bearing most excellently," Faderyn offers diplomatically once he stops laughing.

I curse under my breath and start wrestling myself into this clingy leather outfit *again*, hopping around awkwardly as I try to peel my wet skin from these tight pants.

I yank the sculpted leather top into place and shout over my shoulder. "I swear Axilya's getting a bag of flaming dog shit for subjecting me to these outfits..."

While I'm still fuming about these ridiculous leather outfits that I keep being shoe-horned into, the sumptuous spread laid out for breakfast momentarily sidelines me.

I don't hesitate—I pile my plate high with everything, not even caring when the juice from some weird purple fruit stains my skin bright purple. My stomach is literally growling as I take in all the food—crusty warm bread that smells amazing and just came out of the ovens; bowls of fruit in colors that look too vibrant to be real; pots of rich butter; and roasted meat that smells like it's going to be incredible. Every bite is this explosion of flavor—sweet mixed with tart, all these subtle spices that are definitely some kind of fae magic.

I'm so eager to eat that I don't even care about manners. I'm already reaching for seconds—maybe thirds?—before I've even finished what's on my plate. Erik and Faderyn are obviously trying not to laugh, their hands covering their mouths as they watch me basically demolish this food.

I've never been the type to pretend I don't like eating, which explains my curves. I guess I'm not your poster girl for the waif look—and that's perfectly fine.

I stab another piece of roasted meat harder than necessary, and my fork literally screeches against the metal plate. The sound perfectly matches my mood this morning. I'm probably destroying this fork out of pure frustration.

I look up, and Erik and Faderyn are both suddenly very focused on their own break-fasts. But their lips are twitching like they're trying not to smile.

I kick Erik's shin under the table without looking away from my aggressive meat-cutting. "Go ahead and laugh, it up, boys. Let's see how funny it is when I accidentally singe your eyebrows off later."

Erik's expression goes completely serious, all his amusement disappears—except his silver eyes are absolutely sparkling with barely contained laughter.

They say eyes are windows to the soul, and right now, his are open curtains to a comedy.

"You seem vexed still over garb befitting your station. Was the bath not soothing then?" He manages to keep a straight face even while I'm basically snarling at my food.

"Oh, I got sparkly clean, alright. But it's hard to feel Zen-like peace when you constantly worry your *rack's* gonna spill out for the world anytime you breathe too deep," I shoot back, chugging my coffee.

Shoving away my plate, I fix Faderyn with my most intimidating scowl. "Please inform Her Sparkly Maj that if she tries outfitting me in stripper boots next, I'll shove them right up her—"

"I shall inform Lady Axilya that you most appreciate her curated battle attire," Faderyn interrupts smoothly.

Erik suddenly develops a violent coughing fit. I don't buy for one instant.

I snort into my drink, completely skeptical. "So what time is this sparkly meeting where we discuss why my outfit is basically torture and maybe—you know—save my boyfriend?"

I need to tell Axilya exactly what I think about these clothes.

As I'm voicing my umpteenth complaint about impractical questing wear, I'm startled when the bench suddenly dips beside me. I turn to see this tiny fae kid, probably six years old, staring at me with these bright jewel-colored eyes.

"Hi there," I say, curious since he just keeps staring silently. He's got this adorable round face and messy oak-leaf colored hair.

"You—you is her!" The kid suddenly bursts out, bouncing excitedly closer. "The destiny lady from Mama's stories!"

The unexpected intensity of his words surprises me for a second, but then I soften and smile warmly at him. That gap-toothed grin is absolutely adorable—there's something genuine and unguarded about it that's charming.

I lean forward a bit, keeping my tone playful and curious. "So I'm famous now? Making it into stories?" I say with a teasing edge. "I have to know—do these stories mention my name? Who am I in your mom's version?" I'm genuinely curious how my story's being told around here.

The boy nods so hard I'm worried he's going to fall off the bench. "Mama says a mortal girl-hero comes—an angel comes to fight the Black Fear that steals all the happiness! She says... you very p-pretty and b-brave!"

Hearing "Angel" hits me hard—that's Rhyland's nickname for me, and it makes my chest ache.

The kid's got this serious expression like he's carrying something heavy, so I soften my voice. "I'm definitely just a regular person. But I promise I'll be as brave as I can be," I say, winking to lighten the mood. "Keeping everyone safe is my job. I promise."

I stick out my pinky toward him as a real promise. He hesitates for a second, studying my hand, then understanding clicks. His tiny pinky links with mine, and I curl mine around it playfully. His toothless grin spreads across his face—this simple, pure moment of connection sealed with our linked pinkies.

He seems drawn to the crown on my head like it's pulling him closer. He shuffles nearer, eyes totally fixed on the shimmering thing.

Now that he's close, I can see all the details—his perfect tiny nose, those pointed ears that stick out from his oak-colored hair, soft around the edges. His eyes are so honest and full of belief, and it tugs at my heart.

"Yeah, Mama said a mortal lady blessed by old m-magicks would come and make the monsters run away," he says proudly. "She said you have stars in your skin, that you... f-fall from heaven and b-battle a dark god!"

I blink at how much his mom's exaggerated this, but I nod to encourage him. "Well, the bad guys better watch out now that I'm here. No more scaring awesome kids like you!" I ruffle his hair playfully, he giggles, ducking away.

He waves goodbye and takes off, and I notice Erik and Faderyn watching the whole thing thoughtfully.

Erik claps my shoulder. "It seems tales of your quest already gather devoted followers." His tone is teasing but genuinely warm.

I laugh and roll my eyes at how sincere he's being. "Oh yeah, saving the world means nothing without a fan club first. We should get matching shirts—I Believe in Dani with sparkly unicorns!"

Erik chuckles, moving off to check camp defenses out of long habit.

I watch the little boy cuddle up to his mom nearby, and this ache hits my chest. Could I ever have that? A kid of my own to love? The thought makes me uncomfortable, and I realize how different everything would be with an immortal vampire mate.

Do vampires even conceive normally? And with Rhyland's brooding alpha male nature...would he want more children after the agony of losing his first family?

With everything going on—supernatural wars, his past trauma—I doubt parenthood is on his radar right now...

I mean, it's not as if I could get knocked up even if I wanted to. With my trusty IUD playing gatekeeper, this womb is basically Fort Knox. Getting pregnant would be like winning the lottery without buying a ticket—technically possible, but about as likely as Lucian becoming a monk.

I've got the copper IUD, the one without all those extra hormones mucking up the works. It's like having a tiny bodyguard in my business, ensuring no unwanted swimmers get past the velvet rope.

This reminds me of Aunt Flow, who will be visiting in the next few weeks, and I pray to the menstrual gods that this realm has some decent feminine hygiene gear. Because let me tell you, there's nothing worse than being caught off guard by the crimson tide without the proper supplies.

I let out a long breath, shaking off the rabbit hole of 'what-ifs'—staring down the barrel of an apocalypse isn't the moment for musing about storks or picket fences. Let's pencil in saving the world first, then maybe RSVP to la-la land with a plus one later.

DANICA

17

I walk into the pavilion with Erik and Faderyn, already mentally preparing all my complaints for Axilya. I'm ready to call her out for putting me in this ridiculous leather outfit that belongs in a fantasy novel, not actual combat.

Then I stop dead.

Mental script grinds to a halt, words catching in my throat as my gaze settles on Her Ladyship.

There she is, perched among overstuffed cushions, the very picture of nonchalance—and clad in leathers that mirror my own, down to the last ornate detail.

I let out this frustrated sigh. Of course, she's rocking battle babe couture, too. Axilya notices me doing a double-take and raises one eyebrow like she's waiting to see what I'll do. She doesn't say anything. My heart's pounding, and my frustration is building, but I force myself to smile, even though it feels strained and tight across my face.

I can see Erik's trying not to smirk, which somehow makes me even more annoyed. I'm about to launch into my whole speech about how inappropriate this outfit is and what it says about my status, when something at the edge of my vision catches my attention and completely derails my train of thought.

A plump and undeniably cute creature suddenly stands up and alert. It looks like an oversized ferret, except I've never seen anything like it before. Its fur is glossy and shimmering, colors rippling across it like light hitting a prism.

It's got this fancy leash covered in what looks like gems—basically the definition of luxury. I can't help but let genuine curiosity break through my frustration as I look at this creature's wide, round eyes. It feels like it's offering a truce in the middle of all this tension.

"Aww, how cute!" I can't help but say. "What fascinating little fuzzball is this?" I ask, gesturing toward it with genuine curiosity and amusement. "I mean, what is it exactly?"

Axilya smiles warmly, petting the creature's ears. "This little 'fuzzball,' as you so delicately address her, is a Coatl rescued long ago from poachers seeking their magic fur."

The small creature bounces over and rubs against my leg like a cat. "Ah, I see Syla approves of your company," Axilya says with a mysterious smile.

The little Coatl immediately pushes under my hand, making a continuous musical purring sound that vibrates through my whole arm. Its fur feels rough but silky at the same time, gliding perfectly through my fingers. "How could anyone possibly hurt something this cute?" I ask, genuinely confused.

Axilya's expression goes sad. "Many foolish mages and sorcerers seek pelts still, hoping to bolster waning talents," Axilya continues bitterly. "Magic is not obtained easily these days—despite the practice being utterly forbidden now, poachers persist in trying to locate hidden Coatl dens."

The thought of this beautiful creature being killed for its fur makes my chest hurt. I gently stroke behind its fox-like ears, smiling as Syla makes happy chirping sounds.

Axilya keeps explaining. "Coatl fur has unique magical properties. Pure Coatl pelts boost spellcasting and healing ten times over for people trained to use them. After poachers killed so many, the Coatls retreated far into the Northern Wilds. There are only a few left now, and I've maintained friendships with the remaining packs." Her voice turns fierce and protective.

I crouch down beside this precious creature, still purring under my hand. Those amber eyes are full of both wisdom and innocence. I gesture emphatically down at Syla, now curled up peacefully across my knees. "This is an innocent life. Only completely sick people destroy something this beautiful just for money and power!"

Axilya's smile is tinged with sadness. "You are still young for a mortal heart. Pray such tender outrage endures facing what is to come."

I take a breath and refocus on why I'm actually here, noting Erik's subtle shift—he's got my back. As interesting as Coatl politics sounds, that's not the main reason I asked to meet with Axilya.

I lock eyes with her, pulling up my bootstraps for the fashion face-off. "Before we let the cuteness derail us," I start, my hand gesturing between the two of us and our matchy-matchy leather get-ups, "I wanted to circle back to the topic of my gear."

I notice Faderyn tactfully staying quiet at the edge of the pavilion. I keep going, balancing between being respectful and being frustrated. "With all respect, I'm not showing up to any important meeting looking like I'm about to work at some adult entertainment club. Isn't there something that's actually functional and covers more skin?"

Amusement sparkles in Axilya's sea-green eyes. "You find the battle garb unsuited for the role destiny carved for your shoulders?"

Erik makes an odd coughing noise, quickly masked behind one gloved fist. I swear, steam erupts from my burning ears. Axilya looks at her nails casually. "Peace, small goddess. No soul dictates your fate or self, save you alone. This truth transcends raiment." Her gaze turns genuinely compassionate. "Fear not; I've more decorous attire prepared for when you formally petition the Shadow Queen this eventide."

I let out this reflex sigh, my whole body relaxing like a deflating balloon. "Thank—wait, hold on. Did you say tonight?"

The words hit me like electricity, setting off a cascade of emotions—hope, nervous energy, anticipation, all of it mixed together. Just thinking about seeing Rhyland again, being close enough to see his blue eyes clearly, makes my heart feel like it's going to jump right out of my chest.

"Indeed. After much delicate negotiation, the Shadow Queen will grant you a direct audience tonight. I do apologize for the delay—the Queen is fickle." She almost rolls her eyes. "We merely need to swear temporary loyalty oaths, and she will permit speech regarding releasing your...detained friends." Axilya spreads elegant hands. "I advise accepting any terms provisionally so your petition stands unobstructed."

No shit, it's a delay. It has been almost two weeks! My excitement dims a bit. I don't like making promises I'm not sure about, but for Rhyland? I'll make an exception.

I sigh reluctantly. "Fine, I'll play polite princess for two seconds if it gets my guy walking free, no strings attached."

Already, my brain whirs with ideas for loopholes should Queen Bitch-face try twisting any sworn deals later against us. No way am I kneeling forever for faerie royalty!

Faderyn steps forward like the protective guardian he is, his green eyes surprisingly gentle. "If blessings hold, your absent mate shall stand faithfully reunited before this day ends."

Once I bust Rhyland out and rattle a few glitter-encrusted crowns, maybe these squabbling nobles will snap out of their fairy-tale feud and band together against the real boogeyman.

Wishful thinking? Sure, but hey, a girl's gotta have her fantasies, right?

First things first—there's some serious ass to kick and a certain Viking vampire to reclaim.

There's a quick knock on the tent pole, and a young fae girl slips through the opening. She looks like she's in early adolescence, with brown hair woven with ivy strands. She does an awkward curtsy and hands me a heavy satchel with pretty opalescent stitching.

"Lady Axilya says you should wear this for the meeting, honored guest. She's waiting to escort you herself," she whispers, handing me the bag with this amused, serious expression. She gives me a knowing smirk before bobbing another quick bow and skipping off, her pink and lavender dress shimmering in the sunlight filtering through the trees.

"Not more haute couture surprises..." I grumble under my breath, hefting the bag curiously. What constitutes appropriate garb to wheedle prisoners from notoriously fickle Fae queens anyway?

Given how much Axilya loves fancy clothes, I'm nervous about opening this. But I can't exactly show up butt-naked, so I might as well see what she's put me in this time.

I unwrap the layers of fabric and find a gown that literally leaves me speechless. The material glows with this iridescent shimmer, shifting between periwinkle, seafoam, and blush colors as it moves. The bodice is sheer silver and gold, leaving my shoulders bare, with gold vine cuffs instead of sleeves. The neckline is delicately edged with white feathers. I pull it out completely and hold it up.

My admiration crashes immediately when I see the whole thing. What I thought were modest side panels basically don't exist. From my neck down to my thigh, there's nothing but open skin on both sides. This is basically lingerie. Models would be shocked at how little fabric this is. The panels cascade from the waist and create the illusion of a skirt, but they cover almost nothing.

A sneeze risks utter catastrophe for the remaining shreds of my dignity. I gape stupidly for a long minute before outrage uncorks my frozen vocal cords.

"What the actual hell..." I stammer. There has to be a mistake. "Why in *God's* name...? What part of diplomatic edict insists on baring my entire ass to spiteful Fae Royals??"

I hold up this ridiculous scrap of a dress dramatically, glaring across the tent. I'm deliberately avoiding looking at Erik, who looks like he's about to have a heart attack from how little fabric this dress is. He's slowly edging toward the tent opening like he knows better than to stick around when I'm this angry.

Where the hell am I going to put my daggers?

"This...this Swiss cheese cloth wouldn't cover a Barbie doll, much less any real curves!" My voice climbs several humiliated octaves.

Erik turns questioning glances in my direction but wisely volunteers no risky opinions.

What do they teach regarding propriety and presentation in Fancy Fae finishing schools??

"I swear if Axilya expects me to strut into delicate treaty negotiations with my cheeks *flap flap,* flapping in the breeze for ambiance, she can damn well throw on this joke herself!" I basically yell at the ceiling and any gods who might be listening.

Erik wisely mutters something about checking the armor and quickly walks out, his boots moving fast.

I take a few deep breaths and try to calm down, smoothing out the silk fabric even though there's nothing wrinkled about it.

After some more deep breaths, I finally put the dress on. Damn, Fae likely never endured chafing underwires or pinched back fat—it hardly surprises me that their sense of style prioritizes maximum exposure over functionality.

I look down and try to focus on how little fabric there is, instead of thinking about how exposed I actually am. Even though I'm all about feminist principles, my breath still catches...

Shimmery periwinkle and pink silks drift around like playful fronds scattered by forest winds. Meanwhile, the soft feathers brush around my breasts, almost but not quite covering them. Ditto for currently chilly nether regions barely curtained by sparkly faux foliage, one sneeze away from utter failure.

Peek-a-boo slits parting all the way up my thighs emphasize the ol' stems! At least trailing wisps of silver and gold lace swirl across ticklish skin, distracting from the drafted crotch kite flapping in the breeze situation.

I spin, making the diaphanous garb swirl with every move—one deep breath risks a wardrobe malfunction!

Steeling myself, I finally duck out into the afternoon rays from the tent's modest shelter. My jaw clenches, catching both men's startled double-takes.

Erik openly smirks while Faderyn suddenly pretends to be fascinated by imaginary lint on his tunic.

Wonderful.

Before either can comment on my new airflow-enhancing ensemble, I point a single, stern finger. I press my lips into a tight line to show I'm serious. "Not. One. Word."

Erik just shrugs innocently, but the sparkle in his eyes shows he thinks this is hilarious. "You look absolutely stunning, befitting your position, Little Highness," he says neutrally.

I puff out frustration, muttering, "Thanks," while nudging him with my elbow.

A musical chime heralds Lady Axilya sweeping into view, her eyes glimmering crystalline against the bright day. Naturally, Her Burlesque Highness dons similar diaphanous scraps draped across artery-freezing expanses of violet flesh!

With an eyebrow arched and hands on my hips, I address Axilya with biting sarcasm, "Ah, I see the heavenly exhibitionist committee approves of baring our entire buttcheeks to establish new world orders. Here's to hoping no treaty signings demand twerking rituals, hmm?"

One elegant ebony brow arches. "No idea what 'twerking' means, but such garb graces all court daughters. Nudity appeals equally, of course." Axilya's sharp features soften slightly, observing my discomfort, tugging awkwardly at diaphanous hems. "Come, the day hastens onward—we must be off ere the convocation commences without our shining delegate."

Biting my tongue against another word volcano, I gather yards of slippery silk, trying not to tear Axilya's artsy scrap pile, and carefully hoist myself up into the carriage.

RHYLAND

18

"Damn these ancient scribbles to hell!" Meadow snarls, throwing down the crumbling parchment pages that nearly fall apart in her hands. Her jerky movements kick up clouds of choking dust, swirling through the stale cave air. "Is it really so hard for dead crazy wizards to write legibly?" she bitches loudly, viciously kicking a loose stone. It clatters against the rough walls, the noise hitting my pounding skull like a sledgehammer.

Nearly two weeks since we escaped feels like an eternity in this forsaken hellhole. My nails dig into my palms, fighting to hold onto what's left of my patience. Snapping Meadow's neck might feel good for five seconds, but it won't break the curse strangling me.

I force my voice to stay level, addressing Meadow's hunched back. "Complaining won't decode ancient spells any faster, Mouse. Either figure out those moldy pages or shut the fuck up."

She flushes slightly under my glare, carefully gathering the scattered parchment pieces back together.

"He's got a point there, pint-size!" Lucian, our resident food pilferer, pipes up in his usual blithe manner, completely unbothered by the obvious tension. "Brain-work's bust on an empty tank, pixie! Chow down, power up the noggin!" He flings a chunk of bread and some jerky at Meadow, who catches it like it's the holy grail.

I tear into another piece of stale bread, forcing it down past the bile rising in my throat. I need to eat something to keep the beast from breaking loose. Trapped in here like a caged animal—it's shredding what's left of my sanity.

And this piss-poor excuse for shelter? It's more of a fucking crypt than a cave with each passing minute.

We dove into this hellhole after tearing through this cursed realm, playing hide and seek with death after bolting from the castle. Without Dani's essence throwing me a lifeline from that hellfire above, Lucian and I are toast the minute we brush against those damned rays.

We've had a couple of close calls with Amara's guards on our heels. But we managed to stay in the shadows, invisible and off their radar. So here we are, collared like dogs, while Meadow—this scrawny little servant girl—plays mechanic with the silver noose draining me dry. My head's stuck on repeat, screaming for my mate in dead silence. Doubt's a brutal weight, and the shadows keep closing in.

Hunger's tearing me apart, a beast clawing to break free and slaughter something. After centuries of holding it back, numbing myself, that monster's sliding out of its cage. Finding our mate makes it worse—our bond turns this internal war into absolute hell. Fighting not to lose myself to that void, that desperate need for blood, is exhausting. Dani's light kept the darkness in check, but now? I'm wound so tight, I'm one second away from losing it completely...

Meadow's frustration keeps building as time slips away without any progress on breaking the collar's cursed spellwork. She turns to me, her voice tight but determined. "My Lord, I beg you; standing here brooding in the dark won't help us! I know your stare alone can't shatter these wicked enchantments, but—"

She stops dead under my glare, promising death. The girl's lucky—my last bit of restraint is the only thing stopping me from ripping her throat out.

Meadow drops her head again, suddenly very interested in those moldy pages. But her shaking hands and white-knuckled grip reveal how scared she really is, how much her hope is bleeding away just like mine. The tension is suffocating, and this mountain's too steep for her to climb.

A sharp crack tears through the air—the old grimoire suddenly smashes against the far wall. Lucian and I jump to our feet, caught off guard by the tiny girl's sudden outburst. Meadow's seething in the ringing silence, anger and despair written all over her face.

Lucian whistles low and impressed. "Holy shit! Who knew our little mousey friend was a badass wildcat in disguise?" He flashes a wicked grin. "Talk about looks being deceiving. This one's got claws, and she's not afraid to use them!"

Meadow snarls in frustration and glares hard at Lucian.

He raises his hands in mock surrender. "Whoa, easy there, killer. I'm just the joke machine around here. No need to rip me to shreds... unless you're into that?" He raises his eyebrows suggestively. "In which case, your angry side is actually kind of turning me on."

I shut him down with a brutal glare. There's no time for his bullshit—not when our only shot at freedom is lying in pieces. "Get the damn book, Mouse—your little tantrum didn't fix anything," I snap viciously, my temper hanging by a thread. "Assuming those old pages even survive another hard throw."

I keep my eyes locked on her, every muscle coiled tight as she moves across the rocky ground. And that's when it happens—Meadow lets out a shocked cry just as she disappears behind a jagged outcrop of rocks. A scream of pain cuts through the silence, and the smell hits me—*blood,* fresh and telling.

In a blind burst of speed, I'm at her side in a heartbeat, my last shred of reason obliterated by the primal hunger consuming me. Her shriek is piercing, pure terror, but it's nothing compared to the deafening roar of blood pounding in my ears, my fangs fully extended by pure instinct.

"Rhyland, no!" Lucian's panicked scream barely breaks through the red haze drowning my vision—the urge to kill and feed erases everything else.

Lucian's iron grip clamps around me, his wiry strength like steel chains, dragging me back inch by brutal inch against the monstrous pull. I let out a feral snarl; every muscle fights, reaching toward the trembling victim just out of reach.

Lucian squeezes viciously, shouting right in my ear. "Are you fucking insane? She's our only way out of this shithole, you bastard! Get yourself together, Rhyland! I know you're still in there somewhere, so fight through it!"

Lucian's desperate voice cuts through the haze, piece by agonizing piece. With a guttural roar, I force the raging beast back into its cage. My breathing comes in ragged gasps, my vision still stained red with the hunger for blood that I'm desperately fighting to control.

"I know being separated from Dani is destroying you inside, brother," Lucian says, his sarcasm completely gone. "But you've got to keep it together, damn it. Hold on tight, and don't let this place drag you under." His words hit like a sledgehammer, cutting right through me as I stare at Meadow's terrified face.

Shit, I'm more monster than man right now... How long before even Dani can't drag me back from this black void swallowing me whole?

I rip my fangs back and shove Lucian hard, a low growl tearing out of me. Without looking at either of them, I stalk across the cavern to its darkest corner, driving my fists into the rock wall until my legs give out.

Elbows on my knees, I drag my clawed fingers through my hair, the beast inside roaring like a caged animal, fighting to break loose. It's like I'm drowning in hell's deepest pit with no light—Dani's warmth is gone, and everything's falling apart.

Lucian's urgent whispers and Meadow's muffled crying are just background noise against the screaming in my head. Jaw locked, spine rigid as steel, I'm holding onto sanity by the thinnest thread, fighting for control with every breath.

Without knowing where the hell we are in this cursed realm and unable to feel her, I'm flying completely blind. I can't search this entire place hoping to find her by accident; she could be anywhere. And with this collar, I'm powerless—no vampire abilities. My hands are tied.

"Angel..." I call out Dani's name into the darkness, reaching for even a hint of her, but I get nothing. Silence. Cold. Empty.

"We made a promise—nothing would separate us. But here I am, choking in the dark, with no light from you to guide me, baby. The madness is spreading fast, and I'm losing myself."

How long before there's nothing human left?

Heavy footsteps echo across the cavern floor as Lucian approaches, his voice cutting through my rage like a blade. "Well congratu-fucking-lations, asshole! We're not dead yet, thanks to your insane bullshit!"

I lift my head slowly. Lucian's tight jaw and hard eyes burn with fury, but something worse lurks underneath. Raw fear at what I'm becoming stares back at me. I can't fault him for it.

"You can't go full beast on the one pixie genius who can get these magic choke collars off us," Lucian's voice drops slightly. "I know being separated from your mate is driving you crazy, bro. But you've got to hold it together."

"Sorry for nearly ripping our little mouse to shreds," I grit out. "But we're fucked without..." My voice trails off, my entire body screaming to hunt my mate through hell itself.

Lucian's sharp laugh cuts without a trace of joy. "We're fucked, alright, if that's your idea of an apology!" He roughly forces my chin up, scrutinizing my blown pupils. "Earth to the Braindead Idiot—we need her to crack this curse shit off us! Then we find your suicidal Juliet together, got it?"

His words light my fuse again. With a snarl, I shove him away hard. "One more minute in this cave, and I'm going to lose my goddamn mind! I need Dani—"

I'm clawing at my scalp, the cave's dampness seeping into my hands like frozen death, the stench of rot coating my throat. The constant drip of water somewhere nearby grates on my nerves, a harsh contrast to Lucian's fading scent against the reek of mold and decay.

This fucking cave—it's not just a hole in the ground, it's the void tearing open inside me.

I catch Lucian's heavy sigh. There's no wit, no cocky grin—just raw honesty cutting straight through. He sees the abyss that'll swallow us if we don't succeed. Maybe he also feels the cold shadow of death creeping closer behind us.

I choke back a sound that's half snarl, half sob. "You think I haven't been fighting with everything I've got?" The words come out like venom before my jaw locks shut. Can't let him see how broken I really am. But this is Lucian. After centuries together, some truths can't stay hidden.

My voice drops to barely a whisper, raw fear bleeding through every word. "She's just a dying light in an endless darkness," I admit with a harsh growl. "This cursed separation is tearing what's left of me to pieces, brother. If Dani's fire goes out before we find each other..." I can't finish it. The dread is too heavy, too real—a monster of its own, getting hungrier with every second that passes.

A loud crack echoes as Lucian snaps a tree branch against his knee in frustration. "That's not happening, Rhy. You're going to get back to her, period." Lucian's voice is absolute. "I didn't deal with your brooding ass just to watch you quit now. We're getting out of this hellhole, no matter what."

His fingers dig hard into my shoulders, leaving bruises. "You're the most stubborn, hardheaded son of a bitch I know," Lucian says flatly. "This magical bullshit isn't strong enough to break you. You have to keep fighting."

I nod, the burning in my chest a reminder that I'm still alive. Still fighting. For Dani. For us.

"One way or another," I echo, raw determination flooding my voice like a vow.

Hours blur together, a sick joke, while we get absolutely nowhere on breaking these damn collars.

I'm barely holding on, bloodlust chewing away at what little control I have left, when something massive slams into me like a truck. I stagger, slamming my hands against the cave wall to stay upright. Every nerve is screaming.

What the hell is this?

The scent hits me like a hammer—sickeningly sweet—*cotton candy*. My fangs burst out, and I'm sliding into pure savagery.

Everything snaps. I feel the shadows twisting in my head, clawing for control. Nothing else matters except that intoxicating smell, that irresistible scent I'm desperate to sink my fangs into.

Finally!

I'm moving before I can even think. There's this pull straight from my core, dragging me toward that incredible smell.

A feral roar tears out of me, cutting Lucian off mid-sentence. His eyes lock on mine like he understands exactly what's happening.

I can practically taste this divine creature; it's right there.

Lucian's face goes pale with shock and horror. "Oh shit... Meadow, run!" He moves toward me, hands up like he's trying to cage a wild animal. Meadow bolts into the corner. "Brother, your eyes—Rhy—get control! You could kill her. Self-control, remember? Don't you fucking dare—"

I let out a roar and explode out of the cave, driven by a single ravenous hunger to drown in this creature, to bury my fangs and drink its blood dry.

Thoughts war inside me like titans battling for supremacy.

My bloodlust destroys everything else—fuck the danger, fuck what happens next. Switch is flipped—sweet relief in finally giving in to what I need.

Lucian screams something vicious behind me, Meadow's voice a thin cry on the wind. The primal pounding of my starving heart drowns out their words.

Reason is gone—I'm a weapon tearing through the night, not giving a shit about branches, darkness, nothing.

I'm so fucking hungry.

DANICA

19

This rickety redneck carriage screams the opposite of fairy tale transport. But somehow, I get crammed between two armored fae warriors wearing a crotch kite, pretending it's a real dress.

The problem is, no matter how cold it is, my ass hurts like hell from sitting on these uncomfortable benches for so long.

My butt aches almost as much as my teeth from getting bounced around on this carriage as it hits every bump and hole in the forest path.

At least jostling provides a temporary distraction from Lady Axilya cooly lecturing basics on creative ways to kiss shadowy ass once we roll up to her frosty majesty's chilling throne.

But the creepy woods passing by the window make me really uneasy. All the twisted branches and shadows are making my anxiety worse. Rhyland's in danger, and the thought of losing him keeps eating away at me. Every moment we're not together feels like he's slipping further away. Nothing anyone says helps calm me down—it's just noise compared to the panic building up inside me.

The carriage jostles over another unseen root or stone, throwing my balance and shattering any pretense of grace. I careen awkwardly to the side, any semblance of ladylike poise long forgotten.

I run my hands through my hair out of pure frustration, and my fingers get tangled in the mess, which pretty much sums up how I'm feeling right now.

I groan and let it out. "Seriously, all this bowing and scraping just to get permission to do this mission feels completely ridiculous!" My voice is full of frustration, matching how knotted my hair is—both are completely out of control.

Axilya looks at me with those sharp green eyes like she's sizing me up. "Mind yourself, presenting the Shadow Queen, child. She's powerful—Amara denies trivial wants on passing whims and owns pride in matching dragons." Her tone makes me instantly defensive.

"Let me be clear about something—Destiny doesn't care how powerful you are. I'm not going to stand around being quiet and polite, not for anyone, not now, not ever."

Axilya raises a knowing eyebrow. "Courts of Night and Light throw more tea parties than follow human codes, young queen."

Codes, my ass! I'm here to get Rhyland out, and I'm not going to act submissive.

I know Axilya's giving me good advice, but I can't help showing how impatient I am. "Yeah, yeah, blow smoke up the collective rectum 'til we get our way. But make no mistake—Rhyland is breathing fresh air before we leave by any means necessary." I cross my arms, standing firm despite the tiny straps on this stupid dress.

Out of the corner of my eye, I see Faderyn trying not to react. He makes this weird sound like he's choking and trying to laugh at the same time. Erik stayed back at WhisperVale, and I'm feeling the loss of Mr. Stoic more than ever.

The carriage hits another pothole, and despite trying to stay composed, I yelp as my sore tailbone slams into the hard wooden seat.

"We shall reach the Shadow Court by this evening. Maintaining conservative speeds en route will best avoid unintended territorial disputes," Axilya tells me.

I barely stop myself from groaning out loud. But then Syla, the little Coatl, wraps around my exposed legs affectionately. Her soft, soothing purring sounds go right into my chest and calm me down. Her velvety fur feels amazing against my skin—so much better than all the tension I've been carrying since Rhyland disappeared.

My curiosity is getting the better of me, though. "Okay, so what's the deal with Amara? Why's everyone falling over themselves to kiss the ground she floats above?" I ask, mixing sarcasm with genuine interest.

Axilya stiffens, taking a moment to gather herself before she starts explaining. "Amara commands the arcane of shadows, its lineage veiled in enigma as profoundly as the occurrence that heralded its arrival—the encapsulation of the realms," she starts, her voice measured yet imbued with a hint of apprehension.

She pauses and adjusts her skirt like she's organizing her thoughts. "Our arcane might, as Fae, is inexorably linked with the unicorns' fealty. Upon the advent of calamity, as they receded into seclusion, our magical essence waned, rendering us desolate." Her gaze hardens, reflecting her resolve. "All but Amara, whose faculties endured unscathed, morphing into something malevolent and formidable. Such corrupt power has given her a sinister edge, skewing the balance ever since that fateful descent."

"So she just magically got more powerful, and nobody knows why?"

Axilya looks off into the distance like she's remembering something heavy. "We do not," she admits. "Solely the Sun Court has succeeded in repelling her incursions. Their domain remains shielded by sustained ancient magical wards, a bastion of powerful spells that, thus far, Amara has failed to penetrate."

She drops this lore bomb like it's just a tidbit, casually noting how the Sun Court basically has the ultimate cheat code against Amara's shadow magic—no wonder they're strutting around as one of the big two in the power pageant.

But there's something she's not telling me. I can see it written all over her face. She's holding back parts of this story. I won't push her to tell me, but my gut's telling me there's way more to this than what she's saying.

I must have fallen asleep because suddenly I'm bouncing around the carriage like a pinball as we stop hard. It feels like we've hit something major. The driver apparently got his license from a box of cereal. Men are yelling outside, their voices getting louder and more confused. Syla, still in my arms, looks up at me with those big amber eyes, worried.

"What the hell was that?" I ask.

Axilya pulls back the heavy brocade drapes, the moonlight caressing her refined features. "A wheel has been lost to us. We shall take respite here for the night and resume our journey come morning." She glides effortlessly outside before I can process her stiff words through my mental fog.

When I step out of the carriage, one of the guards grabs my hand to help me down as my legs almost give out. I'm unsteady from sitting for so long. The ground in this clearing is solid and flat, which is way better than that torture seat in the carriage.

I can barely stop myself from crying out as I hop awkwardly, trying to get feeling back in my feet—they're all pins and needles from the long ride.

Once I can stand properly, I look around and stretch out my legs. There's a spring surrounded by moss-covered stones, with water bubbling gently. Firelight flickers across the camp, and I can see fae soldiers moving quietly, setting up supplies. Everything feels calm and peaceful, which is surprising given everything that's happening.

My numb legs need to move, so I wander into the forest to clear my head. My brain won't stop racing with worries, but having Syla draped across my shoulders helps. I run my hand through her soft fur and feel myself calming down, my anxiety easing with each beat of her heart.

We walk silently through these strange trees and glowing plants. Vines covered in this ghostly green light wrap around the massive trunks, pulsing like they're alive. Even the moths here have butterfly wings that shimmer with rainbow colors.

I run my fingers over the soft petals of these flowers—they feel like velvet, and they're warm. The alien blooms lean subtly into my touch. Double-take—they move, responding to stimulation against my skin. Syla purrs happily as this strange energy flows between us.

We walk into this clearing that looks almost too perfect to be real—tall crystals and prisms catch the moonlight and break it into colors like an art gallery. Water trickles through streams reflecting all that light.

I lie down on a smooth crystal rock and look up at all the stars scattered across the sky. My feet dangle, and I just breathe, soaking in this peace that's been missing lately. Syla curls up on my chest, and the steam from the hot springs carries the smell of cedar and wildflowers. I breathe it in deeply.

As I pet Syla's soft fur, her calm breathing hits me emotionally. I whisper, "I wish you could see my world while it's still good and untouched..." She may be a creature of this realm, but right now I really want to show her where I come from.

I realize that if I ever go back home, my whole idea of what's normal will be completely different. Syla shifts and presses closer to me. She makes this soft rumbling sound with musical notes in it, like she's encouraging me. Even though I don't speak this realm's language, I understand what she's trying to tell me.

The stars shine above us in this hidden grotto, the crystals and water making everything look like a dream. As Syla starts falling asleep, I feel it happening to me too.

For a hot second, it's like the entire multiverse decides to throw us a bone, putting the cosmic chaos on "pause."

I am sinking into this blissful silence when suddenly I'm pulled in a direction that is as foreign as it is deja vu. My body goes full marionette, and out pops a yelp that sends Syla bouncing off me as if I'm her personal trampoline.

"Syla, wait," I say, not wanting her to get hurt.

My heart's pounding, and I'm scanning the glen that suddenly looks dangerous. Those blue lights are casting shadows everywhere, turning my peaceful spot into something scary. Every bush and ripple in the water looks like it could be hiding something.

But then reality hits—there's no monster. Nothing is attacking me. The gut-punch of truth lands—it's not an external attack; it's my panic button in a magical chokehold. That gut-wrenching homesickness comes from being away from Rhyland for too long. Our connection is like a rope pulling tight, and I'm feeling everything he's feeling—his emotions are hitting me hard.

"R-Rhyland...?" I say his name, throwing it out there like I'm hoping for a miracle in the middle of all this chaos.

What are the odds my crummy luck could flip to a fairy tale ending?

DANICA

20

Hugging the idea to my chest feels like trying to cuddle a porcupine—prickly and kinda insane. Is it really possible to snatch back my vampire knight in less-than-shiny armor?

But here I am, my heart daring to leap out of my chest, betting all my chips on the chance to win back my brooding, solitary Viking stud.

There's no answer in this glowing garden. But something invisible pulls my head toward the north. I can't see him or hear him, but I sense the big idiot's grumpy essence heading bullheadedly toward me across leagues deemed impassable 'til now.

I bolt off the glittering boulder, warm, soft grass molding underfoot, as my internal GPS locks unerringly onto his signature. I spin in circles, trying to glimpse him for the first time in... forever.

I'm spinning like a makeshift ballerina when—WHAM!

I'm suddenly eating turf like it's my last meal, courtesy of an out-of-nowhere, linebacker-style tackle from the rear. We slam into the green beneath us—my breath leaves me faster than common sense at a clearance sale, but at least the arms wrapped around me are cozier than the collision suggests.

A gulp of air brings a familiar scent that kicks my heart rate up a few more notches—it's spiked with danger but still undeniably Rhyland. The aroma has a sweet undertone with a spicy edge and a hint of 'wrong side of the tracks'—totally intoxicating, totally him.

We're a chaotic mess on the ground, all limbs and adrenaline. His hands find me a bit roughly, clamping down on my face with a grip that borders on frantic. And then there it is—his gaze, intense enough to knock my thoughts clear out of my head, leaving nothing but tumbling dominoes in its wake.

I gawk stupidly, anxiety rising. My vampire wears recent bullshit badly—harsh new lines bracketing his mouth and haunted hollows around those now almost black eyes. Dark scruff shadows his rugged jawline, upping the ominous danger vibes. He scans my face with blistering hunger, barely leashed, sending warning prickles along my spine.

"Rhyland..." I breathe prayerfully, confused, moved by his ravaged state. But only a remote void stares back down, behind devouring eyes, and a painful grip locks us together. Worry spikes when his hold tightens further until breathing grows labored.

His eyes are like black holes threatening to suck in all the light, and he's drinking in the scent of my skin like it's his lifeline. I'm trying to keep the panic from tap-dancing on my vocal cords, but it's hard when every breath from him is like hearing nails on a chalkboard.

"Rhyland?" The name is a bullet I shoot from the gun of my lips, aiming for whatever's left in there of my vampire Viking. I will my voice to be ironclad, trying to summon back the man—my guardian, my rock—within those now eerily hollow pits staring back at me.

But no such luck. All that greets me is a sound that no language class prepared me for, a growl so deep and guttural it could vibrate my soul clean out of my body. To put it mildly, my survival instincts are waving red flags.

My nightmare of him taking the front seat, and panic kicks in. I start thrashing, throwing everything I've got to get free. It's like trying to dislodge a boulder—my desperate squirms are no match for him. With a ruthless shove, he flattens me back to the ground. I clamp down on my lip to hold back the screams, tasting the harsh tang of fear and determination.

That's when I spot it—this nasty silver collar wrapped around his neck like some kind of possession tag. It's dug deep into his skin and locked tight, and just seeing it makes my stomach turn. Anger and fear mix into this awful feeling because, seriously, who does this? Who thinks they can cage my free-spirited warrior and turn him into some broken puppet?

I'm mid-rant, trying to unleash verbal hell, when he pushes down on me hard. His whole body goes stiff and cold, and it doesn't feel like him at all. My brain is screaming that something's seriously wrong. Because this coldness and lack of care—it's nothing like my Rhyland. It's like he's been replaced by someone wearing his face.

His iron fingers grip my jaw, straining my neck cords, baring my frantically throbbing pulse. Things slow to nightmare speed, watching his lips peel off noticeably long fangs, now a mere breath from my jackhammering heartbeat.

Poised at my throat's fragile altar, Rhyland hesitates...and I glimpse the inner war waging behind those dark eyes. Somewhere, my mate—my man—battles encroaching madness and bloodlust even now.

I see a chance and twist away as his grip loosens just a tiny bit. I try to drive my knee up hard into anything that will hurt. But Rhyland's faster—he sees it coming and shifts, pinning both my legs under one massive thigh like they weigh nothing.

Before I can even react, my hands get slammed above my head. His grip on both my wrists is crushing, holding me down against the ground like I'm locked in chains.

I'm terrified and weirdly excited at the same time, which is a messed-up combination. I can feel his arousal pressing against me, and my body is responding even though everything about this situation is wrong. But my little moment of fighting back seems to kill whatever's left of the real Rhyland. He turns back into this stranger wearing his face, his fangs showing as he leans over me, staring at my neck like he's hungry.

"Rhyland, please! I'm right here—come back to me!" I'm basically begging, and yeah, I'm being extra dramatic about it.

Fear shoots through me like acid when suddenly Rhyland's face goes blank. He looks confused, like he's staring at things that aren't there. He's not seeing me, not recognizing me, even though I'm right underneath him, shaking.

His fangs catch that eerie blue light, and they're so close to my neck. I close my eyes tight, trying not to cry, terrified about what's about to happen.

Will he snap out of it? Or is this it? Am I about to become vampire chow?

My heart pounds as I wait—

Then he bites. His teeth sink into my neck, and I scream from the sudden pain. He pulls hard, draining my blood into him like he's starving. This isn't like his normal bites. This is aggressive and desperate.

But then the pain shifts into something else—that familiar burning heat that feels almost good. My blood warms against his mouth. He's pressed against me, grinding into me as he drinks. Fire floods through my body, and I feel myself getting turned on, which is seriously messed up right now. He definitely feels it. His hips move against me. I cry out as his fangs go deeper. He's destroying me and putting me back together at the same time.

I'm his.

He's marked me as his.

I'm completely under his control.

I'm scared, aroused, and in love all at once.

Rhyland pulls back just enough for our eyes to meet. I can see him fighting something inside—like madness and heartbreak are battling it out across his face.

"Don't leave me. Stay with me, Rhyland." Summoning a desperate force, I jolt up and seal our fate with a kiss to his blood-stained mouth. I funnel every last drop of my fear-fueled need into the kiss, the sole lifeline for two lovers adrift in a storm.

He growls low in his throat and kisses me back with this intense, desperate energy. His grip on my wrists slackens, and I seize the moment to draw him even closer. My fingers weave through his silky hair, and a wave of relief washes over my nerves as he kisses me back.

He's back—he's really back with me. His hot breath fans across my skin when he finally breaks our kiss, and his eyes roam the untamed expanse of the meadow, bewildered, as if seeing it for the first time.

I breathe in his scent and feel his heart pounding against mine. When he looks back at me, his eyes are full of confusion and uncertainty. My heart's racing as I stare into those beautiful, icy-blue eyes that I've missed so much.

"It's me, Dani." My voice shakes because I need him to understand. "You're safe. Everything's going to be okay."

His voice breaks, and he reaches out to touch my face with a shaky hand. "Angel?" He barely whispers it, like he can't believe I'm real.

Hearing his voice—really hearing it—wakes something up in me that I didn't know had gone cold. Tears run down my face as I nod, my heart so full it might burst. Relief, love, and fear are all crashing into me at once.

"I'm right here," I say, grabbing his hand and pressing it against my cheek so we can both feel that this is real. "I'm right here with you."

Rhyland stares into my eyes like he's trying to figure out if I'm really there. "Fuck..." he looks down at my bleeding neck, and his face goes panicked. "Did I hurt you?"

I nod and try not to cry. "But it doesn't matter," I tell him firmly, pulling him closer. "What matters is right now—you're here, and we're together."

His whole body shakes against mine as his voice cracks. "Fuck... I'm so sorry," he says like he's in pain. "I hurt you..."

But all I feel for him is love, even though he's broken and damaged. "It's okay," I whisper. I kiss him without thinking, pouring all my love and forgiveness into it.

He doesn't hold back. He kisses me like he's starving for me. He moans into my mouth, and I pull him even closer, desperate to keep him here with me.

I'm getting turned on, and all I can focus on is wanting him inside me. "Rhyland... I need you right now. Please..."

He pulls away from the kiss, his ice-blue eyes burning with want. "I need you too, Angel."

That cocky smile I love so much appears on his face, and it sets me on fire in the best way.

His hand slides down between my thighs, and heat floods through me. This thin dress isn't going to survive this. His calloused hand cups me, and I can already feel how wet I am, how ready my body is for him. I move against his palm, desperate for more friction. "Gods, I've missed you," he growls and tears the fabric of my dress away. "So wet and ready for me," he says with that teasing tone, running his fingers through my slickness before pushing two fingers inside me without warning.

I gasp at how fast he moves, my body tightening around his fingers as they sink deeper. I want more. Rhyland starts moving his fingers in and out, his thumb working my clit like he knows exactly what I need, like my body is a map only he can read.

"Yes," I cry out, my whole body building toward something intense. "Please..." I can barely breathe.

"You're mine, Angel," he growls, not stopping for a second. "Say it."

"Yes," I gasp as the pressure builds and builds. "I'm yours!" My body arches up, ready to go over the edge.

"Good girl." His thumb leaves my clit, and his fingers curl, hitting that perfect spot inside me as he keeps going relentlessly.

One more push, one more touch—I scream as my orgasm hits me hard and fast. I shake and tremble under his hand as he keeps moving, drawing it out. My hands grab his hair and pull him into a rough kiss. Our teeth bump together, and I taste my own blood mixed with him.

I need more. I need everything he has to give me.

I'm still catching my breath, my body slowly coming down from the high of my orgasm, when my gaze catches on the stupid band circling Rhyland's throat. Anger sparks hotly. "What is this damn thing? Take it off!"

He grimaces, fingering the rune-etched collar. "A damn muzzle from the Shadow Queen. It cut off our connection and killed our magic, too." Rage burns in his cold stare. "Her way of making sure I stay her loyal bloodsucking hound."

I grab that disgusting collar, fury giving me strength I didn't know I had. "Like hell! Let's rip this crap off right now and shove it up her—"

"It resists removal by force, Angel," Rhyland interrupts gently, stilling my hands. "The queen's magic secured it beyond even my strength."

Frustrated tears threaten me as I stare at the symbolic shackle stealing precious time together. Then sparks flicker unexpectedly at my fingertips, where they grasp the etched silver. I gasp as raw power surges down my arms, responding to my fierce emotion. "Stay still," I command, aiming a sharp look at Rhyland.

Heat builds in my hands, getting more focused and intense. All those times I've practiced, all those moments learning to control my power—they all come down to this. I pour everything I have into that collar, my eyes shut tight, picturing the metal breaking apart under pure light.

There's this sharp cracking sound—like ice breaking. The metal splits and shatters, the silver melting away and falling to the ground with a soft clink. We both stare in shock as the magic fades from my hands, still glowing from what we just did.

"I gotta remember never to piss you off," Rhyland murmurs before crushing his lips to mine.

I laugh, tears of joy mixing with everything else. He nips at my lip playfully, and suddenly all the darkness is gone, burned away by this bright, perfect feeling that I never want to fade.

"Thank you." His voice fills my mind like a whisper through our connection. That missing piece—it's back. Our bond is whole again. I feel this rush of completeness wash over me, like I've been broken and now I'm finally fixed.

I bite his lip back. "More... Rhyland. I need—"

He kisses me hard, shutting me up. His hand moves down between us, and he unzips his pants. His eyes promise me everything.

"I'm aching for you," I say desperately. Our bond is screaming for this, like an itch I can't scratch on my own. It's not just me wanting him—it's us, our connection demanding to be whole in every way.

He groans as I feel him hard and hot against me, right where I need him. "God damn, Angel, I'm burning for you—I swear it's more than you'll ever fucking know." Then he pushes inside me in one deep thrust.

"Fuck." As he bottoms out within me.

"Heaven," he groans into my neck, his fingers digging into my hips like he's trying to pull me even closer.

"More..." I demand, my nails dragging down his back.

"I know, baby," he grunts. "I know."

Rhyland starts moving his hips, my body rising to meet every thrust. I feel him grin against my neck, that wild, hungry grin that makes my whole body ache for him. "I swear, Angel, there's no end to what I'd give you. Always more, baby, always fucking more." He doesn't slow down, driving into me harder. "Fuuuck..." His hips move faster, deeper, more demanding. I feel him getting thicker and longer inside me. "I'm yours, Angel... always."

"Rhyland." I moan as he hits that perfect spot deep inside me, his fingers gripping my ass like he never wants to let go.

"I love it when you moan my name," he groans against my neck. I cry out louder as he stretches me.

Rhyland's head drops to the curve of my neck, his teeth grazing my collarbone. *I love you so damn much,* he admits, his voice raw and sincere. Our connection pulses through both of us, burning hot in my mind. He's everywhere inside me—not just physically but in every part of my soul. I'm drowning in this feeling of being completely whole, like I've transcended everything human. This isn't just sex—it's love, absolute and all-consuming.

My heart feels like it's going to explode from his words. A surge of emotion tears through me, making my whole body shake and tremble like I'm shattering into pieces.

His cock throbs with need as he slams me into the soft, cool grass. Every impact sends waves of pleasure rocketing through me. He grabs my leg and pulls it over his shoulder, finding another spot inside me that sends fire through my veins.

I can't help but moan, my hands gripping his neck as I pull him down to kiss me rough and savage. His mouth devours mine as he pounds into me relentlessly.

"Come for me again, Angel," he demands, his need driving every forceful thrust. "I need to feel you come undone around me. I need to feel you explode, baby."

He slams into me hard, and I shatter again, like a thousand tiny explosions happening all at once inside me. My body goes rigid and trembles as pleasure crashes over me in waves, my moans turning into raw screams. Rhyland's grip on my hips gets tighter as I drench him with my release.

He groans in satisfaction, his voice rough against my skin as he watches me fall apart. "Gods, you're so fucking beautiful."

My eyes roll back as I keep moving against him, lost in the intensity of our bodies joined together. Rhyland follows right after, spilling himself inside me as I hit another orgasm.

I need more.

I never want this to stop.

"I love you," I whisper against his neck. "I love you so damn much. I tried... I was trying to get to you—" Rhyland cuts me off with a kiss that steals the words right out of my mouth.

Everything feels perfect and complete as the taste of my blood sits on my tongue, and I realize I could never get enough of this man. Our bodies fit together like we're made for each other, taking us somewhere safe where nothing else matters—just us, just this love, just safety.

"I didn't think I'd ever see you again," Rhyland whispers once we can breathe again, his fingers gently tracing my cheek.

I lean up and kiss him softly. I give him a look that's half teasing, half serious. "Did you lose your memory along with your mind? We promised nothing would tear us apart. Some magical nonsense isn't going to let you off the hook for forgetting those vows, Vampking."

Rhyland runs his hand across my cheek, that smirk and dimple I love showing up. "We did." His expression shifts to pain. "I fought like hell for what felt like an eternity, almost got swallowed by the dark for good 'cause you weren't there to light my fuckin' way, Angel. Can you look past my moment of weakness?"

I shake my head, hating that he's torturing himself. "There's nothing to forgive! That evil witch played dirty, tearing us apart like that. But we will always find each other."

Rhyland nods seriously, darkness still flickering in his ice-blue eyes. "Fuck... I was so goddamn lost, baby," he says, like the words hurt him. "So lost I thought I'd never see your face again," his voice breaking with all the pain he went through.

I smile through my tears, looking at my brooding, protective vampire. Always so darkly romantic, even after nearly dying. "Well, here I am, Big Guy—ready to mess with destiny one more time with my oh-so-special Chosen One blood," I say, giving his perfect abs a playful poke.

Rhyland smirks and rolls onto his side, his hot gaze shamelessly scanning my mostly naked body. "What the hell are you wearing... or not wearing?" He tugs at the tiny leaf clasp that's barely covering my chest. "Not that I'm complaining about the view, baby."

I let out a loud sigh. "Don't blame me for this ridiculous forest outfit! That's all, thanks to our sparkly friend Axilya and her weird fashion taste."

Rhyland's fingers trace along the mesh fabric that's barely clinging to my skin, making me shiver. "Mmm, you look good enough to eat." A low, possessive growl rumbles from deep in his chest—pure vampire. "But hell if I'm letting anyone else get a look at what belongs to me."

"Well, take it up with Miss Loves-Attention and her leafy lingerie fetish!" I mock glare at him while his hand keeps playing with those useless straps.

"Who the hell is this... Axilya? And these definitely need a closer inspection..." Rhyland practically growls, laughing when I smack his wandering hands away.

"Cut it out before you tear this cheap costume completely off!" I grab his hand firmly, and I can feel that electric connection between us firing up again now that we've made it through the impossible.

"Maybe you won't need that dress much longer if I decide to have my way with you again," Rhyland teases, giving my ear a light bite.

I laugh and flip on top of him, pinning his hands above his head and straddling him. "Oh no, you don't! I can take you down now, Mister."

Rhyland's eyes go dark as I settle my weight on him. But with one quick move, he flips us over, pressing me back into the soft grass.

"I gotta admit, you've got guts for taking on creatures way out of your league; it's fucking adorable, Angel," he purrs. "Just don't forget who's got the real strength advantage here."

If he knew what I could do now—the power I've got flowing through me—he'd know I took his own brother to the ground like he was nothing.

His smirking face leans down toward mine, his warm lips finding the pulse racing in my neck. I tilt my head back, breathing out shakily, which makes him chuckle against my skin.

"Don't start something you can't finish—"

My half-hearted protest turns into a long moan as Rhyland kisses me hard and deep, like a starving man who's just found his greatest treasure again.

RHYLAND

21

"I'm not about to promise my hands will stay to themselves with you strutting around in these little cocktease scraps, baby." A wicked grin slashes across my face, deep chuckles rolling out as my fiery angel slaps away my roaming hands again.

She's on about gentlemanly manners—as if that shit matters now!

Unable to resist another second, I roll us swiftly, pinning soft curves along the length of me. I grind against barely-there barriers, craving sweet skin-on-skin again. "No fuckin' chance of playing the gentleman when my sexy mate's here, squirming around half-naked like some live-action fantasy."

I match her fierce gaze with my own, a raw need boiling over to pick up where fate's cruel joke left us off

I take Dani's lips hard, my kiss a mix of raw demand and reverent worship as I savor every eager gasp and moan my hunger coaxes from her. Every inch of me thrums with a heated sense of rightness, feeling her pressed against me after what felt like forever of missing her.

It's absolute perfection...

Our lips part, both of us breathing hard, but I keep her clutched close, not letting an inch slip between us. "To hell with the damn prophecy and all—that can take a backseat for now," I state, my voice fervent as I speak against the rapid beat of Dani's pulse. "We got some major sexual reunion dues to repay first, baby."

Her eager moan urges me on readily enough. Chuckling wolfishly again, I haul Dani close, soaking up the salvation of her softness pressed against my hardness. But there's a gnawing pang of guilt—I almost lost my shit completely without her heavenly touch keeping the remnants of my soul from going to shit.

If this angel hadn't found even a spark of light in the darkness of my soul, I'd be nothing but a monster drowning in bloodlust by now. I can feel the shadows retreating now, chased away by the blazing light that is everything Dani is and represents.

Tasting her blood is like injecting liquid sun, jolting life back into my dead veins and burning away the frozen emptiness from my cursed heart. Nothing compares to her, that sweet lifeblood that can drag a dead man's soul back from the edge, pushing back the worst horrors buried deep inside me.

"Wait—Where's Lucian?" Dani asks, her voice tinged with concern.

"He's fine. He's with Meadow—We'll get them... after I take care of you properly," I reassure her, my voice soft but firm.

"Meadow? Who—?"

"I'll explain later; don't worry about it."

I know Dani's worried about Lucian, and she should be—he's family, and we don't abandon our own. But right now, my focus is making damn sure my mate is safe and solid, both body and mind.

With lethal grace, I rise to my feet and pull Dani up with me. The moon's soft light hits her face, and a desperate, consuming need floods through me to tear away the thin fabric covering her silken skin. Our eyes lock and don't break as I run light fingertips along the edge of her clothes, carefully working through the fastenings and pressing whispered kisses to every inch of skin I expose.

As the thin material falls away from her breasts, her nipples are already hard from the cool night air. My fingers keep moving, circling and teasing each peaked tip until Dani gasps with pleasure. I lean down and take one into my mouth, working it until it hardens even more. She moans and buries her fingers in my hair, pulling me closer.

My hands trail up her sides, mapping every curve and hollow of her body before settling on the full swell of her ass, squeezing it hard and possessively. She throws her head back in pure bliss, but I can't get enough of her. She's intoxicatingly delicious, my angel.

I peel out of my clothes in seconds and before she can react, I haul her up into my arms, eating up the distance to the grotto in long, purposeful strides. Her startled gasp melts into breathless laughter.

"It's like a dream," she smiles as we enter the hidden paradise.

"Yes," I whisper against her lips. "Just like you."

With the moon as our only light, the whole place feels magical. The tiny waterfall casts a romantic glow, and the small flowers and vines climbing the walls sparkle like fairy lights in the darkness. I gently lower Dani into the warm, steaming water, her body pressing tight against mine as she sinks into the bubbles. The feel of her soft curves against me drives me absolutely wild with hunger. As the water caresses our skin, I can't help but groan in pure pleasure.

Christ, I already had her just moments ago, and I still can't get enough. The bond screams inside me, demanding more, demanding everything. It's like our connection is clawing at my chest, begging me to bury myself in her and never stop. The separation was too long, too brutal. Every moment apart carved pieces out of me, left me hollow and starving. Now that she's here, touching me, the bond demands I claim her over and over until that void finally disappears. Until there's no distance, no gap, nothing but us fused together.

My hands glide over every inch of her body, ensuring she's clean and safe. Every touch reassures me she's still here, still mine.

Her hands explore my body in return, tracing every contour and plane of muscle as if committing my form to memory. Each gentle caress is filled with tenderness and affection, a physical expression of our deep bond. In this moment, the outside world fades away, and all that exists is the love and comfort we find in each other's presence.

She lets out a throaty moan as the hot water tickles her sensitive spots, but it only amps up her lust. She grabs my neck and pulls me in, our lips smashing together in a desperate, lust-filled kiss. Her limbs are wrapped around me tightly.

Our tongues battle for dominance, igniting a fucking inferno between us. I sense her craving for me, her insatiable hunger, and it's driving me wild with a heady mix of my own dirty desires.

My tension starts to melt away as I lose myself in the moment. Dani's hands roam over my chest, tracing every line and curve before descending lower. Her tight little legs grip my hips, tightening as she squeezes around me, causing my already hard cock to throb against her stomach. She grins wickedly, her eyes filled with lust and longing.

"The ache of missing you has been nothing short of brutal," she breathes out, her hot breath fanning across my skin.

Brutal doesn't even begin to cover it, Angel. Her words mirror exactly what's been eating me alive. The bond between us has been screaming in agony this entire time, every second apart feeling like a lifetime.

The separation carved holes in me that only she can fill. My cock's already straining, desperate to be buried in her heat, to remind us both that we belong to each other in every possible way. The bond won't settle for anything less than complete and total connection.

I nibble on her earlobe, eliciting a shiver from her. "I know, Angel—every damn ache, I felt it tear through me like nothing else. But I swear on everything, I'm never fucking letting you go." I growl huskily, consumed by emotion.

I capture her lips in a searing kiss, our tongues dancing together in a slow, sultry rhythm—gods—her lips. I could kiss her forever. Her hands are all over my body, massaging and kneading my skin. I lean forward to nip at her perky, rosy nipples, eliciting a soft moan from her.

I devour her body, relishing the flavor of her skin. The aroma of her arousal overwhelms my senses, igniting a desperate lust within me. I yank her toward me, forcefully turning her around and pressing her against my chest. Her hair tickles my bare torso, sending electric tingles straight down to my throbbing cock.

Her ass grinds against me, driving me absolutely insane with desire. I can feel every muscle in her stomach contracting and quivering as she rubs herself against me like she's starving for it.

She throws her head back, her body flush against mine as she moans in pleasure. She grinds against me harder. "You want my throbbing cock deep in that tight little ass again, don't you, baby?" I growl in her ear.

She gasps and shudders at my words, bucking against me even harder. My hands move to the front, groping and squeezing her delicious, luscious breasts. Their weight fills my palms, driving me to absolute madness. "That tight little ass can wait, baby. Right now, I want this dripping cunt."

I move us to the nearby rocks, keeping her tight against me. My hand slithers down her stomach and finds her wet and ready. Pressing my body against hers from behind, she moans at my touch, her arms reaching back to grip my neck and thrust her breasts forward. I gaze down at the sinful sight of my angel, her ass grinding against me as my fingers slide over her soaking pussy. "You're such a dirty girl," I growl as I slide two fingers deep into her. She clenches around my fingers, her breathing heavy and ragged. "You're always so fucking wet for me, aren't you?"

"Always—for you."

Her head falls against my shoulder as I push a finger inside of her, hitting that spot that makes her see stars. A loud moan escapes her lips as she rocks her hips against my hand. I alternate between circling her clit and fingering her tight cunt until her breath quickens. Her moans grow louder and louder.

She reaches back to grab my hair, pulling my mouth to her neck. "Please, *gods*, I need you. I need you inside me again, Rhyland," she begs.

"You realize what begging turns me into, right?" I growl, my breath hot on her neck. She nods frantically, her hair tickling my face.

I slowly remove my hand from her slick, swollen center and gently bend down and lift her onto the edge of the steaming hot springs. Droplets of fairy pool water cling to her skin, glistening like diamonds in the moonlight filtering through the trees. Her flawless skin takes on a radiant, almost ethereal white-golden glow.

Her chest heaves with anticipation as I gently spread her legs, my warm breath tickling the sensitive skin of her inner thighs. My lips hover just inches from her glistening, wet petals, and a shiver runs through her body at the thought of what's coming.

"I am famished, Angel," I growl, hunger pulsing through me. "And all I crave is you."

DANICA

22

As I gaze down at the rugged, spicy Viking between my thighs, a deep ache awakens within me. No matter how often we come together, my body always craves his touch.

Rhyland's damp hair clings to his forehead, enhancing his wild and captivating allure. His rough beard grazes my skin while his muscular, tattooed body glistens in the dim light. Every inch of him radiates pure masculinity, igniting my desire. I can feel the wetness pooling between my thighs, a mixture of him and me, and proof of the powerful effect he has on me.

He leans in, his gaze dark and ravenous, as if he's about to devour me. I can't help but arch my hips, pressing myself against his face. A low growl rumbles in his chest as he grips my hips, holding me firmly in place. His tongue darts out, tasting my exposed and swollen clit, sending a jolt of pleasure through my body.

He doesn't seem bothered by the taste of himself mixed with me, and that realization sends heat flooding through me. The warmth of his mouth and the way he savors our combined flavors sends a thrilling jolt straight to my core.

He teases me by slowly dragging his tongue up my slit, licking and nipping at my sensitive skin. My body writhes and trembles with need, my fingers tangling in his hair, pulling him closer. His long, thick lashes brush against my skin as his warm breath surrounds me. He keeps tormenting me, circling my clit with slow, deliberate strokes that make me lose my mind.

A gasp tears from my lips as I throw my head back, my neck arching as pleasure washes over me. The damp moss under me feels electric, building my anticipation. The waterfall nearby mixes with Rhyland's groans and the wet sounds of his mouth on me, creating this perfect symphony of nature and pure pleasure.

"God, baby, you taste like the sweetest candy," he murmurs against my skin, his voice thick with desire. "Want to know my favorite place to bite you?"

I nod, barely able to breathe or think.

He trails kisses along my inner thigh, leaving heat in his wake. "Right here," he growls, his teeth grazing the soft flesh. "And here," he adds, flicking his tongue over my throbbing clit.

My heart pounds at the thought of him feeding from me like that, so intimate and intense. My cheeks burn, and my eyes go wide with shock and arousal at the same time.

A seductive smile spreads across Rhyland's face as he leans in close, whispering, "You'll love it, baby. You might even beg for it." Then he drives his razor-sharp fangs into my thigh, and a moan rips out of me. Pleasure and pain mix as he drinks from me, his hands roaming everywhere on my body.

He growls against my skin, sending shivers racing down my spine. The feeling of his fangs piercing me, combined with his hands exploring me, drives me absolutely wild. I can feel myself getting wetter, my hips bucking up against him as he keeps drinking. Heat builds intensely in my belly, my clit throbbing with desperate need.

Oh, god...

Then he suddenly pulls away, licking his lips clean. My body automatically reaches for him, but he grabs my wrists and pins them above my head. A low, feral growl rumbles from his chest as he locks eyes with me, his lips stained red with my blood. The sight of him like that sends pleasure crashing through me, making the ache between my thighs even worse.

"Not yet, baby," he whispers, his voice husky and dangerous.

Can I really come just from him feeding off my thigh? The thought thrills me, and I realize I want so much more.

His voice drips with danger and seduction as he speaks against my ear. "See? I knew you would." I shudder at the feel of his hot breath on my skin.

"Yes... more than anything," I reply, dragging my tongue up the side of his neck, tracing the intricate tattoo patterns. He tenses, groaning as his hardness presses against my stomach. "Rhyland," I whimper, my whole body burning with need for him.

The air around us crackles with electrifying energy. His eyes burn with intense hunger as he growls, "You're fucking mouthwatering, baby. You have any idea what you do to me?"

He slides his hand between my thighs, cupping me and rubbing his palm against me in this sinful, tempting way. "You want me, baby? You want my thick cock inside that tight cunt?" His voice is a gravelly demand, thick with arousal.

"Fuck yes," I breathe, my body throbbing with need. "I want you. All of you."

His mouth crashes onto mine, consuming me with a kiss that makes it crystal clear he owns me completely. It's fierce, demanding, and utterly intoxicating.

He pulls back, his eyes burning. "Say it again."

I respond with a guttural growl of frustration and desperate need. He knows exactly what I want, and he's loving every second of this game.

A fierce grin spreads across his face, and in one smooth motion, he flips me onto the rough, moss-covered rock, pinning my hands behind my back. My breasts press against the cool stone, and I can feel his cock against my ass. With his free hand, he wraps his fingers around my throat, making me arch back against him in complete surrender.

His dominating presence overwhelms me, his large hand easily circling my throat. I crave more of his passionate intensity, my body desperate for him to claim every inch of me.

A menacing growl rumbles from deep in his chest, sending electricity coursing through my entire body. "You have no fucking idea how much I love your defiance," he teases, his voice dripping with lust. "I can feel your frustration, baby. That desperate hunger coiled tight inside you."

His words are a promise, threatening to destroy every last bit of my control. How does he do this to me? My body aches for him in ways I never imagined possible.

"Stop teasing me, Rhy—" My words cut off as his grip tightens, cutting off my air. My pussy throbs, arousal coating my thighs.

His satisfaction surges through our bond, a two-way street of connection. He tightens his hold on my throat, an erotic moan escaping him. "So fucking beautiful," he murmurs.

He releases my throat, but before I can catch my breath, he slams into me with brutal force. A cry of pain and pleasure tears from my lips as he fills me completely, stretching me to the absolute limit.

I writhe beneath him, my arms still pinned as he grabs a handful of my hair, forcing my head back. His touch sets every sensitive nerve ending on fire, making me feel like I'm at his complete mercy. He exposes my neck, driving into me with relentless force.

"Is this what you need?" he asks, his voice low and dangerous as he hammers into me. "My cock...fucking you...hard and deep?"

My sensitive nipples drag against the rough surface, sending spikes of pleasure and pain through me. They harden, tight and peaked, the friction adding to the flood of delicious sensations overwhelming my body.

The sounds of our bodies colliding and the rush of blood in my ears drown out everything else. The intense, animalistic noises escaping my throat reveal just how consumed I am by him. Every nerve in my body is electrified as he claims me, his words driving me closer and closer to the breaking point.

"Answer me, Dani," he commands.

I can barely form words as pleasure consumes me. "Y-yes...oh, fuck..." I gasp between thrusts.

"Fuck, you look so fucking beautiful taking my cock," he growls, his voice rough like gravel. "My dirty angel, all mine." *Slap, slap, slap.* Our bodies coming together.

I cry out, my body arching, begging for more. He pistons into me like a wild claimed beast. "You love it when I pound into you, don't you, baby?" His voice is demanding and commanding. "You're gonna be my cock-hungry whore Dani? My dirty girl?"

The words shiver through my body, and I know he owns me completely. I am his depraved plaything, and I want nothing more than to be his whore.

The force of his thrusts takes my breath away, stealing any ability to speak.

"Answer me," he demands, pulling my hair harder.

"F-fuck...*yes,*" I moan, giving in to my desires.

"That's a good girl," he praises. "That's it, take it all," he urges, his voice fierce. "Take my cock; take everything I give you because it's all yours, baby. Every. Fucking. Inch."

Every nerve in my body feels like it's on fire as Rhyland fills me, his cock driving into me with an intense, overwhelming force. I scream his name, my orgasm crashing over me like a tidal wave, threatening to drown me in its intensity.

"Fuuuck, baby," he groans, "I love how you drench me." He revels in the way I soak his cock with my release, fueling my pleasure even more.

I can feel him throbbing inside me as he releases hot, potent streams of desire deep within me, igniting another wave of pleasure.

An intense moan escapes him as he collapses onto me, both of us completely spent from the passionate encounter. I can feel our combined releases trickling down my thighs, marking me as his.

We lay there, panting and tangled together, as the cool night air brushes against our sweat-damp skin. The waterfall continues its soothing melody, a stark contrast to our fierce, all-consuming passion.

Rhyland rolls onto his side, pulling me close to him. His arms wrap protectively around me, and I rest my head on his chest, listening to the steady beat of his heart. The realization that I'm completely naked and exposed to the elements makes my skin tingle with heightened awareness.

"Angel," he whispers, his voice lazy with satisfaction.

He gently kisses my forehead, and I laugh softly, my voice still colored with contentment. "Rhyland," I whisper, my eyes fluttering closed.

I can feel his lips curve into a smile against my skin. "You're so fucking beautiful when you come," he murmurs, his voice tender and full of affection.

A chuckle escapes me at his words. It's hard to believe that fate brought my long-lost vampire lover back into my arms after everything that kept us apart. I resist the urge to touch him more, knowing that we need to talk about what happened during our time separated.

"What did she do to you, Rhyland?" I ask softly, my finger tracing lazy patterns on his chest.

I can feel him tense beside me, his jaw going rigid. He begins to recount the horrors he endured at the hands of Amara, the Royal Freakshow, as he calls her. The details pour from his lips in a flood of anger and pain, each new revelation making my blood run cold. I can't help but feel a burning rage build inside me, a fierce need to protect him from any more suffering.

Rhyland's rough palm settles on my cheek, his ocean-blue eyes searching mine. Despite the horrors he endured, his gentle touch still grounds me. "Dani," he says softly, his hand cupping my cheek. "Don't let her cruelty darken your light."

I nod, tears collecting in my eyes. "I'm so sorry she hurt you," I whisper, my voice thick with emotion.

"Nothing she did can truly harm me, not while I have you," he assures me, his thumb brushing away a stray tear.

His words strike deep into my heart, filling me with renewed love and determination. I press a tender kiss to his palm, moving closer to him. We lay there in silence, lost in our own thoughts as the waterfall's melody soothes us into a peaceful calm.

Rhyland's voice rumbles softly in the darkness. "I never stopped trying to reach you—"

I smile, remembering his promise to me, which feels like a lifetime ago. "Well, you did promise me forever."

"I meant it, Dani," he insists, his voice hardening with resolve. "I'll keep that vow, no matter what obstacles or enemies stand in our way."

I lift my head to meet his gaze, my voice filled with certainty. "I know, and we'll face them together."

His hand slides to my neck, threading through my hair as he pulls me in for a fierce kiss. "You're my everything, Dani. My mate, my heart, my existence," he whispers against my lips.

Tears gather at the corners of my eyes as I hold him close, grateful for the man who entered my life and healed my broken heart. "You're mine, too. Forever and always."

Just then, Syla emerges and settles between us. Her bright, amber eyes look up at me with concern. Thank the gods, she's okay.

Rhyland practically jumps out of his skin. "What the hell is that?"

Ever the charmer, Syla snuggles up to him like a cat, purring happily.

"This adorable fuzzball is Syla; she's a Coatl and the sweetest creature you'll ever meet. Aren't you, my little cutie patootie?" I coo, scratching her ears in that ridiculously high-pitched baby voice.

Rhyland relaxes and slowly pets Syla's head, earning a deep purr from her.

"I think she likes you," I whisper, a smile spreading across my face.

"Well, that makes two of us," Rhyland says, his voice low and sultry.

I raise an eyebrow, a smirk playing at my lips. "Oh, really? I had no idea you were so fond of yourself, RhyPie. But I suppose that explains the excessive preening."

He growls, then laughs, pulling me in for a heated kiss that sends heat racing through my body. He slightly pulls back, "RhyPie? I don't know if I will allow that pet name, Angel."

"Oh, come on, it's adorable!" I protest, my eyes sparkling with amusement. "Besides, you call me Angel. I think it's only fair I get to give you an equally cute nickname."

Rhyland raises an eyebrow, a smirk crossing his face. "Cute? I'm not sure that's the word I'd use. Dashing, perhaps. Or devastatingly handsome."

I roll my eyes, unable to hide my smile. "Fine, how about... Sailor Stud? Vike Spice? Ooh, I know—Fjord Lord!"

He chuckles, shaking his head. "You're such a brat, you know that?"

"And you love it," I retort, pulling him in for another kiss, Syla purring contentedly between us.

DANICA

23

Well, *that* was one steamy fae forest reunion to remember! Still tingling all over in places magical glitter can't reach, I finish wriggling awkwardly back into the barely-there overshare pixie costume while watching Rhyland's unfairly perfect ass disappear back into those snug black jeans.

Hellooo lover!

We meander back to the encampment, basking in the warm afterglow of a reunion that only soulmates divided by time could share, all under the approving shimmer of the stars above.

Emerging from the shelter of the trees, we're abruptly bathed in the flickering torchlight. My smile solidifies into a picture-perfect 'oh no' as the realization hits me square in the face. My cheeks blaze with heat under the camp's collective gaze. Their stares and half-hidden smirks tell me they caught the forest performance of our passionate encore.

Syla curled safely in my arms; she peeks her head up at the staring faces, her bright amber eyes wide with curiosity.

Here walks Rhyland, my shirtless Viking vamp, oozing nonchalance while I am shrinking into myself, wishing I could vanish out of sheer embarrassment.

"That was a hell of a homecoming, don't you think, Angel?" Rhyland's voice echoes, strong and commanding, across the hushed camp.

I jab him with my elbow, face on fire, "Zip it, will you?" I whisper. Casting a glance at the sea of smirks around us, I'm mentally shopping for a nice invisibility cloak.

Rhyland chuckles, clearly enjoying my embarrassment. "Don't be ashamed to let the world hear just how much I make you scream my name, baby."

"Ugh, you're impossible," I mutter, quickening my pace toward Faderyn and Axilya's tent—anything to escape the prying eyes and knowing looks. Rhyland's laughter follows me as I duck inside, my heart pounding.

Syla jumps from my arms and heads over to Axilya, snuggling up to her. Axilya looks down at the little Coatl with a soft smile, gently stroking her fur as Syla purrs contentedly.

Axilya raises one elegant brow. "Welcome back. I trust you and Rhyland have...reconnected?"

I groan, covering my beet-red face.

Faderyn smiles sympathetically. "Do not worry, Danica. We are simply glad you and Rhyland have found each other again."

Rhyland's blue eyes have turned into frosted daggers of resolve aimed straight at Faderyn. Every sinew in his body is pulled tight, his aura practically humming with fatal wrath. "Who the hell is this?" he growls, his voice rolling deep like thunder on the horizon.

Cutting off Rhyland's looming threat with diplomatic urgency, I jump in quickly. "Rhyland, meet Faderyn," I interject, positioning myself between them. "He's on our side—a friend—he's the one who came to my rescue—"

"A friend?" Rhyland curls his lip into a sneer. "Is that what we're calling it?"

"What?" I blink at him, taken aback.

"Don't fuckin' play dumb, Dani," Rhyland growls. "I can smell that bastard's lust for you all over him."

My jaw drops, and disbelief splashes across my face. "What...? You can actually *smell* his lust for me? No, Rhyland, hold up—you're way off base here!"

"Then enlighten me," he challenges, crossing his arms over his broad chest.

I snap back at Rhyland, my anger igniting. "The nerve of you—throwing accusations at Faderyn without knowing what went down!"

"Do I?" His eyes pierce Faderyn, the uncomfortable outsider caught between us.

Faderyn's lips remain sealed, staying quiet, but those emerald eyes speak to me—gentle and calm against the storm of rage that is Rhyland right now.

"Cool your jets," I exhale sharply, pivoting to Faderyn. "Faderyn's been the good guy here, a friend and then some. He was there for me when it was a party of one." Spinning back to Rhyland, my words come pouring out. "I don't know what the hell has gotten your fangs in a twist... but let's get one thing straight—there's been zero funny business between us!"

My face is burning, probably glowing brighter than the flickering fae campfires as I stand my ground. Rhyland's got that look—fury blazing so intensely it could rival the most powerful fae magic, his entire body coiled tight like a spring ready to snap, barely containing his rage. It's like facing down a thunderstorm that's desperate to break loose.

I manage to keep my eyes from rolling. Rhyland's ancient possessiveness is definitely getting postponed for a serious conversation later.

"That's enough." Axilya's voice cuts through, sharp and commanding. "I would appreciate it if you could keep your hostility towards my people to a minimum." Her warning lands, and Rhyland backs down.

For now, the storm has passed. Taking a step back, I give both men my 'let's focus on what matters' expression.

"Alright, with that mess untangled, let's turn our attention to the actual bad guys, shall we?"

The room goes quiet as Axilya outlines her plan, her pale green eyes sharp and calculating.

I turn to Axilya, confusion creasing my brow. "Wait—you still want us to meet with Amara when we have Rhyland?" I give Axilya a firm look. "Instead of walking straight into Amara's trap, why don't we head back to Whispervale? Rhyland's free; meeting Amara now puts a target on our backs."

"She knows we've escaped. Dani's right." Rhyland confirms.

Axilya pauses, her strategic mind working through the possibility. "Amara won't take kindly to being stood up, but... yes," she concedes reluctantly. "It may be wiser to strengthen our position away from her attention. I will come up with an excuse—perhaps the carriage malfunctioning—for our absence." Axilya walks back and forth across the floor. "Very well, back to Whispervale," she decides, though clearly with some hesitation.

Rhyland's voice burns with intensity, a rough edge to his urgent words. "Damn straight. We need to get as far from that bitch as possible. We need to focus on Dani's quest for that fucking stone. It's time to take control and push this prophecy forward."

"Indeed, moving quickly would be advantageous in addressing this matter—the sooner, the better," Axilya agrees.

I turn to Rhyland, laying out everything Axilya told me—that Amara's loaded with serious dark magic, hoarding power like it's her personal treasure, and how the Sun Court's got this special magic barrier that's blocking her evil energy.

"I know all about that hag's twisted dark magic. Looks like compulsion shit to me—but that crap doesn't work on us vamps." Rhyland sits down in a nearby chair. "She's messing with serious shadow magic too—almost as bad as Azrael's level."

"Compulsion?" Axilya asks, horrified. The color drains completely from her face. "She can force others to do whatever she commands?"

"From what I've learned, yeah—but it's hard to pin down. As I said, that kind of magic has no effect on us." I move to Rhyland's side and run my fingers through his hair. "Looks like she's got everyone under her control, whether they want to be or not; that's the real question." Rhyland states.

"What of Alinar?" Axilya asks quickly. I notice her expression and her glassy eyes.

"He was there, playing up to that disgusting hag," Rhyland confirms.

Axilya moves toward the back of the tent, and I sense it—she's not just upset; she's carrying deep pain. I start to follow her, maybe to listen, but Faderyn holds up his hand. "We should get some rest tonight. We have a long journey back tomorrow."

I fill Rhyland in on everything that happened while we were apart—his face shows worry and curiosity as I tell him about my near-death experience in the water and how Faderyn saved me.

"And here's the kicker—Erik found me afterward. He's been training me," I say with a hint of pride in my voice.

Rhyland smiles knowingly. "Ah, Erik schooling you, huh? Should've known he'd take you on as his new protégé."

I put my hands on my hips and flip my hair over my shoulder dramatically. "That's right, I've picked up a few tricks. So watch it, don't push me, or you might find yourself flat on your ass, Viking." I give him a playful but serious look.

Rhyland's laugh is deep and rumbling. "I'm dying to see these new moves of yours, baby. Maybe we should set up a little sparring session later." He gives me a heated look that makes my cheeks flush.

His face hardens, the playfulness slipping away. "Listen, about that shit with Faderyn earlier... I'm sorry I got so riled up. When mates are bonded, we can legitimately smell it when someone else hungers for our other half. It triggers some fierce protective bullshit in me."

My eyebrows arch high with intrigue. "Well, that's a new one."

Rhyland sets his jaw as he nods. "Yeah, it's like an extra sense that activates." He takes my hands with surprising gentleness despite his rough exterior. "I'll confront any asshole who dares to want what belongs to me."

I give Rhyland a heated smile, my heart pounding with excitement I can't ignore. As much as I don't need his possessive nature, it stirs something untamed inside me.

My hand rises, fingers softly tracing the lines of his face. "Listen to me, Captain Complicated. There's only you. Being apart has turned me into an emotional mess. Yeah, Faderyn's been a good friend, but that's all it is." I lean closer, my kiss barely touching his. "This heart right here? It beats for you, *only* you, forever and always."

Rhyland's tension eases, the stress draining from his powerful shoulders. I step back and rest against a tree, still feeling the intensity of Rhyland's attention on me. "So tell me, how's that stone-faced brother of mine keeping his shit together?" he asks, concern threading through his voice.

"He's been Mr. Serious, as always," I smirk. "You know Erik—he acts like he's unbreakable but melts when someone needs him."

Rhyland's mouth quirks in amusement. "That's Erik for you, always dependable. He's been looking after you?"

"Looking after? Come on, I've been the one keeping him busy with intense training sessions," I say with a confident smirk, feeling proud of how far I've come. "But I'll admit it—through all the chaos, he's been solid as stone."

Rhyland nods, his bright blue eyes flashing with approval.

"He was the one who kept me breathing when the bond felt like it was crushing me," I say with a gentle smile, remembering how Erik's unwavering support carried me through so many nights. "He'd chase away the nightmares that threatened to consume me, wipe my tears, and remind me to keep hoping." I pause, collecting my thoughts, "But honestly? His intense training sessions—they were my anchor. They kept me from drowning in my thoughts; they kept me from completely falling apart while missing you."

In seconds, Rhyland's in front of me, his strong hand tilting my chin upward. My eyes meet his deep ocean blue gaze, "I'm so damn sorry you had to go through that, sweetheart. It destroys me knowing I caused you that pain. I swear I'll do everything in my power to make sure nothing like that ever happens again." His lips gently touch mine. "And then I'm going to tear Erik a new one for laying a finger on you."

I raise an eyebrow playfully. "What, you jealous that your scary right-hand man—brother turned out to be a cuddly teddy bear? Maybe I should be the one getting territorial over him." I punctuate it with a playful wink. "I could watch you two wrestle it out...preferably shirtless and covered in oil." I gesture up and down at Rhyland, "my smoldering, alpha-licious Viking."

Rhyland flashes a wicked grin, his eyes full of mischief, before letting out a low growl as he buries his face in my neck. "You're just asking for trouble, aren't you?" he growls against my neck, his teeth gently nipping my skin, "begging for me to remind you who's in charge with all that attitude." He emphasizes his point by gripping both sides of my ass and squeezing firmly.

A laugh bubbles up from me as Rhyland's teeth playfully nip my skin, the man radiating jealousy and possessiveness like it's second nature. Honestly, I wouldn't want him any other way.

I quickly change the subject, "We need to go find Lucian."

Rhyland nods, his expression becoming focused. "Come on, Angel."

As we move forward, I keep pace with him, my resolve driving me. It's time to rescue the wiseass known as Lucian and maybe come up with some additional funny nicknames for Rhyland along the way.

RHYLAND

24

We push through thick trees and brush, the moon's silver light casting long shadows across the forest floor. The cold night air cuts against the heat pouring off Dani's body. I feel her hand in mine, her grip strong and reassuring.

"Meadow," I start, figuring it's time to fill her in. "She's complicated, that one. We ran into her deep in Amara's fortress. The girl's got this fire in her, even though she's basically a nobody in the fae hierarchy."

Dani nods, her golden eyes bright with interest as we keep moving through the trees.

"She's the reason Lucian and I didn't die in that shithole, or worse," I say, genuine appreciation in my voice. "And the girl's got some kind of ability—visions or something. She sees shit before it happens."

"A seer?" Dani asks, tilting her head slightly.

"Pretty much, yeah. But the part she played—it was damn critical."

I stop talking as we get close to the cave where I left Lucian and Meadow. We step inside, and the stale cave air hits us, but there's nothing. No sign of either of them.

"Lucian!" My voice bounces off the stone walls, and nothing comes back. "Mouse!" Just our own breathing and the steady drip of water from the ceiling fill the silence.

Dani raises an eyebrow at me, her eyes asking the question she doesn't say out loud. "Mouse?"

I manage a weak smile, but unease is already crawling up my spine. "That's my nickname for her—tiny, sneaky, and quick, just like a mouse."

Dani remains quiet, picking up on my growing anxiety.

Closing my eyes, I send out a silent call, probing for my brother with our instinctive connection. I stretch my senses, searching for Lucian. Suddenly, I sense his unmistakable signature coming from directly overhead. Opening my eyes, I meet Dani's probing gaze.

"They're up the mountain," I tell her bluntly.

I study Dani, looking for any sign that she might be balking at the plan, but I see only determination—the same resolve coursing through me. "It looks like we're scaling a mountain," I state plainly.

Her nod is firm as we mentally prepare for what challenges the mountain has in store for us.

Under the full moon's light, we tackle the upward path. I watch Dani as we climb, her movements confident and graceful. The moonlight plays off her figure, dressed in an outfit that accentuates every curve, and my thoughts start to stray.

I force my eyes to look up and meet hers. "You know," I say, pulling back from those dangerous thoughts, "you still haven't filled me in on Axilya."

Dani rolls her eyes at the mention of her name. "She's been helpful," she admits, hoisting herself over a rock. "But I swear, her taste in clothing is designed to torture me."

I arch an eyebrow. "Oh?"

"Let's just say her taste in attire for me has been more suited for a burlesque show than battle or diplomacy," Dani says, a note of frustration tingeing her voice but her lips curling in amusement.

"I gotta say, I like the view," I can't help but respond.

She playfully swats my arm. "You would. It's bad enough having Faderyn and Erik gawking without adding you to the mix."

Ignoring the comment about Faderyn, I ask quickly, feeling a sudden flare of possessiveness, "But she's on our side?"

"Yeah, she is," Dani replies. "She believes in what we're fighting for."

The back-and-forth between us feels natural, each word closing the gap that was torn between us. Dani opens up about unicorns, legendary creatures with untamed magic and incredible power, each color representing different aspects of what they can do.

Finally, we reach the top of the mountain, the climb feeling like it took forever and no time at all. I call out, "Lucian, you here?"

Lucian drops from a tree branch above, landing with precision.

"Jesus Christ, Lucian!" Dani yelps as she stumbles back into me. "You scared the shit out of me." She swats his arm.

Lucian grins, aiming his smirk squarely at us. "Who, me? Scary? Never," he quips with mock astonishment, then bursts into a bout of chuckles, clearly amused by Dani's reaction.

"Scare is putting it mildly," she shoots back, her eyes thin slits of mock indignation, but the corners of her mouth betray her, twitching with a smile.

Lucian cocks one eyebrow, his dark brown eyes dancing with impish glee. "Damn, I was going for more of a 'holy shit, I just soiled myself' level of abject terror," he quips, a cocky smirk plastered across his face.

I roll my eyes while Dani scrambles to find her footing again after the shock. "Always the pain in the ass," I toss out with a gruff chuckle.

"And you're always ugly as sin—some things never change," Lucian fires back.

Dani can't help it; she laughs despite herself. "You're such an asshole, you know that?" she says, humor clear in her voice.

Lucian's voice oozes with his signature snark, "So this is what you were chasing when you put on your grumpy face." He shakes his head, amusement in his voice. "Should've known. But hey, Princess, I'm glad he found you. Dude was a bee's dick away," he holds up his fingers, barely apart, "from completely losing his marbles."

Dani sighs and looks up at me with concern in her eyes.

Having Lucian here, real and solid, eases the tension that's been sitting heavy in my chest.

Dani fills Lucian in on the last few days—the allies she's pulled together, the fights she's been through, and the political moves she's had to make in this fucked-up game of courts and power. Respect shows in Lucian's eyes as he listens, his gaze landing on Dani with something that looks a lot like admiration, recognizing the strength in her.

"Where's Mouse?" I ask as Dani finishes, still worried about the small fae who helped us escape.

Lucian calls out, "Mouse, time to show yourself. The coast is clear—no nasty wolves lurking around."

Meadow lands softly among the leaves. Her big, round eyes lock onto mine before shifting to Dani.

"You're Dani," she says, her voice barely above a whisper, like she's speaking about something holy.

Dani responds with a smile as kind as summer. "And you're Meadow, I take it."

Meadow steps forward, wide-eyed, her breath coming out shaky. "The Light, you're the Light in my visions."

Dani's brows furrow in confusion, a silent question for me to explain.

"Meadow here's got some tricks up her sleeve," I say, pulling Dani against my side. "Those visions I mentioned? You're front and center in them, sweetheart."

Meadow nods eagerly. "I saw storms and lightning, and you were right there in the middle of it all."

As I'm about to dive deeper, Dani's attention snags on something else—Meadow's hold on the book, which looks like it's seen better days.

"What do you have there?" Dani asks, gesturing toward the worn tome.

Meadow looks down like she just noticed the book was there. "Oh, this? It's... I thought it would have the spell to break the collars." Her gaze lifts to mine, then drifts to my neck. "Your collar—it's gone!" Her voice shoots up with excitement.

My hand moves on instinct, my fingertips brushing against the smooth skin where that fucking collar used to dig into me—no more cold, hard metal.

A smile spreads across my face as I turn to Dani, who's so much more than she realizes—hell, my savior in every damn way. "Magic didn't stand a chance," I say, pride flooding my voice. "Dani got me out with something that hits way harder."

Meadow moves closer, her eyes bright and full, staring at Dani like she's looking at a living legend.

Lucian cuts in, all diplomacy gone as usual. "Hey, maybe we could put a pin in the heavenly reunion moment?" he drawls with sarcasm. "Because there's just the small, tiny issue of this fancy-ass hellhound collar situation." He grabs the collar and shakes it. "That disappearing act you just pulled with my brooding pain in the ass? Think you could do that magic trick one more time for the stubborn blonde asshole in back?"

Dani raises an eyebrow, a smirk tugging at her lips. "Oh, look who's getting his knickers in a knot over an accessory. Hate to break it to you, Lucy, but this isn't a drive-thru service." Her expression turns serious as she locks eyes with Lucian. "First things first, you need to drink my blood."

Lucian's face lights up. "Oh, *hell* yeah," he drawls, that signature smartass tone that turns everything into something dirty kicking in. "If that's an open invite to get up close and personal with a gorgeous woman like you—"

"Dial it back, Casanova," Dani interrupts sharply. "There's nothing remotely sexual about this unless you're into getting your ass kicked by light magic."

Lucian's eyes shine with wicked amusement as he cuts in, "Listen, I've been stuck drinking rat blood and whatever other fairy garbage I could sink my fangs into for weeks now," he complains with that trademark sarcasm. "So if that's your way of offering me a taste of the good stuff..." He pauses on purpose, his eyes glinting as he leans in with a cocky grin. "Well then, I'm definitely not turning that down, sweetheart."

I clench my jaw hard, my gut reaction firing up at the thought of Lucian's fangs anywhere near her. Before I can let him know how pissed I am or say anything, Dani spins around to face me with a defiant look burning in her eyes.

"Hold up, Mr. Overlord—put a sock in it," she snaps. "Or are you keen on your sibling sporting that chic throat bling permanently?"

Her words slam down like a final verdict; she isn't about to put up with any of my shit while she's set on saving Lucian.

Lucian, the insufferable smartass that he is. "Oh, my fuck, that's the absolute best!" He crows, clapping his hands together like an overexcited toddler. "Mr. Overlord? That's like the most perfect nickname ever. Of all time."

He sidles up to Dani, slinging an arm around her shoulders and grinning like a lunatic. "Dani, baby, you are officially my new favorite person. Seriously, can I just, like, carry you around in my pocket? Pull you out whenever I need a sick burn to lob at Rhy-Rhy?"

Ignoring Lucian's bullshit, "I'll be damned if I let that bastard sink his fangs into you, Angel," I growl through clenched teeth. "We'll figure out another way to give him your blood, but not straight—"

"Oh, absolutely not. Our fancy gear? Stashed away in good old Whispervale. And look at Lucian, turning more and more into a ghost right before our eyes—practically a stiff breeze away from being next week's gossip. Plus, sunbathing isn't exactly in his repertoire unless we plan on toting around a king-sized parasol."

With a pissed-off growl, I snap my jaw shut tight and throw her a dark nod, keeping my damn objections to myself.

Dani's toned arm reaches out toward Lucian, her blood singing a damn near irresistible tune for the monster he's got caged inside. Lucian closes in, every step screaming lethal intent. He locks eyes with her, some playful devilry dancing in those brown depths, then snatches up her wrist, pressing her flesh to his lips with a deceptive gentleness.

As I watch this play out, a fierce rage boils up inside me, demanding that she's mine and only mine. Maybe it won't affect her like it does everyone else—maybe she's immune. I step up, sliding my arms around Dani's waist, locking her in like she's the last damn thing

I'm ever gonna let go. I feel every fiber of my being scream in protest as Lucian's fangs puncture her flesh—a sharp intake of breath from Dani sends a shockwave through me.

Lucian's moans vibrate against Dani's skin as he feeds. The sound alone should be enough to set me off, to send me into a fucking frenzy, tearing him off her. But reason overrules instinct. I get why he needs this. Her powerful blood is like armor to him—he'd be straight-up fucked by her divine glow.

Dani's body softens against mine, her tension melting away as the vampire's aphro-disiac venom seeps into her bloodstream. Her head lolls back onto my shoulder, and I take advantage of her exposed neck. My lips graze her earlobe, nibbling gently before whispering dark promises meant only for her. "You have no idea how beautiful you are and how bad I want you again," I murmur into the shell of her ear. *"How I'm going to take you—hard and unrelenting,"* I speak through our mental bond.

Her pulse flutters wildly under my tongue as I trace it down her neck. My hands slide over her abdomen, pressing her closer until my body fully traps her— my presence.

"Imagine all the dirty fucking things I'm gonna do to you," I growl into her mind, my teeth sinking into her soft lobe. *"I'm gonna make you ride my cock while I leave my dark kisses all over you. I'm gonna slam my cock so deep inside you and fuck you senseless."*

Dani moans, her body melting against mine as I claim her with every word. *"And when we're done,"* I growl hungrily, feeling the possessive need coursing through me, *"I'm going to claim every inch of your delicious body... again and again—starting with this perfect little ass that you've been teasing me with."*

Lucian lets go of Dani's wrist after a final, greedy drag that sucks another sharp breath from her. His gaze cuts to me over her shoulder, a whole conversation in that look, silent but clear as day.

When he backs off to clear the air, I ratchet my grip on Dani, staking my claim while calming the storm in her.

She spins around in my embrace, her honey eyes deep with desire.

I crush her lips with mine, all raw and hungry, savoring that sweet taste. The rest of the world can go to hell; it's just her and me and the goddamn fire we've got between us that's burning everything else away.

Tonight is about survival, but once we're done with all this bullshit, I'm making good on every dirty promise I've whispered into her mind—until she can't breathe and I'm buried deep inside her.

As Dani kisses me back with equal hunger, the intoxicating taste of her lips makes me want so much more. But I force myself to pull back, painfully aware that my brother and Meadow are standing right there. This isn't the time or place to completely lose it, no matter how badly I want to consume every inch of her body.

I lean in, my mouth brushing her ear, and whisper hot against her skin, "Don't worry, Angel. I'm gonna make good on every dirty promise... later. But right now, you need me to heal you."

I gaze at the brutal gash on her neck, a result of my hungry bite, and the two wounds on her wrist inflicted by Lucian. Wasting no time, I sink my teeth into my wrist and press it against Dani's lips.

She doesn't hesitate for a second, greedily latching on with her soft mouth, moaning in sheer pleasure, her eyes closing as she drinks from me.

The sensation sends blood rushing straight to my cock, making it rock hard once again. "That's it, baby." Her honey-gold eyes latch onto mine, swirling with raw desire and unmistakable lust. I can practically taste her craving, mirroring my fierce need.

A visible shiver runs through Dani's body at my words. I pull my wrist away, the wounds already healed.

She takes a steadying breath, clearly affected by the heady effects of arousal from my blood and the venom. Turning, she glances at Lucian and Meadow, conversing in hushed tones beneath a towering tree.

Dani swats my chest, giving me an exasperated yet amused look. "Really, Rhyland? Getting me all revved up while your brother has his fangs in my wrist?"

I offer a shrug, a half-hearted, sorry smile on my lips. "My bad, I just couldn't help myself. Wanted you clued into my headspace—and to dodge the bullet of you going all hot and bothered from his chomp." I snap my teeth together playfully, as I downplay the truth, keeping the deeper motives to myself. She doesn't need to know all the whys... yet.

Dani's eyes go wide, a mix of shock and sly humor dancing in her honey-golden gaze. "Wait, you're serious?" She bursts out laughing, the sound full of disbelief and a hint of challenge. "You couldn't have saved those dirty promises for somewhere more private? And what the hell are you thinking—that I'd throw myself at Lucian like he's the last piece of chocolate on earth? Come on."

I growl at the image, pulling Dani tight against me possessively. "Hey, I can't take any chances with you, baby. You're fucking irresistible."

Dani flicks a dismissive glance, the faint hint of a blush betraying her quickened pulse. She steels herself before she strides back to Lucian. My gaze stays locked on her, a mix of fierce desire and admiration churning inside me. She's a force to be reckoned with—my formidable, stunning mate.

Dani inches toward Lucian, her expression softening. Her fingers hover near Lucian's collar as if touching something delicate. Her brow is knitted in deep focus. Her hands are hesitant, barely grazing him, like she's tapping into a secret place—that is hers alone, nudging the dormant brilliance inside.

I'm spellbound, witnessing her transformation—it's magnetic. The air crackles with life, weighty with the thrum of power.

Her typically warm honey-gold eyes now shine with a fierce, ethereal light. It's as if her core is rising to the surface, the long-slumbering force within her coming alive, manifesting in a spectacle of light and life.

I've never seen her eyes glow. Did my blood do that?

From the gentle pressure of her palm, a soft glow spreads, bathing us in its comforting embrace. It's not mere light; it's living, throbbing with the same cadence as our hearts, weaving around Lucian's collar in a dance of pure gold.

Dark shadows squirm under its guise, vestiges of old curses scrambling for retreat against the relentless advance of her light. The collar heats up, glowing an angry red, then seems to dissolve, defeated by her radiant energy.

Lucian, motionless, gazes at Dani with unflinching trust. There's a silent accord in his eyes, a faith that she'd wield this formidable power without harming him.

The heavy collar around Lucian's throat crumbles to dust, disappearing like it never existed. As the last piece of the collar vanishes, so does the glow from Dani's palm. She steps back slowly, her breathing deep and labored as her eyes shift back to their natural honey-gold color.

Her gaze flicks up to mine, searching for some kind of confirmation or maybe just wanting to share in the shock of what she just did. Without a word, I close the distance and pull her into my arms, my chest flooding with pride and love for this incredible woman who just obliterated that collar with nothing but her own damn power.

"Oh... thank fucking God!" Lucian exhales dramatically, rolling his neck with an exaggerated stretch. "Mental note—keep my ass on the good side of the celestial badass over here." He shoots her an appreciative look through half-closed eyes, his mouth twisting into that signature smirk. "Wouldn't want to piss off the 'Angel of Fucking Mercy' herself. That holy rage underneath the halo? That shit's real."

"The Light," Meadow repeats, a whisper of realization in her voice.

DANICA

25

My lips still tingle from Rhyland's fiery kisses, the memory of his seductive words lingering like a heady perfume. How could I forget the intensity of that moment? As Lucian fed on me, Rhyland's embrace and whispered obscenities drove me wild—a sensory overload that threatened to consume me entirely.

My thoughts wander into unfamiliar and potentially risqué territory, my barely-there attire doing nothing to conceal my arousal. It's a good thing vampires can't read minds, or Rhyland would be getting an eyeful of the X-rated movie playing in my head right now.

We slip back into camp as stealthily as shadows, our secret little rendezvous going undetected by the clueless crew. And here I am, cozily ensconced between Rhyland's legs—my personal throne—basking in the heat he's giving off more than the fire itself.

Enter Lucian, plonking himself down with that eagle-eyed gaze that's too perceptive for my liking. It's like he's got a sixth sense for sexual tension, and right now, he's picking up on it like a bloodhound on a scent trail.

I look at him in exasperation, letting out a practically audible eye roll. "What's with the hawk eyes, Lucian?" I fire back, my tone as sharp as a razor's edge.

He leans in, elbows propped on his knees in a casual slouch as that trademark panty-dropping smirk plays across his lips. "Not a thing, sweet cheeks," he purrs, his tone equal parts smooth and smart-ass. "Just wondering if maybe you got a little too into the whole 'vampiric lifeforce happy hour' back there." He arches one brow salaciously. "Not that I'm bitching, mind you. Having a bodacious babe like yourself offer herself to me like that?" He lets out an exaggerated chef's kiss. "Fucking. Dream. Come. True."

Rhyland lets out an intense, growly rumble from deep within his Viking-vampire nature, a flash of fang visible.

I glare at him, "Asshole," I hiss under my breath, because subtlety? Who needs it?

Lucian throws his head back with a rich, rumbling laugh, shaking it slowly as if savoring the moment. "That's rich coming from you, Princess," he shoots back. Fixing me with a look through hooded eyes, he smirks. "The holier-than-thou routine is cute and all, but we both know you've got a deliciously wicked streak under those pristine feathers."

But then his playful demeanor shifts, his gaze sweeping over us and grounding into something more solemn. He tosses me a softer look, the smart-ass façade momentarily shelved. "Thanks," he murmurs, the weight of his sincerity hanging between us like a tangible thing. "For helping me."

I feel a pang of something in my chest at his words, a flicker of warmth that has nothing to do with the fire or Rhyland's body heat. Because beneath all the snark and sass, Lucian's a good guy. A loyal friend. And hearing him express his gratitude so openly and honestly means more than I can say.

So I nod, my lips curving into a small smile. "Anytime," I say softly. "That's what friends are for, right?"

Lucian's answering grin is blinding. "Friends who let friends drink their blood?" he quips, his eyebrows waggling suggestively. "Sounds like a pretty exclusive club." He leans back, draping an arm over the back of the tree trunk. "Count me in as a charter member if it means indulging in delicacies like you more often, Angel Cakes."

I roll my eyes again but can't quite keep the laughter out of my voice. "Shut up," I mutter, tossing a twig at his head. "Before I change my mind and rescind your membership."

Rhyland's growl rumbles from behind me, "Not on my fucking watch, Lucian. You got that? Not ever again."

Lucian holds his hands up in surrender. "Loud and clear, boss. Though you know I never could resist pushing a few buttons here and there." He shoots Rhyland a conspiratorial wink, the brotherly affection clear despite his smartass tendencies shining through.

Needing to change the subject before things get too heavy, I quickly state, "So, big brains on deck—let's hash out our master plan."

Rhyland nods in agreement, pulling me closer in a protective embrace. "What do you suggest?" he asks, his voice low and serious.

"We're taking a field trip to the Sun Court," I say, like I'm announcing the next big road trip destination.

The guys freeze, doing a classic double-take. Rhyland's the first to reboot, his brow furrowed in confusion. "Why the Sun Court?"

Snuggling into Rhyland's muscle-bound embrace is like being cuddled by a living, breathing fortress. "The first time we entered fae-land, something inside me went all 'Jack Sparrow's compass' straight toward the Sun Court," I explain, my voice tinged with excitement.

Rhyland tightens his grip, part protective, part 'tell me more.' "And our good buddy Faderyn? He spun a yarn about the Sun Court's shiny origins and their knack for keeping big shiny things."

Fingers trace along my arm in that unmistakable Rhyland way—half comfort, half conversation. Like he's trying to unravel every mystery the universe ever kept through nothing but the language of skin against skin.

"And you think this Faerite Stone's part of their fancy stash?" Rhyland murmurs in my ear, sparking a shiver that snakes down my back like a lightning bolt.

"It's worth a shot!" I say, my voice bright and determined. "It's our only breadcrumb on this wild goose chase."

Lucian snorts softly, though not out of disbelief. "And you're just planning to waltz into the Sun Court and find this thing?" He arches an eyebrow skeptically, shooting Rhyland a look of pure incredulity. "Correct me if I'm wrong, but isn't that place supposed to be heavily guarded and damn near impenetrable? Not exactly a casual stroll through the park we're talking about here."

The corner of my mouth twitches upward, a smirk playing at my lips. "Something like that," I reply, my tone dripping with mischief.

Rhyland's chuckle resonates from behind me, deep and comforting. "She doesn't 'waltz,' Lucian," he quips, a teasing lilt in his voice. "She storms in like a force of nature."

Before I can reply, Meadow appears at the edge of our circle, her delicate frame barely disturbing the grass as she settles beside us. Her large, doe-like eyes meet mine momentarily before she speaks, her voice as soft as a whisper. "Darkness has many faces," she murmurs, her tone heavy with warning. "Some are closer than we realize."

Lucian's voice slices through the air, "Yeah, like Adrian's epic douchebag move? Turning to the dark side on us?" He shakes his head in disbelief, jaw clenched. "Seriously, I mean, I know the kid always marched to the beat of his own drum, but I didn't see that monumental betrayal coming at all."

I find myself nodding, the sting of it all still fresh, like a wound refusing to heal. "It blindsided all of us," I admit, feeling a hollow ache at the mention of Adrian's name. "One moment, he was our ally, the next... It's like we never really knew him."

Rhyland's response comes from somewhere deep and dangerous—a low, guttural growl that vibrates through his chest like something inside him just broke. The sound of a man gutted, his trust torn apart at the seams. His pain bleeds into me, his anger echoing through my own ribs like a second heartbeat. Without thinking, my hand finds his, fingers threading together in a quiet promise that he's not alone in this.

Rhyland shatters the silence, his voice razor-edged. "I'm going to fucking kill him when I see him—but what's eating me alive is whether he can break back into the realm using your powers."

A frown takes up residence between my brows, and a sigh whispers out, a silent flag of truce in our war against the unknown. "Got a crystal ball? 'Cause that's about what I'd need to tell you when his power-leeching holiday ends," I admit, feeling the weight of our shared anxiety. "Navigating this power of mine is like reading a map with half the landmarks missing."

Lucian leans forward, elbows resting casually on his knees as he fixes me with that steady, piercing gaze. "Alright, so what's the grand plan here, Angle Cake?" He arches one eyebrow skeptically. "We're just gonna storm the Sun Court, lay on some thick charm to dazzle the Fae royalty, and hope they feel generous enough to point us in the right direction?"

A wry smirk tugs at the corner of his mouth. "Because something tells me those pretentious fairy dust snobs aren't exactly gonna be lining up to lend a helping hand out of the goodness of their hearts." He lets the sarcasm linger a beat before adding dryly, "Call it a hunch."

"Amara mentioned they're not what they seem," Rhyland says, his skepticism echoing through me.

"That hag would say anything to make you believe otherwise," Lucian scoffs. "I mean, come on. She's got 'lying sack of shit' written all over her in big, sparkly letters."

He leans in closer, eyes narrowing like he's about to share classified intel. "Seriously, though. I wouldn't trust that bitch as far as I could dropkick her. And given the sheer density of evil packed into that woman, we're talking maybe three feet. *Tops.*"

I can't help but snort out a laugh.

Lucian's commentary aside, Rhyland's unease about the Sun Court still radiates off him in waves. I can feel it sitting heavy between us—a tension thick enough to chew on..

I come to life slowly, cocooned in Rhyland's secure hold. His presence is like a hearth, radiating a deep, bone-deep comfort that seeps into my soul. For a heartbeat, the daunting journey ahead blurs into nothingness, fading away like a half-remembered dream. His thumb gently strokes my cheek, and I press my face into his hand, inhaling the grounding blend of his earthly, salty sea scent that is uniquely his. Our limbs intertwine beneath a canopy of furs, his lips kissing my forehead softly like a whispered prayer.

"Time to stir, sweetheart," he murmurs, the sound breaking the morning's stillness like a spell.

I pull myself from his arms reluctantly, and the morning air bites at my skin—a sharp, unwelcome trade for the warmth we'd built between us. Around us, the camp is already alive with movement, Axilya's people bustling and organizing as they prepare for the trek back to Whispervale.

Axilya's voice cuts through the air, crisp like the morning itself. "Lucian, Dani, and Rhyland, you will take the carriage. Faderyn and I will accompany you and the crew on horseback."

With the carriage now repaired, the trek to Whispervale looms like a day-long marathon of sitting, and I cringe inwardly, flashing back to the last time we rocked 'n' rolled in that rickety carriage and the souvenir buttache I scored for my troubles.

Encore? Hard pass. Nevertheless, it's not like Rhyland can swoop me off to safety with his vampiric speed—not with him in hiding and Cruella De Mean on the warpath. So 'safe' is my middle name for now, even if it means dealing with a case of sore buttcheeks!

We gather our gear, the weight of our quest settling over us like a second skin. I haul myself into the carriage and my stomach immediately does its signature backflip, but bitching about it won't buy us any extra hours in the day, so I swallow it down and keep my mouth shut.

Lucian's the eternal poster boy for 'cool as a cucumber,' flaunting his chill factor like he's daring the universe to mess with him. I shoot him a side-eye special as I plop down, mentally strapping in for the bumpy ride ahead.

Beside me, Rhyland's deep voice booms out to Meadow. "Mouse, grab your shit and saddle up. You've earned your spot with us."

Meadow's eyes are like twin flickers of candlelight in a drafty room—shy, somehow still daring to shine. She nods, barely louder than a breath, "Yes, I'd like that very much."

You can practically hear the boulder of worry tumbling off her shoulders—relief isn't just a word for her; it's a life raft.

Meadow teams up with Faderyn on his horse, giving me a reassuring smile just as the carriage doors swing shut with a resounding thud.

The carriage lurches forward, rattling and bouncing like it has a personal vendetta against my spine. I suck in a steadying breath and latch onto Rhyland's hand, grateful for the quiet anchor of his calm.

We're headed to Whispervale, and every bump and jolt hammers home the weight of what we've chosen. This isn't just distance we're covering—it's the first chapter of something bigger, a story we're writing mile by shaky mile.

DANICA

26

Hours later, as I sit in the cramped carriage, my thoughts drift back to last night's encounter with Rhyland and Lucian. The memories of his touch and whispered promises send a shiver down my spine. I can't help but glance over at him, catching his gaze as he shoots me a sly smile.

"That sweet ass doing okay, Angel?" he asks, his voice low and seductive.

I catch his gaze and see the desire burning in his eyes. "No, actually," I reply with a sassy bite in my tone. "It's like my ass is begging for a break from this damn hardwood and jostling."

Rhyland reaches out and takes a firm grip on my thigh, leaning in close to my ear. "Want to trade that hardwood for mine?"

My heart races as I realize what he's planning. I shoot a look over to Lucian, who's just staring at me with that shit-eating grin.

I inhale sharply; the thought of doing something provocative in front of his brother baffles me. "You're joking?" I whisper. "You can't be serious...?"

He nods, determined to make his move as he pulls me onto his lap, my back against his chest. "There, that's better."

I take a breath, trying to steady the jitters dancing through me. Rhyland's hands start their ascent, tracing the bare skin of my thighs exposed by the whisper-thin dress that's barely there, caressing as if I'm the most precious treasure.

With a simple thought, he reminds me, *"We don't need to speak aloud, baby."*

I pause, glancing at Lucian, who's serving me a full course of 'come hither' looks.
Seriously, what's the deal?

"What are you doing?" I whisper back through our bond.

With Rhyland typically guarding me like I'm the last piece of chocolate on Earth, the idea of Lucian eyeing us like we're the night's premium show both thrills and freaks me out.

"It's okay, baby. I know you want him to watch. Lucian is a filthy fucker. Let's give him a show, shall we?"

Part of me is going, *'Is this for real?'* because, let's face it, my 'normal' meter broke miles back. Yet here's this wild, wicked whisper in my head urging me to ride the crazy wave. There's a twisted thrill in pushing the envelope, in flirting with the forbidden.

And damn if I'm not tempted just to toss caution to the naughty winds.

I lean back into him as he begins to touch me gently, slowly running his hand up my inner thigh, his breath and lips on my neck. His fingers find me already wet as he reaches my pussy.

"So fucking wet. I know this turns you on, Angel," he says with satisfaction as I moan quietly.

Teasing my clit, he alternates between gentle and fast movements, causing my breath to quicken. With my legs spread wide, I sit on his lap while he holds me tightly from behind.

Lucian's positioned to get an eyeful, with nothing obstructing his view.

With Rhyland's other hand, he pulls down my top, revealing my aching, plump breasts and hard nipples. He begins to pinch and flick them while continuing to tease my clit.

Lucian's piercing gaze locks onto mine, that trademark smirk playing at his lips as if he's discovered something absolutely delicious. "Well, well, well..." he drawls smoothly, his eyes traveling over me with clear appreciation. "Isn't this just a stunning sight?"

His smirk transforms into a wicked grin. "Damn, Princess...you're so fucking beautiful like this." He lets the words hang—gaze moving deliberately. "All flushed and breathless and radiating pure temptation." Lucian leans in close, dropping his voice to a low rumble. "Makes a guy wonder what other pretty sounds I could pull from that gorgeous mouth."

His words wrap around me, and I feel like I've been placed on some intoxicating pedestal, adored and worshipped by both of these men like I'm the ultimate prize in their game of seduction.

Rhyland's finger enters me, and I can't help but groan at how thick it feels inside me. My head falls back against his chest as I respond to his touch.

"Fuck yeah, you're all mine now," he snarls possessively in my ear. "Every damn inch of you belongs to me."

I push back into him, my voice barely audible, "Yes...more," I plead.

"Such a needy fucking whore, aren't you, Angel?" Rhyland growls out loud.

I moan at his crude words.

"Seriously, this is like the best show my eyes have ever witnessed," Lucian exclaims shamelessly, completely absorbed in the sight. His gaze flicks back and forth between Rhyland and me. "I mean, hot damn, you two are putting on one hell of a scorching performance."

He gives Rhyland an exaggerated pout, eyes wide with playful desperation as he begs, "C'mon, bro, give me something here! Don't hoard the angel cake—let your favorite brother get a piece of the action." Lucian slowly licks his lips, letting the suggestive motion linger as he grins. "I promise to behave *very*, very well...for the first few minutes anyway."

Rhyland then slides two fingers into my pussy, ignoring Lucian completely. I moan and gasp in pleasure as he works both fingers inside, knuckles deep. He pulls them out, glistening with my arousal, and rubs them across my swollen clit. The slickness and friction push me closer to the edge of climax.

Lucian's eyes blaze with hungry anticipation as he slowly licks his lips. "Ooh, darling, would you be so kind as to grant me the honor of a delectable taste?" He casts a pleading look, visibly restraining himself from reaching out. "Just a little sample?" he wheedles teasingly, flashing that roguish smile. "I promise to savor every delicious moment like a true connoisseur."

I'm so aroused that my body is literally dripping with need, and I can feel it flowing out of me, wetting the carriage floor beneath me.

Rhyland gently presses his fingers against my waiting lips and commands me, "Suck."

I obediently take his fingers into my mouth, sucking with such intensity that I feel myself spiraling out of control.

"You're such a filthy girl," Rhyland growls, "I'll have to keep this mouth occupied later."

Nearly vibrating with hunger, Lucian chimes in with mock innocence, "Oh, dear mother of darkness. Rhy, pal, it's time to share the wealth, don't you think?"

He releases my breast and reaches down to unzip his pants. I shift slightly and reach down between us, wrapping my hand around his thick, throbbing cock. Veins engorged and prominent.

He gasps as I position myself over him. My wetness drips down onto him.

"You ain't seen nothin' yet, brother. Have you ever heard an angel sing? It'll make your fucking balls ache, I swear." Rhyland tells him with heavy breaths.

Rhyland's waiting for me to take the plunge—the growl of his warning vibrates through me, "Sit your needy cunt on my cock now, Angel. I won't ask again."

Rhyland's filthy mouth is like poetry to my ears—a secret language between us, a promise of pleasure and pain that makes my entire body hum with electricity.

With a loud grunt, Lucian pulls his massive cock out of his pants and begins stroking it slowly. The sight has me panting in anticipation, my body burning with fervor.

He's not small by any means—Veiny, corded, and girthy. But Rhyland still surpasses him in that department.

"Do what he says, Princess," Lucian commands, his voice deep and growling with need. "Show me what heaven sounds like."

My whole being is consumed, aching for what's to come.

I can feel Rhyland's hard, bulbous head against my soaked entrance, and without hesitation, I take a deep breath, my eyes locked with Lucian's, and then I obey Rhyland's command. I slowly lower myself onto him, feeling his hard length fill me completely, stretching me open—the exquisite pain and pleasure mingling in a way that only he can bring.

"Oh, she's into the filth, isn't she?" Lucian leans in and tugs at my nipple with gentle twists and pulls. "And so beautiful."

Suddenly, his mouth is on my nipple, hot and insistent. His lips suck and tug, sending electrifying jolts of pleasure through my body. At the same time, Rhyland thrusts into me with a force that takes my breath away. The combined sensations are overwhelming, and I can't help but release a loud moan, unable to contain the pleasure coursing through me.

I hear Rhyland take a sharp breath and sigh in pure yearning behind me. His soft sounds are like an intoxicating elixir, arousing my desire even more.

My body thrums with want—this aching need to please Rhyland and, in some deliciously twisted way, to give Lucian exactly what he's asking for.

Lucian is still fisting his cock while I begin to move, my hips roll in a rhythm that's equal parts raw and reverent—a push and pull of need and want that knots us together in this moment.

"Dani..."

As Rhyland picks up the pace, driving into me with increasing force, I can feel myself succumbing to the overwhelming sensations.

"So... fucking...good...Angel," Rhyland pants in between thrusts, his voice ragged with intensity.

With a tight grip on my hip, he pulls me down onto his massive cock as he thrusts up, sending waves of pleasure through my body. Hearing his moans of delight behind me only intensifies the approaching orgasm that I know is about to consume me.

"Angel..."

I lose myself in the moment and let out a guttural moan as Lucian's mouth bites down roughly, teasing and pulling at my pebbled nipple. *"*Oh, god...*"* My thoughts trail off into a silent plea; as waves of arousal crash over me, I'm left wordless, my eyelids fluttering shut, surrendering to the sensory tide.

With each grinding motion, I feel his pulsing cock pressing deeper and deeper inside of me.

Lucian shifts, his fingers teasing my swollen clit with practiced precision, and a wave of pleasure rips through me. His mouth moves between my nipples—licking, sucking, teeth grazing—each shift sending another jolt of sensation crashing through me until I can barely think straight.

My moans climb higher with every thrust, my body shaking as pleasure slams into me in relentless waves. Heat floods my veins, white-hot and consuming, until there's nothing left in my head but the feel of both of them taking me apart.

"Shh...Angel," Rhyland whispers, but I can't hold back any longer.

"I can't...you feel so... *fucking* good." Rhyland takes a handful of my hair at the base of my neck—my kryptonite and tugs me back, forcing me to arch my back as he slows his movements.

"Fuuuuck," he growls, lost in the intense sensations consuming us both.

Lucian then dips his head down, "I can't take it anymore—I need a taste." his lips scorch my clit, licking and gently sucking as Rhyland slowly moves inside me.

Oh, sweet Jesus! Lucian is an expert at working my clit with his skilled tongue, flicking and sucking it just right.

"Ohh, *god*..." I moan as I grip Lucian's hair—ready to explode on Rhyland's cock at any moment.

"So, damn good..." he chants in a low, seductive voice that makes me shudder. But then he surprises me. "I need more of this pussy. Rhyland, move your fucking dick."

To my astonishment, Rhyland pulls out, leaving me empty and desperate. I'm dripping with arousal all over his cock, and pelvis—so worked up.

Lucian takes charge and commands Rhyland to hold my legs, but Rhyland has other plans. Instead, he pushes against my back entrance, making me gasp as I feel his big head nudging against me.

"Gonna be a good girl and take my cock here?" He pushes and rubs against my ass, massaging the tight ring of muscle. "I've been dreaming about retaking this ass." Rhyland pants in my ear, making me weak.

Lucian sounds shocked and turned on at the same time. "Oh, fuuuuuk... You like anal, Princess?" he asks, his voice heavy with lust.

"Oh, yeah, and she takes it so *fucking* good. Don't you, baby?" Rhyland murmurs in my ear, pulling my head back with a fistful of my hair. "My dirty girl, gonna take it in the ass?"

I nod numbly as Rhyland reaches under my knees, spreading my legs wider and pulling them up. I'm literally spread-eagled, and my pussy is in Lucian's face at this position.

"I need some lube, brother." Rhyland demands.

Lucian doesn't miss a beat. Bending down, he sucks Rhyland's cock into his mouth, slurping, moaning, and gagging. Thick drool and spit glide out the sides of Lucian's mouth down Rhyland's colossal cock.

I'm completely speechless as I watch him deep-throat Rhyland, his cheeks hollowing out as he moans like he loves it.

Oh my fucking god!

Knowing full well that they aren't brothers by blood, only by their maker, makes me curious—have they teamed up like this in the past? It's an interesting dynamic that definitely piques my interest.

Watching Lucian suck Rhyland—It's so hot that I can feel my orgasm building. My clit tingles, and I whimper.

"Fuuuck, yeah," Rhyland rumbles in approval. "I told you he's a filthy fucker."

"Umpffhh," Lucian moans around Rhyland's cock.

After a few minutes of watching probably the hottest thing of my existence—Lucian gagging and choking himself on Rhyland's fat dick—Lucian pops off, spreading my cheeks—spitting drool into my ass, and positions Rhyland at my entrance. It takes a few tries and some breathing before Rhyland works himself in. I moan at the fullness of him, stretching me open.

"Oh, sweet lord above. She's swallowing your cock." Lucian sounds even more aroused. "Now, let me clean this fucking mess you made." Lucian wastes no time and dives back in, my pussy on full display to his ravenous mouth—licking and sucking my clit, spearing his tongue inside my pussy, like a man possessed. I scream out loud at the intense sensations, writhing under their skilled touch.

Lucian purrs with pleasure, "Damn, I've never tasted anything so delicious." His words make me feel wanted and desired, and I start losing control. "She tastes like—"

"I know exactly what she tastes like," Rhyland pants. "Fuck...Angel. Your ass—so tight. I'm gonna fucking explode." Rhyland groans behind me; his voice strained with effort as he thrusts in and out of me. I can feel the pressure building inside me; I am burning up, and my mouth is agape.

"I'm gonna shoot my load all up in this ass. You're going to be dripping with my cum" Rhyland growls behind me.

Lucian then adds two fingers inside me, expertly massaging my inner walls while simultaneously sucking and flicking my clit with his talented tongue.

"Oh, *FUCK*...I'm gonna..." I'm about to reach my peak...

"Umpffh—yeah, give it to me," Lucian says huskily.

"DANI!"

I snap awake, shooting up straighter than an arrow.

There's Lucian, rocking that signature smug grin like he's got all the secrets, and then Rhyland, glaring with a fury that says he's about two seconds from wringing my neck.

Holy shit!

Quite the wake-up call.

DANICA

27

Mother of god, it was all just some twisted, steamy dream. But seriously, brain, what's with the after-hours XX-rated reel?

Lucian's expression morphs into a smug, knowing smirk, as if he possesses some X-ray vision that directly penetrates the deepest recesses of my subconscious. Arching one eyebrow mischievously, he throws out an offhand "Hey princess... have a nice dream?" in a tone with implication and innuendo.

That sounds *exactly* like he peeked into my head and had a front-row seat to the scandalous show.

Rhyland's growl vibrates through me, practically shaking my bones. "We've arrived," he clips out, a no-nonsense note in his voice.

Before I know it, he's got my wrist in a vise grip, yanking me out the door like a caveman claiming his prize. I let out a squeak of surprise as he slings me over his shoulder with all the ceremony of hoisting a sack of potatoes, my skimpy excuse for a dress doing absolutely nothing to hide my backside from the universe.

Lucian's chuckling is the soundtrack to my upside-down, head-pounding protest; his amusement is as infuriating as it is contagious. "Dammit, Rhyland! Put me down!" I demand, my voice climbing an octave as I pound my fists against his back.

Rhyland, ever the man on a mission, barks at Faderyn, "Where's her tent?"

Without missing a beat, Faderyn points the way, and off Rhyland stomps with me slung over his shoulder like a sack of flour. I thrash and holler, my fists drumming against Rhyland's back, but to him, it's likely just the pitter-patter of an irate, miniature human throwing a tantrum.

Inside the tent, Rhyland lands a stinging swat on my rear, and I can't hold back a yelp of frustration. The next thing I know, I'm plopped onto my bed, piled with furs, my hair a tousled mess, and my cheeks flushed with indignation. I swipe my hair from my eyes and shoot him a glare that could scorch his skin off, my voice a mix of anger and disbelief. "What the hell, Rhyland?"

He looms over me, caging me with his arms, his face so close that I have to tilt my head back to escape the furnace of his fury. "I'd like to ask you the same question, Angel," he rumbles, his voice low and dangerous.

Heat creeps up my cheeks, and suddenly, I'm burning up, the warmth having nothing to do with his proximity. A hard knot forms in my throat, and I force it down, my mind racing with the implications of his words.

Could he possibly know about the scandalous theatre my subconscious just staged? The thought sends a shiver, equal parts thrilling and terrifying.

As if reading my mind, he answers, "Oh yeah, sweetheart. I know all about what went on in your pretty little head. Lucian's little gift, and he filled me in with every detail after I nearly choked it out of him." He says this with barely contained rage, his eyes flashing with a possessive fury that takes my breath away.

Oh, for the love of—this is just fucking great! When did Lucian add mind-reading to his bag of tricks? And more importantly, when did he decide to use that particular talent to spill the beans about my dirty dreams?

Rhyland's eyes look like roiling, turbulent seas, and I'm grasping for something to steady myself, my mind reeling from the magnitude of his words. "I..." Words abandon me entirely, my tongue completely tangled. "I—I don't know why I dreamt that, Rhyland."

My response blends honesty with a sharp edge of defensiveness, my bewilderment churning within me like a violent storm. As much as I despise admitting it, even silently, a part of me thrills at his jealousy, at the possessive rage that emanates from him like scorching heat.

But there's also a part of me that's livid, that resists being held accountable for the random productions of my sleeping mind. I mean, who's the dream whisperer anyway—able to dictate their nocturnal narratives?

Not me, that's for damn sure.

Rhyland's rumble hits a bass note that practically vibrates the space, and I'm half-convinced there's a puff of smoke swirling out of his ears. "I'm going to fucking kill him," is all he says, his voice low and deadly.

Confusion crosses my face like a big, fat question mark. But Rhyland, catching onto my bewilderment, decides to fill me in on Vampire Biting 101. Apparently, their venom is like a cocktail of chill-out and turn-on, a potent mix of relaxation and arousal. But here's the kicker: it's all about the dosage—just a dash does the trick. And Lucian, being the generous soul he is, overdosed me, leaving me stuck with a side of steamy X-rated specials playing on repeat in my subconscious mind.

"That... asshole," I mutter, simmering in my own irritation sauce. I can't believe he would do something like this, knowing full well the effect it would have on me.

No shocker. He was throwing around that smug grin earlier, fishing for the effects of his little nip. My eyes dart to Rhyland, silently begging him to reel it in. He's a storm barely holding together—every muscle coiled tight. His arms are rigid, fists clenched white at his sides, each breath punching out of him like he's one wrong word away from leveling the room.

I inch forward, my hand tentatively reaching for his. "I thought only your... venom did what it did?" I ask, my voice small and uncertain.

Quick as lightning, he's on me, his hand wrapped around my throat in a grip that jolts me into shock. "I fucking told you not to let him drink from you, Dani," he growls, his voice a low rumble that makes my entire body tense. "Now look at the mess we're in."

It's like trying to swallow with a noose around my neck—courtesy of Rhyland's iron grip. But damn if my body isn't responding with its own defiant rebellion, heat blooming and arousal climbing to a frenzied peak despite the spike of fear coursing through my veins.

God, I'm a twisted bitch.

Now, I get the whole 'straight from the source' deal with Erik. Why the big secret, though? Couldn't he have spelled it out for me instead of being all cryptic and mysterious?

Annoyance flares up inside like a match to kindling, and I narrow my eyes at Rhyland. "I didn't know it would do... that!" I snap, frustration clear in my voice. The last words practically sizzle as they leave my lips, my anger warring with the desire that thrums through my veins.

Rhyland loosens his hold on my throat, his fingers softening even as his eyes burn with something feral and possessive. "I know you didn't know," he murmurs, voice low and shredded. "But now, I'm gonna remind you of the only man you'll ever fucking dream about."

Without warning, he lunges forward and captures my lips with his own, his mouth hot and demanding against mine. My body responds instinctively, releasing a low, guttural moan that is quickly devoured by his insistent kiss. His lips are warm and soft, yet beneath his touch is an underlying hunger that leaves me breathless and wanting more.

I melt into him, my hands fisting in his hair as I pull him closer, desperate to feel every inch of his body against mine. The world falls away until there's nothing but the two of us, lost in a haze of desire and need.

Rhyland's hands roam over my body, his touch leaving fire trails in their wake. His hands close over my breasts, thumbs dragging slow circles across my nipples until they stiffen under his touch—each pass sending a sharp bolt of heat straight between my thighs.

"You're mine, Dani," he growls against my lips, his voice rough with possessive need. "Only mine. And I'm going to make sure you never forget it."

"Bite me... please," spills out of me, desperate and raw. It's the only way I can scrub away Lucian's lingering mark, to rewrite my body's memory so it only screams for Rhyland.

With a quick and forceful motion, Rhyland violently pulls down the top of my dress, baring my heaving breasts to the cool air.

"Already ahead of you, baby," he rasps, eyes dark and starving.

Without another word, his teeth sink into the delicate flesh of my breast, causing me to gasp sharply at the sudden pain. But as quickly as the pain comes, it transforms into an intense wave of pleasure that leaves my body trembling.

My hands tighten around his head, my fingers tangling in his hair as he relentlessly sucks and draws my life force into him. No doubt he's giving me an extra dose of his potent venom. My body becomes liquid fire, my arousal spiking to new heights even though I'm already dripping from my weird sex dream.

His mouth is hot and demanding against my breast, each pull sending a current of electricity skating down my spine. My body arches into him, every nerve lit up, my need ratcheting higher with each second that passes.

With forceful hands, he tears away the delicate fabric of my dress, leaving it in tattered shreds. My head spins as he pulls me upright and whirls me around with lightning speed.

I'm bent over, and the sound of his pants hitting the ground echoes through the tent as he positions himself behind me.

Rhyland lifts my leg effortlessly and places it on the bed. With a sharp smack, he spanks my ass, causing me to wince and let out a surprised whimper. The sting rips through me, blooming into a sharp rush of pleasure. He grabs my hair, pulling me back roughly, and I can't help but moan at the sensation of his rough handling. My mouth falls open, and I can feel my body responding to his dominance.

I'm completely turned on.

"This is your fucking reminder, Angel," he growls before plunging his impressive length deep inside me.

Rhyland and I turned the tent into confetti in the heat of our unrestrained fervor. I love how aggressive he can be sexually. Now we're sprawled out here, savoring the afterglow. Sweat-streaked and panting, riding the waves of our shared breaths.

"We need to get up, Angel. As much as I would love to lie here with you all night, I gotta take care of something."

I let out a begrudging mutter at his nudge to rise, but I cave because, let's face it, duty calls. Axilya and Faderyn are waiting, and we've got serious brainstorming on the docket.

Rhyland slips into his attire with that vampire swiftness. Then there's me, rummaging around to unearth the leathers I can't escape. With a groan about the irritation bubbling up, I face the music. Because really, my options are limited to this—suiting up in the 'come at me' battle leathers or going the prehistoric route and draping myself in furs.

Rhyland bolts from the tent, a blur of urgency, while I'm left wrestling my boots into submission. I finally catch up, darting out of the tent flap just in time to see Lucian ambling over with a troublemaker's grin.

"Well, well...the two love—"

His jab is cut short as Rhyland's fist becomes an impromptu introduction to Lucian's face, promptly sending him on a one-way trip to the dirt. I cringe and hold my hands up to my face. Lucian had it coming, though.

"You fucking prick. You just had to be an ass and do the unthinkable." Rhyland reprimands Lucian.

Lucian drags himself up from the dirt, jaw already swelling from Rhyland's fist. He swipes a thumb across the blood trickling from the corner of his mouth, and even now—even with his brother standing there like a lit fuse—that insufferable smirk doesn't so much as flicker.

"Okay, I'll admit," he draws out the words with a dramatic wince, "That one stung a little. But was the sucker punch really necessary?" Lucian arches an inquisitive brow at Rhyland's thunderous expression. "It was just a harmless prank—no need to get your fangs in a twist, bro."

"Are you shitting me right now, Lucian? You see all this as one big fucking joke, huh?" Rhyland shoots back, pissed off.

Lucian's smirk takes on a more taunting edge as he jerks his chin toward me. "Although I can't blame you for being a tad... overprotective of your precious angel's innocence after that little venom slip-up." Lucian tsks mockingly. "My bad for giving her such deliciously naughty dreams. You're right; I really should learn some restraint."

"You worthless fuck." Rhyland's gaze turns wild, the beast within unleashed as he hurls himself forward.

Lucian swings back at Rhyland, landing a solid punch to his face, and then it's just chaos. They're nothing but a blur of motion before us, fighting it out like a couple of unleashed wild animals.

Before I can take the next breath, Erik has pulled his signature move, zipping up beside me so fast it's like he teleported. My hair is a testament to his supernatural entrance, fluttering in the gust he's left in his wake.

"Jesus, Erik," I blurt out, trying to tame the wild strands. "How about a heads-up next time, huh? Give a lady a fair warning?"

"My apologies, Little Huntress. What's going on?"

I exhale a drawn-out breath, then lay it all out—the wild saga: Lucian's venom overload, the wild dream, Rhyland's green-eyed monster moment. Erik is standing there, gobsmacked, taking in the full soap-opera-worthy recount.

"You permitted Lucian to drink directly from you?" His voice carries a trace of mirth. "It astonishes me that Rhyland would consent to such an act. Lucian has a notorious penchant for stirring the shit pot."

"No doubt about that," I say, head bobbing in firm agreement. As the fury of fists and vampire speed unfurls before me, I start to suggest, "Should we—"

But Erik quickly shuts that down, interjecting a decisive "Nope." His word lands like a full stop, and we're clearly sideline spectators to this supernatural scuffle for now. "These two are no strangers to clashing; it's best to let them work through it. Lucian's error in judgment was grave, and Rhyland's reaction is entirely justified in my eyes."

Standing there, nodding silently with Erik's words still hanging between us, I can't tear my eyes away from the ferocious ballet of their brawl. Rhyland throws punches like sledgehammers, but Lucian's no slouch—dodging and weaving, he lands some sharp jabs in return.

Then, what seems like an eternity passes, and there's a change in the tide. Rhyland, with the ferocity of his age-old Viking roots, secures the upper hand—grabbing hold of Lucian in a way that's sure to sing soprano.

There's a moment of absolute stillness before Rhyland's deep and commanding voice cuts through: "Do you yield, little brother?"

Lucian shakes his head, and Rhyland releases him. "Good, now fucking apologize to me and Dani," he says, pointing in my direction. "And don't you ever fucking do something so goddamn sleazy to my mate. She was helping you, you son of a bitch!"

It's as if the entire camp has come to a standstill, everyone's gaze glued to the drama unfolding. For a moment, the world narrows to the spectacle of the two vampire brothers locked in their fierce and personal battle. It's a scene drawing the collective breath of onlookers, all waiting to see the outcome of this intense familial showdown.

Lucian's usual bravado seems to deflate somewhat as he turns his gaze toward me, his expression sobering. "Alright, alright, I'm genuinely sorry this time—no jokes," he says, raising his hands placatingly. He meets my eyes directly, his own holding an uncharacteristically sincere look. "It was stupid of me to pull that stunt, I'll admit it. Forgive me, please?"

The air around me is practically electric with anticipation, every pair of eyes fixed on me as I weigh the gravity of the moment. Rhyland's gaze burns with an intensity that's hard to read, holding still amid chaos like the eye of a storm. And Lucian, brought to his knees—quite literally—is looking up at me with a mixture of contrition and hope, awaiting my verdict like a man on trial.

"Yes, I forgive you," the words fall from my lips, smoothing over the jagged edge of the tension that's encasing us all like a suffocating blanket.

Rhyland approaches me, and I reach out to hold his hand, feeling the tightness of his muscles beneath my fingers. But as I gently squeeze his hand, I can feel them start to loosen, like a knot slowly unraveling.

"He's lucky I didn't give him the ultimate death for that," he growls, his voice low and menacing in my mind. *"And you... I wouldn't have forgiven the shit; I would've made him beg!"*

"Oh, come on, Rhyland! You whooped his ass. I think he gets the idea," I venture, frustration lacing my tone with playful reproach.

It's a blend of challenge and disbelief, hoping to coax him away from any lingering anger he might be harboring toward me for offering Lucian forgiveness. The underlying message is clear: Let's move on from this, shall we?

Rhyland reaches back through our bond, his thoughts tinged with a stubborn edge. *"Yeah, but the fucker doesn't deserve your forgiveness."*

I throw my hands up in exasperation, letting out a huff of frustration that's half sigh, half growl. *"It's Lucian!"* I exclaim, my voice rising in pitch. *"Honestly, do I even need to elaborate? He's your brother—You know how he is!"*

Rhyland huffs and clenches his fists, his jaw tightening with barely contained irritation. *"He should've known not even to think—"*

But before he can finish his rant, Lucian interjects, cutting him off with a pointed cough that draws attention back to himself. "Uhh—should I be privy to this little Professor Xavier mind-chit-chat or what?" he asks, his eyebrows raised in a look of mock innocence.

Without missing a beat, Rhyland and I snap back in perfect harmony, our voices ringing like a double-barreled shotgun. "NO!"

RHYLAND

28

I storm into the tent like a hurricane, the flap rustling in my wake as my anger from the confrontation with Lucian still simmers under my skin. That fury, that raw fucking rage at what he's done, it boils within me like a volcano ready to blow. Erik's already here, his expression a mix of concern and understanding like he knows the shitstorm that's brewing inside me.

"You know?" I ask, my voice rough with emotion. I barely hold back the snarl threatening to rip from my throat.

He nods, his gaze unwavering, a fucking rock amid my chaos. "I do."

I rake my hand through my hair, frustration boiling over until I can't contain it anymore. "He's a born troublemaker, but this is some next-level shit," I growl, with venom.

"It's low, even for him," Erik agrees, his features hardening into a stone mask. "But we've dealt with worse."

I scoff, a harsh, bitter sound that scrapes against my throat. "Not from our fucking kin."

Erik shrugs, his shoulders a tense line beneath his armor. "Family or not, he crossed a line and needs to be dealt with."

I let out a long sigh, trying to calm myself before I fucking explode. "He never learns," I growl, my voice trembling with the effort it takes to keep my shit together. I start pacing, my boots wearing a hole in the ground. "He took advantage of her—of me, Erik! Knowing what it would do to her—she was only trying to help him, for fuck's sake!"

Erik winces, shaking his head like he can't quite believe the level of fuckery we're dealing with. "I'll talk to him, Rhyland. I promise."

I'm straining to hold my shit together in front of Erik; he doesn't need to catch any fallout from the shitstorm raging inside me. "Thanks," I grind out between clenched teeth, my jaw aching with the effort.

Erik shrugs nonchalantly, like it's no big deal, and goes back to sharpening his weapon. "Don't mention it, brother."

Despite the anger still coursing through my veins, I can't help but feel a surge of gratitude for Erik's presence, for the way he's been there for Dani when I couldn't be.

My voice softens as I thank him—the words sincere and heartfelt. "No, I meant...thank you for watching over Dani, for being there for her when I was stuck in that hellhole."

Erik adjusts casually, like it's just another day at the office, and keeps working on his blade. "It was an honor and a duty, brother."

His words hold weight, a sincerity that cuts through the bullshit and makes me feel both grateful and proud to call him family, to have him by my side through all this fucking madness.

"Care to explain what the hell happened? Dani filled me in on Lucian's...antics. However, I'm still at a loss for how she got you out of Amara's clutches."

I briefed Erik on the whole damn mess—the way we busted out, that gutsy little maid—Mouse, finding Dani, and how we ditched those Shadow Court bastards for a new play—hitting up The Sun Court.

"Yes, Faderyn, Dani, and I are inclined to affirm that the stone resides nearby. She alluded to perceiving a peculiar sensation upon our initial arrival. Faderyn insists that we receive a formal invitation before we embark there." Erik imparts to me.

A formal invitation?

"How the hell long is that gonna take?" I demand to know.

Erik shrugs, "The Shadow Queen dallied two weeks before granting Dani an audience—who can say, brother? One can only hope they extend invitations for tea with greater alacrity."

This damned realm is getting under my skin; it feels like we're wearing out our fucking welcome, and we've barely made a dent in what we came here to do. Moretemis and Azrael are buzzing around in my head like hungry vultures, a non-stop reminder of the shitshow we've left on standby.

Then there's the council. Azrael's joke of a welcome wagon has been ringing alarm bells since we landed in this cursed hellhole.

What the hell's been happening back home while we're stuck here? Not knowing is choking me up like a goddamn death grip tightening around my throat, squeezing the life out of me bit by bit.

I plop down, my arms braced on my thighs, and drag my fingers through my hair with a frustrated growl. The scent of her fills my senses before she even enters. The tent flaps open, and my cock springs to attention at the sight of her— a fucking goddess in leather, every sexy curve and delicious part of her skin on display, tempting me beyond belief. My sweet little battle babe, driving me wild with desire. I didn't clock her outfit before, too blinded by rage dealing with Lucian's crap.

"Fuck, baby," I groan, drinking in every inch of her inside the makeshift tent. She's a goddamn work of art, the tight leather clinging to every curve like it was poured onto her. She catches me gawking and hits me with an eye roll that's equal parts amused and exasperated.

"Yeah, this getup is all thanks to Axilya and her wicked sense of what passes for battle attire," she quips, implying that Axilya's idea of gearing up for a confrontation includes a rather... unique sartorial twist.

Erik tries to stifle a chuckle, but it's damn clear Dani's fiery spirit amuses him as she goes off about her clothes. "Little Huntress, you might as well get used to it."

I stand up and stride toward her with determination, unable to resist any longer. "Fuck, Angel, you're stunning," I growl before giving her ass a hard smack. The noise reverberates through the quiet tent, causing her to let out a surprised yelp.

"Well, at least someone appreciates the vibe," she retorts playfully as I eye her hungrily.

"I wouldn't mind seeing you wear this all the time," I admit.

"Why does that not surprise me?" she shoots back, her quip laced with dry humor and resigned expectation.

That smirk's still playing on her lips, telling me that even if she isn't sold on the getup or the moment, she knows it turns me the fuck on, and that knowledge is power in her hands.

"Sorry for butting in," she starts, "but we were about to dine and thought maybe you boys would want to tag along."

Hell, 'dining' takes on a new meaning, far from whatever's served. But I pocket those dirty ideas for now and seize two generous handfuls of her plump ass, hoisting her up.

She lets out another squeal, clinging onto me for dear life like a koala.

I start moving us out of the tent, "Time to eat—but you're the main course later," I promise with a wink.

DANICA

29

Rhyland saunters into the clearing, that wolfish grin already plastered on his face like a billboard advertising his cocky confidence. "Ready to get your cute little ass kicked again?" he taunts, with playful arrogance.

I roll my eyes but can't help mirroring his smirk, the thrill of the challenge already coursing through my veins. Twirling my daggers with a flourish that's half skill, half showmanship, I sass back, "Keep dreaming, Nordi-licious. I'm so gonna wipe that smug look off your face."

We've been going head-to-head all week, sparring and honing our combat skills to a razor's edge while awaiting that fateful summons from the Sun Court. And now, with the arrival of that golden envelope at dawn, the stage is set for today's battle—a final test of our mettle before we embark on the next leg of our journey.

Keeping the crown concealed is second nature now, the weight of it a constant presence in the back of my mind. I've also woven it into my hair on days I want to show it off. The glimmering strands plaited into some badass warrior braids that make me feel like a damn Valkyrie. This power has become a part of my very being, as much a part of me as my own heartbeat.

Rhyland circles me, his eyes roaming over the daggers, spinning through my grip with a predatory gleam. "Those little knives won't save you, sweetheart," he taunts.

"We'll see about that, won't we?" I pivot on the balls of my feet, mirroring his predatory movements with a grace born of hours of practice and a healthy dose of adrenaline.

The forest seems to hold its breath as we stalk each other, the air thick with tension and anticipation. My pulse thrums with the intoxicating fusion of fear and excitement that only Rhyland can inspire—a heady cocktail that makes me feel alive in ways I never thought possible.

He strikes first, his sword cutting through the air with blinding speed. But I'm ready for him, deflecting the blow with an upraised dagger. The clang of impact reverberates through my bones like a bell.

"Too slow, baby," Rhyland rumbles, grinning as he unleashes a furious combination—jab, cross, hook—that would have laid me out flat a week ago.

But I'm not the same girl I was then. I weave away from his blows like a dancer, his knuckles hissing past my cheek with a whisper of displaced air. Twisting at the last second, I rake my blade toward his ribs, seeking to slip past his guard and score a hit.

But he's already clear, the deadly arc of my dagger finding only empty space. Damn, his lightning reflexes.

"Gonna have to try harder than that," he tsks, circling again with that damn sexy swagger of his that makes me want to kiss him and kick his ass in equal measure.

Fine, if he wants to play, then we'll play.

I charge with a feral yell, my daggers whirling in a blur of silver death. Rhyland backpedals, deflecting each lethal slice with his lightning reflexes, his own blade a streak of gleaming steel in the dappled sunlight. Our blades clash and part, the staccato rhythm of combat echoing through the trees like a savage symphony.

Then Rhyland overcommits on a swipe, exposing his flank for a single, precious breath. I seize the moment and drive my heel toward his exposed ribs, putting every ounce of strength and speed into the blow.

Rhyland twists away, but not quite far enough—I feel the solid thunk of impact against his side, a glancing blow that nonetheless sends a thrill of satisfaction through me.

"Sonuvabitch!" he grunts, stumbling back a step, his hand going to his ribs. A fierce thrill surges through me at drawing first blood, so to speak—pride burning hot and wild in my chest.

Of course, I should've known better than to let my guard down, even for a moment. In a heartbeat, Rhyland recovers and charges back like an enraged bull, his fists thunderous pistons loaded with enough force to shatter bone.

I duck and dodge, curving away from the onslaught with a dancer's grace. Still, he's inexorable, driving me back toward the treeline with a relentless fury that's both terrifying and exhilarating.

A vicious fist cuts past my ear, the rush of displaced air ruffling my hair. Rhyland closes the distance, his body a wall of corded muscle and Viking fury, eyes lit with something dangerous enough to make my blood hum.

I feint left, then cut right, aiming desperately for his face with a slashing blow that would lay open any normal man's cheek to the bone. But Rhyland is no normal man, and he bats my blade aside like an annoying gnat, a dismissive gesture that only fuels my determination.

And then, with a grunt, he's on me, his body slamming into mine with the force of a freight train. We crash together, all tangled limbs and grappling, our breaths mingling in harsh pants as we struggle for dominance.

His iron grip captures my wrists, pinning them apart as I struggle against his overwhelming strength, my muscles burning with exertion. Our faces are mere inches apart. My breath comes in ragged pants that brush across his carved features. His eyes pierce into mine with an intensity that robs me of oxygen.

"Not...bad..." he rumbles, his voice a low growl that reverberates through my body. "But I'm still holding back, baby."

"Oh yeah?" I bare my teeth in a feral grin, my heart thundering with a wild exhilaration. "Well, I'm not."

And with that, I tap into that awakening power within me, that extraordinary and remarkable gift that's become as intrinsic to me as breathing. I feel the world shift beneath me, time thickening into molasses as my awareness stretches outward, absorbing every nuance with vivid precision.

Rhyland's crushing grip now moves at a snail's pace, his preternatural speed rendered impotent by my newfound abilities. With almost languid ease, I twist free of his grasp and whirl behind him, a ghost slipping through the frozen flow of combat.

As the moment reasserts itself, I drive my elbow toward the base of Rhyland's spine with every ounce of momentum I can muster, putting my body's full force and power behind the blow.

He lurches forward with a grunt, stumbling as the world snaps back to full speed, his hand flying to the small of his back. When he spins to face me, disbelief and delight battle across those sharp features—his eyes wide, caught somewhere between shock and open admiration.

"Well, shit!" The curse is tinged with a breathless laugh. "Where'd you pick up that nifty little trick?" Rhyland shakes his head, a rueful chuckle escaping his lips. "Damn, woman," he says, his voice tinged with a fierce pride that warms me to my core. "You never cease to amaze me."

I blow a stray lock of hair from my eyes, grinning at his reaction. "Just one of my many talents, babe. You should see what else I can do."

"Oh, I can't wait." Rhyland shakes off the momentary shock, hunger flaring in those azure depths as he stalks toward me again, his movements low and coiled like a panther.

Our dance resumes with fevered intensity, attacks and counterattacks unfolding in a lethal ballet—the kind that could only exist between two warriors so intimately attuned. I channel that strange power, manipulating time to eke out the slimmest advantages, while Rhyland counters with sheer ferocity and preternatural reflexes honed over centuries of combat.

We're both heaving, sweat-slicked and gleaming as we trade blow after blow, testing each other's defenses. But underneath it all, there's an electric pull—a tension coiling between us that has nothing to do with the fight.

With a well-timed pivot, I manage to slip inside Rhyland's reach. My dagger flashes up in a decisive arc, the razor edge drawing a thin line of crimson against the sculpted plane of his chest.

He sucks a sharp breath through his teeth—more surprise than pain—his eyes flaring wide for a split second. I hesitate, a beat of regret cutting through the adrenaline, wondering if I've pushed too hard, gone too far.

But then his lips curve in a slow, sexy smile, and the hunger in his gaze robs me of breath, stealing the air from my lungs and the thoughts from my head.

"Well, well..." That velvet rumble caresses me like a physical touch, sending shivers through my entire body. "Looks like my angel has some fire after all."

I open my mouth to respond, to fire back some clever quip or sarcastic jab, but any words evaporate as Rhyland closes the distance between us in a heartbeat, his body a blur of speed and power.

My daggers fall to the ground, abandoned, as his muscular arms pull me against that sculpted expanse of muscle and blazing warmth, his heat consuming me like an inferno.

Our mouths collide in a fierce kiss that tastes of urgency and need, of passion and commitment, and something profound that burns with the promise of so much more. I surrender into him, melting beneath the flood of sensation—the wet heat of his tongue, the intoxicating taste of him, the relentless strength that holds me captive yet threatens to undo me completely.

When we finally break apart, I'm breathless and unsteady, my thoughts scattered and my heart hammering like thunder. Rhyland's forehead rests against mine, his breath's coming in heavy gasps that echo my own desperate attempts to catch my breath, our bodies heaving in sync.

"I've got you," he murmurs softly, his voice a deep rumble meant only for me, a vow and a promise all in one.

And I get the weight in those words, the unspoken pledge that extends way beyond our playful exchange and into devotion, loyalty, and connection. A promise that says he'll always be there and always have my back, no matter what obstacles we run into.

I give his chest a playful push, overdramatizing my annoyance with feigned irritation that contradicts the smile I'm struggling to hide.

"So it seems," I concede, even as I work to stifle my grin, my mouth fighting against the urge to break free."But only because you cheated with vampire speed."

He flashes me a satisfied smirk, brimming with self-satisfaction. His eyes glint with playfulness and something deeper, something that makes my pulse quicken.

"All's fair in love and war," he quips, echoing a truth as old as time yet never quite so literal—or thrilling—as it is in this moment between us, this perfect, shining moment that feels like a gift. "Not bad for a cute human," he husks out, the words both teasing and reverent, a contradiction that sends a thrill through my veins.

Mustering what little defiance I can, I shoot him a look from under my lashes, my eyes narrowed in a playful glare. "I'll show you cute, Mister Fang-and-Claw," I purr.

His only response is a low, rumbling laugh—the kind that's so damn sexy it's contagious, pulling a grin across my face before I can stop it. And I know, in this moment, that this game is far from finished between us. This is just the start of something wild and incredible and completely ours.

In the distance, the trees sway in the cool forest breeze, witnesses to the next thrilling round of our eternal spar, our endless dance of love and war, and everything in between. As I look up at Rhyland, the man who holds my heart and my future in his hands, I feel a fierce, wild elation blooming inside me, a joy born of love, laughter, and the rush of the fight.

DANICA

30

I uncurl in the squishy comfort of the bed, hissing a bit as my muscles throw a fit—the morning sun slinks in, turning the tent into an amber sanctuary. I'm basically one big bruise thanks to yesterday's boot camp—Rhyland style—each twinge a not-so-subtle nod to his no-mercy training methods.

But under all that ouch, there's this new power simmering in me, this raw energy that's itching to show the world it's not just about survival anymore; it's about kicking some serious ass.

Rhyland's all snuggled up to me, his body heat cranking up like my private little sun. I scooch even closer, taking a deep breath of that rich sandalwood and ocean blend that's all him. It's downright intoxicating how he's bottled up the whole Norse coastline in his vibe.

He's got that born-out-of-a-storm-on-the-high-seas aura, my very own Vike Spice. I let my hand wander over the landscape of his chest, my fingers dancing across each intricate ink stroke like they're reading braille stories of his past.

His reaction's instant—a tightening embrace that melds me to all those hard planes and edges. His grip takes a tour on my hip, and shivers sprint down my spine.

"Good morning, Angel," he rumbles, his voice raspy with sleep and sexy with that husky morning allure.

My insides start doing acrobatics, a full-on Olympic routine, just from a few words.

"Morning," I echo back, pressing a trail of eager kisses downward, ensuring each tattoo feels the love. I lavish them with attention, treating every inked line like a guide leading straight to my chest—right to the very spot where my heart beats a rhythm for him alone.

"Mmm...baby, I could get used to this," he purrs, that deep voice vibrating straight through me all the way to my toes.

The evidence of his excitement is pretty hard to miss, with the sheets pitching a not-so-little tent. A cheeky idea flickers to life, and I can't help but want to explore just how much 'morning glory' this Viking's hiding under there.

I kiss his chest, then work my way down to those hard, defined abs. I'm not just kissing, though—I'm giving them a little lick, too, tiny flicks of my tongue that seem to make him moan in delight.

I peel back the sheets, revealing more of his glorious form, and continue my slow, sensual descent.

I can't help but be astounded by the sheer size of him every time I see his glorious member. His hands are all over my head and hair, eagerly grasping and pulling as I take him into my mouth.

His groan meets my eager moan as I wrap my lips around his veiny shaft, savoring the salty-sweet taste of him. With practiced skill, I swirl my tongue around the length of him, taking my time to relish every bump and ridge, a slow torture for us both.

When I reach his manscaped balls, I pause, letting the anticipation build before taking them into my mouth, one at a time, and rolling my tongue over them. I feel his body tense, his breath catching, and a surprised groan escapes his lips. "Fuck," he gasps, his hips jerking involuntarily.

Eager for more, I take them both into my mouth, sucking gently as my hand strokes his thick cock. He tastes and feels exquisite, and I relish the power I hold in this moment.

"Goddamn, baby," he grunts, his voice gravelly and raw. "Keep going, Angel. You're driving me fucking insane."

After a moment, I pop off with a wet sound, savoring the sharp hiss of his breath and the way his body tenses. I slowly lick back up his length, my tongue tracing every inch before I take him deeper into my mouth, my tongue dancing and swirling as I increase my pace. He's overwhelming—all primal power and control, dominating me with nothing but his sheer size. His hands tangle in my hair, pulling back with just enough force to expose my throat, and when I gag slightly around him, it only intensifies the heat between us, driving us both higher.

"That's it, Angel," he commands, his voice a low, sexy growl. "Take it all, take every fucking inch. Show me how much you love being my cock-hungry slut."

His words sear into my skin like a brand, heat pooling low in my belly. My body trembles, lust spilling through me unchecked, and I moan my consent.

His eyes burn into mine, holding me captive, "You love it, don't you, baby?" he demands, his voice low and rough, his hand tightening in my hair. "You love getting fucked in that pretty mouth."

I moan, my throat constricting around him as tears well from the slight sting.

"Fucking say it, baby," he commands, his grip becoming fiercer. "Say it, baby. Admit how much you love my cock in your mouth—how dirty you are."

He pulls out of my mouth, a slick, wet sound, and smacks my jaw with a stinging slap. "*Words,* Angel. Let me hear them."

"Yes," I finally gasp, my voice raw and hoarse. "Yes, I love it. I'm your dirty girl."

"Yeah, you are."

He rewards me with a swift thrust back into my mouth, his length hitting the back of my throat. I suppress my gag reflex, determined to take him, please him, my thighs slick with my desire.

His sexy groans fuel my fire, spurring me on as I increase my pace, eager to taste his release.

"That's it, baby," he praises, his voice strained. "Fuck. That's so good."

I'm nearly choking on him now, tears streaming freely down my cheeks, and I couldn't care less. It's gloriously messy—spit slicking my chin, his cock impossibly hard as iron as it fills my throat completely. I moan around him, the vibration drawing the most devastatingly erotic sounds from deep in his chest—raw, animalistic sounds that unravel me completely, pooling heat between my thighs until I'm absolutely desperate.

His body coils with tension, those impossibly carved abs flexing and contracting as he teeters on the razor's edge, every muscle straining with the effort of holding back. His grip tightens in my hair—a silent demand for more, for everything, for all of me. I've never felt more undone, more completely owned in my life.

The rush of excitement takes over me, knowing I'm about to push him over the edge.

"Oh—fuuuck, Angel—I'm—"

Lucian bursts into our tent, his golden blonde hair sticking up in every direction like he just stuck his finger in an electrical socket. But the moment his eyes land on me and Rhyland in our—ahem—compromising position, his jaw drops so fast I swear I hear it crack against the ground.

"Sweet baby Jesus on a pogo stick! My eyes! My innocent, virgin eyes!" he yelps, slapping a hand over his eyes like he's just been blinded by the sun. "But damn, guys, at least put a sock on the tent flap or something!"

He stumbles backward, tripping over his own feet in his haste to escape the scandalous scene. "I'm sorry, I'm sorry, I'll just—I'm gonna go bleach my eyeballs now, okay? Okay. You two just... carry on with your little game of hide-the-salami. Pretend I was never here."

And with that, he scurries out of the tent like his ass is on fire, leaving me and Rhyland staring after him.

Rhyland curses, then yells, "Anyone ever teach you to fucking knock?"

I giggle, wiping my mouth as Rhyland looks at me, half-pissed off and half still turned on, breathing hard. It's a sight to behold this Viking god of mine, all flushed and wild, his eyes gleaming with irritation and desire.

I flash him a playful smirk, "Now, where was I?"

Axilya announces, "Today we set forth to the Sun Court," her voice like wind chimes in a gentle breeze, melodic and soothing. "Prepare yourself for a two-day ride to the north, adjacent to the Crystal Peaks."

I groan inwardly at the thought of another carriage ride, and the memory of my last journey's discomfort—and the fiasco between Lucian and Rhyland—makes my decision swift and final.

"I'll pass on the carriage," I say firmly, my voice brooking no argument. "I think I'll manage better on horseback."

Axilya arches an eyebrow but nods in understanding, a small smile playing at the corners of her lips.

When we arrive, the stables are bustling with activity. Horses whinny and stamp their hooves, sensing the excitement in the air. I stand awkwardly among them, painfully aware of my lack of equestrian knowledge, feeling like a fish out of water in this sea of horseflesh.

But then Rhyland appears beside me, his presence like a warm cloak enveloping my senses, his signature scent of salt and sea instantly putting me at ease.

"Are you sure about this?" he asks, a mischievous twinkle in his azure eyes. His lips curve into a smirk that is half challenge and half invitation.

I nod, mustering up a bravado I don't quite feel. "I've got a gentle grasp on horseback riding—just the cliff notes, really," I say with a half-shrug, trying to play it cool even as my heart races in my chest.

He chuckles—a deep, resonant sound that rumbles through his chest like distant thunder—and reaches out to stroke the mane of a majestic black stallion. His fingers glide through the silky strands with a casual grace that makes my mouth go dry.

"No worries, Angel," he says with a confident and charming grin. "You'll ride with me."

Before I can protest, he effortlessly swings onto the horse's back, his muscles rippling beneath his shirt like a work of art. Then he extends a hand to me, his eyes glinting with a challenge that I can't resist.

With a deep breath, I accept his help and hoist myself up in front of him, my body molding to his like a puzzle piece snapping into place. His arms encircle me as he guides me into position, his touch gentle but firm, and it feels good, so good, to be pulled snugly against him like this.

His chest is a solid wall against my back, his thighs pressing against mine as he adjusts our seating, and I can feel the heat of him seeping into my skin like a brand.

"Comfortable?" he murmurs into my ear, his breath warm against my skin, sending heat through me.

Okay, sure. Horseback riding semi-virgin here, but guess what? I'm perched on this equine giant with a Viking god strapped to my back like the world's most muscular safety feature. So yeah, I'm feeling pretty damn comfortable right about now.

But then the beast beneath us decides it's the perfect moment to shimmy, and my fingers instinctively latch onto Rhyland's, my nails digging into his skin as I fight to keep my balance.

"As I'll ever be," I toss back sassily, slathering on a layer of courage like the final touch of war paint, determined not to let him see how much his proximity affects me.

A chuckle rumbles out of Rhyland, doubling as my personal back massager, as he coaxes our four-legged Uber into gear without breaking a sweat, his muscles flexing beneath me with every movement.

And then Meadow slides to a stop beside us, her timing impeccable as she reaches us and our steed, her delicate features creased with concern.

She offers a deferential bow, her eyes lowered in respect. "My lady," she acknowledges softly before lifting her gaze to Rhyland with a respectful inclination, "My lord, may you both journey safely. Thank you for being so kind and..." She hesitates, her expression clouded by contemplation as if weighing her words carefully. "I foresee...trials ahead—whispers. So I urge you to proceed cautiously."

Her ominous words raise the hair on my arms, chilling me to the core, despite my efforts to remain unaffected and project an air of calm confidence.

"Thank you, Meadow," I manage, though my voice quivers barely, betraying the unease that coils in my gut like a serpent.

"No worries, Mouse. No harm will come to her or me," Rhyland announces confidently, his voice a low rumble that vibrates through me like a second heartbeat, strong, steady, and sure.

With a respectful nod, Meadow retreats, her lithe form melting back into the bustle of the stables like a shadow.

There's comfort in knowing that we've aided her, securing her refuge in Whispervale, where her safety is all but guaranteed. One less weight on my shoulders, one less burden to bear as we set out on this journey into the unknown.

As we ride, the rhythm of the horse's hooves against the earth creates a potent cocktail of calm and thrill; each beat hitting like a bass drum tuned by the gods. I can't help but feel a sense of excitement bubbling up inside me, mingling with the nerves that flutter in my stomach like butterflies.

"You're doing great," Rhyland reassures me, his voice low and playful, his breath tickling the shell of my ear. "Just relax, baby, and let me take care of you," he says, and I can almost hear the wink in his words, the promise of something more than just a ride through the forest.

Eye roll incoming—Mr. Alpha Male has a one-track lexicon, but let's be real—there's a fortress-level of safety vibes with Rhyland playing my personal shield, his body a barrier between me and the world.

"And I plan to do it while having a little fun in the process," he adds, his hand squeezing my inner thigh with a teasing lilt to his words as we fall in step behind Axilya and her crew, the promise of adventure and excitement hanging in the air like a tangible thing.

My face is on fire from his little hint-drop, but I'm dishing it right back at him, my lips curving into a smirk. "Keep your eyes on the road, hands on the reins, Big Guy. It'd be a shame if we took a tumble and your ego ended up with a boo-boo."

Rhyland tosses me another one of his chuckles, the sound warm, rich, and full of promise. He pulls me tighter against him, like he's wordlessly vowing not to let me so much as stub a toe on this journey, to keep me safe and sound no matter what trials may lie ahead.

RHYLAND

31

Already a day into our trek, nature's untamed majesty blossoms around us like a masterpiece. Thick woods that would put the finest manicured gardens to shame flank us on either side, and the hills roll out before us like a lavish spread of emerald and gold, basking in the glow of sunrise and showing off every vivid color in its arsenal. This place is a chorus of old magic, a landscape that's wild and eternal, that doesn't give a single flying fuck about the march of time or the petty concerns of mere mortals.

The rhythmic thud of hooves against the earth is as steady as a drumbeat, a slow march that syncs up perfectly with the wild symphony around us. It's like the very land itself is alive, pulsing with an energy that I can feel thrumming through my veins, setting every nerve ending on fire.

Dani's heat is pressed up against me, a solid anchor that reminds me why I'm in this fight, why I'm willing to go to the ends of the earth and beyond to keep her safe, to claim what's ours. I pull her in closer, my arms like steel bands wrapped around her, while I handle the reins with an ease born of centuries of practice, not even breaking a sweat.

She's nestled right between my thighs, fitting there like she was made for it, like every curve of her body was designed to mold perfectly against mine. It's a feeling that sets my blood on fire, that makes me want to forget about the mission, about the fate of the realms, and lose myself in her, in the way she makes me feel alive in ways I never thought possible.

That blowjob this morning completely blew my fucking mind. And I can't stop thinking about all the filthy ways I'm going to make it up to my dirty little angel.

I'm holding Dani tight against me, her scent—like sunshine and honey mixed with a hint of spice—slamming into me hard, making my head spin with need. I can't help but bury my face in that sweet spot on her neck, breathing her in deep, letting her essence flood my lungs and ignite my blood.

Dani's decked out in her battle gear, and fuck me sideways if she doesn't look like a goddess of war. The leathers are snug, really fucking snug, in all the right places—skimpy enough to make a man's mind wander to all sorts of sinful shit, but not so much that they don't mean serious business. They're like a second skin, outlining every delicious curve of her body, screaming both 'Touch me' and 'I'll kick your ass six ways to Sunday.'

Each strap, each buckle, is placed just so, showcasing her strength and power. The way that dark material sets off her golden, sun-kissed skin has me on edge. She's walking art, a lethal package wrapped up in one hell of a tempting package, and I'm the lucky bastard who gets to stand at her side to call her mine.

Her hair, twisted into intricate war braids by the local fae girls this morning, has my cock throbbing non-stop, straining against my leathers like it's got a mind of its own.

She's a goddess, a warrior, my mate, and I'll be damned if she isn't going to conquer this battle just like she conquered my heart, claiming it as her own.

This morning, before we hit the road, she fed Lucian and Erik with her blood, using that ancient-as-fuck blood-drawing gear that Faderyn handed over. A sacred ritual, a bond forged in crimson.

Lucian and I, we've put our shit to bed... for the moment. Dani, in all her infinite wisdom, pushed us to 'kiss and make up,' and I went along with it, though not without a metric fuck-ton of grumbling. She laid it out clear as day—we've got to pull in the same direction, to have each other's backs. We can't let the petty stuff trip us up, not now, not with so much at stake. And as much as it grinds my gears to admit it, she's got a point.

Watching her fight, seeing how she moves, the grace and power in every strike, every blow? It's a fucking intoxicating mix of desire and pride that burns deep inside me. She's picking up the skills fast, my little warrior.

Off to our flank, Lucian and Erik ride easily, their mounts tearing gently through the soft grass, leaving a trail of flattened blades in their wake. Hanging back, Axilya and Faderyn are lost in their conversation, their murmured words getting caught up and carried away by the wind, secrets whispered on the breeze.

"Remember," Axilya calls ahead to us, "the Sun Court is not one to be trifled with. They value beauty, peace, and elegance above all else."

Lucian's scoff reverberates, his golden hair shimmering in the fading sunlight as he flings his head back with dramatic flair. "Pfft... beauty and elegance?" He echoes the words with obvious disdain, upper lip curling. "In other words, a total snoozefest." He punctuates this dismissive assessment with an exaggerated yawn and eye roll. "You know how I operate—any hint of pretentious stuffiness or mind-numbing propriety, and I simply must counteract it with a deliciously sordid spectacle."

Lucian's usual bullshit has me smiling. "Figures. You thrive off chaos," I throw back, tossing him a look.

Flashing me a roguish wink, "Oh, yeah. So prepare yourselves, ladies and gents. Things are about to get wildly, outrageously inappropriate." Lucian ends with irreverent charm. "You're utterly welcome in advance for the entertainment."

Dani stirs in my arms, turning her head to join the banter. "So, what's the deal with the Light King and his Radiant Queen?" she asks, her voice laced with curiosity.

"The King is cerebral and detached," Axilya replies. "He views his rule as a sacred duty."

"And the Queen?" Dani presses on.

Axilya's voice softens. "She's warm, nurturing... but carries a secret sorrow."

Dani's interest is lighting up; she's got one hell of an empathetic streak in her.

Erik's silver eyes catch some light, sparking to life as he pipes in, breaking his silence from the start of our ride. "They say she lost something precious to her—a sorrow that lingers like a shadow despite her eternal youth."

"The court holds beauty and nobility in high regard, so we must present ourselves accordingly." Faderyn chimes in, his tone heavy.

Lucian lets out a theatrical groan, "What, no brawls or love bites on the agenda?"

"Only if you're aiming to ignite yet another conflict with the Fae," Erik counters, his tone laced with dry sarcasm.

I catch a look at Dani, who's biting back a grin at their back-and-forth.

"Keep your eyes on the prize," I break in, bringing them back on track. "We're here to score some goodwill and backup from the Sun Court, not kick up a damn storm."

Dani gives me a nod so subtle it's more felt than seen. "Alright then, what's the etiquette? How do we hail the glow-in-the-dark royalty?"

"With respect," Axilya answers promptly. "Address him as 'Your Majesty' and her as 'Your Radiance.'"

Lucian's eyes roll dramatically skyward.

Erik keeps his mouth shut, but his eyes are all over the place, soaking up the scene like a sponge—always the watchful warrior, ready for whatever might come our way.

Chatter fades to nothing when we hit the edges of the Sun Court's domain. The Light Lands stretch out before us, a never-ending canvas of greens and golds, like some artist lost his damn mind and just splattered his whole kit across the landscape.

After a spell of quiet that settles over us all, Faderyn clears his throat, breaking the stillness with his announcement. "We're nearing the Ivory Tower; we will rest tonight and should arrive by tomorrow's eve."

I gaze up to see what lies before us—an ancient palace that has stood the test of time but has surrendered some pieces. On the horizon, it holds on to the final traces of its fading glory.

"It was magnificent in its prime," Axilya says wistfully. Her eyes glint with memories of a past age.

Dani leans into me, just a fraction, and I know she's vibing with what Axilya's laying down about this place. It doesn't escape me that she's finding beauty in all this decay—classic her, always catching a glimmer of light in the darkest shit.

Erik's voice cuts through with a warning note. "Do not forget that despite their current peaceable facade, the Sun Court has been at odds with the Shadow Court for centuries."

"We won't forget," I tell him with a firm edge to my voice. "Maybe we can even turn that to our advantage."

Lucian lets out a soft, mocking snort, "Yeah, right. Like that will happen when they're cozied up next door to—"

"Enough," I snap, cutting off his smart-ass comment. Then I swing back to Faderyn and Axilya, my face all business. "Is there anything else we need to have on our radar?"

Faderyn exhales deeply before speaking. "They may ask you to demonstrate your worth through knowledge, combat skill, or magical ability."

I feel Dani exhale a weary sigh, as if she's had it up to here with having to show everyone what she's made of since she gained her abilities.

Dani tips her head back with a playful glint in her honey-golden eyes. "Sparkle duty? Pssh, consider me the queen of glitterati," she retorts with a sass-laden grin.

Faderyn laughs, and Lucian chimes in with cheeky commentary, "Oh, sure. They'll flip their lid completely when they get a load of Miss Firecracker Fingers here."

Dani's all business with a dash of sass. "I'm gonna lay it all out—give them the full Blockbuster trailer of the doom that's about to RSVP uninvited to their magic cottage. But top of the to-do list? That stone. They've gotta have some information on where that gem's hiding."

I pull her in closer, savoring her warmth and sweet scent. "We'll get it, Angel," I whisper against her ear so only she can hear. "Do you feel it? The pull?" I need to know about her connection to that stone.

She gives a little head shake, firm and sure. "Tough to pin down, but there's this subtle pull—a sixth sense or GPS for the mystical, I guess. One thing I do know? We're headed in the right direction," she asserts with confidence.

DANICA

32

Butts numbed to oblivion and sporting a second skin of trail dust, we haul our road-weary selves off at a clearing that unfolds like a scene from a painter's wildest dreams.

The Light Lands stretch out below, a breathtaking panorama of luminescent meadows that seem to radiate with an otherworldly glow. The forests murmur secrets on the breeze, their leaves catching the fading sunlight like emerald shards. And the rivers—oh, the rivers—capture the last golden rays of the day and turn them into liquid gold, a stunning sight that almost hurts to look at.

"Here," Axilya declares with a sweep of her arm, "we make camp."

Rhyland, ever the considerate warrior, is at my side in a heartbeat, his strong hands lifting me from the saddle like I weigh nothing. "Easy there, Angel," he murmurs, his voice a low rumble that sends warmth flooding through me.

Of course, I'm about as graceful as a newborn giraffe, sliding down his muscular frame like a sack of potatoes. Meanwhile, Axilya's crew dismounts with an effortless elegance that screams, "I could do this blindfolded." And here I am, legs wobbling like jelly after our marathon riding session. Totally nailing it.

As we set about pitching our tents, the diamond-dusted trees stand guard, their branches glittering in the twilight. The fireflies put on a show that would make Vegas jealous, their flickering glow a perfectly choreographed light display that fills the air with magic. And the flowers—they basically throw a party, unfurling like they're giving us a standing ovation, their perfume drifting on the breeze like nature's own air freshener.

I pitch in where I can, but honestly, I'm mostly just standing here in complete awe. This is the deep magic of the Light Lands, untamed and pristine, a force so powerful it literally steals the breath from my lungs.

Dead center of the camp stands this massive tree that looks like it's been standing guard since the beginning of time. Its roots sprawl everywhere, basically doubling as nature's own built-in seating, and the leaves rustle with this hushed conversation that has me dying to know what ancient tree gossip they're sharing.

As the last tent peg gets hammered into the soft earth, I take a second to just stand here and soak it all in. The beauty of this place, the sense of belonging that washes over me like a warm hug—it's a feeling I've never really experienced before, this connection to something way bigger than myself.

As night wraps its arms around us, we huddle close to a campfire that pops and hisses, its flames dancing with colors that would make a rainbow look basic. Axilya's fae crew spreads out this incredible spread of fruits and vegetables that practically glow from the inside out, each bite like a flavor explosion—equal parts new and weirdly comforting at the same time.

I'm all cozied up in my go-to spot, sandwiched between Rhyland's linebacker thighs, soaking in the double warmth from my personal heater and the crackling campfire. It's a moment of pure bliss, a respite from the chaos and uncertainty that seems to follow us wherever we go.

"How's my Angel holding up?" Rhyland murmurs, his breath warm against my ear as he plants hot kisses along my neck, working his way down with clear intent.

It's so typical Rhyland—thoughtful as hell, with that possessive vibe wrapped around me like a security blanket. His presence is exactly what I need, a reminder that no matter what goes down, I've got him watching my back.

But our peaceful moment gets obliterated by a violent rumble beneath us. Gentle tremors suddenly explode into bone-shaking quakes, sending the fireflies scattering everywhere. Their once-beautiful light show turns into a chaotic dance of panic; the insects dart and weave desperately trying to escape whatever's coming.

A massive roar tears through the air, deep and booming like something straight out of a monster movie. It's a sound that freezes my blood, a raw cry that screams violence and death.

"They're coming!" Axilya's guard shouts over the deafening noise, his voice tight with fear and urgency.

They? I'm mentally running through my mental list of potential threats when hulking silhouettes crest the hill—massive stone-skinned creatures with arms thick as tree trunks, each step they take shaking the ground beneath us. Behind them, serpentine horrors slither forward, a nightmarish tangle of deadly claws and fangs that drip venom.

"Ogres!" Faderyn's warning cuts through like a knife, his eyes wide with shock and dread.

"Everybody, battle formation!" Axilya's command rings out, her voice sharp and authoritative as she draws a blade that gleams like moonlight. It's a weapon that screams power and control.

Rhyland and I move instantly, muscles locked and ready for war. Of course, he positions me behind him, playing the overprotective wall, his body solid and immovable between me and the incoming horde.

Erik's broadsword screams as he rips it free from its sheath, the steel humming with anticipation. "Stay behind us, Little Huntress!" he barks, his tone a mix of gruff affection and deadly intent.

His blade becomes part of him, moving fluidly before tearing into thick ogre flesh. Blood sprays in arcs as skin and bone split like rotting fruit under each vicious strike. Erik carves through the creatures with the intensity of a hurricane—limbs fly, heads roll, and gore splatters across the ground in rivers of crimson.

The night explodes into a symphony of snarls, shrieks, and the brutal clash of steel against bodies as the monstrous horde tears into our camp. The reek of death and decay floods the air, thick enough to choke on as I watch the slaughter unfold.

Lucian becomes a blur in the chaos, his movements sharp and precise as he ducks between snapping jaws and grasping claws. His fists and feet crack bone and tear flesh in a rapid-fire sequence of devastating hits, each one placed perfectly. He uses the ogres' own weight against them, slamming them together with brutal efficiency, their pained howls ripping through the night.

Amidst the chaos, Rhyland stands tall and immovable, a tower of strength in the heart of the storm. His outstretched hands crackle with telekinetic power, the raw energy visible only through its gruesome aftermath. With a casual flick of his wrist, he sends an ogre hurtling skyward, its massive body twisting helplessly before it crashes down in a sickening explosion of shattered bones and spraying viscera that paints the ground in blood.

The stench of death is suffocating, a putrid wall that threatens to turn my stomach inside out. But I force it down, my eyes locked on the massacre unfolding before me.

Seizing the moment, I let out a scream, the sound ripping from my throat as I launch myself into the thick of it, my daggers gripped tight in my sweaty palms.

The blade plunges into an ogre's bloated belly, sinking deep into the fetid flesh with a sickening squelch. A fountain of partially digested slop erupts from the wound, drenching my face and chest in a nauseating spray of bile and blood.

"Eww... fucking gross," I mutter, my face twisting in disgust as I wrench my dagger free with a wet, sucking sound that makes my skin crawl.

But I'm not done yet. With a surge of power, I summon a searing orb of light, the energy pulsing and writhing in my palm like something alive. With a grunt, I hurl it at the wounded ogre, watching as the creature's flesh blackens, blisters, and melts away like wax. Its agonized shrieks reach a fever pitch before cutting off abruptly into dead silence.

A serpent's mouth gapes wide, its fangs glinting wickedly as it strikes for my throat. I spin hard to the side, my heart hammering as I grab one of its thrashing tentacles and yank with everything I've got. The sickening pop of dislocating joints echoes in my ears as the creature slams to the ground, its body convulsing in agony.

With a wild growl, I move in for the kill, my dagger slicing through the serpent's soft underbelly. Blood and guts spray with each vicious thrust, coating me in a grotesque collage of gore. The blade cuts deeper and deeper, a brutal, unrelenting dance of steel and blood until the creature's hisses fade into nothing but silence.

The air reeks of copper and decay. Blood drips from my hair, smears across my face, and soaks through my clothes. The creature's insides ooze and seep, a repulsive tangle of organs and putrid fluid that clings to me, mixing with my own sweat and dirt.

"We need to push these bastards back!" Rhyland roars over the screaming and clashing steel, his voice cutting through like a command that sends adrenaline flooding through my veins.

"Behind you!" Erik shouts, his blade flashing in a lethal arc as he ducks under a club swing to bury his steel deep in an ogre's throat. The creature gurgles violently, black blood spilling from its mouth as it staggers and collapses, its massive frame hitting the ground with a thunderous impact that shakes the earth.

Lucian's laughter rings out, wild and pumped up, a jarring contrast to the screams and snarls filling the air. He moves like a tornado, his fists and feet a blur as he takes down creature after creature, his face lit up with this fierce, almost feral excitement. Classic Lucian—probably having the time of his life while the rest of us are actually struggling here.

I can feel the heat of battle burning through my blood, the rush of adrenaline and magic coursing through my veins like wildfire. My heart pounds in my chest, each beat a defiant drumbeat against the encroaching darkness.

We keep fighting, our blades and bodies a wall of steel and muscle against the relentless assault. The ground turns slick with blood and gore, the rotten smell hanging thick in the air. But we don't break, don't back down.

The sight that hits me as I glance to my left stops my heart cold. An ogre, its massive club dripping with blood, swings with bone-crushing force at one of our fighters. The sickening crunch of bone against wood steals the air from my lungs, the sound reverberating through me like a death knell.

The warrior crumples into a twisted heap, limbs bent at impossible angles, blood pooling black in the moonlight. It's straight out of a nightmare, a grotesque scene that makes my stomach flip. Bile rises sharp and bitter in my throat as I fight the urge to lose it.

There's no time to process what I'm seeing because razor-sharp serpent claws come slashing toward my gut, ready to rip me open. I barely dodge, my heart exploding in my chest as I feel the rush of air from how close that was.

Rhyland's right there, his wrist flicking casually as he sends the serpent flying upward. Its screams pierce the night until it crashes back down with a sickening thud.

"Danica! On your six!" Rhyland shouts, but his warning comes about a second too late as an ogre blindsides me, materializing out of the darkness like something out of a horror movie.

I drop and roll, feeling the rush of air as its club swings past, missing me by inches. Rhyland lets out a furious roar, his hand moving sharply as he sends the beast crashing into a nearby tree trunk with a wet, bone-breaking crunch.

I scramble back to my feet just in time to face down two serpents, their eyes gleaming with hunger as venom drips from their fangs. I scream and charge at them, my white light exploding outward to fry them with raw arcane power.

But even as they fall, more snapping jaws and glowing eyes surge forward in this endless wave, a never-ending tide of nightmares threatening to crush us all.

I can feel myself wearing down, my hits getting weaker with each second that passes, but these things just keep coming like some kind of endless monster assembly line. How much longer can a handful of fighters hold out against this never-ending horde?

Sensing my exhaustion, Rhyland unleashes a massive surge of telekinetic fury, a crushing wave of invisible force that blasts the encroaching creatures back, shattering bones and pulping bodies into a disgusting mess.

"Damn," I can't help but breathe out, my eyes wide with a mix of awe and horror at just how destructive he really is. "Show-off."

Lucian's voice rings out, full of unhinged excitement. "Keep that Obi-Wan Jedi shit coming, bro! Now toss me that mind-forged lightsaber! I wanna show these slimy bastards where the sun doesn't fucking sparkle."

Erik tears through the thinning enemy ranks, his sword singing a deadly song as he leaves trails of crimson across the ground. "We've got them on the run!"

With hope flickering back to life, I dig deep for every last bit of strength I've got left, scorching serpents to ash with blazing orbs of light. Their numbers are dropping now, their broken bodies scattered across the ground in gruesome pieces.

An ogre lurches forward, its club raised high for one last, desperate swing. But Faderyn's suddenly there, a blur of motion, his blades plunging deep into the monster's gut. With a vicious twist, he spills its steaming insides all over the blood-soaked earth.

"That's the last of them!" he shouts in triumph, his voice cutting through the sudden, heavy silence settling over the battlefield.

DANICA

33

My lungs are burning, my muscles are screaming, and I can taste blood coating my mouth. Rhyland's solid presence towers beside me like a rock, his chest heaving from the effort of keeping me alive through this nightmare.

I collapse to my knees, barely processing that we actually won. We just fought our way through a brutal mess of ogres and serpents, and now their lifeless bodies are scattered all over the clearing. The scale of the carnage is almost incomprehensible.

Hands grab me, and suddenly Rhyland's pulling me into a crushing embrace, his whole body shaking with what I can only assume is the aftermath of adrenaline and relief.

"Come here, Angel," he breathes out between gasps. "You okay?" There's this desperate note in his voice, like he needs to know with absolute certainty that I'm not hurt.

I lean into him, my body trembling from exhaustion and the adrenaline crash hitting me hard as a ton of bricks. He wraps an arm around me, holding me tight as we take in the carnage surrounding us. The reality of what just happened settles over me like a heavy blanket.

It's like something straight out of a slasher film—the ground is basically a graveyard of twisted, broken bodies. The stench of death is suffocating, mixing with the metallic reek of blood and the burnt smell of charred flesh. It's almost too much to take in.

But underneath the horror, there's this rush of relief, of actually pulling this off. We survived. We took on these monsters and came out the other side, battered and covered in blood but still standing. That counts for something.

I latch onto him, taking a deep, dramatic whiff. His scent is like an oceanic forest spa mixed with sandalwood and danger. "Yeah, I'm good," I say, my voice steadier than I feel. "Are you okay?"

I untangle myself from Rhyland's iron grip and scope out the scene. Everyone's still in one piece, which is honestly miraculous considering what we just went through. Erik's there, casually using a deceased ogre as a napkin for his sword—gross, but efficient. Lucian's strutting over with the glee you'd expect from someone who just won an arcade jackpot. Faderyn and Axilya are playing medic with the wounded troops, moving between injured fighters with practiced efficiency.

I catch Faderyn's eye, and he gives me a silent nod—like a mystical "we're all good" stamp of approval. It's reassuring, though I can tell some of Axilya's crew didn't make it.

"Well, that was... unexpected," I let out, my voice dancing between amused and utterly gobsmacked. It's an understatement, but what else can you say when you've just faced a horde of nightmarish monsters and lived to tell the tale?

Rhyland's hand slides through my gross hair, his fingers finding one of my braids and giving it a playful tug. "You kicked ass, Angel," he says, his blue eyes lit up with admiration, love, and this ridiculous amount of pride that makes my chest actually swell.

I rise on my tiptoes, my hands cradling his bearded face as I reel him in for a kiss that's straight-up fire. Sure, he's sporting the latest in ogre blood and grime, but who's paying attention to a little battle splatter? Not me, that's for damn sure. All I care about is the feel of his lips on mine, the way his arms tighten around me like he never wants to let go. This moment—this connection between us—feels real in a way nothing else does right now.

Lucian comes barreling over, this wild grin plastered across his face like it's Christmas morning and he just got everything on his wish list. "Oh my... FUCK! That was incredible, right? It's like we just went toe-to-toe with Shrek and his entire swamp crew!" he shouts, his voice high on adrenaline and pure joy. Only Lucian could make a joke about literal ogres at a time like this.

I pull back from Rhyland's kiss and can't help but laugh at Lucian's take on the absolute insanity we just survived. "Lucy, what the hell is wrong with your brain? 'Fun' is literally not the word I'd use for nearly getting crushed into a pancake by a monster," I say, shaking my head at his ridiculousness. "That was survival, not a theme park experience."

Lucian just shrugs casually, but his mouth betrays him with that signature impish grin—the classic Lucian move that's equal parts mischief and undeniable charm. It's infuriating how he can find humor in everything.

"Come on, Princess. Don't act like you didn't feel that rush," he teases, his dark brown eyes crinkling with amusement as they lock onto mine. They're sparkling with the same energy as a hyperactive puppy, except this one knows exactly how to wrap you around its finger. "I saw your face when you were throwing that light around. That was pure joy."

I mentally shrug, conceding a point to Lucian's oddball take on the situation. As much as I hate to admit it, there was a certain rush, a buzz that came with letting my powers loose without worrying about accidentally torching an entire forest. It was exhilarating and terrifying all at once.

Maybe I'm finally inching toward a truce with the magic that flows through my veins—mastering the mayhem could be my new party trick, a way to turn the tables on our enemies and give us the edge we so desperately need. Power without control is dangerous, but power with purpose could change everything.

With a flick of frustration in my tone, I toss the question out like a Frisbee at a picnic, "So, anyone wanna explain what that was about? Because last I checked, ogres and serpents weren't exactly on the guest list for this little camping trip."

Axilya walks over, her violet skin catching the firelight and casting these creepy shadows across her delicate features. She looks at us with those pale green eyes that seem to hold centuries of pain and knowledge—the kind of depth that makes me feel like a kid playing dress-up in her world of ancient fae politics.

"Long before the fae courts fell apart," Axilya begins, her voice a haunting whisper that demands you listen, "Ogres were gentle giants roaming the fertile plains of our realm. They worked the land, tended to the crops, and respected nature's gifts with a reverence that was almost spiritual. They lived in harmony with everything around them, building a civilization based on peace and cooperation."

Rhyland's eyes bore into Axilya with this intensity that could slice steel. "What the hell changed?"

Axilya's eyes go dim like the memory is physically crushing her, weighing down on her shoulders like an ancient burden. "When the realm descended into chaos, power struggles tore us all apart. Different fae courts began vying for control, and in their quest for dominance, they saw the Ogres as expendable. Ogres were enslaved, beaten, and forced to fight in wars that weren't even theirs, wars between courts that had nothing to do with them. The brutality they suffered—it was systematic, deliberate, and unforgiving. It twisted their hearts into stone, turning them into the monsters we just fought."

I squeeze Rhyland's hand so hard my knuckles turn white as this unexpected wave of empathy hits me for the creatures we literally just slaughtered. "So their violence is basically a reflection of what was done to them? They became what their tormentors made them?" I ask quietly.

Axilya nods, her expression heavy with the weight of history. "Yes, Danica. Once they broke free from their chains, their need for revenge became everything. It consumed them. They attack any fae they encounter, seeing them as reminders of the ones who hurt them, who enslaved them, who broke them."

Rhyland exhales sharply through his nose, his jaw clenching visibly. "Violence breeds violence," he mutters, speaking like someone who knows that truth way too well from his own centuries of existence.

"We can't justify what they did," I say firmly, my voice steady even as my heart aches for the tragedy of it all. "They made their choices. But understanding their suffering... it changes how I see them. It paints them in a different light, doesn't it? They're not monsters by nature; they became monsters by circumstance."

Axilya reaches out as if to touch the air between us all, her gesture graceful and measured. "Compassion is a powerful weapon, Danica. One that can heal more than just physical wounds. It can heal the rifts between people, between worlds, between past and future."

We stand there for a long moment, each lost in our own thoughts about Axilya's account of how the ogres became corrupted by centuries of brutality and oppression. This burning need to make things right starts settling in my chest, like an itch I can't ignore. The injustice of it all weighs heavily on me, pressing down like a physical force.

This is so not right. There has to be a way to fix this.

Pity settles deep within me for the ogres, though they didn't exactly give us much choice in how things went down. War leaves no room for nuance.

Rhyland gives my shoulder this soft nudge, a gentle reminder that he's always watching out for me, even in complete chaos and carnage. "Come on, Angel," he says low, his voice just for me. "Let's get you cleaned up."

We dig out fresh clothes from our bags and head away from everyone, throwing Axilya a quick nod as she stands there lost in thought, her forehead creased like she's carrying the weight of everything she just told us. The sparkling lake calls to us in the distance, its peaceful rhythm promising exactly what we need after the bloodbath we just survived.

As I sink into the cool water, I feel all the tension draining out of my battered body, the blood and gore from the battle washing away in these pink and green swirling clouds. The water is almost therapeutic in its coolness. My fingers work through my braids, undoing the tight plaits that are basically cemented with today's chaos and dried blood. It takes patience and effort, but slowly they come loose.

"God, this is exactly what I needed," I murmur, letting the water flow through my hair and work out all the tangles and knots that have taken over. The sensation is almost meditative.

Rhyland looks like he walked straight out of some ancient warrior painting. His tattoos, a bold contrast against his skin. Intricate designs that tell stories of battles long past, and the moonlight hits him just right, making him look like he belongs in a museum or something. Seeing him like this takes my breath away, reminding me just how powerful and graceful the man I love really is beneath all that brooding intensity.

Rhyland flashes me this smile that literally messes with my heartbeat, his teasing words cutting through the night's heaviness. "You're still breathtaking, even covered in ogre blood and guts," he jokes, his eyes sparkling with genuine amusement. There's a lightness to him right now that I rarely see.

I splash some water his way, laughing at how ridiculous he's being. "Smooth talker," I call out, but I'm grinning because, honestly? I love it when he gets like this—playful and present instead of brooding and distant. This version of him is addictive.

In two seconds flat, Rhyland's pulling me against him, his massive frame wrapped around mine like he's claiming me for all eternity. His fingers thread through my wet hair, and his eyes—those ocean-blue eyes—hold mine with this look that stops my breathing entirely. "You were incredible out there, baby. My badass angel," he says, his voice rough with emotion.

I open my mouth to volley a sassy reply, but before I can utter a word, his lips capture mine in a kiss that sets my soul on fire. It's intense and passionate, demanding and giving all at once. Melting into him, my arms loop around his sturdy neck, returning his passion tenfold beneath the moon's ethereal glow. The rest of the world falls away, and there's only him, only us, only this moment.

But then—*whoosh*—I'm flying through the air with a shriek that's somewhere between thrilled and absolutely pissed. "Are you serious right now?" I sputter as I hit the water with a splash, scrambling to my feet all tangled up and laughing despite myself. "Dirty play, Mr. Norseman!"

Swiping a soggy curtain of hair from my face, I fix my gaze on the culprit of my impromptu dive, narrowing my eyes in mock outrage. "Oh, you are so gonna pay for that,

Mr. Mighty Mead," I threaten, but the effect is somewhat ruined by the grin splitting my face from ear to ear. He knows he's won this round.

I charge at Rhyland like I'm actually gonna take him down, arms outstretched and ready for combat. But it's an epic fail; my efforts are as effective as a kitten trying to take down a lion. I'm completely outmatched, and we both know it.

In a flash, I'm airborne again, completely at his mercy as this ancient Viking tosses me around like I'm weightless. It's infuriating and exhilarating all at once. Rhyland's laughter echoes across the water, this deep, joyful sound that's somehow both infectious and maddening. It's like he's having the time of his life while I'm out here getting tossed like a ragdoll in slow motion.

Hearing that laugh does something to me, though—it makes my heart skip, spreads this genuine grin across my face that I can't suppress no matter how hard I try. Getting to see this playful, unguarded side of Rhyland is something truly special. I'm completely here for this fun, laughing version of the ancient warrior I love, the one who lets his guard down and just enjoys life.

But underneath all the laughter and splashing, I understand what's really happening. This is his way of keeping me grounded, like he's anchoring me before the real chaos hits. He knows the days ahead are gonna be brutal, that moments like this are gonna be hard to come by, and he's making damn sure we soak up every second we have together while we still can.

With this sudden burst of speed, Rhyland grabs me and pulls me flush against his chest, his movements swift and sure. "Fair warning, Angel—I hold the 'Water Warlord' crown. Undefeated champion," he teases, his voice a deep rumble that sends goosebumps over my entire body, his dimpled smirk making my heart race uncontrollably.

"Oh, I bet you say that to all the girls," I shoot back, my eyes playful as I stare up at him, my hands settling on his chest where I can feel his heartbeat thundering beneath my palms.

Rhyland's eyes ignite with this mix of raw desire and tenderness that's absolutely devastating to witness. "Nope. You're the only one," he murmurs, his gaze holding mine with an intensity that steals my breath completely. "You've always been the only one for me."

I can only grin like an idiot.

"Why can't I ever get enough of you?" he says right before his lips set on a collision course with mine. The kiss is electric, this searing explosion of heat and passion that ignites my whole body, my form completely melting into his like wax under flame. It's all-consuming, demanding everything from me.

His hands move over my curves with reverent touches that border on worship, gentle yet demanding all at once, silently asking for more without speaking a word. I match his intensity, my fingers tangling in his hair, my nails scraping down his back as I pull him closer, desperate to feel every part of him pressed against me.

In this moment, nothing else exists but us—our bodies intertwined beneath the stars, the world completely falling away until there's only the heat radiating off his skin, the taste of his lips, the synchronization of our hearts pounding in perfect, unbreakable rhythm.

DANICA

34

After our epic splashdown showdown, we're both refreshed and changed into clean clothes we'd brought along. We return to the campsite, where Axilya and our companions have settled in their tents for the night.

Rhyland lays our furs next to the crackling campfire, inviting like a bear's den. I snuggle in close to him, my back to his front, folding into his arms as if I'm the missing puzzle piece designed to fit right there—in the nook of his embrace, my forever spot.

Rhyland's warmth rivals the campfire, teaming up to banish the ghostly chills left from our makeshift lake shower. His arms cage me in a fortress of security while we both get lost in the ballet of sparks that leap toward a sky glittering with celestial sequins.

"You okay, baby?" he asks softly.

I crane my neck to lock eyes with him, giving him a mini smile. "Yeah—just shook up from the ruckus, and I want to fix the wrongs...but I'm not sure how," I admit.

Being 'okay' seems like a ship that's sailed. How those ogres stormed us, fury-fueled for the hurts they've carried, tightens my chest fiercely. I'm stuck in the middle of this seven-realm hot mess, the one they say I've gotta sort out, and I'm winging it without a how-to guide.

"Hey," Rhyland pulls me close, squeezing tight enough to press the assurance into my bones, "I know this shit's heavy, and you want to fix everything—it's a fucking burden that's not meant to be carried alone. But, baby, I'm right here, stride for stride with you. You're not in this solo for a single moment."

His words are a tether, his resolve an anchor, and I let out a sigh, letting them wrap around me. "I know," I whisper back, feeling the warmth of his conviction.

But inside, doubt and fear are persistent shadows, heavy on my mind. The path ahead is long, and what I've tackled is barely a mark on our vast expanse of challenges.

Rhyland presses his lips to my neck, a brief sanctuary in the chaos of emotions swirling within me. "I can feel the storm brewing inside you, baby. Remember? Your feelings are mine to share. And this doubt festering in your pretty head—it's gotta end."

His words are an attempt to steady the storm inside me, reminding me of our unbreakable bond.

"I've got my ways to take your mind off this, even if just for a bit," Rhyland's voice is laced with a smirk I can all but see without looking. The playful undercurrent of his tone promises a temporary escape from the weight of my concerns.

I whip my head around to meet his mischievous gaze, shocked. My eyes dart around the makeshift campsite—the fae camp sprawled in uneasy sleep, mostly in tents, but some are sprawled out on makeshift beds.

"Oh, no, no, no...we can't—" I protest.

Rhyland cuts off my words, his lips landing gently on mine. He kisses me softly, a promise in the brief contact, and then pulls back with a finger to his lips.

"Shh... don't rouse the others," he whispers into my mind, a sly grin playing at the corners of his mouth. "Just relax and let me take care of you."

I roll back onto my side, a huff escaping me as I shake my head at Rhyland's boldness. Yet, there's a smirk tugging at my lips—because, damn, the audacity of this man is somehow endearing.

Who doesn't want a man who's hell-bent on showering you with pleasure, ceaseless in his devotion to your happiness?

I can't help but glance around again, ensuring the soft breaths and still forms around us remain undisturbed. As I confirm everyone's deep in slumber, Rhyland's hand moves with quiet deliberation toward my pants, fingers deftly working at the clasp with a slow, tantalizing intention.

His voice, a low velvet murmur, floats through my mind like a lover's caress, *"I'm gonna make you feel so good, Angel. Consider it a debt I'm more than happy to settle."*

The flirtatious promise in his tone sends a shiver of anticipation down my spine.

"Rhyland, come on..."

My brain detours as his hand slips into my leathers and locates my sweet spot, as if it's his personal GPS. His other hand snakes up from underneath me, yanking the leather aside and exposing my breast to the cool night breeze. My nipple stiffens and aches. Then, his warm hand takes control, covering it like a protective shield.

"Yeah, baby. You can't deny this is what you crave. I know your body, Dani, and what it needs," his voice is like a lover's tender touch in my mind. *"See how fucking slick you are."*

His body melds with mine, his hard cock rubbing against my ass, his fingers playing my clit like a maestro with his violin, hitting all the right notes.

My eyes roll back, and now there's only one thing on my mind—more of him. He knows exactly which strings to pluck, making my body sing.

"I will always crave you..." I moan out loud at his touch, lost in the moment.

"Shh..." he reminds me.

His fingers thrust inside me, a rough, possessive claim that sends a jolt of pleasure-pain through me.

"Mmm... I need more." His voice is a low growl with a rough edge that promises satisfaction.

I bite my lip to stifle my moans, my body arching with each thrust of his fingers. The sensation is overwhelming, a whirlwind of pleasure that's taking me higher and higher. He continues to pinch my nipple, twisting and pulling. It's driving me mad.

He quickly withdraws from me, yanking my leathers down my legs.

"Get these off," he growls.

I do a shuffle-and-shimmy routine as I wage war with the constricting embrace of my leathers under the covers. The thought of Rhyland's next move has me all aflutter. After what feels like a gazillion years of grappling with the pesky fabric, I kick them off.

Rhyland moves like lightning, flipping me quickly, tossing the blanket over us like a cloak of secrecy, and finding his cozy spot between my thighs before I can catch my breath.

He's going for it right here, smack-dab in the middle of camp, where anyone could take a peek. Talk about being on display—I might as well have gills and fins with how exposed I feel!

"Rhyland! Keeping it down isn't exactly my strong suit when you're doing... that!" I whisper-yell into his mind.

His chuckle is a low vibration in my thoughts, *"I know, baby—that's precisely why I adore you. You're not shy about hitting those high notes, and I fucking live for hearing my Angel sing. But if you don't want to be caught, I suggest you keep that beautiful voice on mute."*

Crap. He's on his own wavelength, immune to my caution.

Bracing to interject and squeezing my legs shut out of sheer reflex—this is madness, *"Rhyland—"*

But just like that, my protests evaporate, and every coherent thought zaps away, leaving me utterly without words as his searing tongue glides up my clit and his lips wrap around the tight bundle of nerves—

Sweet Jesus!

"Mmm...cotton candy." His voice rumbles through my thoughts, describing how I taste—a decadent concoction of sweet, sexy, and downright intoxicating.

I surrender, hoisting my imaginary white flag high as my resistance crumbles and my legs part like the Red Sea.

Here I am, shamelessly sailing the seas of pleasure aboard the good ship Rhyland.

DANICA

35

We proceed on horseback for the entire day, our backs aching and butts numb. Around dusk, a seemingly miniature metropolis unfolds before us. Curious Fae emerge from their dwellings, keen to glimpse our entourage threading through their domain.

"What is this place?" I query aloud, the words hanging in the air.

Axilya seizes the opportunity. "This is Sun City, the sanctuary of all the Fae from the Sun Court."

It strikes me how many Fae call this place home. It's like stepping into a children's fantasy, with each house appearing as if lifted from a fairytale illustration.

As we pass, a young girl beams a smile in our direction. Her sunny blonde hair modestly conceals the tips of her pointed ears, and her violet eyes glitter with the deep purple luster of amethysts.

"How beautiful," I manage to utter, utterly awestruck by the enchanting scene and the little Fae girl.

Rhyland's arms encircle me from behind. "Not as beautiful as you," he whispers, and I can feel the heat of a blush color my cheeks in response to his flattering words.

We journey through the city in silence, the whispers of the wind barely audible over the gentle clip-clop of our steed's hooves. More and more Fae pop out to steal glances, their eyes wide with wonder as they observe our passage through their luminescent Sun City.

As the last vestiges of daylight slip away, we finally approach the Sun Court Palace. Every inch of me aches from the long ride.

Rhyland, my Norse companion, has been the epitome of love and care. He murmured sweet nothings and epic sagas into my ear all day, spinning yarns of his heydays back in the land of fjords and fearless warriors.

We approach the Sun Palace gates, a jaw-dropping moment. The gates look like they've been dipped in liquid sunbeams, casting a mystical light show on the stones beneath. The palace itself, with its towering spires, is illuminated and exudes pure-hearted opulence, making my pulse quicken.

As we pull up to those regal doors, I shift around, trying to find some relief from the saddle's unforgiving embrace. "If I don't get off this horse... I swear I'm gonna—"

The ancient hinges groan, introducing a scene so enchanting it silences my complaints. The expansive gardens resemble a vibrant explosion of colors, with blooms practically buzzing with inner light.

Wings and whimsical creatures flit past, like living dreamcatchers. Birds sing tunes so sweet and clear that I believe it's what happiness must sound like.

"Welcome to the Sun Court," a gentleman announces. "I am Baelen, your escort," he strides forward with practiced decorum that could rival any diplomat.

He bows deeply to Axilya, who nods in return. "We thank you for your gracious welcome," she replies with equal formality.

"Our stables await your noble steeds," he says, extending a hand for our reins.

Rhyland is off our horse in a flash, scooping me up like I weigh nothing. With a groan, I slide off and melt into the ground, my legs feeling like jelly after hours in the saddle.

"Oh, thank god," I mutter, each wince a silent plea as I straighten out. The sensation returns to those nameless places that have gone numb from the relentless ride.

Lucian leaps off his horse with grace and agility, handing his reins to the guard with a rakish grin. "Well, isn't this just paradise wrapped in sunlight?" His voice drips with sarcasm, but his eyes dance with excitement.

Rhyland does the same but stays coiled tight, his gaze cutting through the surroundings in search of anything that doesn't belong. "Pretty things often hide sharp thorns," he mutters, voice low and edged with suspicion.

You can almost see the wariness rolling off him; Rhyland stands there, every inch the alpha male, ready to defend against any threat, real or imagined.

Then, Fae folk emerge from every corner, adorned in fabrics that defy reality. Their movements are so fluid and graceful that even the simplest gestures seem like performances worthy of an ovation. Their attire is extravagant, robes and threads shimmering and dancing as if cut from the night sky, all moonbeam sheen and cosmic glitter.

Servants glide towards us, offering assistance with our belongings. Their expressions are serene and inscrutable, and their demeanor is so far removed from normalcy that it sends my head spinning.

It feels like we've wandered onto the set of some fantastical production where every extra is fighting for the spotlight, the air thick with otherworldly beauty and danger.

"Can you believe this place?" Lucian grins, his eyes wide with wonder, his excitement palpable even through his trademark snark and sass.

"Nuh-uh, this is... unbelievable! It's like nothing I could've dreamed up," I say, the words tumbling out as I soak in the staggering splendor around us. Even in my wildest imaginings, I never could have conjured a place like this—a realm so far removed from anything I've ever known that it feels like a dream come to life.

A servant approaches me, her eyes sparkling like twin sapphires set into her flawless face, pointy ears peeking through golden-spun hair. "May I assist you with your gear?" she asks, her voice a melodic lilt that makes me think of wind chimes on a breezy day.

I nod dumbly at first, still taken aback by everything, my mind struggling to process the sheer scope of the splendor surrounding us. Then, my wits snap back into place, and I manage a smile. "Yeah. Yes, thank you." The words stumble out of me, awkward and clipped, as I hand over my satchel.

Something about her quiet composure settles even my frazzled nerves, a calm radiating from her like something I could reach out and touch.

Rhyland keeps close behind me as we walk through this garden of living wonders toward what promises to be an equally spectacular palace, his presence a solid and reassuring warmth at my back.

"Keep your eyes open," he murmurs just loud enough for me to hear, his breath tickling the shell of my ear—a reminder that not all is as it seems in this realm of beauty and illusion.

The guards gently lead our horses away while Baelen guides us further into this world where every turn reveals another impossibility—a tapestry woven from pure sunlight here, a fountain spouting liquid diamonds there.

Rhyland's hand finds mine, his fingers intertwining in a comforting squeeze.

As we step through the grand entrance, a hush falls over me. It's like crossing an unseen threshold into a world where the impossible becomes possible, and the boundaries of reality blur and shift like smoke.

Rhyland tightens his grip on my hand, leaning in close, his breath hot against my ear. "If you keep gaping like that, I might have to find something to fill it with."

My jaw snaps shut, heat flooding my cheeks—equal parts embarrassment and arousal from his R-rated comment. I nudge him with my elbow, giving him a look that can't decide if it's a scolding or an invitation.

"Behave," I hiss under my breath, trying to keep my expression neutral, even as my heart races at the promise in his words.

Rhyland grins, his eyes glinting with mischief and something darker. "Where's the fun in that?" he murmurs.

I roll my eyes but can't suppress the smile tugging at the corners of my mouth.

"The Hall of Sunbeams," Baelen says.

The entrance is a cavernous space, the ceiling arching high above like a perfect dome. Crystals hang suspended like stars, casting soft light across polished marble floors that reflect our images at us.

A chandelier of crystalline flowers hangs overhead, casting a soft glow. Its petals pulse with an inner light, bathing us in warmth.

Living vines creep along the walls and columns, blooming with flowers that release a subtle perfume.

Staircases curve up on either side, their railings crafted from gold and silver, twined into intricate patterns. The balustrades are entwined with flowering vines, nature, and artifice, blending seamlessly.

"The King and Queen will meet with you tomorrow," Baelen informs us as we take in our surroundings. "You must be weary from your travels; tonight, you shall rest and restore."

I can feel Rhyland tense beside me at the mention of a royal audience. It's a tension mirrored in my own chest, a fluttering unease.

Axilya nods her acceptance of these arrangements. Faderyn smiles in agreement while Lucian leans against a pillar with feigned nonchalance, his curious gaze betraying his interest. Erik stands like a statue, his eyes scanning every detail with precise attention.

"Each of you will be assigned personal attendants," Baelen announces grandly.

My very own personal attendant? Slap my ass and call me a duchess. This is straight out of a Regency romance novel. The Bridgertons would absolutely shit a fancy porcelain brick over this lavish treatment.

Baelen claps his hands, and more attendants appear as if by magic. "We have prepared rooms for each of you," he continues, motioning for us to follow.

Lucian's voice slices through the quiet like an uninvited guest, with mock astonishment and the kind of snark that makes you want to throw something at his head "Well, call me a lucky bastard!" he exclaims, eyes widening comically. "Did I seriously just score my own pimped-out bachelor pad in this swanky joint?"

I roll my eyes, feeling the weight of every gaze in the room as they turn to stare at Lucian as if he's just floated in from the Netherworld or as if he's sporting an extra head, their expressions ranging from shock to disapproval.

I shoot him a look that could freeze hell and silently shape the word "STOP," hoping to caps-lock his manners into place before he gets us all thrown out on our asses.

Lucian grins without an ounce of remorse, and damn him, I can't help the wave of affection that hits me even through my frustration.

I'm led down a corridor lined with tapestries so lifelike I half expect them to come alive and walk off their looms, their threads sparkling with beautiful light. We stop before an elegant door carved from shimmering wood and inlaid with intricate designs that seem to move.

"Your quarters, my lady," says one of the attendants, who introduces herself as Alina, pushing open the door with a graceful flourish.

My room is like something out of a dream—a massive, moonlit bed dominates the space, the canopy dripping with gossamer curtains that flutter in an unseen breeze.

"You will have everything you need here," Alina assures me as she flits about the room, lighting candles that fill the air with a sweet, heady scent. "If you desire anything else, do not hesitate to ask."

I nod mutely, taking in the details—from the paintings on the ceiling that seem to move to the lacework on the curtains that look like it was spun from starlight.

Two other attendants stand at attention, holding fresh garments for me to change into and a tray laden with fruits and sweet treats.

"You must be exhausted," Alina observes, her voice soft and sympathetic.

"I'm fine," I manage, though my body suggests otherwise, still throbbing from the ride.

Rhyland lingers at the threshold until another attendant offers directions to his room. He declines, his jaw tightening.

"No—I'm staying here." His voice leaves no room for argument.

The attendant hesitates before nodding. "Of course, sir," he replies, and then leaves.

Rhyland turns to me, concern etched into his features. "Are you alright?" he asks, his voice low.

"I'm overwhelmed," I confess, flopping down on the bed. It's like sinking into a cloud.

He sits beside me, taking my hand. "This place... we can't trust it yet." His intense blue eyes hold mine. "Don't let it blind you to what's important."

"I won't," I promise, though part of me wonders if I can stay focused amidst such splendor.

How can something this beautiful be bad, be wrong? Maybe these people are good; they're not a threat like their counterparts—the Shadow Court.

Alina and the other attendants clear their throats, nodding toward the bathing chamber. "My lady, a bath has been drawn at your convenience, and we have arranged fresh attire."

We both rise, and I make my way toward the bathing chamber just as Rhyland's attendant slips back into view, waiting silently by the door.

Rhyland gives him a curt nod before closing the distance between us in a few long strides, moving with a fluid grace that defies his size. He tips my chin up with a gentle hand, drawing my gaze into the oceanic depths of those brilliant blue eyes. His touch sends warmth rippling through me.

"I'm gonna be right down the hall, and I'll catch up with you soon, Angel." He kisses me quickly, his lips soft and warm against mine—a promise and a reassurance all in one—before turning to leave, his shoulders squared and his head held high.

RHYLAND

36

The hot water works wonders, sinking into my worn-out muscles after two days of travel and sleeping on the ground. Steam wraps around me, caressing my skin like a submissive lover. I recline, my thoughts drifting to Dani—her tough-as-nails journey and the shit she's pulled off. She faced down those ogres and monsters without breaking a sweat, her power and determination shining like a beacon in the darkness. Then there's the crap we might face next with these royal assholes—I've had it up to here with fae royals ever since I crossed paths with that queen shadow bitch.

My trust in them is as worthless as a pile of dog shit. I'd rather wipe my ass with poison ivy than put my faith in their scheming hands.

And hell, it's been days since I've buried myself in Dani's tight heat, felt her clench and squeeze around every inch of me while I drag her to the edge of oblivion. It's fucking maddening—this gnawing ache to pin her down and wreck her the way my body is screaming for. Every waking thought is consumed with bending her over and fucking her stupid, making her scream my name until her throat gives out and her legs are shaking so hard she can't stand.

I'm addicted to her—the way she toys with me, that wicked glint dancing in her eyes, daring me to make a move. And when I buried my face between her thighs, delving deep into her sweet, slick petals, tasting every drop of her—it only made the hunger worse. A craving that claws at me from the inside out, one that no amount of her will ever be enough to satisfy.

Hoisting myself out of the bath, water beads slide over my ripped muscles. Every droplet traces the contours of my build, highlighting the raw power and strength that lies coiled beneath my skin.

I wrap a cloth around my waist and step barefoot onto the chilly stone, striding to the mirror. My beard has grown thick and wild, a testament to our days on the road, while my hair hangs damp around my head.

I look like a fucking savage, a beast ready to tear into anything that stands in my way. And right now, the only thing I want to tear into is Dani, to bury myself inside her until she's writhing beneath me, her nails raking down my back as she begs for more.

"Sir, may I assist?" My attendant gestures toward the chair, where scissors and brushes sit, waiting for a much-needed trimming.

"Yes, thank you." I nod, settling into the seat, my muscles still loose from the bath. "What's your name?"

"My name is Quillars. But please, call me Quill." He offers a slight bow.

"Alright. Thanks, Quill." I lean back in the chair and let him do his thing, his fingers deft and sure. As he starts with my beard, the gentle scrape of the scissors has a soothing rhythm against my skin.

"How would you like your beard, sir? Shaved or trimmed down?" Quill asks softly.

I pause, wondering what Dani would say. She hasn't complained about the rough look and seems to like how it feels against her skin. "Just trim it, keep it neat," I say gruffly.

Thirty minutes zip by, and I gotta admit, Quill knows his shit. He's got the sides of my head buzzed down tight, left the top with a bit of length to run my hands through, and my beard? Fucking masterpiece. It's cropped close but full—like a damn boss, ready to take on the world and claim what's mine.

I eye the pants they've prepped for me with curiosity and disdain. They're a far cry from the rugged leathers I'm used to, ghostly white and shimmering in the candlelight. The fabric is light as a feather, fanning out at the hems and floating around my legs with every stride—they're strange and ethereal, yet not entirely shitty. The waist clinches right below my hips, kept in place by nothing but a basic drawstring that gives a nod to the warrior lying underneath, ready to spring into action at a moment's notice.

The shirt's just as odd—white cotton that clings to my chest like a second skin, with a deep neckline that flaunts the cut of my chest and a peek at my ink. There are no sleeves, the fabric ending at the shoulders and throwing my arms and their inked-up muscle into the spotlight.

It's different from my usual attire, but I can't deny it makes me look like a fucking god, my body on full display. Catching a glimpse of myself in the mirror, I imagine Dani's face when she sees me like this, cleaned up and ready to play the game.

Because that's what this is: a game of power and politics. And I'll be damned if I let these fae bastards get the upper hand. I may be dressed like one of them, but underneath, I'm still the same ruthless warrior who's fought and bled for everything I have, who's claimed Dani as my own, and will stop at nothing to keep her safe.

An hour's all I've got before dinner, and every inch of me is screaming for release. Dani's the only one who can quench this raging hunger before it devours me.

Determined, I walk purposefully toward her quarters, my strides long and quick, driven by a need that is all-consuming. The hallway is dim, with torches flickering and dancing shadows on ancient stone walls. The eerie play of light and dark mirrors the turmoil inside me.

Getting closer to her room, anticipation winds up inside me, tight as a damn spring, ready to snap. When I finally reach her door, I don't bother knocking; I push it open and step inside.

The moment I walk in, I freeze—holy hell, she's breathtaking, a vision of pure, unadulterated temptation that hits me like a punch to the gut.

She's wearing a tight white cropped shirt that clings to her, no frills, just straight-up sexy. Her breasts strain against the fabric, and I want to squeeze them, feel their weight in my hands as I tease her nipples into stiff peaks.

The shirt bares her shoulders, teasing with curves that my hands are itching to explore, and the flash of her waist begs to be touched. Her pants flow like mine over her legs, soft but hugging all the right places, accentuating the swell of her hips and the roundness of her ass.

And the gold jewelry—fucking perfect against her caramel-gold eyes, turning them into molten pools of desire. With every move, her bangles chime a challenge, calling to the beast inside me. Those necklaces draw the eye, nestled in the valley of her cleavage like a treasure waiting to be claimed.

Her hair tumbles down to her waist, bouncy and wild, just like her. I'm itching to thread my fingers through it, to grip it tight as I tilt her head back and devour her mouth.

She's standing there, making it clear that she's both a force to be reckoned with and a sanctuary to be cherished.

And me? I'm all kinds of fucked, my body thrumming with a need that's urgent and all-consuming. I want to rip her clothes off and give in to the urge, to bury myself inside her and lose myself in her heat.

But I hold back, my fists clenched as I drink her in, my eyes roaming over every inch of her perfect form.

"Well, hey there, Thunder Throb," she purrs, floating up to me with a sultry smile that makes my blood run hot. Rising on the balls of her feet, she plants a soft kiss on my lips, her scent invading my senses and making my whole body tighten with barely restrained need.

I clasp her waist, yanking her close until every inch of her is pressed against me, and growl low in my throat, "You look fucking delicious, baby—I could devour you right here and now, attendants be damned."

"And you..." She reaches up and tugs at my beard. "I love this." Her fingers thread through the coarse hair. My eyes damn near roll back in my skull, and I let out a rumbling moan as she keeps pulling, the sensation shooting straight to my cock.

The soft coughs from her attendants slice through the moment like a bucket of ice water, reminding us that we're not alone. "My lady, this way, please," one of them murmurs with a neutral tone.

Damn. There goes my chance to have her all to myself before we have to play nice at dinner.

"Hold up, where do you think you're going?" I demand, my voice a near-snarl of frustration. "Dinner ain't for another hour, and I'm not done with you yet."

Dani flashes me that knowing smile, the one that says she's reading me like an open book. "Drinks in the formal room," she tells me. "We have to make an appearance, Rhyland. You know the drill."

I grunt, knowing she's right but hating it all the same.

Dani places a soothing hand on my chest. "Down, boy," she murmurs, her eyes all sexy with mischief and promise.

Easy for her to say. I'm riled up, every muscle in my body coiled tight with the urge to grab her, toss her over my shoulder, and carry her off to the nearest secluded corner.

But I know I can't. Not yet. We have appearances to maintain and a game to play. So I take a deep breath, fighting to get myself under control.

Fuck. This is going to be a long night.

DANICA

37

I was halfway to cloud nine when Mr. Viking Temptation himself, Rhyland, strutted in. The man's the spitting image of every girl's Norse god fantasy—his hair cut just right, those sculpted features, delicious muscles, and that scruff he's rocking, all a downright siren call to my fingers.

I let out a soundless "wow"—the man is downright edible.

My pulse picked up the pace as the vibe between us hummed with his craving—it's like a fiery spark just waiting to catch, and boy, is it contagious. I caught his smoldering gaze and let my lips curve in a sly little smirk, knowing I was pushing all his buttons without saying a word.

We saunter into the formal room, and it's like walking into a scene from a Bridgerton episode. Laughter and chatter float over the clinking of glasses, and gorgeous fae folks are dressed to the nines in casual and chic attire everywhere I look. It's like the Fae of this court decided to let their hair down and throw one hell of a soirée.

Lucian is lounging with a glass in hand, looking like the cat that got the cream, while Erik stands nearby, all brooding elegance and mysterious allure. Axilya radiates regal confidence beside them, and Faderyn's hanging out in the corner, talking it up with another noble fae.

Rhyland takes my hand, his touch sending delicious heat through my body as he guides me into the room. His charisma and smoldering looks are like magnets, drawing every eye in the place to us.

We settle into our seats among the group, and our attendants swoop in with drinks that look like something a magical mixologist brewed. The glasses are iridescent and filled with a golden liquid that seems to glow from within.

"What's this?" I ask, eyeing the enchanted concoction with curiosity and wariness.

Alina, ever the font of knowledge, gives me a conspiratorial wink. "It's our specialty, My Lady. Brewed from the finest grapes kissed by the sun in our vineyards," she explains, making it sound like the nectar of the gods.

I bring the glass to my nose, taking in the aroma—it's like distilled sunlight, zesty with a hint of lemon.

Tempted, I take a small sip; a symphony of flavors bursts onto my taste buds. "This is delicious!"

"Thank you, My Lady. It's... got a special kick to it," Alina responds with a chuckle. She gives me a gracious curtsy before making her exit.

"Wait," I call out, my curiosity getting the best of me. "Who are all these people?" I ask hurriedly, hoping to snag an answer before she can leave.

Alina pauses mid-step, turning back to face the gathering with sparkling eyes that practically glow with excitement. "My Lady, feast your eyes on the resplendent Fae of The Sun Court," she says, her voice brimming with a mix of reverence and pure, unadulterated joy. "They've gathered here to extend a heartfelt welcome to you and your friends. It's in your honor that they've conjured up this magnificent feast and party," she explains, looking like she might burst with pride at any second.

"Oh..." I breathe, the sound escaping my lips in a simple utterance that somehow manages to convey my complete astonishment. These fae sure know how to roll out the red carpet.

Ever the opportunist when it comes to a well-timed wisecrack, Lucian sidles up with a conspiratorial gleam in his eye. His signature smirk is firmly in place. "Well, well, well, looks like the grapevine in this joint is faster than a speeding bullet, huh?" he remarks with playful mirth. "Congrats, Princess—you've already got your own cheerleading squad. Groupies included, free of charge!"

He punctuates the quip with an exaggerated wink—the kind that somehow manages to be both utterly charming and completely infuriating.

I roll my eyes at him, but I can't quite keep the smile from tugging at the corners of my mouth. "Watch it, Lucy," I warn, my tone playful but with an undercurrent of steel. "This *princess* might just have to put you in your place if you're not careful."

Lucian's laughter bursts forth, a vibrant, irresistible sound. "Aw, you know you can't resist my devilish charm, Your Worshipfulness," he quips, dipping into an exaggerated bow. "Admit it. Life would be a total snooze fest without my sparkling wit and dashing good looks."

I shake my head, unable to argue with that. Lucian may be a pain in the ass sometimes, but he's our pain in the ass, and I wouldn't have him any other way.

Turning my attention back to the gathered fae, I take a moment to really drink in the sight of them. They're a stunning bunch, all ethereal beauty and otherworldly grace, and I can't help but feel a little awe. It's humbling to think that they've gone through all this trouble just for us. I make a mental note to find a way to thank them properly later.

The room is washed in a buttery light, reminiscent of a swanky, bygone era. The buzz of chit-chat's a masterclass in polite murmurs, spiced up now and then by the tinkle of some seriously fancy glassware.

In the corner, a string quartet plays tunes so smooth they could calm a thunderstorm. These musicians could give Mozart a run for his money.

And smack dab in the middle of it all, there's little ol' me, rubbing elbows with the Fae elite like it's just another Saturday night. These folks are a different breed—all finesse and grace on the outside, but I'd bet they've got their share of melodrama behind closed doors.

Meanwhile, anticipation and whispers zip around me like they were born to party in the fast lane. It's exhilarating.

Rhyland's deep blue eyes lock onto mine, serving up a stare so intense it could give the night sky a run for its money. Just that one look sends my pulse skyrocketing, and I have to take a deep breath to keep from melting.

His steadfast hold on my hand anchors me in the middle of this swirling social whirlpool, full of faces I don't know and secrets they're not telling. He's my rock amid all this chaos.

Suddenly, a lithe Fae with hair like spun moonbeams and eyes as blue as the sky glides over to me. "Lady Danica," she greets me with a nod that holds centuries of tradition. "I am Elowen. Pray tell, how did you find your journey to our Sun Court?"

I blink, momentarily taken aback by her formal tone and the weight of her gaze.

I nod to Elowen, feeling all eyes on us. "Hey there, Elowen. My rear might file a complaint about the hike, but I gotta say—the beauty of this realm is so stunning, it almost made me forget about my aching ass," I quip, my mouth running ahead of my brain as usual.

Oops, did I just let that slip out? Classic me, with a filter as reliable as a sieve. Sometimes, the words pirouette right off my tongue before my brain can send the red alert.

Elowen's lips twist up in a smile that could light up the gloomiest dungeon, and a laugh spills out of her, all sparkly like fairy dust in the sun. "Truly, our realm is a tapestry woven with the threads of wonders and enigmas," she muses with amusement at my less-than-delicate phrasing. "My apologies for the tribulations endured by your... ass, as you have so quaintly put it."

I feel my cheeks heat up, but I grin. And if my little faux pas helped break the ice, I'll chalk it up as a win.

With a knowing smile, Elowen drifts through the throng, engaging with other attendees. I watch her go, marveling at her ease and grace.

Me, on the other hand? I'm more of a bull in a china shop at these kinds of shindigs.

I glance over at Rhyland, who's watching me with this mix of amusement and exasperation written all over his face. "Smooth, Angel," he murmurs, his voice low and rough in a way that makes my stomach flip. "Real smooth."

I stick my tongue out at him, feeling a bit like a petulant child, but not caring. "Hey, at least I'm being authentic. These fae types could use a little dose of reality, don't you think?"

Rhyland shakes his head, a smile playing at the corners of his mouth. "You're something else, you know that? Never change, baby. Never change."

I grin at him, feeling warm in my chest at his words. "Wasn't planning on it, Berserker Brat," I assure him, squeezing his hand. "You're stuck with me, sass and all."

As the evening progresses, Rhyland's thumb keeps up its soothing orbits on my skin—a warm, grounding Morse code that keeps my insides melting at his constant touch.

I catch Erik's silvery eyes scanning the room, his gaze as sharp and alert as a hawk on the hunt. The guy is like a human alarm system, always on guard and ready to spring into action at the first sign of trouble.

Meanwhile, Axilya exudes a zen-like command, her presence as serene and unruffled as a still pond on a windless day. And Faderyn? He's deep in conversation with some Fae in fancy threads, the two of them going at it like they're hashing out plays at the Super Bowl.

Then there's Mr. Smart-Ass himself, the charmer extraordinaire, already dishing out his grade-A flirt game like it's going out of style. He's got a Fae lady practically parked on his lap, giggling away like he's the funniest thing since court jesters. Lord knows what line he's fed her—probably something about her eyes being like starlight and her laugh like music to his ears. Classic Lucian.

Out of nowhere, a new noble parts the sea of bodies—a guy tall enough to shadow a statue, with skin gleaming like a moonlit lake on a calm night. His presence commands attention, and the room seems to hold its breath as he approaches.

His voice rings out, smooth and melodic, as if he's about to serenade the lot of us. "Forgive my intrusion," he says with an elegant bow straight out of a fairy tale. "I am Aelius. There are whispers among us about your intentions for gracing our court."

Before we can respond, Rhyland's deep voice fills the space. "We come seeking understanding and perhaps aid," he states firmly, leaving no room for doubt about his conviction.

Erik leans forward slightly, deliberate and precise, like a general outlining a battle plan. "We recognize your court's sovereignty and wish to discuss matters that concern not just us but all realms."

"We indeed seek your court's counsel—there are shifts in the fabric of our worlds that require unity," Axilya adds.

Aelius considers this momentarily, his brow furrowing in thought, before turning back to me with keen interest sparking in his gaze. "And you, Lady Danica," he starts inquisitively, his eyes boring into mine as if trying to read my soul, "are you indeed the one foretold in ancient prophecies? The mortal who will stand against encroaching darkness?"

All eyes shift to me, and the room goes still as I straighten my posture, feeling the weight of their gazes. Rhyland's silent encouragement flows through our bond like warm sunlight, bolstering my resolve and giving me the strength to face this moment head-on.

My voice doesn't waver when I reply, "Yes, I am she." My affirmation resonates through the room—a declaration to Aelius and all present, a statement of fact that brooks no argument.

The posh Fae crowd goes quiet like they're chewing on my words, feeling the heavy aftertaste of destiny hanging in the air. It's like they're trying to decide whether to believe me—to put their faith in a mortal girl with a big mouth and an even bigger destiny.

The band keeps up their gentle melody, but it's now hushed and suspenseful, waiting for the next scene to unfold. We are all holding our breath, waiting to see what Aelius will say next.

"Marvelous! We earnestly anticipate that you are indeed the personage you profess to be. The evidence you bear is keenly awaited with great interest," Aelius says, and just like that, the buzz of chatter and ripples of laughter crank up again as if he's just pressed play on the soirée.

I exhale a breath that's been sneakily squatting in my lungs, feeling like I've just passed some test. But before I can fully relax, Alina signals it's time for dinner. "My Lords and Ladies," she announces formally, "dinner is served."

The crowd starts drifting towards the dining hall, their laughter and conversation flowing like a river as they go.

As we migrate to the dining hall, I'm nearly bug-eyed at the spectacle before us—it's like stepping into a fantasy epic where grandeur takes on a whole new definition.

The dining chamber is an expansive sea of elegance stretched beneath a ceiling lost in the soft golden glow of a twinkling chandelier constellation. The walls sparkle with inlaid gemstones that glint like stars, their light reflecting off the polished surfaces until the whole room shimmers with an otherworldly radiance.

And the table—good lord, the table—is a wooden beast so long you'd expect one end to be in a different time zone, with room left over for a dragon to nap at the end. It's draped in golden linens, dotted with crystal goblets, silverware that out-sparkles the stars, and blooms so lush it's like a rainbow crashed right into the centerpiece.

Thrones masquerading as seats line the sides, their high backs adorned with sunbursts that make each Fae noble seem like an emperor at a war council, albeit armed with silverware instead of swords. It's a display of power and prestige that's as subtle as a sledgehammer but damn effective.

This isn't just a meal; it's a feast for the senses, a courtly dance of splendor and anticipation, where each mouthful is a vow of the Fae's enchanting opulence. It's enough to make a girl feel like she's stumbled into a dream.

"My god..." I breathe, my mouth hanging open as I try to take it all in.

Rhyland slides up behind me, and his arms find my waist with the precision of a hawk on the hunt. His touch gives me goosebumps, and I lean back into his solid warmth, feeling grounded by his presence.

He leans in, his breath tickling my ear as he murmurs, "Angel, if I knew a room could steal your breath like this, I would've built you a palace made of stars."

I crack a grin at his line, feeling a flutter in my chest at the raw sincerity in his voice. "Well, if you keep sweet-talking me like that, I might just forget an entire Fae army surrounds us," I toss back, my tone light and teasing.

But Rhyland's voice rumbles in response, low and rough with barely restrained desire. "Don't fuckin' play with me, sweetheart. I'm on the edge right now, and the scent of you and the way you look in this outfit," he grips my ass possessively, his fingers digging into the soft flesh, "is pushing me to the brink of insanity."

I suck in a sharp breath, feeling heat pool low in my belly at the raw need in his voice. "Rhyland..." I murmur, my voice strained.

Before I can say anything else, Alina signals it's time to sit, nudging me out of Rhyland's gravitational pull—man's about ready to toss the rules out the window right here and now.

I clear my throat, trying to regain some semblance of composure as I nod my thanks to Alina. Rhyland's hand slides from my ass to the small of my back, a gesture both possessive and protective, and together we make our way to our designated spots at the grand table.

I can't help but marvel at the sheer opulence surrounding us.

The only thing missing is the scandalous whispers about who's courting whom. I half expect Lady Whistledown to come swooping in with her latest gossip column, dishing the dirt on which fairy lord was caught canoodling with which pixie duchess behind the rose bushes.

But then I catch Rhyland's eye and see the heat and hunger burning in those ultramarine depths. He's not playing—but I remind myself that this is no game. We're here for a reason: to forge alliances and gather information that could mean the difference between life and death for our realms.

I hurry over to my chair, which Alina's already pulled out for me, and plop down with all the grace of a baby deer on ice. She's right there, pouring this golden, shimmery wine into my glass—the kind that's basically liquid courage in a bottle, and honestly? I need it right now. Without thinking twice, I wrap my fingers around the stem and take a long drink, the sweet, intoxicating liquid hitting my stomach and sending this wave of warmth spreading through my entire body. The way Rhyland's affecting me, keeping my self-control in check is turning into a full-time job, and I'm seriously not equipped for this kind of assignment.

Rhyland slides into the space beside me, all coiled power and barely restrained desire, and tosses me one of those smoldering glances that would make anyone's heart skip a beat. It's like he's trying to set me on fire with just a look, and damn if it isn't working.

I try to act nonchalant, like I'm not acutely aware of the rising heat from our bond, the way it's thrumming through my body like a live wire. I tip back another glass of that bewitching golden elixir, hoping it'll cool the flames licking at my insides.

"Take it easy, Angel," Rhyland whispers, his voice a thread of silk against my senses. "Don't need you drunk and unable to keep up with what I've got in store for us later."

I murmur back, a wry twist to my words as I lay down the law with a playful but firm edge, "We're in diplomacy mode, and I'm all about the schmoozing game with the Fae tonight. So do me a favor and quit firing those...sexy bat signals at me through our bond, alright? I need to focus, please."

"Mm-hmm," is all he gives me, noncommittal as ever, like he's only half-listening to my request. The man's got a one-track mind; right now, that track is leading straight to the bedroom.

Snatching up his glass filled with warm amber brew, he sends it down in one go, his throat working as he swallows. I watch, transfixed, as a single drop of the liquid escapes the corner of his mouth and slides down, and I have the sudden, wild urge to lean over and lick it off his lips.

Great, now I'm stirring up my own storm of annoyance and frustration inside, a heady mix of emotions that has me gripping the edge of the table like it's a lifeline. I'm trying to keep my head in the game, to focus on the task at hand, but Rhyland's making it damn near impossible with his heated looks and suggestive comments.

I take a deep breath, trying to center myself, and turn my attention back to the rest of the table. The Fae nobles are engaged in lively conversation, their laughter and chatter rising and falling like the swell of a tide. I catch snippets of their words, tales of courtly intrigue and ancient legends, and I find myself leaning forward, eager to soak up every bit of knowledge I can.

But even as I try to immerse myself in the conversation, I can feel Rhyland's gaze on me like a physical caress; his desire is a palpable thing, threatening to consume me whole. Being so close to him and yet so far is a delicious torture, and I know that the moment we're alone, all bets are off.

DANICA

38

Elowen, bless her timing, slices right through the thickening sexual tension with a question, turning our attention from the silent battle of wills back to the matter at hand. "Pray tell, how have vampires been assimilated into the societal fabric of your domain, and in what manner have your customs evolved from the point of our last knowledge?"

Her brows arc in a mix of curiosity and skepticism, like she's unsure what to make of this motley crew of vampires and humans sitting at her table. I can't say I blame her—we're far from the stuffy, formal delegations she's probably used to entertaining.

Lucian leans in, that familiar smirk dancing on his lips. "Oh, Elowen, you wouldn't believe the plot twist back in the Mortal Realm," he starts, "Vamps and mortals? We're practically braiding each other's hair and swapping friendship bracelets now. A little plasma in your OJ? No sweat, we're all about that inclusive breakfast club life." He grins, clearly reveling in the ridiculousness of it all.

"Protection? We're rocking the buddy system like champs. It's like supernatural Secret Service up in here. Who would've thought—fangs and humans, teaming up to fight the good fight, side by side." Lucian chuckles, taking a nonchalant swig from his glass as if commenting on a mildly amusing sitcom rather than the groundbreaking shift in age-old supernatural dynamics.

I have to bite back a laugh at his irreverent tone, knowing that he's walking a fine line between charming and offensive. But Lucian's always been a master at toeing that line, and I can see some of the Fae nobles hiding smiles behind their hands, their eyes sparkling with amusement at his antics.

Lucian angles his head toward Rhyland, "And this tall, dark, and perpetually scowling glass of water over here?" He stage-whispers conspiratorially to Elowen. "He's the big kahuna, the grand poobah of the fang gang. Our vampire whisperer keeps us all on our best behavior... or at least maintains the illusion of it."

He shoots Rhyland a cheeky grin, clearly enjoying the opportunity to rib his stoic brother in front of an audience. "It's a tough job, but somebody's gotta do it. And who better than Mr. Tall, Dark, and Brooding himself? He's got that whole 'I'm silently judging you' vibe down pat. Keeps us mere immortals quaking in our fashionable boots."

The wink Lucian fires off at Rhyland could power a small city with its impudence, wrapping up his briefing with all the smart-ass charm he's known for. I can practically feel Rhyland's eye roll from here, but I know he's not annoyed. Lucian is his brother, and he's used to his antics.

Elowen, for her part, looks like she's not quite sure what to make of Lucian's little speech. Her brows are still arched, but there's a hint of a smile playing at the corners of her mouth like she's trying to decide whether to be amused or offended. "Are you indeed the sovereign of your people?" Her tone rides the line between respectful intrigue and outright astonishment pointed at Rhyland. "And you, Lady Danica? How do you feel about this new world order?"

I sit up a little straighter, feeling all eyes on me as I clear my throat. "As Lucian said, vampires and humans have come a long way in learning to coexist peacefully in the Mortal Realm. It hasn't always been easy, but we've made great strides in building trust and understanding between our species."

Aelius leans forward, his eyes sharp with interest. "And what sort of issues have you—your realm encountered, Lady Danica? Surely, the path to peace has not been without its obstacles."

I nod, acknowledging the truth of his words. "Of course, there have been challenges along the way. Centuries of mistrust and prejudice don't disappear overnight. But we've found that we can overcome even the most deeply entrenched divides by focusing on our common goals and values."

There's a moment of silence as the Fae nobles digest my words, their expressions ranging from skeptical to intrigued. I can feel the weight of their gazes on me, but I refuse to shrink under the scrutiny.

"I must admit, it is quite a fascinating and unprecedented revelation. Yet, if those within the mortal realm can bridge their divides, it stands to reason that we should also embrace such progress," Elowen elegantly says.

Her words are the starter pistol for a ritual; everyone hoists their glasses up as they've rehearsed them. A sea of shimmering crystal catches the light, a mirror of the respect now bouncing around the room. It's a toast to new beginnings, or at least the hope that stubborn grudges can be loosened and let go of, just like mortals and immortals are learning to get along.

As the attendants set down the spread—a gastronomic dream in front of me—my stomach growls—a silent but fierce battle cry. I am starving, like a wolf in winter.

It's a swirl of lustrous fruits, gleaming meats, and puffed pastries that emit flirtatious steam. The salad looks like a botanical marvel, kissed with morning dew, straight out of a fairy tale. And the roast—it's the grand finale, all sizzle and mouth-watering aroma.

I grin like the cat who caught the canary, my eyes darting from one delectable morsel to the next. My hand itches to dive in with reckless abandon, savoring every last bite. But I clamp down my hunger, reminding myself of where I am—among the fae aristocracy.

I pick up my fork and knife with determination, each slice and bite a study of self-control. I slowly ease into the meal, letting the flavors tease my taste buds.

I eat with polite, measured patience, though every fiber of me yearns to throw caution to the wind. It's torture when everything tastes like a chef's kiss from the divine, but I manage, damping down my cravings with a smile that's only slightly strained at the edges.

"Damn, check you out, suppressing all those wild urges and cravings—and I'm not just talking about what you're stuffing in that beautiful mouth," Rhyland murmurs, his voice low and rough, meant for my ears alone.

I shoot him a knowing smirk, not missing a beat. "What can I say? I'm full of surprises. But don't worry, keeping my cravings in check is a talent—and trust me, it's not limited to the dinner table."

I let my words hang between us, heavy with promise and innuendo.

Rhyland's reaction is immediate and almost comical—his cough is a strangled sound, and his drink doesn't go down as smoothly as planned. As he sputters and recovers, I don't dare let the concern flicker across my face. Instead, I cock an eyebrow and lean in with a half-smile dancing on my lips.

"Is that a threat?" he growls lowly, eyes flickering with that familiar fire that tells me he's already weaving strategies and scenarios in his head, plotting his next move in this dangerous game we're playing.

My response is laced with mischief, a siren's call wrapped in a teasing lilt. "Only if you think you can handle it, Viking."

Rhyland's lips curve into a smug grin, his ocean-blue eyes blazing with a dangerous promise that makes my pulse quicken. "Handle it? Sweetheart, no force on this earth or beyond could stop me from handling anything you dare to throw my way." His voice is a low rumble threaded with the certainty of a predator who's never known defeat, a king who's never met a challenge he couldn't conquer.

I snatch up my glass, its contents catching the light and twinkling like liquid stars, and down it a bit faster than intended. The sweet burn of the wine is a welcome distraction from the heat building between us. The vintage is lovely, with a subtle kick that sneaks up on you, much like the challenge I've just lobbed into Rhyland's court. Setting the glass down, I tilt it expectantly, silently asking for another pour, even as my inner voice screams to slow down.

Shit.

My inner voice reminds me that challenging Rhyland is probably not the most brilliant move, especially here and now, surrounded by the watchful eyes of the Fae court. We're supposed to focus on diplomacy, forging alliances, and gathering information, not on the electric current of desire that crackles between us like a live wire.

It's too late now, though. The gauntlet has been thrown, and the twinkle in Rhyland's eye says game on. I can practically feel the anticipation thrumming through him, the barely leashed hunger threatening to consume us both.

I take a deep breath, trying to steady myself and remind myself of what's at stake. We have a mission and destiny to fulfill, and I can't let myself get distracted. We need to make nicey-nice with these Fae right now.

But even as I try to focus on the conversation swirling around us, the pointed questions and veiled insinuations of the Fae nobles, I can feel the pull of Rhyland's presence like a physical thing. It's like he's the sun, and I'm a helpless planet caught in his orbit, unable to resist the gravitational force of his desire.

DANICA

39

The meal winds down to a close with few words shared amongst us—I'm too wrapped up in my own sensations to contribute much to the conversation anyway. It's like my body has become a live wire, every nerve ending sparking with a strange, effervescent energy that I can't quite place.

That same handsome Fae and Faderyn seem utterly engrossed in whatever world-saving topic they're quietly debating, their heads bent together in intense discussion. Then, they both grab their drinks and head off to another room. Lucian, of course, draws peals of laughter from Elowen, his charm as potent as ever. I can't help but wonder what stories he's spinning to coax such mirth from the usually composed Fae, but knowing Lucian, it's probably a mix of outrageous anecdotes and flirtatious quips.

As for me, I'm trying to pinpoint this peculiar buzz creeping over me, a sensation that's both exhilarating and unsettling. This isn't like the wine back in Whispervale, with its pleasant warmth and gentle loosening of inhibitions. No, this is something else entirely, an almost... magical force.

Each sip I took felt like swallowing a spark of pure energy, and now I'm fizzing inside like a potion about to boil over. Heat creeps up my skin, a flush that starts at my chest and rises to my cheeks until I feel like I'm glowing from within. I resort to fanning myself with my hand, seeking respite from the inexplicable warmth engulfing me.

Glancing around the table, I notice that others seem to be in similar states of merry disarray, their faces flushed and their eyes bright with a feverish light. Some sway in their seats as if caught in the throes of some private euphoria, while others drift off to chase their newfound bliss elsewhere. But Rhyland, he's cool as a cave in winter, his composure unruffled and his gaze sharp and assessing. His iron-clad self-control stands in stark contrast to my rapidly unraveling composure.

Rhyland's gaze pins me—concern edged with something darker, more primal. "Are you okay?" His voice cuts low and rough through the fog in my head like a beacon in the dark.

I pull myself together with considerable effort, determined to keep the strange, bubbly sensation from showing on my face. "Yup! Just need to find the potty," I say with what I hope is a convincing smile, my voice coming out a bit too bright and chirpy to my own ears.

I rise from my seat, the motion slow and deliberate to counteract the dizziness that threatens to send me tumbling back down. Alina, bless her, points me in the right direction with a knowing look, and I stumble off searching for the facilities.

But even as I weave through the crowd, dodging swaying bodies and tripping over my feet, I can feel Rhyland's gaze burning into my back, a tangible force sending liquid heat to my already burning core.

Navigating through the blur, I stay focused on my destination, my mind locked on the singular goal of reaching the restroom before I combust. The path feels longer than it should, a winding maze of corridors that seems to stretch on forever, but soon enough, I've found sanctuary in the blessed privacy of the ladies' room.

After taking care of the necessities, I wash my hands in the ornate basin, and the cool water is a lifesaver against my overheated skin. But the relief doesn't last long, as another wave of that weird, electric sensation floods through me, igniting my nerves with an intensity that takes my breath away.

This time, it's not content with just making me hot and bothered—oh no, that would be too easy. Instead, it stokes a fire inside me, arousal so fierce and consuming that it feels like it's trying to claw its way to the surface, to break free of the constraints of my body and mind.

I grip the counter's edge, my knuckles turning white with the force of my hold, as I try to ground myself against the onslaught of sensation. This unbidden intensity has alarmed and confused me, leaving me reeling and desperate for answers.

What on earth was in that wine?

The realization strikes me mid-shudder, the heat coiling tighter in my belly as understanding dawns. Could it be? It's not beyond the realms of imagination, especially not with Rhyland involved. The man's a landmine of vampire allure, a walking, talking aphrodisiac with a smirk that could melt panties at fifty paces. And knowing our bond, the strange, inexplicable connection that seems to grow stronger with each passing day, it's not a stretch to think he could have sent a sizzling, wordless command through whatever mystical channel we've got going on. Horny bat signals, indeed.

That cheating bastard.

A little voice in my head snickers at the thought, equal parts amused and outraged. How very like Rhyland, to stir the pot and poke the dragon, to fan the flames of my desire without so much as a word spoken aloud. Because if this is his doing, if he's shooting vampiric pheromones down our psychic love line like some supernatural Cupid, then that's one heck of a low blow.

I grip the counter tighter, bracing myself against another wave that threatens to sweep me away. A mental note is firmly made—there will be a 'come to Jesus' meeting on the topic of psychic etiquette—and soon. Because while I'm all for a little spice in the bedroom (or the broom closet or the hidden alcove behind the tapestry), there's a time and a place for these kinds of shenanigans. And in the middle of a diplomatic dinner with the Fae elite? Yeah, not so much.

But first, I have to calm down and get back out there without looking like I'm ready to jump the bones of the next creature I see. Because as much as I'd love to give in to the fire raging inside me, to let Rhyland sate the hunger he's stoked to a fever pitch, I know that now is not the time. We have a mission to complete, a destiny to fulfill, and I can't let a little (okay, a lot) of supernatural horniness derail us from our path.

So I take a deep breath, squaring my shoulders and staring hard at my reflection in the mirror. "Get it together, Dani," I mutter, my voice shaky and seriously irritated. "You're supposed to be the savior of the realms, not some woman who loses her mind every time a hot Viking looks at her."

As I navigate out of the restroom, the fog in my brain makes me take a wrong turn. I find myself in a vast room bathed in the soft glow of candlelight. Shelves laden with books stretch infinitely upwards, and a chaise lounge sits invitingly in one corner. Then, I hear unmistakable sounds.

The rhythmic cadence, the shrouded whispers and sighs of lovemaking weave through the silence, ensnaring my attention. The heat within me simmers, and the noises fan the flames, sending my senses into a frenzy.

My feet seem to have a mind of their own, leading me closer to the erotic scene like a moth to a fuckin' bonfire. The soft pants and sighs dotting the air turn up the room's temperature to 'Do Not Disturb.'

Curiosity gets the best of me, and I find myself creeping closer, hooked on every sound that's both a lullaby and a siren's call. My breath hitches like I'm unwrapped, and this live tutorial utterly captivates me.

I stand there, jaw dropped, eyes as wide as saucers. The scene before me is a complete shock, but should I be astonished in a realm where the expected rarely pays a visit? It seems the word 'surprise' will need a new definition around here.

What unfolds before me is pure, unadulterated gay fae-erotica, and I'm hunching over the sofa like a covert ops agent. Each scandalous sound cranks my internal thermostat, and I'm practically a walking advertisement for 'Hot and Bothered.'

On my knees, elbows resting on the back of the sofa, I tuck myself against the backrest and watch as the taller Fae grips Faderyn's hips tightly. Faderyn leans against the wall, legs spread wide, and the taller Fae takes him forcefully. Their skin is slick with sweat, and the sounds of their flesh slapping together fill the room.

Looks like I just discovered something unexpected about Faderyn. His taste in people is way more diverse than I thought, which means he's either bisexual or just doesn't care about gender when it comes to who he's attracted to. This could imply that Rhyland's detection of Faderyn's interest in me was only part of the picture.

Faderyn moans and pants, begging for more as the taller Fae pounds into him with powerful thrusts. The giver asks, "You like my cock in your ass?"

Faderyn demands, "Ummpfh y-yes... harder."

I've never ventured into the realm of gay porn, but something about this scene and how it makes me feel has me hooked. It's a primal and passionate display of desire that leaves me wanting the same.

Can't a girl indulge in a little guilty pleasure?

The giver's actions become even more forceful, his massive cock plunging in and out of Faderyn's ass like a piston, hitting against that sweet spot deep inside him with each thrust.

Oh, the prostate—nature's little backdoor buzzer. I've flipped through some pages due to my scientific need to know everything, and let's say it's not folklore—it's science with a spicy kick. The "P-spot," they call it, and rumor has it, unlocking that treasure can blast a guy into seventh heaven—no rocket needed. A prostate orgasm? It's like the body's own secret handshake—exclusive club, epic results.

As a curious cat with a taste for knowledge, this particular tidbit piques my curiosity.

Faderyn's mouth is pried open, the other Fae's fingers shoved deep against the back of his throat, choking the air from him as pleasure and desire hold him hostage. Sweat slicks their bodies, mixing with the obscene mess of pre-cum and other fluids smeared between them.

Meanwhile, I watch from my perch on the couch, the sight of these two in an erotic dance making me drip between my legs. The giver's rough handling only adds to the intensity of the experience, reminding me of how Rhyland is with me.

As Faderyn arches his back in ecstasy, his voice becomes hoarse from all the panting and moaning. "Yes, fill me... take me... breed me...!"

Before I can process another thought, I smell him—an ocean breeze envelops me, and Rhyland's arms wrap around my torso, pulling me tight against his solid chest. "There you are," he murmurs, and I'm frozen, caught in the act.

"Aren't you a filthy girl—enjoying the show?" His words are velvet dipped in sin, and I'm trapped in his embrace, my body still buzzing with arousal.

"I... I got lost," I whisper, blurting out a lame excuse.

He chuckles softly, his lips grazing a hot trail along my jaw. "Lost, huh? Damn lucky for me, I stumbled across you, Angel—flushed, panting, and all kinds of fuckable."

His words strike hot and fast, lighting a blaze inside me. I'm ensnared in his dominance, and a part of me doesn't want to escape.

"Prepare to have your cute little challenge blown out of the water, sweetheart."

RHYLAND

40

Fuck—my filthy, gorgeous, insatiable angel. Seeing her like this, so damn worked up, I can't help but think about how her little challenge at dinner is about to go up in flames. I can't wait to have her moaning and begging for me.

Her little voyeuristic streak is doing things to me I can't even describe. My girl's mind never stops spinning, and watching her eyes glaze over while two guys rut like animals only proves what I've always suspected—she's hiding something depraved behind those pretty eyes, and I plan to drag every last bit of it out of her. That dream about me and Lucian sealed it. She's got a mind dirtier than sin, and I'm counting the fucking seconds until I crack her open and find out just how deep that filth goes.

"I asked you a question, baby," I say as I slide my hand around her throat to hold her in place. I tip her neck back and keep my other hand around her body, hunching over her possessively. Her sweet round ass digs painfully into my cock. She takes a shaky breath, feeling me pressed against her back while I keep my grip on her throat. "Tell me what you are doing watching them, dirty girl," I order her gruffly.

She likes to watch, and I aim to find out just how much.

"I...I...don't—" I cut off her rambling, tightening my grip on her throat as I take in the intoxicating scent of her arousal.

All this turns her on. The guy is drilling Faderyn from behind, their flesh slamming together with loud smacks and moans echoing throughout the room.

Faderyn plays both sides, huh? A taker and a bi, I never would have pegged him for it. Not my scene, but Dani's all stirred up about it, so who the hell am I to throw shade? Everyone's got their thing.

I couldn't give a damn about them. I focus solely on Dani and how her body responds to my touch. I've been patient—waited two days too long, but now my patience has run out.

"You want to watch, sweetheart? Then feast your eyes, but know this, I'm gonna do whatever the fuck I want with you..."

"Rhy—" I hush her and quiet her protests. My hand slides up under her shirt, cupping her full, swollen breast. Her nipple tightens under my touch, so I squeeze and stroke it. Her moans escape her lips.

"That's it, Angel. *Moan* for me."

I release her throat and glide my hand down to her pussy. Without hesitation, I slip my hand inside her pants and confirm what I already know—she is dripping wet. "So naughty, Dani."

Her whimpers fill my ears. I hear the men still fucking in the corner, their moans getting louder.

"I bet I can make you scream louder," I growl, my voice low and menacing. "And damn, I can't wait to hear those sinful sounds spilling from your pretty lips."

"No...no...not here..." she protests.

"Oh, yeah, baby," I slowly pull her pants off, still holding her in place, and I guide her to slide back until her knees are balanced precariously on the edge of the couch and her pussy dangles invitingly over the edge.

I sit underneath her, my back to the couch, and I lean my neck back. My face is at the perfect level for what I have planned.

"Rhyland...what....what are you doing?" she whispers. Her question hangs in the air. She's about to find out what I'm about to do.

She can enjoy her spectacle while I devour my most cherished delicacy.

"Sit down," I demand.

She gulps in a sharp breath at my lewd suggestion. "Rhy..." she starts to protest, but I give her ass a swift smack, watching it jiggle and bounce with the force of my hand.

Her squeak of pain and surprise turns into a whimper as I growl, *"I said sit the fuck down on my face and ride my mouth, Dani."* I use our mental pathway to tell her how serious I am.

My angel, so dirty and enticing, is driving me fucking wild with need. I can't contain my arousal any longer. I want to experience all her heart desires and to show her that she can't resist me, no matter how much she tries.

With extreme caution, she lowers herself onto my lips, and I instantly lick her swollen clit passionately.

"Hold on tight, baby."

She grips the back of the couch—gasps, and trembles, savoring the sensation of being so exposed. I suck hungrily on her bundle of nerves, wanting more like devouring my favorite candy. I vigorously massage my hard cock, plunging it into my tight grasp as I hungrily eat her juices.

She rocks and pants above me as her cotton candy-like nectar begins to ooze from her, dripping down my chin and then chest. The sight of her arousal fills me with delight. I growl lustfully as it seeps out of her.

I grab her voluptuous hips tight and yank her closer. *"Goddamn, baby. Bury me alive with your pussy."*

The lewd noises of these bastards pounding each other only grow louder, their skin slapping and their filthy moans and growls providing a downright obscene soundtrack for my angel. The room is filled with the raunchy symphony of their pleasure as she watches, and I can't help but feel possessive as I stake my claim on her.

She grinds hard on my face as I moan in pleasure from the suffocating bliss of her sweetness.

She shouts through our bond a passionate howl, *"Rhyland...oh fuck!"* she moans.

I slide two fingers deep inside her warmth, feeling her clench around them. *"Yeah, baby. Drown me..."*

I flick my tongue quickly against her tight nub, slick and wet, and hold her firmly against me, pushing her closer and closer to the edge until she's screaming out in ecstasy, her orgasm cascading down my throat.

I moan at her flavor.

Her cries of pleasure are muffled to my ears as her thighs clamp down tightly around my head.

The charade's done. No doubt she's snagged the gaze of our unsuspecting company.

Without wasting another tick, I scoop Dani up before our pesky fae porn stars catch sight of us. Our surroundings become a hazy blur as my vampiric speed and velocity catapult us back to her quarters. The door crashes shut with a thunderous noise as I press her slender body hard against it.

"Mmm...cotton candy," I remind her with a hint of hunger before our lips collide, and I ravage her taste, insatiable. She clings to me, legs and arms coiled tight.

"You...asshole," she gasps, tearing her swollen lips from mine, panting and flushed. "What the hell was that for? In front of them?"

I chuckle at her audacity. "Asshole? Mm..that naughty mouth of yours is gonna get a punishment. You loved it, baby. Don't pretend with me. Why were you spying, Angel?"

She gives me that intense, see-into-your-soul kind of look before dropping the bomb, "You totally ninja'd your way in with those horny bat signals of yours. My body's lighting up like a bonfire, thanks to that Jedi mind cheat code you pulled."

A chuckle breaks out, "I didn't fucking cheat, sweetheart. You think I need to play dirty to watch you fall on your ass? Please, I've got more honor in my pinky than to pull a stunt like that."

"Then what the hell?" she starts, clinging to me like a koala on a tree, her fingers twirling through my hair and her body grinding against mine like a freight train. "I don't know what's gotten into me."

I flick her a sly grin, "Probably all that sweet shit you've been knocking back all night. Makes this whole game a hell of a lot more entertaining for me."

She shoots me a no-nonsense glare, "Rhyland, cut the games. I'm in serious need here—" I silence her with a forceful kiss, cutting off her protests.

I fucking know what she wants, and I'm gonna give it to her, but she's gonna have to work for it.

First things first—I'm going to fuck that bratty mouth until she learns some manners. When I'm done, muffled moans will be the only sound.

"You're gonna get what's coming to you, baby. My thick cock is gonna stretch that filthy mouth of yours until you're gagging on it like the greedy girl you are—until you are a whimpering mess. And if you're lucky, I might fuck you."

I roughly grab her by the hair, and with my other hand, I reach between us, and I plunge my fingers into her dripping cunt. "Does that feel good, Angel? Does it make you want me to claim every inch of your body?"

She moans and arches her back as I thrust harder, showing her who's in control. "Don't even think about coming without my permission. Just remember, that move back there—that was a freebie. Next time, you won't be so lucky."

She growls at my dominance, "Dammit, Rhyland... please..."

She knows damn well what begging does to me, "That's right, beg for it, baby. It's gonna be your fucking mantra all night long."

RHYLAND

49

I haul Dani to the bed and nearly throw her on it. She bounces from my lack of gentleness. She tries to bolt upright, thinking she can escape.

I snatch her throat, pressing my solid frame against her. "Where the hell do you think you're going, Angel?"

The chase between us has been a game from the start, and I enjoy indulging her wild fantasies and mind games.

Defiance blazes in her stunning gold eyes as she gazes up at me, lust she can't mask. I tighten my grip on her throat; her eyes widen with unshed tears.

Damn, she's a sight to behold.

I yank off her shirt, tossing it aside carelessly. My clothes hit the floor. I'm fully aroused, all for my angel.

"Stand up and turn around," I command. Surprisingly, she obeys. I bind her hands behind her back with the bed's tassel rope, aggressively restraining her.

She squirms. "What the hell? Rhyland—"

I grab a fistful of her hair and jerk her head back. She gasps at my sudden movement.

My mouth is near her throat. "Stay still, Angel. You've been bad, and now you'll be punished."

I finish binding her, relishing her struggles against the restraints. Her anger and lust mingle, but I see through her facade. Gripping her hair, I draw her body closer. My tongue trails along her neck, eliciting shivers.

She fucking loves it.

"You think you can challenge me, Little Angel? You're just begging to be fucked. Behave, and maybe I'll let you come. Try me again, Dani. But I'm in control here, and you'll do as I say. On the bed," I demand gruffly. "Lie on your back, head on the edge."

Bound, she struggles but obeys, gasping in anticipation. Unable to fight me, she's trapped between me and the mattress.

I hover over her, my hard cock pressing against her soft lips.

Steadying myself, I trap her beneath me. "Now be a good whore, and take my cock in that heavenly mouth."

Greedily, she takes me in inch by inch as I feed her. She lies with her neck bent, and I ravage her mouth.

"That's it, Angel..." I grunt, driving my dick down her throat. She moans in pleasure, gurgling as I press harder. My hands wrap around her slender neck, feeling her pulse.

Gods, her warm mouth feels so fucking good—my cock throbs with pleasure as she expertly sucks me off.

I feel my balls tap her face as I speed up. "Good girl," I praise. "You're doing so good, baby."

The view is filthy and sexy. Her breasts wiggle as I thrust into her throat. Her tight legs spread wide; her mouth stretched as I bury my cock in it... She's gurgling and choking, drool drips down her gorgeous face. I crave to fill her every hole as she gags on me.

Unable to control myself, I burst forth at the sight of her taking me, the dirty thoughts in my mind, and the exquisite sensation of her tight mouth.

She struggles for breath around my thick length, gagging each time I slam deep. Her mouth can't fully take me yet, but she swallows eagerly.

I don't stop my relentless pace even as tears and drool stream down her face. "Take it, Angel," I snarl through gritted teeth.

Dani chokes and sputters, but I keep pumping down her tight throat. When I'm done, she'll only have energy for muffled whimpers.

"You like being a dirty whore? Watching guys fuck?" I ask as I slam deep.

She moans and coughs around my dick, drenched in her spit.

I pull out, hovering over her. She takes in a deep breath, "What's that? I couldn't hear you..."

"Y-yes..." she gasps.

"Hell yeah, you do. My filthy whore gets off watching someone get their ass fucked, doesn't she? Is that what you crave, baby—getting your tight ass pounded?" I don't let her respond, forcefully driving my cock back into her eager mouth.

I want her to confess her dirty desires, her turn-ons, with no holding back or fear of judgment.

I reach between her spread thighs, teasing her throbbing clit roughly. She's soaked, *dripping,* and squirming under my touch.

She moans around me in pleasure as I rub her clit, making her wetter and more desperate.

Breathless, I release her and stumble back, far from done. I aggressively grab her head and slam my lips onto her swollen ones.

"Now..." I growl breathlessly. "Get on your knees and turn that sweet ass around for me." Still bound, she eagerly complies. "Bend down. I want your face in the bed."

Her perfectly round ass, slick and shiny with arousal, begs to be taken. "Look at this mess, baby," I sneer, relishing her pleasure moans.

I lick at her puckered asshole, savoring every filthy taste of her. She squirms and bucks beneath me, face buried in the sheets, muffled moans spilling out as I eat her like a starving man. I rear back and crack my palm across her ass—hard—that rings through the room. The way her flesh ripples under my palm has me groaning against her skin.

"This *fucking* pussy..." I spread her lips and attack her clit with my tongue, "Mmm...*mine.*" flicking it rapidly and driving her wild. "I can't get enough of it." I tease and play with her tight ring with my thumb, feeling her squirm more beneath me.

"Rhy...land..." she moans, "Oh fuuuuck..."

"Do you like that, baby? Do you like me playing with your filthy holes?" I suck and nibble at her back entrance, my tongue delving deep as I rub her clit with my fingers. She's trembling, entirely at my mercy, as she begs for more.

I grip her bound hands, taking a handful of her hair and pulling her tight against me. Her moans and whimpers only fuel me more because she loves this.

"You know what to do, don't you?" I growl in her ear, gripping her tighter.

She nods obediently, trembling.

"That's right, beg me, baby," I whisper, trailing my tongue down her neck.

"Please. Please...Rhyland—" She whimpers desperately.

I tighten my hold. "Beg harder. Beg me to ravage this pussy—that you crave me more than anything, Dani."

She grinds against me, craving my touch. "Please, Rhyland...fuck me. I need you so badly," she pleads with desperate moans. "I'll always want you...I love you."

Those three words break me. I'm aware she enjoys the kink and wildness, but now all I care about is giving her everything she wants.

Without hesitation, I push into her slowly. Her sounds are blissful, nearly driving me over the edge. Her voice and moans are a heavenly melody.

"You're playing dirty, sweetheart." I increase my speed, "This is punishment, but then you say things like that..." I release her hair and grasp the front of her neck, tilting her head to gaze into her stunning honey-glazed eyes.

"You want it, Angel—You want to come?"

"Yes...p-please..." she moans, writhing in pleasure under my thrusts.

I release her bound hands, and she immediately reaches back, behind her—wrapping her arms around my neck, desperate to hold me. She tangles her fingers in my hair, urging me on.

"I will never get enough of you, Angel." I groan, gripping and teasing her breasts mercilessly. "You have no idea how fucking good you feel," I pant, nearing the edge. "Now be a good girl, and come all over my cock."

"Fuck...me...harder," she demands.

So I do, gritting my teeth and slamming into her with brutal intensity. The bed knocks against the wall, shaking from our passion. Her sexy growls and delicious moans fuel my dominating nature, driving me to pound her harder and deeper. My dick stretches her tight pussy, causing her to grip me like a vise, and I swear I see stars from the sheer ecstasy.

Her orgasm crashes through her, clenching tighter around me. Her arousal coats my length as she screams in pleasure.

My own release detonates right behind hers, a guttural roar ripping from my chest as I pump every last drop deep inside her, flooding her tight little cunt until it's dripping down her thighs. We collapse into the wrecked sheets, chests heaving, bodies spent and slick with sweat. I drag her against me, cock still buried inside her, refusing to pull out—not yet. Not when she's still clenching around me like she wants every fucking drop I've got.

After a long moment, I slide out of her and she rolls in my arms, turning to face me. Those honey-gold eyes find mine, brimming with so much love it damn near knocks the wind out of me.

I reach up and tuck a wild strand of hair behind her ear, my fingers lingering against her flushed skin. A cocky grin tugs at my mouth. "You just had to play that card, didn't you?" I challenge.

She grins defiantly, white teeth on show. "All's fair in love and war," she shoots back playfully.

Still laughing, I manage, "Is that so? Well, be ready because I'm rewriting the rules."

DANICA

42

Dawn's light filters through the sheer drapes, casting my chamber in an almost ethereal golden hue. Today, I face the Sun Court's King and Queen, and the weight of it presses down on me like a ton of bricks. Alina flutters around me with her delicate movements and genuine smile, presenting a gown that's actually modest for once—a total change from all the barely-there outfits I've been wearing, and honestly? I'm grateful for it.

The dress is subtle yet undeniably elegant—a cascade of cream-colored chiffon, soft as a whisper against my skin. Embroidered sunbursts adorn the bodice, their rays stitched in gold and palest yellow thread that catch the light with every movement. Sheer sleeves flow to my wrists, cinched in tight cuffs detailed with tiny pearls, and the skirt falls in gentle folds to the floor, each step revealing an underlay of rose gold that shimmers like a sunrise.

Alina snaps the final button into place at my gown's back, and that's when I catch a glimpse of my reflection in the full-length mirror. A surge of reassurance floods through me as I take in the sight—I'm the embodiment of royalty, exuding an undeniable strength that seems to radiate from within. This gown is more than just fabric and thread; it's a suit of elegance, my battle attire for the challenges that lie ahead.

"You look beautiful," Alina breathes out.

"Thanks," I shoot back, pivoting away from the looking glass to face her squarely. "I feel... fitting for the occasion."

And it's true—I do feel fitting like I'm exactly where I'm meant to be, doing exactly what I'm meant to do. This sense of purpose and destiny is a heady feeling that buoys me up like a rising tide.

I pause for a moment, considering Alina with a thoughtful tilt of my head. "You know, I don't think I've ever asked you about your life here at the Sun Court. How long have you been an attendant?"

Alina's eyes widen slightly, surprised by my interest. It's clear that she's not used to being asked about herself and having someone genuinely interested in her life and experiences. "Oh, I've been here for a few years now," she says, a hint of shyness creeping into her voice. "It's a good life, serving the court and being a part of something greater."

I nod, understanding the sentiment all too well. "I can imagine. It must be rewarding, in its own way."

"It is," Alina agrees, a genuine smile gracing her features and lighting up her eyes. "And if I may say so, My Lady, it's an honor to serve you. Your presence brings a new light to the court, a sense of hope and possibility that we haven't felt in a long time."

Her words touch me deeply, striking a chord within my heart that resonates with the truth of her sentiment. I reach out to give her hand a gentle squeeze, feeling the warmth of her skin against my own. "Thank you, Alina," I say softly, my voice thick with emotion. "That means a lot to me. I hope we can become friends during my time here."

Alina returns the squeeze, her eyes shining with warmth and hinting of something that might be tears. "I would like that very much, My Lady."

I quickly switch topics. "Okay, now *please* tell me. Just what in the hell was in that wine?" I ask, my mind replaying last night's uninhibited antics with vivid clarity.

Alina, trying to maintain her composure, smiles demurely. "It's a signature blend of our vineyard. As I mentioned, it comes with a certain... zest."

"Zest? That's like calling a wildfire a spark," I quip, my eyebrows arching. "Felt more like a liquid love potion if you ask me."

With a grace that matches the poise of her giggle, Alina nods. "Indeed, it contains a... passionate additive," she says, her diplomacy shining through her amusement. "It is a treasured essence, one that has kindled fires in our realm for many generations, My Lady."

I can't help but gape at her, my jaw dropping. "Wait, wait, wait. You're telling me you guys have been spiking your wine with some ancient, magical horny juice for hundreds of years?"

Alina nods a hint of pride in her smile. "Indeed, My Lady. It's a closely guarded secret, passed down through generations of our winemakers."

I shake my head, a grin spreading across my face. "Well, damn. You guys sure know how to party.

Alina's laughter rings out, her eyes dancing with amusement. "Indeed, My Lady. It helps...relax, in a sense—keeps the peace."

At this moment, I feel a connection forming between us, a bond of friendship and understanding that transcends our differences in rank and station. It's a reminder that, beneath the trappings of court life and the weight of destiny, we are all just people searching for connection and meaning in this strange and wondrous world.

I smile at Alina, feeling a sense of peace and contentment settling over me. "Well then, my friend," I say, my voice light and teasing, "shall we go and face the court together?"

With the crown in place—the final gleaming touch to my ensemble—I swiftly take a final look at my reflection. This is it—the moment when the mirror tells no lies and the regal figure staring back holds the weight of destiny.

It's showtime.

Alina grins. "Let's do it, My Lady," she says, offering me her arm in a playful gesture of camaraderie.

We strut out to rendezvous with Rhyland, Erik, and Faderyn. The trio looms like towers of power, but their expressions turn all puppy-dog the moment they lay eyes on me.

Erik emits a low whistle as we approach, his eyes widening in surprise as he sees me in my formal finery. "I never thought I'd see you don a gown willingly after our last debacle with courtly attire," he says, a hint of teasing in his voice.

That gets me chuckling—a quick snort that's more about jittery nerves than anything else. "Let's just say it's nice to be sporting a little more fabric real estate today," I quip back, smoothing my hands over the lush skirts of my gown.

"You look beautiful, Little Huntress," Erik says sweetly, his eyes softening with genuine affection.

Rhyland saunters over, all soft gazes and gentle touches, and weaves his fingers through my carefully coiffed locks. "You look stunning, Angel," he murmurs, his voice dipped in honey and promise.

"Thank you," I breathe out, feeling a flush of pleasure at their compliments. But even as I bask in their admiration, I can't help but inquire, "And where's our dear Lucy tucked away?"

"He beat us to the punch, mingling in the throne room with the rest of the crowd," Rhyland tells me, a hint of amusement in his voice. "You know Lucian—he's never one to miss a chance to work the room."

I nod, a wry smile tugging at my lips. "Of course he is. Probably charming the pants off of every Fae in sight."

Faderyn flashes me a toasty grin as we buddy up toward the throne room, his eyes twinkling with mirth and mischief. I toss a quick smile in return, all the while dodging his gaze so as not to spill the beans on my little spying spree earlier.

As we approach the massive double doors of the throne room, I take a deep breath, squaring my shoulders and lifting my chin in a show of confidence and determination. I may be a mortal in a world of immortals, but I am also the prophesied savior of the realms, and the pomp and circumstance of the Fae court will not cow me.

Let the games begin.

The throne room is breathtaking—ceilings soaring sky-high, graced with frescoes whispering tales of ancient Fae mysteries. Light bathes every inch in a soft glow; shadows don't dare encroach here.

Queen Titania Solaria embodies her title—The Radiant Queen. Her hair flows like molten bronze, each strand vibrating with inner light. Summer-sky eyes set into a face that holds centuries of wisdom within an eternally youthful visage. Her gown rivals the morning sky—diaphanous yellow and white chiffon floating around her as if alive.

King Oberon Aurealis is her perfect counterpart—The Light King—tall and sharp-featured, cutting a regal silhouette against his throne. Silver-moonlight hair cascades past his shoulders, and his eyes hold glints of icy blue ringed with gold, otherworldly in their intensity.

The space brims with Sun Court Fae arrayed in pew upon pew—a holy assembly on a supernatural power trip. The moment we enter, murmured chatter cuts off like someone hit the mute button on the entire crowd, the weight of countless gazes locking onto us.

I stride down the grand aisle toward the dais where the King and Queen sit, their eyes fixed on us, keeping my composure under the intensity of it all.

"Lady Danica," Queen Titania declares, her voice resonating throughout the chamber—melodious and warm as sunlight on bare skin. "We eagerly invite you to recount your journey to our distinguished court. Our esteemed Axilya has graciously shared some details concerning you and your passage, yet it is from your own words that we wish to learn. Please enlighten us on the nature of your quest and disclose how we might bestow our assistance upon you."

I mentally brace myself for a scene straight out of a Game of Thrones high-stakes intrigue. I've binged enough to know the drill—smile like you know all the secrets, stand like you hold all the cards, and keep your cool like you're the puppet master.

Here goes nothing—I summon my inner Emmy winner and lay on the performance of a lifetime.

I dip into a curtsy, nailing it despite the gown's theatrics, then look up to meet their royal stares. "Your Highnesses," I start, my voice smoother than expected, given the internal acrobatics. "I stand before you not merely as an outsider from a foreign land but as a bearer of both promise and trepidation for our collective futures."

King Oberon leans forward, his gaze piercing yet not unkind. "Speak plainly, Lady Danica," he commands gently.

Oh, thank god. No diplomatic tap-dancing required.

So I lay it all out—Azrael's scheme, Mortemis and his creeping darkness looking to RSVP to the end-of-world party, and this crown of mine that likes to play peekaboo with more tricks than I can wrap my head around. I spill about Rhyland and our cosmic connection that laughs in the face of Father Time, and I map out my quest across the seven realms to collect the stones—apparently the VIP ticket to beating back the dark and hitting save on all our asses.

"I am, believe it or not, the direct descendant of Elysium himself."

Not exactly your everyday family tree. I half-wonder if they'll buy it or if I'll need to produce some kind of celestial birth certificate.

Their expressions shift like clouds drifting across the sun—curiosity, worry, and comprehension moving across their regal features in slow, telling waves.

"May we ask you to prove your power? That you are indeed who you say you are..." King Oberon inclines, raising his brow in a silent challenge.

I knew this would be a requirement per Faderyn's explanation of these Fae and what they represent. They are beings of power and magic, and they will not accept my claim without tangible proof of my own abilities.

With a deep breath, I reach within, tapping into the wellspring of power thrumming through my veins like liquid starlight. I conjure my white fire first, letting it wreathe my hands in a shimmering aura of pure energy—flames dancing and flickering against the throne room walls, held steady by my will alone.

Then, I shape the light into a sphere, molding it like clay between my palms until it glows with an inner luminescence that rivals the sun itself. With a wink and a playful grin, I blow the sphere towards the King and Queen like a bubble, watching as it floats gracefully through the air before resting above their heads.

The Fae monarchs stare at the sphere in wonder, their eyes wide with awe and perhaps a hint of trepidation. Of course, they have seen magic before—they are creatures of magic themselves—but it's been cut off to all Fae, and they've never seen it like this and never wielded by a mortal with such ease and mastery.

I can feel the weight of their gazes on me, the pressure of their expectations, and their doubts. But I stand tall and proud, my chin lifted and my eyes shining with the light of my own conviction.

There is a moment of stunned silence, broken only by the soft rustling of fabric as the Fae shift in their seats. And then, slowly but surely, a murmur of excitement and anticipation begins to build, growing louder and more insistent with each passing second.

"The prophecy is true," someone whispers.

"The savior has come at last," comes another voice.

This is my moment, my chance to prove myself worthy of the title that has been bestowed upon me.

And I will not let it pass me by.

With a final flourish, I release the sphere of light, letting it dissipate into a shower of glittering motes that rain down upon the assembled Fae like stardust. And as they gaze up at me with a mix of wonder and respect, I know that I have passed their test—that I have proven myself to be the savior they have been waiting for.

Queen Titania leans forward ever so slightly. "You are indeed who you claim to be."

I nod once.

"You bear a considerable weight upon your shoulders," she reflects audibly. "Displaying such fortitude and resilience in journeying today speaks volumes of your courage. We are aware of the Darkness..."

I incline my head in subtle thanks for acknowledging my tale and plight.

"And regarding this stone that you seek," she proceeds, her words emerging deliberately after a pause long enough to draw a collective intake of breath from those gathered, "I regret to inform you that it lies outside the scope of our wisdom and beyond the confines of our realm."

As she finishes speaking, a soft murmur ripples through the courtiers—this mix of shock and disappointment that matches the sinking feeling in my own chest. The room fills with their quiet whispers, each one seeming to echo the heavy weight settling inside me.

Firm in my conviction, I address the queen. "If I may, Your Radiance. I have sensed it—the unmistakable tug of the stone. It resides somewhere within this realm. With your permission," I pause, knowing this will certainly get a reaction... "I desire to venture to the Crystal Peaks."

The air erupts with gasps and the buzz of chatter, a testament to the audacity of my request. The queen's eyes flicker with concern, then questions.

Faderyn leans in, his voice a sharp whisper. "What are you doing? I've told you no one—"

"Silence, please." King Oberon's command cuts through the room like a blade, swallowing Faderyn's warning whole. Every voice falls away, leaving nothing but the weight of anticipation hanging in the air.

If the stone isn't hiding right under our noses, then it's waiting at the Crystal Peaks. Faderyn dropped heavy hints back in Whispervale—something about unicorns moonlighting as top-tier security for a realm-breaking or realm-saving artifact. Connect the dots and it's as clear as crystal—I bet my bottom dollar it's stashed up there.

Oberon's expression carves into a frown that speaks volumes. "Do you grasp the gravity of your entreaty, my dear?" he inquires, his voice tinged with solemn depth. "No soul has ever surmounted those formidable peaks and returned to weave their tale. The undertaking you propose bears the semblance of a death wish."

"I do, Your Highness," I assert with a confidence I hope is convincing.

Rhyland's voice sneaks into my mind, a silent murmur, *"Are you sure?"*

Without missing a beat, I reply internally, *"Without a doubt."*

On the outside, though, it's all poise and purpose, "I'm here on a quest for the stone—It's my destiny, Your Highness. My gut tells me it's up there in the Crystal Peaks, and I intend to get it."

The room erupts in sharp intakes of breath, but as Queen Titania rises, an expectant hush blankets the court. Each step she takes toward me feels like the tick of a grand clock. She's a cascade of radiance—warm, welcoming—her smile a work of art even as her gaze drifts to the crown perched on my head.

"May I?" she inquires, enchanted.

I nod, a bit amused. "It's pretty stuck on there, but you may touch it."

She raises her hand, her fingers graze the cool gold, and the crown sings a note of pure magic in response. "Extraordinary," she whispers with awe, veiling her tone.

Tears shimmer in her eyes, creating depths of emotion that are impossible to fully understand. "We feared you might be a myth," she confesses through a quiver of relief. "I—we..." her hands splaying wide, gesturing to the entire court, "have awaited your arrival through countless turns of the season. Welcome, at long last."

Then, like dawn bestowing light, she graces me with her pronouncement. "You shall have our full support, Danica—the foretold Chosen One, the hopeful Savior of the Seven Realms."

The hall erupts into applause and jubilant cheers—a shot of adrenaline straight to the heart. They get it. They get *me*. Their support is a beacon in the dark, fueling the fire for the road ahead.

"But be certain of this," King Oberon's voice cuts through the celebration, solid as bedrock yet softened by an undercurrent of kindness.

Silence falls. His eyes lock onto mine with unwavering determination.

"Your expedition to that treacherous place will not be devoid of tribulation. The path is fraught with peril, yet rest assured, we shall extend our aid to you in whichever manner lies within our power."

I dip my head, the universal sign for 'I gotcha,' but inside, my scientist's brain is doing somersaults—cartwheeling through every rational alleyway, trying to pin down what boogeyman could possibly be haunting the fabled Crystal Peaks.

DANICA

43

The invitation to remain throws me for a loop—unexpected yet a reprieve that feels like a gulp of fresh air—having a moment to breathe, to prep, and to steel our nerves before taking on the Crystal Peaks? That's a slice of heaven we'd be fools to shoo away.

Shooting Rhyland a glance, I see that telltale arch of his brow, his silent way of saying, 'Yep, we're totally on the same page, babe.' He's got that 'let's milk this for all it's worth' glint in his eye, and frankly, I'm right there with him, ready to squeeze every last drop of advantage out of this little pit stop.

"Your hospitality is appreciated," I say, offering Queen Titania and King Oberon a smile that's equal parts charm and cheek. "We accept," I add, hoping my voice doesn't betray the jitters playing xylophone on my ribs. Because let's be real, this is the Fae court we're talking about—one wrong move, and we could end up as garden gnomes in the royal hedge maze.

With the royal affirmation, the deal is done, and we're whisked away to a cozy little chamber that's like a nook tucked inside a treasure chest. The air is thick with excitement and nervous energy like we're standing at the edge of something colossal—or at least something that could turn us into toadstools if we're not careful.

Our motley crew circles the table, a heady mix of personalities and power, each bringing their own flavor to this pre-quest banquet. It's like the world's weirdest dinner party, with vampires, Fae, and one slightly overwhelmed human all rubbing elbows and trying not to step on any metaphorical toes.

I kick back in my chair, looking as comfy as possible while sizing up the room with a discerning eye. This chamber has a more intimate vibe than the throne room, but it doesn't skimp on the wow factor, with little orbs of light hovering and dipping like a school of glowing sea creatures. It's like being inside a lava lamp if Tim Burton designed lava lamps on acid.

And then there's the table at the heart of the room—Mother Nature's masterpiece of twisty-turny wood, with a tapestry of leaves and vines that could make the finest artist green with envy. It's like something out of a fairy tale, if fairy tales involved high-stakes diplomacy and the fate of the realms hanging in the balance.

Axilya slips into the chair beside me, all regal grace and quiet intensity. There's a grounding vibe about her—a stillness amidst the storm that makes me feel like maybe, just maybe, we might actually pull this off without getting killed.

She flicks a regal nod at the royals, no words needed to convey the depth of meaning in that simple gesture. And then there's the secret eyelash flutters, the subtle quirks of the lips that speak volumes without a single syllable uttered. It's like watching a soap opera without subtitles, trying to decipher the hidden messages and unspoken alliances that swirl beneath the surface.

What's the story here? My mind races with possibilities and potential pitfalls. Because in this game of thrones, knowledge is power—and I'll take every scrap of intel I can get my hands on.

"So," Lucian drawls, his posture relaxed, a mischievous smirk playing on his lips. "Any takers willing to spill the tea on the big, bad boogeyman lurking beyond those picturesque peaks? I promise I won't even charge for the therapy session afterward."

King Oberon leans forward, hands clasped before him. "The Crystal Peaks are not just treacherous because of sheer cliffs and unpredictable weather," he begins, his authoritative voice demanding attention. "They are steeped in deep magic—ancient and untamed."

Queen Titania's piercing gaze locks onto mine, touching my essence beyond the surface. "There are sentinels within those mountains," she continues. "Entities from the darkest dreams, stationed to ward off trespassers."

Erik shifts, eyes narrowing—his warrior's mind assessing threats.

"Sentinels?" I echo, unease prickling my spine.

Faderyn's solemn declaration about the creatures protecting something beyond just unicorns makes my eyebrow arch. It's like trying to digest a boulder-sized chunk of information without any water.

And speaking of hard-to-swallow things, I can feel my cheeks flush at the memory of catching a glimpse of Faderyn's, *ahem*, assets last night.

Of course, Mr. All-Knowing Rhyland has my number, his hand gliding up my thigh with sly confidence and giving me a delicious squeeze. Oh, he knows exactly what I'm thinking, the smug bastard. But two can play at that game, and I shoot him a look that promises all sorts of wicked retribution later.

Clearing my throat, I try to steer the conversation back on track. "Well, I guess that settles it. The stone's tucked away in there," I quip, probably crossing the line of casual banter considering the high-caliber company. But come on, mythical creatures deserve an edge, and if we can't crack a few jokes about their super-secret hideout, what's the point of being The Chosen One?

Axilya's lips curve slightly before she responds, her voice low and mysterious. "Perhaps the true nature remains hidden. Those who have ventured forth have never returned to tell their stories—it is said to be a wellspring of life itself."

My mind reels at that bombshell. Not just the stone? What could they be protecting? A magic mushroom patch?

I glance at Rhyland, running a hand through his hair in frustration. The poor guy looks like he's about to pop a blood vessel trying to understand all this mystical mumbo-jumbo.

"A source of life? That sounds heavy," he mutters before raising his voice. "What are we talking about here? A fountain of youth? A genie in a bottle?"

The Light King's eyes flicker with amusement. "Not youth," he corrects. "Balance."

And just like that, my curiosity is piqued. Balance—what we've been seeking all along—between realms, between light and shadow.

"And these sentinels," Lucian interjects casually, "they just stand around scaring tourists? Sounds like a boring gig."

"Not tourists," Faderyn replies with a faint smile. "But formidable guardians deterring any seeking to disrupt the equilibrium."

Queen Titania's expression turns grave. "Whispers suggest even time itself may warp and twist within those mountains."

Her words send a chill racing through me. Time warping and twisting? That's some Doctor Who level shit right there. And if there's one thing I've learned from binge-watching sci-fi shows, it's that messing with the space-time continuum never ends well.

But then, I'm not just a baseline human anymore. I might have a card up my sleeve, with supernatural abilities that include a nifty little time-warp trick. If this place bends time, I may bend it right back.

Erik's voice resonates with certainty. "We will need more than blades and bravado."

Rhyland leans forward, fixing the royals with a stare that could freeze lava. "So, how do we get past these nightmares?" he demands.

The Light King briefly regards Rhyland before responding."Cunning and purity of intent," he intones like he's reciting a fortune cookie.

"Great," Lucian mutters, rolling his eyes so hard I'm surprised they don't fall out of his head. "We're screwed then."

The tension breaks, giving way to chuckles and snickers. Trust Lucian to slice through the somber mood with his wit.

Faderyn glances at Axilya, then turns back to us, his expression thoughtful. "There may be paths within the mountain that could lead us through rather than over."

"But such paths come with dangers," Axilya warns.

"Dangers?" I prompt. What haven't we faced at this point? Vampires, shadow beasts, ogres, creepy-crawly—just another day at the office.

Axilya hesitates. "There are tales," she begins, her voice like a ghost story around a campfire, "of creatures even the Fae whisper about—Whisperlings."

Rhyland's hand tightens around mine—my thoughts immediately reflect to Meadow's warning—Whispers.

Lucian leans closer, his trademark smirk fading into a look of genuine curiosity. "Whisperlings?" he repeats like he's trying the word out for size. "Sounds like something out of a fairytale, the kind of creature parents use to scare their kids into bed at night."

Axilya nods solemnly. "Indeed, they are the stuff of legends, creatures born of silence and secrecy. They weave illusions so convincing you could wander lost for eternity in their maze of whispers."

The table falls silent as we consider this new challenge. Faderyn speaks softly, with respect. "To face a Whisperling is to confront one's inner turmoil," he says. "They mirror our buried fears and doubts."

Lucian pipes up, recognition dawning in his tone. "That's got 'Morty's mojo' written all over it," he quips, referring to our old nemesis Moretemis. "Sounds like the kind of mind-fuck he'd get off on."

King Oberon interjects. "Runes safeguard our domain, barriers against malicious intent. Beyond these grounds, you embark on a journey relying solely on your own resources. Only those undimmed by deceit and untainted by malevolence may hope to pass unscathed."

A wave of unease washes over me. To face the darkness inside ourselves? That's an entirely different beast altogether.

I glance around the table. Rhyland's jaw is set in a grim line. Erik's hand rests on his sword. Lucian's smirk has faded. And Faderyn looks like he's already steeling himself for the trials ahead.

Axilya meets my gaze, her eyes understanding. We're not just facing a physical journey. We're embarking on a quest to confront our deepest fears and darkest secrets.

Seraphina's caution reverberates, reminding we all have shadows to wrestle with, even Rhyland.

"But there is hope," Queen Titania adds softly, her voice as gentle as a summer breeze. "The Whisperlings are not malevolent. If you are steadfast and true, they will allow you passage."

Lucian raises an eyebrow, his expression as skeptical as a cat eyeing a bath. "So we just need to be honest?" he drawls, with sarcasm. "Well, that's easy. I do that every day in the mirror."

His bravado draws an exaggerated snort and eye roll from me because who is he trying to kid? We all know Lucian's relationship with the truth is about as straightforward as a corkscrew.

"Perhaps," Axilya says, her tone amused but also slightly chiding. "But these creatures will delve deeper than vanity or self-assuredness. They will see into the very heart of who you are."

I feel Rhyland's questioning gaze on me, his eyes boring into the side of my head like a laser beam. I know what he's thinking because it's the same thing that's been on my mind since the Whisperlings were first mentioned.

I inhale deeply, seeking assurance from Rhyland. "We all have shadows," I murmur. "But we're here to save our realms."

"And yet," Faderyn adds, "even noble intentions can be clouded by fear or doubt. You need clarity of self."

The room falls into contemplation. Facing our deepest fears is a daunting prospect. But if that's what it takes to save the realms, we'll do it.

"Is there any way to prepare for a Whisperling?" Erik asks.

Axilya considers. "Ignore them," she says simply.

Rhyland's thumb brushes mine, a silent vow that we'll face this together.

King Oberon rises. "We will offer guidance. Let us break and reconvene."

I ponder what he might offer to help us.

"But know this: The journey will test you in ways you cannot fathom," Oberon warns.

Servants enter with trays of refreshments, signaling the end of our meeting. We stand, an eclectic mix bound by a common goal. The Fae nobility bows respectfully as we take our leave, a sign of the gravity of the task that lies ahead.

Outside the chamber, Rhyland pulls me into an alcove shadowed by prying eyes. His piercing blue eyes hold a direct challenge as he leans in close, his breath hot against my skin. "You sure you're up for this?" he rumbles, demanding my certainty.

His eyes search mine, looking for proof that I'm solid in my determination. I meet his gaze head-on, making sure my eyes don't betray even a shred of doubt. "I'm ready," I say with force, my voice carrying a confidence that I'm desperate is real and not just bluster. It's my own private pep talk, a way to lock down my courage before whatever comes next.

Rhyland nods once, a gesture of acceptance and understanding, before pulling me into an embrace. His arms are like a fortress around me, a shield against whatever fears lurk in my mind's shadows.

Lucian claps dramatically, the king of sass, even in the face of looming danger. "Alrighty then," he declares, a grin plastered on his face. "Time to go have a lovely little chat with some ancient, uptight, mythological assholes. I'm sure they'll be absolutely thrilled to see us."

He rubs his hands together in mock anticipation, eyebrows waggling. "Think they'll offer us some tea and crumpets while we swap war stories?"

Erik steps forward, his gravity anchoring his words. "We take repose tonight," he says, his voice as steady as a mountain. "At dawn, we embark on those mountains."

RHYLAND

44

As Lucian and Erik stride away, a cold dread latches onto my spine like a vise grip, squeezing the life out of me. Dani's stubborn belief that the stone is hidden in the Crystal Peaks cranks up the tension tearing through my body, setting every nerve on fire. The horror stories about the Whisperlings mess with my head—their illusions are as deadly as the peaks are steep, a one-way ticket to insanity.

I'm rooted to the ground like an oak tree, but my head's a war zone, fears storming in like berserkers, ready to tear me apart from the inside out. They say those Whisperlings come at you with the darkest, most twisted fears you've buried deep down, weaving traps so convincing you could lose your mind in them for a hundred years. The beast inside me snarls a deep, guttural rumble that reverberates through my chest, desperate to jump into the fight and surrender to the hunger for blood and that wild, untamed pull of pure instinct.

Dani locks eyes with me, her keen, honey-gold gaze cutting through the bullshit, seeing right to my core. "You okay?" she asks, knifing through the room's dying reverberations, cutting through the chaos in my head like a beacon in the dark.

I falter, my words stumbling out like clumsy, drunken soldiers. "Yeah, I'm fine," I bluff, the lie tasting bitter on my tongue. But who am I kidding? Thanks to our bond, she calls my bluff without a word, her eyes narrowing in that way that tells me she sees right through my tough-guy act.

Her gaze sharpens as she moves in close, putting distance between us and any nosy onlookers. "Rhyland..." she insists, her voice laced with an intensity that cuts straight through the crap, leaving no room for anything but the raw, unfiltered truth.

My defenses shatter, the walls I've built crumbling under the onslaught of dread threatening to drown me. "It's those Whisperlings," I admit, my voice rough with emotion. "What if..." I pause, hating how vulnerable I feel. "They could make me lose control, make me lose you."

But Dani stands firm, undaunted by my towering form, by the fear eating me alive. Her response is fierce, her voice a fortress of certainty. "I thought the same thing back there," she says, her eyes blazing with determination. "But Rhyland, I swear nothing like that's gonna happen. I won't let anything happen to you." It's a pledge tying her fate to mine, a promise she'll fight to keep.

I chuckle wryly, shaking my head at her boldness, at the sheer audacity of this woman. "You've got it twisted, Angel," I tell her, my voice low and rough. "It's my job to protect you, to keep you safe from all the shit out there."

But Dani just smirks, sass practically oozing from every pore as she prods at my chest with a slender finger. "Try and keep up then," she teases, her voice light and playful, a challenge wrapped in jest. Her sass is a godsend when my inner storm tries to tear everything to shreds and the darkness threatens to swallow me whole.

"Keep up?" I let out a low, mocking chuckle, my voice heavy with challenge. "Baby, I set the pace. And you better believe I'm gonna make sure you keep up every step of the way."

Her laughter rings out, a melody as potent as a spell, taming the wild beast raging in my core. "Sure you do, Viking," she teases, punctuating it with a wink that makes my blood run hot.

I lean in close, nearly nose to nose—my voice a low rumble meant just for her. "Is that a challenge, baby?"

Dani's grin turns wicked, her eyes roving over me in a way that makes my muscles tense with want. "Maybe it is," she purrs. "Think you can handle me?"

I bite back a growl, my hands itching to grasp her. But we aren't alone, and I force myself to take a measured step back.

"Careful, Angel," I warn, my tone husky with desire. "You don't want a repeat of last night, do you? Not here."

Before I can react, she's in front of me, grabbing fistfuls of my hair and yanking me down into a searing kiss.

For a moment, my mind blanks, lost in the taste and feel of her. Then instinct roars to life, and I wrap my arm around Dani's waist, hauling her close. I devour her mouth greedily, heedless of our audience. Her soft curves mold to my body, and she moans against my lips. The sound nearly shatters my restraint.

With effort, I break the kiss, my breathing ragged. Dani's eyes are glazed, and her lips are kiss-swollen. Gods—the way she tests my control.

"Minx," I rasp. "What's gotten into you?"

A serious crease forms between Dani's brows, her features hardening with resolve. "I need this, Rhyland. Need you close," she says, her words laced with urgency. She lays a hand over my heart, the warmth of her touch searing through me. "I won't lose you," she vows, her determination unyielding.

She meets my gaze squarely, her voice playful but challenging. "Now, try not to slow me down, Viking," she dares with a sly smile. "I've got realms to save, and I need you at your best."

Fuck me sideways. This woman is a no-bullshit force of nature. She doesn't hesitate to kick my ass into gear when I need it. My cock twitches.

Dani slips out of my hold and struts off, her hips rolling with each step. I'm rooted to the spot, mesmerized, until she vanishes down the hallway. A low chuckle bursts from me. Even with all the beasts around, my mate's the fiercest of them all.

I shout after her, "That's all you got, Angel?"

Her laughter answers, bright and teasing, bouncing back to me. "Wouldn't you like to know!"

DANICA

45

Refueled and refreshed from lunch, we congregate once more in the heart of Oberon's domain after turning the Sun Court's courtyards into our personal racetrack. His vast chambers, echoing with the whispers of countless secrets, welcome us back like the stage awaiting the pivotal second act of a grand play.

I unroll the worn map carefully, its edges softened and frayed by time and touch. A complex network of routes to the Crystal Peaks sprawls before us like the veins of a fated quest, a tangled web of destiny waiting to be unraveled. We huddle around the sacred parchment as if it's a mysterious relic that could inspire avid treasure hunters—and give Indiana Jones himself a moment of awe-struck pause.

King Oberon leans over the map with a knowing glimmer in his eye, his expression as sage as a wizened old oak. "This artifact possesses enchanting properties," he intones, his voice heavy with the weight of unspoken history. "It is imbued with magic."

The statement hangs densely in the air, pregnant with possibilities and secrets. My forehead creases lightly as I try to decipher his meaning, my mind racing with questions and theories. "Magical abilities?" I ask, my tone mingling with skepticism and curiosity.

Oberon's fingers hover above the map, and with a single tap near the ominous Crystal Peaks, the flat expanse suddenly springs to life. It's like watching a magical pop-up book unfold before our eyes, trails stretching upwards and mountains ascending from the parchment-like miniature giants. Valleys dip into palpable depressions, creating a landscape that looks almost real enough to touch.

Our mouths agape, we watch as a mini-world rises from the table as some sort of Hogwarts homework assignment comes to life. It's a sight that leaves us speechless, more gobsmacked than a gaggle of geese in a glitter factory.

I reach out tentatively, half-expecting my hand to pass right through the illusory terrain. But to my surprise, my fingers meet resistance, and the peaks and valleys feel as solid as the real thing. It's like holding a piece of the world in the palm of my hand, a tangible reminder of the quest that lies ahead.

"This is incredible," I breathe, my voice hushed with wonder. "I've never seen anything like it."

Rhyland leans in closer, his eyes narrowing in concentration as he studies the map. "That's new," he murmurs, his tone equal parts admiration and wariness. "But what does it mean for our journey?"

Oberon smiles enigmatically, his expression inscrutable. "The map will guide you," he says simply, "if you know how to read it."

Lucian snorts, "Great, another riddle," he mutters, rolling his eyes. "Just what we need."

But Erik is already studying the map intently; his brow furrows in concentration. "There are hidden paths here," he says slowly, tracing a finger along a barely visible trail. "Routes that could take us through the mountains unseen."

Out of nowhere, a voice cuts through the hushed silence, narrating lore that feels like skipping history classes. It weaves a narrative around the floating landscape, and we're all ears, caught in the story's spell, hanging on every word.

When the voice trails off, my gaze swings to Oberon, my mind dazed and reeling. My face must be a canvas of shock, eyebrows high and eyes wide as saucers because, really, who saw that coming?

"The map bestows understanding of each depicted region," Oberon explains calmly. "Through this magic, we've gleaned knowledge of such a perilous area and the grim fate of those who journeyed there, for none have lived to tell the tale."

Lucian arches an eyebrow, watching the map with a smirk. "Well, that's one way to show off your Google Earth skills, Your Majesty," he quips. "Any chance of a mini-dragon popping up for the full theme park experience?"

"Sure, Lucian, dragons hibernating under the 'Here Be Dragons' sign," I say sarcastically. "And if we're really lucky, His Majesty will throw in a souvenir photo op."

"Well, aren't you sharp today, Princess? I might need to check your pulse—that deadpan delivery is inhuman," Lucian tosses back, unabashed mirth dancing in his eyes. "But you can keep the tacky photo—I prefer my memories non-tacky, and the only shop I want to visit is the one that serves decent Bloody Marys."

I give Lucian a quick eye roll. "You and your damn mouth."

Shaking my head, I return to the now flattened map. It's time to study it—maps, stones, realms to save.

The journey stretches through the Whispering Woods, past Mirror Lake, skirting the Shardfall Cascade before ascending the peaks. It's a route as daunting as it is beautiful, a testament to the wild and untamed nature of the realm we're about to enter.

Erik leans in, his silver eyes scanning the terrain with hawk-like intensity. "We should take the Northern Pass through Eldergrove Forest," he suggests, nodding toward a densely shaded area.

Lucian scoffs lightly. "Oh, sure, more trees than a squirrel convention. What could possibly go wrong?"

"What, you prefer an open field for your tan?" I shoot back sarcastically.

He grins wickedly. "Babe, I'm already golden," he purrs, leaning over the map to point to a narrow strip of land. "Right through here. Fool's Pass. Only an idiot would take that route."

"Or someone with nothing to lose," I quip.

Rhyland chuckles, his hand finding the small of my back. "I think we'll keep our wits about us and take the Spectre Vales around Frost Weaver Hallows."

Faderyn traces a different route. "The path through Silverglade Valley is more direct," he suggests. "Though not without its own risks."

Axilya nods thoughtfully. "The Lynx Eyes coven watches over Silverglade. They are not fond of trespassers."

"Witches? Here?" I blurt out, my eyes widening with shock and curiosity.

Erik's gaze doesn't waver from the map. "Witches are everywhere, Little Huntress. We can handle a few witches."

Lucian snorts, his eyebrows raised in a look of mock horror. "Speak for yourself, Sir Broods-a-Lot. I'd rather not have my handsome face cursed off by some disgruntled hag with a wart collection."

"You're assuming they'd find anything worth cursing," I tease, lips twitching.

He winks at me. "You wound me, Princess. And here I thought you appreciated my rugged good looks and charming wit."

Rhyland grunts disapprovingly but can't hide his smirk. His protective arm tightens around me slightly. "We'll take The Spectre Vales—it avoids confrontations and keeps us out of sight."

"And here I was, looking forward to getting hexed," I say dryly.

"Your disappointment is palpable," Faderyn remarks with a soft smile. "We should prepare provisions and gear," he suggests.

I silently agree, excitement thrumming through my veins at the thought of action.

The king and queen exchange a look before turning back. "We cannot accompany you," Oberon announces solemnly.

"We understand," Rhyland replies with a respectful nod.

"Your Majesty," I ask, curiosity heavy in my voice. "Why entrust me with this map when others braving the Peaks didn't get the honor?"

Oberon nods slowly. "Because I trust you, Lady Danica, will defy expectation and return with it," he states, his voice laced with confidence.

Queen Titania steps forward. "May your bonds remain strong and spirits undeterred."

Axilya stands gracefully. "We depart at dawn on horseback."

I grimace at the thought of *more* saddle hours. My horseback memories are more bruises than wind-blown freedom.

"Great," I grumble with dry humor. "More medieval pony trekking—my ass is filing a grievance as we speak."

Rhyland moves in close, breath warm against my ear. "I'll take care of that sweet ass, baby," he murmurs with a promise that sends my pulse racing.

Heat rushes to my cheeks as I try to compose myself. With a cough, I attempt to banish his risqué words, clearing my throat feebly to steer us back to innocence.

I suggest teleporting to save time, but Faderyn quickly dismisses that idea—it's too "dangerous" without pinpoint accuracy.

I nod reluctantly; I haven't mastered popping in and out anyway.

"No shit," Lucian chimes in. "We don't want to end up in some twisted Narnia."

"So through Spectre Vales, up Whispering Woods, left through Frost Weaver Hallows, and hit the Peaks, right?" I ask, tracing my finger along the faded parchment.

Rhyland leans over my shoulder, breath tickling my neck. "That sums it up, Angel—think you can handle some saddle days?"

I wrinkle my nose. "If it means that stone and saving your fine ass, I'll suffer anything."

Rhyland chuckles, that sexy laugh making my knees weak.

Focus, Dani.

Faderyn's posture radiates resolve. "I'll spare no effort to alleviate this odyssey's burdens."

Lucian cocks a brow, lips curving into a wry smirk. "Damn, Tinkerbell's getting heroic. Just sprinkle some pixie dust when shit hits."

Axilya's eyes sparkle with sass. "Worry not, Lucian. Faderyn's *dust* could teach you a lesson or two."

Lucian smirks, unfazed. "Sweet burn, Ax. But let's hope Faderyn's dust packs a punch. My charm can't do all the work."

Erik remains silent, arms crossed. Mr. Stoic isn't for conversation, but I know he has our back if things get dicey.

Rhyland's voice booms, echoing with command. "It's settled then. We leave at first light."

My big, bad alpha is in battle mode, sights set on victory. And me? I'll be right by his side, ready to face any nightmare. It's us against the world.

DANICA

46

Cracking my eyes open, soft hues of dawn creep through my curtains, painting the room in a gentle, rosy glow. But it's the sight of Rhyland, sprawled across the pillows like a Viking god, that truly steals my breath. I can't resist running my fingers through his jet-black hair, marveling at the silky strands that slip through my fingers like water—hell, who could blame me?

His eyelids flutter open, and that voice, low and raspy with sleep, wraps around me like a warm embrace. "Good morning, Angel." And just like that, I'm melting, my insides turning to goo at the sound of his voice, at the way his eyes crinkle at the corners when he smiles.

He stretches, muscles rolling under his golden skin—the kind of display that's nothing short of criminally divine. I drink in the sight of him, my eyes roaming over every inch of his godlike physique, committing every detail to memory.

Suddenly, he's on me, swift as a predator, his arms tight around my waist as he pulls me against his body. I let out a squeal of surprise that quickly turns into a laugh, my heart racing with excitement and anticipation.

"Seems like you're itching for another round of 'hands-on' with yours truly," I quip, my chuckles vibrating into his torso as I snuggle closer, relishing the feel of his solid body against mine. "Good morning to you, too, ya big lug."

His laugh rumbles against my cheek, a deep, captivating vibration that makes my breath catch in my throat. "Angel, it's not so much an itch as a certainty—a Viking pledges to conquer what's his," he murmurs, his blue eyes glinting with playful light and the unmistakable flare of ancient possessiveness. "And I take pleasure in my victories... especially when they involve you."

Giddy at his words, the promise and threat they hold, my body responds to his nearness with a flush of heat. But before I can lose myself in the intoxicating pull of his presence, Alina's persistent tapping at the door brings reality crashing back.

"Duty calls," I murmur into the nest of Rhyland's neck, smiling against his skin, treasuring our moment even as it slips away.

He responds the only way he can—turning a simple farewell into a kiss that scorches everything from my mind. His lips claim mine with a fierce intensity, leaving me breathless and weak in the knees. The world narrows down to the press of his body against mine, the slide of his tongue, and the overwhelming power of his presence.

Alina's insistence becomes distant drumming as my senses are saturated with Rhyland—his taste, feel, scent, and the overwhelming power of his presence. For a moment, I forget about everything else—about the Sun Court and the trials that lie ahead, about the destiny that hangs heavy on my shoulders.

For a moment, there is only this—only the two of us, lost in each other, wrapped up in a cocoon of passion and desire and something deeper that feels like forever.

Yet duty is indeed relentless, and despite the magnetic chaos of his kiss, we can't ignore it indefinitely. When he finally breaks away, the words "Not until I've had my kiss first" linger in the air like a challenge he's just conquered, his possessiveness wrapped in a smirk that knows no equal.

With a mischievous glint and a sigh for the reprieve that will have to wait, I slide out of Rhyland's grasp and sweep toward the door.

It swings open to reveal Alina cradling a surprise that practically whispers sinful luxury. "Good morning, My Lady. I have something for you," Alina announces, her voice smooth as silk and sharp as polished steel, holding the sartorial equivalent of a decadent secret.

Rhyland sweeps by me with that commanding air he always carries like a cloak, his hand connecting with my ass in a casual yet possessive squeeze. "I'll be right down the hall. Gonna get dressed," he declares firmly, leaving an unspoken promise that he's never too far away.

As Alina reveals the contents, the leather unfurls like a flag of some chic warrior tribe. My gaze takes it all in—a sumptuous, buttery brown leather that looks like it would mold to my body with a tailor's devotion. This is not just any outfit, but a holy grail of badassery, boasting a second-skin fit that promises to accentuate every asset without crossing into R-rated fantasy clichés.

"Damn," I breathe out, a smirk playing on my lips. "Alina, these are—"

"Perfect? I know." Her smile holds a hint of pride as she hands them over. "They're designed for mobility and... distraction."

I duck behind the dressing wall, kissing any lingering leather loathing goodbye. It's funny how Whispervale's swanky, ass-kicking gear can turn a skeptic into a devotee. I had to hand it to those talented fae folk—it turns out that knowing your way around a needle and thread or whatever magic they did makes for some seriously sweet battle wear.

I shimmy into the pants, snug but never stifling. Mobility is the new brown, baby; I'm rocking it. Who knew I'd have a love affair with animal hide?

The zipper on my top, coy and unapologetic in its promise, halts with precision, daring all eyes to wander but not too far. The pockets—those clever little thigh-huggers—begging for the kiss of cold steel. I oblige, slipping my daggers in with a delicious *snick*.

Emerging from my impromptu fortress of solitude, I strut out—daggered, leathered, and dangerously good-looking.

Alina insists on braiding my hair as if the leathers weren't enough to make me feel battle-ready. Her nimble fingers weave through my locks with a deftness that speaks of years of practice. When she's done, my long, brown tresses cascade down my back in intricate braids, some woven into the crown that looks like a work of art, keeping my hair out of my face in a practical and stunning style.

"There," she says, stepping back to admire her handiwork with a critical eye. "Now you're ready."

I turn to look at myself in the mirror and hardly recognize the woman staring back at me. Gone is the uncertain girl who stumbled into this world, replaced by a warrior queen with fire in her eyes and steel in her spine. The braids lend me an air of fierceness, strength, and determination, and I can't help but feel a surge of confidence at the sight.

I give Alina a grateful hug, my arms wrapping around her slender frame. "Thanks, Alina. I don't know what I'd do without you," I murmur, my voice thick with emotion.

She returns the hug with a gentle squeeze, her voice light and teasing. "You'd probably trip over your own hair and fall face-first into trouble," she quips with a wink.

I laugh, the sound bright and carefree. "You're probably right," I admit, shaking my head. "I've never been the most graceful of creatures."

Alina grins. "Well, that's what you have me for," she says warmly. "I'm here to keep you from falling on your face and ensure you look good doing it."

I smile, my heart swelling with gratitude for this unexpected friend, this ally, in a world of uncertainty. "I couldn't ask for a better partner in crime," I tell her sincerely.

She nods, her expression serious for a moment. "I know you have a lot on your shoulders, My Lady. But remember, you're not alone. You have people who care about you and believe in you. We'll be here for you, no matter what."

I feel a lump in my throat at her words. "Thank you, Alina," I whisper, swallowing past the knot. "That means more to me than you know."

She smiles, her eyes shining with warmth. "Anytime, My Lady. Now, let's get you out before they send out a search party."

With a final glance in the mirror at the warrior reflected there, I nod and head out to face whatever lies ahead, knowing I have allies beside me and a destiny to fulfill.

The stables are a hive of purposeful motion and restless energy, a symphony of snorts and hoofbeats serving as the morning's spirited overture. The air practically tingles with anticipation, charged enough to jolt any lingering threads of sleepiness awake.

I navigate the buzz of activity, weaving through the crowd of horses and handlers until I reach our designated stallion—a creature that could rival any of the Fae realms' legends. With a coat mirroring the midnight shades of Rhyland's locks, he's a sight that demands a pause, a little bit of awe, and maybe even a nod of respect.

"Hey there, big guy," I greet the equine beauty, extending a hand to pet his velvety nose with affection. My fingers gently stroke his soft muzzle, and I'm rewarded with a fond nuzzle. His massive head pushes gently against me, his breath warm and sweet against my skin. I can't help but laugh, pure and delighted, the sound echoing through the stables. "Looks like you're a charmer, huh?"

"Seems like someone's taken a liking to you," Rhyland's voice rumbles from my left, low and amused.

I glance up to find his beautiful cerulean eyes glinting with amusement, his lips quirking in a half-smile that sends flutters through my stomach. "He's just buttering me up for extra treats," I quip, voice light and teasing.

Rhyland chuckles and steps closer, his body a solid wall of heat and muscle beside me. "He told me he wants ear scratches," he says, his voice a low rumble that vibrates through me like a physical caress.

"Oh, did he now?" I raise an eyebrow before reaching up to oblige, my fingers finding the soft spot behind his ears and scratching gently. The stallion closes his eyes in bliss, his head drooping in contentment as I continue, clearly loving every second.

"What's his name?" I ask while continuing the ear massage, my voice soft and curious.

"Storm," Rhyland replies with a touch of pride, patting the horse's neck with familiarity.

I lean close to Storm's ear and whisper conspiratorially, my breath ruffling his mane. "Take care of me out there, and I'll take care of you," I promise, my voice earnest. The horse nods as if understanding our pact, his ears flicking forward in acknowledgment before he nibbles playfully at my hands.

"Easy there, handsome," I chide between bursts of laughter. "Save the sweet moves for the mares."

Rhyland watches the exchange, a silent, amused sentinel, his arms crossed over his broad chest, his eyes sparkling with warmth and affection. There's that familiar head-shake, the one that's all affectionate exasperation, and his smile cuts through any residual morning grumpiness like sunlight through a fog. And damn, if that smile doesn't just ratchet up his allure another ten notches, turning him from devastatingly handsome to absolutely irresistible.

Words? He doesn't bother with them, and why should he? The man oozes assurance from every pore—it's practically a crime how he can convey so much with just a look, a gesture, a quirk of his lips. His silent, smoldering presence is my brand of courage serum.

Rhyland is decked out in his battle leathers, the kind that clings to every muscle like a second skin, molding to his body as if made just for him. The ensemble accentuates his formidable build, highlighting his broad shoulders, the taper of his waist, and the powerful lines of his thighs. But it's his backside that really steals the show, the leather hugging his perfectly sculpted ass like a lover's caress, turning it into a work of art.

And admire I do as Rhyland turns to adjust the horse's reins—my eyes lingering on that part of his anatomy for a beat too long, my cheeks flushing with appreciation.

"Ready to mount up?" he asks after a moment, his voice low and rough. His eyes glint with a knowing look that says he knows where my thoughts have wandered.

"Yes," I manage to say, my voice only slightly breathless as I tear my gaze away from his leather-clad posterior and square my shoulders, preparing myself for the ascent.

Rhyland gently lifts me onto Storm's back. His hand lingers on my inner thigh before he swings himself up behind me.

Mounted in front of Rhyland, the closeness is downright sinful, his secure arms bracketing me, our bodies aligning with the kind of precision that speaks of many nights entwined.

"There, safe and sound, exactly where you belong—sitting on my cock."

I laugh. "Well, I suppose that's one way to make sure I'm not going anywhere," I fire back.

A low, satisfied growl vibrates from Rhyland as he squeezes me tight. "Oh, Angel, I've got plenty of ways to keep you right where I want you," he says, his voice thick with innuendo. "But a hands-on approach always works best with a fiery little thing like you."

Round two of this horseback riding journey with Rhyland at my back. My hands rest on my thighs in a position of relaxed readiness—a posture befitting the oddball heroine I've become.

Last night, I handed out my signature O-neg cocktail to Erik and Lucian, ensuring they were fortified—the vampire's equivalent to a knight's shining armor. As for Rhyland, I enjoyed his sips directly from the source. I also enjoyed my own personal 'O' directly from *his* source.

Mr. Stoic gives us a nod, his silver eyes betraying a flicker of amusement.

Lucian, with all the charm of nightclub royalty and sass to match, flashes a grin that says he's probably cooked up a snarky remark he'll share later.

Faderyn, looking like he stepped out of a dream to join us, and Axilya, with a commanding presence that could make a grown man rethink his life choices, all bathed in the burgeoning light of dawn.

The first proper rays of sunlight embrace us, a golden draping worthy of any legendary tableau. And right at the heart of it, there's me—straddling Storm with Rhyland's heat at my back—feeling like a queen about to lead her quirky, powerful retinue into the pages of adventure.

DANICA

47

The ride's rhythm has been my constant companion, Storm's hooves laying down a beat that vibrates through my very core. We become a symphony of motion, a blend of muscle, sinew, and leather—wrapped in relentless purpose. Hours bleed together in a blur of landscapes and the ever-present thrum beneath us.

But then, a shudder ripples across my skin as we hit a glitch in the world, like walking face-first through an unexpected cobweb. It's that moment of ick amplified by a thousand, yet there's no spider, just the eerie caress of magic.

"Did anyone else feel that?" I glance back at Rhyland with raised brows.

"We've just breached the protective runes," Faderyn calls out from horseback, a few paces to our left. "We are no longer covered under their protection." His emerald eyes reflect the sudden alertness that overtakes us all.

The forest around us seems to awaken. Ancient trees stretch their limbs toward the sky, bathed in sunlight filtering through leaves of emerald and gold. It's as if we've entered a realm where nature itself has conjured enchantments.

As the strange sensations ebb, a new one blossoms—the press of Rhyland against my back, his arms forming a bastion of strength around me. He leans in, his voice a gritty thunder against my ear. "How are you holding up, Angel?"

Despite eyes watching us, I allow myself to savor the closeness. There's something grounding about his hold, a quiet reassurance that seeps into my bones.

"If you keep holding me like this, I'll be more than fine," I quip back softly, just for him, angling myself into the solidity of his frame.

But I know what he's asking—how I'm coping with the magical unknown we've stumbled into—so I give a little nod of assurance. "I'm good," I confirm, volume back to normal. "But if this enchanted forest tries any funny business, I'm letting you handle it. You can be my knight in leather armor." It's a gentle tease, my way of saying I feel safe under his protection, even as we venture deeper into a realm ruled by ancient forces.

Rhyland chuckles, the sound vibrating through me. "And deprive the world of seeing you kick ass in enchanted forests? Never." His grip tightens slightly, adding weight to his words. "Besides," he adds, his breath warm on my neck, "you shine brightest when you show me up. How could I take that away from you, kära?"

Curiosity colors my voice as I tilt my head slightly. "And what's 'kära'? You've never called me that before."

He pauses, a teasing in his tone. "It's a term of endearment from my old world, meaning beloved or dear one." His words drip with a baritone richness, a hint of an ancient Norse accent wrapping around the word like a caress. "But for you, it could also mean 'feisty little temptress who has a Viking under her spell,'" he adds with a playful growl, his lips close enough to tease the shell of my ear.

His arms constrict gently, reinforcing the word's weight with his unyielding presence. His tone is playful and dominating, a reminder that he's a force to be reckoned with—a protector from times when the word meant a fierce guardian of heart and body. "Get used to it, kära, because I have a feeling there are many more ancient endearments I've yet to call you."

His words, steeped in affection and a trace of that owning, dominating charm, are enough to heat my cheeks and raise the ante in our playful exchange. If this were a sparring match, Rhyland's verbal volley would have the crowd roaring.

"We'll reach the Spectre Vales by nightfall," Faderyn calls out from ahead. "A day's ride."

Curiosity nibbles at me, and I pull out the map from the saddlebag. I touch the spot for the Spectre Vales, activating its magic. The map ripples, its surface shimmering like a storyteller clearing his throat before weaving his tale.

"In a land cloaked in eternal twilight," the map begins in its 'once upon a time' voice, *"lie the Spectre Vales of Crystal Peaks. Here, pale wisps of mist cradle secrets and confound the senses. Beware the Whisperlings that merge with the fog; they entangle thoughts and lead wayfarers astray."*

A knot tightens in my stomach with each revelation from the map, its whispers painting a foreboding picture. Just the thought of Rhyland and those ghostly Whisperlings sends a cold shiver skittering up my spine.

I tuck the map away, but its warnings stay with me, making me hyperaware of Rhyland's presence.

Sensing the shift in my mood, he dips his head, his breath warm against my neck. "I've got all the protection I need right here." His lips graze my skin in a tender and fierce kiss, a silent oath that my worries are his to bear. He feels each flutter of apprehension through our bond, just as I sense his steadfast resolve flowing back.

I melt into that brief moment of intimacy, drawing strength from our shared connection. Whatever dangers lurk ahead, we'll face them together. He is my shelter in the storm, just as I am his guiding light. With Rhyland beside me, I can face whatever storm comes.

Craning my neck, I find his fathomless blue eyes—calm seas and raging tempests captured in twin spheres. "Betcha your ass," I volley back with a hint of sass. But letting truth slip in, I add softly, "I won't let anything happen to you."

Rhyland's laughter rumbles through me, rich and gritty like aged whiskey. "Angel, it's them who should be worried about me."

"Out of curiosity, does your...power extend to, let's say, invisible entities? Or is it just the tangible stuff you can influence?" My scientific mind itches to know the limits and mechanics of his telekinesis.

Rhyland exhales deeply as if gearing up for a lengthy explanation. "Honestly, as far as I've determined, my power is effective only on physical things. What's got you asking?"

My thoughts circle back to that terrifying day in the forest when Marcus took me, and Azrael joined the fray. I remember the helplessness I felt as Rhyland struggled against the intangible forces. That memory makes my heart beat faster with worry.

What if the Whisperlings can bypass Rhyland's defenses, too?

Putting on a brave face, I try to mask my concern with humor. "I'm basically getting my PhD in Telekinesis 101, courtesy of Professor Vampire."

Rhyland doesn't miss the undertone of distress. "You're about as transparent as crystal, Angel. Spill it. What's gnawing at that brilliant mind of yours?"

I take a deep breath. "You couldn't touch Azrael's shadows," I start, my wit retreating in the face of my fears, "and that scares me. If the Whisperlings are anything like that—I can't bear the thought of anything happening to you." My voice cracks, the final words barely whispered.

Rhyland becomes a solid, reassuring force. His hand lifts my face, making me meet his gaze—his eyes holding a tempest of determination. "Listen to me," he says, his voice a low rumble charged with indomitable will. "I may not have been able to grip those damn shadows, but I've survived a millennium's worth of nightmares. No shadow, no Whisperling, nothing in this world or the next can take me down easily, especially with you by my side." He pauses, his thumb gently caressing my cheek. "I've got you, and I'll tear through whatever I must to keep you. That's a promise, and I don't break my fucking promises." His eyes blaze with fierce protectiveness, a silent vow in that intense gaze.

Leaning into the fortress that is Rhyland, I whisper, "I'll do whatever I can—I will let nothing happen to you."

It's our secret, a feisty pledge in the quiet of our shared moment. My mind races like a sprinter; shutting it off isn't an option.

We ride in silence for a while, his inhale drawing in the scent of my hair, trying to read my emotions. "Angel?" His voice hints at the powerful creature he is. "I can still feel your anxiety. Is there something... I need to do?"

I'm an open book to this man, unable to hide my inner turmoil. The fear that's grabbed me ever since those visions invaded my sleep—of him, consumed by shadows, Moretemis stealing him away, my Nordic Nightwalker is relentless. It's replaying repeatedly, and it's eating me up inside. He's always here, finding ways to steer my mind clear of those dark images.

I trust Rhyland to put an offer on the table as casually as if he's ordering a pint, utterly indifferent to the audience around us.

The mere idea sends a thrill down my spine, yet I can't help but blurt out, "Have you lost your marbles? Right here, right now?"

"If you don't relax, baby," he warns, the corner of his mouth ticking up in that cocky half-smile I know all too well, "then I'm just gonna have to find a way to relax you." The promise in his tone is as much of a caress as his gritty and unyieldingly flirty touch.

Oh no. What is with this man and PDA—X-Rated style?

My body tenses up instantly as I quickly survey our crew. We're spearheading the group, with Faderyn at our six, diligently covering our backs. Erik holds our left side, ever the stoic guardian, while Lucian's on our right, no doubt ready with a quip. And falling into place, Axilya assumes the rear.

"Rhy—" But before I can even get my protest out...

"We're going to ride ahead a bit. Give us some room," he asserts in no uncertain terms, then nudges Storm into a swift gallop, widening the gap between us and our companions.

"Oh, for the love of all that is *HOLY*. Are you for real right now, bro?" Lucian whines.

I hear Erik's voice fading into the distance before it becomes inaudible, "Zip it, Lucian. No one needs to hear your bitchy commentary."

Rhyland spurs Storm forward, leaving a trail of dust and distance. The forest boughs lace together above, dappling us with cool shade speckles as Storm drops leisurely.

"Rhyland, this is hardly the time for....*that.* There are more pressing matters, and let's not forget, we're not exactly alone," I chide him, rolling my eyes.

Rhyland laughs, full of confidence. "Since when the hell does an audience stop me, Angel? You must've forgotten our little escapade the other night and the night in the forest already," he quips, leaning in and kissing my neck. I roll my eyes harder as he pulls me roughly against his chest, "I need you to relax," he growls in my ear.

His hand slowly reaches the front zipper of my vest, "and what better way to do that..." With a quick tug, it's undone. Before I can protest, his hand is cupping my bare breast, and I can't help but let out a soft moan as my nipple hardens at his touch. "Than to make you fucking come?"

My eyes flutter shut as I surrender to the sensation. "Godsdamn, you're so responsive," he mutters, his fingers pinching and plucking at my hard nipple. "You're gonna come for me, aren't you?" he says with a smirk, and I can't help but nod in agreement, my body already responding to his touch.

"Yeah, you are. Here. Hold the reins." I snatch the reins from Rhyland's grip with lightning speed, and before I know it, his other hand is making a beeline for the front of my pants. "You better lean back and give me that pretty pussy, sweetheart," he demands in that rough tone.

All I can do is comply as Rhyland makes good on his promise of pleasure.

RHYLAND

48

The Spectre Vales envelops us like a predatory beast, the thick fog coiling around our legs like ghostly tendrils, almost as if it's got a mind of its own, hell-bent on choking the life out of us.

I swing down from Storm, my boots hitting the spongy ground with a muted thud, the sound swallowed up by the heavy, eerie silence. I help Dani down gently, ensuring she's steady.

That's when the whispers start, needling at the corners of my thoughts, wriggling and clawing to get in, to find a chink in my mental armor. I know I've got to block them out, can't let them get their hooks in me, or I'm fucked. I clench my jaw, breathing deep and centering my mind, focusing on the solid weight of Dani's presence beside me. The whispers intensify, their insidious voices growing louder, more insistent, but I push back harder, fortifying my defenses, refusing to let them breach the walls I've built.

Not today, you slippery bastards. Not on my fucking watch.

I secure Dani next to me, one arm wrapped tight around her waist, while I grab Storm's reins with the other, leading him by hand through this soupy mess of a landscape. I'm hyper-focused on each mundane task, using simple actions to keep my mind grounded to keep the whispers at bay. They hiss and flutter at the edges of my consciousness, testing my walls for weakness, probing for any crack they can slither through. But I'm not having it, not now, not ever.

The cold bites at my skin, a bone-deep chill that seeps into my marrow. Even with my vampire edge and my heightened senses, I can hardly see shit through this dense, ghostly shroud that blankets everything. Each step is silent on this spongy earth, saturated with the weight of untold mysteries.

The whispers continue to tease at the edges of my mind, slithering and insistent, a siren's call threatening to drag me under, to drown me in their lies and deceptions. But I grit my teeth and focus, ignoring their call, refusing to let them sway me from my path.

Dani's soft touch sweeps across my cheek, her voice cutting through the whispers' clamoring drone like a blade through gossamer. "Hey, keep your focus on me, got it?"

Her golden eyes, which somehow seem to glow in this pitch-black abyss, lock onto mine, their warmth a beacon shining through the spectral fog that shrouds my thoughts, threatening to lead me astray. I press into her palm, letting her presence strengthen my resolve, letting her touch anchor me to what's real and matters.

"I've got you, Rhyland," she says, her thumb grazing my jaw in a delicate sweep. The simple touch is a balm to my frayed nerves, a lifeline in this sea of shadows.

I clasp her hand in mine, bringing her wrist to my mouth and pressing a hard kiss against her pulse point, staking my claim, making it clear to the wraiths clawing their way into my head that she is mine, that nothing they whisper can change that unshakable truth. With my woman beside me, I can take on anything—mist, shadows, lies—it doesn't fucking matter. She keeps me steady, guides me through the dark when I need it most, and I'll be damned if I don't protect the shelter she provides, whatever it takes.

A frustrated snarl tears from my throat like a feral growl. "Can't see a fucking thing," I grumble, my eyes straining to pierce the goddamned nothingness that stretches out in front of us, an endless sea of swirling gray mocking our every step.

"It's like wading through a dream," Dani comments, her sunlit eyes capturing the scarce twinkles of starlight that muster the courage to slice through the mist. With a thought, a sphere of light flickers to life in her hand, washing her features in gentle radiance and sending shadows skittering playfully over her body, creating a mesmerizing dance of light and dark.

"Better than fumbling around blind," I admit, as the orb's light slices through the pitch-black, guiding us to a place where we can bunk down for the night. Its glow is a damn sight better than trying to navigate this soupy mess without it, a beacon in the darkness that promises a modicum of safety, however fleeting.

We find a clearing surrounded by trees, their twisted branches stretching out like skeletal hands clawing through the fog. It's not much, but it'll work for now—a brief break from the Vales' constant assault on our minds. I tie up the horses as we settle in, my senses on high alert for anything moving through these cursed mists, every muscle locked and ready to strike at the first fucking sign of a threat. I can't ease up, not for a damn second. Morning's gonna bring more spectral bullshit, another round of mind-fuckery we'll have to fight through. But we'll handle it together, no matter what gets thrown at us. Our connection is our armor against the Vales' poisonous whispers. Right now though, rest is what we need—time to recharge and rebuild our defenses.

Lucian wanders off into the fog, his form swallowed by the swirling mists, only to return moments later with an armful of damp wood and a triumphant grin on his face. "Great," he quips, dropping the wood with a smirk. "Who's ready for some smoke signals?"

I roll my eyes but can't suppress a low chuckle, the sound rumbling in my chest. "You'd find humor in your own funeral, you cheeky bastard." Lucian's mind-tricking magic can probably block out these damn whispers as if it's nothing, as easy as breathing. His ability to compel, to bend others to his will, probably gives him the edge to just slam the door in their fucking faces, leaving them scrabbling uselessly at his mental walls.

"Please," he scoffs, mock offense evident. "My funeral would be the event of the century, a spectacle for the ages. I'd make sure of it."

Erik remains silent as always, his silver gaze scanning the Vales as if he can see through this cursed fog. His keen senses pick up on things the rest of us can only guess at. He's a rock, unshakable and steadfast, a silent guardian watching over us all.

Axilya watches Lucian with an amused tilt of her lips, her light-green eyes sparkling with mirth. "Do you ever tire of your voice, or is it a constant source of entertainment for you?"

"Never," Lucian shoots back with a grin, his teeth flashing white in the gloom. "It's music to my ears, a symphony of wit and charm that I can't get enough of."

Faderyn clears his throat softly, ever the voice of reason amidst the banter. "Perhaps we should discuss our approach to the Whispering Woods come morning? It would be wise to have a plan in place before we venture further into their depths."

I sit down beside Dani on our makeshift bed, welcoming her warmth against my side as I listen to Faderyn's suggestions. His words are a grounding force amidst the Vales' eerie whispers.

"We'll need to traverse the Northern Pass," Erik finally says, his voice calm but authoritative, leaving no room for argument. "It's treacherous but direct, the quickest path through the woods."

"And boring," Lucian interjects while striking flint to steel, attempting to ignite a spark. "We could always scale the eastern ridge for a bit of excitement, add some spice to this dreary journey."

"Or plummet to our deaths," I counter dryly. "Let's stick with Erik's plan, which doesn't involve us risking our necks for your amusement."

Axilya nods in agreement, her expression serious. "The Northern Pass is wise. We should conserve our strength for what awaits us in the Whispering Woods. The challenges there will be formidable enough without us expending energy unnecessarily."

Lucian finally gets a flame going, grinning like he just won the damn lottery as he throws more wood on it, coaxing it into a real fire. The heat is a fucking godsend after the Vales' icy grip, a small mercy in this cursed-ass landscape.

Axilya stretches out her legs with fluid grace, her slender frame elegant even at rest. "Rest is essential tonight; we face more than just physical challenges ahead. The Vales will test our minds and spirits as much as our bodies."

After the meal, with the food we managed to carry along now settling heavily in our stomachs, Dani and I settle down on the scratchy bedroll, our bodies instinctively seeking each other's warmth. I pull her against me, my larger frame fitting against hers as we huddle near the fire, its glow casting shifting shadows across us. Our closeness and the flames are all we've got to fight back against the Vales' freezing grip—a small pocket of heat and life in this eerie silence.

Looking down, I watch the fog twist and coil around us like a nest of cold, writhing snakes, its fingers reaching out like they're trying to trap us in their ghostly hold. This whole damn place is unsettling, a chill crawling across my skin like icy hands dragging down my spine. I tighten my grip on Dani, a silent promise to keep her warm, to protect her from this place's twisted, disturbing presence.

I lift my head to look at her, worry creasing my brow. "Are they... getting in your head?" I ask, needing to know she's not suffering through this alone, that I'm not the only one being tormented by the Vales' sick whispers.

Her brow furrows slightly as she describes the sensation, her voice soft but steady. "It's like a thousand pinpricks against my mind, a constant pressure trying to find a way in. But I'm holding them at bay, so they sound like they're underwater, distant, and muffled. It's all just garbled whispers right now, nothing clear enough to understand." She meets my gaze, her eyes reflecting the firelight, a silent reassurance that she's still fighting with me.

"Good." I kiss her cheek, my lips lingering against her soft skin. "Get some sleep, baby. I've got you." I lay back down, squeezing her close, my arms a protective barrier around her, a silent promise to keep her safe, to guard her dreams against the Vales' ghostly intrusions.

DANICA

49

"Danica!" The voice tears through the suffocating fog like a blade, drenched in terror and desperation—a cry that freezes my blood solid.

Emily.

My heart explodes into a frantic gallop as her scream pierces the heavy mist, a lifeline in this disorienting white nightmare. I jolt upright, eyes wild and searching through the impenetrable haze, hunting for any glimpse of her, any trace of where she is.

"Emily, where are you?!" I shriek, my voice fracturing with panic and dread. But the fog swallows my words whole, muffling them into useless noise, absorbing them into its hungry depths.

Then it comes again—Emily's scream, twisted with pure horror, a sound that liquefies my blood and sends my heart slamming against my ribs. "Danica! Please...help—"

The scream cuts off abruptly.

Panic floods my system, choking me as I lunge blindly into the mist. I'm desperate for anything—a shadow, a movement, *something*—to tell me where she is. Her cries are the only thing keeping me oriented in this blinding void, the only thread stopping me from completely losing it as despair claws at the edges of my mind.

"Emily!" I scream, but the heavy blanket of fog suffocates each plea, swallowing my words before they can travel more than a few feet.

Through the veil, shapes materialize—Rhyland and the others, sprawled out in an unnatural stupor, their bodies completely motionless, their faces eerily peaceful despite the horror closing in around us. Terror wraps around my heart like a fist, squeezing relentlessly.

Why can't they hear her? Why won't they wake up and help me?

"Dani!!" Emily's anguished wail explodes through the fog, a shock of pure adrenaline that catapults me forward. My feet slip on the damp ground as I stumble into the mist.

The fog writhes around me like it's alive—sentient, deliberate, feeding off my fear and confusion as it swallows every landmark in sight. My foot snags on a hidden root, and I eat dirt, hard. Each ragged breath crystallizes into ghostly vapor that the fog devours instantly, just another phantom swallowed by this nightmare.

I have to find her. I have to move. I have to—

Now.

"Emily! Where are you?" I call, cupping my hands around the radiant orb exploding to life in my palms—a tiny sun blazing with golden light. Under its glare, the world snaps into sharp focus—trees weeping with dew, the slick, treacherous ground beneath my feet, the twisted path coiling deeper into the suffocating mist.

"Dani! Oh god... please!" Her scream rips through me—raw, blood-curdling, so drenched in terror it feels like someone just cracked my ribs open.

I shove myself forward, my light tearing a violent path through the fog like a blade. "Emily! Hold on!" I scream back, my voice breaking apart under the weight of my own panic.

Even as I push myself past breaking point, even as I claw at the air for any sign of her, I can feel hopelessness creeping in like poison—the sickening realization that I might be too late, that I might have already lost her.

But I can't stop. I won't.

Despite everything screaming at me, a small voice in the back of my mind whispers—*what if this is Whisperling bullshit?* Some sadistic illusion designed to break me from the inside out? But her terror is too raw, too visceral, too gut-wrenchingly real to write off as a trick.

I reach out with every ounce of power I have, probing the air, hunting for any trace of deception. But all I find is her—her terrified essence, unmistakably familiar and painfully real, cutting through the fog like a scream.

Her shrieks ramp up with each passing second, each one a spike of adrenaline driving me forward, pushing me through the mist faster than I thought my body could move. She's close—I can feel it. Her desperation blazes like a flare through the suffocating white, and I claw toward it with everything I have.

Then I see it—a silhouette materializing from the fog. A lone mirror standing like an open wound in this twisted landscape, pulling me toward it with a force I can't fight.

Dread thrums through my veins as I approach, every instinct screaming that this thing is *wrong*—violently out of place, unnatural against everything around it.

I lock eyes with my reflection, and my blood turns to ice.

My face stares back at me—ghastly pale, hollowed out, eyes wide and drowning in terror. But the horror doesn't stop there. Emily materializes beside my reflection, her face wrecked with tears, eyes wild with desperation as Azrael's claws sink into her hair. He wrenches her head back with brutal force, his face twisted into a mask of pure cruelty, teeth bared in a smile ripped straight from a nightmare.

"Dani... help..." she whimpers, her voice cracked and broken, each syllable a shard of glass burying itself in my chest.

Rage detonates inside me—a supernova of fury that scorches through every nerve ending, consuming me from the inside out. I summon every shred of power I have, the air crackling and spitting with raw force as I lock blazing eyes with Azrael's reflection. My gaze is a promise. A threat.

"Let. Her. Go." Each word hits like thunder wrapped in steel—not a request, not a plea—a command.

But he just sneers—a vicious, contemptuous twist of his lips—while Emily sobs and thrashes in his iron grip, her body convulsing with raw terror. "Dani, open the fucking door—help me!" she screams, her voice ragged and shredded, ripping straight through my defenses.

Adrenaline turns my blood to fire. Without thinking, my palms slam against the cold glass with bone-jarring force. Emily's name tears from my throat in a jagged, anguished cry that echoes through the suffocating mist like a death knell.

But the glass doesn't break. It doesn't even crack.

And more importantly, where the hell is she?

The Playful Pint materializes like it heard some unspoken command—achingly familiar and utterly terrifying in its surreal normalcy. Power surges inside me, warm and insistent. I can shred this veil. I can tear through this barrier. I can get to her.

"Emily!" I bellow, hands splayed against the shimmering surface, my reflection warped and fractured by the portal. *Please see me. Please reach for me.*

Then Azrael's voice slices through everything—cruel, mocking. "Open the damn door, bitch, or your friend dies!" he snarls, his eyes glinting with something beyond malice, beyond darkness.

In a blink, he drives his fangs into Emily's neck, tearing through flesh like hot knives. Her scream pierces the barrier between us—pure, raw anguish—and it drops me to my knees. Blood pools beneath them in a spreading crimson tide, and the memory of his bite hits me like a freight train—that searing, excruciating burn I know all too well.

Vengeance surges through me like a tsunami, my power rising with it—the air humming and spitting with volatile energy. A storm inside me howling for blood.

"Let her go. *Now.*" My voice thunders across the barrier. Not a request.

Fury ignites me as I double down, forcing the portal wider—a luminescent threshold nearly ready to cross, a gateway to the hell that awaits me on the other side. But darkness slams down like a curtain, snuffing my light cold. A crushing weight anchors me in place as the air fills with Rhyland's grounding essence—that familiar, intoxicating scent that's both comforting and absolutely maddening in its steadiness.

"No, no, NO! Emily! NO—Let me go! She needs me!" I thrash against the iron grip pinning me in place, fighting like a wild thing, desperate to break free, to reach her, to tear Azrael apart with my bare hands before he destroys her.

But his grip only tightens, holding me back, trapping me in this nightmare while my best friend screams for help I can't give.

"Angel...stop. Listen to me..." His calm voice cuts through my panic, pulling me back from the edge. It's a lifeline in the chaos. "This isn't real, Dani."

I blink—and reality crashes back into focus. Only Rhyland stands before me. No dying, Emily. No Azrael.

The dam breaks.

I collapse onto the dewy grass, my body giving out completely as the sobs tear through me—violent, uncontrollable, tearing screams from my throat. Rhyland pulls me into his arms, wrapping me in a cocoon of solace and protection, holding me as I come apart, as my body convulses with the force of my grief and overwhelming relief. I cling to him desperately, my fingers digging into his shirt, needing to feel that he's real, that he's actually here, that this—*him*—is the truth and not another cruel deception.

For a long moment, I can't do anything but break in his arms, the weight of what I've just experienced crushing down on me with suffocating force.

"Are you s-sure?" I grip him tightly, searching for certainty.

His eyes lock onto mine. "Sure of what, Angel?"

"The mirror—Emily? D-did you not s-see them?" I stammer between shaky breaths.

"No, baby. There was nothing. You were opening a portal—I had to stop you."

But as the weight of my near-mistake crashes down on me, a sinister sound pierces the quiet—the black portal snapping open like a wound, a gateway to darkness that swallows the air itself.

Instinct propels Rhyland and me to our feet as Azrael and Adrian step through the swirling darkness into our world. Their faces are twisted with malice, their eyes glinting with something absolutely venomous and wrong.

I'm raging at myself for falling for the Whisperlings' mind games, for letting my guard down long enough for that traitorous bastard Adrian to slip through my defenses. Delving inward, I summon my power, white-hot flames wreathing my hands in crackling energy, a promise of retribution and vengeance.

"The hell with you," I snarl, launching my light to send them back. But it finds only empty air as Azrael's smoke bomb cloaks them in churning shadows. The cowards disappear like a noxious fart!

Shit!

Azrael's too cunning to let me own his ass a second time—not after I chucked him and his pet sorcerer through the portal before, a humiliating defeat he's sure to be itching to avenge. And now the bastards have pulled their disappearing act—no telling where they've scurried off to.

What fresh hell are they planning to unleash?

I catch my breath, ready to unleash profanities, but Rhyland's somber expression gives me pause. He's strategizing our next move.

Keeping my mouth shut and my temper reined in is wise for now. No sense fanning the flames of the dumpster fire we're currently standing in. I lift my gaze to Rhyland; he's just like a damn statue—unmoving.

Is it shock?

I stretch my hand out, brushing against his. "Rhyland...?"

His head tilts, eyes meeting mine—his beast rising to the surface.

Oh, shit, he's *pissed*.

"We've got a serious fucking problem."

RHYLAND

50

I'm absolutely boiling inside, each step back to camp heavy with rage. Dani can feel the silence between us, charged with the fury that's got my hands clenched tight at my sides. She let Azrael and Adrian slip through a fucking portal right in the middle of these damned Vales as if she laid out a welcome mat for those bastards.

How could she be so reckless?

I don't care what kind of mind tricks those Whisperling bastards pulled; she ought to have seen through it. If anyone was going to fall for their bullshit, I'd have thought it'd be me. But Dani?

The second we step into camp, it's clear everyone's on edge. Their heads snap up, alert and ready for a fight—proof they'd heard Dani's screams cutting through the Vales like a knife.

"What the hell happened?" Erik demands, his gaze sharp as it flicks between Dani and me, searching for answers. His stance is tense and vigilant, like a damn statue poised to spring into action.

I suck in a deep breath, reigning in the torrent of cuss words itching to break loose on Dani. "She opened a fucking portal. That's what," I spit out through clenched teeth. "Azrael and Adrian—they're here now because of it."

The group's reaction is instant—a shared intake of shocked breaths as they all grasp the gravity of the situation I've just laid bare. Dani starts to open her mouth, probably to let a flood of sorries spill out, but I cut that shit off quickly with a look that could slice through steel.

"Not now, Dani," I growl, my words like shards of ice. The fury simmers just beneath the surface but is held in check, barely. "You've put every single one of us at risk with...this."

I gesture widely with my arms. "Do you even realize the shitstorm you've just called down on us?"

Erik moves to speak up, "Rhyland, she—"

I silence him with a glare before he can say another damn word. Not his place.

Her eyes flare as she glares daggers at me. "Screw you and your sanctimonious bullshit! You don't get it at all," she jabs her finger into my rock-hard chest to emphasize each word. "Those slithering Whisperling turds totally screwed with my head, making me think Emily needed rescuing from that smog-chugging asshat." She throws her hands up, adrenaline and fear boiling over. "What the hell was I supposed to do? Let my best friend get tortured in Shadow Fuckwad hands? Like hell."

Her voice hits a fever pitch, her words erupting in a shout. It's like throwing gasoline on the embers of my anger. I can feel my hands balling into tight fists, my nails digging into my palms as she ramps up with her mouthy tirade. My patience frays thinner with every word she spits out.

"Don't feed me your 'portals have consequences' crap right now, Mister Know-It-All. I don't need a lecture from Professor High-and-Mighty." She steps closer, eyes blazing. "So stow the pompous vampiric wisdom and get the hell off my back."

"It doesn't fucking matter," I roar, my control snapping like a brittle twig. "You know damn well not to listen to those wraiths and their poison whispers. But you let them twist your mind, and now look at the catastrophe you've landed us in."

I'm seeing red, blind to anything but the ravenous urge to unleash the full force of my wrath. Consequences be damned. She needs to understand the severity of her mistake, which could cost us everything. My fury feeds on itself, an inferno blazing out of control. All I can do is let it burn.

"Fine, I'm sorry—alright?" she shouts back, matching my volume. "How many freaking times do you want me to say it? I screwed up, but I was trying to save my best friend. So don't you dare get all high and mighty on me, Rhyland—we both know you're not exactly perfect either, Mister Broody Bloodsucker." She jabs her finger at me again, feeling my temper rising. "Yeah, that's right, I went there. Go ahead, keep lecturing me. But don't pretend you haven't made mistakes, too. I'm sure you've got centuries of screw-ups under your belt, so get off your damn high horse."

From behind me comes the faint sound of Lucian making a mocking "Ohhh, buuurn," as if Dani just won some verbal sparring match instead of royally screwing us all.

The urge to whip around and knock that smug look off his face surges hot within me. But I clench my jaw and ignore the baiting, keeping my focus locked on Dani. She's the one I need to deal with right now, the source of this mess. Lucian and his bullshit can damn well wait.

I move in closer, using my height to loom over Dani as I stare her down. "A mistake? This goes way beyond just some little screw-up, kära," I say, my voice low but edged with steel. "You might've doomed every last one of us—doomed the whole damn future of the realms. And for what? Because you were foolish enough to listen to those spirit freaks—for Emily?" I'm in her face now, our noses nearly touching.

Part of me knows I need to rein it in, but the words keep spilling out in an acidic torrent fueled by fear and anger—the whispers in my damn head—for the situation she's put us in. We're all in danger now because of her lapse in judgment. No matter how much I wish I could, I can't just shrug it off. The stakes are too high now.

Dani stands her ground, refusing to back down. "You think I don't know that? They were crazy convincing, down to the last detail. In the heat of the moment, I genuinely thought I was doing the right thing." She steps closer, arms folded across her chest. "But hey, if you'd rather stand here chucking petty insults instead of hatching a plan, then be my guest. Go ahead, keep telling me how stupid I am. That's *clearly* so productive right now." She meets my glare defiantly. "Or we could spend our energy figuring out where those smoke-stacking assholes went and how to kick their asses back out of here. But I guess berating me takes priority. So get it out of your system and then get your head back in the game, Rhyland. Because we've got bigger problems than my screw-up."

We stand there, chests heaving, anger crackling in the scant space between us. I try to keep my temper in check, but the thought of what's coming has me raging, thrashing like a wild beast. And it pisses me off even more that her defiance and that damn bratty mouth are getting me hard.

"Well, this is quite the predicament," Lucian drawls, ever ready with a quip even in a crisis. "I'd say we're up shit creek without a paddle on this one."

I shoot him a withering glance. "Not helping, Lucian."

"Enough," Faderyn interjects firmly. "What's done is done. Arguing will not change it nor help us respond." He looks pointedly between Dani and me. "The Whisperlings are feeding off your emotions, and we need level heads now, not heated tempers."

I release a harsh breath and give a sharp nod. He's onto something. These assholes are cramming my brain with crap, trying to provoke me into turning on Dani. Losing my cool won't scrub away this mess. I crossed the line.

I grit my teeth and shove that mental noise the hell out of my skull. It's a bitch of a fight, but I muscle through until my thoughts are mine again, and I can finally take a damn breath without feeling choked.

"Dani, I'm guessing you were asleep when you went looking for Emily, right?" Faderyn asks.

Dani shrugs. "I don't think so. Felt too real. Why?"

"If you had been wide awake, we would've picked up on it early—Rhyland would've sensed you were up," Faderyn suggests.

Scratching my head in befuddlement, I press, "Spit it out. What are you hinting at?"

Hoisting his bag upon his shoulder, Faderyn thoughtfully observes, "If she indeed accessed her abilities to open a portal whilst, in a state of slumber, it is a testament to her formidable strength. This revelation presents us with many more pressing concerns to consider."

Dani's expression shifts from confusion to sudden insight. "Given how you lot were sawing logs through my scream fest, you might just have a point."

"Can those blasted mind-pokers actually jab into your subconscious?" Lucian asks, almost surprised.

"That's precisely their aim," Axilya confirms. "They ensnare you in a dream world and hold you captive within it."

Dani's brow furrows, irritation lacing her voice. "Hold on a second—are you telling me I was dreamwalking and popped open a portal? What in the world does that even mean?"

"As I've indicated, the realization that even your subconscious harbors such immense power necessitates that we prioritize our concerns accordingly," Faderyn elucidates.

Honestly, this info's got my head spinning. And now I feel like an even bigger asshole for ripping into Dani when she wasn't conscious—something I promised her I would protect. Faderyn's got a damn good point—My temper got away from me, and I never should've been so rough with Dani. She was just following her damn gut, doing what came naturally. I'm the one at fucking fault here. I know better than most how strong instinct can be.

Axilya steps forward, her expression grave. "Azrael and Adrian are on the loose, which is our darkest fear come to life. We must act quickly before they have an opportunity to strike."

"Agreed," Erik says. "We should rest here for no more than an hour, then be on our way. The longer we linger, the more danger we face."

We fight like we fuck—fierce, unrestrained, full of fire. Our connection only amps up what the other one's feeling, making us wilder. It's a raw, primal dance fueled by passion.

Her slender arms encircle her frame, a shield she doesn't even goddamn need. "I'm so sorr—"

The world slams into a halt with her half-spoken apology, and I can't—I just fucking can't let that stand. My fingers clamp around her, hauling her to me with all the restraint of a damned hurricane. Our mouths crash together, a cataclysm of lips and unspoken promises. Her apologies slice through me like a blade, and I can't stomach another syllable of guilt from her. Me? I'm the bastard here. My chest is a vault of regret, and she's got no cause to feel any of this shit.

This kiss is more than just a merging of lips—it's the bearing of my soul, every fuck-up I own. It's my silent plea for absolution, wrapped in a feral desire that roars louder than the words I can't find.

"Forgive me?" spills out, raw and ragged, from the depths of my chest, pressed into the sanctity of our kiss.

Then she—my fiery angel—kisses me like the world is ending, and this is our last chance at salvation. "I forgive you," she breathes, bringing life to me, her words feather-light, and yet they're everything.

Thank fuck! I can't have her upset with me.

The shadows—that cesspool where I was wallowing—and those godforsaken Whisper bastards gnawing at my sanity need to be drowned out. And she—my angel—she's my damn lifeline.

"Let me make it up to you," I breathe out the words against her mouth, a murmured vow.

Her smirk is a spark in the dark, full of promise and sly delight, as she draws back just enough to lock onto my gaze. Her voice is a tease dipped in honey. "Well, since you're offering... I'll consider it an IOU. But Rhyland, I'll be collecting with interest," she quips, that sass of hers fanning the flames in me even higher.

And her wit—it's the goddamn cherry on top.

All I can do is smile before I claim her mouth again.

DANICA

5I

Rhyland's kiss crashes into me, a full-on make-out hurricane that blows away all the Whisperlings' icy bullshit. I wrap my arms around his neck and kiss him back hard, taking out my anger at myself on his lips.

My mind races, lashing at myself for succumbing to the Vales' treacherous illusions. I should have known better; I should have been stronger. Emily's phantom screams still echo in my ears, a reminder of my momentary lapse.

Damn, I love his taste—a sexy ocean breeze. It yanks me back to reality quicker than a Jägerbomb. I'm lost in the storm of his kiss, reminding myself this is real—no smoky asshole illusion could replicate Rhyland's smoking hot mouth devouring mine.

The weight of his remorse gnaws at my core. We clashed and tore into each other with the ferocity lovers sometimes show. I get it—it's not all going to be smooth sailing—but that's not the soil where a strong relationship grows.

When we finally come up for air, foreheads touching and breathing hard, I know I'm back. No more falling for fake trapdoors for Shadow Dickwad and whatever messed-up tricks he pulls next. From now on, I'll remember what's real—Rhyland lighting me up like a pinball machine. His love guides me home like a lighthouse when I'm adrift.

Rhyland's eyes shimmer, and an apology is already on his lips. "Don't," I manage to say before he can speak. "Don't apologize. I'll fix it."

I'm breathless from more than just the kiss; the weight of responsibility presses on my chest like a physical force. He searches my face, and for a heartbeat, I worry he'll argue. But instead, he nods, understanding the promise in my words.

We linger there until the sun begins to rise, casting a pale light that struggles to penetrate the dense fog. It's not much, but it gives us a semblance of visibility—a white canvas that hints at shapes and shadows rather than the complete obscurity of night.

"What of Azrael and Adrian?" Erik inquires. "Do you have any thoughts on where they might have ventured off to?"

Channeling my inner DNA whiz, a lightbulb flicks on—they are sitting ducks without my blood. They must be laying low until dusk blankets everything. I waste no time in bouncing this theory off Erik.

"Seems the sun is in our damn favor for once," Rhyland growls.

Mounting our horses feels like an act of defiance against the night's events. We're still here; we're still moving forward. I take out the map again—a piece of parchment that holds more than just directions—and lightly tap the following location.

The map comes to life under my fingers, as if waking from a slumber. A delicate glow emanates from its surface as it begins to illustrate our next destination: Whispering Woods.

The voice accompanying the map's animation is ethereal, a whisper yet clear enough to cut through the fog, which clings to us like a second skin.

"Whispering Woods," it intones as though confiding a secret meant only for us. *"It is a place where ancient trees weave a canopy so thick that daylight fears to tread. Here lies the domain of the Whisperlings—spirits born from profound silence and keepers of secrets untold."* The animated lines on the parchment form an intricate dance of gnarled branches and paths that appear and disappear in mere moments—a maze meant to ensnare unwary travelers. *"The paths are many,"* continues the voice as if reciting lore passed down through ages uncounted. *"Yet most lead not where they promise but into confusion and ensnare-ment."*

Even I can't help a little involuntary shiver—there's a real, creepy truth bomb in those words. Deep down, I know that whatever freaky Friday we're about to march into in those woods will be more than just some throwdown or fancy footwork challenge.

"To traverse these woods unharmed," concludes the map's narration, showing a glowing path cutting through deception, *"one must be sharp of mind—beware, for things are not what they seem."*

Crap. After the dumpster fire of last night, my faith in my own head game is seriously shaken. I better strap on those mental blinders tight, or we're booking a sequel to disaster—this time, with more encore.

And a cryptic riddle to boot!

Just freaking great!

"Oh, Princess, what porous mental shields you have," Lucian drawls with a smirk. "Pro tip—Might want to patch those up before your thoughts become public domain."

"Alright, smart-ass," I shoot back, my words laced with a pinch of sass. "What's the big, dark vampire secret that has you speaking in riddles?"

"Newsflash: Your mind has fewer defenses than a cardboard fort. Even a charming intruder like myself can stroll right in without knocking."

The rumble of Rhyland's growl vibrates through me from behind like a subwoofer of pure irritation. It's his not-so-subtle way of telling Lucian to choose his next words wisely—unless he's looking for a one-way ticket to a vampire-style ass-whooping.

"Ha! Relax, brother. I've retired my Peeping Tom days—swear on my fangs." He smiles with all fang. "One traumatic mental stroll was one too many. But don't blame me when your thoughts come blaring through like a freaking stadium PA system. Your brain's a wide-open broadcasting station."

"Wait...You're telling me you can *actually* eavesdrop on my thoughts, like...right this second?" My voice is a cocktail of shock and outrage, shaken and stirred.

"Yeah, it seems like when you're freaked out, stressed, or asleep," he winks. "Your thoughts go into overdrive stereo mode," Lucian says casually, as if reading minds is no big deal. "It's like your emotions turn up the volume knob in that head of yours."

Rhyland exhales deeply, clearly mustering all his willpower to stay calm. It's crystal clear he's very familiar with Lucian's supernatural eavesdropping, but it seems he's not too thrilled about how I'm practically broadcasting my thoughts like a morning radio show.

"So, what's the genius plan, oh Enlightened One?" I ask, tilting my head, all ears for his next slice of wisdom—or whatever you call it when Lucian's wheels are turning.

"I've got a couple of nifty tricks up my sleeve... You know, to fortify that whimsical brain castle of yours. But only if Captain Brood-a-lot gives his royal nod of permission." Lucian offers with a smirk.

"Okay, I'm genuinely curious," I say, curiosity gnawing at me like a mouse in a cheese factory. "What's the full scoop on your mind tricks? Seeing my—*ahem*—dream is one thing, but what else have you got stashed in your mental magic hat?" Lucian chuckles at my mention of that; "Rhyland only gave me the teaser trailer for your brainy superpowers."

"Consider me a cerebral hustler. If I fancy, I can shimmy into people's noodles, see their thoughts—dreams," he says with a smirk, and I can't help but roll my eyes, "and even make them dance to my tune. But that specific little trick is a mortals-only club. It seems like the supernatural crowd's immune to my charms—they must be slathering on some mental bug spray."

"Over the millennia, the Fae have cultivated a resistance to vampire charm," Axilya supplies. "We consider this a strategic evolution—our means of fostering an innate immunity."

"Is that right?" Rhyland's voice is a low purr as we shift on the saddle, Storm walking steadily. "It's sort of like you are evolving to be top dogs over other creatures, huh?"

"One might say so," Axilya consents. "View it rather as an apparatus of survival. Our progenitors instituted this measure eons past to shield our kind from extinction."

The endless enmity between the fae and vampires is a saga of conflict older than the stars.

"This is precisely why your mention of Amara employing 'compulsion' strikes me as odd, given our immunity," Axilya adds.

Rhyland's shrug rolls off behind me, his tone nonchalant. "Beats me. This is news about you guys being immune—that mind fuckery isn't my thing. Whatever the hell Amara's pulling, it's not the same shit your forebears were guardin' against."

I can't resist tossing the question to Lucian, "Ever pulled that mind-whammy on me? The compulsion number?" I feel Rhyland tense up behind me, ears perked with interest.

"Yup," Lucian quickly answers with no remorse. Rhyland rumbles in that gravel-pit voice of his, but Lucian cuts in before he can unleash the thunder. "And, for the record, it's a big ol' dud on you—might be that halo in your family tree buffering you up—not that I've nailed down the why. And before Mr. Scowl-In-Boots over there goes full-on beast mode, let the record show I only gave it the old college try that day you came sniffing at my club about Max—worked on Emily. But—surprise, surprise—it ricocheted right off you. That's when yours truly clocked you as something special."

The memory of that day and Emily floods my mind, missing her most. "Huh, interesting. But you've still got access to my mental diary?" I quip back. "And hold up a second! You went all mind-magic on Emily?"

Lucian rolls his eyes, a smirk playing on his lips. "Look, Princess, your mental barriers are flimsier than Grandma's Metamucil farts. I can show you how to build up those defenses, especially if we're about to tango with the Whispering Anus Brigade. Just a little brain armor 101, no biggie." He adds, "And let's be real, it was just to get her to stop busting my balls—nothing to write home about."

I flash a quick grin just thinking about that time with Emily and her epic meltdowns, serving Lucian a grade-A ball-busting he's not likely to ever wipe from his memory.

Whipping my head around to Rhyland, I catch his ocean-blue stare, all heavy with that wordless determination. He tosses me a nod, no need for a pep talk, and that's my cue—the learning marathon is officially on.

With the Whispering Woods a couple of hours out, we've got a chunk of time perfect for a brain-boosting binge. "Okay, Lucian, teach me."

"Picture your mind like a fortress," he instructs, his tone a mix of authority and reassurance. "Your thoughts are the priceless treasures kept within those walls. To reinforce your defenses, you've gotta make those walls thicker and the ramparts higher. Mentally build an impassable barrier, solid and unbreakable, to guard your inner world."

"So, I've got to build a fortress in my head, right?" I ask, seeking that clarity I crave in and out of the lab.

He nods, and I close my eyes, trying to conjure up the strongest, most daunting walls I can imagine encircling my mind. I conjure up my lab's familiar, comforting confines in my mind's eye. The door is locked—firm and final—a barrier to the outside world. The blinds are drawn, casting the room in soft, secure shadows. The scent of antiseptic, sterile, and sharp drifts to my senses. There's an intimacy to the quiet, an echo of my focused, solitary work with beakers and petri dishes.

It's just me and the quiet hum of my thoughts, a symphony of hypotheses and discoveries. With this peaceful, private image as my foundation, I take Lucian's guidance and start to build my mental fortress. Each detail of my lab—from the cool metal surfaces to the rows of meticulously labeled specimens—becomes a brick in my shield. This haven, where my science thrives, is now the stronghold safeguarding my thoughts. With Lucian's words as mortar, I fortify the walls, confident and cocooned in the safety of my inner sanctum.

Lucian's voice breaks through again, coaching and steadying. "Visualize a shield holding firm, Dani. That's your space, your sanctuary. Trust it."

I stay fixed on that mental image, reinforcing the vision of my lab. Each detail bolsters the walls a bit more. Oddly, I find a soothing solace in this picture I've painted in my head; it roots me. A sense of readiness settles in as I solidify the last brick in my mind's fortress.

"Okay, I've got it," I announce, surprisingly firm. "Do your worst."

"Swing and a miss, Sugar. Your walls wouldn't even stop a horny chihuahua, let alone a mind reader." Lucian sasses with his signature sharp wit. "Gonna take more than some lacy lingerie layering your pretty head. Try harder, Princess."

I exhale in a puff of frustration, feeling the sheen of sweat as a testament to this intense cerebral gymnastics session. But surrender? That's not in my vocabulary. I grit my teeth, determined to push through. Mind over matter, just like in the lab. I will get this.

Rhyland's arms encircle me from behind, his presence a silent pillar of strength as I labor through the mental workout. Words are unnecessary; he knows the level of concentration this demands. His occasional squeeze is a wordless communication, a reminder of his unwavering support right here with me.

We're only an hour deep into Lucian's brain boot camp, and I already feel the mental burn. He keeps penetrating them with ease. This stuff is intense and draining. Gaining this skill, this mental muscle Lucian wields, gives me a whole new level of respect for him. He's not just a master of witty comebacks and nightclub domains—he's honed a trait that demands every ounce of my will.

The fortress of my mind needs bolstering, something—someone unbreakable. Instinctively, my thoughts turn to Rhyland, my steadfast protector. I close my eyes tighter, and there he is, a tangible presence within the sacred confines of my mental lab. With his strength and assurance, he is beside me amidst my vials and equations. I sense a shift then, a newfound solidity in the barriers of my mind.

Feeling the shift, a surge of confidence courses through me. "Alright, Lucy," I taunt, squaring my shoulders. "Give it your best shot."

"Well, I'll be damned...you're a star pupil, Princess. Your walls are solid." Lucian laughs, and I can't help but grin. "Just keep 'em up. Takes practice and some serious brain juice, but I'd say you've got this shield thing on lock." He finishes with a wink.

As our group rides deeper into the territory of Whisperling whispers, I feel a determined surge within me—I'm ready. I'll protect us all, starting from the labyrinthine corners of my own vulnerable mind.

DANICA

52

The coldness of the Whispering Woods bites at me, the frosty air a far cry from the heat emanating from Rhyland's body against mine. I keep Storm steady, navigating the maze of paths, all shrouded in mystery.

Swirls of fog slither through the air, wrapping around us in ghostly tendrils while an eerie silence swallows the woods whole. Trees loom like ancient sentinels, their gnarled limbs reaching toward us as if hungry—ready to either whisper the forest's darkest secrets or drag us into their wooden embrace.

Then the path splits without warning, fracturing into a tangled web of trails that bleed into the shadows. Each one is a gamble. Each one disappearing into nothing. The air grows heavy and still, holding its breath as we stand at the crossroads of this twisted game.

"Which way now?" Faedryn's voice cuts through the foggy haze.

Erik moves forward, his silver eyes scanning the murky surroundings. "Left," he asserts, pointing to a path shrouded in thicker mist.

Axilya shakes her head, her crown of pale flowers and thorns catching droplets of mist. "No, we must take the right fork. It leads to higher ground."

Lucian scoffs. "And what? We'll just fly over this damned fog from there?"

Rhyland's authoritative voice rumbles behind me. "Enough! We can't waste time bickering."

Tension crackles around us like the prelude to a tempest, but deep down, there's a flicker in me—a knowing without words, a compass in the chaos.

"Hang on—" I announce. My companions fall silent, their eyes fixed on me.

I close my eyes and breathe deep, holding the silence of the woods in my lungs before releasing it slowly. Storm remains still and patient beneath me, as though he senses exactly what I'm doing.

Inside, something pulls—a visceral, bone-deep connection to the stone that cuts straight through the fog and shadows surrounding us. It tugs insistently, growing stronger, more undeniable with every passing second. A tingle blooms at my crown, a physical confirmation of the certainty taking root within me.

"This way," I murmur, my voice carrying a quiet assurance that surprises even me. That invisible tether guides me as surely as a compass needle chasing north. With a gentle press of my heel against Storm's flank, we move forward onto a narrow, less-traveled path—a thin thread cutting through the darkness, whispering of both promise and peril in equal measure.

Lucian's voice drips with a know-it-all tone. "Obviously, I was about to choose this very route."

My crown vibrates as though it's coming alive.

"Your crown," Rhyland's voice is hushed and thick with awe, right behind me, "the glyphs are glowing... shifting."

We enter a clearing. Beneath us, Storm's restlessness grows; he shifts his weight, his body wound tight as a bowstring, as though he's picking up vibes we can't. Suddenly, he lets out a piercing whinny, and his hooves hammer a nervous tattoo into the forgiving earth—his unease is contagious as the other horses follow suit.

"Easy, boy..." I try to soothe him, but before I can even start, something zips by—a blur of speed that's anything but natural. Storm's reaction is immediate and explosive; he's up on his hind legs, powerful and magnificent but utterly terrified, pitching wildly beneath us.

My fingers tangle in Storm's mane, desperate for anchorage, but the force defies my grip. Like ragdolls in a typhoon, Storm launches us off his back, proving that gravity's got nothing on a spooked horse in a supernatural forest.

The impact is brutal—a crushing blow that detonates through my entire body, slamming every last molecule of air from my lungs. I open my mouth in a silent scream, desperate for oxygen that seems to have abandoned me entirely. Pain erupts from shoulder to spine, searing and unforgiving, as the world spins sickeningly above me.

I can't breathe.

For one terrifying moment, I genuinely cannot breathe.

Then, finally, air staggers back into my lungs in ragged, sharp-edged gulps, each one tasting of damp soil and cold fear.

The moment I wrangle control over my breath and will, Rhyland is right there instantly to lift me off the unforgiving earth. That's when it hits—an unearthly scream that detonates through the silence, shredding through the trees like a blade. It isn't just a sound. It's a declaration. A warning. Something terrible announcing its presence in the darkness.

Every hair on my body stands on end.

My hands dart for my daggers, their solid heft both calming and empowering—a tactile promise that I'm not defenseless against whatever horror is about to emerge from the Whispering Woods' deceiving tranquility.

Lucian's question pierces through the heavy mist. "What the fuck was that?!"

My eyes snap open to our new reality. Everyone's dismounted, poised for combat, turning a wary circle to face the unseen threat.

The horses bolt away in a frenzy as though fleeing from flames. The map sits at my feet, enclosed in its leather case, dropped and forgotten.

That's when the nightmare crew decides to make their appearance, stepping right out of the fog. These ugly fucking things? They stand tall and foreboding, silhouettes knitted from the woods themselves with limbs of gnarled branches and a maze of thorns protruding dangerously from their humanoid forms. They move in a freaky lockstep that feels like they're dancing to the tune of the seriously unhinged.

Thorns as sharp as daggers jut menacingly from their limbs while their faces remain veiled in a tapestry of moss and leaves. Only their eyes are visible—glowing orbs radiating pure loathing.

I plant my feet, my resolve steel. We're not the all-you-can-eat buffet they're craving. Rhyland's at my side in an instant, every inch the vampire Viking fortress he is, and our fingers brush—a promise of battle to come.

"Anyone wanna clue me in on what these freaky fuckers actually are?" Lucian asks, his voice tight, slightly panicking.

My heartbeat explodes into overdrive, hammering so hard I can hear nothing else, feel nothing else. Adrenaline floods my veins like poison as they close in—moving with an unnaturally fluid grace that makes my skin crawl. The forest itself seems to shift and contort around us, twisted trees leaning inward like skeletal fingers reaching to pluck us from existence.

Then the whispers start.

They slither into my mind uninvited, oily and insidious, coiling through my thoughts with lies and deception designed to fracture me from the inside. I don't hesitate—I slam my mental barriers shut with violent force, locking them out, sealing my mind like a fortress under siege. "Shields up!" I command, my voice cutting through the chaos.

Power surges beneath my skin—electric, urgent, absolutely ravenous. It crashes through me like a living thing, demanding release, begging for blood. The anticipation is suffocating, intoxicating. This is what I was made for. This battlefield is about to become my domain, and every single one of them is about to learn exactly what I'm capable of.

I'm ready to burn this entire forest down.

"Ax! Care to fucken' enlighten us?" Lucian calls out, his voice piercing through the uneasy atmosphere.

Axilya's face is etched with concern as she replies, "I believe...these...are Thicket Shades—these woods, sites of ancient betrayals and battles, now give rise to physical forms born from the land's deep-seated pain and anguish. They will stop at nothing to bury you alive."

I shoot Rhyland a look, our eyes sparking a wordless pact in an instant—we'll be damned if we let that happen.

Lucian's brow furrows as he asks urgently, "Alright, so we're dealing with some spooky-ass tree spirits? What's the strategy, Ax?"

"Beats the hell outta me," Axilya snaps.

The first strike comes without warning—a Thicket Shade unfurling an arm like a sentient whip, vine-thick and dripping with venom, aimed directly at Erik's throat. Even with vampire reflexes that should be impossible to match, Erik can't dodge it completely. The blow catches him across the ribs, and the sound that tears from him is pure animal fury—a feral snarl that echoes through the trees.

His retaliation is instantaneous and savage. His sword arcs through the air in a blur of silver vengeance, moving with surgical precision and absolutely no mercy. Every motion is calculated brutally, death incarnate, as Erik tears into the creature with ruthless efficiency. The collision is deafening—steel meeting gnarled flesh and woody armor, a violent symphony announcing that something far more sinister has begun.

"Battling bitchy bark," Lucian deadpans with a derisive snort, his own twisted version of a battle hymn. Then he's airborne—launching himself into the chaos like he owns it, tapping into his supernatural speed and strength with the casual confidence of someone who was born for exactly this. He coils and releases, driving a devastating kick into the nearest Shade with the force of a battering ram. The creature crashes to the forest floor with a ground-shaking boom that reverberates through the roots beneath our feet, rattling the very bones of the forest itself.

Lucian flashes a devil-may-care grin and drawls, "I can play Paul Bunyan."

Faderyn plunges headlong into the melee, blade unsheathed and slashing with precision. He dances through the conflict, an artist severing limbs, each move cloaked in shadow and silence.

Yet the Shade, unfazed, seamlessly regenerates its limb, drawing from the sylvan energies around it as if the forest itself conspires to mend its form.

Right there with Faderyn, Axilya steps into the dance, her sword harmonizing with the clash of battle, a symphony of steel as she meets her foes.

Rhyland, with his subtle command, the very air becomes his weapon. A casual flick of his wrist sends a Thicket Shade reeling as effortlessly as if he'd tossed aside a pebble, revealing the might of his telekinetic prowess—an unseen titan at play. The Shade shatters into fragments as if it were torn to pieces by a wood chipper.

I take a breath, and suddenly time becomes my bitch.

Everything around me lurches into molasses—the Shades transforming into sluggish puppets jerking on invisible strings. I explode into motion, my body a calculated blur of acrobatics and pure, unapologetic sass.

One of the creatures stretches its limbs toward me with greedy desperation, branches hungering for sunlight they'll never touch. I slip beneath their reach like smoke, my body flowing through the thick air with the grace of someone who just rewrote the rules of physics. I'm untouchable. I'm unstoppable.

I crane my neck to look past one of the creatures and—there. A core embedded deep in its back. A smoldering red beacon pulsing like a diseased heart. My analytical mind locks onto it instantly. A hypothesis crystallizes.

Gotcha, you bastards.

My daggers sing through the warped air—one finds its mark in the creature stalking Rhyland from behind with lethal precision. I flick it away with a wink, sending it flying straight toward its date with oblivion. Before it even hits the ground, I'm already scanning the battlefield for my next target.

Who needs regular feet when you can teleport?

In what feels like a leisurely stroll inside my time bubble, I'm suddenly everywhere at once—materializing behind another Shade with my dagger already buried in its back. The creature doesn't even have time to scream.

As time snaps back like a rubber band, my fingers wrap around the hilt, pulling it free with a flourish. My 'dance partner' lets out an ear-splitting shriek, a sound so piercing it feels like my eardrums might burst.

I hit the ground hard, palms clamped over my ears as that unholy wail detonates through the forest like a sonic bomb. Around me, everyone drops—all of us brought to our knees by the sheer, devastating force of it. The sound is a weapon. The sound is agony.

Then, as violently as it started, it stops.

The Shade collapses in on itself, its form withering and rotting at an impossible speed, crumbling to dust like centuries are passing in seconds. What remains isn't even recognizable as something that was once alive.

I'm already moving before its companion can process what happened.

I slip through the fractures between moments, bending time to my will like it's made of clay. The battlefield warps with my rhythm—slow, then lightning-fast, then slow again—leaving the Shades flailing and disoriented, completely unable to match my deadly choreography.

There are so many of them.

Rhyland's eyes lock onto mine across the chaos, burning with raw pride and something far more possessive, far more consuming. I'm already pivoting, already striking—dispatching a Shade that was seconds away from blindsiding Lucian.

The air reeks of death—rich, moist earth and decay, nature's suffocating death grip made manifest.

Then Lucian drops.

His body convulses violently, seizing as the Shade releases a cloud of toxic gas that spreads like poison through the forest. My heart stops.

I gag violently, twisting away as my stomach lurches and burns. I can't breathe. Can't think. I clamp down on my breath, fighting every instinct screaming at me to inhale, and dive back toward Lucian's convulsing form. I drag him out of the toxic cloud, away from the spreading poison, pulling his dead weight across the forest floor with desperate strength I didn't know I possessed.

It's already too late.

Hallucinogens are ravaging his system as he mumbles disjointed, incoherent nonsense that chills my blood. I haul him behind a cluster of gnarled trees, away from the worst of it, my lungs screaming for air as the poison hangs thick in the atmosphere.

Then I see it. A Shade heading my way.

Rhyland's fingers flex, and the air itself seems to contract. The Shade, heading toward me, suddenly launches skyward as if caught in an invisible vice, suspended and helpless. Its limbs thrash desperately before he crushes it downward with devastating force, slamming it into the earth with enough power to shatter it into splinters and dust.

The Shade begins to reconstruct itself, the wooden shards melding back together as if drawn by a dark and twisted spell of enchantment.

Shit!

"Lucian—" I don't hesitate. My palm connects with his cheek hard enough to rattle his brain, a shock tactic designed to obliterate the narcotic fog drowning his mind. His eyes lock on me, clarity striking like a lightning bolt's comeback tour, and bam! He's a vampire blur, hurling himself back with the grace of a caffeinated ballerina into the fray.

"You're welcome, jerk!" I toss over my shoulder, not pausing to see if his ego's bruised. Time is ticking, and I've got more Shade goons to introduce to my daggers. "Eyes peeled for their gas!" I yell into the bedlam, tossing a lifeline into the sea of madness to keep us from going under.

Axilya battles with ferocious determination, her form a blur of motion perfectly attuned to the rhythms of combat. She slices through limbs that regenerate as swiftly as they are severed, but she is relentless, a tireless warrior who refuses to abandon the deadly dance.

"The heart core!" I yell out to the others. "It's on their back!"

I can't help but wonder how these tree-hugging pricks would feel about a taste of my angel fire.

My pulse becomes a war drum in my ears as I dance between the Shades—slow, twisted things groping to snare me in their gnarled claws. I drop and slide beneath one, driving my blade up to the hilt in its wooden hide. It unleashes an otherworldly shriek—my very bones seem to quake in protest. Channeling my power as I've practiced, I concentrate on setting this bastard ablaze. Sparks dance from my fingertips, erupting into a searing white inferno that engulfs the Shade, reducing it to charred remains.

A flash to my left shows Faderyn trapped in the coiled embrace of a Thicket Shade. Its twisted limbs bind him, crushing his breath.

"Faderyn!" Already rushing forward, fear grips my heart. In desperation, I focus my power, willing time to slow. The world around me syrups. I dart forward, a blur of motion.

Faderyn's face twists in pure agony, each breath a ragged, desperate gasp as the Shade squeezes with relentless, suffocating force. I pour on every ounce of speed I have, my blades flashing as I close the distance, ready to slice through woody flesh and free him. But I can see it in his eyes—that crushing desperation. He knows I won't make it in time. He's already accepting it.

His body goes slack. Resigned. Dying.

No! I howl inside, the scream tearing through me like a physical wound. I will not lose him like this!

I launch myself at the Shade with raw, unfiltered fury, screaming so hard my throat burns. My daggers carve deep gouges into its twisted bark, but every strike feels useless against something so ancient and unyielding. I hack at the appendage strangling Faderyn, but it's like attacking solid stone—immovable, indifferent. I hold my flames back, terrified of incinerating him along with the creature.

"Let him go, you bastard!" I scream, my voice cracking with desperation and rage. The creature stares at me with those glowing, heartless eyes, completely unmoved by my demands. I don't waste another second on words. I pivot and drive my dagger deep into its back.

It shrieks.

The sound is ear-splitting as it whips a branch toward me like a club. The hit sends me flying backward, but the creature's grip on Faderyn finally loosens. It crashes to the forest floor and begins to wither, collapsing into nothing but ash and rot.

The impact is thunder—knocking the wind out of me—I hit the ground hard, breathless. Twice, seriously? That's two helpings of face-planting gourmet with a side of 'oomph' sucked right from my lungs. Faderyn drops to the ground, coughing and gasping. His eyes meet mine, filled with torment but also resolute trust.

Before I can react, I'm snared, woody limbs coiling around to pin my arms. My feet leave the ground, suspended helplessly in its clutches as they tighten like a vise, crushing the breath from my lungs.

Erik's cry, "Dani—!" ends in a guttural grunt as a Shade punts him across the clearing like a rag doll. He hits the ground and rolls bonelessly, silver hair falling across his face.

Across the clearing, Rhyland's face contorts in torment. He surges forth but is battered back by two more Shades.

"Danica!" Rhyland howls across the clearing.

I gasp for air, stars bursting across my vision as the creature's grip grows ever tighter. Each breath now requires a Herculean effort, hard-won and fleeting.

Rhyland fights with savage determination to reach me—he tries to blur, but a Thicket Shade impales his stomach, and Rhyland crumples to the ground. Though mute, I try to cry out at his anguish, feeling the phantom agony lance through my own body.

Wood—it's like kryptonite for Vampires.

My pulse pounds relentlessly, the rapid thunder of my heart desperate to sustain me. Struggling to summon my fire, my hands flicker with feeble sparks, but it's useless when air refuses to fill my lungs.

Everyone is in battle, fighting them off as they continue to close in.

His eyes—those endless blue depths—are flooded with torment and desperation, silently begging me to hold on, just a little longer, as he fights to push himself up off the ground. But the darkness is closing in. Suffocating. Swallowing everything—light, sound, hope.

No. This can't be happening.

I can't find the strength to fight back. Can't summon my light.

Below me, Lucian is a blur of movement, his blades flashing as he tears into the Shade. "Piece of fuckin' shit, let her go!" he roars.

The Shade constricts harder.

My ribs crack under the pressure, white-hot spikes of pain shooting through my chest. I can't breathe. I can't—

A tendril moves so fast I don't even see it coming.

It punches through my leather vest and into my chest in an explosion of crimson. For one suspended, surreal moment, there's only pressure. No pain. Just the sickening sensation of something foreign tearing through muscle and tissue. I watch my blood bloom across the fabric, staining everything red.

Then the pain hits.

It's apocalyptic. Agonizing and all-consuming, lancing through my entire torso like molten steel. A ragged, broken scream tears from my throat—a sound I barely recognize as my own. The tendril withdraws with a sickening squelch, my blood dripping from its tip like a grotesque trophy.

I'm thrown away like garbage.

My body hits the ground hard enough to shatter, the impact driving what little air remains from my lungs.

Through blurry vision, I see Rhyland's face contorted in anguish and fury. Time slows to a crawl—with a roar, he tears through the Shades separating us, eyes blazing cobalt fire. He hurls the Shades aside as if they were mere trifles, but they continue to swarm.

A silent scream claws its way up my throat, voiceless and desperate. I glance down to see the ragged hole in my own chest, blood pouring out in thick, crimson rivers. My vision whitens at the edges, reality fracturing into fragments.

Through the descending veil suffocating my senses, Lucian's face suddenly swims into focus. His mouth is moving, words forming urgently, desperately, though I can barely hear them through the roaring in my ears. "Fuck...Hold on," he's saying, his dark brown eyes wide with anguish and terror. "I got you...stay with me."

I try. *God, I try.*

"RHYLAND!" Lucian screams, but it sounds muffled, like I'm underwater.

Somewhere in the distance, Rhyland unleashes an anguished cry that pierces my fading consciousness. He is a man possessed, fighting through the Shades, telekinetic power hurling them aside like leaves in a gale.

But even his strength cannot hold back the tide rising to swallow me. Each breath is a fire in my chest. My life spills hot on the damp earth beneath me.

"Luc—" His name bubbles past my lips, drowned in bouts of blood rising from my ruined chest and lungs. I cough violently, blood spraying, feeling as though I'm drowning on dry land. Lucian's face swims sickeningly before me as he tries to stem the relentless flow. But we both know it is futile.

"Shh...don't talk," he tells me. "RHYLAND!" Lucian's cry resonates through me, a thunderclap rending the shroud of silence.

The shadows continue their insidious march, consuming my vision by degrees. Soon, only a tunnel remains, framing Lucian's anguished eyes.

"Fuck...I'm so sorry...for what I'm about to do. Please forgive me," Lucian pleads.

I'm confused— lost in the void. I blink; time's a twisted joke here. It could be minutes, seconds, or a freaking eternity.

Rhyland's face appears above me, shouting words I can't understand. I feel like I'm being lifted. His voice fades, and a bone-deep cold creeps through my limbs.

"Rhyland..." I cling to one final shred of light, determined to imprint his face on my heart.

Darkness creeps into the edges of my vision, beckoning me into its embrace. My eyes fall shut, too heavy to keep open. Rhyland's frantic voice echoes from somewhere far away as oblivion rises to claim me.

RHYLAND

53

I crush Dani to my chest, the weight of her body is both delicate and unbearably heavy, a precious burden that threatens to shatter me. The gaping hole in her chest sears into my vision, a vicious wound that no mortal should survive, a testament to the cruelty of fate. Blood froths at the corner of her lips, and the scent of iron fills my nostrils, a sickening reminder of how close I am to losing her. Her punctured lung heaves with each shallow, labored breath, a wet gurgle twisting my insides, a sound that will haunt me for eternity.

"Dani, you're not going anywhere," I growl, my forehead pressed against hers as if I can anchor her to this world through sheer force of will. "Stay with me, or I swear to all the gods, I'll tear this whole fucking world apart."

But Dani remains unmoving, still in my arms, her life force ebbing away with each passing second. Terror rages within me, a beast unchained, howling in despair at the thought of losing her.

I whip my head around, a snarl ripping from me, directed at Lucian. He's there, stained with the act—crimson at his mouth, his wrist marred by his own bite, indisputable proof of his blood feeding her. "What the fuck did you do, Lucian?" I demand, fury laced with dread at what this could mean.

Lucian swipes at the blood on his mouth, a defiant glimmer in his dark eyes. "What had to be done, Rhyland," he retorts, his tone a mix of defensive snark and solemnity. "I fuckin' waited, Rhy—waited as long as I bloody could." His voice is raw with emotion. "But you couldn't get here in time... She was dying, man. What the hell did you expect me to do, watch her take her last breath? So, yeah, I stepped in—" His voice holds a biting urgency, indicating the difficult decision he faced.

Lucian's response is a blade twisting in my chest, offering no relief from the anguish that has seized hold of me. I can't exist without her—if she transforms, I'll handle her after. If it happens due to Lucian's blood, I'll kill him. Silently, I rip open my wrist with a fang, embracing the sting, anything to distract from the agony shredding my spirit.

"Come on, Angel," I urge Dani as I shove my bleeding wrist against her lips. The blood flows thick and heavy from the wound, dripping down her chin in a dark stream—a final offering, my last shot at pulling her back. "Drink, baby. Please, just fucking drink."

I'm torn, knowing I'm not giving Dani a choice as I had. I'm forcing this on her, thrusting her into a world she never asked for. But call me selfish—I can't exist without her, can't bear facing eternity alone, without her light to guide me.

She's motionless, her heart gone fucking silent, but I'll be damned if I accept that if I let her slip away without a fight. I plead to the Norse gods I've long since abandoned, begging Dani to return to me, to come back from the brink.

"Odin! Hear me!" I roar to the heavens, my voice breaking with the agony of a man on the verge of losing everything. "Please, I need her back...I'm n-nothing without her!" As she lies motionless, doubt creeps in, a sinister whisper insisting it's over—that she's lost to me, that I've failed her in the most fundamental way.

I'm too fucking late. The voice hisses, a cruel taunt. I've let her down, let the one person who matters most slip through my fingers, and now I'm left with nothing but the bitter ashes of what could have been.

Still, I clutch her tight, bringing my wrist against her lips again, silently demanding she drink. My heart fractures imagining life without her light, without her tenacious spirit. "Don't leave me, baby," I implore, my voice breaking. "Not when we've only just found each other." I stroke her hair, cherishing its softness, praying this isn't the last time. "Please come back, Angel. Please..."

Everything outside this moment becomes meaningless—the fight raging on, the screams of fury and pain fading to nothing. My entire world shrinks down to this: holding Dani like she's the only thing keeping me from drowning in a violent storm.

Lucian lingers nearby, his features warped with regret and remorse, the weight of his actions etched into every line of his face. I know he was attempting to save her—but if his fucking blood succeeds where mine falters...that is a nightmare I can't confront.

I shut him out, shutting out fucking everything except the woman I cradle against me—my reason for existing. "Drink, baby," I plead once more, my wrist pressed to her mouth, my lifeblood dripping, waiting for her to respond. But her lashes don't stir, and her lips remain still, a cruel mockery of the vibrant woman I know and love. Despair crashes over me, a bottomless darkness clawing at me, trying to drag me down.

She has to come back to me.

She has to...

Lucian's gaze darts between us, his eyes filled with anguish and uncertainty, torn between the ongoing fight and the unfolding tragedy before him. "Rhy, I think..." He lets out an anguished gasp, his voice barely above a whisper. "I think it's too late."

"No!" I roar, my voice a howl of denial, of rage against the very fabric of fate. "Come on, baby..." I plead to Dani, my words a desperate litany, a prayer to any god who might be listening.

Lucian comes to a swift resolution, spinning away without another word, leaping back into the thick of war, leaving me alone with my grief.

Dani's breaths are now non-existent—the rise and fall of her chest, a terrible, unnatural stillness that threatens to break me. My voice fractures as I keep pleading for her life—for the future we're meant to share, now dangling by the most delicate strand.

But as the seconds tick by, each one an eternity of agony, a sickening realization begins to dawn, a truth I can no longer deny.

We were too late.

I was too late.

And now, as I hold the woman I love in my arms, her body shattered and motionless, I feel the last threads of hope bleeding away, swallowed by a crushing void of despair.

Then...warmth floods through us, radiating a light that doesn't come from me or any magic I know. It's pure and ethereal, a glow that seems to pour straight from Dani herself, a radiance that breaks every natural law. Her lifeless body rises from my arms like invisible hands are lifting her, a gentle but undeniable force I can't fight.

Awe and hope ignite inside me as I watch her limp form suspended before me, wrapped in a soft, pulsing light. Her hair moves in an unearthly breeze, each strand flowing like invisible fingers are touching it, and her skin glows from the inside out, shimmering with a light that seems to come from her very core. I want to reach for her, to pull her back against me, but something stops me—this isn't normal, isn't anything I've encountered in centuries.

"Dani?" I whisper, barely able to believe what I'm seeing, my voice rough and shaking with disbelief and desperate hope. Is this her power? Some hidden part of her she didn't even know existed? My broken heart is terrified to believe what's happening in front of me

"She must come with me," an otherworldly voice commands, power resonating through every word, making my skin crawl and sending ice down my spine.

It's a voice that seems to come from everywhere and nowhere, a presence that fills the space around us.

A growl rips out of me, raw and uncontrolled, pure instinct overriding everything. I reach for her—my grip on Dani tightens like a vice—I won't let her go, not to anyone or anything, not to whatever the hell this is.

"No!" I roar at the unseen force, yanking Dani back against me with all my strength, every ounce of power and will I've got. "She stays with me!"

My fangs are out, muscles tensed and ready to strike at whatever tries to take her from me. Dani is my mate, my reason for breathing, my entire world. I have no fucking clue what this thing is, and I don't trust a goddamn thing when it comes to her.

"You must trust me," the voice insists again, a note of urgency threading through the words, a plea that seems to resonate in the very marrow of my bones.

But how the fuck can I do that? How can I trust anything or anyone when it comes to Dani, when the mere thought of losing her threatens to shatter me beyond repair?

Before I can respond, before I can voice the torrent of emotions raging within me, Dani begins glowing brighter and brighter, the light intensifying until it's almost blinding, a supernova of pure, radiant energy. Then she's gone, vanishing in a flash like she never existed at all.

"No!" A tortured roar tears from my throat, raw and agonized. She was here, in my arms, and now she's been ripped away by forces beyond my comprehension.

I whip around, seeking the owner of the voice. "Bring her back, now goddammit," I demand, ready to tear apart anything that keeps us apart. Dani is my mate, my reason for existing. And I'll burn the world down to get her back.

Our bond, the intangible tether between us—it's gone. Snuffed out like a fucking candle in the wind. Her light, her essence, everything we share—all gone, as if she never was. My chest tightens, pressure crushing my ribs. I drop to my knees, my hand clawing at where my still heart resides.

No. No. No. This cannot be happening.

Without her, I'll spiral into madness, losing myself to the damn demons inside. She is my anchor, my redemption. Futility and devastation threaten to fucking drown me. I failed her—wasn't fucking strong enough to protect my mate. "Fucking bring her back!" I bellow again into the empty space where Dani just was. But only silence answers. No sign or trace of her remains.

Rage boils inside me, violent and scorching. She's been stolen from me, and I'm fucking powerless. Helpless. Weak. I drive my fist into the ground, welcoming the pain. It's better than feeling the wreckage of my heart. I need her. Need Dani like oxygen, like blood. She's my light in the endless dark. And now she's gone.

"Give her back!" My roar echoes through the chaos, a desperate shout that no one hears, swallowed by the madness around me. I'm moving, spinning around, hunting for something—anything—to channel the inferno burning inside me. The Shades. Those bastards want blood? I'll give them hell itself, a reckoning that'll haunt them forever.

Power explodes from my hands, fiercer than it's ever been, a force that tears through my veins like liquid lightning. Thunder cracks overhead, the sky bleeding black, and lightning splits the air, casting the battlefield in jagged, harsh light—that's fucking new. But there's no time to figure out why.

I tear through those Shade bastards with my telekinesis and lightning, striking with just a thought—the skies answering my call. The air reeks of ozone, and the stench of smoke fills my nose.

The winds scream, mirroring the agony clawing through me. Rain hammers down, a vicious downpour that drenches me, but I don't give a damn. The elements are wild, uncontrolled—a reflection of the chaos tearing me apart. She was my anchor, the only one who could hold back this storm.

More Shades burn to nothing, obliterated by my pain. It's never enough until she's back where she belongs. I'm a hurricane of destruction, demolishing everything in my wake.

My roar matches the thunder, a guttural sound that bleeds raw from my throat.

She has to come back to me. She fucking has to...

She is my everything; I am lost without her. Wholly and utterly fucking lost, adrift in a sea of despair with no anchor, no guiding light to lead me back to shore.

DANICA

54

I gasp for air, my eyes snapping open to a brilliance threatening to sear my retinas. I squint against the glare, the taste of iron still thick on my tongue. Panic claws at my chest, memories of the woods—the Shades—flashing like a nightmare's afterimage. Rhyland's arms, Lucian's grip, both desperately holding me, their faces a study in terror.

Then... nothing but the abyss.

I'm sprawled out like a jigsaw puzzle, missing half its pieces, noodling through the scattered snatches of time before the Big Blackout smacked me upside the head. My fingers start dancing all on their own, hunting for that searing hot souvenir—the tree limb that decided to play skewer with my chest.

But all my fingertips find is a blank canvas. Zilch in the way of scratches or scars. And this gown I've got on—so freaking white it's practically radioactive—doesn't have a single splatter of red. Which makes zero sense considering the state I last remember being in.

I haul myself upright, feeling about as disoriented as a cow on Astroturf, my brain scrambling to make sense of this absolute mindfuck. One second, I'm getting skewered like a kabob, the next, I'm waking up pristine and unblemished in what looks like heaven's waiting room?

Something is seriously, catastrophically off.

I slide my legs off what I can only describe as a bed fit for the gods themselves. The sheets are softer than a baby bunny's fur and so white I have to shield my eyes. My feet hit the floor, which is warm and smooth like glass but not slippery.

I take a few cautious steps, wincing at every sound I make. The noise gets swallowed up almost immediately in this massive, glowing chamber. The silence is suffocating. Eerie.

I half expect something to come screaming out of the shadows—some nightmare-fuel jump scare designed to stop my heart.

Columns rise like silent guardians along a pathway that seems to pull me forward, almost hypnotic in their beckoning. They're carved with intricate figures frozen in eternal conflict—angels locked in brutal stone combat with demons, a silent war carved into marble and trapped in time.

Where the hell am I?

Am I dead? Is this it? Did I actually kick the bucket, cross over, hop the rainbow bridge, take the final bow? All those stupid euphemisms people use when they're too scared to say the word "death"?

My stomach twists. Because if I'm dead, then Rhyland—

No. I can't think about that right now.

I stumble upon a mirror framed in ornate silver vines. It's like gazing into perfectly still water, and my reflection stares back at me. My hair falls in that effortlessly sexy way, not a single tangle or blood-matted strand in sight. But my eyes—they're different. Brighter. Deeper. Like they're holding onto knowledge I haven't earned yet.

I gotta say, mirror-me looks like she knows some secrets the old me didn't.

I hear a little swish behind me and spin around so fast I nearly drill a hole in the floor. But no one's there, just a fancy dress laid out on a stone bench by the bed. It's a serious gown, like something Athena would wear to the Greek God Met Gala. My heart hammers against my ribs like it's trying to escape, which is ridiculous given how serene this place feels. One meditation room isn't enough to undo the "survival mode" that's hardwired into my bones right now.

I give the dress a little touch, and it's like stroking distilled moonbeams, smoother than silk and probably with a price tag to match. Makes me wonder who left it here for me. Is it formal wear for meeting some gods over tea and ambrosia? Or maybe it's battle gear for some unseen big bad?

A soft breeze tickles my skin, smelling like rain kissing the sun-baked stone. It's weirdly comforting, but in an unfamiliar way, I can't put my finger on it. This whole place has my head spinning more than that merry-go-round ride from hell at last summer's carnival.

I take the gown carefully off the bench, holding it up to admire the intricate embroidery stitched into the bodice and sleeves. It looks like it was made for me, and the fabric drapes and flows perfectly to accentuate my curves. I slip it over my head, the material cool and silky against my skin. It's lighter than air, almost weightless. I smooth out the skirts that cascade to the floor, the color shifting from pearlescent white to a shimmering silver, depending on how the light hits it.

Twirling in front of the mirror, I can hardly recognize myself. The dress transforms me, making me look powerful yet ethereal, as if I could command armies or dance among the stars. Running my hands over the bodice, I notice delicate designs stitched in, constellations and planets in swirling patterns. It's like wearing a piece of the night sky.

I don't know who left this for me or why, but wearing it makes me feel brave, beautiful, and ready to face whatever awaits me in this strange, luminous place.

The taste of pennies fades as I hoof it through this megamansion, eyeballing every detail like evidence in a crime scene. Each footfall feels dreamlike, disconnected from reality. I half expect a hidden panel to collapse beneath me or some powerful angelic figure to materialize and render judgment.

But the further I go, the more this place starts giving me major sanctuary vibes—all hushed and peaceful, with an undercurrent of ancient mojo power thrumming through the walls.

Ahead, I spot a fountain carved from marble that practically screams wealth and divinity. Crystal-clear water cascades from some invisible source into an elaborate basin, pristine water lilies floating on the surface like they just bloomed this morning. I dip my finger into the cool liquid and watch the ripples distort my reflection into something almost unrecognizable—something more than I am. The water is cool against my skin, radiating a magic fountain of youth energy.

Maybe I'll wake up looking ten years younger if I take a dunk; who knows?

I'm creeping down this endless hallway like a ghost, hyperaware of every sound I make. My dress whispers against the marble with each step, the fabric swishing in a rhythm that feels almost orchestrated, like invisible hands are guiding my movement.

My heart pounds out an erratic cadence, like it's jamming to its own beat—probably Morse code for "WTF is happening?"

I have to give props to my ticker, though—its incessant drum solo is proof that I'm still kicking—or at least I'm pretty sure I am. The jury's still out on the alive vs. dead question until I find some cosmic receptionist to check me in.

This place is quieter than a library right before closing time. I keep padding through—maybe the next hall over will have a directory or a freakin' help desk—an angelic barista ready to offer cappuccinos and directions!

A macchiato would really hit the spot right about now.

The hallway seems to go on forever, lined with towering columns and walls etched with an endless battle. Angels and demons clash in stone, their struggle so raw and detailed I can practically hear the screech of metal and the desperate screams tearing from their throats. It's brutally gorgeous—all that violence crystallized and trapped in marble.

The craftsmanship is undeniably brilliant, but it's also deeply unsettling. So much savagery frozen in time. So much rage and suffering locked in stone, forced to relive the same brutal conflict for eternity.

I stop to admire one carving of an angel wrestling it out with a big, bad demon dude. Tracing my finger along those stone wings gives me the chills—the marble's freezing, but it lights a fire in my veins, too.

It feels oddly familiar, like I've traced these carved figures with my own hands before. But it's more than just a vague sensation—it's visceral, like my body remembers what my mind has forgotten. My muscles know this place even if my brain refuses to cooperate.

The cloud of recognition is suffocating, thick as fog. I push deeper into it, desperate to break through to something concrete, something real. So I forge ahead through this otherworldly passage, letting my fingers drag across the stone carvings as I move. Hoping the angels and demons etched into this place will guide me where I need to be.

What's waiting for me at the end?

A gift shop with novelty halo keychains?

A cosmic DMV to renew my soul license?

I have to be fucking dead.

A laugh escapes me—a hollow sound that bounces off the marble and is lost among the angels' wings.

Heaven? If so, where's Saint Peter with his keys or his checklist?

Where's the heavenly choir or the loved ones gone before me?

At this point, I'm just following the fancy stone breadcrumbs and hoping they don't lead me off a cloudy cliff. With each step, more questions unravel inside me. The familiarity isn't just in what I see—it's in what I feel, an echo of something profound and unexplainable.

The hallway seems infinite, as if each stride takes me both closer and farther from some unseen destination. Angels and demons blur past me now as I pick up pace, their silent war becoming a background to my own inner turmoil.

"Hello!" I shout into the void. There's only silence—an all-encompassing silence that fills every crevice and corner of this corridor.

I round a curve, and the hall opens into a vast rotunda, ringed by soaring columns that seem to stretch into infinity. Their marble surfaces gleam in the soft light that filters down from above. Filtered sunlight falls across the mosaic floor in dappled patterns, a kaleidoscope of color and texture that dances beneath my feet like a living thing.

I'm zoning out on the pretty decor when a voice resonates behind me, shattering the silence like a brick through a window—

"Dani..."

It stops me dead in my tracks, every muscle locking up tight, every nerve ending singing with a sudden, electric awareness. I know that voice.

I spin around so fast that my hair whips me in the face. My dress swirls dramatically around me, the fabric rustling like the whisper of a thousand secrets.

Now, without a shadow of a doubt, I know I'm dead.

RHYLAND

55

Anger fucking burns in my blood like a raging inferno that won't be tamed. I'm panting like a beast, the air heavy with the smell of burning wood and ozone. Those fucking Shades, the bastards that touched her, they're demolished now, obliterated. My might, unleashed and wild, turned them into ash and wreckage scattered all over the foggy wooded ground.

Trees that are left from my rage stand like blackened sentinels, their trunks split and smoldering, their leaves reduced to ash. I barely recognize this place now—a grim canvas of my wrath. The ground is scorched earth where my telekinetic energy ripped through it, tearing at the roots and soil. And the sky above—a witness to my onslaught—crackles with the remnants of the lightning I somehow commanded.

Each blast nailed those Shade fuckers dead-on. Watching them disintegrate into nothing felt pretty damn good for a second, but now there's just a hole where victory should be.

I'm hollowed out, scoured clean by the intensity of the magic I apparently wield.

What the fuck did I just do?

How did those deadly volts answer my call like eager hounds at my heels? I don't recognize myself anymore. My hands still tremble from the power that coursed through them.

What have I become?

Erik cuts through the chaos toward me, his steps slow and deliberate over the ruined ground. He's the eye of the storm—unshakable, steady, exactly what I need right now.

His hand lands on my shoulder like an anchor. He says nothing for a moment, silver eyes scanning me with the kind of quiet intensity only Erik can pull off. When he finally speaks, his voice is low and even, but there's a crack in it—barely there, but enough.

"Brother." A beat of silence. "I have seen you level armies. Tear through battalions without blinking." His grip tightens. "I have never seen anything like that."

I peer at him through eyes hazed by rage and an emotion too close to hopelessness. His silver stare locks with mine, sharp and lucid, piercing through the mess in my head. "You need to get this shit under control. Whatever it is."

His words help deflate the storm within. He's right. I need to leash the magic—now wild and unfamiliar—before it damn near controls me completely. I force my fists to unclench and my frame to relax. The energy simmering under my skin slowly settles as I breathe deep and release the lingering vestiges of that deadly tempest.

"I don't get it," I grind out as the final lightning sparks fade into nothing. "The skies—it fucking obeyed me."

Erik's hand tightens on my shoulder, grounding me further as I struggle to rein in this strange new power.

"Since when can I command the sky?" I ask, anger and confusion still churning inside me. The scent of ozone hangs heavy in the air, echoing the havoc I've wrought.

"We'll figure it out together," he assures me. "But right now, you need to focus on calming down."

His words hit me like a rope tossed into a raging storm. I grip it like my life depends on it, getting my shit together for Dani's sake—for all our damn sakes.

Lucian strides over with Axilya and Faderyn on his heels. Their faces are a picture of worry and befuddlement as they scan the chaos we're standing in.

"Where's Dani?" Faderyn demands, his voice sharp. The mere mention of her name ignites a fury in me, and it's all I've got to wrestle that anger down. My hands ball into fists, then relax, over and over, while my teeth are damn near grinding to dust, my jaw popping from the strain.

Axilya's pale green eyes sweep across the clearing, searching every inch for some hidden hint amidst the ruin. Lucian's quiet steeliness is tangible even as he observes the scene, those dark brown eyes cuttin' through the chaos like they're on the hunt.

Before I can pull my thoughts together to spill the ugly truth, Lucian's got his lips moving, ready to lay it all out. But hell, if I'm letting him drag it out—not when every fucking tick of the clock without her is a slice of forever lost to the void.

"She's gone," I snap, shutting Lucian down mid-sentence. My voice is rough, but it grabs everyone by the throat. "Someone, some voice—they took her."

"Took her?" Lucian asks with pissed-off confusion. "Who the fu—"

I'm on him before he can even finish, "I don't fucking know," I bark back. "Some...thing snatched her away." I lay it all out, everything I saw and the shitshow that ended with Dani just disappearing into thin air.

Lucian pales and doesn't say anything—it's a wise move. He's got the sense not to prod the raging beast that I damn well am right now.

I can't tear my eyes away from where Dani had been sprawled lifeless in my arms just minutes ago. That patch of earth is forever marked, the grass still bearing the bloody imprint of her body.

My fists ball up tight, her blood's metallic tang still clinging to my skin—a goddamn monument to how I failed her.

Axilya's voice pierces through the turmoil. "What did it look like when Danica was taken?" she asks, her tone sharp with urgency.

I lift my head, locking eyes with her. Even fucked up as I am, I can see that same terror staring back at me from those light green eyes of hers. "Some golden glow was all around her," I growl, my voice rough as hell. "It lifted her off the ground..." My words choke off, and I'm slammed again with that torturous memory.

"Azrael?" Erik asks, his silver eyes narrowed in thought.

I snap my head, dismissing that shit instantly. "No. This was way stronger than that damn serpent."

Azrael's all about his shadowy bullshit, his lies, and his tricks. But whatever snatched Dani, something else shone like a blazing sun, full of power and authority.

I turn back to lock onto Axilya's intense stare. "You've seen anything like this around? Some force in this place with that kind of serious muscle?"

She shakes her head slowly, her brow furrowed. "No. Nothing in this realm could manage such a feat."

"Perhaps something...or someone...from Atheria?" Lucian suggests quietly.

Atheria—that legendary heavenly place that's been blocked off from all the rest—Dani's true home.

I scoff at the idea, a hard, biting laugh escaping me. "They haven't stepped in before—why the hell would they step in now?"

Understanding dawns on Axilya's face. *"Because* of Danica," she breathes. "She has the power to cross between realms. Whoever took her must have tapped into that ability while she was..."

Dead. That silent word weighs a ton in the air. Dani had taken her last fucking breath in my arms right before she vanished. Some force had to make its move in that brief moment, twisting her realm abilities without her say-so.

"Remember Seraphina, Dani's guardian angel? She's got that realm-hopping trick up her sleeve. She popped into our world to see Dani before," Lucian remarks, connecting the dots with a hint of intrigue threading his voice. "What if she pulled the same stunt again just now?" His suggestion hangs in the air, hinting at a celestial interference that could change the game.

The reality of it drapes over me, cold and suffocating. It makes perfect sense they'd come for her, their child, scooping her back home when she died.

Lucian raises an eyebrow, the playful edge in his voice replaced by genuine curiosity. "So what's the play here? What the hell does this mean for us?" He crosses his arms, waiting for an explanation to piece together the implications of the unfolding events.

While my mind's spinning, Faderyn cuts in, "My bet? It was to save her. She's the one the prophecies are all about—she can't..." He hesitates, giving me a look like he's weighing his words before he drops the one that's going to haunt me to my grave: "Die."

I gotta get my head straight—she's in Atheria, or so we're guessing.

What the hell does that mean for me stuck down here? Are they gonna haul her ass back or what? Are they gonna cling on to her?

Fuck this. No way I'm letting this shit slide. She's got a damn destiny, and it's with me, right by my side. They better send her back. But the clock's ticking—how fucking long do I have to hold out before I lose my mind? I've gotta keep my cool and stay sharp. No way in hell am I losing Dani because I couldn't keep my head straight.

The fog creeps back, winding around our boots like it's slinking home after recoiling from my unleashed fury.

As if on cue, Erik's there, cutting through my internal crap with his trademark blade-sharp insight. "You have to tough this out, brother. We can't afford to lose you too," he says. He's got that unyielding, no-bullshit look in his steel gray eyes—the one that doesn't waver, doesn't doubt. "For now, we keep our heads down until Dani comes back. Without her, our hands are tied." His gaze locks on mine, steady and unwavering, "She will come back, brother."

That's the lifeline I gotta cling to, keep it buckled tight to my soul. But damn, if that hollow emptiness doesn't creep back in, that dark abyss that I can't shake off.

The Whisperlings start their crap again, buzzing in my skull. I push back, "We gotta move, find some higher ground."

DANICA

56

Seraphina—my very own celestial bodyguard. Her locks are like strands of pure sunshine, and those eyes? Gleaming gold, like she has a pair of miniature stars plugged in. Standing before me with major main-character energy, her aura practically screams, "I'm here, I'm divine, get used to it!"

"Hello, Dani," she croons, and it's like my soul just scored front-row tickets to the concert of a lifetime—a siren song I never knew I needed until now.

She moves toward me, and her golden wings unfurl, making her look like she's stepped right out of a Renaissance painting. With her dress catching the light, it's a full celestial spotlight effect—fancy.

Instantly, we're in a full-on hug, all jasmine and storm-scented drama, our bodies pressed together in a fierce embrace of joy, desperation, relief, and longing. "Seraphina, it's so good to see you," I say, and I mean it. Her presence is like a balm to my battered soul, a light in the darkness threatening to consume me.

"You too, dear. Although it's not quite as planned," she says, her voice tinged with that wry amusement I've always loved about her, admired, and envied in equal measure.

And it's true—this isn't how I imagined our reunion, not in a million years. I mean, who plans for their own death, for the possibility of waking up in some celestial waypoint, caught between worlds, realities, and destinies?

But then again, when has anything in my life ever gone according to plan? When have I ever been able to predict the twists and turns that fate has in store for me—the challenges, triumphs, and heartbreaks that have shaped me into the person I am today?

"I know this isn't what you expected," she states matter-of-factly.

I'm trying to process this. It's like my brain's buffering at the worst possible moment. When I manage to find words, they come out all high-pitched and whimsical, like I'm floating somewhere between disbelief and the ceiling. "I'm dead, aren't I?"

Saying it louder might break the enchantment and wake me from this dream.

Her smile is as soothing as hot cocoa on a cold day. "No, dear heart. You're very much alive. You're in Atheria," she tells me as if we're discussing the weather.

Okay, so the cheese has officially slid off my cracker. I'm not supposed to be in Atheria. Thanks to all the lore I've waded through, I know it's a real place—my home, per se, but it wasn't penciled in for today's itinerary on the grand realm-hopping tour.

I had my route all planned out, one stone at a time, methodical and calculated. Atheria was supposed to be a future adventure—a 'season finale' destination—not a random Tuesday pop-in.

"I brought you here because... well, I think you know." Seraphina's voice fades as memories wash over me. I'm back in the Whispering Woods, hanging onto consciousness—

I remember the Shades, followed by a sharp, searing pain. Lucian was screaming for Rhyland, then begging for forgiveness.

I'm teetering on comprehension when Seraphina brings the pieces together. "I had to prevent you from... turning," she begins, the gravity of her words slowly descending. When my face registers nothing but question marks, she adds, "Into one of them—creatures of the night."

There it is—a statement that holds the weight of this new world's sun.

Did Lucian and Rhyland feed me their blood?

It dawns on me that my rescue from the clutches of death was also sparing me from eternal life in the shadows, an existence she implies would come at the cost of something much more significant—perhaps my humanity itself.

"So you brought me here to..." I trail off, the implications swirling. "Wasn't I... dead?"

"Nearly," she affirms with a tender touch of reassurance. "I halted your transformation—I pulled you back from the precipice. I purified and restored you to health."

I'm trying to understand this whole back-from-the-dead plot twist, trying to make sense of a world where death isn't the end, where the rules that I've always taken for granted no longer apply. Because if you've got divine blood, if you've got a destiny that's written in the stars and a fate that's been foretold since the dawn of time, then death is just a timeout—a brief intermission in the grand drama of your existence.

"Please understand that my actions may have strayed from the path of rules, but my sacred duty is to watch over and protect you. I willingly embrace any repercussions that await me." Her voice carries the weight of solemnity, yet it's touched with gentle resolve.

I'm gawking at her, my mouth hanging open so wide you could park a celestial chariot in there, and I'm about two seconds away from turning on the waterworks. If there's one thing I've learned, it's that playing fast and loose with the cosmic rulebook—especially regarding the higher-ups and the divine crew—never ends well. "Seraphina, you can't be serious—"

"Fortuitously, your presence remains concealed; your father remains unaware," Seraphina imparts with gentle assurance.

"Hold up, what if he catches wind that I am here? Seraphina, I feel like you're holding out on me. Spill the tea, sis."

"I have dared to interfere with destiny—your destiny—which is an act the Gods see with disapproval. I have exceeded my mandate, yet at this moment, my only concern is fulfilling my responsibility to you. That is the entirety of my conviction," Seraphina expresses with serene confidence, devoid of any regret for her choices.

My eyes are brimming with tears now, the gravity of her selfless act hitting me like a celestial sucker punch. "If the powers that be catch wind of this, what's going to happen to you?"

"We must set aside those concerns for now, Dani. We have much to address, and our moments together are swiftly ebbing."

"My mother?" The words spill from my lips in a frantic gush. Our previous soul-baring chat in my corner of the great cosmic tapestry replays in my head—the part where I was meant to bring this up with the paternal figure. But I refuse to let this lead go cold; I'm desperate for the truth. Especially in light of Azrael's earth-shattering reveal—I have to know!

"That is a matter you will need to discuss with your father, I'm afraid," Seraphina deflects, her tone gentle yet firm.

Nope. Nah-ah. I'm done playing the waiting game. "Seraphina, just tell me...Please," I beg, my voice teetering on the edge of desperation. "I have to know."

She eyes me for a heartbeat, probably debating if I'm ready for the truth. Then, as if she can't resist the urge to spill the tea like a high school gossip queen, she let's it all out.

She quickly tells me the tale of my mother and my father—Elysium—weaving the words like threads of gold through the tapestry of my heritage. He came from Atheria, descending on currents of pure luminescence, a figure of myth-made flesh. With him, he brought the glow of the upper realms to Earth, capturing my mother's mortal heart with his divine light.

Then, boom—passion ignited, and—bam—I'm the spark.

"But Azrael," Seraphina's voice falters, her eyes darkening with sorrow. "He discovered their secret when she was eight months along with you." Her hand trembles as she reaches for mine. "He sought to end the prophecy before it could begin—to extinguish the light that would unite the realms and defeat the Darkness—Moretemis."

I can feel the sting of tears, the kind that sneaks up on you, as Seraphina unfolds more of this staggering history. She recounts how grim and ruthless Azrael decided to play for keeps, cutting my mother's life thread short while I was still part of her, nestled safe inside.

The guy was betting on a two-for-one deal—an exit strategy so cold it could freeze the sun. But here I am, the 'still-standing' testimony to a plan that didn't pan out as intended.

In that instant, with clarity sharp as a dagger, I swear a silent but deadly promise to myself: Azrael's days are numbered, and I'm the one holding the calendar.

"I had to do what I could," her voice trembles with gratitude. "I blasted him with my light and saved you—hid you among the mortals."

My mind's eye paints a vivid picture—Seraphina bringing me into this world, then spiriting me away to the hospital where I was abandoned.

Catching Seraphina's eye, all brimming with emotion like she's about to star in a tearjerker, I give her a glance that's pure gratitude—no additives. Grabbing her hand because sometimes words need a little hand-holding action, she tells me, "It was my honor, dear heart."

"And my mom? What happened with her...after?" The words claw their way past the boulder lodged in my windpipe.

Seraphina's response hits me like a celestial freight train. "Her soul was stolen."

I'm pacing, my feet moving on autopilot as I try to process this bombshell. "Moretemis?"

Seraphina nods in confirmation, the motion rigid. She swallows hard like the truth is a jagged pill. "Yes."

I stop pacing as she reaches for me. Her touch is like a warm blanket, chasing away all the chills. Her following words slam into me, "You are our hope, our light, Dani."

I melt into her embrace, the floodgates within me shattering as I release a lifetime's worth of anguish. She held the pieces to my mom's story, the key to understanding it all—she's the reason I escaped Azrael—Moretemis.

The noise that tears out of my throat is unfiltered and visceral—the type of soul-deep catharsis you don't even know you've bottled up until it shatters the silence. And now, the brutal reality hits—my mom's essence is stolen, ensnared by a grade-A nutjob who has no right to claim her.

I cling to Seraphina like she's made of mist, terrified that if I dare to relax my hold, she'll dissipate into nothingness. I'm mourning a mother ripped away before her time, a woman I never had the chance to know truly and now never will—all because my existence ignited a murderer's twisted obsession.

After a moment, Seraphina gently eases back, her hands tender as they cup my face, her thumbs brushing away the salty trails of sorrow. "Shh... don't cry, dear heart. There's still hope," she soothes, her voice a melody against the cacophony of my emotions. Her tears shimmer, betraying the depth of her feelings even as she radiates strength and comfort.

I echo her gesture, my fingers gently brushing against her face, snagging the crystalline droplets. My words stutter as I grasp at a glimmer of levity in our shared heartache. "No, you stop first," I quip, a wobbly smile surfacing despite the tempest raging within me. "How is there hope knowing my mother is damned for eternity? What's the hope in that?"

Seraphina dabs away her tears with tender gestures, and we find ourselves enmeshed in a maelstrom of emotions. "Salvation is within reach for her."

Just like that, the brief moment of levity evaporates—talk about a narrative curveball I didn't see coming.

"Follow me." Seraphina's fingers lace with mine as she leads me out of the room—a lifeline amidst the storm of revelations.

RHYLAND

57

We find the horses huddled together in the woods—they hadn't gone far.

I jump onto Storm, gripping the reins tight enough to make it clear we're done fucking around. It's time to move. I cast a look back at the crew. They're mounting up fast, their faces giving away a silent understanding. We're hauling ass back to the Sun Court and sticking around for Dani there.

We've overstayed our welcome in this shitshow of Whispering Woods and creepy fog.

Our horses don't need coaxing. Their instincts scream, 'Get the hell out,' and we're in tune with that plan. The map and meticulously prepped gear? Torched, thanks to my uncontrollable blaze of fury. It's my ass on the line in front of the Light King for scorching his prized possession.

The fog clings to us—whispers nagging at the edges of my mind, trying to get in. I throw up a mental fortress; thoughts of Dani become my ramparts and shields against the onslaught.

Lucian pulls up next to me, and I can see his usual bullshit confidence has taken a nosedive. He's all somber and shit—like he knows he messed up big time. "Look, Rhy... I fucked up, okay? Whatever you're gonna throw at me, do it. I'll take the fall," he says, bracing for whatever hell I decide to dish out.

"What did you do, Lucian?" Erik asks from my left.

"I..." He hesitates, and even through my seething, I notice the gravity of his confession. "I gave Dani my blood."

Erik is just staring, trying to piece together the shitstorm about to rain down on us.

"Fucking hell," is Erik's only response. Two quiet words, but they speak volumes.

My hand drags down my face as I try to contain the monster inside me, roaring for blood—Lucian's specifically. This brother of mine could have just messed things up royally. No one should mess around with the sacred bond we share with our mates. Now, Lucian's bound to feel everything she goes through—from her darkest depths of despair to her peaks of joy, it will slice through him.

"What do you want me to say, Lucian?" I growl, forcing myself to shove all thoughts of Dani's body tied to Lucian's to the depths of hell from where they came.

His face is all desperation and dumbassery mixed into one as he speaks. "I couldn't just stand there and watch her die, Rhy. I'm sorry, man—I shouted for you, I did. But fuck, letting Dani slip away wasn't an option! I had to act." Lucian's turmoil is clear, and a part of me understands the reasoning, even as another part wants to rip into him.

I nod tightly. "I know, little brother. I know," I reply, trying to keep my voice level over the damn cacophony of beastly rage in my head.

The ride through the night feels like the pre-show to a storm that's been brewing for ages. Axilya's getting twitchy—something about the woods being edgy tonight—and Faderyn's got his 'I sense a disturbance in the force' look going on. He thinks we're strutting into a trap. Hell, I've been feeling that for miles now.

"Feel that?" Axilya's voice is low, a whisper barely carrying over the rustling leaves.

Then the thunder rumbles, way off but closing in, the kind of sound that promises it ain't bringing anything but danger—an omen.

Erik's getting his usual 'time to whoop ass' vibe, "Stay sharp," he barks out.

The air turns ice fucking cold—like a wave of bad blood just curdled the night air around us. I don't need to see jack shit to know who's out there; we sure as hell aren't alone anymore.

"Adrian," I bark into the thickness, trying not to betray the shitstorm brewing inside me.

The silence that meets me is a little too pointed, and then out strolls the traitor himself. There's a war going on in his eyes, but he stands there, stoic as hell.

"I'm sorry, brother," he spits out, and that's my cue; Azrael, the bastard, materializes out of nowhere.

The forest mood shifts, and it feels like everything is holding its breath.

With his trademark infuriating arrogance, Azrael begins to spew his verbal diarrhea. "Oh, Rhyland, isn't it just tragic how far this pitiful little realm has fallen in such a short span? It's almost enough to bring a tear to my eye," he sneers, with sarcasm and disdain.

I clench my fists, refusing to rise to his bait. "If by 'short span' you mean the four shitty weeks since you last fucked things up, then yeah, things were fine before your ugly mug decided to show up again," I snarl, showing a little fang for effect.

His warped, grating laughter scrapes against my nerves like razor blades on a blackboard. "Oh, I suppose—more like an agonizing four years, give or take," he muses, his tone laced with perverse amusement.

I don't give a damn what he's on about with time—I know time flows differently here.

"Now, where, oh, where could our dear, sweet doctor have scampered off to? Her presence is so urgently needed," he wonders aloud, his eyes sweeping the area with exaggerated movements. A contemptuous sneer curls his lips as he searches, his every gesture a biting mockery.

I'm on a knife-edge, my beast ready to rip right out of my skin and dance on his grave. "She's out of your reach, Azrael. So fuck off."

Azrael's voice oozes venom as he mocks me mercilessly. "What's the matter, Rhyland? Did you fuck up keeping your mate under your wing—some guardian you turned out to be," he spits, his eyes glittering with malice. "So, where's our darling little songbird flown off to now, hmm? Surely you've got her tucked away somewhere safe and sound, right?"

I'm fighting to stay on top of the anger I'm about to unleash, the fury threatening to consume me whole. "Not now, asshole—" is all I manage to grunt before the shadows yank me from Storm's back, slamming me to the ground with all the grace of a wrecking ball. The impact knocks the wind from my lungs, leaving me gasping for air as I struggle to regain my footing.

Shadows and ghostly figures swarm us, their ethereal forms dodging our blows and laughing at our attempts to bust through their ranks. It's like trying to fight smoke: Our fists and weapons pass harmlessly through their insubstantial bodies, meeting nothing but empty air.

We're punching shadows, our efforts futile and ineffective, while Lucian's and Erik's desperate swings go right through them, their blades slicing through the murky darkness without finding purchase. Axilya and Faderyn are in the same predicament, subdued by the relentless onslaught of the shadow horde. The damn shadows absorb everything we throw at them like a black hole, leaving us drained and powerless.

Then, as if to add insult to injury, I'm met with chains—no matter how much power I summon, how much strength I pour into my struggles, these chains are like the ones I faced with Amara—fucking fae-cursed, sapping everything I have, leaving me weak and helpless.

Out of nowhere, a horde of these shadow pricks wrenches me to Azrael. Their ghostly hands hold me fast, their grip like iron despite their insubstantial forms. Suddenly, my face becomes intimate with the dirt, the grit, and rocks scraping against my skin as they force me to the ground.

Azrael's boot collides with my jaw in a nauseating, bone-shattering crunch, an explosion of white-hot agony radiating through my face as he viciously grinds his heel into my battered flesh. "Know your place, you miserable, crawling maggot," he snarls, his voice as frigid and unforgiving as the icy kiss of a steel blade pressed against my back, slicing through the fabric of my clothing to bite hungrily into my skin.

Adrian steps forward, carrying that smug 'I-got-secrets' look. My pulse hammers a warning, and Adrian's gaze is full of shit I don't want to see—like apologies, he doesn't mean that feels like a slap.

Azrael, the sadistic puppet master orchestrating this hellish circus, delivers the coup de grâce with a twisted flourish. "I must extend my gratitude, dear Viking, for so graciously providing the perfect bait. Your precious Dani will come sprinting straight into my waiting embrace like a moth to a flame," he purrs, with perverse anticipation. "And oh, the delightful surprises I have in store for her when she arrives."

I sneer at Azrael, my lip curling in defiance even as the shadows hold me fast. "The hell you playing at?" I spit, glaring up at him as he leans over me, all cocky and self-assured, the shadows he's whipped up swirling around him like a living cloak.

"There's someone positively writhing in anticipation of being reunited with you," Azrael hisses, his eyes smoldering with pure, unadulterated malevolence. A vicious, warped smile contorts his features into a nightmarish visage of sadistic glee.

I can barely follow his gloating as the shadows yank me through the abyss, their icy tendrils wrapping around me like a vice, dragging me into the heart of darkness. Zipping through the shadows is a goddamn gut-twister—my stomach churning, the pitch-black void pressing in on me from all sides, an aroma of sulfur thick enough to taste coating the back of my throat.

We slam to a halt, and I'm dumped unceremoniously on the ground. My body hits the unforgiving stone with a bone-jarring thud. I hurl up nothing but blood, the coppery taste mingling with the lingering sulfuric stench, courtesy of that hellish ride we just blasted through.

His shadows yank me up like they're Azrael's own damn hands, their grip bruising, and I find myself staring at a nightmare I never wanted a replay of. Amara's perched on her throne, her eyes cold as the ice queen she is, and she loves every moment of my humiliation, drinking in my pain like it's the finest vintage.

Azrael struts his victory, convinced that Dani is coming for me and that he has the perfect bait to lure her into his trap.

Amara throws me a frosty look, and her voice drips with mock warmth, a sickly sweet poison that coats every word. "My pet, what a treat it is to have you back. You're like a walking, talking riot wherever you go." Her words slice through the chilly air as she lords over me from that nightmare of a throne, carved out of terror—a monument to her cruelty.

"Yeah, a real fucking pleasure to see you too," I sneer back at Amara.

Azrael barks out an arrogant laugh."Oh, he's the ideal little maggot to dangle on the end of our line," he remarks with a smug, self-satisfied smirk. Laying it all out there, no bullshit. "Our dear, heroic savior won't be able to resist rushing to his rescue. And when she takes the bait, we'll be primed and ready to spring the trap."

Amara gives me a look that could freeze hell over, her eyes boring into mine with a malevolent intensity that sends a shiver down my spine. "Oh, pet. Such secrets. Have you forgotten all about my lovely lessons?"

DANICA

58

As I step into the massive room, I feel like I've walked onto the set of *Gods Gone Wild*. The jaw-dropping glitz makes the Sun Court look like child's play. The celestial decorators really went all out here—it's part renegade architect's magnum opus, part cosmic exhibit. Every glint and glimmer here hollers "opulence" loud enough to make the most pampered royals blush.

Seraphina's hand is a lifeline as we wade through this tsunami of splendor. Crystals compete for attention with their prismatic tango, lighting up every inch of the place. You know the ones I'm talking about—they're not content, just being fabulous. They're throwing a full-on luminescent rave.

Under our feet, the marble gleams with a polish so fierce it's nearly blinding. Heck, I half-expect to find cherubs detailing the corners. Look up, and the ceiling dissolves into stars, which brings about a minor existential crisis—am I inside or somehow space-walking?

"This is just—" The words die on my tongue as my gaze snags on another ethereal presence—a male. He is breathtaking, with chestnut locks cascading to his shoulders and eyes so luminous they could be forged from molten gold. He commands attention at the chamber's far end, an object cradled in his grasp. Towering, sculpted, the very essence of divinity, his wings are pristine, the hue of freshly fallen snow.

Seraphina nudges me on, her voice a cocktail of pride and a pep talk. "Come, Dani, meet Jophiel," she encourages, nudging me from trepidation to determination.

I shuffle forward, my feet barely obeying me. Jophiel has this vibe that's half 'wisdom of everything' and half 'cool uncle who knows all the best jokes.' His good looks are timeless. His aura is less intimidating and more friendly than I expected.

"Dani," he rings out the word—it's epic yet somehow tinged with 'let's grab a coffee.'

Jophiel awaits, his expression one of anticipation, as I navigate forward, wading into the sun-strobe display of light and warmth.

"I trust Seraphina has already informed you of the pressing reason for your unceremonious arrival. We had to step in lest your beloved—your 'mate,' if that's the term you prefer—commit an act so astoundingly foolish we feared the worst."

At the mention of Rhyland, defensiveness spikes within me, and I am ready to defend my vampire against an onslaught of sanctimony. They may hold dominion over the realm of light, but I will not let him disparage the man who lives in the shadow of my heart.

"He did what was necessary. He felt he had no other option," I defend him fiercely.

"Your love tethers you to darkness. It is a dangerous bond," Jophiel warns, his words a celestial breeze that could snuff out stars.

"Then consider it tethered," I counter, the bite in my response undiluted, a symphony of conviction for Rhyland's worth.

The tension between us crackles like static in the air—a celestial being grappling with a mortal choice.

"Then you must seek the means to make sure you have completed the Soul-Tie," Jophiel drops the reference casually, as though I'm already well-versed in the subject matter.

"What exactly is a Soul-Tie?" I ask.

I'm completely in the dark about this divine stranger's identity or how he fits into this cosmic puzzle.

Apparently attuned to my unspoken questions, Seraphina chimes in: "Jophiel is one of Elysium's most trusted confidants. He is an angel renowned for his profound wisdom and boundless compassion."

"A Soul-Tie is precisely what it sounds like. It is an act of willingly giving and tying your soul to another, and they, in turn, offer and tie theirs to you. It shields you, safeguarding your soul from being seized by another."

His gaze locks with mine as the pieces snap together in my mind. He's referring to the horrifying possibility of Moretemis stealing my soul or, even more unthinkable, Rhyland's.

"Okay, but how? What do I need to do? I thought I already accomplished that by bonding with him. I sensed it at that moment—my soul entwining with his." The words tumble out in rapid fire.

"I—We—are not well-versed in vampire blood-bonding. A Soul-Tie is far more enduring and intricate," Jophiel states with unyielding authority, his words resonating with absolute conviction.

Isn't that the same damn thing? I'm so confused.

Seraphina faces me, her expression conveying the gravity of our situation. "You must seek the one who holds the knowledge of this ancient rite, someone to guide you through the process. This practice was lost when the realms were sealed away from one another. I yearn to give you the answers you need, dear heart, but alas, I do not possess them."

Realization dawns on me like a divine epiphany. This is precisely why Moretemis has been able to plunder souls with impunity—because they remain unclaimed, ripe for the picking.

"Then why didn't my father tie his soul to my mother's?" I blurt out, desperate for answers.

"Elysium sought to achieve precisely that," Jophiel explains with firm resolve. "However, he was unable to find the means to complete it before your mother's untimely demise. This is why we need you to see it through to prevent such a tragedy from happening again."

I stand there, shock and confusion coursing through me. If my parents had performed this *soul-tie*, my mother's soul would have been protected, safe from the fate that claimed her. The realization hits me like a punch to the gut, and a deep sense of loss washes over me. But amidst the grief, a fierce determination takes root. I can't let the same happen to Rhyland. I won't lose him, not to Moretemis. Whatever it takes, I'll ensure our souls are bound, forever intertwined, so that we'll never be torn apart.

"Very well." Jophiel clears his throat, signifying the shift in focus. "Let's proceed to the heart of the matter for which we've beckoned you here. We are running out of time."

The implications of that statement elude me. The longer I linger here, the more I feel like a disobedient child, sneaking out and dreading the inevitable moment when the parental figure catches on to my misdeeds.

Talk about divine grounding.

He opens his hands to reveal a diamond-studded box, exquisite and captivating in its craftsmanship. This box, no doubt, carries something significant within it.

"Be ever mindful that Rhyland's path of shadows may yet be your undoing, Dani. Until we know for sure that your souls are, in fact, tied, hold fast to your path and cradle your luminescence."

A final warning.

As the diamond-studded box opens with an almost celestial whisper, Jophiel presents the Atherite stone—a crystal that seems to throb with the very essence of his realm.

My breath catches, stolen momentarily by the pure grandeur before me. The stone's facets are mesmerizing, each appearing to cradle swirling galaxies within their depths, a dance of cosmic light and shadow playing across its surfaces.

"This is the legacy to which you were born," Jophiel proclaims, his voice harmonizing with the essence of the universe. "The Atherite stone harbors formidable powers—forces of creation and annihilation intertwined in its heart."

"What does it do?" I can't help but ask, curiosity laced with awe as I reach out tentatively toward the stone.

My fingers barely graze its surface, but even that feather-light contact sends a shiver of warmth through me. The stone feels almost alive, pulsating with an energy that resonates at the same frequency as my heartbeat.

"The Atherite embodies the very essence of Atheria—light and creation," he explains with a gravity that seems to make the air around us thrum with importance. "It can heal, cleanse, and bring clarity where there is darkness. For you, Dani, it will resonate with your gifts, allowing you to access the light within and manifest it in ways the realms have yet to witness. It is not just a symbol of power but a token of your destiny."

I hold the stone in my hand, admiring its impossibly beautiful appearance—how it seems to drink in the light around it and refract it into a million dancing colors. But when I think this moment can't become more awe-striking, the unexpected happens: the stone breaks free from the confines of my palm, levitating with a mind of its own.

It hovers for a heartbeat, a suspended spectacle of sparkling wonder before it moves—deliberate and sure—toward my crown. The stone gently embeds itself, finding a home among the ornate metalwork as if it were always meant to be a part of me.

My head buzzes, alive with a new power that feels alien yet familiar. Tingling sensations race down my spine, spreading to the rest of my body as the Atherite syncs with my essence.

"And you," he asserts with a grave tone that bears the weight of eternal truths, "are now protected, untouchable, and possibly even transcend mortality."

Immortal—the word echoes in my skull with a reverberation that might as well be a bass drop at Lucian's nightclub.

"So you mean... I can't die?" The question tumbles out of me before I can stop it, and I instantly feel like a newbie at a supernatural convention.

Jophiel's reply is patient—a lesson in cosmic custodianship. "Mortality's embrace remains, ever looming, for the stone's judgment is not ours to command—it chooses when, how, whom it aids, and indeed if it chooses at all."

My confusion is evident as I try to understand the idea of an inanimate object that decides, judges, and discerns. It's not just a 'get out of death free' card.

"This stone is imbued with the breath of the ancient gods, entwined with the very fabric of existence itself. It is not merely a tool to be wielded but a divine entity with its own will. It is no gatekeeper to immortality but a sovereign of restoration, guided by a wisdom far beyond your mortal grasp."

Well, alrighty then. We're dealing with a choosy stone with a sense of self—or at least a discerning taste in life paths. Noted!

I take a deep breath, steadying my nerves before finally voicing the question that's been burning inside me. "I need to know why I have been given this task—why Elysium himself couldn't defeat Moretemis?"

"Danica, Elysium's strength and his light are vast but not infinite. As he is bound by the very fabric of Atheria and its need for balance, there are limits to what he can do against Moretemis."

"But still," I press on, frustration lacing my voice, "he is a God. How is it possible that Moretemis, banished and shadowed, could be beyond his reach?"

Jophiel's gaze, as warm and expansive as the sunlit heavens, meets mine. There is sorrow there and the weight of unspoken eternity. "Danica, if there were a way for Elysium to vanquish Moretemis himself, he would have gladly done so. But the balance of our realms, the intricate fabric of power that binds everything, prevents him—us—from acting directly against him."

I become defensive, the frustration gnawing at the edges of my resolve. "So the realms get to stay 'balanced' while my life gets turned upside down? What kind of balance is that?"

He smiles, a gesture both melancholy and tender. "Balance does not mean an absence of strife. The shadows exist as a counterpart to light. We are bound by cosmic laws, restrictions that Moretemis relentlessly seeks to exploit. His banishment and locking of the realms were the extent of Elysium's influence. But the bastard's playing dirty, trashing the rules and tipping the scales—just like the old gods and prophecies said he would."

A laugh bubbles out, all sharp edges and irony. Here's Mr. Holiness himself, slinging slang like some street corner prophet, and here I am, yanked into this celestial tug-of-war.

Universe, your sense of fairness is seriously whack.

"Danica," he says, his voice resonating with the undercurrent of creation itself, "your destiny is not merely chosen. It is forged by who you are, by the light you carry within. You are born of two worlds, and this unique lineage is the key to transcending the limitations that bind Moretemis and Elysium."

I shake my head, disbelief shadowing my thoughts. "And if I can't do it? If this power I'm born with isn't enough?"

He approaches—the light of his being casting no shadow, an awe-inspiring reality I struggle to accept. "It will be enough, for it must be. There has never been another like you, Dani. You embody the hope of all seven realms, the promise of renewal. Your journey will awaken all the power that slumbers within you. When you collect the stones and face Moretemis, it will be as an equal—light to his darkness."

RHYLAND

59

Here I am again. Rotting in some black pit, only this time that bastard Azrael is banking on using me as fucking bait to lure Dani to him.

These damn stone walls might as well be bleeding black, trapping me in a pitch pit stinking of death and old shit.

Shadows slink around like live things, a thick blanket of darkness choking out any speck of hope. I can almost hear the ghost of my old self, that green kid, rattling off prayers to my Norse gods, who have turned a deaf ear. Now? I don't bother wasting my breath on begging. My trust is in the toughened core of my endless vampire soul.

Nothing but heavy silence down here, broken up by the screech of these rusty-ass chains every time I try to suck in some air. Suspended from the ceiling, arms wrenched above my head—chained up tight. Can barely brush the ground with my feet.

I've lost track of time, being suspended down here, trapped here with nothing but my own thoughts for company. Time down here bleeds together into one endless, nightmarish stretch of existence.

Days?

Weeks?

I have no fucking clue anymore.

Time has lost all meaning in this hellhole, each moment stretching out into an eternity of pain and despair. The darkness presses in on me from all sides, a suffocating blanket threatening to smother the last embers of my sanity.

I drift in and out of consciousness, my mind playing tricks on me, conjuring up visions of my worst fears and deepest regrets.

The pain's intense, like a motherfucker, with my body stretched tight, and I can barely draw a breath against the crushing weight on my ribs.

This is some hardcore bullshit. But I'll be damned if I give these assholes the satisfaction of hearing me complain. Just gotta ride out whatever sick game they've got planned next. Not the first time trying to break me, but I swear it'll be their last.

The beast inside is clawing its way out, raging in the fucking darkness now that Dani's vanished—haven't been fed in days, weeks, I don't know anymore. The bloodlust is reaching its peak. My fangs ache for flesh. But I'll be damned if I lose my grip. I've gotta keep the faith that she'll come back to me. I know it in my soul.

I've weathered some shit, but this place wants to swallow me up and spit out whatever's left. Can't let that happen. Gotta dig deep and hold on—for her.

"Azrael! You piece of shit, let me the hell out!" I'm not gonna let whatever twisted game they're playing drag Dani into this go down.

Minutes tick by, then the door of the cell grinds open, and a flood of torchlight damn near blinds me. Amara struts in, Azrael—her damn enforcer—right on her heels. They're both grinning like they've cornered me, and it churns my gut to see it. But I lock eyes with them, not giving an inch.

"Seems my pet's getting antsy in his pen," Amara drawls, running a pointed nail down my chest. I keep my stare dead ahead, not giving her the satisfaction of reacting to her bullshit.

"Where's my brothers, you ugly bitch?" I demand.

Azrael's fist plows into my face. The coppery, metallic taste of blood floods my mouth in an instant. "Tsk, tsk, Mr. Eriksson. Didn't anyone ever teach you that it's rude to speak out of turn?" he chides, with mock disapproval and sadistic amusement.

Amara's icy cackle bounces off the walls. "Mmm....your filthy tongue only fuels me more. You ready to give in to my desires yet—my pet?"

I raise my head and spit blood at her feet. She snarls, her claws twitching to tear me apart. But she smiles slowly instead, a viper waiting to strike. "Alright then. We'll keep this little game going a while longer."

"Fuck you."

"Oh, I'm just waiting until you do." She cracks her palm against my bare chest, curiosity burning in her eyes. "I'm really itching to find out if what you're spouting is true or not," she snaps at Azrael.

He grins back, "There's only one way to find out."

What the hell are they on about?

She tears into me with those claws, shredding me up like a piece of meat, then goes to town, sucking down my blood 'til my head's spinning and my legs are shaking.

She purrs, her tongue darting out to lick her bloody lips. "Mmm...delicious," she moans, her hands sensually caressing my body. "Your blood is like an aphrodisiac. I can feel it coursing through me."

I want to fucking puke.

"But I can't help but wonder...what other fluids of yours would satisfy me in more...intimate ways?" Her eyes gleam with a wicked hunger as she leans in closer, ready to explore all the dark desires that linger within her.

"Fucking kill me now, damn it," I growl, a sneer of disdain aimed right at her.

"Didn't I tell you?" Azrael says, eyeing her like I'm not even in the room.

"My dear, your information never fails to arouse me. The notion of vampiric essence being so intoxicating never crossed our minds—we saw it as a mere poison, a toxin. It is nothing short of pure ecstasy."

She grinds herself on me, staking her claim like I'm her damn prize, and in this moment, nothing tempts me more than the thought of sweet, dark nothingness.

Her seductive gaze meets mine as she whispers, "It's lust in a venomous bottle." I can feel her twisted desires seeping through every word.

In a split second, she yanks down my pants, and they hit the floor with a thud. Bound and strained to the fucking max, I keep fighting against her, but every tug just amps up the excruciating agony pulsing through my arms.

"You have no idea the things I'm gonna do to you, pet," she growls, high as a fucking kite and buzzing from my blood. Nothing can stop her now, and my gut twists with nausea at the thought.

She grabs my balls with a firm grip, then takes hold of my flaccid cock and starts to pump it roughly. I feel a surge of disgust and anger as she touches me, and I have to fight the urge to vomit.

"Oh, my, my... The rumors about men of your stature appear to hold water—well endowed, indeed," she purrs.

Azrael's voice cuts through the air like a serrated blade, heavy with disdain. "For fuck's sake, Amara, I don't have time for your incessant, horny shit right now. I assure you, there will be ample time to indulge your depraved little fantasies later," Azrael scoffs, his voice laden with exasperation and contempt. "Keep your hands off the merchandise for now," he demands, his lip curling contemptuously.

Amara's body locks up rigid as hell, like some invisible force just slams the brakes on her. She's forced to release her grip on me, and I let out the breath I'd been choking back.

Even Azrael can tell this is one fucked-up situation.

Azrael forcefully inserts himself into my field of vision, his iron grip seizing my jaw in a bruising hold as he pries my eyelids apart with ruthless fingers. "Well, well, well, just as I suspected... the clock's ticking, Rhyland, and it won't be long before that savage beast inside you takes the reins. And when it does, your soul will be served up to Moretemis on a silver platter—now that's what I call a truly delectable prize," he gloats, his laughter ringing out like a demented hyena reveling in the twisted hilarity of his own sick joke.

I am not letting this bastard get to me. He won't fucking break me, no way in hell. My brain is spinning, trying to figure out how these two are in cahoots and what twisted game they're playing. I cock an eyebrow, glancing between these two dipshits. "So what's the story with you assclowns anyway? Bumpin' uglies?" I spit, my words dripping with venom.

Azrael's icy stare bores into me, his eyes narrowing with barely contained rage. "Mind your tongue, Rhyland, or I'll slice it clean off," he hisses, his voice a deadly whisper.

My laughter echoes through the room, a harsh, manic sound that borders on hysteria. Am I losing my mind? Possibly. But I couldn't care less, not when I'm facing down these two sadistic fucks.

"Oh, did I piss you off?" I quip with a smirk, my split lip stretching painfully with the motion. "Hey, if you're into pussy that reeks of rot, who am I to judge?"

Another damn fist slams into my face, the taste of blood flooding my mouth, coppery and thick. I spit it out, watching with grim satisfaction as it splatters across the floor.

Then Azrael makes a beeline for the door, Amara in tow—both of them strutting out like they couldn't give a damn, smug in their belief that time and goddamn solitude are gonna break me, that I'll crumble under the weight of my own thoughts.

Left in the dark, naked and bleeding, my mind can't help but wander to Lucian and Erik. Are my brothers locked up close by, or have they been dealt a shittier hand? That bitch and that bastard have their fates hanging over my head like a juicy carrot, just another mindfuck in their twisted game.

What if my brothers are getting screwed over while I'm rotting in this shithole? The last time I saw Erik, he was chained up just like I was, his silver eyes burning defiantly. And

Lucian...that smartass is still my blood, no matter what shit we've been through. If I've lost them, the blame's on me. I should have fought harder, should have protected them better. But here I am, screwing up with them just like I'm screwing up with Dani.

Dani, my fierce, gorgeous angel. The thought of her in Amara and Azrael's clutches, suffering as I am, makes my blood run cold. "If they get their claws into you like they have with me, I'll never fucking forgive myself," I whisper, my voice hoarse with emotion.

I try talking to her, sending my words through our mental link, but it's like shouting into a damn black hole—nothing echoes back, just a yawning emptiness that threatens to swallow me whole.

I'm bleeding out, and this godforsaken collar has fucked up my healing, leaving me weak and dizzy. My sight's getting fuzzy, my grip on consciousness slipping away like sand through my fingers. I'm flickering between moments of peace and some fevered, hellish dreams, my mind a kaleidoscope of nightmares.

I'm watching my brothers getting cut down as some shadowy motherfucker with eyes like firestorms tears through everything I give a damn about. Adrian's icy warnings are repeating in my mind, a haunting soundtrack to the horrors unfolding before me. And Dani, she's caught like a fly in Amara's web, struggling and screaming as the Shadow Queen's poison seeps into her veins.

I'm pulling at these damn chains, desperate to save her, but she's fading further and further away until all that's left is the dark, a suffocating void that threatens to consume me. And my fuck-ups, they're right there with me, hounding me, even as I slip into the abyss, a chorus of accusation and recrimination that follows me down, down, down...

DANICA

60

Ever in tune with my emotional currents, Seraphina offers a light touch to my arm—her presence reassuring amidst the celestial vastness. "There is a subtlety in the flow of time that you must come to understand," her voice carrying a soft power that belies the depth of her words.

I pivot toward her, absorbing the comfort of her presence. "What about time?" I inquire.

She reveals how time meanders differently across the realms—it isn't the linear march I've always known. Here, days could translate to moments elsewhere or stretch into years.

That revelation trips my heart into double time. *"Years?"*

The prospect of such temporal dissonance sets my head reeling.

Acknowledging my concern with a solemn nod, she elaborates, "Indeed, the nature of time is unique to the realms. Consider it a fabric we traverse with utmost caution and respect."

Jophiel offers to elaborate, flicking his lush brown hair over his shoulder, painting a vast, intricate picture of existence's timelines. "Imagine each realm as a chamber in time's grand palace, each with its own pendulum of moments. While navigating your native temporal river, remember the other parallel streams, each fundamental to the cosmic ballet."

The mind-bending complexity of this multi-tiered reality sucker-punches me. I wring my hands, anxiety spiking. "How long have I been stuck in this celestial time-out corner?"

Bewilderment laces my tone as flashes of lost moments with Rhyland flicker through my thoughts. Did I accidentally hit the cosmic fast-forward button on our life together?

Jophiel doesn't hesitate, "Four weeks by Luminara's measure."

My chest constricts like a heavyweight is crushing it, and my stomach takes a sickening plummet. But I've barely been in this realm, right? An hour at most if I go by my watch's time.

"How long have I been here?"

"A day," Seraphina answers.

A tidal wave of sheer panic crashes over me, lodging a suffocating lump in my throat. Visions of Rhyland's safety—or lack thereof—slice through my core like razor blades.

"I need to get back to him—*now.*"

I don't waste a second—the air shimmers with the summoning of my portal, Seraphina swiftly interjects, her voice laced with a prudent warning, "Not advisable."

"Why not?" I snap.

Seraphina's voice carries the weight of the heavens as she addresses the gravity of the situation, "Portals are unpredictable elements; they can be as wild as gambles cast in the dark. Creating an opening here could provide Azrael a direct path to our location, a danger we cannot entertain."

My resolve is ironclad, even as my insides contort in anguish at the mere thought of what he might be enduring. "But Rhyland—"

"I will send you back," Seraphina interrupts, sensing my urgency.

Before I can protest or thank her, Atheria's light evaporates, and the opulence fades into grim shadows.

My feet hit the hard stone with a thud, and suddenly, I'm choking on the dank, stale air instead of breathing in Atheria's sweetness—real nice move, sis—no heads up, no goodbye, just a famous celestial Uber.

My eyes struggle to pierce the darkness shrouding this place like a living entity.

What kind of voodoo shit did she pull? Is there some cosmic fine print that's going to bite me in the ass for her superhero catch and release? Or even more terrifying—what's the karmic blowback for Jophiel slipping me the Atherite stone at this juncture in my epic quest, assuming that was even part of the grand master plan?

No time to fret over the potential divine ramifications now, though.

I notice I'm back in my leathers, hugging every curve. I feel the weight of the daggers strapped to my thighs, cozy as ever in their sheaths.

Then, a familiar scent hits me, stopping my breath. Rhyland. His scent is faint but unmistakable, cutting through the stale air. I wave my hand, summoning a ball of light, desperate to lay eyes on him.

The cell flickers into view, harsh and unforgiving. And there, chained up like a slab of meat in a butcher's fridge, hangs Rhyland. My heart lurches. They've got my Viking trussed up and suspended from the ceiling. Anger flashes hotly through my veins.

"Rhyland," his name—only a whisper in this dark cell.

His once strong form is now a canvas of pain—battered, bloodied, and bruised. The sight makes something inside me crack, and my heart doesn't just break. It shatters. Splintering into a thousand tiny pieces, each one crying out in anger and hurt for him.

"Oh my god—Rhyland!" His name bursts from me, tearing through the silence of the cell as I sprint to him. I reach him in what feels like a heartbeat, hands shaking as I grip his face, urging him to look at me. "Please, Rhyland, look at me." My plea is a whisper against the cold stone and colder reality we're facing.

His injuries are severe—this isn't just flesh and bruises; there's a torment here that runs deeper than skin. He's unresponsive and doesn't even flinch at my touch when I'm used to at least getting a growl.

I can't—I won't—lose him. Not like this, not when we've only just started rewriting our forever.

Determination ignites within me, a fire fueled by love and desperation. I summon my light, that raw, instinctive magic that thrums in my veins, and focus it into a ball of pure intention. My arm arcs forward, the light responding to my unspoken command, and I hurl it at the damned chains suspending him.

With a force that vibrates through the chamber, the light collides with the cold metal. The chains shatter, the sound of liberation ringing loudly in my ears, and his body drops. He lands with a heartbreaking thud on the hard stone, and I'm there, scrambling to his side even before the echo fades.

"Rhyland, sweetie...wake up." My voice softens, brushing against the hard lines of desperation. With newfound energy coursing through my being, I coax the remaining chains around his wrists to surrender. This time, they fall away with less ceremony, clinking against the dungeon floor.

The collar around his neck—that cursed piece of iron and evil—snags my gaze, and I see nothing but red. A surge of fury tightens my grip, and my other hand is already moving toward my wrist, offering the one thing I know can mend more than just his physical wounds.

I press my wrist to his pale lips, the warmth of my skin stark against his colder-than-night kiss. "Rhyland, come on, drink... please," I plead, my voice a tight whisper of urgency. "You need this. I need you."

My heart races as I watch him remain still, unresponsive to my pleas. With desperation clawing at my chest, I grab my dagger and slice open my wrist, blood spurting out in thick rivulets. My hand shakes as I press it against his lips, urging him to drink from the wound.

He doesn't move as my warm blood trickles down his chin. I begin to panic. But then, *finally,* he begins to wrap his chapped lips around my bleeding wrist, slowly sucking the life-giving liquid into his mouth. "Yes," I whisper with relief. "There you go."

He gulps down my blood with reckless abandon, his body shaking. I reach out with my free hand to brush back his unkempt hair, but he suddenly grips my wrist like a starving man. A soft whimper escapes his lips, and the sound threatens to break me as I witness the depths of his anguish.

Just as I'm convinced he's had enough of what I am giving him, I yank my wrist away and quickly wrap it with a torn cloth, my eyes narrowing on that cursed collar. With a surge of will, I call forth my light, unleashing it once more upon the accursed device, and witness it shatter, crumbling to the dungeon floor.

"Hey..." My voice is gentle. Rhyland's eyelids finally lift, and I breathe a sigh of relief to see the familiar, beautiful, stormy blues of his eyes, silently whispering thanks to the heavens.

"Angel—" he rasps out, his voice coming through shredded and gritty as if each syllable were being forced through a gravel bed.

"Yeah, I'm right here," I respond, and faster than a pulse, he's up and lifting me with him, wrapping me in an embrace as unyielding as steel, pressing me against the distant wall with exhilarating force.

His hold is intense and unwavering. I hold him just as fiercely, our arms locked in a desperate grip, my legs wrapped tightly around his waist. Through the conduit of our bond, a torrent of emotion floods into me: starvation—his longing, his relief—each moment without me magnified a hundredfold from his perspective.

He engulfs me as if imprinting my scent on his very being, and I match his fervor, devouring his presence in turn. In a swift, unyielding motion, he withdraws just enough to let our eyes lock, and in that sliver of a moment, his lips ambush mine, plundering the breath from me with a Viking greed. A sharp hint of my blood on his tongue intertwines with the fierce tenderness of his kiss, a passionate declaration scrawled in the language of urgency, painting his longing, adoration, and fierce claim over me in the boldest of strokes.

He traces a searing path with his kisses down my chin, descending to the vulnerable expanse of my neck. "Fuck...I... thought...I thought the worst—" he confesses, each word laced with such raw longing that it wrenches tears from my eyes.

"I'm here. I'm here," I whisper, trying to soothe his fears. Sensing the depth of his need, I lean into him, granting silent permission to claim what sustenance he requires, as I know what I fed him is not nearly enough for what he's endured.

His fangs graze my skin before sinking in with a sharp, electric bite. The pain blooms into pleasure as he pulls me closer—impossibly closer—his arms turning to iron around me. One hand threads through my hair, cradling my head with surprising tenderness as he drinks from me, savoring every drop like it's the most precious thing he's ever tasted.

He drinks deeply, a moan vibrating against the curve of my neck as his venom ignites an immediate blaze of desire within me. I become liquid fire, my arousal scorching through me.

"Your flavor... fuck... I could drain you to the last drop," Rhyland's voice is a whisper in my head, laced with a deep hunger.

I draw him in tighter, driven by the urge for him to feed, to satisfy his craving, me being the sole source of his long-denied hunger. Draining me dry right now is the least of my concerns. My destiny is cradled in his grasp, and fear is nowhere to be found in me.

As Rhyland presses against me, his cock springs to attention like a soldier reporting for duty, and I can't help but let out a soft, seductive whimper. With a devilish grin, I clutch his hair, pull him closer, and grind against him with an intensity that leaves no doubt about my desires.

Then, with great reluctance, he ceases his intoxicating feast and presses his forehead to mine, inhaling my presence like a man starved of air. "I never fucking quit... I hung on—fought—for you."

"I know... I am so terribly sorry. Time twists differently in Atheria; I had no clue I'd been away for so long," I say, my voice trembling with emotion as I pitch my plea to him. I hope he grasps the truth of my words—that abandonment was never in my stars nor a part of the destiny that I've embraced with every fiber of my being.

I never wanted him to suffer through losing me, to experience that sharp, cutting pain of my absence like a wound that won't heal.

Never wanted him to know what it feels like when someone rips away the one person who makes the world bearable, leaving behind only emptiness, hunger, and cold. Or for him to taste that bitter poison of abandonment, to feel how suffocating loneliness becomes when the person you love most simply vanishes.

"No 'I'm sorry' bullshit; you never have to say you're sorry to me, ever." He wipes away the tears streaming down my face, his own eyes swimming with conflicting emotions—grief and happiness warring with each other, relief so tangible I can feel it radiating off him. In this moment, a promise crystallizes in my chest: I'll move mountains, burn down the world, do whatever it takes, never to put him through this kind of agony again.

"I'm just so damn relieved you're alright. I was losing my mind over you—I had you in my arms, and then you fucking stopped breathing—" his forehead drops to mine. "Then you just...disappeared. I couldn't sense your presence, your essence, your light—just everything—gone."

I silence his fears with a kiss, pouring every ounce of my love into it. "I know..." I whisper between the fervent kisses. "I'm here... I'm alive," I reassure him, each word punctuated with another kiss.

The terror that must've gripped him as he cradled what he thought was my lifeless form is unfathomable. Were our roles reversed, I'd probably be on the fast track to a padded room in the nearest madhouse.

I notice he is already healing and looks ten times better than he did a moment ago. His skin has regained its healthy glow, and his muscles ripple with renewed strength. It's a stark contrast to the battered and broken man I held in my arms just moments before, a testament to the incredible resilience of his vampire physiology and my blood.

"We need to fucking leave, now." Rhyland's voice brooks no argument, the hard-ass Fjord Lord in full command.

RHYLAND

61

The moment my eyes locked onto Dani, it was like a damn revival kicked off in my chest. I was hit by a rush of pure fucking euphoria, the kind that could wake a dead man—or in my case, a starved vampire who's felt nothing but the cold grip of loss for too long. This agony of being apart has been like living in a never-ending night, but seeing her now, it's the dawn, bright and blinding and oh so welcome.

Her blood hit me like a wave, chasing the shadows out of my soul with a vengeance. It's a wild, untamed sensation that sets every nerve alight—her essence, vibrant and essential, igniting the embers of my being with the promise of renewal. I'm breathing her in, and it's like my lungs remember what real air tastes like. Her presence is the fucking spark I've needed, awakening me, reminding me what it's like to feel truly alive.

Her touch is a brand, searing right through my skin, and fuck if it doesn't feel like coming home. I'm overwhelmed by love, fierce and possessive, and it grips me with the certainty that I'd tear the world apart before I let her go again. This is where she belongs—in my arms, now and always.

We go to leave, and in waltz, Azrael and Amara into this shitty underground cell—my personal slice of hell—with their entourage of her Shadow Court Fae army on their heels; I know it's about to get messy. They circle us like a couple of vultures eyeing their next meal, but Dani—she's standing beside me like she's ready to take on the whole damn army.

Azrael's lips twist into that infuriatingly smug, shit-eating grin that makes me want to rip his face off. "Well...if it isn't the esteemed Doctor Pierce! How gracious of you to finally bestow upon us the honor of your presence," he drawls, with biting sarcasm. "And I must say, your dear Rhyland has been an absolutely delightful guest, savoring every moment of our warm hospitality. Isn't that right, Rhyland?" He turns to me, his eyes glinting maliciously as he delivers the taunting question.

I shoot him a death glare; no fucking way am I letting him haul my ass back to that dark cesspit in my mind. He's been keeping me in it like some trophy for weeks. The thought alone of spending another second in this hellhole with him and that cold-hearted bitch makes my skin crawl.

"Going somewhere?" he mocks, his gaze flickering between Dani and me.

Dani's got her game face on, chin jutted out, and her stance screams she's not to be messed with. "Actually, Azrael, we're off to a party," she quips with a sharp edge of sass. "Strictly VIP. Too bad your invite took a detour to the trash."

Amara slinks in, all high and mighty, a sneer plastered on her face like we're the dirt under her boots. "Feeling optimistic, are we, darling?" she taunts, scornfully. "Hate to break it to you, but there's no exit ticket from this."

Dani cocks an eyebrow and fires off a wry grin. "Well, damn, if it isn't the Queen Bitch of Bullshit of Oz herself. You bet your ass I'm all sunshine and rainbows, knowing I'll get front-row seats to the fireworks show where you're the sparkler, paying up for all the shit you've dragged my man through."

Dani whirls her daggers like a damn maestro, that smirk on her face screaming one thing loud and clear: you're fucked.

"That's not gonna happen, My Dear." Azrael's voice is a sneer wrapped in an echo. His steps toward us are measured and filled with a malevolent grace.

Then, his face flickers with an instant of shock, his usually impassive eyes widening as if he's just spotted a ghost. It's rare to see such a master of darkness taken aback, and that look—it's a goddamn Christmas present. Whatever's got Azrael looking like he's seen the devil himself, I'm here for it and ready to use it to our advantage.

"The stone..." Azrael's voice trails off, hitting a wall of disbelief mid-sentence. He stops dead in his tracks, his hand, spindly fingers like midnight itself, raising to point squarely at Dani's crown. There's a glint in his dark eyes that I've never seen before; it's apprehension mixed with a dawning realization, and it gets the blood in my veins pumping even harder.

I follow his gaze, shifting ever so slightly to keep him within the periphery of my vision, ready to throw down should any of their tricks aim her way. I see the glimmering jewel set front and center into the metal of her crown, a stone resonating with the purest light, pulsing like a heartbeat of life itself.

A smirk splits my face as I lock eyes with Azrael—this fucker just slipped up, showing a crack in his usually unbreakable mask. Now, I'm not just prepped; I'm hungry to take this asshole down a notch. Whatever magic this rock's packing, it's got Azrael rattled in his grimy, worn-out boots, and that alone's got me tasting a sweet slice of triumph.

Dani plays it cool, casual as ever, with her signature wit. "Oh, this thing?" She lifts a hand, waving it dismissively at the crown perched atop her head, baiting her enemy with feigned innocence."It's nothing much—just a heavenly upgrade courtesy of the big guy in the sky."

Azrael's growl rumbles low, the kind of sound that promises nothing but pain. I'm locked into every sound, every shift of the shadows—they're all telltales of the incoming storm.

Azrael's head swivels toward Amara, his eyes devoid of any sympathy or concern. "You're flying solo on this one, sweetheart. Consider it a test of your mettle," he informs her, his voice as flat and unyielding as a slab of cold granite. Then, his piercing gaze locks onto Dani, a steely determination etched into every line of his face. "Mark my words, little girl, this is far from over. We've barely scratched the surface of what's in store for you," he warns, his voice low and menacing, the weight of his threat hanging in the air like a suffocating fog. With a flick of his wrist, he gathers the tendrils of smoke and shadows around himself, his form dissolving into the inky darkness as he takes his leave.

I keep my senses primed and muscles coiled, not trusting the shadowy bastard as far as I can throw him.

But the cell is still; the coward has retreated... for now. Dani stands strong, haloed in the light of her magic, eyes scanning for any lingering threats. I meet her gaze, and relief crashes over me in a dizzying wave. We're both still standing, still fighting.

Amara's bunch is just standing there, gawking, unsure of what to do next. Shocking the shit out of Azrael really got them scratching their heads.

"Get them, you fools!" Amara orders.

Seizing this fucking moment—I gather my strength, focusing on the enemies that encircle us. I gather up my power and let the telekinesis well up until it feels like it's gonna burst out my skull, a pressure building behind my eyes that threatens to split my head in two.

"Dani, get behind me!" I bark, my voice rough with urgency.

It's the only warning I give—and Dani is behind me instantly, trusting me implicitly, her faith in me unwavering. With a roar that shakes the very foundations of the room, I release the pent-up energy, slamming it right into the horde of sorry bastards around us.

Their bodies fly, smacking into the walls with a sound that makes my inner Viking grin, a savage joy welling up inside me at the sight of their defeat. The sickening crunch of bone, the groans of the fallen, they're the sweetest fucking lullaby to my ears, a symphony of vengeance long overdue. As they crumple to the floor, looking like a pile of broken dolls, I feel a sense of grim satisfaction—a dark pleasure in seeing them brought low.

Dani's gaze drifts past me, locking onto Amara, who is cowering against the wall like the pathetic wretch she is. The shadow queen's usual arrogance is gone, replaced by naked fear in her eyes as she meets Dani's stare, like a rabbit caught in the sights of a wolf.

Amara turns to run, a last-ditch attempt to save her own skin—I don't even see Dani move, her speed a blur of motion that my eyes can barely track.

Suddenly, she's got Amara pinned, dagger at her throat, a snarl of rage twisting her beautiful features into a mask of righteous fury. Amara struggles, but Dani's grip is iron, unyielding, and unbreakable.

"And just where the hell do you think you're going?" Dani hisses, eyes flashing.

Amara unfurls her smoke and shadows, trying to compel under Dani's hold.

"Yeah, that crap's useless on me, you know that, right? Chosen One and all that shit," she retorts with a fierce grin packed with snark and defiance.

Amara chokes out something, pleas or curses, but Dani's having none of it. She presses the dagger tighter, just enough to draw a bead of inky blood from that pale, cursed neck.

I watch, pride surging in my chest as Dani overpowers her. Fuck she's a sight. She's an avenging angel, wreathed in celestial light, passing judgment on these creatures of shadow and malice.

Amara deserves no mercy, and I know Dani will have none to give. This is only the beginning, the first taste of the reckoning we will bring upon our enemies. And any who stand in Dani's way—in our way, will soon learn that even the light can fucking burn when provoked.

"You don't get to run, not after what you've done," Dani says, her voice cold and sharp as the blade she wields. "You wanted a war, bitch? Well, now you've got one."

DANICA

62

I can't help but smirk down at Amara, her once-powerful demeanor now reduced to pleading and squirming beneath me. "My, my, how the high and mighty have fallen," I taunt, pressing the dagger against her neck with a wicked grin. "Karma's finally caught up to you, hasn't it? And who better to deliver the blow than little old me?"

Amara masks her irritation with a mocking smirk, "Oh, so you're the grand trophy my pet obsesses over?"

Her words land like a slap, and I flinch—the implication that Rhyland belongs to her, that he's nothing more than her possession, ignites something fierce inside me.

Without missing a beat, I fire back, "A trophy? More like the grand jackpot — and 'your pet'? I didn't realize we were back in preschool, Amara, playing pretend. But sure, in your make-believe world, keep thinking Rhyland's on a leash. In reality, though, he's the king of the beasts, and honey, he's all mine." I lean in closer, relishing the fear in her eyes. "You know, you should consider this payback for every hellish moment you put my man through. Your reign of terror ends here, by my hand."

Amara's eyes widen, her lips parting in a frantic bid for leniency. "You need me! I have information, power—"

"Oh, spare me the performance, Amara. Your lies couldn't sway a gnat, let alone me," I snap, with disdain and leaving no airspace for her excuses.

She tries again, her words growing more desperate. "I can help you! Spare me; I'll give you everything you need to defeat the Dark Demon!"

I can't help but chuckle, sharp and biting as if I am chewing on broken glass. "Strike a bargain with the devil in heels? Please, Amara. I'd rather eat dirt. Your little hourglass has run out, and your words? They're worth less than the damn breath you spent spitting them out."

I press the blade harder against her throat, taking satisfaction as a bead of black wells up. The fear in her eyes fuels that dark thrill within me. "Any last words before I send you back to the hell that spawned you?"

The dagger's hilt digs into my palm as Amara writhes futilely beneath me, her panicked breaths a haunting reminder of Rhyland's agony—agony she inflicted with twisted glee.

But now, raw power surges through my bloodstream, blazing from the Atherite stone embedded in my crown. Its celestial light floods everything around us, even giving the Angel of Death pause. The stone amplifies my abilities tenfold, transforming me into something far more dangerous than I've ever been. This is just the beginning of what I'm truly capable of.

Amara's eyes dart wildly, seeking any shred of mercy. But my resolve is iron-clad; her cruelty ends here—I alone decide her fate.

Amara's words drip with toxic delight, "You'll never locate them. Your beloved vampires are well out of your clutches."

Amara's jab stops me cold, chilling me to the core. My thoughts race... has she shackled Lucian and Erik, giving them a taste of her own brand of crazy?

I notice a shiver run through Rhyland, his concern for his brothers seeping into me through our emotional wiretap.

I keep my voice steady, betraying none of the dread coursing within. "Where are they, Amara? What have you done with them?"

"Oh, you'd love that piece of information, wouldn't you? But my lips are sealed, even with your blade kissing my neck. Do your worst because you'll learn nothing from me."

I see it in her eyes then—raw fear that her ruse will fail. I press the advantage. "Tell me where they are, or you'll face a fate far worse than death."

Amara's expression shifts, desperation melting into cunning. "Could you do it, *Chosen One?* Could you end a life in cold blood?" She throws her head back, her laugh sharp and empty.

My eyes lock onto hers, my will as unyielding as iron. "I've suffered losses you can't even fucking imagine." Flashes of John, my parents—Emily—my brother, and the past life I left behind weave through my head, stark against the ties I've formed here with Lucian, Erik, and Rhyland. "I'd tear apart the heavens for the ones I love. This? This isn't just killing—it's vengeance biding its time." My voice is rock-solid as I set the ultimatum. "Spill their damn location, Amara. I'm hanging on by a thread."

The dagger glints wickedly as I press it into her throat. Her pulse thrums wildly under the blade's kiss. But her silence persists, her final gambit.

Just as anxiety begins to take hold, a voice floats through my mind, soothing the whirlwind of worry—it's Rhyland. *"They are safe. I just reached out to them. They're at the Sun Court,"* he assures me through our private psychic channel.

I barely manage to keep my expression neutral, the wave of relief threatening to crack my stoic facade. She doesn't have to know that I'm one step ahead, aware of the reality behind her charades. She's bluffing, dealing lies like worn-out cards, and I'm all in, ready to turn her deception into my ace.

Amara's arrogance lights a fire in me, a swirling hurricane ready to redecorate her face with a taste of my newfound power.

She sneers, "I knew it. You're pathetic, just like your pitiful mate." She motions to Rhyland with a flick of her head. "You'll always be a feeble weakling who can't even manage a proper kill. What kind of savior are you?"

I hover dangerously close to giving in, the line between justice and sweet, sweet vengeance thinner than the plot of a bad soap opera.

I burst into a mocking laugh. "Seriously? That's your best shot? Hold on, let me scribble that down in my diary of lame-ass comebacks, right in between 'you're a poopy-head' and 'I know you are, but what am I?'" I shake my head, feigning sorrow. "And you're going with 'weak'? That's rich, coming from the chick who resorts to kidnapping, compelling, and torture to puff up her fragile ego. Seems to me that speaks volumes about you, not me, sweetheart."

I land a solid punch right in her perfect little face, and I'm almost mesmerized as black liquid starts oozing from her nose. She tries to cup her nose, but it's too late—blood is already spewing from her broken face.

Ah, sweet satisfaction.

With a rough yank on her hair, I drag Amara away from the wall and into the center of the cell like a rag doll. Before she can even blink, I have her cuffed and chained like the nasty bitch she is. "Make yourself at home, honey," I say with mock sweetness. "I'd love for you to experience Rhyland's five-star accommodations firsthand. And don't worry, I'll be back once I figure out a more permanent living situation for you."

I give her a sarcastic little wave as I head for the door, savoring the look of shock and outrage on her bloody face.

She whines, "You can't leave me here! Stop! I know where—"

"Save the dramatics, Amara." I slam the cell door shut with a loud clang. "Make yourself comfortable in your new home. I'll be back to check on you soon." I give her one last sarcastic smile as I turn the lock, leaving her chained inside.

The second the cell locks, Rhyland is on me, his mouth crashing into mine as his fingers tangle in my hair. I return his fevered kisses, pouring all my love, devotion, and empathy for his suffering into it.

He went through hell at Amara's hands—twice! Simply ending her sadistic life would be too merciful. No, she needs to endure every ounce of anguish she inflicted on him and then some. I deepen our kiss, a silent promise that we will make her pay in the most excruciating ways imaginable.

He pulls back, locking his gaze with mine, intensity burning in his eyes, "Fuck, I am so proud of you for not getting sucked into her bullshit trap—for not going to a dark place I'd have dived into without a second thought. You kept your dignity and held onto your honor."

I gaze into Rhyland's mesmerizing blue eyes, dark and churning like a storm at sea. "Amara's earned a fate worse than death," I say firmly. "I can't give in to blind vengeance. My purpose is greater—to unite the realms and heal the divisions."

I caress his cheek, steeling my voice with resolve. "We'll make Amara suffer for what she's done in ways she can't even fathom. But we'll do it right—paving the path to justice."

Rhyland's forehead meets mine, his embrace firm, "Damn right—"

Footsteps sound to our left, "I have to admit that bitch doesn't deserve your pity. But it sure warms my heart to see her rotting in a cell. Been wanting her behind bars for ages, but couldn't do squat with her deal with Moretemis."

Rhyland and I turn around at the voice echoing down the dim passage.

"Sorry for the fright, I'm—"

"King Alinar Cimmerian," Rhyland interjects.

I pause, caught off guard by his words. Amara's husband? This revelation leaves me momentarily bewildered.

"I'm sorry—a deal with Moretemis?" I finally ask, unable to contain my curiosity. "I don't understand—?"

I search Rhyland's eyes questioningly. This changes everything—I need to know more about Amara's connection to our sworn enemy. What sinister arrangement does she have with the Demon of Shadows? My mind races with the implications of this unexpected twist.

Alinar peers through the bars and then pivots to face us. "Amara's been in cahoots with that Shadow Bastard for ages. She's let him corrupt this kingdom—this entire realm—scheming together, feeding him souls through her twisted games and vile perversions."

"Alinar, you fool! Cease this madness at once! He's going to hunt you down—and when he's finished with you, he'll come for me!" Amara spits venomously from behind the bars of her cell.

Disregarding Amara's jeers, Alinar continues, "That's the root of the split between our kind, the war, the division. I've been playing along with her charade, waiting for the prophesied savior to come and redeem us all." His gaze locks on mine, determination burning in his eyes. "You."

Rhyland closes the distance, his presence commanding, "I had my suspicions, but you stood out like a sore thumb that day in her chambers. Now, it all makes fucking sense."

"Indeed, my sincerest apologies for the display. I recognized the righteousness of your intent, yet I had to uphold appearances. I trust you understand," Alinar explains.

Rhyland shrugs.

"Wait, so her compulsion doesn't work on you?" I quickly ask.

"It did, but I've found a way to repel her compulsion," Alinar explains.

"So, Amara's been dancing with Moretemis this entire time?" It's like discovering the quiet librarian secretly runs a dragon fight club—scandalous yet oddly fitting.

"Since the realm was cut off," Alinar confirms.

Rhyland folds his arms across his chest, deep in thought.

As if a light bulb goes off in my head, I recall seeing Amara wearing something—something that makes everything fall into focus."Hold up—" Unlocking the door, I kick it open and strut back inside.

"Danica, wait—" Rhyland calls out, his voice tinged with concern and caution, but I'm already storming into the cell with determination, my focus narrowed to a laser-sharp point on the task at hand.

Amara is sobbing, her hands covering her blood-soaked face in a futile attempt to hide her tears and her shame. But with a flick of my wrist, I blast a ball of light into the cell, illuminating the space with a blinding brilliance that cuts through the gloom and the despair.

Her gaze snaps to me, eyes blown wide with terror and desperation. And there it is—a black stone dangling from a chain around her neck, no larger than a pea, yet radiating such toxic, poisonous energy that my skin prickles and my teeth clench involuntarily.

Without hesitation, I snatch it from her neck, my fingers closing around the cold, hard stone with a sense of grim satisfaction.

Amara screams like a banshee, her voice high and shrill with panic and despair. "No, no, no! Give that back, you bitch!" she wails, her hands scrabbling at her throat as if she's been robbed of her very lifeblood.

But I pay her no heed, storming out of the cell with the same determined stride that brought me in, slamming the door shut behind me with a resounding clang that echoes through the stone walls.

I hold up the necklace to Rhyland and Alinar, a triumphant grin spreading across my face as I dangle it before them like a trophy, a prize hard-won and well-earned. "Looks like someone's been shopping at the inter-realm Costco for magical knick-knacks," I say with a smirk. "This explains her connection with Moretemis."

Rhyland gently takes possession of the necklace, his eyebrows raising in recognition as he turns it over in his hands. He examines it from every angle with a critical eye and a knowing expression. "Is this what I think it is?"

I confirm with a confident nod, "Indeed, it's a fragment of the Soul Stone."

RHYLAND

63

The necklace dangles from my hand, its dark gem pulsing with an eerie, subdued power that sets off alarm bells in my head—just a shard of the Soul Stone—Amara's tool for bending wills and shattering spirits. Dani figured out that puzzle. I swell with pride; her sharp eyes and even sharper mind put this shit together before the rest of us dumbasses.

"Looks like the witch only had a sliver of this thing," I growl, rolling the necklace between my fingers as its sinister weight rests in my palm.

Dani slides up to me, her eyes alive with mischievous triumph. "Which means Azrael is only getting a taste of this stone's full potential. If I had to guess, that's why he looked like he'd been thoroughly pegged when he spotted the Atherite Stone. Poor bastard probably felt like he was the one bent over, not the other way around."

I can't help my grin, wrapping an arm around her. "Baby, you have a way with words that could make a sailor blush." Her humor is a bright spark, even as our situation grows dire.

She laughs, unfazed by the gloom. "Just channeling that rainbow energy I've picked up along the way."

King Alinar approaches, an enigma shrouded in darkness, his aura shifting—a silent admission of a game forever changed. "Thank the Gods you got that from her. Your achievement rings through the courts," he intones, a resonant sound in the silence. "Amara's days of manipulation are done. My allegiance and my blade are yours."

I brush off his statement about nabbing the stone and can't help wondering—why the hell didn't he snatch it himself if he knew its bullshit tricks?

Eyeing Alinar carefully, trust isn't granted—it's earned, hard-won through fire and fate. But his forces? They could tip the scales our way.

I acknowledge with a terse nod. "We can use all the help we can get."

Dani chimes in, embodying the voice of reason. "We need to regroup. Lucian and Erik are waiting—and heaven knows they need my supervision."

Her attempt at humor doesn't mask her worry. We're in unison there; I can't stomach the thought of leaving my brothers in the lurch.

Dani pivots to Alinar, asserting command. "You take charge here while we're gone. We need someone strong and someone we can trust on that throne."

He bows, a silent oath made manifest. "Consider it done. My forces stand at the ready."

With Alinar keeping order here, we can face the trials ahead. I yank Dani tight against me; her presence steadies the storm within. The path ahead's a murky, treacherous bitch, but with her as my anchor and Alinar ruling the roost here, it seems like we're set to tackle the hellfire coming our way.

"It's time," I whisper, urging her toward our next destination. "Stones to find, wrongs to right, and cravings for you that just won't quit," I admit, my desire for her making itself known.

Her cheeks pinken as my words land precisely where intended.

She's all business, opening a portal that pulls the Sun Court into view. The fresh scents of rain-drenched flowers and sunbeam-touched earth reach us, starkly contrasting the shadow's grip.

"Alinar," Dani's authority echoes in the space, her final command cutting through the stillness. "Keep Amara locked up—she won't evade my judgment for long."

Even though she's spitting out words laced with determination, I can tell she's wrestling with herself inside. She hates the thought of bloodshed, but gets that sometimes you gotta serve up justice cold. This tug-of-war inside her cements her reputation as a true leader—she's got heart, but she's also steady as a rock.

Alinar lowers his head, assenting. "By your word, my lady."

She turns back to me, honey-gold eyes glinting with determination. "Let's go."

Dani gave me the quick lowdown as we ascended the steps to the imposing palace. How Seraphina stepped in, and some angel dude named Jophiel tossed her the stone that had changed everything. But before she could say any more, the grand doors of the Sun Court fly open, and I am practically blinded by gold and crimson light streaming in, bouncing off marble like it is made of sunbeams. Alina, in her dress woven as delicately as cobwebs, is already making a beeline for us, relief etched on her pretty face.

"My Lady," she almost gasps, directing a mix of respect and urgent worry at Dani. "After the incident, the Court was rife with whispers that you'd—"

Dani is quick to act, pulling her into one of those reassuring hugs that say, 'Everything's under control.' "I'm fine," she asserts. "And just so we're clear, it's going to take a hell of a lot more than some twiggy little booby traps to knock this chick down for the count."

Alina's laughter tells me she's relieved enough to ignore royal decorum.

I clear my throat, an itch of urgency nipping at me. "Alina, where are my brothers?"

She steps back, gesturing like she's presenting a grand prize toward the gilded study door. "Inside, My Lord. They've been longing for your return."

I toss her a quick nod, firming my grip on Dani's hand as I steer us toward the study. The door glides open smoothly, revealing my brothers looking like someone had just canceled the apocalypse.

Curtains are drawn shut, plunging the room into darkness with only the weak glow from tallow candles and fae lights to cut through the gloom.

Alina snaps the door shut right on our heels.

Lucian practically hurdles out of his chair to wrap Dani in his arms, hugging her like she's the damn life raft after a shipwreck. Even though my skin's crawling seeing him get that close, I swallow the snarl, itching to break free—Lucian's damn near losing his mind with relief.

Dani is clearly fighting to keep from laughing as air is squeezed out of her. "I can't breathe," she taps his shoulder.

Lucian's still got her in that death grip of a hug. I give him a nudge on the shoulder, a silent 'Enough already.' He takes the hint, easing off with a step back. His eyes are glossy, a stormy mix of relief and whatever else he's got churning inside.

"I'm so fucking sorry; it was my fault for what happened to you. I should've—"

She cuts him off cold, leveling him with a look that could stop any man in his tracks. "What happened to that cocky, wise-cracking vampire who could take life's sucker punches and still come out swinging? I miss that guy." Lucian manages to crack a smile, but the guilt still hangs heavy in his eyes. Dani's expression softens, driving home her point. "Listen, Lucy. No more of this self-flagellation bullshit, you hear me?"

A low growl rumbles from deep in my chest, enough to get Lucian to take a step back. Dani turns to me, her eyes clouded with confusion. She's clueless about what Lucian's blood has possibly done. That's a talk I'm dreading, one I sure as hell ain't ready for.

Dani rolls her eyes as if annoyed. "I know, I know—Seraphina mentioned I could have... changed, or whatever it is, you vampires call it. But look, I'm fine; nothing's wrong," she tries to reassure us, brushing it off. But it ain't that simple, and that's not what's eating at me.

The room falls dead silent, the air thick with unease.

Erik moves in, breaking the ice. Encircling Dani with his arms, he pulls her into a quick but hearty hug. "I'm glad to see the Little Huntress hasn't lost her touch. Your training shines through."

From a corner, cloaked in shades of violet that contrast with the room's somber tones, Axilya rises. "I knew you'd find your way. I never gave up hope," she intones, her voice echoing like a prophecy fulfilled.

Leaning against a shelf heavy with leather-bound tomes, Faderyn breaks into a reassuring grin. "Few doubted the Savior would falter," he winks. "Welcome back, Danica."

Once greetings and back-patting taper off, I cut straight to the chase. "How'd you break out of that shadow-infested hell?"

Grateful as I am, the curiosity gnaws at me. This whole situation was one massive clusterfuck.

Lucian meets my gaze, his smug smile cutting through the tension. "Adrian—" The shock's gotta be written all over my face 'cause Lucian keeps going. "Yeah, that's right. He's the magical badass who blasted those damn shadows to oblivion and yanked our asses back to the land of the somewhat living."

I'm lost, and my gaze darts around like an idiot, waiting for Lucian to continue.

Lucian's expression shifts, a hint of seriousness creeping into his voice. "After that grim reaper wannabe Azrael got his shadowy mitts on you and pulled a vanishing act, Adrian suddenly grew a conscience. So, that's why we're in this delightful predicament now."

Silence descends, heavy as a shroud, uninvited and cold. I can feel Dani's grip clamp down on mine, her head swiveling my way. Our eyes lock—hers swimming with shock, mine clouded over with a storm of rage.

"I ain't swallowing that shit. You think he pulled this stunt out of the goodness of his damn heart?" The words come out as a snarl from me, each syllable laced with a pissed-off vibration, rough around the edges with fury. The flavor of treachery, especially coming from my own kin, is one hell of a nasty pill jammed in my throat.

Lucian's shoulders lift and fall in a carefree shrug, but his eyes are sharp, betraying the serious intent behind his laid-back facade. "Well, you know Adrian; dude's got a flair for the dramatic," he says casually, yet the firm set of his jaw reveals the iron will underlying his seemingly nonchalant comment.

Erik's silver gaze narrows, a silent threat all on its own, mirroring an unspoken understanding. Nobody's saying shit, but the room is practically crackling with the tension.

"What?" I ask. "What is it?"

Slipping back into his trademark persona, Lucian arches an eyebrow with sarcastic amusement. "Oh, he's currently enjoying the luxurious accommodations of our five-star dungeon suite," he quips, a sardonic smile playing on his lips. "Apparently, he's decided to audition for the role of the repentant prodigal brother, hoping for a callback on the whole redemption arc. Guess Azrael didn't deem him worthy of a guest spot on this particular adventure."

A deep growl churns up from my gut, my fangs itching to break free as betrayal burns in my veins. "He's still here? Figure's he would grovel. The bastard's got no one left now that Azrael's ditched his ass." I spit the words out like venom. "Or maybe this is some new level of hell—a damn trap."

Lucian leans back, crossing his arms with a bitter and satisfied smirk. "Hey, at least he's got plenty of time to perfect his groveling skills while he rots in that cell. Maybe if he's convincing enough, he can earn himself a participation trophy in the 'too little, too late' category."

Then Axilya, cool as you please, slices through the bullshit with that regal bearing of hers. "We must address this matter carefully," she says, every word dropping like ice into a glass of whiskey, cool but sharp.

Faderyn keeps his mouth shut and gives a somber little nod. He seems to agree with Axilya's 'play it smart' approach.

Dani's hold on my hand is like a vise, her eyes a mirror of my own fury, laced with a damn dose of disbelief at the crazy-ass twist our story's taken.

Erik moves closer, his voice a blend of firmness and allure. "We must proceed cautiously; Adrian is privy to our vulnerabilities."

Lucian lets out a low, ominous chuckle. "I say we let the backstabbing prick marinate in his mess for a change," he suggests, a wicked glint in his dark eyes. "It's high time he gets a five-star serving of betrayal straight from the chef's special menu of karmic retribution."

Dani cocks her head to the side, that fiery spark lighting up her eyes without so much as a peep. She's standing there, all fired up, defiance radiating off her like she's ready to take on the world.

My heart's pounding a rhythm of rage and resolve—Adrian's gonna pay. He's gonna answer for every last fucked-up thing he's done to us.

DANICA

64

The door closes behind us with a definitive click, sealing us away from the chaos beyond. Sandalwood fills the air—that unmistakable scent that clings to Rhyland like a second skin. He moves toward the window, his broad frame backlit by the fading light, shoulders rigid. His eyes remain fixed on the darkening sky outside, as if searching for answers in the shadows.

My head is spinning with all the mind-blowing revelations from my Atherian crash course, but right now, Rhyland's well-being eclipses everything else. I can sense his inner turmoil through our bond, and it's gnawing at my very soul.

"Alina," my voice carries gently through the chamber to where she stands alert. "Would you be so kind as to prepare a bath for Rhyland?"

Her response is a quiet nod, her slight form barely stirring the air. Observant and perceptive, her wide eyes dart from me to Rhyland and back again, a silent witness to the unspoken tensions rippling between us. With a quick, almost fluttery motion, she vanishes to set the bath in motion, leaving me to focus fully on Rhyland's brooding figure.

Rhyland, remaining at the window, carries the burden of his thoughts like a bulwark against an invisible tempest. I encircle him from the rear, my arms wrapping around his sturdy frame, and lay my cheek softly against the muscle of his back.

"Talk to me," I whisper gently, coaxing the words into the silence that hangs between us.

Rhyland's answer carries a distant, hollow quality, his voice traveling across an invisible gulf of secrets left unspoken. "There's nothing to tell, Angel."

He's shutting me out—I can discern the unsteady tremor beneath his words, sensing the trouble simmering beneath the surface.

I maneuver myself to stand before him, my hands reaching up with purpose to cradle his scruffy face, guiding his gaze down to meet mine. "Look at me, Rhyland," I say, seeking connection through the windows of his beautiful blues. Observing the muted turmoil, I recognize there's more than he's willing to admit.

My heart aches to imagine the torment Rhyland must have suffered while I was gone, locked up and chained by those two monsters. Just thinking of the cruelty he endured during his last imprisonment by Amara is enough to ignite a firestorm of fury in me, making me want to watch that sadistic bitch burn.

And now the presence of Adrian, his own brother by blood, shackled and imprisoned before him, must be tearing Rhyland apart from the inside out. The bitter sting of betrayal, the agonizing realization that someone he trusted, someone he called family, has turned against him—it's a pain that cuts deeper than any physical wound ever could.

I can see the conflict raging behind Rhyland's eyes, the tempest of emotions threatening to consume him whole. His mind must be a battlefield, a landscape of shattered abuse, trust, and fractured loyalties, as he grapples with the harsh reality of what has happened.

Rhyland remains frozen, clearly lost in the labyrinth of his own haunted thoughts. I know he's not only grappling with the fresh wounds of his recent captivity and Adrian's treachery but also the unrelenting anguish of not knowing if or when I would find my way back to him—an endless cyclone of turmoil and dread that must have ravaged his mind and soul.

Alina's presence is discreet, her voice barely more than a murmur from the doorway. "The bath is ready, My Lady."

Grateful for her service, I reply without turning, "Thank you, Alina." She retreats with a hushed grace that speaks of her understanding, leaving us alone in our private sanctuary.

The steam from the bath fills the room, weaving through the air like ethereal wisps, setting a mystical stage. Alina's meticulous work is evident in the large, inviting tub, where the hot water sends ribbons of heat that curl into the cooler air of the chamber.

Facing Rhyland, I gaze into his eyes and find only turmoil churning beneath the surface. "Let's talk while you soak," I coax softly, suggesting both an invitation and solace.

His nod is quiet, a silent acknowledgment of the need for conversation, yet his lips remain sealed. Rhyland stands before me, a paragon of restraint, but I feel the subtle cracks threatening his composed exterior.

Perched on the tub's rim, I watch as Rhyland discards his garments one by one with mechanical precision.

He's an absolute vision, a breathtaking spectacle that seems almost too perfect to be real.

Standing there, he's the living, breathing embodiment of a Norse deity—powerful, raw, and so damn captivating it hurts. He's covered in blood and dirt, but it only amplifies the rugged, primal sexiness that draws me to him like a moth to a flame. His very presence commands attention, demanding worship and reverence with every perfectly chiseled inch of his godlike form.

His cut abs are a masterpiece, each muscle expertly carved, forming an alluring V that points like an arrow to my favorite toy. The striking black ink of his tattoos spans his chest, arms, and neck, each intricate design hinting at untold chapters of his past. The bold lines stand out against his skin, a testament to his strength and the darkness he's conquered. His raven locks fall carelessly over the jagged scar on his brow, the rugged stubble along his jaw accentuating his handsome features.

He's devastatingly magnetic—a portrait of raw power and dangerous appeal. Just looking at him knocks the air from my lungs and sends my heart into overdrive. Every part of me gravitates toward him, helpless against the sheer force of his presence.

He steps into the steaming water completely bare, sinking down with a long, heavy sigh that carries the burden of everything weighing on him—a sound caught between relief and dread.

Snatching up a nearby cloth, I squirt a dollop of soap onto it and start the task of cleaning my Tattoo Titan. My hands, guided by intent and tenderness, begin their journey across the landscape of his chiseled chest, meandering to his brawny arms and the column of his neck.

I'm meticulous, leaving no inch of him untouched by the cleansing ritual, ensuring every bit of him is refreshed and cared for.

Extending a hand, I gently sweep back the damp strands of his hair, clearing his forehead. "Rhyland," I begin, voice barely above a whisper, eyeing him with concern and care, "I want to understand what happened... what they did to you."

His eyelids fall shut, a curtain drawn over those deep, expressive blues as if to shut out the world. Minutes pass before he gives a feeble shake of his head, murmuring, "It's not worth remembering."

Despite his dismissal, I can sense the fleeting play of darkness that flickers across his closed lids. It's clear to me that he's already transported back to the depths of that grim cell, reliving the memories he desperately strives to keep at bay.

"Please," I persist, unwilling to let him retreat inward to cut himself off from me. "Tell me."

He resists with a shake of his head, his muscles in his jaw tightening as he tries to remain closed off. "You don't need those memories in your head," he argues, his voice laced with the pain of recollection.

"I'm not asking because I need them," I assert firmly. "I'm asking because you need to share them. Let it out, Rhyland. Let me help you, please." I'm well aware of the effect my pleading has on this man—there's a twist of shame for playing that card, but damn it, I need answers.

Rhyland surrenders, his gaze lifting to meet mine. His stormy blue eyes hold mine captive, swirling with equal parts anguish and devotion. He reaches out, resting his hand over mine, his touch conveying a plea for understanding. "Close your eyes, and let me in your mind," he directs with a voice that leaves no room for dispute.

Obedient to his request, my eyelids fall shut, forming a blank canvas for his revelations. The physical world fades, and abruptly, I gaze not merely into Rhyland's eyes but into the very essence of his haunted past.

The memory engulfs me—

Azrael looms over Rhyland, a dark monolith that swallows what little light filters into the cell. His black eyes—twin voids of pure malice—pierce straight through to Rhyland's core, threatening to devour him whole. Poisoned words spill from his lips, promises of power designed to break him, to make him kneel.

But Rhyland doesn't shatter. His body is ravaged, his spirit tested to its limits, yet one fragile thread keeps him tethered to sanity—thoughts of me. He clings to those memories like a lifeline: my laughter, the softness of my touch, the unshakeable strength in my spirit. They burn inside him, a beacon against the encroaching darkness.

Azrael's shadows writhe through Rhyland's mind, hunting for cracks to exploit. But each tendril is met with blinding recollections of us, and Rhyland uses them to anchor himself, to fight back. His mind becomes a battlefield, but he refuses to yield.

Enter Amara, a walking contradiction of glamour and malevolence. She glides through like poison dressed in silk, determined to strip away his last shred of dignity—her hands touch him without permission, seeking to reduce him to nothing. She feeds on his blood like a junkie chasing a high. The grotesque display turns my stomach inside out with revulsion. I can taste his disgust as clearly as if it were my own—bitter, metallic, suffocating.

Starved.

Whipped.

Assaulted.

He was brutally beaten, over and over, tortured relentlessly by Amara's goons. It's as if the horrors are stuck on an endless loop, day in and day out, while I am off in another realm. And through it all, he clung to hope, never letting go.

Rhyland survived each cruel, agonizing moment because he understood the stakes—if he broke, he didn't just lose himself, he lost us. The possibility of a future together became his anchor, the one thing keeping him from sliding into the abyss. That fragile thread of hope was everything. He clawed through hell itself for me, for what we could be.

Rhyland pulls back from my mind, and our eyes collide. The exhaustion etched into every line of his face cuts deeper now—raw, bone-deep weariness that comes from reliving those horrors. Sharing that memory has drained him, left him hollowed out and fragile in a way I've never seen before. He watches as I struggle to contain the tears threatening to overflow, and something shifts in his expression.

I'll earmark how he just shared a memory with me in my mind for another time.

His voice drops to a harsh whisper, all torn up with emotion. "I never fucking lost hope," he rasps out. "I knew you'd come back—to me."

His voice cracks with raw emotion, and my heart splinters in response. I watch his anguish unfold like a wound reopening—layers of suffering and fierce resistance all tangled together—and I feel every bit of it as though it's happening to me.

Tears spill over my cheeks for him—for all he endured alone in that cold darkness for weeks.

My words tumble out, choked by my own crying: "I'm so...s-sorry," each syllable heavy with regret. "You shouldn't have had to go through that... because of me."

Rhyland sits up, and the water sloshes over onto the floor with the sudden movement. His hand's slick and wet—cradle my cheek. "No," he says—voice solid as a rock. "Don't you go hauling that burden; none of this shitstorm is on you."

Despite my best efforts, my tears have a mind of their own—each one a reluctant salute to the battles he fought and the scars I couldn't shield him from.

Grief hangs thick in the air between us, mingling with the curl of steam rising from the water. Our combined sorrow settles over everything like a physical presence—so tangible I could almost lean against it.

"Angel, stop." Rhyland yanks me right into the tub with him; more water spills out the sides. I land smack on top of that hard, tattooed chest of his. He gets a firm hold on my hair at the nape, making damn sure I'm staring straight into those deep blue seas of his. "This ain't your load to bear—Gods, I knew I should've kept that shit to myself," he exhales long and hard, his eyes losing that fierce edge, going all gentle like a calm after the storm.

Tears are winning the battle, turning me into a sob-fest extraordinaire, every bit of his past torment echoing through me. "No—don't ever keep things from me, Rhyland." The pain starts again, and tears have a mind of their own, "I-just. I hurt...it hurts....so much for what happened to you."

It's the damn bond; I'm feeling every high and low of his, and he's riding the waves of mine—A bond that, as it turns out, is solely the product of his magic and blood—a crucial detail I need to hash out with him—the whole Soul-Tie situation. Rhyland's eyes search mine, and he's holding me tight against him, fingers of one hand buried in my hair, the other hand firm on my chin, and then—his lips crash against mine. It's like he's out to consume all the air I have. His kiss is a fierce mix of agony, love, loyalty, and recognition.

"Then I'll just have to make you stop," he vows, breaking just long enough to steal my breath and give it back in the space between us.

"Y-yes, plea—" My words are abruptly snatched away, severed before they can fully form as Rhyland's growl rumbles through his chest as he rises, clutching me to him like I'm the last solid thing in a spinning world, striding into the bedroom. My clothes are nothing but tatters in seconds, shredded by hands that can't bear a second more of separation. His kisses are fervent, charged with a hunger born from too damn long a wait. I'm there, matching his urgency, giving as good as I get because hell, I'm done waiting, too.

DANICA

65

His lips blaze a path across my skin, his tongue mapping every curve and dip of my body. I'm burning alive from the heat pouring off him. He finds my nipple and draws it into his mouth, and the sensation shoots straight through me like a livewire. My back arches off the bed as I fist his unruly hair, silently begging him to take everything.

He pushes me back onto the mattress, spreading my legs with his own, settling between them like he was made to be there.

"Don't cry for me, Angel. I will endure any pain, any suffering, for you—for us."

My heart splinters for what he went through. The thought of Rhyland tortured, broken by unspeakable cruelty, guts me. His love—his absolute, unwavering devotion—has claimed me entirely. My heart isn't mine anymore; it lives in his hands, and I wouldn't want it anywhere else.

What he survived for us humbles me to my core. He chose agony over surrender, chose our future over his own peace. That kind of love transcends everything—pain, fear, logic itself.

I understand now that I belong to him as completely as he belongs to me. Our souls are tethered by something that can never be undone. Looking at this man who bled for us, I make a silent vow: I will cherish and protect what he's given me—his heart, his faith, his unbreakable spirit.

"The only tears you're gonna shed," he says, voice thick with a promise, and kisses my lips. "Will be from nothing but pure pleasure."

I'm craving his pleasure like a junkie fiending for a fix. I'm talking about that mind-blowing, earth-shattering, panty-dropping kind of love that devours every inch of your being—I swear, those lips must be laced with something illegal because one taste and I'm hooked, desperate for another hit.

And his promises? The way he murmurs those filthy-sweet nothings against my ear, his hot breath sending shivers cascading through me... It's enough to make a girl's knees buckle. I need those whispered vows of devotion like I need oxygen, clinging to them like a lifeline in the middle of all this chaos.

His touch, his presence, his relentless devotion—they're the anchors holding me steady when everything else threatens to drag me under. He needs this as much as I do. Control was ripped from him—stripped away piece by piece in that hellhole—and I will gladly, willingly surrender every part of myself so he can reclaim it. This is his love language. Dominance. Command. Possession. And I'm fluent in every word.

I'm ready to lose myself in everything that is him and let our bodies do what our words can't—put us back together.

His mouth consumes me, lips and tongue painting wet trails down my neck. With one hand, he pins my wrists above my head, his grip iron-tight as he worships every inch of exposed skin. I moan helplessly as he devastates me with those punishing kisses, stoking a blaze inside me that nothing can tame.

Jesus. I'm already soaked just from his mouth alone. This man has a direct hotline to my libido, and he dials it to eleven without even trying. He could probably undo me with nothing more than a smoldering look and a well-placed whisper. It's almost criminal how effortlessly he wrecks me, how fast he has me desperate and aching for more.

His hand slides between my trembling thighs, fingers finding my throbbing center with devastating precision. "Fuuuck," he growls, low and filthy. "You're dripping, baby." He circles my swollen clit with expert pressure, sending rolling waves of pleasure crashing through me.

Without warning, he drives his cock deep inside me, filling me with every thick inch until my breath is gone. Our eyes lock—his blazing with need and love so fierce it undoes me completely.

I wrap my legs around his hips, pulling him deeper, begging without words. This is our language—raw, unfiltered, primal. But he sets the pace, moving slow and deliberate, making sure I feel *all* of him. My breath catches as he hits that perfect spot buried deep, and white-hot ecstasy detonates through my body.

"You're the only thing keeping me from drowning, Angel. My salvation. The love I never thought I'd ever fuckin' find or deserve." His ocean-blue eyes burn with raw hunger as they cut straight through me. "You're the light that pierces my darkness, my fire—and you're all fucking mine."

"Yours," I whisper against his lips.

His possessive words detonate something inside me, each command and claim feeding the inferno already raging beneath my skin. His dominance is intoxicating—a drug I have zero interest in quitting. Power and surrender, all tangled together until I can't tell where he ends and I begin.

I crave his mark. I want him to brand me with every growled *mine*, every fierce declaration of ownership. These aren't just words—they're proof of what we are, a reminder of how completely we belong to each other.

Being claimed by him is everything. I hunger for it—the surrender, the freefall, the feeling of being utterly possessed by this man. His words wash over me and I arch into him, wordlessly offering him more. In this dance of dominance and devotion, I've found exactly where I'm meant to be.

His mouth crashes into mine, urgent and wild. His tongue finds mine, moving in perfect sync, matching every desperate pull and twist. I want all of him—the raw power, the untamed force beneath his skin. This tender version of Rhyland is intoxicating, but I'm starving for more. I know he's holding back, trying not to crush me, trying to soothe my fears and pain. But I don't want his restraint. I want the unfiltered passion of him unleashed, his love without apology or caution.

I wiggle my hands out of his tight grasp and clench his hair tightly, pulling as he teases me with slow, torturous strokes. "Rhyland," I moan, my voice needy and impatient, "stop playing games..." I hope he's catching on to what I want—what I *need* from him.

He chuckles, the rumble vibrating deep within his chest. "Look at you—getting all demanding on me?" He teases, his voice low with alpha dominance. "You want to get fucked, baby? Hmm? Want me to take this pussy and own it?" He thrusts his hips, stealing my breath away with the slow, deliberate motion. This man has honed my body to crave rough, degrading, primal sex. "Want me to treat you like my whore?"

"Fuck. Y-yes, please." I plead, my arousal surging at his filthy words.

I know I should feel degraded and disgusted by his crude words and possessive behavior. But instead, I'm the polar opposite—completely turned on and willing to be anything he wants me to be. It's like he's cast a spell over me, making me feel safe and cherished with his filthy talk. I'm putty in his hands, ready to be molded into whatever shape he desires, and god help me; I've never wanted anything more in my life.

In one swift motion, he hauls me off the bed and pins me against the wall, my palms flat against the cold surface like a criminal under arrest—Rhyland's hard cock giving my backside a friendly nudge.

"Mmm...you know what that begging does to me, sweetheart," he says. "It makes me *feral.*" That last word is a whisper against my ear, and I'm covered in goosebumps.

Good.

"Don't hold back," I murmur against the wall. "Take what you need from me, Rhyland." I bite my lip, heat crawling up my cheeks, but I push through it. "Use my body however you want. Fuck me in every dirty, sinful way you've been craving—"

Rhyland's fingers cut off my words, gripping my hair and digging into the sensitive spot at the base of my nape, giving me a delightful yank—his other hand, with a bruising grip on my hip, has me praying for some deep purple bruises come morning.

There he is.

Here's the man I crave more than anything—raw, rough, and undeniably the epitome of a Viking alpha.

"You're treading on dangerous ground, baby—you sure you know what you're getting into? Think you can handle the beast inside?"

I nod eagerly, my body already responding to the command in his voice.

"I've been dreaming about you, Angel, for *weeks.* Dreams of feeling your tight pussy clenching my cock, of pounding into you so hard and deep you're fucking breathless and senseless."

His chest presses into me, forcing the air from my lungs in a sharp gasp. His hot breath ghosts over my neck as he grinds his hips into me, reducing me to a mute, aroused mess. My arousal drips down my thighs, a testament to the intensity of the moment.

He releases my hair. "Stay put. Don't you dare move," he commands, his voice thick with authority.

His lips press against my skin, gliding down my spine with a trail of wet kisses. His mouth finds my ass, teasing and nibbling at it roughly, eliciting moans of pleasure from deep within me. I can't help but push back into his kisses.

"Now, bend down and grab your ankles," he demands, and I do.

He drops to his knees and spreads my ass cheeks apart, eagerly devouring me from behind, his tongue delving deep into the tight ring of muscle. I gasp at the sudden pleasure, unable to resist his boldness any longer. I give in to the sensation of his mouth on me, my body igniting as he expertly licks and teases me.

This man has got a thing for my ass, and I'm not complaining one bit.

I push into him, offering him access as he spreads me open more, and his mouth lavishes attention on my most sensitive area. I moan at the filthy sensation—my head buzzing from this position. His hand travels up my inner thigh, rubbing my arousal and then finding my clit. He rubs it slowly, finding just the right rhythm as he continues to eat me out from behind—going from clit to ass in long licks and slurps.

I'm being devoured, igniting the most intensely erotic sensations that set my entire being ablaze with wanton need.

His moans, growls, and slurps only intensify everything. My mind goes blank from the intense sensation, and my breaths are shallow and ragged.

"You like getting your ass eaten, Angel?" He asks between licks, his voice thick with power.

I can't answer. I'm consumed by him entirely, my body and mind surrendering to his dominance.

"Answer me, Dani—You like being my filthy whore?"

It's one thing to experience it, but another to actually admit to it. But that's Rhyland, always pushing my boundaries and making me voice what I want.

He slaps my ass hard, the sound echoing off the walls. I scream at the contact, the pleasure and pain melding together. "Yes...Y-yes!" I answer, my voice trembling with want.

Rhyland is up, his hand wrapped around my throat before I take my next breath. "You fucking crave it, don't you? My cock filling up that tight little hole of yours," he growls, pressing me harder against the wall. His rock-hard dick teases at my entrance, sending shivers down my spine.

His vise-like grip on my windpipe swallows my nod, the lack of oxygen heightening my pleasure. He knows he has complete control over me, and it only turns me on more. I grind against him, begging him to claim me. He firmly grips my pussy with his other hand, then coats my ass with my own arousal.

"You're gonna come hard with my cock deep inside you. And I can't fucking wait to hear you scream my name," he demands against my throat.

He leisurely pushes his cock into my dripping center, making me wait in agony. His thick thumb finds its way to my ass, no doubt remembering how he prepared it earlier. His thumb enters me slowly, pulling out and thrusting back in, teasing me mercilessly and causing deep moans to escape my throat.

"Rhy—"

His hand tightens around my throat, cutting off my words as his cock rams into my drenched pussy. My body spasms with each thrust, the lack of air adding to the overwhelming pleasure. Blinding white flashes fill my vision, but I am lost in the sensation of him filling me. He slams into me relentlessly, taking me to the brink of ecstasy before pulling back and starting again. The vulgar sounds of our bodies meeting fill the room, consuming us both in our lust.

The sensation of suffocation teases my senses as Rhyland pounds into me, pushing me to the brink of consciousness. I never knew depravity could turn me on so much, but being fucked while struggling for air is an irresistible and intoxicating kink, and I crave every filthy, dirty moment of it.

I'm losing it, teetering on the edge of an orgasm that'll split me in two. Both holes are occupied, and the feeling is utterly mind-blowing.

"Godsdamn, you're so fucking tight, baby," he groans. "Fucking come on me, Angel. Come all over my cock." My body coils tighter, desperate for oxygen. But I don't give a damn—he finally lets go of my throat, and I gulp in a lungful of air as my orgasm takes over, screaming his name in ecstasy.

At my earth-shattering orgasm, I'm pretty sure I squirted like a geyser. I'm drenched in my own juices, and they're trickling down my legs.

"That's it, Angel. *Christ.* Drown me..." Rhyland has a thing for my squirting. He's a master at making me explode like a damn fountain.

"Fucking scream louder—let everyone hear how beautiful you sound coming on my cock." He smacks my ass hard. "That's one..."

I'm sure I sound like a wailing banshee because my voice cracks, and my throat feels like it's been sandpaper-sandwiched.

Rhyland roughly spins me around, lifting me with ease as he slides effortlessly back into my pussy. He slams me against the wall, biting my lip hard enough to draw blood as he ravages my mouth with his tongue. His hips thrust forcefully, matching the rhythm of our passionate kisses. I grind and ride him with a desperate need for another release, but he knows how to make me wait, teasingly slowing his pace just when I'm about to climax.

"Is this what you fucking want, baby?" he grunts, "Huh?" his tongue lapping at my neck as he thrusts deeper. "For me to own this pussy—to fuck you hard?"

I gasp and moan, my body trembling beneath him, powerless against the primal need he unleashes in me. "Yes!" I cry out. "Always... just like this!" My body surrenders completely to the savage hunger Rhyland draws out of me—the kind that lives in my bones, in my blood. I'll never get enough of this. Never tire of his unrestrained, all-consuming passion. He can have every piece of me, and I'll beg him to take more.

"Good girl," Rhyland grunts against my skin. "That's all you'll ever get from me." His hips drive into mine relentlessly, each punishing stroke igniting a new wave of ecstasy that ripples through my entire body.

Suddenly, his teeth are in my neck, and he bites down hard, his instincts taking over as he fucks me relentlessly against the wall. I feel my blood trickling down my breasts—a mixture of pain and pleasure courses through my body as I surrender to him completely. My orgasm builds again; my pussy flutters and tightens around Rhyland's cock, and I explode again in an earth-shattering release, coating us both in a slick layer of my cum.

That's what Rhyland does to me—consumes and ravages me until I am nothing but a quivering mess at his mercy.

"Fuuuck. I love it when you come undone around me," he growls, licking my neck. "That's two, baby. I've got some catching up to do." His lips devour mine, taking my breath away.

I melt against him, every inch of me yielding to my Viking's raw dominance. My body, heart, and soul are his to claim, and nothing thrills me more than surrendering completely to his darkest wants.

His hands slide possessively over my curves, and I arch into his touch, silently pleading for more. I want to be the vessel for every ounce of his pent-up hunger, the canvas for his most savage urges. I crave the sharp pleasure of being utterly owned by him, of letting him use me however he wishes.

I'm drunk on the idea of being his plaything, his whore, his goddess—his everything. The only one who can give him both peace and ecstasy in a world that keeps trying to rip us apart.

I let go of all control and drown in the wicked bliss of being conquered by my blue-eyed berserker. There's nowhere else I'd rather be than here, wrapped in his powerful arms, surrendering to the devastating pleasure only he can give me.

He sinks his sharp fangs into the plump mound of my breast, eliciting a throaty cry of pleasure from me. As he sucks and pulls, his fat cock continues to thrust deeply into me, driving him closer to the brink and pushing me onto yet another mind-blowing orgasm.

I moan, clinging to him desperately. He lifts his head briefly, allowing a trickle of my blood to drip between us as he resumes his relentless assault on my senses. "I can't get enough—you're so sweet, Angel. So addictive." He latches onto my breast again—sucking and feeding. His venom only sends more waves of pleasure through me, signaling my next climax.

"Rhyland..." I'm left with only whimpers.

Rhyland's pace turns punishing, each powerful thrust slamming into me so deep it steals the air from my lungs. His thick cock strikes that perfect spot inside me over and over until my vision whites out with overwhelming pleasure.

"Shiiiit, baby—I'm—" he growls, burying himself as he comes hard, flooding me with pulse after pulse of hot cum. "Fucking fuuuck."

His sexy, guttural moans push me over the edge for the third time, my body clenching around him as ecstasy crashes through me, leaving me completely at his mercy.

When it's over, we stay tangled together, chests heaving, bodies slick with sweat. The air hangs thick with the unmistakable scent of sex—musk and need still clinging to our skin.

As our racing heartbeats gradually settle, Rhyland leans in, pressing his lips to my temple in a kiss so tender it almost doesn't match the man who just wrecked me. That gentle contrast sends a fresh wave of warmth flooding through my veins.

He pulls back just enough to rest his forehead against mine, and the quiet intimacy of it says more than words ever could. Our breaths mingle, skin still flushed, and I feel it—deep in my chest—two souls perfectly, irrevocably locked together.

Gazing into his eyes, I see a reflection of my own emotions—the love, the devotion, the unwavering commitment that binds us together.

"Three down, and I'm fucking far from being finished with you, Angel."

Well, shit! This man is going to be the death of me. Death by orgasms—it's a great way to go.

DANICA

66

The underground cell greets us with a chilling embrace, the air thick and cloying like a ghostly veil. It's a stifling space, walls weeping with the earth's tears; moss and lichen are the only adornments on the cold stone surfaces. The faint *drip-drip-drip* of water echoes a melancholic metronome in the dimly lit chamber.

Thin slivers of light bleed through the cracks above, throwing restless shadows across the walls and deepening the cold, forsaken feel of the space.

Post-sex marathon, it's the next morning, and every little ache hums a sensual anthem courtesy of Rhyland's thoroughness—five blissful orgasms later, I'm sporting the kind of 'loved' soreness you wear with a smirk. My body is a tapestry of bruises and love bites, a testament to being thoroughly and utterly cherished.

Armored back in my skin-tight leathers, hair braided and fortified by a warrior's breakfast, I join Rhyland on a mission below ground—to the cell that cages his turncoat brother, Adrian. With each step into the depths, my heart swims in a storm of emotions. Adrian's deception has cut to the bone, risking everything sacred. Now, it's time for him to spill his secrets.

Adrian's cell sits at the heart of this heavy silence, a confinement of despair where comfort and warmth are strangers. There, cowering in shadow and regret, he's the picture of defeat. Adrian's eyes catch the dim light, a twinkle of 'I fucked up' in the depths of his midnight gaze as it meets ours. I mentally zip up my sassiest armor, braced to slice through the thick tangle of his treachery with razor-sharp wit.

The dude's clearly seen better days—when was the last time he fed? His face is sunken and ashen, like he'd been moonlighting as a ghost in a haunted house gig. The hair that once proudly screamed 'sorcerer-shampoo-commercial' now whispers 'dungeon life.' It's time to decode the enigma wrapped in a riddle, smothered in betrayer sauce that is our dear Adrian.

"Why?" I serve the single syllable into the chill of the cell, letting it ping against the stone like a siren call for truth. "Why pull a Judas on us after everything?"

Adrian's hands dance a nervous ballet, weaving a tapestry of second thoughts in his lap. After what feels like an eon, he throws his voice into the void, and it lands like a lead balloon. "I had no choice. Azrael promised me the one thing I desire most—my family's souls."

Surprise rockets my eyebrows skyward—I didn't anticipate that curveball. I instinctively retreat a step as Rhyland puffs up beside me, a scowl etched on his face so intense it could pierce metal. "Moretemis has your family? How can you be sure—what evidence do you have?"

"I just know," Adrian snaps. "Azrael claimed Moretemis holds their souls captive, damned for eternity. He said if I helped him capture you, Moretemis would free them." His voice cracks. "I had to try..."

A twinge of something slices through my irritation—a wave of empathy? Would I have played the game differently if I were in his no-good-traitor shoes? After all, the stakes are family souls. And after what Seraphina just shared with me, my mother is in the same boat.

"Spill it," I demand, my patience with riddles as thin as tissue paper. Adrian's got the exclusive scoop on Moldy-Wart, and it's high time he broadcast the full saga, minus the cryptic bullshit.

"Moretemis, he's the demon ruler of the Shadow Realm—the Underworld—and holds my parents—my sister captive in the Abyss, among thousands of others," Adrian says, meeting my gaze. "Centuries of torment while I'm powerless to save them."

This isn't new. Moretemis has been aggressively amassing souls, almost as if he's trying to build up a vast collection, like a twisted Pokémon card collector. But now, Adrian is painting an even more ominous picture, making it sound like Moretemis is angling to take on a role akin to the Greek god Hades—the ruler of the underworld who lords over the souls of the dead.

The burning question claws its way up my throat, demanding an answer. I must know if Adrian is in on Azrael's dirty little secret. What would it say about him if he knew all along?

"Did you know?" I demand, my voice razor-sharp. "Azrael killed my mother?"

Rhyland goes rigid beside me, his fury radiating off him in palpable waves. He doesn't know yet—the truth I've discovered.

"What?" he snarls, a guttural sound that speaks volumes.

Adrian's head droops, shame pouring off him in tangible waves. I can feel the sting of tears pricking at my eyes, but I staunchly refuse to let them fall.

"Azrael filled me in only after we knew for sure you were the foretold one. I swear," he confesses, his voice heavy with regret.

I'm at a loss for words, unsure how to process or respond to this revelation: Adrian's betrayal and the pain it brings slice through me like a serrated blade.

"Did you also know that he took my mother's soul, and now it's in Moretemis's filthy hands?" I manage to choke out, my voice quavering.

Rhyland is at my side instantly, his hands cupping my face, compelling me to meet his gaze. "Are you certain about this? Where'd you get this intel?"

"Seraphina," I breathe, and that single word carries the weight of a thousand unsaid things.

Rhyland's eyes glaze over, a mirror reflecting the storm raging within me. He feels what I feel—the searing hurt, the bitter betrayal, the aching loss, and the desperate need for redemption.

"I did," Adrian confesses matter-of-factly.

I clench my eyes shut, desperately trying to dam the flood of emotions threatening to overwhelm me. When I finally trust my voice not to betray me, I force the words out, each laced with urgency. "How?" I ask, worry lines etched into my forehead. "How can their souls be redeemed?"

Adrian leans back, his composure fracturing as the desire to assist shines through. "I've been trying to find the answers—I'm close. What I do know is that there must be a path to redemption. No soul deserves to languish in Hell unjustly or endure a fate more harrowing than death itself."

Seraphina's words echo in my mind—the souls are indeed redeemable. But the burning question remains: how? That's the elusive jackpot answer we so desperately need.

"I understand that this may be unexpected for you. But, as the savior..." Adrian begins.

"Enough with the savior crap," I cut in. "We need to unravel this mystery. My mother's soul is at stake."

"I believe...It has to do with you, Dani."

"Don't you dare put this burden on her," Rhyland growls, his tone low and dangerous—a clear warning directed at Adrian.

Adrian leans back in his seat, a hint of resignation on his face. "I'm just stating the facts here. Dani's the one with the power to take on Moretemis. If anything, she's the *only* one who can free them."

I glare at Adrian.

"Now you want to play the fucking hero and help us? After everything you've done, all the betrayal and lies, you expect us to welcome you back with open arms?" Rhyland's tone is nothing but pissed off.

Somewhat chastened, Adrian's gaze drops to the floor as he mumbles, "No, I don't expect that. Just hope." He lets out a long breath. I can feel his remorse. "I messed up, okay? I admit that."

Rhyland's jaw locks, eyes blazing. "You let that bastard Azrael work me over for *weeks* for what? Some bullshit hope to free your family, with no real plan? Put me through Amara's twisted games? And that shit hole where Cade had his fun torturing me—explain that, you piece of shit."

Adrian flinches. "I'm sorry, it wasn't meant to be that way. All I did was give Azrael your location before everything got messed up. He swore he'd only keep you under Cade's watch until..." he looks to me with guilt in his eyes, "until he secured Dani." His eyes plead for understanding as he meets Rhyland's gaze. "You must understand—I had to take the chance..."

Rhyland quits the statute act and paces the cell like a caged predator; each breath heaves out thunderously against the silence.

My voice releases the building tension. "What changed? Why all the smoke and mirrors?"

Adrian dips his head, something like defeat flickering across his face. "Right—he wasn't counting on your power, so we had to pivot our plan—thus the reason we pulled you out of the bunker." He motions to Rhyland.

The big picture snaps into focus like the last few turns of a Rubik's Cube. The memory hits me afresh, raw and searing—Rhyland vanished, leaving me thinking I'd been left in the lurch, only to learn he was trapped in a hole, taking a beating that would've killed a lesser man. It was all part of Azrael's grand scheme to keep him off the board while trying to grab me. When that flopped, plan B was to parade Adrian in, playing the hero, all to tap into my still-under-wrap powers.

"Nice move, though," I say with enough sarcasm to peel paint. "Play the double-agent game, hand us over on a silver platter, and for what? Your little choice there didn't just backfire. It gave Azrael all he wanted on a silver stake. Ever think maybe you were just a pawn in all their bullshit?"

"Of course I did." Adrian bursts out. "But the damned have few options." His head drops wearily. "I was a fool. Now, we all may pay the price."

Rhyland's words cut through the air, fierce and unforgiving. "Nobody's footing the fucking bill but you. I've paid enough for your betrayal—bled for it, suffered. That debt's been settled in full by me, and me alone!"

Adrian's head bows as if carrying the weight of the world. "I know, brother—"

"Stop calling me that." Rhyland snaps. "You lost the right to call me brother. Family doesn't pull the kind of shit you did."

Adrian shakes his head. "I was a fool to trust Azrael's word. But when you've endured endless grief, any glimmer of hope is blinding."

Internally, I'm struggling to understand Adrian's limits—his pressures and decisions. Outside, my face is an unreadable mask. I nod slightly, showing the world a pillar of strength amidst the storm of betrayal and conflict.

I switch gears before Rhyland goes full-on Pompeii. The Soul Stone—that's the next breadcrumb. "Alright, enough about who betrayed whom for now. Let's slice into something meatier—the Soul Stone. Enlighten us, Adrian."

Adrian, the human shrug emoji, offers up his shoulders in a half-hearted lift. We all know there's much more to unravel about the Soul Stone, and it's high time he started spilling.

"Right, let's cut the dramatics and talk turkey about Azrael's pet rock. I'm not entirely in the dark here—we're dealing with a 'Humpty Dumpty' situation; it's all in pieces, and Amara's played keep-away with a chunk. So spill—how does this glorified gravel ramp up Azrael's mojo?" Arms crossed, I have zero patience for the long version. "Give me the Cliff Notes, Adrian. How does it give Azrael power?"

Adrian straightens, a scholarly light entering his eyes despite the dire topic. "The stones draw magic from the realm of Unbra. Shadow magic, illusions, mind control, necromancy. In the wrong hands, it corrupts."

"So the stone controls the user?" I ask.

"Not exactly," Adrian says. "It exploits flaws already within someone. It heightens their worst impulses—cruelty, deception, hubris. It makes them a vessel for destructive powers."

I consider this carefully. The stone reveals someone's true nature. "Can the magic be harnessed for good?"

Adrian tilts his head thoughtfully. "Perhaps, but the temptation for personal gain is too great for most. The magic demands a steep price for use. Azrael's strength grows with each piece he acquires; they amplify his dark abilities, making him a force that stands opposite the essence of creation you wield, Dani. It's a chessboard of cosmic forces, and he's been playing a long game to gather them and ascend to unchallenged dominance."

Cutting through the niceties like a knife through a fog, I lay down the crux of our quandary. "How many pieces are we talking about, and how many has Azrael already snagged?"

"Azrael has only gotten his hands on one so far—the one from Marcus. It's a larger shard, which means it's giving him a significant boost in his abilities," he explains.

I tilt my head, a slow smile playing on my lips. "So, if Azrael's after Amara's fragment, what's with the buddy act? Why not just five-finger-discount it from her? Unless they've got some weird 'frenemy' thing going on that I don't know about?"

Adrian nods, his voice carrying an edge of solemn knowledge. "The stone has to be handed over willingly. It can't be taken by force, like your crown and the stones you control. Azrael's goal was to win Amara over to give him the shard freely so he could boost his power. But—"

"Then why the hell was it so easy for me to snatch Amara's piece right off her neck?" Realization dawns on me.

Adrian looks at me, shocked at first, then thoughtfully nods. "I think it's because you wear the crown—the stone recognizes its rightful place is with you."

The gears turn in my head, pieces of this maddening puzzle slotting together.

I need details now. Every second counts. "Where's Azrael's stone?"

Adrian hesitates before answering quietly. "In a ring on his right hand. But breaching his defenses would be suicide."

I lift my chin, a steely edge shimmering in my eyes—determination and defiance blended. Turning to Rhyland, I take in the silent storm brewing in his stance, every line of his body a testament to barely restrained fury.

Rhyland's voice is firm as he breaks the silence. "We're going to get it, make no fucking mistake about that."

I take in Rhyland's internal battle, the visceral churn of conflicting emotions within him. Love isn't a switch; you can't flip it off even when betrayal cuts deep. He might never forgive Adrian. Yet, standing in Adrian's shoes, what lengths would I go to for those I cherish?

I need to know how souls are captured and sent to the underworld. "How does the Soul Stone work—how does it capture them?"

Adrian explains, "The Soul Stone is more than a mere gem; it's a trap for wayward souls. It lures them with a glow only they can see and uses ethereal chains to pull them into Moretemis's realm. Once absorbed, their essence bolsters his power."

Wayward souls. Untethered—the Soul-Tie. "What do you know about the Soul-Tie?" I blurt out.

Rhyland goes rigid next to me, and I can practically feel his eyes boring into me, silently demanding an explanation. But he keeps his lips zipped, letting me handle this one.

Adrian leans in. "You know about the Soul-Tie?"

"It's a straightforward question, Adrian. Either you know what it is, or you don't. Which is it?" I shoot back.

"Yes," he replies, as simple as it is frustrating. "But I'm not aware of anyone capable of completing it. It's a lost cause."

Great. Another impossible task. But I signed up for this whole "savior" gig, right? Might as well embrace the chaos.

"Does a blood bond hold the same meaning—the same connection?" I ask, my voice urgent, needing to understand.

Adrian shrugs, "I believe it is similar, but our kind hasn't engaged in the mating process for centuries, so it's difficult to ascertain if the experience is precisely the same."

I let out a frustrated sigh. Rhyland has remained silent, and I can sense his confusion, knowing he must be wondering what on earth I'm talking about.

"If there's even the slightest chance I can help your family, consider me on board."

Adrian's eyes glisten with fragile hope. "I don't deserve your grace. But... thank you, Danica."

Rhyland's warning is laced with command. *"Angel, stop. Don't feed him hope."*

A sigh escapes, heavy with the burden of uncharted truths.

How can I paint a picture of the possibility for him to see?

I ponder, imagining the roles reversed. The thought solidifies my resolve—understanding dawns that in love, sometimes the unknown and the unseen are worth every perilous step into the void.

"What would you do if it were me?" I send the thought into Rhyland's mind.

He snaps his head, eyes burning with a fierce, predatory fire. *"Stop. Don't you ever fucking think that way... This—us—is a whole different game. I'd gladly take a one-way ticket to hell and sell my soul if it meant saving yours. What that fucker did is beyond forgiveness, Dani."*

I throw a sidelong glance at Rhyland. *"Rhyland, no one's downplaying the backstab bingo we're in. But humor me with a 'what if.' What he says is true—I'm getting my mother out of the pit. Let's not tunnel vision on the betrayal. The truth is, we're neck-deep in bizarre, babe, and I'd wager we haven't even scratched the surface on this episode of 'As the Otherworld Turns.'"*

Adrian glances at us, his expression a mixture of uncertainty and amusement. "Um, should I give you two a moment alone? I'd take off and let you talk, but..." He raises his wrists; the sound of chains clinking together punctuates his predicament. "I'm not exactly free to move around."

I slip some reprieve into my tone, easing off the throttle. "No, it... It's fine. We're on our way out as it is. We've got realms to save and villains to thwart, remember?"

Adrian looks earnest, his request carrying the weight of his earlier actions. "I realize this might sound insane, and you have every right to say no, but could I come with you? I want to help. I need to make things right, Danica, please. Give me that chance."

Before I can even grasp the full meaning of his question, Rhyland's roar shreds the air, "Hell fucking no! Totally out of the question! You think I'm an idiot? To let you waltz back into our—"

"Yes," I say. "That's mighty big of you, Adrian. All hands on deck, right? We're not exactly swimming in allies—so your help? We'll take it."

A quick, coy sidelong peek at Rhyland's handsome face twisted in ire, and despite the gravity of the predicament, I can't help but let a rogue smirk play across my lips. Overruling the Viking vampire's verdict adds an unexpected thrill to this perilous chess game. With a buoyant step, I pivot and ascend the stairs, leaving behind the cell—and his simmering dominance.

As I contemplate the future, a flicker of devilish anticipation sparkles in my thoughts.

Will there be repercussions for this bold move? Abso-fucking-lutely.

I'm practically betting on it, counting on Rhyland's own brand of impassioned retribution. It's a price I'm willing—and secretly eager—to pay.

RHYLAND

67

I burst out of the cell, the heavy metal door slamming shut behind me with a resounding clang that echoes through the dank, stone corridor. The sound mirrors the fury surging through my veins. Adrian's words and audacity linger in the musty air, but I shove them aside. My focus is solely on the woman who dared to challenge me.

Dani, with her bold defiance and nerve to question my authority, sets my thoughts ablaze with a violence fiercer than hell itself. I storm forward, muscles coiled tight, every alpha instinct sharpened by the inferno coursing through my veins. I'm a man possessed, a predator on the hunt, tracking her with single-minded determination.

Her footsteps echo through the stone passages, each one drawing me closer. But this flame isn't born of desire; it's a raging wildfire of pure anger. She appears on the staircase, her lithe figure exuding strength and grace that normally ignites a different hunger within me. But not now. Now, the sight of her only fuels my fury.

In three long strides, I close the distance between us. My hand shoots out to grab her arm and spin her around. I yank her close, forcing her to face me, my eyes blazing. She meets my gaze, defiant and unafraid, which only serves to fuel my rage further.

"What the hell do you think you're doing?" My voice is a dangerous growl, each word sharp.

Dani, ever defiant, doesn't even flinch. She stands her ground, her honey-gold eyes locking onto mine. "Giving him a chance—"

"A chance?" I spit out the word. "After that traitor sold us out? Are you out of your mind?"

Even in the face of my anger, her gaze never wavers. "Love makes people do crazy things," she counters, her voice a calm blade slicing through my anger.

I'm a hurricane of fury, a tempest of wrath, and her damned tranquility only serves to fan the flames. I want to grab her by the shoulders and shake some fucking sense into her—or maybe shake the insanity out of her. But I can't. My hands, my heart, they're tied. No matter how infuriating or maddening this woman can be, she's the one I love with every fiber of my being, the one who brings me to my knees.

"How can you think about trusting him after the torment he put me through?" The words rip from my throat, ragged and raw.

Dani's eyes gleam with emotions, twisting a knife of pain deep in my chest. Seeing her tears threaten to fall has always been my Achilles' heel.

"I know—but what if he can help?" Her voice fractures, each word a shard of glass piercing my heart. "I have no clue how to save my mother from Moretemis, Rhyland. Adrian has knowledge that I don't."

My hands ball into fists, every muscle in my body coiled. I can't fucking believe it—she's buying into this crap? She's willing to gamble it all on some slim chance Adrian isn't lying again. But I get why she's hooked—her mother.

"We'll sort this out together, kära, without any traitors."

"Rhyland, please..." she implores. "This isn't the time to be picky about our allies."

It's my responsibility to shield her—from every fucking threat out there, and she's ready to toss caution to the wind, banking on the word of a traitor. Wordless, I turn and stride away, leaving Dani in the gloom.

I storm into the study, each step a thunderclap against the polished floor. The others are gathered, their faces a mix of curiosity and concern. They don't know the nightmare about to unfold.

I don't bother with formalities. My eyes sweep the room, commanding silence. I take a deep breath, the words spilling out like acid.

"We've been duped," I growl. "Adrian's been sitting on critical intel about the Soul Stone—how it's in pieces, and Azrael's on the hunt. Dani's mom is in literal hell with Moldy-Ass. Now it's on Dani to free those damned souls. No pressure, right? Fuck."

I pour a stiff drink and toss it back, the burn searing my throat. "Amara's involved, and Azrael ran the second Dani flashed the Atherite Stone."

The room falls silent. Even Erik's stoic face flickers with surprise.

"And you know what really fucking kills me?" I spit out. "Dani thinks we should let Adrian back in and let him tag along on our quest for the Faerite Stone. After all the betrayal, she wants to hand him a shiny new star."

Lucian, the epitome of a cocky smartass, leans back in his chair. "Well, shit, I gotta say, I'm almost impressed. This whole clusterfuck is shaping up to be better than my usual Friday night entertainment. All we need now is some popcorn and a few more plot twists, and we've got ourselves a bona fide blockbuster."

Adrian's deceit sits like bile in my stomach, echoing my own torturous past. That Dani would even consider trusting him again... it's a fucking slap to the face.

A memory of Adrian's grief over his lost family surfaces. At the time, I didn't think twice about it. But now, a new realization dawns on me, like a punch to the gut.

In all my centuries of existence, through all the battles I've fought and the horrors I've witnessed, never once did I think Adrian would be so fucking stupid, so desperate, as to fall prey to the temptation of trying to win back what he lost. Unbra, that accursed realm of shadows and despair, has been sealed off and impenetrable for as long as anyone can remember—until now. And it's all because of Dani, because of the power she holds within her, the power that could tear open the very fabric of reality and unleash untold horrors upon the world.

What if Adrian's telling the truth, and there's a slim chance that we could save those lost souls—Dani's mother—from an eternity of torment and despair? The very thought of it is enough to make my head spin, to fill me with a sickening mixture of hope and dread that churns in my gut like a writhing mass of serpents.

And yet, despite the tiny sliver of doubt that gnaws at the edges of my mind, I know one thing for certain: I can't trust Adrian, not after everything he's done, not after the way he's betrayed us repeatedly. The risk is too great, and the stakes are too high. If we're going to have any chance of stopping Moretemis and protecting the realms from his insidious grasp, we can't afford to be led astray by false promises and empty hopes.

Dani walks in, radiating confidence and sass.

"Well, well, well, if it isn't our resident paragon of virtue," Lucian chimes in. "Trouble brewing in the land of rainbows and unicorns, eh, Princess?" He can't help but poke the proverbial bear; his mischievous nature compels him to fan the flames of drama.

I'm gearing up to verbally bitch-slap Lucian when Dani offers up a breezy, unfazed response. "Nope. No trouble at all."

I shoot him a glare that could freeze hell over, warning him to tread lightly. "Watch it, Lucian," I growl.

Lucian smirks. "Whoa there, easy now. I'm just calling it like I see it. There's no need to get your boxer briefs in a bunch, tough guy."

I clench my fists, fighting the urge to smack that snarky grin off his face. "Stow it, Lucian. Keep running that smart mouth, and I'll decorate it with my fist."

Lucian lets out a low chuckle, obviously taking great pleasure in pushing my buttons. "Tsk tsk, someone's got their fangs in a twist. Is that any way to speak to your loving, supportive brother?" He shakes his head in mock disapproval, tongue clicking against his teeth. "And here I thought we were engaging in a friendly, wholesome family chat. My, how quickly the tables turn."

From his position removed from the center of the conversation, Erik's voice cuts across the room. "Lucian, enough," he commands, his tone unyielding.

The smug jackass is practically begging me to deck him. I've got bigger problems. "Dani, if you honestly believe I'm going to—"

"Rhyland." Dani's voice cuts through my rage. "Moretemis is holding souls—my mother—hostage in Hell. Adrian can help, and we need it," she implores, her caramel eyes—swirling—pleading. "If there's a chance to save them, we must take it." She looks to everyone for approval, "All of us."

Ax, in her usual unflappable way, tilts her head. That icy stare doesn't give anything away, but she isn't dismissing the plan outright. Lucian tosses out a shrug like he couldn't give two shits. Erik's giving Dani the hard eye, sizing her up like she's some fucking riddle he can't piece together—and Faderyn? That mystical fae bastard lets out a weary sigh as if he's had it up to here with our bullshit. "We should get our asses moving toward the Crystal Peaks," he pipes up, steering us away from this shitshow.

DANICA

68

The quiet that stretches between Rhyland and me is more oppressive than the iron shackles clamped around Adrian's wrists—Rhyland, a fortress of seething anger, paces at the edge of our motley crew. Not a syllable has broken free from him since we stepped out of the portal I conjured—a forest smeared with our most recent conflict, the familiar sight imprinted in my memory like a scar.

Adrian shuffles ahead, sporting the latest in fae fashion—shiny cuffs that don't just sparkle. They put the 'less' in 'powerless.' Ensorcelled wristwear, stripping him of his magical mojo one trudge at a time. Rhyland gets a nugget of satisfaction from that—a peace-keeping compromise on my part. Call it couples therapy, medieval style.

As we navigate through the haze-shrouded labyrinth of the Whispering Woods, time seems to stretch and warp, leaving us unsure how long we've been wandering through this eerie, murmuring landscape. The forest appears alive with secrets, each rustling leaf and snapping twig carrying whispers of half-truths that dance just out of reach. The snow-blanketed ground soon greets our boots, each step accompanied by a satisfying crunch. The crisp, invigorating scent of fresh pine and pristine snow wafts through the air, tickling my senses with its refreshing purity.

Lucian, our charismatic shit-stirrer of pots, is having himself a grand ol' time surfing the waves of angst. As we navigate the misty enigma that is Whispering Woods, he throws me a grin that's all shark in a sea of minnows. "Surely you haven't forgotten our last little escapade in this neck of the woods, particularly the, ah, shall we say, 'gesture of brotherly love' I so graciously gifted you with."

Oh, for the love of...

"What're you yammering on about this time? Do you seriously think I've developed amnesia about what went down in this very spot? Please. If you're referring to that whole 'feeding me your blood' thing, then color me utterly unsurprised."

Lucian never backs down from a challenge—grins wider. "Oh, I don't know, Dani-girl. Do you feel anything from my token of graciousness?"

I roll my eyes so hard I'm surprised they don't get stuck in the back of my head. "Lucian, I swear to god—"

"Or maybe," he interrupts, waggling his eyebrows suggestively, "you're feeling a little... different? A little more... dare I say it... Lucian-esque?"

I shoot him a glare. "The only thing I'm feeling right now is a burning desire to punch you in the throat—"

"That's enough, Lucian," Rhyland's voice slices through my rant like a blade through silk.

I can feel my annoyance spiking—not at Lucian's playful ribbing, but at Rhyland's uncanny ability to butt in at the most inopportune moments. Seriously, what's his deal? Something is amiss, and I plan to find out what that is.

But my chance to interrogate Lucian is ripped away as we step into a massive cave opening, its gaping maw ready to swallow us whole and plunge us into the silent depths of the earth.

"I do believe we've arrived at Frost Weaver Hallows," Faderyn announces, his voice bouncing off the icy walls in an eerie echo.

The moment I cross the threshold into the cavern, a bone-chilling cold slams into me like a freight train, wrapping its icy fingers around my body in a vice-like grip. We've stumbled into a new world where the Frost King reigns supreme, and the chill is his faithful consort. I half-expect to see a chandelier of icicles dangling from the ceiling, like some grand ballroom for abominable snowmen. And don't even get me started on this handsy fog, with its icy caresses that seem to seep through my clothes.

Each breath I take comes out in a swirling, ghostly puff, dancing away into the frigid air before vanishing into nothingness. For all I know, we could be time travelers, suddenly transported to some ancient, frozen historical moment when the sun's warmth is nothing more than a distant, half-forgotten dream.

As we venture deeper into the icy cavern, my body seriously considers drafting a strongly worded complaint to the management about this impromptu polar expedition. But just as I'm about to start composing my scathing review, my power decides to crash the pity party and flex its independence. Suddenly, my hands burst into flames, a dazzling display of white-hot defiance dancing and flicking between my fingers.

The cozy glow of my hand-held inferno chases away the frosty bite, warming me from the inside out like the sun decided to give me a private spotlight.

Lucian's eyebrow shoots up, and he hits me with a smirk. "Well, slap my ass and call me a s'more; look who's gone and become a walking, talking flamethrower!" He quips, with enough sarcasm to drown a small village. "How delightfully convenient of you. Should I pack the marshmallows and graham crackers for our next little jaunt into the arctic wasteland, or will you charge me a fee for basking in your radiance? *Oh, Great One?*"

I roll my eyes.

He chuckles, the sound somewhere between amused and exasperated. "To think, last time we found ourselves in a similar predicament, I was rubbing two sticks together like a fucking boy scout on his first camping trip, praying to whatever sadistic deity was listening for a spark."

I meet Lucian's gaze with a grin as sharp as the icicles above. "A flamethrower? Please, I'm more of a portable sunbeam," I counter, with mock grandeur. "Consider the s'mores a mere taste of my boundless benevolence—a freebie from my magnanimous heart." I flutter my lashes in an exaggerated display of innocence. "And that campfire performance? Quite the showcase of your rugged determination—adorably valiant, I must say."

Adrian's voice cuts through the frigid air, "As much as I hate to interrupt this delightful little exchange, we need to move on before we all turn into human popsicles."

"Agreed," Faderyn chimes in, his teeth chattering as he wraps his arms tightly around his torso. "Time is of the essence, and I, for one, would prefer not to become a permanent fixture in this frozen hellscape."

Erik is the picture of fortitude, the very image of stoic strength, but even he can't deny the creeping bite of the cold—his silver eyes betray a glimmer of discomfort. Rhyland is no stranger to the frost either. His brawny arms fold over his chest in an attempt to shield against the relentless chill. Even a Viking vampire can't scoff at the cold's insistent embrace.

Feeling the weight of urgency pressing against the bitter cold, I give a sharp nod. "Let's move."

Axilya huddles into herself, punctuating her statement with a shiver, "I was n-not c-counting on it being so... so absolutely *f-frigid.*"

An unspoken rule in adventuring is always to respect a place named after something cold. Frost Weaver Hallows—honestly, it sounds like a delightful spot for penguins, yet here we are, dressed for a fall festival rather than a foray into Frostbite Central. Note to self: pack a coat next time we visit a place with 'frost,' 'weaver,' or 'hollows' in the name. Or six.

With resolve, I march on, my internal compass fixated on the stone's silent beckoning through the cavern's twists and turns.

As we venture deeper into the heart of the cavern, the walls, clad in their icy finery, come alive with an ethereal dance of light courtesy of the fiery glow emanating from my hands. The azure luminescence bathes the frosty interior in an otherworldly hue, transforming it into a gallery of natural art, each frozen formation a testament to the raw beauty and power of the elements. The scene is breathtaking in its stark elegance, a symphony of ice and shadow that steals the air from our lungs, as if the cold hadn't already done a thorough job.

Stalactites hang from the ceiling like frozen chandeliers, threatening to drop at any moment, while stalagmites claw upward from the ground like the jagged teeth of some ancient buried beast. It's a world of breathtaking danger, where wonder and terror share the same razor edge.

We pick our way carefully across the ice-slicked floor, our breath curling into small ghosts of mist that vanish almost instantly. Then a sharp crack splits the silence, fracturing through the cavern like a gunshot, a stark reminder of just how unforgiving the ground beneath us truly is.

Panic prickles at the base of my neck as Rhyland's sharp command slices through the howling wind, "Stop!" His voice carries the weight of impending doom.

I don't need to be told twice—his deep, authoritative rumble never signals anything less than critical. A peek down confirms our predicament; the ice below is a fractured canvas of imminent betrayal.

"Fantastic," I mutter, the sharp edge of my sass barely masking my alarm. "Let's backtrack with all the grace of Bambi on ice, shall we?"

The others heed my words, cautiously backtracking with the precision of a bomb disposal unit, except me. I'm the statue in this perverse game of red light, green light, staring down the beast beneath me.

Rhyland's grip on my hand is the only anchor in a sea of shifting ice. "I've got you," he vows.

Our joined hands are the only warm thing in this icy hellscape as we tiptoe across the treacherous crust. I shoot him a sidelong glance, raising a brow, and say, "Next date, let's do something less life-threatening. Dancing, maybe?" Attempting humor feels like clutching at straws as another crack reverberates underfoot, sending my stomach into a nosedive.

The piercing sound of the fracturing ice is a chorus of warnings. "Careful yet quick—like pulling off a band-aid," he reminds me, the strain evident beneath his composed exterior.

Rhyland nods once, decisively. "I'm gonna blur us across," he states, poised to propel us across with vampiric speed.

The ice gives without warning.

One second, Rhyland is beside me—the next, a sickening crack splits the air, and the ground simply ceases to exist beneath him. My stomach drops with him as he slams onto a narrow shelf of ice, his body jerking to a violent stop. Below him, nothing. Just a yawning black throat of darkness so deep it seems to pull the light down with it.

My lungs forget how to work.

A column of frozen air breathes up from the abyss, hitting me like a wall—sharp, vicious, stripping the warmth from my face in an instant. My gaze drops to my boots. The ice beneath them is alive with movement, thin black lines racing outward in every direction, branching and splitting like shattered glass in slow motion.

Crack.

Crack.

Crack.

The sound ricochets off the cavern walls, each one closer than the last.

"Go! Now!"

His voice slams through the cavern. But his eyes—those ocean-blue eyes—aren't searching for an escape route. They're locked on me.

My jaw tightens.

Even now, dangling at the edge of oblivion, his only thought is me. Any other time, that would melt me completely. Right now, it just makes me furious.

Something inside me slams shut—the part that listens, the part that retreats. I drop to my knees, the ice biting through my clothes like broken teeth, and throw both hands around his jacket. Every muscle in my arms screams as I wrench backward.

"In case you haven't noticed, I'm not exactly an obedient damsel," I grit out, my teeth clenched so hard my jaw aches. "And you're not getting out of this date that easily."

His fingers claw at the ice beside him, desperate, searching, finding nothing but smooth, merciless surface. My knees slide forward an inch. Then another. The fractures beneath me bloom wider, a web of destruction spreading in every direction I look.

Another crack.

A deep, resonant groan rises from somewhere far beneath us—the sound of something ancient and enormous shifting, surrendering. The shelf beneath Rhyland shudders violently. The ground beneath my knees splits open with a sound like a cannon shot.

There is one weightless, terrifying second where everything simply stops.

Then the darkness takes us both.

DANICA

69

As we fall, Rhyland's instincts kick in—he pulls me close, his arm locking around me like iron bands. His body becomes my shield; his embrace is a fortress as we tumble into the void, bracing for whatever comes next.

In an agile maneuver that defies his size, Rhyland twists midair, an act of preternatural reflexes ensuring his body bears the brunt of our uncontrolled descent. Rhyland hits first, his body slamming into the packed snow with a brutal thud. I crash down on top of him a heartbeat later, and a rough grunt punches out of him as my full weight drives the air from his lungs. His body takes everything—the impact, the force, the fall—absorbing it all so I don't have to.

For a suspended heartbeat, relief floods me, warm and dizzying. I'm unscathed, cocooned in the arms of my vampire who's just cheated death—or at least grievous injury—for us both.

"Nice catch!" I quip, the irony of our situation not lost on me. "But next time, let's aim for a feather bed, shall we?"

I brush the hair from my face, trying for levity even as the echo of our fall fades in the strange, dark void we've found ourselves in.

Rhyland's groan is half in discomfort, half in exasperated affection. "I told you..." He grunts, trying to sit up, "to get to the other side. Why don't you ever listen?" he chides.

"I'm sorry—I couldn't just let you fall! Besides, where's the fun in always doing what I'm told? Admit it—you're secretly thrilled to have played hero again, even if it means a few more bruises," I retort with a playful edge to my voice, unable to resist poking fun at the situation even as we lie sprawled in a heap of snow at the bottom of who-knows-where.

Rhyland's agitation sears through his usually cool demeanor, a fiery protector chastising my recklessness. "I'm immortal, *woman*. I could've taken that fall and walked away without a scratch. But you—shit, if I hadn't done what I did, you could've died!"

His fury is a tempest, fierce and justified. I realize it's time to fill him in on my recent celestial power-up courtesy of the Atherite stone and its restorative gifts.

"Yeah—about that..." I trail off, acknowledging the conversational bomb I'm about to drop on him.

The darkness enveloping us is as thick as ink. I conjure an orb of radiant light which blooms from my hand, pushing back the shadows.

With the impromptu lantern illuminating our cavern, I focus on Rhyland, eager to assess his condition. The light reflects off his rugged features, giving his ocean-blue eyes an ethereal glow. Now that I can see him clearly, I start looking for any injuries that might have gone unnoticed in the adrenaline-fueled tumble.

"Yo, you still breathing down there, or has the allure of the underworld finally seduced you into its cold, clammy embrace?" Lucian shouts, the sound bouncing off the walls like a drunk acrobat on a trampoline. "Give us a sign if you haven't kicked the proverbial bucket yet, or I'm calling dibs on your worldly possessions! Finder's keepers and all that happy horseshit."

From our unintended landing spot, I raise my voice, "I swear to god, Lucian, if you touch my stuff, I'll haunt your undead ass for all eternity!" I holler back, my voice echoing through the cavern like a pissed-off banshee on steroids. "And for the record, we're still very much alive, you asshat."

"About what?" Rhyland's tone is a mix of confusion and vulnerability. He tugs gently, bringing me back down to his steady frame, his hand brushing my hair from my face, his gaze locking with mine in search of clarity.

Nestled atop him again, I take a deep breath and launch into the tale of my heavenly intervention and the Atherite stone's enchantment. "So, it turns out the new stone blessed me with a bit of an upgrade," I start, with a knowing look that says 'brace yourself.'

I divulge everything—the glowing power of the Atherite Stone, its healing capacities, and my newfound connection to it. His eyes reflect every facet of the story, a mix of incredulity and dawning awareness as the pieces fall into place. "Basically, I'm not as fragile as I used to be."

"And you figure *now* is the goddamn time to tell me this?" he shoots back sharply.

Everything happened so damn fast when I was given a celestial Uber back to Rhyland. "I know...I know. But with everything that happened once I was brought back, it literally slipped my mind—I was going to tell you, but..." My voice trails off, the excuse sounding feeble even to my ears.

After all, how often does one get a divine lift to the heavens and angelic upgrades?

I search Rhyland's face for a hint of understanding, hoping he'll grasp the chaotic whirlwind that upended any chance for a proper debrief. It's not every day you get handed a heavenly lifeline, and you'd think someone might cut me some slack for not shouting it from the rooftops the second I touched down.

Rhyland's silence stretches out, his eyes devouring mine, but it is broken instantly. His lips crash against mine with an urgency that steals my breath away. It's like he's pouring every ounce of frustration and relief into the kiss, a silent conversation between our hearts that words can't capture.

"You drive me fucking crazy, kära," he murmurs, pulling back just enough to let the words tumble out, a growl threaded with vehement passion. "You know that?" Without waiting for an answer, he claims my lips again, more fiercely this time, and I respond with equal ferocity, our kiss becoming a battleground of raw emotion. "Fucking crazy. I want to punish you for what you do to me," his words dance between breathless kisses, each one landing like a spark on dry tinder.

With every searing kiss, I'm spelling out silent apologies and declarations of love, a torrent of pent-up feelings being released in how our lips move together.

Rhyland's voice is a raging roar of emotions. "You fucking push me to my limits, woman. Disobey my every command, make me go mad with worry." His fingers grip tightly in my hair. "My heart belongs to you, and you're the only one who can make my damn cock ache like no other—all at the same time."

His eyes lock onto mine, fierce and aflame, each syllable a testament to his unguarded truth—a cocktail of frustration, fear, love, and overpowering attraction that I seem to stir up within him effortlessly. With every word, his grip tightens as if he could merge our very beings to quell the storm of feelings I evoke.

There's a thrill, a delicious sense of power in knowing I can melt this formidable, age-old Viking vampire into a puddle of longing with just the right amount of teasing and defiance. Yet, in equal measure, there's a profound comfort in his dominance, a heady desire for the strength and protection his vampire nature so ardently provides. This dynamic, a dance of push and pull, makes us who we are—two halves of a passionate, fiery whole.

A war rages behind his deep blue eyes—fury and betrayal tangled together, every bit of it aimed at Adrian.

"I know you're mad at me about Adrian," I start cautiously but determined. "But I truly believe he can help us—redeem himself. I love you, and I'm sorry for going against—"

I manage to sputter, but the rest of my confession gets cut off as he takes my words hostage with his lips again.

"Do me a favor and shut that pretty mouth, Angel," he murmurs in a low rumble, lips brushing against mine.

His kisses are a force of nature, a relentless tempest that hijacks my senses. It's a full-on, no-holds-barred assault that doesn't waste time with flowery speeches or long-winded declarations. Nope, it's all about the raw, pulsating desire and an unspoken 'I know' seared into every sizzling touch.

I can read Rhyland like an open book—he's not the type to hold grudges or stay mad at me for long. He's more of an 'actions speak louder than words' kind of guy, and right now, his actions are screaming, 'I can't keep my hands off you, and I don't give a damn about our little tiff.' It's clear that fighting with me is way down on his list of priorities, somewhere between watching paint dry and attending a snail race. He'd much rather channel all that pent-up energy into more...pleasurable pursuits.

"No apologies. And believe me, Angel, your ass is in for some serious punishment," Rhyland delivers the promise with unmistakable authority, leaving no room for argument.

Before I can retort—

"Hate to be the proverbial turd in the punchbowl, lovebirds, but the rest of us up here are slowly morphing into ice sculptures while you two are busy making goo-goo eyes at each other!" Lucian shouts down, the sound echoing through the cavern like a smartass yodel. "Any chance we could crash this little lovefest, or is it a strictly VIP affair reserved for the horizontally inclined?"

I can practically hear the smirk in his voice as he continues, "Also, exactly how deep is this little love grotto of yours? Just trying to gauge whether I need to fetch a ladder or a fucking bungee cord to join the party."

Rhyland groans, burying his face in the crook of my neck. "I swear, one of these days, I'm going to strangle him with his own intestines," he mutters, his breath hot against my skin.

"Get in line, babe," I chuckle, pressing a quick kiss to his temple before reluctantly untangling myself from his embrace. "Looks like we've got company, whether we like it or not."

"It's a stone's throw away," Rhyland barks out.

I crane my neck to peek at the gap we'd plunged through, channeling a beam of my light upward to gauge the distance what I'd optimistically estimated as a stone's throw stacks up to forty feet. That's a mini cliff, but I bet it's practically a hop, skip, and a casual leap for a vampire.

Lucian, Erik, and Adrian drop in with thuds that scream 'action heroes.' They carry Faderyn and Axilya, aiming for tough but probably scoring a perfect ten in unintentional comedy.

I rise to my feet, brushing off the chill of the snow, and extend my hand to Rhyland. With a solid tug, he's back on his feet beside me.

"Stick tight to my side; I'm fond of that...heat you're giving off," Rhyland commands, seizing my waist firmly.

My flames may have flickered out, but my internal wellspring of power hasn't stopped radiating warmth like a miniature sun burning bright inside my core.

"Of course, you've snagged prime real estate next to the mystical space heater. Must be nice, basking in the glow of your own personal inferno while the rest of us plebeians are left to freeze our asses off in the metaphorical cheap seats." Lucian jeers, rolling his eyes with a scoff that echoes his disdain for missing out on the warmth.

The collapsed trail above seals our fate, and the icy cave below is our reluctant new path. "We need to move." I glance at the others, their breath curling in thick clouds, lips edging toward blue. "There has to be a way through these tunnels."

I pause, shutting my eyes to concentrate, casting out my inner senses like a net, searching for the stone's magnetic tug. It beckons me to the left with a nearly imperceptible pull, guiding me with invisible threads. Satisfied with the direction, I conjure a glowing orb of light and hurl it ahead into the gloom.

It bobs gently in the air, transforming the suffocating dark into a landscape of shadows and ice. The cavern ahead, narrow but manageable, unfurls before us. My homemade beacon is a makeshift flashlight, illuminating uneven walls and frozen formations.

We edge forward, tentative but resolute, my light leading the way deeper into the heart of the cave.

Traversing this frozen domain, we find ourselves ensnared in a world that time seems to have forgotten, an icy sepulcher untouched by the sun's warmth. It's a realm of eternal winter, where the heavy shroud of silence is so profound you become aware of the rhythm of your heartbeat, a solitary drum thumping in your chest, echoing in your ears.

We press forward, carving a path through the serpentine passageways of this wintry labyrinth. It's as if we're tracing the ghostly path of a river, long since surrendered to the cold's embrace. In places where the ceiling dips low, whispering secrets of eons past, we duck our heads, forming a tight procession, following the soft luminescence of my light.

Time turns elastic down here, each hour feeling like a marathon in slow motion, with nothing but the steady crunch-crunch of our boot-clad feet against the frosty floor to keep any semblance of time. Every now and then, I half-expect some ice-loving boogeyman to pop out for a "gotcha" moment—this place is prime real estate for a monster mash. But there's zip, zilch, nada; not even a snow flea to break the monotony. Guess the cave's cold shoulder is too much for the local wildlife.

Occasionally, I play my own version of tag, laying a fleeting touch here and there among my frost-nipped friends. It's my personal brand of 'warm-up service,' a little heat 'n' run to take the icy sting out of the air.

"May I speak?" Adrian pipes up after a long stretch of silence.

I glance over at Rhyland, searching his face for clues about his thoughts. He meets my gaze with a look that screams he couldn't give a shit about Adrian's two cents, but he catches the hopeful curiosity in my eyes. With the slightest lift of his chin—a silent, begrudging yes—he gives me the nod. It's my go-ahead to listen to whatever Adrian's got to pitch.

"Sure," I toss the word to Adrian like it's my last piece of gum.

"The Soul Stone," he launches in, all matter-of-fact. "It appears to be split into three pieces."

I knit my eyebrows together, puzzled. "And how did you trip over that tidbit?" I probe, curiosity piqued.

He exhales, the sound carrying the weight of ancient tomes. "It's in the Book of Shadows," he reveals as if talking about some bestseller.

"The Book of what now?" I raise an eyebrow; I can't say I've seen that on any bookshelf.

He's unfazed. "There's a book for every realm," he says with the ease of someone discussing the weather.

"Okay..." I say, egging him on.

Adrian obliges, "In its pages, it speaks of the Soul Stone—a powerful entity tied to the essences of shadows, souls, and darkness. The text alludes to a secret: He who reunites the three will wield the ultimate power."

My scientist's curiosity, ever the driving force, kicks into gear as Adrian's words sink in. The Soul-Shadow Stone—shadows, souls, darkness—is the trifecta of power every good story warns you about.

Adrian speaks with a blend of reflection and realization. "At first, I didn't grasp its significance," he admits. "I assumed it referred to three separate stones or perhaps three powerful individuals. But now it clicks, especially after learning Amara had a piece and considering Azrael's pursuit of it. We couldn't connect with the realms until you came along... And with Azrael tapping into the realm here and discovering the shard—"

"It all adds up," I say, completing his thought with a cheeky nod. "Three shards, one whole stone—one big power-up. Classic!"

"You hold one piece," Adrian reminds me, his voice as calm as a steady current.

Ah, yes. The little malignant jewel I've been safeguarding—a trinket of darkness, Amara's shard. It's just one part of the equation, like the initial ingredient in a cosmic recipe. Now, to secure Azrael's piece of the stone and sniff out the final shard, then—voilà! The stone is complete, and there is another notch in my tiara.

"Do you think this piece I've got will pull any stunts for me?" I casually toss the question to Adrian as my foot skids on a treacherous patch of ice—swift as a shadow, Rhyland's there, his reflexes keeping me upright. "Thank you," I murmur to him, my appreciation whispered like a secret between us.

"Have you tried slipping it into your tiara?" he counters, a sliver of suggestion in his tone.

The notion had only just grazed the edge of my consciousness. "No... I haven't," I admit, feeling the cogs in my mind begin to whir at the fresh possibility. "The last thing I want is for that object to go soul-snatching—mine or anyone else's." My eyes shift to Rhyland as I ponder the implications, seeking reassurance or a shared sense of concern in his gaze.

"Hmm..." Adrian intones, leaving his thoughts to hang in the air, cryptic and open.

But here I am, tangled in a knot of worry, cramping my style. What kind of wickedness could this gem dish out? Is it the soul-sucking type that can leave a girl feeling utterly unfabulous? And the big question: does someone have to give the go-ahead for it to vacuum up a soul, or does it work on some sick autopilot?

Then there's that sly little voice in my head—what if I'm the wild card? Adrian said this thing's a personality amplifier—it could turn me into the diva of darkness or the saint of sunbeams. And let's face it, if anyone could rock an unholy relic with a side of sass, it's me. So, as my brain does the mental tango with a conga line of 'what-ifs,' I've got to wonder if each new thought is a door to disaster or just another walk-in closet waiting to reveal a universe of killer potential.

"Don't even think about playing hot potato with that wicked pebble. Not until we've given that piece of gravel the full Sherlock Holmes treatment, complete with a magnifying glass and a pretentious-as-fuck deerstalker hat," Lucian snaps sharply, his advice laced with his characteristic blunt wit.

"I agree, Little Huntress," Erik finally interjects, his voice cutting through the silence after what feels like an eternity. His rare contribution, stoic and measured, carries a weight of solemnity.

We approach a fork in the tunnel, the bracing wind playing with my hair—a harbinger of the open air nearby. I sense the tug, an almost magnetic draw from the stone, guiding me. Instinctively, I veer to the right. "This way," I assert, trusting in the strange compass I've become.

Our footsteps echo with a crisp crunch against the frost-laden ground; the tunnel walls glisten like crystalline glass, yet are as unyielding as rock-hard ice. Drawn by a morbid curiosity, I press my light against the transparent barrier and peer through. A chilling tableau meets my eyes—figures' faces etched with ageless expressions of terror and sorrow, forever captured within their icy prison. I can't help the gasp that escapes me, drawing the others to huddle around me for a closer look.

"These must be the Forest Fae," Axilya's voice breaks the heavy silence, a note of somber realization in her tone. "They disappeared centuries ago."

I can't tear my gaze away.

They're everywhere—dozens of them—suspended within walls of ice so thick it would take an axe days to break through. Their faces are pressed close to the surface, eyes wide and unblinking, mouths frozen mid-scream, mid-sob, mid-plea. Every expression is a portrait of terror, caught and kept like insects trapped in amber.

My throat tightens.

"How?" The word barely makes it past my lips. "How did this happen?"

"When the realm split, it shattered the tranquility and equilibrium within this place. Thus, it earned the name Crystal Peaks—a moniker born of the expansive frost that claimed this area and all who dwell here," Axilya explains.

Axilya's deep knowledge sends ripples of intrigue through me. She's a repository of ancient truths, by the looks of it. Yes, she's been here long before our time, but there's a depth in her understanding that hints at more than mere longevity. It asks what her place in this realm's tapestry truly was before the schism that tore it apart. With histories stretching back eons, her experiences could be a key to untold secrets of the realm's past.

"Axilya, what exactly was your role before the realm fractured?" The question leaves me before I can think to stop it.

I have never been able to help myself. Put me in front of something ancient, something unexplained, and every instinct I have shifts into overdrive—cataloging, questioning, pulling at every loose thread until the whole picture unravels into something I can understand.

Axilya gives a little theatrical shiver, not so much from the cold as for effect, and averts her gaze with a flourish of drama. "Shall we continue?" she suggests, her voice lilting with a hint of impatience. "I am rather chilled to the bone and would quite prefer to depart from this frosty gallery of the damned."

Her deflection from my probing question is almost as smooth as the ice encasing the Frozen Fae—almost.

Right, enough staring contests with the ice prisoners. With a dramatic flick of my hair, I pivot away from the eerie exhibit of frozen regrets, lead the charge through the icy labyrinth, and start our chilly trek. The ice tunnels? Zero trouble. Call it a lucky streak or just a boring hike, but it seems we're too cool for school—or at least too cool for cave drama.

Busting out from the sub-zero labyrinth, we crash-land into some enchanted tree party in the forest. These timber titans are so close together, I half expect them to start doing the wave. The fog's been ditched, and now we've got this whimsical mist threading through the trees, giving off some severe fantasy vibes—as if we've stumbled onto the set of the next big-budget fairy tale flick. Who directed this place, Mother Nature or Spielberg?

My eyes scan the area, and then...there it is, a sight for sore eyes—just beyond the literal edge of our woody enclave stands the majestic Crystal Peaks. A grin breaks across my face before I can stop it, as I take in the sight.

"We made it."

Two words. But they carry the weight of everything—every stumble, every close call, every frozen, breathless moment that tried to swallow us whole. We crossed the finish line, and somehow, against every odd stacked against us, we're all still standing.

RHYLAND

70

The Crystal Peaks loom up front, a jagged masterpiece shining like a hoard of diamonds under the relentless sun. Light refracts off their surfaces, casting prisms onto the frost-covered pines that shiver under winter's unyielding grip. The beauty of it almost steals my breath—if I were the kind of man to get lost in the scenery.

Dani strides next to me, her eyes blazing with fire and life. I catch the fierce resolve sparking inside her. That's my Angel—lighting up the damn way, it doesn't matter if she's sure where it's heading.

Her damn apologies nearly fucking gutted me back there in that cave, but she's got no need to beg forgiveness for anything she does. Dani's got a mind of her own, always charging ahead, and I wouldn't have her any other way. I am curious about her so-called "angelic upgrade" and this Soul-Tie shit she spoke of with Adrian now.

I know she wasn't ready to spill the news right away, with all the chaos of her return, but I can't stop pondering the implications of my blood inside her. It keeps me connected to her, and I figured she'd always need a touch to keep her engine running. Now that she's *almost* immortal, she doesn't need my blood to keep her alive.

I'm not thrilled she brought Adrian along and gave this asshole another shot—it chafes my ass just thinking about it. But if it makes her happy to have him help in freeing her mother—I'm willing to swallow that bitter pill and let it ride... so long as she's prepared to pay for it in other ways. I'm happy to discipline my little Angel; she seems to enjoy the consequences.

Axilya glides through the snow like it's her ballroom, damn fae grace in every step. She draws close to Dani, her voice soft but carrying over the hushed whispers of the forest.

"Do you know where we're going, Danica? No one has ever reached this far into the Peaks," she asks, all regal and shit.

Dani shakes her head, her golden eyes fierce and determined. "I don't have a damn clue. Just following this pull inside me," She confesses, raking her hand through those chocolate-brown waves. Her knuckles accidentally rap against the circlet atop her head, which thrums a response."What I do know is we're getting very close."

We march through the snowy forest with intent, our breath fogging up in front like ghostly escorts shoving us on. Every step is quiet except for the muffled crunch underfoot—the cold's practically lickable, like a sharp, icy blade on my tongue.

The trees split like they're showing us to our seats, unveiling their big act—the clearing between the peaks looms huge and quiet before us. As far as the eye can see, it's just a stretch of snow and ice. But shit, something's off; a nagging feeling is pulling at my gut.

To our left stretches an endless field blanketed in white—pristine and undisturbed snow save for where our boots mar its perfection. Dani pauses, head cocked as if listening to a voice only she can hear.

"We go this way," she says with certainty, pointing across that virgin expanse.

Lucian snorts from behind me, his tone laced with sarcasm as usual. "There's nothing there but snow and more fucking snow," he says with a dismissive wave of his hand.

But Dani doesn't budge an inch. "The pull is this way," she insists, steel underlying her words.

I shoot Lucian a glare that screams, 'Back the fuck off,' and then I give Dani a quick nod. "We follow your lead then."

She flashes a smile that's quick but damn near blinds you before she strides off across the field, us tagging along in her wake.

To our right, there's this towering building jabbing at the sky—like a damn lighthouse for the poor bastards stuck in this icy wasteland. The light bouncing off that thing is so intense it's a bitch to even glance at it.

I'm all for chasing that glare like moths on a death trip, but Dani isn't having any of that. She's dead set on veering left, and hell, that means we go left.

Then the shit hits the fan. The deeper we go into this frosty field hell, the crazier it gets. Images start to pop up in front of us like some twisted reflections in a mirror, stretched over this gaping snow coffin that's the ground and sky. There's this buzzing noise; it could be power or my pulse hammering in my head.

We all slam the brakes at this unseen wall as our own faces look back at us, all warped and skewed like we're in some screwed-up carnival mirror.

Lucian's voice cuts through the air with his signature sarcasm. "What fun house hell have we stumbled upon here?" he inquires, half-expecting the answer as absurd as the situation probably is.

Dani takes a stab at it. "A portal, possibly?"

Instinctively, I reach out to it, and holy hell, if it doesn't scorch like grabbing a chunk of live coal! The cold bites into my flesh—so damn vicious I snap my hand back, hissing like It is some venomous serpent.

"Fuck!" I grumble, trying to shake off the burn from my stinging hand.

Lucian chuckles from his perch beside me—the smug bastard revels in others' misfortune. "Didn't your mama ever warn you not to play with strange objects?" he quips, wearing that infuriating smart-ass grin I'd love to smack off his face. But not today, since I know he's got a point this time. Even when he's being a dick, Lucian doesn't mince words.

I shake my head and shoot him a dirty look, all while my pride stings almost as much as my palm does—but I'd be damned if I'd concede he's got a point.

Dani, ever the worrying and caring type, snatches up my hand for a closer look. It's healing up already. "Are you okay?" she asks, her eyes swimming with concern.

"Yeah, Angel, I'm good," I throw back at her, trying to ease her mind.

"This is decidedly significant," Faderyn comments from my left. "There's something beyond this barrier; it intends to mislead anyone at a distance—no one has managed to venture this deep into the peaks before."

"Well, I'm down for trying it out," Dani declares, solid as stone. She reaches for that mirror-like barrier, and instead of frying her like it did me, her hand slips through, sending ripples across it like it's water. Fluid and freaky as hell.

She yanks her hand back in a hurry, sucking in air sharply. I'm right on her, tense, thinking maybe she got hurt, but she only smiles. "It's warm on the other side," she spills to all of us, her face lit up. "Feels like the sun's shining, and I swear, there's the scent of flowers."

"Alright, let's make a move already. My ass is about to chip off from this cold," Lucian quips with a roll of his eyes.

"It's a magical barrier," Adrian calls out, explaining its purpose. "A protective wall that's shielding the entrance to the Hidden Valley."

"How the hell do you know?" I can't help snapping at Adrian.

Before Adrian can respond, Axilya interjects, "Yes, it's concealed from all. This mirror, or whatever it may be, must serve as a gateway into the Hidden Valley."

"And I can feel it, Rhyland. The stone... it's pulling me this way," Dani says, laying it out straight while she locks me with gorgeous eyes.

If it zapped me, how are we all supposed to get through this? Is it some magic door that only swings open for Dani? Like hell, I will chill out here while she steps into who-knows-where.

"I'm coming with you," I state with a growl.

"Ahem, I think you mean to say that every single one of us is tagging along on this little adventure, whether you like it or not," Lucian deadpans. "No ifs, ands, or buts about it, buttercup."

"Alright, let's join hands," Dani instructs while she takes hold of mine. We all clasp hands, forming a line, facing whatever awaits us. "Here goes nothing," she says decisively. With those words hanging in the air, we move forward as one.

DANICA

79

When we thought frostbite was about to become our newest and least welcome buddy, the universe decides to lay out a red carpet into Eden itself. My eyes are doing double takes – once, twice – trying to wrap around the technicolor switch-up from Ice Queen's castle to Summer's personal VIP lounge.

We're smack in the middle of Mother Nature's parade float, surrounded by a sea of green so lush you'd think it's photoshopped. Hills roll around us like lazy emerald giants at rest, decked out in the season's finest floral bling. And that sky – somebody's dialed it up to 'heavenly,' with the sun beaming down on us like it's our spotlight.

Then there's the breeze, sauntering like a charming rogue, all warm and full of sweet nothings scented with honeysuckle and lavender whispers. I let myself... pause.

Eyes closed, breathing deep, soaking up that solar hug—a stark *see ya never* to the bone-chilling cold we left behind. It's like the universe flipped some cosmic switch from frozen hell to pure bliss. This slice of paradise proves we've punched our tickets to somewhere spectacularly otherworldly.

When I finally pry my eyelids open, it's to a sight that'd give any rainbow a run for its money. Birds decked out in a blinding array of blues, greens, and golds are cutting shapes through the air, pirouetting and gliding like they're auditioning for "Avian Idol."

Below is a comedy routine of round-bodied, horned bunnies giving their best impression of rambunctious ram-rabbits, barreling through the brush and tangoing with the tall grass. This valley is an outright bonanza of vitality and radiance, a haven that seems to have ghosted the rest of the universe and done a vanishing act off ole Father Time's map.

"Holy shit, did we just stumble into fucking Narnia or what?" Lucian blurts out, his voice echoing through the ethereal forest like a verbal record scratch. "Because I'm pretty sure I didn't sign up for any magical wardrobe bullshit today."

"Such eloquence as always, Lucian," Erik says dryly from behind us. I glance back and see a hint of wonder in his metallic eyes as he surveys the valley. Even Mr. Stoic can't entirely hide his awe.

My gaze drifts to Axilya and Faderyn.

The shift in them is immediate and undeniable. They've dropped to their knees among the wildflowers, heads bowed low, shoulders curved inward—every line of their bodies folded into something that looks like reverence. No words. No signal. As if the ground itself pulled them down.

A quiet understanding settles over me. Whatever this place is, it is not simply beautiful. It is sacred.

And just as I'm piecing this mystical jigsaw in my head, out of the corner of my eye, something shimmies into focus, a bright, impossible silhouette against the lushness.

No freaking way...is that what I think it is?

I watch, awestruck, as a something so beautiful steps delicately into the meadow. My heart forgets to beat for a second, and my jaw drops as what can only be described as the most beautiful, majestic unicorn I've ever imagined trots into view. Its coat shimmers pearlescent white in the sunlight, and the spiraled horn rising from its head looks to be made of pure silver that matches the silver of its mane.

It's like time decides to take a coffee break. We're all statues, practically hypnotized. Beside me, I can hear Axilya's sob as a teardrop scores a trail down her cheek—And Faderyn, well, he's so shellshocked he's practically communing with the spirit of silence.

My eyes grow to the size of dinner plates as the vision of equine elegance comes to an expert stop before me, its movements embodying grace and poise. Then, with an almost regal dignity, the unicorn lowers itself, bending one leg in an unmistakably inviting gesture.

"I think he wants you to get on..." Axilya says, her voice laced with a hint of amusement at my apparent astonishment.

Well—that's not something you do every day. Ride a unicorn? Without any saddle? This is uncharted territory.

I look into his light blue eyes, which are beautiful like the sky. Hesitantly, I reach out, resting my hand on his neck. The feel is indescribable, smoother than the finest silk, warm and luxurious under my touch. With a mix of awe and care, I swing a leg over, finding my place atop his strong back, situating myself snugly between his majestic shoulder blades.

As I settle, the unicorn stands with such swift elegance that I'm surprised, grasping at his mane to anchor myself. Each strand is as soft as a spider's silk but firm as woven destiny and sparkles like glitter in the sunlight.

Now, astride this magnificent beast, I understand that this ride won't just be an ordinary trot through the woods—it will be a journey unlike any other.

My eyes drop to Rhyland.

He's watching me with that look—the one he thinks he hides but never quite manages to. Worry carved into every line of his face, yes, but beneath it, something warmer. Something that moves through his ocean-blue gaze like light through water. Pride, quiet and unguarded, there and gone in a single breath.

It settles over me like warmth just as the unicorn turns, poised and purposeful, ready to embark on what promises to be an epic exit.

Rhyland steps forward as if to accompany me on this enchanted escapade, but Axilya and Faderyn intercept, their hands gently outstretched to still his stride.

"No—she needs to do this herself," Axilya says, her voice slicing through the thick tension with resolute clarity.

Though it's no easy feat for one so possessive as Rhyland, her words ring with a truth that goes beyond want or protection. There's a part of this narrative, a part of this magic and growth, that is mine to navigate, atop the silent strength of a unicorn. It's a leap of faith, a test of trust, and the start of a journey all rolled into one profound moment. And in that silent exchange of looks, I know he understands.

The majestic creature turns and begins to slowly trot away.

Lucian cups his hands around his mouth, his voice carrying through the enchanted forest like a smartass foghorn. "Yo, try not to get your ass shanghaied to some magical land of sparkly rainbow farts and unicorn glitter while you're gone!" He calls out, his smirk so sarcastic it could wither a houseplant at twenty paces. "And if you do, bring me back a souvenir! I've always wanted one of those 'My friend went to Fairyland, and all I got was this lousy t-shirt' shirts."

I'm laughing. Then my magical beast decides to go full gallop. I'm hanging on, my hands aching from the tension, not expecting him to take off, "Whoa...whoa, there, big guy." But he ignores me and shifts into a higher gear, leaving a gust in his wake.

I grip his mane tightly, my thighs squeezing his rib cage as the magnificent beast gallops at full speed. The exhilarating ride overwhelms my senses—the scent of open fields, the warm air lashing my face, my hair blowing wildly in the breeze.

A smile spreads across my face as he continues to pick up speed. I squeeze my legs tighter against his sides to keep my balance firm and begin to release my tight hold on his silky mane. I feel comfortable and secure atop this mystical creature as we fall into a rhythmic gallop. With growing confidence, I stretch my arms out and close my eyes, giggling and whooping joyously as he runs ever faster.

There is no feeling more liberating. I surrender completely to the magic of the moment.

As we nuzzle up against the edge of the woods, he downshifts to a leisurely pace, his hooves drumming a soothing rhythm on the earth. My heart's still doing cartwheels, and I'm grinning like a kid with too much birthday cake. "That was..." I gasp, every breath a sip of pure, wild air. "Amazing!"

Now, my magical steed dials it back to a gentle amble, easing us into the forest's embrace. A carnival of butterflies dances around us, their wings a cascade of moving art, while tiny luminescent critters turn the forest into a live fantasy nightlight. Hitting a patch of open sky between the trees, he pauses and takes a knee—like a four-legged Sir Galahad offering his palm—my hint of sliding down from his celestial back.

My feet have barely touched the ground when movement pulls my gaze to the right.

Another unicorn emerges from the tree line, its coat the white of untouched snow, its horn catching the light like poured gold at dawn. Its mane shimmers with the same warm hue, each strand sparkling as it moves with a grace so absolute the forest seems to hold its breath around it.

It glides closer, and that's when I see it—a collar, though to call it such seems near blasphemy. But it's what rests at its center that rips the air straight from my lungs.

The Faerite stone.

Unmistakable. Radiating a deep, living green that drinks in the sunlight and throws it back tenfold, glowing as though it has been waiting—specifically, privately—for this exact moment.

The unicorn stills, close enough that I can feel the warmth radiating off its coat. The stone glows at its throat, inches from my outstretched hand.

Then it dips its head.

The gesture is slow, deliberate—a nudge so gentle it barely qualifies as pressure, yet it moves through me like a current. My hand lifts on instinct, fingers trembling, and the moment my fingertips graze the stone, it releases.

No resistance. No force. It simply lets go, as if it has been waiting for precisely this touch and no other.

It hovers between us, suspended in the air, pulsing with a slow, rhythmic light—like a heartbeat. Like recognition.

Then it rises.

It drifts upward in a quiet, unhurried arc and finds its place in the crown with a resonance I feel more than hear—a deep, bone-level hum that begins at the top of my skull and rolls downward through my spine, my chest, my fingertips, all the way to the soles of my feet. Ancient and immediate all at once, like remembering something I was never taught.

The buzzing doesn't fade. It settles into me, steady and alive.

Something shifts inside me—a quiet unlocking, like a door I didn't know existed, swinging gently open. The emotions of every living thing around me rush in all at once, not as noise but as feeling—pure and unfiltered, flowing directly into some wordless place beneath my ribs. Joy. Relief. A warmth so genuine it has no agenda behind it.

"Welcome, Danica, Daughter of Elysium—Savior of the realms—we have awaited your arrival," says a deep male voice.

DANICA

72

I jolt, shaken by the sudden intrusion of a voice that wasn't mine inside my head. Frantically scanning our surroundings, seeking the source, the realization dawns on me—it's the beautiful unicorn. He says nothing aloud, yet his thoughts move through mine like music through an empty hall—wordless, seamless, as natural as breathing.

Rhyland's concern slips into my mind on another mental line—a whisper, both intrusive and curiously reassuring. *"What's happening? I sense your unease,"* he inquires, his mind gently prodding at the source of my tension.

"Nothing. I'm fine," I shoot back almost reflexively, tucking away the ripples of unease. I offer him a mental facsimile of reassurance despite the churn of new magic and unearthly encounters still vibrating through my core.

"Uh, h-hi there," I stammer out loud, feeling as eloquent as a duck with a stutter. "You know who I am?"

With his silver horn, the beautiful beast gives me an affirmative nod, then goes full-on cuddly, nuzzling against me like an overgrown lap cat.

Guess we're bonding now.

"Yes. We all know who you are," his mellow mental voice returns. *"I am Calimero, leader of the unicorns and guardian of the Faerite stone. But you can call me Cal. And this is my mate, Lunaria."*

With an ease that betrays none of the shocks I'm feeling, he gestures nonchalantly toward his companion—the one adorned with the gold-kissed horn, the very unicorn who bore the Faerite stone.

"Hello, sweet Danica," a gentle female voice whispers inside my head. It's like an auditory caress, and my tension melts away under its warmth.

Their tones are casual, even amused, like they get a kick out of catching me off guard. Which is fair enough—it's not every day a unicorn strikes up a telepathic conversation. I'm quick to roll with it, though, giving my brain a shake and my wits a rally.

My heart thumps a victorious rhythm. I've made the journey, braved the trials, and here stands my reward, with a mane softer than silk and a disposition more serene than a monk in meditation. Now, it's time to see how this stone fits into the grand puzzle of saving the realms.

I extend my hand, a little hesitant but too charmed not to make contact. My fingers brush against Calimero's nose—warm and smooth, more real than anything I could've ever imagined.

"Thank you. It's been quite the journey, to say the least," I confess, giving a soft chuckle that cuts through the weight of my adventure.

It's a little puff of laughter, almost a disbelieving snort. If anyone had told me I'd be nose-bopping unicorn royalty when I woke up this morning, I'd have recommended a strong cup of reality with a side of sanity check. But here we are, and it's wonderfully, magically real.

"And just so you know, we had anticipated your arrival a tad sooner." Calimero's telepathic tongue-in-cheek confession brings a grin to my face as I continue petting him.

It seems even ageless beings can get impatient waiting for prophecies to unfold.

"Ah, yeah, sorry about the mix-up," I shrug. "Had a little scheduling mishap and popped up at the wrong place too early. You know how it is." I let out a playful huff, masking any frustration with humor. "And if that wasn't enough to fill my dance card, I've been playing referee back home—it turns out my personal dream team has a few opinions about my mate choice." I roll my eyes for effect.

Calimero practically does a sly little mental tap-dance next to me. *"Time, my dear Danica, doesn't play by anyone's rules but its own. It loves a good zigzag,"* he says, the rich humor in his telepathic voice making the air around us seem to wink. *"And your mate? In life's grand epic, he's your unexpected plot twist—that dash of irreverent charm amidst the solemn verses."*

"What do you mean by that?" I ask, my curiosity piqued. I want to unravel the riddle wrapped up in his lighthearted commentary.

Calimero's sky-blue eyes shimmer with unspoken laughter, and he continues with a note of jest, *"I meant precisely as I said—we unicorns had marked the calendar for a slightly earlier prophecy fulfillment. I suspect some unforeseen escapades delayed your grand entrance. As for your mate, you could say that, in the grand tapestry of fate, not everyone appreciates the... eccentric stitches,"* he muses cheekily, a quip veiled in wisdom.

Calimero doesn't miss a beat, and his spirited wit is still going strong despite being the astute beastie he is. *"Hence, you carry the Atherite Stone in your crown,"* he notes, with the air of solving a particularly juicy riddle.

"Sharp as ever," I respond with a smirk, appreciating his ability to piece together my tangled journey with just a few puzzle bits. Thinking about it, I'd expect nothing less from a creature who's probably seen more plot twists than the stars themselves.

The combination of his intellectual jest and the half-mocking, half-teasing light in his gaze makes it impossible to feel offended. His tone echoes the unseen smiles, combining comedy and cosmic timing.

When I don't think things could get any more magical, more unicorns emerge from the forest, slowly peeking out. My eyes go wide, hardly believing the scenery unraveling before me. Unicorns, with coats so white it's almost blinding, but it's their horns and sparkly, colored manes that make me gasp—painted every hue you could dream, and then some, are stepping out shyly. Their horns and manes are not just textbook white—they look like they've been dipped in pots of sky blues, sunset oranges, deep sea greens, and then some. Even the baby unicorns are toddling out—pure cuteness overload.

"Wow," escapes me, a breathy whisper of sheer wonder. "How many—"

"Thousands of us," Calimero cuts in, and his pride is as tangible as the forest air. With a flick of his beautiful mane, he continues, *"Indeed, the time has come for us to emerge from the Hidden Valley, to mingle with the Fae as we've yearned for countless moons. Your being here signals the moment to resume our place in the realm—we place our faith that the Shadow Queen has been sufficiently thwarted to allow for this. It is then essential to restore the realm to find itself again in an era of wholeness and prosperity."*

"Yes, they mentioned that you are needed, and nothing has been the same since the fracture," I admit to him, acknowledging the weight of the past and the hope pinned on the now. "Amara has been detained," I confirm, a matter-of-fact edge in my voice, as if I'm reporting on mundane court bureaucracy rather than the fate of a powerful adversary. "Until I find a more permanent solution for her...that is."

The words carry the weight of decisions yet to be made—decisions that will shape the future of the realms. But for now, Amara's chapter is written in stone, leaving us to script the next with the fresh ink of newfound alliances and the hope that comes from the turn of fate's tide.

The weight of it all presses in around the edges of the conversation—ancient lore, tangled destinies, and somewhere in the middle of all of it, me. The point where broken roads are supposed to meet and become whole again. The thought alone is staggering.

There are rifts to heal. Alliances to build from nothing. And a road ahead that has no map.

"Right...now that we've cleared up the Shadow Court Queen situation, I trust you are prepared to learn of the Faerite stone?" Calimero inquires as if we're swapping something as mundane as borrowed books.

I nod, resolute. "Yes."

"Very well. With this stone, you hold the authority to commune with creatures and beings touched by magic, along with an empathy deep enough to dive into their souls."

It's an empathy so profound that it's nearly overwhelming, but in the same beat, it feels like coming home—a connection to the pulse of the magical world, an intricate, invisible thread now tied to my essence. This is the gift of understanding, the purest form of communion with the magical heartbeats of the Seven Realms.

"So I can talk to any creature, animal, or magical being with this?" I question the notion, almost too grand to grasp. A door to endless possibilities swings wide open before me.

"Exactly," Calimero states it with quiet certainty, as though the matter was never in question.

Words almost fail me as the reality sinks in: with the Faerite Stone, I've just been handed the universal passcode to converse with the heartbeats of the wild and whimsical. A new dimension of dialogue awaits—every whisper in the woods, every murmur of the meadows, is now an open book. The world just got a whole lot more conversational.

Calimero chauffeurs me through the mystical woods and returns me to my motley crew. Upon entrance, I catch Rhyland's face lighting up like I've just returned from a one-woman mission to Mars. Everyone gets to their feet, playing it cool, but eyes are glued to us. Calimero hits the brakes, and with a slick dismount, Rhyland's there to snag my waist with a 'you're-never-escaping-me-again' kind of hold.

I sidle up in front of Calimero, petting his neck, slipping in alongside Axilya, who looks ready to burst into tears. Then Calimero takes a knee, bowing to Axilya like she's fae royalty, and I can't help but raise an eyebrow.

What's the deal here?

"Thanks for the lift," I say, gratefully glancing at Calimero with the kind of nod you'd give a cabbie after a clean getaway.

My face scrunches as a twinge of 'oops' creeps up. "There's a teensy detail I might've glossed over..." I half-mumble, suddenly finding an interesting speck of dirt on my shoe.

Calimero perks up, all ears. *"Speak—"*

So I drop the bomb: "Azrael, my personal stalker from beyond—yeah, he hitched a ride through my DIY portal, and now he's here crashing the party. You might want to hold off on any plans to ditch this fairytale hideout until I've shooed him back to his nightmare."

Calimero releases a puff of air that's a billboard for frustration. I'm picking up on his vibes loud and clear with this shiny new stone. *"Ship him back to Mortalis. Let's keep the theatrics in your backyard. Snag that little shard of his, and he'll vanish from our list of headaches."*

I quirk an eyebrow and let a wry chuckle slip. "That simple, huh?" The words roll off my tongue, drenched in a heavy coat of irony.

A hint of a smirk plays in Calimero's tone; his voice touched with both amusement and gravity. *"Indeed, it is. Think of yourself as the wielder of an unseen scepter, with powers that multiply his by leagues and lengths. Employ it, and never play down the might at your fingertips. And your mate? Ah, he's a veritable trove of untapped potential—has this not been a topic of fireside whispers between you two?"*

I swivel my gaze toward Rhyland, locking eyes with his sea of confusion for a brief moment. Pivoting back to Calimero, I plant my feet and declare with resolve, "I'm clued in on his mojo."

But beneath that certainty, I can't help but wonder, *What's he driving at?*

Calimero's words are laced with a playful note, a knowing twinkle in his eye. *"The storm brewing within him is more than just for show—Lightning Wielder. Do you know of his heritage? I think it's high time for you two to curl up and unravel some of those hidden volts and rumbles."* A thread of amusement winds through his voice, suggesting revelations await in the space of quiet conversation.

My mind kicks into overdrive, zipping back to Meadow's cryptic sneak peeks of Rhyland—those snippets she painted with words about lightning and thunder.

Lucian's voice cuts through the air like a verbal chainsaw, his words laced with enough incredulity to choke a horse. "Hold the freaking phone, are my eyes deceiving me, or are you seriously shooting the breeze with a flippin' unicorn right now?" He pipes up from the back, his tone suggesting he's about two seconds away from checking himself into the nearest mental institution. "Because if so, I'm gonna need a moment to process this level of weird."

"He's not the brightest of your companions, is he?" Calimero's voice slides through my mind again, dry and pointed—less a passing comment, more a verdict.

The comment catches me off guard, sparking an irrepressible giggle that bubbles out. The audacity! I mean, Cal's not wrong, but his sass is so unexpected it's hilarious.

Lucian narrows his eyes, his voice sharp enough to cut through steel. "Oh, it's funny? —*HA HA*. Excuuuuse me for being a little fucking confused when Princess here starts chatting up a creature that, up until about five minutes ago, I thought only existed in Lisa Frank sticker books and the wet dreams of prepubescent girls."

The moment hangs in the air, each face swiveling toward Lucian, wearing an expression equal parts disbelief and 'Oh, come on, dude.' In all his glittering grace. Cal's elegant headshake is all the answer anyone needs, and then that celestial whinny lifts into the air—unmistakably the sound of equine laughter.

"Well, no shit, she's talking to him, dumbass," Rhyland finally speaks up.

Lucian throws his hands up, "Obviously, I'm the only one here who hasn't completely lost their grip on reality. My bad for attempting to apply logic to a situation that's about as logical as a fucking Escher painting."

"The stone, Lucian. Try to keep up," Erik remarks.

"Ah—yes. Makes total sense now!" Lucian says, rolling his eyes with enough force to generate a small gravitational field. "Because clearly, the only thing standing between us and total annihilation is a shiny rock that allows a one-sided conversation with My Little Pony over here. Clearly, I'm the one who's not operating on the same plane of existence as the rest of you enlightened fuckers."

He scoffs, "You know what? At this point, I half expect a talking mushroom to pop up and start reciting Shakespeare."

"Why are you so frazzled, Lucian?" Faderyn inquires, his ethereal features etched with genuine curiosity.

"Duh—I'm jealous she," he motions to me, "gets to chat it up with a unicorn when I'm the one with the big brain here." He taps his head with the side of his finger, "Cerebral Hustler, remember?"

I can't help but snort at that, shaking my head in amused disbelief. "Cerebral Hustler? More like Cerebral Bullshitter, if you ask me."

Lucian gasps, clutching at his chest in mock offense. "You wound me, sweet cheeks! I'll have you know that this brain of mine is a finely tuned machine, capable of processing complex thoughts and ideas that would make your pretty little head spin."

"Complex thoughts? Like what, exactly? The best way to style your hair for maximum douchebag effect?" I shoot back, unable to resist the urge to poke at his overinflated ego.

"Oh, *haha*. Very funny," he deadpans, narrowing his eyes at me. "I'll have you know that I've got a mind like a steel trap, baby. Nothing gets past me."

"Except for the fact that she's *literally* talking to a unicorn right now," Erik chimes in, his voice dry as the Sahara.

Lucian whirls on him, jabbing a finger in his direction. "Hey, I'm processing, okay? Forgive me for needing a minute to adjust to the fact that we've apparently stumbled into a fucking Disney movie."

Rhyland pinches the bridge of his nose, letting out a long-suffering sigh. "Can we please focus on the task at hand? In case you've forgotten, we've got a world to save."

"Right, right. The world. Saving. Got it," Lucian mutters, waving a dismissive hand. "Lead the way, oh, wise and glorious unicorn. Take us to the promised land or whatever."

Axilya, Faderyn, and Adrian are all doing their best to stifle their laughter at the brotherly banter these three are infamous for.

Calimero snorts, tossing his mane in a gesture that somehow conveys both amusement and exasperation. *"Your friend is quite the character—"*

"You have no idea," I reply, unable to keep the fondness from my voice.

"There is one last thing I must mention before you depart," Calimero says. The gravity in his tone sets my nerves on edge.

The anticipatory uh-oh chorus kicks up in my mind. Good news or bad, when a unicorn plays the 'there's one more thing' card, you listen. "Okay—I'm all ears," I say, steeling myself for anything.

What he says next hits me like a stone dropped into still water—rippling outward in every direction at once. It shouldn't make sense. And yet it does, snapping into place with a clarity so sudden it nearly winds me.

I stare at him.

The silence stretches.

Then I can't help but blurt out in disbelief, "You've got to be kidding."

RHYLAND

73

I plunk down next to Dani in this extravagant-as-fuck dining hall of the Sun Court, still trying to make heads or tails of this new intel. She's damn near gleaming now, proudly wearing that Faerite Stone perched in her crown. Christ, the woman already looks like a queen.

I lean back as she talks about how the glittery rock allows her to speak to magical creatures and read emotions. Supposedly, the unicorn king, Calamari, or whatever his high-and-mighty name is, dropped some big-time gossip about me harboring hidden powers.

The suggestion confuses me, leaving me bewildered. I shake my head, emitting a chuckle. "Baby, you and that overgrown My Little Pony were huffing some serious fairy dust back in the hippie valley—I'm just a regular, badass vampire who can move shit with his mind. No special powers are hidden up my sleeves over here. You already know what I can do."

It isn't until Dani brings up lightning that my mind is catapulted back to that horrific day in the Whispering Woods—the agony of losing her. Her death fueled my anger, sent me spinning out of control, and unleashed the skies and elements in my fury.

"I don't know what that was... the Whispering Woods, after you..." I can't even say it, "When something...happened," I confess haltingly. I dismissively wave a hand, wrestling with the painful memory that stabs deep into my gut. Reliving the nightmare of watching Dani die right before my eyes is a torment I'd not wish on anyone.

"So let me get this straight," Dani says, eyeing me with that fiery look. "You can just whip up lightning storms now, and you didn't think to mention it?"

Mistaking her momentary distraction, I mention that she didn't spill the beans about her immortality upgrade or this Soul-Tie thing she still hasn't explained. "Looks like we're even, huh?" I say with bravado, instantly regretting the words as her expression shifts. Her eyes shift from warm honey gold to something molten and blazing, burning with a fury that should probably concern me. It doesn't. If anything, it makes me want to grin. My feisty, fire-blooded angel wants a fight? I'm more than happy to give her one.

Leave it to Lucian to take a tense situation and crank it up to fucking max with his special brand of verbal diarrhea. The asshat's wearing a grin that practically screams, "I'm about to make everything worse," and I can already feel my blood pressure skyrocketing in anticipation of the impending shitstorm.

"Oh, man, you should've been there!" He crows. "Picture this—Armageddon rage-fucked a Michael Bay film and their love child came out swinging—everything went up in flames faster than my browser history after a bad night on the internet. By the time the smoke cleared, total devastation. Like Godzilla showed up, ate everything, shit it out, then stepped on it for good measure. Absolute *chef's kiss* level destruction. Ten out of ten."

He laughs, the sound grating on my nerves like nails on a chalkboard. Clearly, the concept of "read the fucking room" is about as foreign to him as quantum physics is to a goldfish. I swear, sometimes I wonder if he has a secret death wish or if he's just too damn stupid to realize when he's about to get his ass handed to him on a silver platter.

I shoot him a glare, my jaw clenched so tight I'm half-surprised my teeth haven't shattered. "Lucian, I swear to god, if you don't shut your fucking piehole, I'm going to shove my foot so far up your ass, you'll be tasting leather for a week," I growl, my voice low and dangerous.

Dani shoots me a triumphant smirk like she's just kicked ass and taken names.

"Angel, whatever shit that went down was a one-time thing, okay?" I try to shrug it off like it's nothing. "I was deep in some dark-ass hole... And you, you were..." My words choke off, the grim thought too intense to put into words.

Dani crosses her arms, cocking her hip to the side. "Oh, really? So you go all Storm from X-Men and summon lightning after I died, and it's no big deal to you?"

"Listen, it was a one-off, alright?" I rake a hand through my hair, pissed off. "Why the hell does it even matter?"

"Alright, get this—Meadow, our very own seer-in-residence, had one of her vision deals," Dani explains, fishing for clarity within the mystical forecast. "She saw you encased in lightning, Rhyland. That's gotta mean something, doesn't it? It feels like a clue, some prophetic nudge we shouldn't ignore."

I shake my head, cutting through the crap. Meadow's visions are like a fucked-up jigsaw puzzle. Me, with some special lightning powers? That's horseshit. But Dani's latched onto this idea like a stubborn hound with a bone.

I give her a steely glare, sidestepping those inquisitive eyes. "It was a damn fluke, alright? Who's to say I was even the one in control? I ain't no goddamn Thor... X-Men, or whatever with lightning powers."

"Oh, of course, how silly of us," Lucian drawls, rolling his eyes so hard I'm surprised they don't get stuck in the back of his thick skull. "Because obviously, every other fucker on that battlefield had the power to summon a lightning storm straight out of a high-budget disaster movie. My bad for not realizing that controlling the weather is a standard-issue superpower these days."

He fixes me with a look that's equal parts exasperation and 'Are you fucking kidding me?'

"I mean, it's not like you're the only one here with a direct line to the Force or anything, right? Oh, wait..." Lucian taps his chin in mock contemplation; his eyebrows raised so high they're practically merging with his hairline. "Wouldn't it make sense that the guy with the telekinetic mojo would pull the strings on that little light show? Or am I just talking out of my incredibly toned and perfect ass again, Obi-Wan?"

I'm grinding my damn teeth because this is batshit insane. I've never played puppet master with the skies, and since that one freak day, I haven't given it a second thought. My Gods have been radio silent for centuries, and this idea that sky-wrangling's a part of me is enough to make my head spin out of control.

"Seriously, though, who else could it have been? The tooth fairy? Santa Claus? The ghost of Christmas fuck-you? Come on, man, you're not fooling anyone with this whole 'who, me?' routine," Lucian finishes.

"It's not exactly a giant leap when you look at it with a smidgeon of common sense," Dani quips, a twinkle of mischief in her eyes.

This woman is poking at my last nerve, and damn if my dick doesn't stand at attention at her defiance and sass—going on about this baseless shit that I possess some elemental control power.

My chest receives a prod from Dani's insistent finger. "Quit denying this like it's nothing," she retorts. "Calimero's waving around the idea that you've got some serious juju bottled up. The sort of 'storm god ancestry' flair comes with it. Is that stirring any memories or shaking any family trees? Or do I need to knock harder?"

I never knew the bastard who contributed half my DNA. And it's not a memory I'm eager to dive into. Dani and I have this crappy common ground with our mysterious parentage, and this crap is spiraling out of control. That day threw me in a loop just as much as it's messing with me now. My mother did the single-parent gig, spinning yarns about the Gods visiting her and giving her a gift—a blessing—which was me. As for my old man, the story always was he'd never show his face again. She filled my head with legends of my Gods in Valhalla, keeping an eye on me.

"No, it damn well doesn't," I snap at her. "Drop it, Dani."

Jesus, she's not playing nice. I fight to keep my temper in check.

Dani plants herself firmly, eyes on fire, her look fucking challenging me. I meet that dare head-on—this is a showdown, and we're both dug in, neither backing down. She's got zero tolerance for lies, deception, and all that shit; I respect that. But what the fuck am I supposed to spill?

Teetering on the edge, my patience shot to shit—I hoist her up and toss her over my shoulder like a damn sack. She unleashes hell, kicking and hollering, but I move fast, charging into a private room and throwing her feisty ass onto the couch.

Dani puffs up indignantly, her eyes blazing with the fierce independence I've come to know so well.

"Stop doing that!" she huffs, flipping her hair out of her face as it tangles in her crown. She's staring up at me with that challenge in her gaze. "I'm not some cavewoman; you can just heft over your shoulder on a whim."

Her voice crackles with that don't fuck with me attitude, the feisty spirit that refuses to be treated as anything less than an equal.

Unleashing a low growl, I force my point, "I don't want to entertain this any longer, Dani. Do you understand?"

Dani moves to duck out—hell no—she's not slipping away from me. It doesn't take a second to snatch her by the throat and shove her back against the wall, my body crushing hers. There's no escape, no way out, until I know she's good and ready to end this damn standoff.

Dani holds her ground, staring back at me with that fierce steel in her gaze; she somehow isn't afraid to show. Damn, this woman, she's got me dead to rights—she damn well knows I'd never lay a finger on her in anger. But fuck, I need her to get that I ain't entertaining whatever nonsense that unicorn filled her head with.

Yeah, I'll give it to her. The sudden lightning control was uncanny that day in the woods, but that was just a fluke. It didn't make a peep when I tangled with Azrael that night, so there's no way this apparent power is a "calling" or anything to fuss over. But, fuck, what if Lucian's onto something—with my telekinesis and all? I mean, I can move shit with my mind, right? What if there's truth to it?

Dani relaxes a smidge under my grip, her throat bobbing as she swallows. Her arousal floods my senses, and I can't help but growl. She's getting turned on by this, and damn if I'm not just as riled up as her. This woman's got a thing for heated encounters, and hell, if I'm not ready to stoke the fire.

Her tone softens from confrontational to genuinely puzzled, the sass yielding to concern. "Why are you in denial?" Dani probes gently, her honey-gold eyes searching mine for truth. "Why can't we just look into this more, Rhyland?" There's a plea in her voice, an invitation to unravel the mystery together, and a call for transparency that she hopes I can't ignore. "Open up to me..."

"Dani, fuck the powers. I've got everything I need right fucking here." I yank her to me, rough but right, and she cracks a grin that could light up the darkest corners.

Fuck, this woman's gonna be the death of me. She feeds off this challenge as much as I do, two peas in a pod, and hell if I don't want to bend her over and fuck her into submission to show her who's running shit.

"Nice try, Mjolnir's Muse. We're getting to the bottom of this."

Her voice cuts through me like a blade, sharp and unforgiving. She stands there burning with fury, golden eyes blazing with determination. My fierce, feisty angel doesn't back down from anything.

"Oh, aren't you just fucking cute."

My self-control snaps, and I crush my lips onto hers, stealing a moan that tells me she's all in and wanting more. She tangles her fingers into my hair, tugging tight and making a hiss escape my lips. I tear into her clothes, unzipping her leather tunic, and her beautiful breasts spill free. Moaning at the sight, I can't resist squeezing them in my hands, twisting her nipples just as she loves.

She gasps and pulls me closer, "Yes... I need you, Rhyland." The raw desire in her voice sends my need soaring higher.

I kiss a trail down her chin and throat, finding her hard nipple and sucking it into my mouth. Need pulses through me as I pull her tighter, her moans driving me wild. My cock strains and aches for her—for me to have her wrapped around me.

"Are you gonna let this go?" I murmur, pressing kisses down her neck.

"Not a chance—you're holding out on me, and I'm not having it," she retorts with a firecracker snap.

"Dani, let it go," I warn. "I'm done talking about this," I insist, trailing my tongue across her collarbone, eliciting shivers and raising goosebumps on her skin.

She shakes her head, stubborn as hell, grinding her tempting body against mine, breathing hard with want and need.

There's no way I'm folding. I'm not about to plunge headfirst into this mess of un-tapped lineage or play pretend with some make-believe elemental talent she's convinced I'm hiding. And after the stunts she's pulled—with Adrian's crap, defying me right in front of him, and holding back info—there's a score to settle. I made a vow. She's in for it now.

Diving my hand into her pants, I find her soaked and ready, dripping with arousal.

"Yes," she whimpers breathlessly.

I start working her clit, teasing circles that makes her need build. While I devour her mouth with a demanding kiss, she can't help but moan in response.

"You want this, baby?" I grunt, my voice thick with lust. "Want me to fuck you hard and raw, like you crave?"

"God—*yes*—please," she breathes out, almost a whisper.

I can sense her winding up as I keep grinding her clit, her grip on my neck tightening, and her body quivering under my touch. I know her like the back of my fucking hand, and I can tell she's just seconds away from detonating. My cock is begging for its release, but I won't give in. This game is gonna be one hell of a ride.

"Fuck, baby, you're so close... You gonna come for me?" I mutter, knowing I'm working her up.

Her breathless whimpers, her golden eyes blown from pure lust, and the desperate grip she has on me tell me that she's hanging on by a thread.

"Y-yes...I need you inside me, Rhyland—fuck—" She pants as she tries to regain control of her breath and her body.

I make no apologies as I pull my hand away and slowly suck her arousal off my fingers, giving her a smug look that says, loud and clear, 'I fucking win.'

Then, as if it is nothing more than a minor distraction, I change the subject, "Sorry, baby—we'll have to continue this later. We gotta chat with King Alinar, make damn sure Amara's keeping her ass right where it's supposed to be."

Dani stands there in shock, trying to process what just happened. Seconds later, her face morphs into pure anger. I can't help but smirk, anticipating her reaction.

"You..." she starts while zipping up her tunic, but I cut her off, fully aware of what's coming.

"You what, Angel?" I look her right in the eyes, challenging her, ready to put her fiery temper on full display. "Let's hear it; I'm dying to punish that filthy mouth of yours again."

Dani's expression shifts drastically; her face is etched with unmistakable frustration, a result of my deliberate edging game. It's a look I know all too damn well and a testament to our unique dynamic. The underlying tension only heightens the anticipation, ensuring that when release finally comes, it'll be fucking explosive.

She might surrender to her fury momentarily and let loose a torrent of curses. But then, she pulls it back, seething as she fixes me with a glare full of suppressed wrath.

"Oh, we're playing with fire now, is that it? *Fine.* Let's dance, babe, and see who burns up first. Just don't be surprised when it's not me."

The challenge is issued with a sizzling combination of ire and sharp wit that leaves no doubt she's up for whatever confrontation this game may bring. She glares daggers before storming out of the room, leaving me with a satisfied smirk.

I practically sprint after Dani, my feet moving faster than my brain can keep up. As we burst out of the room, we were greeted by Lucian's shit-eating grin, his expression practically screaming, "I'm about to say something stupid."

"Well, well, well, if it isn't the lovebirds themselves," he coos, with mock sweetness. "Did you two finally kiss and make u—"

Lucian's words choke off the second he clocks the look on Dani's face—a glare so scorching it could incinerate a man on the spot.

Lucian's eyes widen, and he takes a step back, holding his hands up in a gesture of surrender. "Whoa, okay, backing up now," he laughs nervously, his self-preservation instincts finally kicking in. "I'm taking that murderous expression as a hard 'no' on the reconciliation front."

I shoot him a look that clearly says, "No shit, Sherlock," but he just shrugs, his grin never wavering. "Hey, can't blame a guy for trying to lighten the mood, right?" He chuckles, utterly oblivious to the fact that he's about two seconds away from getting his ass handed to him.

I let out a heavy sigh, silently praying for the patience not to strangle him with his own intestines. "Lucian, I fucking swear if you don't—"

"Let's go," Dani says, her voice firm as hell. She shuts down any more talk and flips the switch to go-time.

Striding through the castle dungeons, the foul stench and the wails of the caged bastards corrupted by Amara grate on my nerves. She's huddled like a beaten mutt against the cell bars at the row's end.

"Well, well, ain't karma a bitch," I sneer.

Amara's head snaps up; her eyes blaze with pure hate. "You'll pay for this humiliation."

Dani doesn't hesitate; the air hums with her iron-clad will. She locks eyes with Amara, her voice sharp and unyielding. "Game's up. Count yourself lucky we're not stooping to your level of barbarity."

Her cool-headed stance knocks me back a bit—gotta give her props. Amara continues to mouth off, hurling every dirty word she's got, but we leave her behind. She's just a toothless tiger now, as screwed over as the poor bastards she used to crush.

Dani's still fuming with me, giving me the cold shoulder as we climb back to the surface. There's Alinar in the throne room chatting up some glittering Fae straight out of the Sun Court.

We stop dead in our tracks, then Alinar clocks us and gives us the nod. "Ah, at last, you've returned. I must admit, a twinge of concern for your journey had taken hold. It pleases me greatly to see you both safe. Rest assured, my word stands firm—Amara remains untouched by sunlight, as she will for all days to come.

"We appreciate it, Alinar," Dani states. "Got a report for you," she spills the whole deal from Cal—those ethereal creatures are game for a comeback to stand with the Fae again—but only if we can kick Azrael to the curb and make sure Amara rots in her hellhole.

Alinar rejoices, clapping his hands with a hearty laugh echoing through the chamber. "Splendid news! Indeed, the reign of this vile sorcery is at its breaking point. You have my solemn vow, Savior—she shall never step beyond the walls of her prison cell."

Dani shifts on her feet, almost worried, before speaking again, "There is one more issue that needs to be resolved, Your Highness."

What is she doing? What other issue?

"Anything!" Alinar says with a gleam in his eye.

"You're going to allow Axilya to reclaim her throne—as the queen of Luminara," Dani insists, her voice carrying a playful yet stern cadence that leaves no doubt she's serious. "You know, her rightful place?" She punctuates the demand with a cocked eyebrow, daring any challenge to her declaration.

Swiveling my head her way, I flash all the surprises a vampire has in his arsenal.

"What?" My voice cuts sharp and quick, demanding an instant rundown. "What's this about?" But she ignores my prodding.

Alinar's face slips and becomes severe, "I had already planned on it, my dear. For she is my true mate," he confesses.

My brain's scrambling to catch up—what the fuck is happening here?

Dani's composure falters momentarily, and a gasp slips through her lips. "W-What? I—I don't understand?" Her voice trembles, the once-steady rhythm now caught on the edges of stupefaction and disbelief. Her wide, golden eyes mirror the shock of her halted words.

I'm just as blindsided here. I'm groping around in the pitch-fucking-black, trying to figure out what the hell has been dropped on us.

Alinar squirms in his throne, looking all antsy and shit. He takes a deep breath and winds up, "By the treacherous hand of that damned harpy, I was rent from Axilya's side, and she has held me captive—usurping the throne that was never rightfully hers. Envy coils in her black heart; she loathed my dear Axilya, coveting what was ours with poison in her soul. The moment she clutched the Soul Stone, her power surged, ungodly and malign—and she compelled me away, along with over half the Fae of this realm, the dearest prize to wound Axilya most grievously. Yet, within this darkened cage, I've played the knave, biding my time and clinging to the slender hope of your arrival to mend the fractured lands."

"You've been that bitch's obedient little pet for centuries, just waiting around and praying Dani would pop up one day?"

I'm floored, and that's rare for me. This dude could stomach rolling with such wickedness for so long when his mate was just a stone's throw away.

"How the hell could you do that to yourself—to your damn mate?" I ask incredulously, shaking my head. This whole fucked-up situation doesn't make any goddamn sense.

Dani's been dead silent, just as blown away as I am. She's standing there gawking at Alinar, waiting for him to explain his ass.

"I gave nary a piece of my heart to that enchantress—it was all a performance, a mere masquerade to appease her dark hunger. As the moon climbed and her ceremonies of decadence unfurled further into the abyss, my essence remained untouched by her corrupt desires. 'Twas Meadow, a servant of subtle craft, who brewed an elixir to shield me from her bewitchments."

I freeze. My Mouse, doing the unimaginable, explains why she was so strong-willed—it's her and those damn magic potions of hers.

Alinar continues, "She craved naught but to wound my Axilya, spreading falsehoods that I had betrayed our bond. I played the part only to protect myself while captive in this dreadful place, though it shredded my soul for Axilya to think me unfaithful. My love, my heart, is Axilya's alone. This I swear upon my life."

"Alright, time out..." Dani exhales in exasperation, "Does Axilya have the full scoop on this epic tale? Does she know any of this?"

I don't know Axilya, as well as Dani, but it's always struck me how reserved and melancholy she comes across. And now I think I get the damn reason why.

Alinar's countenance darkens with sorrow as he confesses, "No, Axilya knows not the truth. Since my—our—captivity began, all paths of contact have been severed. I've been unable to reach her to tell her that my heart remains true. All she's filled with is what Amara feeds her and the land—I abandoned Axilya for Amara. When word came that you were journeying to parley, I saw my chance—I would reveal everything to Axilya when you arrived. But you never came. Axilya still believes Amara's web of lies, and it eats at my soul that she may doubt my faithfulness. We must find a way for me to tell her, for her to know I am still hers, in heart, mind, and spirit. I will not rest until she understands it was all Amara's vile ruse, and my love for Axilya never faltered, not for a moment."

Now it clicks. The way Alinar brushed off Amara like garbage in her room that day when she was interrogating me about Dani. How that sadistic bitch got off on keeping me as a 'pet,' knowing damn well my heart was with someone else. She thrives on shattering hearts and souls into pieces. Why? 'Cause that psychopath is jealous; she'll never have that bond for herself. How she would compel anyone for sleazy hookups every night 'cause no one in their right damn mind would willingly sleep with that miserable cunt by choice.

"Leave it to me," Dani chimes in with determination. "I'll have a heart-to-heart with Axilya. Here's hoping she has the patience to hear me out and grasp the gravity of the situation. It's high time she reclaimed her throne—the queen bee of this realm is overdue for her comeback."

"Indeed, my dear, you've sized it up perfectly. You have my sincerest thanks for playing matchmaker on my account, and rest assured, I'll be here, playing the patient suitor until she bestows upon us the honor of her company," Alinar says, his voice a blend of polite sarcasm and genuine appreciation. "And for the record, I've set up a rendezvous with King Oberon at the Sun Court to hash out these pressing matters."

DANICA

74

The bombshell we learned yesterday is still sizzling in my brain, repeating like the rumble of far-off thunder that I've gotten used to. Those words are doing the mambo in my brain, throwing down some soap opera-level severe drama. Alinar and Axilya, an item? Now that's a spicy turn of events that's got me all kinds of dizzy.

I could tell there was more to Ax than her zen vibes and strategist smarts. Every hint of majesty that slipped through her chill facade totally made sense now.

Setting up shop in Whispervale, giving court life the big ol' middle finger—she wasn't just hanging out; she was sitting on an invisible throne. Suddenly, it's like, 'Hello! Here comes the queen! She's been hiding in plain sight.'

So, what's the deal with Faderyn? Did he have the inside scoop this whole time? It's like this annoying tic I can't shake off.

He had to know, right?

How could he not see it? But then, why play keep-away with that kind of need-to-know intel? Flashbacks of our talks and those sneaky looks he shared with Axilya are all adding up, and I'm feeling the sting of being double-crossed, big time. Trust is like gold in this high-stakes mystical mess, and I'm starting to feel like I got played.

Rewinding to the moment, Axilya's ice queen act cracked when she found out Rhyland got snagged by Amara. It's hitting me now—her soft spot wasn't just random feels. Alinar didn't just get nabbed; she thought he bailed by choice. Talk about an emotional minefield right in her chest.

A flash of rage hits when Rhyland's antics cross my mind—his latest tease-a-thon, acting nonchalantly about his freaky new lightning tricks. Whenever he shrugged it off, my irritation with him cranked up another notch. But simmering beneath that irritation is a realization: our powers are as knotted up as our destinies—mine with its sway over light and the stuff of life, his cracking with this stormy energy. Calimero's mysterious hints about the one who commands lightning being aware of his ancestry echo in my mind. Just how deep does Rhyland's understanding of his bloodline go? It's a puzzle piece that may unravel many mysteries, but it's not the day for solving riddles.

So, game on—I'm gonna freeze him out, flip the script, and see how he likes a taste of his own meddlesome medicine. But let's be honest, who the fuck am I kidding? This is Rhyland, Mr. Irresistible himself. Whether I can hold out against his charms... well, only the tick-tock of the clock's gonna spill that secret.

And as if summoned by some twisted universal scheduler, right on cue, my monthly visitor decided to join the already chaotic party. Seriously, timing is everything—and mine has a wicked sense of humor, deciding to make its grand entrance amidst all the mayhem. Just another variable in the complex equation that is my life right now.

Thank the heavens for Alina—what an absolute gem! She swooped in like a fairy godmother and saved the day with her stash of lady essentials.

Strutting down the hall to Axilya with my game face on, it is high time to straighten out this knotty mess of secrets and fibs wrapping around us. We are blowing the lid off this thing, and whoever isn't ready for that conversation should probably make themselves scarce.

I've got questions, I want answers, and I'm fresh out of polite.

The vibe in the Sun Court is mystical. The air practically sparkles with happiness and sunshine as I hustle down the halls to Ax's room, a cocktail of jitters and boldness bubbling up inside.

My knock lands on the door with enough force to make my intentions crystal clear—subtle was never really my style anyway.

"Enter," Axilya's voice floats through the wood, smooth and unbothered, as if she's been expecting me since breakfast.

I push the door open and step inside. The room breathes with that signature Whisper-vale calm—warm, hushed, wrapped in the kind of quiet that makes the rest of the world feel very far away. Axilya is positioned by the window with what I can only describe as deliberate elegance, the sunlight carving her into a silhouette of someone who absolutely knows more than she's letting on.

How very on-brand.

"Danica," she hits me with a welcome, not even bothering with a peek, as though her Axilya-senses told her I was dropping by.

"I need answers," I cut right to the chase, shutting the door behind me.

That's when she swivels, locking me down with her pale green eyes, which somehow manage to be super intense and weirdly reassuring.

"You probably have a list," she says, poised and ready to spill the tea.

I nod, and funny enough, I find my motor mouth on pause—just for a hot second, though. Then, it's like the floodgates open. I blurt out everything: my head-scratchers about Calimero dropping the truth bomb on her, the sneaking feeling Faderyn kept secrets, not to mention Ax's own story wrapped in mystery.

Axilya doesn't make a peep; she gives me the serene queen look while I unload.

After my spill-the-beans monologue, she exhales gently, "Well, I figured you'd stumble onto the big reveal sooner or later."

"But seriously, what's with all the mystery?" I press, cutting straight to the point. "Why not just lead with it—that you're the rightful queen of this place?"

Axilya looks away momentarily, gathering her thoughts before meeting my gaze again. "I...I gave it all up. So no, not anymore. I wanted to stir away from enemies—from making choices out of obligation rather than free will." Her voice is steady but tinged with regret. "I wanted you to carry out your cause because you believed in it, not because of my title or crown."

I shift gears, my tone edged. "And what about Faderyn? Did he know all along?"

"Faderyn knew only as much as he needed to," Axilya replies gently. "His loyalty was always to our cause first—to ensure your safety and success."

Gotta say, even when it's dressed up with good intentions, that sting of betrayal still tastes like shit.

"So, this entire time..." I grapple with the mixed feelings, trying not to let the cracks show.

Axilya reaches out, her hand touching mine in a rare gesture of comfort. "I am sorry for not telling you. But you've proven yourself more than worthy, Danica. Your strength and heart have brought us closer to unity than we've been in ages. I gave up on the throne long after..."

She pauses and looks away again, another secret she's been hiding. She's offering a balm here, but it's not entirely taking the edge off the burn of those hidden truths.

My head's damn near spinning with a whirlpool of thoughts ready to take me under, but one fact stands out through the chaos—I've got a laundry list to hash out with Axilya.

Gripping that nugget of clarity, I plop into the chair facing her. This isn't your garden-variety chitchat—nope, we're about to dive into a talk that'll probably map out our next moves in wild, unpredictable ways.

The quiet in the room is heavy, like a blanket of snow untouched by footprints, waiting for something big to happen. Axilya's eyes are on me, solid and deep—I might as well be staring into the abyss. I hiccup a breath, trying to herd my swirling thoughts into something coherent.

"Amara," I spit out; the word is straight-up venom. "She's been the fog machine, the spider spinning her fib-fest that's muddled up the whole picture."

Axilya's eyes darken, a tempest brewing in their depths. "What do you mean?"

I edge forward, dropping my voice. "It was the Soul Stone, Ax—her gateway to Moretemis and illegitimate power, compelling Alinar and everyone else to her side.

"Alinar didn't bail on you for some shiny throne or epic tales. Amara was pulling strings because she was green-eyed over the legit, unshakeable thing you two have going—a thing she can't get her grubby mitts on."

Axilya sucks in a quick breath, her eyes widening just a tad. "You know about me and... Alinar?" It's like I've just dropped a plot twist she didn't see coming.

"He just confessed everything to me," I say, not missing a beat.

Axilya perks up, all regal-like, but I can see the twinge of hurt slicing through her typically unshakeable, fae-fancy facade. "How do you know this... for sure? We—our kind can't be compelled," she quizzes, a wisp of vulnerability peeking through.

I can almost visibly see the gears grinding away as she recalls Rhyland's words about the compulsion. She's putting two and two together, and you best believe she's not about to settle for an answer of bullshit.

"Because," I lay it down with all the gusto I've got, "That stone is more powerful than what you or your ancestors could ignore, and Amara used that. Alinar's been in your corner, duking it out with that witch and holding his heart for you. But Amara, she's put a lid on him—tight. He's head-over-heels for you, Ax. He found a potion to guard his mind from her compulsion, faking it. He's stuck it out and is now waiting for you to catch wind of the truth and make your move—even now."

That hope in Axilya's eyes? It flares up quickly before she snaps her ice-queen mask back into place.

"You imply that he has harbored affection for me all these years—retains his love? And all the while, I believed he had forsaken me," the quiver in her voice reveals an aspect previously concealed—a vulnerability she's trying to hide. "And what of Amara?"

"Because that's what Amara wanted you to think. The real stuff—like what you've got—doesn't go poof from time away or a few miles in between." I feel that pang in my chest 'cause Rhyland, and I live the same epic love story. "Amara is awaiting judgment," I confess.

I lock eyes with her as she starts to let her guard down, walls toppling over to show the real deal—her heart, craving something lost but not forgotten. There's something about watching a queen come undone—like the most powerful storm showing its eye.

"He's been in contact with King Oberon," I toss in, watching her closely. "They're set to discuss handing the crown back to where it belongs—to you, Your Highness."

She draws in a sharp breath—I might as well have said the magic words. It's like I've unlocked the chest where she's kept all her wishes stashed.

"Why?" The word tumbles out of her, wrapped in a whole tangle of dazed and hungry emotions. "I gave it up."

"Because you're born to wear the crown of Luminara," I shoot back, cutting through the fluff. "And because let's face it, Luminara is itching for its *one* and *only* queen."

You can almost hear the destiny gears grinding, setting things into motion with a hum in the air that screams 'epic moment.'

We're looped back into the silence—a thick blanket of nothingness lingering in the air as we each take turns on this wild ride of feelings.

"You know, just between us, Calimero is basically holding his breath for you to waltz back and take up that crown. They're ready for an encore, and who can stand in the way of your triumphant return, Ax?" My tone is equal parts jest and challenge, a feisty spur to action.

A glimmer appears in Axilya's eyes, a tide of unshed tears at the invocation of Calimero's name. "He belonged to me, once upon a time—before this chaos," she states, her lips curving into a poignant smile.

"Oh, brilliant. Sneak up on me with a twist, why don't you?" I say, with mock astonishment and a playful roll of my eyes. Kinda figured that little surprise.

"Alright, 'Your Highness,' lay it on us—what's the next move in your regal playbook?"

"I will go to Alinar," Axilya declares, her face all lit up with that royal 'never-say-die' vibe. "The hour's come for me to step up and wear that crown again of Luminara like I was born to."

"As for me," I pipe up, feeling that adrenaline pump, "I'm hightailing it back to the mortal scene. Gonna lure Azrael out into the open so you can get the house in order around here."

"And Ax...Amara—you call the shots on that one. Your decision, your rules." My words are laced with the unsaid—give 'em hell. But it's Axilya's call to make, not mine. This is her arena, her face-off—her payback.

Axilya gets to her feet, and the room seems to straighten up as she rises. She's got that look, all majesty and power, like she's ready to step up and rule it all.

"Hand in hand," she nods, confirming the game plan, "Luminara will be whole again. Our magic restored." Ax smiles at me, the genuine, no-strings-attached smile I never figured I'd see from her. "Thank you, Danica—Savior," she says, and just like that, she's wrapping me up in a hug that could squeeze the fight out of a bear.

DANICA

75

The library greets me with the hush of a thousand untold stories, but I'm not here for the quiet. I'm all fired up, purposely charging my steps. "Pack up," I break the silence, "We're going home."

Rhyland nods in agreement. "I'm more than ready to get the hell out of here."

Lucian leans against the bookshelf like he's posing for some magazine, that infuriating smirk of his plastered across his face like a neon sign screaming, "I'm an asshole; ask me how!"

"For the love of FUCK and praise be to whatever sadistic deity finally decided to take pity on me," he drawls. "If I have to spend one more second prancing around this Lisa Frank fever dream of a wonderland, I was going to shove a fucking pixie stick so far up my ass; I'd be shitting glitter for a week."

He pushes off the shelf, sauntering to us with that trademark Lucian swagger. "But hey, at least now I can finally get back to the comforting embrace of civilization, where the only magical creatures I have to deal with are the crackheads behind the 7-Eleven and the occasional stripper with daddy issues."

I roll my eyes so hard I'm pretty sure I strain something. "Oh, cry me a river, Lucian. You act like you're the only one who's had to deal with this bullshit. News flash, jerkface, we're all in the same boat here."

He shrugs that infuriating smirk, which never leaves his face. "All I'm saying is, if we could wrap this up sometime before the heat death of the universe, that would be fan-fucking-tastic. I've got a bar to run and a reputation as a snarky asshole to maintain, you know."

Despite the gravity of the situation, I can't help but snort at his tirade, shaking my head in a mix of amusement and exasperation. Leave it to Lucian to find a way to bitch about our world-saving mission like it's a minor inconvenience.

"Careful, Lucian," I warn, my lips twitching with barely suppressed laughter. "Keep talking like that, and people might start to think you actually care about something other than yourself."

"Bite your tongue, Princess," he retorts, clutching at his chest in mock offense. "I'll have you know that I am a deeply complex and multi-faceted individual with a wide range of interests and concerns."

He pauses, his brow furrowing in thought. "They just happen to mostly revolve around booze, sex, and being a pain in everyone's ass."

I can't help it; I burst out laughing, the absurdity of the whole situation finally getting to me. Here we are, on the brink of a catastrophe that could destroy everything we know and love, and Lucian is still finding a way to make it all about him.

Erik frowns, crossing his arms. "Are you certain returning now is wise? Azrael will surely follow us."

I shoot Erik a grin, amped up and raring to go. "I'm banking on it. Luminara's got no shot at patching things up with that jackass running loose. We gotta punt his ass back through the portal—one-way ticket style."

No time to lose, I grab some vials of my O-neg elixir for Erik, Lucian, and Adrian.

"Drink up, boys," I say, passing out the vials.

Rhyland's eyes blaze with fury when I offer a vial to Adrian. "Absolutely not," he snarls. "That traitorous piece of shit doesn't deserve an ounce of your blood after what he did."

Rhyland is scowling like a thundercloud, grumbling about giving Adrian a vial. It's like dealing with a grumpy toddler.

Rolling my eyes, I place my hands on my hips, fully loaded and ready to tear into him. "You've got to be kidding me. Your brother's about as flammable as a gas station, and I'm not about to turn this trip into an episode of 'Vampire Roasts.' Give him the blood so we can get out of here without unnecessary barbecue sessions."

"Fuck that," Rhyland spits. "Let the bastard burn. I warned you what would happen if you crossed me—over him again," he says, motioning to Adrian.

"Oh, please, give it a rest!" I retort as I meet Rhyland's gaze head-on. "You don't get a say in what I do with my blood, big guy. Since when did you become the blood police, huh? Newsflash: I'm a grown-ass woman, and I can make my own decisions—including whom I give a vial of blood to."

Rhyland steps closer, eyes burning with dominance. "Keep running that smart mouth, and you'll regret it later, Angel. I keep my promises, remember?"

I stand my ground, eyes locked on Rhyland, refusing to be intimidated. "Are you seriously trying to threaten me over a tiny vial of my blood?" I say with a sarcastic smirk. "Because that's, like, the most vampirey thing ever. I'm still waiting for you to break out into a dramatic cape twirl. Give me a sec; my popcorn's in the microwave."

Lucian laughs behind me, "Oh, yes, please. Do the cape twirl! And while you're at it, why don't you throw in a 'I vant to suck your blood' in your best Transylvanian accent?"

Rhyland's eyes narrow dangerously, his jaw clenching with barely restrained irritation. "You two think this is a fucking game?" He snarls, his voice low and threatening. "It's a promise, baby." Rhyland's voice drops an octave. "You're playing a dangerous game defying me like this."

The air between us grows thick, practically crackling with tension as neither of us backs down. Rhyland's eyes blaze that unmistakable shade of vibrant blue—a warning sign that he's reached his breaking point. My heart races, and I struggle to suppress my arousal. I'm still wound up from his damn edging game.

Dammit, why does this alpha-hole behavior make me hot? I must be certifiably insane, but I'm not about to let him see that. I take a deep breath, willing to stay calm and keep my game face on.

With a huff of frustration, I cave and shove the vial back into my bag. "Fine, you overbearing ass. You win this round," I grumble, glaring at him through narrowed eyes.

Rhyland can't hide his triumphant smirk, and it takes every ounce of my self-control not to punch it right off his face. Oh, I'll find a way to make him pay for this later. But let's be honest; I'm pretty much screwed when it comes to going up against this sexy-as-sin vampire.

He's got me outmatched in every way—strength, speed, and centuries of experience. But one thing's for sure: there's nothing sexier than a powerful man who knows how to get under my skin. Now, how do I turn this weakness into an advantage? It's time to devise a plan to make this immortal bad boy eat his words and maybe some humble pie.

Rhyland swings his menacing glare towards Adrian. "Take this as a warning if you even entertain thoughts of double-crossing us again. You're lucky we are even taking you with us."

Adrian looks up from his book, resignation etched into his features. "It's okay, Dani," he says softly. "Don't worry about it," ignoring Rhyland's threats.

My heart sinks at his acceptance of exclusion, but the decision is made. I'll have to find a safer route.

"Mmm, *fuuuuck,*" Lucian breathes, sinking his teeth into his bottom lip like he's watching something he shouldn't be. Then his head drops back against the wall, and the theatrics kick into full gear. "Somebody hand me a towel because I am *sweating* over here." He fans himself with one hand, tongue pressed to the inside of his cheek. "The sexual tension in this room is so goddamn thick I could choke on it. Pretty sure I just developed a kink I didn't have five minutes ago."

He waggles his eyebrows like a man with zero shame and even less self-awareness."D on't mind me. Front row seat. Living my best life. You two keep doing... *whatever the hell this is.*" He makes a crude gesture between us. "Mommy and Daddy are fighting, and honestly? It's doing things for me."

I roll my eyes and feel my face turning a shade of red that would make a fire truck jealous. But of course, Lucian cackles like the unhinged lunatic he is, clearly getting off on my discomfort. "Hey, don't shoot the messenger, sweet cheeks! I'm just calling it like I see it. You and Tall, Dark, and Brooding over there have the kind of chemistry that could set off a fucking nuclear reaction. Embrace the hate-fuck, I say! Ride that angry dragon all the way to O-Town!"

Oh, for the love of all that is *holy,* I cannot believe Lucian. It's like he has a direct line to the gutter and no shame whatsoever in sharing the filth that spews forth.

He's got a point, though—our bedroom acrobatics are top-tier. I cut Lucian a withering look, my patience for him officially running on fumes.

Rhyland steps in, his voice low and threatening. "Lucian, I'm only going to say this once: shut your fucking mouth before I shut it for you. Permanently."

Lucian raises both hands like he's backing away from a crime scene, but that shit-eating gleam in his eyes tells me he's already loading the next round.

Erik chuckles, trying to hide his laugh.

I spin away from the jury, zeroing in on Mr. I-Prefer-My-Own-Company, Faedryn, who, like magic, drops his cup and pulls the stand-and-impress move.

"Faderyn," I choke out because my vocal cords are auditioning for a tragic opera.

His gaze meets mine, and there's a deep sorrow that wasn't there before.

"Why?" My voice is barely above a whisper. "Why did you keep Axilya's identity hidden?"

He sighs deeply before speaking. "Dani, it was never about deception for deception's sake." He pauses as if searching for the right words. "I didn't want Axilya's truth out before she was ready to—"

"But you kept it from me," I interject softly.

"I'm aware." His voice fractures a tad. "And I seek your forgiveness. My actions were guided by reasons, Dani. Reasons I am confident you will comprehend."

And I get it—I really do. I get the whole 'loyal to the queen' bit and the need for secrets. That doesn't mean it doesn't sting like hell, though. Here we are, tossing each other one of those long, loaded glances—the kind that says we've been through the wringer and back together. It's like a silent montage of our own personal dramedy, complete with every nasty curveball life pitches our way.

"I've watched you grow," he continues, voice laced with pride and sadness intertwined like vines around an ancient tree trunk. "From that mortal woman who fell into our world by chance... to this incredible force who has fought for our realm with every breath."

My eyes prickle as feelings bubble up, threatening to spill over in a salty waterfall of tears.

"I'm so proud of you," he whispers earnestly.

His words envelop me like a cozy hug on a blizzardy day—all warm and fuzzy yet prickly with the harsh truth that this is a goodbye.

His tone softens appreciatively as he speaks, "You've transcended the role of merely a savior; you've woven yourself into our fabric—into the essence of Luminara. And you've become a valued friend to me."

A lump forms in my throat, leaving Faderyn feels like I'm tearing away a piece of myself that has taken root in these magical forests and skies painted with stardust. "Thank you—" I whisper, my voice faltering as emotions swell.

Faderyn was the first person I met when I came here, the first friend I made in this strange new world. He was the first to see me, to truly understand my unchecked powers. From that moment by the riverside when he saved my life, his kindness and wisdom have guided me through the darkness. He trained me, yes, but he did so much more—he gave me hope when all seemed lost, strength when mine failed, compassion when I needed it most. On this journey, he became the brother I needed.

And now...Now, I have to find the words to say goodbye to him.

"What for? The gratitude is mine to express, Dani," Faderyn encourages soothingly.

"For saving me, that day by the river. For becoming a friend when all I was to you was a stranger," I confess, my voice a soft murmur between us. The enormity of what lies ahead casts a long shadow—a blur of what's to come shot through with streaks of hope and threads of fear.

Faderyn moves to reach out but hesitates, a dance of second thoughts. Finally, his hand finds its way to my shoulder, a touch laden with a deep understanding and the warmth of friendship, anchoring me in the now, even as we stand on the precipice of tomorrow.

"It was my pleasure," Faderyn replies, his voice loaded with layers of unspoken camaraderie and kinship.

We stand there a beat longer than we should—the scholarly fae who chose my side when he didn't have to, and the human who stopped being ordinary somewhere between the first disaster and the last. I wrap him up in a bear hug, breathing him in like I'm memorizing him.

When we finally step apart, the ache is there—quiet but sharp, the way goodbyes always are when they matter. But it's not an ending. Not for us. Not for two souls stitched together by chaos and magic, tethered by something that doesn't care about distance or time or the borders between worlds.

Sneaking a final peek at Faderyn—rocking that bittersweet 'you got this' grin—I whirl around to face Rhyland, Lucian, Erik, and Adrian. The squad's all here. The checklist is done, and we're a team with our eyes on the prize. So we're bidding adieu to Luminara's cuddly clutches, but hey, we're pocketing some of that glow for the road. It's our secret weapon against the big bad lurking in the wings.

Mentally, I'm already sprinting back to Emily and Damon, eagerness bubbling up inside like a fizzy drink. It feels like I left them way back in the Stone Age—and judging by ol' Father Time and his infuriating puzzle clock, I may as well have.

Are they alright?

How much has shaken up around them while I've been on this wild goose chase?

I pull myself out of my own head.

Gotta buckle up for the next installment of the ongoing saga: getting Azrael back to mortal town and figuring out where this magic crown will lead us next.

RHYLAND

76

Dani had us twiddling our fucking thumbs in Luminara, waiting for the damn night to fall. This was all 'cause of the blowup with Adrian—a damn nuisance, but whatever.

The second we strut through the portal, time itself jerks around us, something you'd feel down to your bones. It's a weird-ass sensation, jumping through realities and ending up further along the timeline. Yet, in this mind-bending mess, time's still straight as an arrow across every damned realm. It makes zero sense, and it's disorienting as hell.

With a loud crack, the portal clamps shut.

One whiff of this world's air, and I am damn near ready to hurl—it's the polar opposite of Luminara's crisp atmosphere. Catching a glimpse of Erik, I can tell he is feeling the same damn thing.

And then there's Lucian, the little shit, who's acting like he just walked into a goddamn candy store. He takes a deep, exaggerated breath, a look of pure bliss spreading across his face. "AHHHH... the sweet, sweet aroma of piss, shit, and desperation. Oh, how I've missed the subtle nuances of this world's unique perfume."

He spreads his arms wide as if embracing the very essence of the place. "Breathe it in, my friends. Let the heady musk of human misery fill your lungs and invigorate your soul. It's the fragrance of life, of reality, of—"

"Of a fucking sewage plant," I cut him off, wrinkling my nose in disgust.

We're loitering in the back alley of Karma, and bam, memories of this shithole alley with Dani come flooding back. Can't forget this is the exact spot where I had to step in and save her from that dickhead Max. A warm rush of sweet realization floods through me, and shit, if I can't keep a grin from spreading across my face.

Dani pipes up, saying we should hold tight right here, banking on Azrael to show up any minute now.

She tosses a glance at Adrian, quirking an eyebrow. "Okay, explain—the big mystery. What's his deal with my portal popping? Does he have some sixth sense or what?" she quips.

Adrian tells her thoughtfully, "Yes, exactly—he can detect its presence. He can determine exactly where it is and harness the leftover energy it emits to replicate one of his own with the stone."

Dani nods in agreement, and we all settle in to wait.

And just like clockwork, here comes the leech.

From the corner of my eye, I see that black and oily portal start to take form. The scumbag Azrael slips out, the real fucking piece of work he is.

Danica's hands light up, ready to rain down a storm of hell.

The stench of rotten eggs and sulfur almost knocks me over as Azrael emerges from the portal, his tiny rat-like eyes bulging in surprise. In the blink of an eye, that cowardly son of a bitch has Adrian tangled up in a shadow tendril and using him like a damn human shield.

Damn it, Dani pauses, her angel fire temporarily held back. If she let it loose now, Adrian would be toast—literally. Those magic-nulling cuffs he's wearing leave him as helpless as a goddamn fly caught in the web, Azrael using him like some fucking disposable meat shield.

"Adrian, you disloyal snake," Azrael sneers, with contempt. "First, you turn your back on your own blood, and now you try to play me for a fool? I should've known better than to trust someone who betrays their own kind."

Adrian's eyes flick over to us, desperation reflecting in them. And honestly? I can't seem to rustle up any fucking sympathy for him at the moment. Azrael's right—though it makes my gut churn to even think that.

Something in me's switched off, dead cold, and all I can feel is the urge to do fucking damage.

"You know how this goes," I growl at Azrael, my voice slicing through the tension like a razor-sharp knife. "Let the traitor fucking go, or you'll feel my wrath."

It's no idle threat, not here and now. If he doesn't untangle himself from Adrian, I'll unleash hell on Azrael's sorry ass, and no one's gonna be there to pull me back.

Dani's firm voice slices through the tension. "Drop him, Azrael." The flames in her hands dance wildly, ready to be unleashed. "He's not part of your twisted collection."

"Oh, come now." Azrael glares at Dani, dark, pitiless eyes narrowing. "Turns out you can't blast your holy flames my way while dear Adrian's my shield. Seems to me the kid's untouched by your special blend—what's the name you gave it?"

How the hell does Azrael know about Dani's blood and what it does?

My mind's racing, trying to piece this shit together, when it hits me.

In a flash of fury, I realize—fucking Adrian, who spilled the secret. My temper flares like some uncontrollable wildfire. "You son of a bitch," I snarl, barely managing to hold myself back from ripping Adrian's throat out with my bare hands.

And right on cue, I see that same flash of guilt in Adrian's eyes. So, he knows he fucked up, he knows the shitstorm he just brought down on us.

But it's not enough; it's never fucking enough to make up for this betrayal.

As my eyes lock onto Adrian's, the silent promise of vengeance hanging heavy in the air, I feel my power surge, ready to do whatever it takes to save Dani and bring that bastard Azrael down.

Because fuck this, I won't let anyone get in the way of protecting her, not even my own brother.

"How—?" Dani starts, but I cut her off in her mind.

"Adrian told him, isn't it obvious?" I seethe.

The sting of that damn betrayal hits me like it's ripping through my chest all over again. My gut is twisted up, echoing every damn knot Dani's got carved into her heart—spilling her deepest secret about her blood.

"Dani, I'm so sor—" Adrian starts, but Azrael silences him with a quick lash of a shadow tendril before he can say another word.

"Don't even bother with your sorry-ass excuses, Adrian. It's damn pathetic," Azrael spits venomously. "Everyone's got an earful of your treachery already, and if you look at your so-called big brother," Azrael looks right at me, "it's clear as hell he gives zero fucks about your fate."

Dani shrugs, trying to brush off the gravity of the situation, her resolve hardening against the asshole threatening Adrian. "Rewind, Azrael. Do you really think you can just waltz out of here? Just so you know, I'll hunt you down to the ends of the earth to snatch that shiny rock off your finger—if I have to chop it off, so be it."

"Oh, I'm looking forward to it, darling," he sneers maliciously. "Since your precious blood holds the source of light and day itself, I'll have every last vampire lining up at your doorstep, thirsting for a taste." He breaks into a sinister, maniacal laughter. "And when they finally catch you—because, oh, sweet girl—every last one of them is working for me—I'll enjoy your 'special sauce' first-hand, as you so endearingly put it!"

I glare at Azrael, barely holding back the fury seething inside me. His sunken eyes lock onto mine, filled with pure hatred. The urge to tear him apart is almost overwhelming, considering what he's already done and the chaos he's about to unleash. Fucking opening Pandora's box is an understatement; this will screw everything up.

"Ah, yes, our dear Adrian has been quite enlightening," Azrael confesses, a devious smile curling his lips. "He's shared a wealth of information about your magical little secrets, most notably the special blood that flows through your veins—a precious gift from dear ol' daddy that I'm simply dying to taste... again."

"Give Adrian and his never-ending blather a massive 'fuck you.' Do it, Dani—maybe then we can all catch a break!" Lucian hollers from behind us.

But I know Dani—she's got a heart of gold, and her empathy is her biggest and most powerful weakness. It makes her vulnerable, but it's also what drives her to do what's right, even when it's damn near impossible—and Azrael knows this.

My patience shatters like a goddamn twig. "Enough of this bullshit!" I bellow, unleashing a tidal wave of telekinetic rage. Azrael and that traitorous prick Adrian are blasted back like ragdolls, their bodies smashing into the wall with a sickening crunch. The impact is so brutal that it fractures the bricks, sending chunks of debris raining down.

But even as I bear down on them with the full force of my powers, Azrael, the slimy bastard, clings to Adrian like a fucking parasite. He's using my own brother as a meat shield in this fucked-up standoff. The audacity of this manipulative piece of shit knows no bounds.

The air crackles with energy around us as I clench my fists, every fiber of my being screaming to destroy Azrael and rip Adrian free from his sadistic grip. If anyone is going to deal with Adrian, it's me—my brother, my blood, my responsibility. But even as the wrath burns through me, a darker thought creeps in—charging in could make this worse, plunging us into a war none of us are ready to fight.

My jaw locks, face twisted with barely restrained violence as I weigh my next move—uncertainty and dread clawing at my insides. This standoff can't hold forever.

Azrael's smug smile pisses me off even more. He thinks he's already won, this asshole. "Ready to give up yet?" he taunts.

"Not by a fucking long shot." I bellow—my anger and determination more than matched by my ability to focus my powers with laser precision.

"Rhyland—no!" Dani shouts, "Stop!" but it's too late.

I slam my energy into Azrael once more, intending to end this once and for all. But he anticipates my move and quickly surrounds himself with an impenetrable shroud of darkness, teleporting out of harm's way just in time.

My heart sinks as I watch with horror as Adrian, caught in the line of fire, takes the full brunt of my blow. Unable to dodge or defend himself, Adrian is slammed against the nearby wall with lethal force. The sickening sound of shattering bone fills the air as his skull cracks upon impact, and my stomach roils at the sight of his limp form crumpled on the ground.

"ADRIAN..." Dani's cry rips through me, her voice raw with pain, scratching at my guts.

In a flash of dark energy, Azrael reappears on the other side of the alley, a smug grin spreading across his face as he watches me struggle with the heavy weight of my guilt and fury. His vampire blurring is erratic, popping in and out of existence with a familiar, disorienting sound. I can't help but feel the bitter taste of defeat at the back of my throat as I realize the depths of Azrael's cunning and cruelty.

"Ah, such a pity about dear Adrian," Azrael coos with mock sympathy. "But no worries, he'll likely still be useful after he...heals. Or, even better—"

"Dani, now!" Erik's voice bellows through the chaos, urging her to strike while Azrael is momentarily distracted.

Dani calls upon her power with a fierce cry, crackling energy at her fingertips, unleashing blinding bolts of white light that streak through the alley. But Azrael, always cunning and elusive, seems to anticipate her moves. With a sinister smile, he shadows himself again, narrowly dodging Dani's attacks with a blink of dark energy.

Despite the frustration of missing her target, Dani's resolve remains unwavering. Fueled by anger and determination, she hurls waves of radiant power at Azrael, determined to land a hit no matter the cost. Her failed hits hit the alley walls, scorching and crumbling at impact.

Dani's time warp mojo kicks into high gear, and she's zipping around the alley like a superhero, hot on Azrael's heels as they both blink in and out of existence. Dani's hurling her light like it's going out of style, while Azrael's countering with his shadow bullshit, trying to snuff her out.

Silence crashes down like a hammer. We stand frozen, the air thick enough to choke on, every breath held, every muscle locked.

Then my world fucking ends.

No...

Azrael materializes from the shadows like death itself, coalescing right behind Dani. His hands are already reaching for her before I even process what's happening.

Everything inside me combusts. I explode forward, every muscle screaming as I launch myself toward her. "DANI!" Her name shreds from my throat, a guttural sound ripped from somewhere broken. I'm moving faster than I've ever moved, power coursing through me, but then something invisible slams into me like a freight train mid-stride. The impact throws me backward—hard. My spine cracks against the brick, mortar exploding around me, and all the air punches from my lungs. Stars detonate across my vision, but I'm already fighting back, clawing my way up, desperate to reach her.

I watch in horror as those shadow tendrils wrap around Dani's body, suffocating her, squeezing the life from her lungs. Her eyes are blown wide with terror, her mouth open in a silent scream.

But before any of us can move, before we can even fucking breathe, Azrael yanks the shadows tight around me, and my brothers. We're slammed against the wall a second time, pinned and gasping as that choking shadow wraps around our throats. Helpless. Trapped. All I can do is watch as that bastard turns his attention to Adrian, who's still reeling from the last impact. Adrian fights back with everything he's got, grappling with Azrael looming over him, clutching his arm in a death grip as Azrael goes for the unthinkable, the twisted fuck.

"You won't win, boy." With a brutal, swift movement, Azrael plunges his hand into Adrian's chest and rips out his heart. The sight of it sends a wave of nausea through me—the true death.

Dani's suffocating scream pierces the air, a sound so full of anguish and despair that it feels like it'll shatter my soul. My chest feels heavy; I can't breathe as I feel her heartache reverberate through our bond. Erik and Lucian are in the same struggling choke hold as I am; their expression is equally pained, knowing that Dani's grief over Adrian's death is mirrored in my agony.

We are held here in shock and horror, unable to react as Azrael carelessly tosses Adrian's heart. "Let this be a lesson to every last one of you," Azrael sneers, spitting on Adrian's heart. "Cross me, get in my way, and you'll suffer a fate far worse than this pitiful excuse," he kicks Adrian's body. "Time for me to exit. And I think..." Azrael looks at Dani, still struggling. "I'll take a trade," he says, moving toward Dani.

Out of fucking nowhere, we all drop to the ground like a bunch of limp noodles. We're all sprawled on the ground, gasping for air like fish out of water. Dani's coughing up a lung, clutching her throat, desperately sucking in oxygen. Lucian, Erik, and I are right there with her, massaging our necks, trying to get our shit together. I glance at Azrael; even he looks like he's been sucker-punched.

He tries to summon his shadow fuckery again, but something's not right. The confusion on his face says it all. Then, before anyone can react, he's on Dani in a flash, trying to haul her up over his shoulder like she's nothing. Dani's barely standing, but she's a fighter, clawing and thrashing with every ounce of strength she's got left.

They keep going at it, trading blows like there's no fucking tomorrow, but it's plain as day that Dani's running out of gas. She's not about to throw in the towel, though. She whips out her daggers and starts twirling them like a damn ninja, ready to carve Azrael a new one.

My heart's pounding out of my chest, adrenaline surging through my veins. We've got to make a move, and fast, before that son of a bitch gets away with my girl.

I'm consumed by an overwhelming urge to protect her. The memory of losing Dani in the Whispering Woods—rips through me like a serrated blade. Never. Not fucking again. Not while I'm still breathing.

I channel every ounce of rage, every shred of anguish into this single moment. The air ignites around me, crackling with raw, untethered power. Storm clouds barrel in like an invading army, ozone burning my lungs. Lightning tears the sky to pieces in a blinding assault, and that same volatile energy surges through my hands, desperate to break free. Thunder builds in a bone-rattling crescendo that drowns out everything else.

A feral howl tears from my chest so violent it cracks the ground beneath me. I release it all—a devastating torrent of light and energy aimed straight at the bastard. The blast is so intense it leaves me temporarily blind and deaf, my ears popping and ringing like crazy.

As that raw power drains from me, the acrid scent of burnt metal hangs heavy in the air. I'm left gasping, hollowed out, not even sure if I made a dent in that bastard.

Did I put an end to this nightmare once and for all? I don't know.

All I know is that the strength to protect Dani and have my brothers' backs is what's keeping me going. It's all I've got left in this fucked up world.

My legs buckle, and I crash onto the concrete, furiously looking for any hint of Azrael—no sign or trace.

Dani bolts toward Adrian's fallen form in a flash, collapsing to her knees beside him. Time warps strangely around me; the only anchor in the chaos is the rise and fall of my own breath. Lost in a fog, I have no damn clue how much time slips by before I spot Dani—with her face streaked in tears—rushing in my direction.

She lunges at me, and I nearly lose my balance. Her tears flow freely, and I can feel her anguish searing through me. How can she still hold such a tender spot for Adrian? He backstabbed her—he betrayed us. Yet, I wonder if he deserved a gruesome death like that.

Before I can react, her hand connects with my face in a resounding slap.

"Why did you do that? I told you to stop!" she cries between sobs. Though my ears are still ringing, her agony is etched on her face. "We could've spared him, Rhyland!" she screams at me through her tears, her voice thick with pain and anger. "Now, I'll never be able to find my mother! He knew how!"

My heart's being ripped to fucking shreds, torn apart by the whirlwind of chaos churning inside me. It's gotta be that new stone she's rocking, cranking her emotions up to the stratosphere while she's drowning in everyone else's bullshit too.

With vampiric speed, Lucian grabs hold of her, effortlessly pulling her away from me. He maintains his grip despite her thrashing and protests, attempting to ease her fury. "Whoa there, Princess!" Lucian chuckles, his usual tone with that special brand of conde-scending snark that makes me want to knee him in the balls. "Let's take a deep breath and count to ten before we regret something, like, say, rearranging Rhy's pretty-boy features into an abstract art piece."

Dani kicks and screams like a wildcat.

"Come on, Dani, we all know that traitor had it coming," Lucian informs her, with his no-bullshit tone.

Dani's anger flares, her eyes blazing, as she turns her fiery temper toward all of us. "He's your brother! How could you treat him like he's disposable?" She spits the words, "He made mistakes, sure, but he was trying to fix them!" Dani is beside herself with anger and sorrow, yelling and crying as her words tumble out. "Why couldn't you listen to me? Azrael wanted us to react—to hit first. And you fell right into his trap! He didn't need to die." The torrent of her emotions, raw and unfiltered, leaves me reeling as I struggle to come up with an answer that could ease her pain.

I watch Lucian scoop up a thrashing, cursing Dani, hauling her against his chest as she unleashes a torrent of creative obscenities. I knew exactly what my outburst would cost me, but in that moment, I didn't give a shit. Betrayal, protecting Dani and unthinkable rage had taken the wheel, and I was just along for the ride.

"Whoa there, Spitfire!" Lucian grunts, narrowly avoiding a fist to the face. "Let's get you inside before you go full 'Woman on a Warpath' and start laying waste to the innocent landscaping."

Dani snarls, her eyes blazing. "Fuck you, Lucian! Put me down before I scorch your dick off!"

But Lucian tightens his grip, his expression uncharacteristically serious. "Not gonna happen, sweetheart. You're hurt, you're pissed, and you're about two seconds away from going nuclear. So why don't you take a deep breath, let me get you inside, and we can figure out how to make that bastard pay?"

I can see the fight drain out of Dani at his words, her anger giving way to a bone-deep exhaustion that makes my heart ache. With a shuddering sigh, she slumps against Lucian's chest, silent tears streaming down her face.

As they disappear into the club, I run a hand through my hair, feeling like the world's biggest asshole. I should be the one comforting her, the one helping her through this nightmare. But instead, I'm out here, wallowing in my own guilt and self-pity like a fucking coward.

Her sobs become distant as I stay kneeling on the cold concrete, my mind racing to make sense of the chaotic shitstorm that just went down. The fucking lightning answered my call *again,* and now I've lost one of my own in a battle that could've been prevented. My emotions are reeling—that son of a bitch Adrian screwed us over royally! Now, Azrael is aware of Dani's blood and the power it holds—I can only imagine how many vampires will be hunting her down when Azrael decides to let the bastards loose.

As Lucian takes care of Dani, the intense pressure of guilt and responsibility crashes over me.

"Come on. We can't spend all night out here," Erik urges, extending his hand to help me up. As my brother, he's always been a steadfast presence in my life. With a heavy heart, I reluctantly tear my gaze away from him and glance down the deserted alley, where Adrian's lifeless form lies, grayed and decomposed, as is the fate of our vampire kin in the throes of true death.

I can't shake the disappointment and anger simmering within me, and as I take Erik's hand, I let out a heavy sigh.

"I need to take care of Adrian's body and..." I begin—feeling a deep sense of responsibility toward my younger brother despite his betrayal.

"Don't worry about it, Rhyland. I'll handle Adrian," Erik reassures me, his voice steady and resolute as he steps forward to take on the grim task. "Go inside and be with Dani. I'll join you as soon as I'm finished," he adds, giving me a reassuring nod.

At this moment, I am grateful for Erik's support, and with a curt nod, I turn my attention toward the looming challenge ahead: facing the wrath of my Angel.

RHYLAND

77

As I barge into Karma, the relentless pulse of the bass beats against my skull while strobes slice through the dim like a blade. I'm here for one reason—to track down Dani after that clusterfuck in the alley.

I walk into Lucian's office. "Where is she?" The words come out sharp, like a cracked whip.

"Relax, Rhy!" Lucian chuckles, holding up his hands in a placating gesture as I practically vibrate with barely contained rage. "Take a chill pill before you pop a blood vessel. Your little spitfire is safe and sound, probably scrubbing the crazy off in my deluxe shower as we speak."

I glare at him. "You think this is fucking funny, Lucian? Dani just watched our shitstain of a brother get murdered by that psycho. She's probably scarred for life!"

Lucian rolls his eyes. "Cry me a fucking river, Rhy. We both know Adrian got what was coming to him after the stunt he pulled. Karma's a bitch, and so was he."

I clench my fists, barely resisting the urge to punch the smirk off his face. "That's not the fucking point. Dani wanted to save that ass—*him*—to free his family's souls—her mother's. She's too goddamn good for all this."

Lucian snorts, shaking his head in disbelief. "Yeah, well, I hate to break it to you, but I don't think 'negotiating' was ever on Azrael's to-do list. Fucker is crazier than a shithouse rat on crack."

I take a deep breath, trying to rein in my temper. "I don't give a flying fuck what Azrael's agenda was. All I care about is making sure Dani's okay."

Lucian waves a dismissive hand, his trademark smirk slipping back into place. "Then go check on her, oh great and powerful alpha. I've got shit handled here—already working on scrubbing some of the security footage. Can't be too careful."

I shoot him one last glare before I'm hauling ass after Dani, my heart threatening to beat right out of my damn chest. I'm praying to every fucking deity out there that Dani's okay, that her unbreakable spirit and fiery resolve are still burning bright. Because if she's not... there'll be hell to pay, and I'll be the sorry son of a bitch footing the bill.

My fury at my screw-ups burns hot, but I can't deny Lucian's knack for slicing straight to the heart of the matter. And damn him for it. Adrian had it coming after what he pulled. There was no two ways about it, but I wanted to be the one to dish out his dues, not to watch him take the *true death.*

I prowl down the corridor, every footfall heavy with intent, toward Lucian's private sanctuary. Echoes of that night when I ended Max and his friends resurface like some twisted déjà vu. Without hesitation, I shove the door open and step into the dim. My eyes cut through the shadows, scanning for any trace of Dani.

"Dani?"

As I follow the sound of water trickling, a previously unnoticed door at the far end of the room catches my attention. I steel myself for whatever awaits on the other side and push it open. My eyes adjust to the sight, and I can't hold back my reaction to the unexpected scene that unfolds before me.

"What in the ever-loving fuck, Lucian? You twisted son of a bitch." The words roll through my mind directly to Lucian's through our mental link, laced with disbelief and admiration.

I step further into the room, my eyes widening in surprise and reluctant intrigue as I take in the sight before me. It's like I've stumbled into a fucking sex dungeon on steroids, every conceivable toy and piece of BDSM equipment laid out like some kinky buffet. Swings, whips, chains, floggers, leather—you name it, it's here, along with a collection of dildos that would make a porn star blush.

"Ah, yes," Lucian drawls in my mind, with smug satisfaction. *"Look who's discovered my little den of debauchery. Welcome to the pleasure palace, brother!"*

I shoot him a glare through our mental connection, trying to ignore the heat creeping up the back of my neck. *"Jesus Christ, Lucian. Do you ever think about anything other than getting your rocks off?"*

"Hey, don't knock it 'til you've tried it, Rhy. A little bit of kink never hurt anyone. Well, unless they wanted it to, of course."

I roll my eyes, but can't help how my gaze is drawn back to the array of toys and equipment. It's like a fucking car crash—I know I shouldn't look, but I can't seem to tear my eyes away.

"Feel free to take anything for a spin," Lucian offers, with innuendo. *"I promise, everything's cleaner than a virgin's conscience. My crew is very thorough."*

I scoff, shaking my head in disbelief. *"Yeah, I think I'll pass. Unlike you, I don't need a fucking arsenal of sex toys to get the job done."*

Lucian laughs, his tone full of mischief. *"Sure, sure. But let's be real, Rhy-Rhy—we both know you've got a kinky side. Don't be afraid to embrace it. Who knows? Maybe you'll find something to make your little firecracker's toes curl."*

I mentally flip him off. Lucian and his fucking sex dungeon. I swear, one of these days, I'm going to strangle him with one of those leather straps.

But even as I make my way back to Dani, I can't shake the images from my mind—the swings, the cuffs, the fucking whips. And God's help me, a part of me can't help but wonder what it would be like to use them on her, to watch her come undone beneath me as I—

No. Fuck, no.

I shut that train of thought down before it could go any further. The last thing I need right now is to be thinking with my dick. Dani needs me, and I'll be damned if I let her down again.

As I enter the adjoining room, my mind races with thoughts of Dani and what she's going through. She's always been so strong, so fucking resilient, but losing Adrian like that... It's enough to break anyone, even a fiery thing like her.

But that's where I come in. If there's even a chance that I can be the one to help put her back together, to show her that I fucked up and try to fix the broken pieces, then I'm sure as hell going to do it.

I push open the door to the bathroom, and I'm immediately hit with a wall of steam, the air heavy with the scent of jasmine and vanilla. And there, standing under the double shower like a fucking goddess, is Dani. The water cascades down her curves, highlighting every dip and swell, and I feel my blood run hot with desire.

I know I need to tread carefully here—she's in a vulnerable place, and the last thing I want to do is push her too far. But at the same time, I know that sometimes, the best way to heal is to let yourself get lost in sensation and forget the pain and the heartache, even if only for a little while.

So I strip off my clothes and step into the shower behind her, sliding my arms around her waist and pulling her back against my chest. She tenses for a moment, but then I feel her relax into me, her body molding to mine like it was always meant to be there.

"I'm sorry, Angel," I murmur, pressing my lips to the shell of her ear. "I'm *so* fucking sorry."

She shudders in my arms, and I tighten my grip, letting her know I'm here and not going anywhere. She presses her hand to my forearm, her fingers trembling slightly, and I feel my heart clench.

I trail my hands up her body, mapping out the curves and planes I always dream about. I cup her breasts in my palms, feeling the weight of them, the way her nipples pebble against my palms. She lets out a soft gasp, arching into my touch, and I know that no matter what happens next, I'll do whatever it takes to make her feel good, to chase away the darkness and the pain, even if only for a little while.

Because that's what you do for the people you love: You fight for them, even when they can't fight for themselves. And Dani? She's worth fighting for—always.

Finally, after what feels like an eternity, she speaks up, her voice barely a whisper. "I know you are," she admits, her words filled with an unspoken vulnerability. Dani's voice trembles, her fiery exterior cracking just a little, "I can feel your pain too. I-I just wish you hadn't fought with me and allowed me to give him my blood—this all could've been avoided." She pauses for a beat, "I'm sorry... for reacting that way. It's just... I wanted to help him, to save him. My Mother—" She takes a deep breath to regain her composure.

As I gently run my fingers through her soaked tresses, I can't help but be captivated by the feeling of wet silk against my skin. The vanilla scent of the shampoo she used fills the air, adding to the intoxicating mix of emotions coursing through me. Her crown is absent now, leaving behind the vulnerable and beautiful woman I can't help but be enamored with.

The words tumble out of Dani's mouth on an uneven breath, the revelation still raw. "I'm not blind—I see it in your eyes. No pardons for his kind of betrayal." She pauses, steadying herself. "But now, what's our play? Azrael's sitting pretty with the secret Seraphina swore should never fall into enemy hands." Her voice carries the weight of the predicament we're faced with, a hint of determination simmering beneath the uncertainty.

The icy tendrils of fear grip my heart; the same terror I know is coursing through Dani's veins. Her deepest, darkest secret is now in the hands of our most dangerous enemy.

I press my lips to her pulse point, feeling the frantic beat beneath my tongue. "I swear on my life, I will protect you, Dani. I will fight to my last fucking breath to keep you safe." My words are a solemn vow, a promise etched in steel.

"That bastard will never lay a finger on you or any of his minions. I won't let them get within an inch of you." My voice is low and fierce, brimming with unwavering determination.

I feel the tremble in her exhale, the fear still clinging to every fiber of her being, radiating from her mind like a distress beacon. It breaks my fucking heart to see her like this, so vulnerable and shaken to the core.

I can't resist the urge to tangle my fingers in her silky tresses, giving them a mischievous little tug. "Listen up, baby. I won't let a single fucking thing harm a hair on your head," I say, my voice caught somewhere between ironclad certainty and quiet tenderness. "I'll tear apart anyone who even thinks about messing with you."

A smirk tugs at the corner of my mouth as I lean closer, my breath hot against her ear. "And let me remind you, sweetheart—what have I told you about apologizing to me? I'm pretty damn sure I've made myself clear on that front countless times. Your feelings were valid."

She lets out a deep, tantalizing moan when I tug her hair, and my damn cock responds instantly. I know she's been on edge since I left her wanting more the other day. I was planning on punishing her by teasing the fuck out of her again, but now I have a whole new set of ideas—ones that only involve loving her and caring for her—giving her what she needs.

"Are we going to revisit that dazzling little lightning stunt you pulled off—the one you tried to pass off as a one-hit wonder?" she prods.

"Baby, I'm here for you. Right now, the only thing on my mind is making damn sure you feel safe and cared for. Whatever you need, I've got you. We'll get through this other shit later, okay? You're not alone. I'm right by your side every step of the way."

I take a deep breath, trying to rein in my swirling emotions. I know what I'm doing, even if I don't want to admit it to myself. I'm deflecting, plain and simple. This new power that's somehow awakened within me... It scares the ever-loving shit out of me. I don't understand it, I can't control it, and I sure as hell don't want to face what it might mean.

I can feel her body slowly unwinding, the tension seeping out of her as she allows the topic to drift away, at least for the moment. But I know my girl. Dani's not one to let things go easily. Before long, that brilliant scientific mind of hers will be itching to dissect every damn detail, to pick apart what happened and analyze it from every angle.

That's just who she is—a force of nature, relentless in her pursuit of understanding. It's one of the many things I fucking love about her. But for now, I'm content to hold her close, to be the rock she can lean on as she navigates the aftermath of this nightmare.

Dani stands firm, "I just need... I need you, Rhyland, but don't treat me like I'm going to shatter—I won't. I'll manage. But give me a moment here; it's...it's just a mountain of stuff to wrap my head around all at once," she says, her voice a mix of strength and the vulnerability of being swamped with overwhelming truths.

I squeeze her tighter in my strong arms, pulling her closer until there's no space between us. My nose grazes the soft skin of her neck as I inhale her intoxicating scent, letting it wash over me like a soothing balm.

"I've got you, sweetheart. I'm right here," I murmur against her skin, my voice a low rumble. "Whatever you need, whatever it takes to make you feel whole again—it's yours. Take whatever you need from me, baby. I'm all yours, body and soul."

The water continues to pour over us, the sound of our heavy breathing mingling with the rhythmic drumming on the shower tiles. My hands roam over her soaked body, and I can feel her trembling beneath my touch. I can smell her arousal and taste it on my tongue.

Her whisper cuts through the tension, a soft plea with yearning and the desperate wish to escape the torrent swirling in her mind. "Distract me," she breathes out. "Bite me, please. Make it all go away—the pain, the chaos in my head. I need you to take the reins, Rhyland." She tilts her head back, and her eyes search mine, silently begging for the reprieve only I can grant.

I smirk mischievously. Oh, she needs a distraction, does she? Well, lucky for her, distraction happens to be my specialty.

I lean in close, my voice low and playful, "Alright, Angel, you want me to take your mind off all this heavy shit? Consider it done. I've got more than a few tricks to make you forget your name, let alone anything else."

With a firm grip on her hair with one hand, I twist and pinch her nipples just the way she loves it with the other, causing little hisses of pleasure to escape from her. Her ass eagerly grinds against my rock-hard cock.

Tugging her hair more forcefully, I demand, "Come here, baby. I'm fucking famished."

Wasting no time, I sink my teeth into her neck, drawing her sweet, warm blood into my mouth. My eyes roll back in their sockets as the delicious taste overwhelms me. I swear she's gotten sweeter, if that's even possible.

Her body stiffens in surprise, and she sucks in a deep breath. Still, almost instantly, the sensation switches to one of pure ecstasy as my venom courses through her veins, flooding her entire being with a euphoria that only a vampire's bite can provide.

As I continue to pull her blood into my mouth, our moans mingle in the steamy confines of the shower, the sensual sounds echoing off the walls. Her taste is otherworldly, intoxicating me further with each draw. The warmth coursing through me is a welcome relief after the massive drain from summoning that lightning storm earlier.

Her hand snakes its way between our entwined bodies, finding my eager and insistent cock. The sensation of her soft hand against my hot, hard flesh nearly sends me over the edge. Before I can react, my hips instinctively buck, pumping into her tight grip as I continue lapping up her sweet, replenishing blood. The dual sensations are almost too much to bear, and I cling to the edge of my self-control.

Tearing my mouth away from her neck, I growl, "Fuck, Angel. You're driving me crazy." With a surge of strength and determination, I spin her and lift her effortlessly, slamming her back against the shower tiles. She releases an involuntary "oomph" at the sudden impact, which quickly morphs into a wanton moan as she wraps her legs around me.

Wasting no time, my mouth is on hers, eagerly claiming her lips and battling with her tongue, exerting my dominance as the primal need to possess her consumes me.

Breathless and hungry for more, I break away from our heated kiss just long enough to utter three little words, "Fucking. Beg. Me."

DANICA

78

The whirlwind of events leaves me reeling. In what feels like mere minutes, I've watched the door to finding my mother—and freeing countless others—slam shut. Adrian, my bright spark of hope, was ruthlessly taken from this world in a way he never deserved. To top it off, our greatest adversary now knows my deepest secret, meaning the vampire brigade and anyone else with a nose for intrigue will be on my scent, chasing me through all seven realms.

This new stone hasn't just handed me the universal code for communication; it also cranks up the emotions, feelings, and pain of every magical being around me to max. I felt Adrian's agony, both internally and physically, before he died. It was excruciating—like the stone made me experience every bit of his suffering firsthand.

When Azrael fled, I rushed to Adrian's body, channeling the Atherite Stone's power to no avail; his silence was deafening. I pleaded with any god that might spare a glance my way, tears and fury spilling out uncontrollably. But as reality set in, all that was left was to turn my seething rebuke to Rhyland.

Now, he throws himself into the battle to help me survive this storm. He's laying out his devotion, love, and remorse-like armor to shield and keep me standing. Deep down, I recognize the torment within him; he never intended for Adrian to die. It was rage, unbridled and fierce. But here he is, trying to make amends, showing me he's more than the fury that once overtook him.

The longing for his bite has become more than a desire; it's a chant that loops endlessly in my mind. I yearn for it, for him, with an intensity that borders on obsession. It's my calming salve, the singular force that can unwind the coiled tension within me like nothing else.

But Mother Nature's untimely entrance effectively dampened any activities Rhyland might be considering, no matter how much my hormones throw a full-blown, tempest-like tantrum. The raging internal battle is fierce, yet here I am, at the mercy of biology's impeccable timing.

The moment for revenge has arrived. It's time to watch and see how he'll respond.

"Not happening," I declare with unwavering conviction, locking eyes with him—my stare blazing with pure, unshakable will. His growl rouses my insurgent side, urging me to hold firm even as it kindles a separate hunger within me. "You won't win this one with a growl and a glare."

My breath hitches as he murmurs against my lips. "Angel, I'm losing control here. Tell me what it is you want."

"I—I can't right now," I stammer, the message clear in my head but tangled on the way out.

His brow furrows in confusion at first, and then he smells the air. A switch flips, illumination washing over his features as realization dawns—clear and unmistakable. Embarrassment creeps up hot and sudden at his recognition of my condition. It's one thing to deal with biology privately, but something else entirely when laid bare before someone else, especially Rhyland, in such a raw moment.

The dirtiest smirk crawls across his face. His eyes drag down my body and back up again, slow and deliberate, making it abundantly clear that he knows exactly what time of the month it is—and couldn't care less. Not even a little.

"You can't be serious." The words leave my lips, punctuating the absurdity of the moment—a question, a challenge.

His tone is laced with a teasing edge; the words practically ooze sarcasm, as sweet and thick as honey. "Hi. Have we met?" He tilts his head, that mischievous gleam sharpening in his eyes. "I'm a *vampire*, baby." He lets that word hang in the air, watching it land. "What do vampires love?"

My eyes blow wide, locked on him in pure disbelief. The sheer *audacity* of this man steals every word right out of my mouth. My brain short-circuits somewhere between *absolutely not* and *wait—is he actually into this?* Because Rhyland isn't just unfazed. He's not just tolerating the idea. The bastard looks genuinely *thrilled*.

"No. You can't—that's just—"

Effortlessly, Rhyland moves us to the shower bench—a mere blur. Once settled—I'm seated and Rhyland kneels between my legs—his question is direct and practical in its intimacy. "How many days are you in?"

"Two," I snap back quickly.

"And you're in pain."

I look at him, my nod loaded with a silent, 'Well, congratulations, Sherlock—cramps aren't exactly a secret womanly joy.' His perception might be sharp as a tack, but right now, it's just another reminder of the unwelcome guest cramping my style—and everything else.

Without a word, he yanks my thighs apart, baring me to his expert mouth. He nips at my inner thigh, causing me to buck on the bench. His tongue finds my clit, circling and sucking with urgency. A blush of embarrassment washes over me at the intimacy of the act.

Holy hell! Thank goodness I'm showered and not a heavy bleeder; otherwise, this would be a crime scene.

As good as it feels, every instinct tells me to push him away, to preserve some decorum. I don't know if I'm prepared to plunge into these forbidden depths just yet.

I gracefully close my legs and rise, heading back to the shower sprayer. Rhyland, ever attentive, encircles me with his strong arms, his skilled hands finding my breasts. He massages them tenderly, pinching my erect nipples as I release a soft moan. His lips and tongue dance along my neck, causing my body to melt into his embrace.

He trails his hand down to my clit, circling it slowly and gently with his fingers, testing me.

Suddenly, I sense Lucian's presence in my mind, his thoughts reaching out. There's a hint of jealousy, but he knows I belong to Rhyland. His thoughts project into mine, imagining himself with me—still, he can't help but appreciate the passion, wondering when he might find his own mate.

This cannot be fucking happening right now!

Amid my confusion and the exquisite pleasure Rhyland is bestowing, I try to connect with Lucian mentally. I focus on a different frequency—one I've never explored before. It's faint, but I sense it.

"Lucian?" I call out to him mentally. *"Why am I hearing you?"*

"Dani? What the hell? You can hear me?" His surprise is evident in his thoughts.

Panic washes over me, and I swiftly erect my mental walls, blocking him out.

My mind races, struggling to make sense of the unexpected connection.

And why now?

Rhyland must sense my little mental escapade. He stops, flips me around, and locks eyes with me. "What is it?"

I play the stupid card, "Nothing, just um—"

Rhyland gives me a pointed look, clearly not buying my attempt at a quick excuse.

"I'm just... not ready for you to..." I fumble for the words, heat climbing my neck. "You know. Not while I'm... while this is happening," I finally manage, gesturing vaguely downward.

"Hmm," he hums, threading his gentle hands through my hair. He's still not buying it, and I know I need to distract him. And what better time to dish out my payback for that bullshit edging game he left me in earlier? Two can play at this game.

I press my body against his, feeling the hard planes of his muscles slick from the shower. I tilt my head up, my lips brushing against his ear as I whisper, "There are other things we can do. Something that will make you forget all about your questions."

I lock eyes with him, a smoldering look promising a world of pleasure and sin.

"But first, I think we should finish getting cleaned up." My voice purrs as I reach for the soap. Lathering it between my palms, I drag my hands across his massive chest, shoulders, and arms.

Steam rises like a cloud of forbidden desires as the warm water cascades over us. My fingers trail down his chiseled chest, teasing and tempting. A mischievous grin crosses my lips.

His breath hitches, his desire tangible. "Oh, yeah? What've you got planned, baby?"

I rinse the soap from his chest and trail open-mouthed kisses down his neck, savoring the taste of him. I work my way lower, paying special attention to his hard nipples—flicking them with my tongue, biting gently. A groan rumbles through him as he tangles his hands in my hair, pulling me closer.

I gather more soap in my hands and wrap them around his hardness, stroking slowly. He moans with each movement. "Gotta make sure every inch of you is clean," I murmur against his skin, smirking at how quickly he falls apart for me.

His rough hands grab me, his kiss feral and demanding, his tongue claiming mine. My strokes become bolder, my touch teasing as I move faster.

He hisses as I cup his balls, sending jolts of pleasure through him. His reaction fuels my boldness.

"Fucking hell, baby," he grunts. "Keep stroking, just like—fuck—don't stop."

The suds froth with the friction, building as I work him faster. His mouth hangs open, his breathing ragged, his hips thrusting into my fist.

"You want to come, big boy?" I tease. "Want me to milk this big fat cock of yours?"

The dirty words spill from my lips, spurring him harder. Every muscle in his body draws tight, his need rolling off him in waves.

"Goddamn, yes." His voice is raw. "That filthy mouth is going to be the death of me."

A naughty smile plays on my lips as I stroke him faster. "You like your girl filthy? Going to paint me with your cum?"

He bucks at the image. "Fuck, yes, I want you to swallow it," he grits out. "I'm close, Angel. So *fucking* close."

Now it's *my* turn.

"Ow—my *hand!*" I gasp, selling it like I deserve an Oscar. "It's just so... cramped. What a shame." I pull away in one swift move, leaving him stranded right at the edge, chest heaving, breath ragged.

I flash him a wink and a grin dripping with pure evil as I slip out from under him. The look on his face—jaw slack, eyes wide, caught somewhere between shock and outrage—is worth every second. I bite my lip to keep from laughing, smugness settling over me like a crown.

"Oops." I blink at him, the picture of innocence. "Did I leave you hanging?" My smile is saccharine sweet, but the wicked gleam behind my eyes gives me away completely. "How *terribly* rude of me."

I turn my back to him like nothing happened, resuming my shower routine with the casual ease of someone who didn't just yank the rug out from under him mid-freefall.

The growl that tears out of him is *feral*—pure frustration tangled with a hunger that hasn't gone anywhere. It bounces off the tile walls and rolls straight down my spine. But when he finally speaks, there's a dark thread of amusement woven through the ragged edges of his voice, a low rumble of laughter vibrating deep in his chest.

"Fucking hell, woman," he grits out, his eyes narrowing as they lock onto mine. "Playing dirty, are we? I see how it is."

He shakes his head, a wry smile tugging at the corner of his mouth despite his obvious irritation. "Payback's a bitch, isn't it, baby?"

My grin stretches wider, eyes lit up with mischief and the unmistakable glow of victory. "Oh, you have *no* idea, babe," I purr, letting every word drip with challenge. "But don't worry. I'm sure you'll figure out how to... settle the debt."

His eyes flash—irritation and admiration crashing together in a combination that only makes the air between us hotter. "Oh, I'll settle it," he says, voice dropping to a low, lethal rumble that curls around me like smoke. "And when I do, you'll be *begging* for mercy, little girl."

The mood shifts like a record scratch, the playful tension evaporating in an instant. Rhyland towers over me, his eyes narrowing as he pins me with a look that sends a shiver down my spine. "I'm glad you had your little fun," he says, his voice low and dangerous. "Now, when you're ready to come clean about what went on up here..." He taps the side of my head, his touch gentle but firm. "I'll be waiting."

With that, he turns on his heel and leaves me alone, gaping after him like a fish out of water—my heart pounds in my chest, a mixture of excitement and trepidation coursing through my veins.

Fuck.

I lean against the wall, my legs about as reliable as wet paper. I can't keep this from him forever—the truth about my connection with Lucian is a ticking time bomb sitting right in the middle of my chest. The thought of telling Rhyland sends a wave of anxiety churning through my stomach.

How will he react? Angry? Jealous?

Oh, who the hell am I kidding? He's going to be *fucking furious.*

DANICA

79

A growl rips out of me—more urgency than anger—as I rinse off in record time and haul myself out of the shower. What's my play here? How the hell did Lucian worm his way into what's supposed to be a private, Rhyland-and-me-only mind link? That's not how this works. That's *never* how this worked. Something is wrong.

Could the new stone be amplifying my connections, casting a wider net, and pulling in every vampire within range? Honestly, I have no fucking clue. I'm a rookie fumbling through a game where no one bothered to hand me the rulebook. Whatever this is, none of the pieces fit together the way they should, and the not knowing is eating me alive.

Storming out, towel-clad, I hotfoot it after him. Planting my hands on my hips, I snap, feigning ignorance. "Come clean about what?"

Why am I dancing around the truth instead of laying it out?

He stares at me, ignoring my question.

Frustrated, I slap my hands on my thighs and whirl around, ready to bolt and throw on some clothes.

With vampire swiftness, Rhyland closes the distance in a heartbeat. He grabs my hair, spins me, and tugs just enough to lock my gaze with his.

"I want the fucking truth. Do you hear me?" Rhyland's eyes blaze with rage. "Where did your mind wander off to? I could sense your confusion—your fear." Rhyland growls.

My body stiffens, but I stay cool despite my pounding heart. "I..." Damn it, why is this so difficult? Just spit it out, Dani! "I don't know," I say, trying to sound casual, but the effort flops.

Rhyland's eyes narrow, sensing my fear despite my flimsy act. He knows me too well. Nothing gets past him.

"Don't lie to me, Dani. I can smell a lie on you. Now spill it; who were you talking to when I was," he grabs my pussy, "feeling you here?" His tone is menacing, and jealousy sparks in his eyes.

He's nailed the one thing that bugs me—spinning tall tales. And here I am, tangoing with untruths. But can I spill the beans? Is this dance all to shield Lucian?

"It was nothing, I promise! Just a random brainwave hit me out of nowhere." A half-truth—my words tumble out, a silent plea for him to let it go. But Rhyland, being the shrewd Viking vamp he is, isn't buying what I'm selling.

DAMN IT! What's tying my tongue in knots?

"Don't fuck with me, Dani," Rhyland growls, leaning in close enough that I can feel his breath hot on my face. "I know when something's off with you, so don't try to feed me any lies. Tell me the damn truth right now, or I'll get it out of you myself."

I inhale a lungful of resolve, weighing my next move. Confession might win me some mercy points, or I could keep up the charade and pray Rhyland's detective skills fail. With a resigned exhale, I settle for the truth.

"It was Lucian," I concede, staring at the wall as if it were the most fascinating sight. "Somehow, his thoughts and voice just... popped into my head. He was watching us, jealous—or so I gathered—before I shut that door in his mental face. I swear, it wasn't me inviting him."

The silence that follows feels like walking a plank blindfolded. I shuffle awkwardly under his looming presence until he breaks the quiet.

"Fuck, I knew it!" Rhyland explodes, letting go and storming across the room.

My eyebrow arches, and my arms wrap around my chest. He's so ticked he's practically drilling a path into the ground. "You knew what, exactly?" I toss back, frustrated.

"Nothing," he dismisses me, raking a hand through his locks.

This is where I draw the line. He can't just unload this and zip it like it's top secret. If I'm expected to lay it all on the table, he'd better be ready to join the sharing circle.

"So you're pissed because Lucian chatted telepathically with me—as if I dialed him into my headspace on purpose?" I cry out, my patience frayed.

"Yes," he bites out.

My mouth hangs open. "Seriously? Look, it's not like I summoned him to—"

In a flash, Rhyland's right in my face again. "You should've told me immediately, Dani," he growls. "Why am I always pulling info out of you? What Lucian did is screwed up, and you're covering for him?"

He's got a point. Maybe I should've clued him in, but come on, talk about bad timing. It's not exactly sexy to hit pause and say, 'Hold up, your bro's hitching a ride in my thoughts.' Total mood killer.

"I'm not his damn keeper, Rhyland. It caught me off guard—and considering you're bouncing around with a fuse shorter than a matchstick, that moment didn't feel like prime sharing time," I snap back.

"Oh? Would you have mentioned it if I hadn't cornered you?" Rhyland tosses back, full of accusation, giving me pause.

Would I have let him in on it or gone full lone-wolf detective as usual, letting my obsession with cracking the code get in the way of simple couple transparency?

"Exactly," Rhyland remarks, turning his back. "How can there be trust, any real depth between us, if you're holding back bullshit bombshells? It's supposed to be us against the world, Dani. How do we navigate this crazy if you're unwilling to share with me?"

Crap. He's right. Before I can stop them, the tears start falling. I've hurt him without intending to. Lucian is more than a friend; he's practically family. After his last little circus act, Rhyland almost went full Viking slaughterhouse on him. I feared Rhyland would go off the deep end over this latest psychic party crash.

Rhyland exhales heavily, looking beaten down. "I'm partly to blame here," he admits.

Surprised, I dab the tears. "How's this on you? How is his telepathic eavesdropping your fault?"

Rhyland wraps his arms around me, jerking my chin up to meet his gaze. "Because I should've been straight with you about how our blood plays out in humans. How we forge those mind links."

I lock eyes with him, seeking answers. That's when it clicks—the memory of that day in the woods, Lucian's blood, his plea for forgiveness. Apparently, they didn't cleanse me as thoroughly as they thought.

"Are you telling me *any* vamp's blood can do that mind-meld thing?" I connect the dots out loud.

Rhyland lays out the facts—it's not just about blood, but the relationship with the drinker. And it's more than psychic chitchat. The vampire gets it all, every quiver, every desire.

He spells it out: it's not just fear. It entwines with desire, too.

"Don't twist this into something it's not, Dani. What we have is written in the fucking stars. You're *my* mate, and that's a bond no one—nothing—can touch," Rhyland says, his voice absolute. "That's why, once we claim our mate, we keep our blood to ourselves and—"

"And not let someone else turn them into a personal snack bar," I finish for him, the pieces clicking into place. I exhale hard through my nose. "So why the hell didn't anyone tell me this?"

"I was banking on his blood being a bust, and I didn't want to even entertain the thought that he could mess with you." Rhyland's forehead thumps against mine, emotion in his eyes. "I prayed it didn't stick."

His distress twists my stomach into knots. The last thing I need is Rhyland fretting over Lucian and his invasive trick. I've gotten a crash course in psychic self-defense—I'll have to maintain my mental fortifications.

"We need better communication. Seriously, what's our next step? How long does Lucian's blood grant him access?" I prod for clarity.

Rhyland shakes his head, uncertain. "I don't know—it's uncharted territory. It takes a single drop."

He's got enough on his plate. And Lucian? He's not my type. I get that he acted to save me from the Grim Reaper, but knowing we've got a psychic peeper isn't sweetening the bitter aftertaste.

"This doesn't change anything between us," I assert. "I'm good at shutting him out, and I'll keep it that way until his vampire hotline fizzles. Maybe more of your blood could drown out his echo. It's been a while since I had..." Halting, I rack my brain to pinpoint the last time I had his blood.

Rhyland freezes, considering. "Maybe. Just swear you won't chat with him in your head. I get you have a soft spot for Lucian, but I don't like it. I know he's sorry for what he did. We've just been waiting to see if it kicked in." His hands sweep through my hair, his voice fervent. "Just swear, Dani."

Firm and resolved, I nod. "Yes, I swear. Now, can you please give me your blood so we can move on?" The words roll off my tongue, demanding and laced with impatience.

Rhyland's signature smile breaks through; his dimple is deep and charming. "Ask, and you shall receive. Just remember what this does to you." That message rings with a reminder and a warning.

His blood? It's sin, distilled to its essence. Facing what's to come, I'm either about to practice self-restraint or succumb like an overcharged hormone machine.

Trust Lucian to be the ultimate nightclub-owning vampire with a touch of thoughtful host. Lo and behold, what do I find when I rummage through the bathroom drawer? A stash neatly packed with all the essentials, including period underwear.

Who knew Lucian was so up with the times?

Once Rhyland and I swap our getups for something less 'Fae cosplay extravaganza' and more 'mortal chic,' we reach Lucian's office. The moment we step in, there's Lucian, arms raised in surrender.

"Whoa there, trigger! Before you go all 'pew pew' on my ass, let me say this mind-meld thing? Totally unintentional. Our brain signals got scrambled, capiche?"

I hold up a hand, cutting off his excuse. "Zip it, Lucian. Look, I appreciate you having my back in the spooky forest, but this 'sharing is caring' with our gray matter? One-time deal. My skull's in lockdown. That's how it stays."

Glancing at Rhyland, it's clear he's a second from going full Viking on Lucian. His knuckles are white, his fists like granite, and there is a storm inside him—the clash between brotherly affection and Lucian crossing *another* line.

Lucian holds up his hands placatingly. "All right, no harm done. But let me make one thing clear: this whole mishap? Not on my bucket list. Never was, never will be. Understand that."

I study him, searching for deception. Lucian seems sincere. I nod. "Fine. But from now on, keep your vampire mojo to yourself. My head's off-limits."

"Hey, no arguments here. Trust me, the last thing I want is a front-row seat to the Rhyland and Dani show."

I roll my eyes, but can't help the small smile. Even in a crisis, Lucian can't resist being a smartass.

Moving to practical matters, I look at Lucian. "Give me a phone, please. I need to connect with Emily and Damon—they're probably climbing the walls by now."

I'm itching to talk to my bestie. My life hit pause, and for all I know, my apartment's a spider haven, Emily's a cat lady, and my brother... well, who knows? Time's a weird beast.

Lucian, ever the dramatic benefactor, sends a phone spinning my way. "Catch," he calls. Reflexes don't fail me, and I grasp the device.

The phone is an enigma, cold and sleek—past meets future. It's like Apple's finest, given steroids and sorcery.

Realization shivers down my spine as I turn it in my hands. Time has been a trickster, warping and stretching. Now, this gizmo makes me realize just how far reality has pitched forward.

"Thanks," I say, thumbing through to dial Emily's number, praying to the gods of unchanged contact info. The line trills, "Come on, come on, pick up." I mutter, heart hammering. Another ring, "Please..."

Two more rings—then, a familiar voice, "Hello?"

"Emily!"

RHYLAND

80

I wanted nothing more than to punish her for the secret she'd tried to hide from me—for the way she'd nearly kept it all buried if it wasn't for me pushing the damn issue. The fact that Lucian had been the one to creep into her head, pulling off that unauthorized telepathic bullshit, has me on the fucking edge.

I lock eyes with Lucian, gaze fierce, as I stand over the chaos of his desk. Tension coils in my jaw, tight and ready to snap. "You never should've given her your blood," I growl. "Even if Dani were on death's fucking doorstep, we could've found another path. You don't have a damn clue what kind of fallout this might trigger."

Lucian flashes his patented 'I don't give a fuck' grin, lounging back in his chair, "Well, excuse me for not wanting to watch her kick the bucket. How was I supposed to know she had a one-way ticket to the pearly gates? I did what any devastatingly handsome and heroic vampire would do in that situation. And as for the whole mate thing, I tried to wait for you, bro. Knowing full well the possible outcome."

His careless jabs, designed to get under my skin, hit their mark. I can feel the beast inside me clawing to the surface, desperate to tear into him. "She's not your fucking responsibility, Lucian. You sticking your nose in could screw things up in ways you can't even imagine. You have no goddamn clue what this could mean."

Lucian's eyes gleam with mischief as he takes in my growing irritation. "Whoa there, Captain Overreaction! Are you seriously getting your panties in a bunch over a little bit of my blood? In case you haven't noticed, Dani is head over heels for you, you giant meathead. She's your mate, not some timeshare. So how about you dial back the possessive alpha male routine and realize that I'm not trying to put the moves on your girl? What happened tonight was a freak accident, plain and simple. It won't happen again."

That comment Dani dropped has my blood boiling. "Then why the hell would she say you're jealous, Lucian? What's got her thinking—or feeling that shit—with you, huh?"

Lucian pauses, carefully considering his next words. "Listen, I'm not entirely sure what Dani may have felt or heard, but there's a part of me that is... jealous. Not of you specifically, but of what you two have together. That connection, that bond... It's the kind of thing every vampire dreams of finding someday—a mate to call their own, you know?"

I understand it's the insane twist that none of us could have ever imagined. But now, here I stand, with the love of my life—my mate. It's what every one of us bloodsuckers hopes for, that one soul who can hold back the beast inside.

"So how about you climb down off your high horse and cut me some slack, you overgrown man-child," he says, rolling his eyes. "I'm not trying to steal your girl. That's not how I roll."

He's on the money. I've gotta rein in the rage, quit obsessing over bullshit that's dead in the water. Yet, this whole mate circus is uncharted territory, and my gut-deep protective streak for Dani ain't gonna quit. Lucian already stepped over the line once with intent, but this round was instinctual—I get that. "Good. Remember, you're skating on thin fucking ice from round one, Lucian. Just wanna drill it into your head so you're damn clear on my take."

Lucian waves his hand dismissively, "Yeah, yeah, got it. Message received loud and clear, chief."

Feeling the edge slip away, I sink into a chair and drag a hand down my face, the tension slowly easing out of my muscles.

Lucian smirks, "One more thing, big guy. I'm not just gonna sit on my ass and watch Dani go down in flames; you've got another thing coming. I've got a built-in 'damsel in distress' radar, and when it goes off, I'm not gonna let your possessive caveman bullshit stop me from swooping in to save the day. Capiche?"

He leans forward, resting his elbows on the desk, his eyes locked on me. "She means something to me, too, even if she's not my mate. I'll keep her safe whether you like it or not."

The itch to vault over this desk and put Lucian in his place in the pecking order is damn near irresistible. I grit my teeth hard, pulling back the tidal wave of anger. "This shit ain't a game, Lucian. Consider this a fucking warning—watch your step." The words rumble out, a snarl cloaked in a veneer of control, a threat lurking right under the skin.

"Dude, you've got more trust issues than a politician at a polygraph test. Dani needs all the backup she can get, and if you can't count on your own brothers, who the hell can you count on? Seriously, take a chill pill, alright?"

Before I can fire back, Erik strides in, cutting the tension. "What are you two idiots bickering about now?" He's got that knowing look like he can smell the drama from a mile away.

Lucian throws himself back in his chair, arms flying up. "Oh, you know, just the usual chaos. Rhyland's got his fangs in a knot because I had the nerve to save his girl's life." He gestures wildly. "The absolute audacity of me, right? The fucking ingratitude is astounding."

Erik sighs, shaking his head like he's dealing with two unruly toddlers. He settles into a nearby chair beside me, shooting Lucian a glare. "You're a fool. Never had much taste for rules, did you?"

"Oh, so it's totally cool for tall, dark, and stoic over here to play bodyguard and sensei to Dani, but the moment I try to lend a helping hand, I get a big, fat 'fuck you' for my troubles? How's that fair, huh?"

Without skipping a beat, Erik and I chime in perfect unison, "Because you're an asshole."

"*Wow*, really feeling the love here, assholes. You sure know how to make a guy feel special." He turns his attention back to his paperwork, waving off the tension in the room like a bad fart. "You know what? Screw it. You two can return to your little 'no girls allowed' clubhouse. I've got more important shit to deal with."

I can't help but roll my eyes. Classic Lucian, always playing the victim card when he gets called out on his crap. But as much as I hate to admit it, the bastard has a point. If I can trust Erik to watch Dani's back, then maybe I need to extend that same trust to Lucian, even if he is a walking, talking migraine.

I take a deep breath, trying to rein in my frustration. "Look, Lucian, I appreciate you looking out for Dani. I do. But you've gotta understand this whole mate thing... It's new territory for me. I can't help but be protective of her, especially after everything that's happened."

Lucian leans back in his chair, a smirk playing at the corners of his mouth. "Aww, look at you, being all mature and shit. I think I might just shed a tear." He mimes wiping away an imaginary tear, sniffling for added effect. "But seriously, I get it. You're in uncharted waters here and scared of losing her. Believe me, I know the feeling."

I arch an eyebrow, not entirely buying this sudden shift. "Do you?" The words come out slow, measured—like I'm waiting for the catch.

He nods, his expression turning uncharacteristically somber. "Yeah, man. I mean, I may not have a mate of my own, but I know what it's like to care about someone so much that the thought of losing them makes you want to tear the world apart. It's fucking terrifying."

We stare at each other momentarily, a silent understanding passing between us. Then, just as quickly as it appeared, the moment is gone, and Lucian's signature smirk is back in place. "But hey, enough of this sappy shit. We have a world to save and a damsel to keep out of distress. So, what do you say we bury the hatchet and get back to being the badass motherfuckers we are?"

I can't help but chuckle, shaking my head in amusement. "You're a real piece of work, you know that?"

Lucian grins and gives me a wink. "And you wouldn't have me any other way, big bro."

Erik digs into his pocket and tosses a small object in my direction. Instinctively, my hand snaps out, snatching it from the air. I roll it between my fingers, a flicker of recognition in my eyes. "Found this on Adrian—he was clenching it tight."

"Is this—is this what I think it is?" I demand, surprise overtaking me.

Erik nods, "I believe it is."

I swallow hard, pushing past the lump in my throat. "How the hell?" I narrow my gaze, growing more determined to unearth the truth.

"Guess this sheds light on his hasty exit," Erik remarks dryly, the understatement highlighting his inherent stoicism.

Dani bursts through the door, her grin fucking radiant enough to light up a continent. "Emily's on her way over," she pants out, teetering on the edge of excitement. "Girl time is long overdue, so I'm gonna need you gentlemen to occupy yourselves with... whatever manly endeavors you've got on the docket."

I spring to my feet and bolt to her side in an instant. Clamping my hand around her waist, I yank her toward me, "We gotta hash out some shit about Azrael—" I start.

"Can this please take a rain check? It's been ages since I've seen Emily—I have to see her, Rhyland." I start to argue, but then she stands on her damn tippy toes, sucks my bottom lip into her mouth like she owns it, and says, "Please?"

Fuck, this woman is gonna be the end of me. How the hell am I supposed to say no to her, to *that?* My cock is still rock solid from her little teasing, never fully softened from our earlier encounter.

"Fine. Afterward, we've got serious shit to talk about," I admit reluctantly.

Her face brightens as she turns to leave again. I snag her wrist and pull her back into me, a soft "oompf" escaping her lips. Those honey-gold eyes find mine, and I hold her there. "Don't stray too far—stick around this bar, will you... Please?" I press my mouth to hers before she can argue.

"I promise," she breathes. And then she's gone, spinning on her heel and darting out the door before I can blink.

DANICA

81

Perched at Club Karma's bar, my foot's rhythmic tapping broadcasts my impatience. The phone call's barely over, and the anticipation of reuniting with Emily has me practically vibrating in my seat.

Dressed in a sultry little black ensemble found in Lucian's secret stash, I feel both sexy and like I'm in my own skin—a familiar echo of my style. Knee-high boots complete the look.

Concealing my crown with a thought, I sit engulfed in emotions—a whirlwind of chaos clashing within me, unseen yet overwhelming.

Adrian's loss weighs on me like a stone in my chest, and now dealing with Lucian's blood and our telepathic link is a headache I didn't sign up for. Every thought of the night sharpens the sting of guilt and regret. Combine that with the anticipation of reuniting with my best friend, and I'm teetering on a razor's edge of raw nerves.

Oh, and let's not forget about Rhyland and the delectable revenge I served up. The look on his face? Priceless. I've got that memory filed away for safekeeping. And I just know he's plotting his retaliation for when Aunt Flow packs her bags. The thought of what he might have in store sends a tingle of excitement through me, and I can't help but grin like the Cheshire Cat.

Can you blame me for feeling triumphant? After all the times he teased and edged me, it was about time I gave him a dose of his own medicine.

But I'm not naive. I know there will be consequences for my stunt. And you know what? Bring it on. The anticipation of his revenge is almost as delicious as the act itself.

So, Rhyland, my love, my mate, my partner in all things naughty and nice... Game on.

I catch the bartender's eye, signaling for another drink. The alcohol burns a fiery path down my throat, but it's nothing compared to the inferno raging inside me, an all-consuming need threatening to devour me whole.

Damn, Rhyland and his sexy vampire blood. It's like liquid Viagra, igniting every nerve ending in my body with an insatiable hunger. Indeed, there was a distinct zing, an added kick to his taste this time around. I can feel it coursing through my veins, a pulsing, throbbing ache that settles deep in my core, making me squirm on the barstool—anything to counter Lucian's blood, which seems set on sticking around like an unwanted parasite.

I cross my legs, trying to find some semblance of relief, but it's like trying to put out a wildfire with a water pistol. Every brush of fabric against my skin is torture.

After months in Luminara's magical embrace, the contrast hits—I've missed the mortal world, its pulsing music, and its vivid chaos more than I would have guessed.

As my eyes sweep across the club, it's impossible not to notice security has ramped up since my last visit. Shadowy figures indulging in illicit sips from donors are absent tonight. In fact, I don't see one vampire.

I wonder if it's just an off night for Karma or if something else is at play beneath the veneer of tranquility.

Slamming back the last of my drink, I scan the crowd. Suddenly, like a gust of fresh air, Emily whirls into the scene. She hones in on me with precision. I'd pick her out of a lineup with my eyes closed. Time's etched its story a little deeper into her features, casting her in the light of a seasoned thirty-something—still gorgeous, but now with an added layer of fierceness.

The moment we're within arm's reach, it's all systems go for the most epic of bear hugs. We clutch each other with a ferocity that spells 'soul sisters' in a language only we understand.

"Oh my god, Emily!" I sigh, steeped in raw emotion, joy, and relief. "I have missed you so much!" We stay entwined until we need to truly see each other. I slacken my grip and step back to drink in her changes.

Emily's vibrant presence is undeniable. Her blonde hair is streaked with pastel rainbows, and her fire-engine red lipstick makes her electric blue eyes pop. She's a burst of color and life.

"Holy shit, babe—did you start training with the Avengers or something?" Emily gapes, eyes wide with exaggerated disbelief. "Look at you, walking around here jacked like you just graduated from superhero boot camp!"

I chuckle, "Guess I owe it to a diet of twigs and berries and my own smokin' personal trainer—a total Matrix makeover." Clasping her hands, excitement bubbles over. "Oh my god, it's insanely good to see you!"

"Okay, you need to start talking right now," Emily demands, eyes lighting up with barely contained nosiness. "You ghost us for five whole years—just disappear off the face of the earth—and now you're back looking like that? Start spilling everything. And I mean *everything*—like, is the person responsible for all those gains stupidly gorgeous or what?"

The whole time-hopping between realms thing is a cosmic mindfuck that makes my head spin. According to my watch, barely a month has passed, which means the portal jumping must be tethered to *my* timeline—not whatever calendar the realms are running on.

I visualize Erik and nearly laugh—good old Mr. Stoic. There's no denying his looks, but he's not my type. But Emily and Erik? Now, that's a thought. My inner cupid does cartwheels. "He's a solid ten," I comment with a playful wink. "Six-one, chiseled like he's from an ancient myth, and rocking silver hair with a serious vibe. But trust me, he's strictly no-nonsense."

Emily rolls her eyes. "Ugh, cut the cautionary bullshit, will you? I'm dying for a hit of that supernaturally spicy romance action in my life."

Laughter bubbles out, a reminder of the good old days with Emily. God, how I've missed her sharp wit and risqué humor.

"You've met him, Em. Remember? And Erik's not the only eye candy in the eternal aisle," I hint mischievously. "Not sure about his stance on casual hookups, though—you've got Lucian to consider..."

Emily's grin spreads like wildfire. "Oh, right. He's the guy who took me home that night or whatever. Hold on—" Her face scrunches, nose wrinkling like she just caught a whiff of something rotten. "*Lucian?* The night king who used to run this place?" She waves a dismissive hand. "He reeks of fuckboy energy. And I'm not talking about his revolving bedroom door—I'm talking about *nail-me-to-the-wall*, write-sonnets-about-it, legendary kind of love. The total sweep-you-off-your-feet saga, like what you've got with Rhyland."

A warm smile spreads across my face as I look at Emily. Being in love with Rhyland is nothing short of a miracle—an epic, once-in-a-lifetime kind of story—and I'd want nothing less for my best friend. But her words pull a thread in my mind, rewinding to that quiet ache I felt from Lucian. That unspoken longing for someone of his own. The thought lingers, tugging at something deeper. How does vampire mateship even *work*? How did Rhyland and I end up tangled in something so ancient and cosmic?

"Honestly, girl, if only I had the recipe to give you this fiery passion and deep connection. It's like a thunderbolt to the soul—you know it when you feel it vibrate through every part of you."

Emily waves her hand dismissively. "Alright, enough with the romance crapola—I want the nitty-gritty, the down and dirty. Spill it, girl. What the hell went down in that otherworldly neck of the woods?"

I let the story unravel, spilling every last detail to Emily. Five drinks and a slew of astonished exclamations later, she's fully briefed, her mind swirling with 'oh my gods' and 'holy shits.'

"Now that we're back, Azrael's slipped the leash again. I had to bring him back." I explain the gravity of the situation. "Next on the agenda? Aquaria seems like the logical stepping stone."

Emily's jaw unhinges. "Okay, wow," she breathes. "That is a seriously unhinged amount of chaos to unpack." The energy rolling off her is practically vibrating. "Babe, Azrael is not someone you want to play games with."

"Yeah, tell me about it."

The conversation shifts, focusing on my brother. "How's Damon doing? I've tried his number, but it's a dead end."

Emily knocks back her shot with finesse, then slams the glass down. "Oh, girl, he's good—real good. After you left, he flipped your folks' house and jetted off on some 'Eat, Pray, Love' bullshit to find himself. Last I heard, his soul-searching ass was chillin' in Bora Bora, probably getting sunburned. And, believe it or not, he's hooked up with some beach babe. Look." She flashes the pics at me with a gossipy grin.

Peering down at her phone, there's Damon—grinning, looking every bit the embodiment of joy beside a stunning girl against a picturesque backdrop. A smile pulls at my mouth, and I feel a sting of tears at the happiness in his eyes. I'm relieved and thrilled to see Damon content.

Emily leans in, emphasizing every word. "He thinks you're out kicking ass on some job venture—that's the line I've been feeding him." She gives a conspiratorial wink. "He knows how much of a workaholic you are, so he's not sweating it. He's living it up."

The tears spill, tracing warm paths down my cheeks. The knowledge that Damon is chasing happiness tugs at something deep within, unlocking a wellspring of emotion. It's a mix of joy for him and an acute sense of the distances life creates.

Noticing the tears, Emily quickly nips them in the bud with her mix of soft heart and sharp tongue. "And hey, no waterworks, okay?" She dabs my eyes gently. "Keep your angel-freakish eyes dry for me, alright? And just for the record, I moved into your place. I've been keeping up with the rent and everything. Why shell out for a second pad when yours is top-tier?" She punctuates with a playful wink.

With a teasing grin, I laugh. "Absolutely. My pad—galaxy away from your joint in comforts." My affection for Emily swells—her thoughtfulness and her ability to lift my spirits are irreplaceable.

Emily keeping her number unchanged just on the off chance I'd come crawling back? That's some next-level best friend intuition right there. She probably marched straight into the phone store and said, 'Keep the line hot, folks; she'll dial me from another dimension.'

"So, what's the latest in Emily's world?" I inquire, shifting gears to catch up.

Emily signals the bartender for a refill, her enthusiasm undimmed. "Oh girl, you won't believe the circus town this place has turned into," she muses, leaning closer. "Freakin' werewolves are strutting their stuff out in the open now! Just popped up like daisies right after you took your little sabbatical. Claiming territories like it's 1862—Homestead Act! Oh, and witches, too—they're not just for Halloween anymore!"

I swallow hard at the mention of werewolves—a stark reminder of the heartache, the brutal loss of my parents. I push past the discomfort, and try to focus on the other bombshell.

"Witches?" The word hangs, charged with electricity, sending my thoughts into a frenzy.

"It's a whole new level of batshit here. And they've slapped stringent new laws on us, targeting this place. No more open feedings at Karma, hence the beefed-up security." Her eyes gleam as she nods to the bouncers.

That *aha* moment dawns. "So that's why I'm not swatting vamps away—my blood being their crack deal."

"Yup. The world's done a full one-eighty since you took your jaunt through the Twilight Zone. It's like Seattle turned into Diagon Alley—witch shops sprouting up faster than Starbucks, covens rolling deep like the new neighborhood watch. Werewolf packs are out here claiming territory, basically acting as their own law enforcement minus the badge. The whole thing plays out like a reality show nobody asked for but can't stop watching. And meanwhile, the government is scrambling to slap legislation on all of it under the guise of 'equality.'"

"Shit." The word falls out of me on a breath, equal parts wonder and disbelief. Everything has shifted—tilted on its axis into something I barely recognize. And somewhere in the middle of all of it, I'm left standing here trying to figure out where the hell I fit.

"Come to the table in the back. Bring Emily with you." Rhyland's rich voice booms within my skull, nearly startling me.

"Get a move on, girl. Looks like the high court has summoned us." With playful sarcasm, I toss the words over my shoulder.

Emily scoops up our cocktails with an eye roll. Together, we make our way through the club. In a dimly lit corner, like Norse gods, sits my man—all dominance and allure—flanked by the equally imposing figures of Lucian and Erik.

RHYLAND

82

We've claimed a booth in the darkest corner of the club, and I watch like a predator as Dani and Emily sashay their way over. Dani's got that tipsy swagger, her steps all out of sync, and giggles spilling out of her—it's hot as hell. She's lit just right for the dirty shit I've got planned. The girls reach our table, and Dani slams her drink down like she owns the place.

"Gentlemen," she nods, her eyes finding mine, that sassy grin on her lips. "You summoned, *Viking Lord*?"

Christ. The way she purrs *Viking Lord* with that seductive lilt and those devastating eyes dragging me under—it's taking every ounce of restraint I have not to throw her over my shoulder like the feral, possessive bastard I am and remind her exactly who she belongs to.

After what she pulled in that shower, payback is more than warranted. Dani loves to push—and I push back harder. Always. "Oh, I summoned you, alright," I growl, holding her gaze with dark promise. "Sit." I pat the space beside me—not a request. Not even close.

Lucian takes one look at them and his expression cycles through annoyance, disbelief, and unholy amusement in about three seconds flat. "Oh, fantastic. It's the Sloshed Sisters." He crosses his arms, surveying the carnage. "Okay, I need a full damage report—how many drinks deep are we? And before you answer, know that I *will* be judging you." He pauses, tilting his head. "Actually, scratch that, I'm already judging you. How are you both still vertical?"

Emily raises her voice, words slurring together like a drunk text, "Seriously? Who's keeping score at this point? What do we look like, mathematicians?"

Lucian's smirk goes full voltage. "You're right, you're absolutely right." He holds up his hands in surrender. "Math is hard. Especially when your blood alcohol level *is* the math."

I can't help but chuckle, enjoying the show. It's not every day that I get to see Dani let her hair down like this, and even though I should be concerned about her level of intoxication, I can't help but find it adorable. There's something about seeing her so carefree and uninhibited that makes me want to... take her hard and claim her repeatedly.

Whispering in her ear, "Keep this up, sweetheart, and you might find yourself at my mercy. Wouldn't that be a predicament?" I tease, a sly smile playing on my lips as I hold Dani's gaze with confidence and challenge.

She shoots me a playful glare, her cheeks flushed from the alcohol (and maybe a little something else). "Oh, please. Like you're one to talk, Mr. 'I can drink an entire liquor store and still bench press a Buick.' Besides, we're just having a little fun. No harm, no foul."

I lean back in my seat, a smirk tugging at the corners of my mouth. "Oh, I'm all for a little fun, baby. But let's say I have a different kind of party in mind."

Lucian makes a gagging noise, pretending to stick his finger down his throat. "Ugh, get a room, you two. Some of us are trying to keep our dinner down over here."

I flip him the bird, not taking my eyes off Dani. "Jealousy is a disease, Lucian. Get well soon."

He laughs, shaking his head. "Please. Like I'd ever be jealous of you two lovebirds. I prefer my women with a little less 'happily ever after' and a little more 'happy ending,' if you catch my drift."

I roll my eyes, but can't help but chuckle.

I pull Dani closer to me and gently trace my hand up her exposed thigh. She takes in a sharp breath, clearly aroused by the combination of the drinks, my blood, and our earlier activities. She's not fooling me. "Are you girls all caught up?"

With another tilt of her cocktail, Dani confirms, "Yup, just like no time's passed. Emily's clued in on everything."

"Good, that means we can speak without any bullshit filters," I state.

Dani nods, then waves to Emily. "Go ahead. Tell 'em everything you dumped on me. Get these guys up to speed."

Lucian's expression is puzzled. "Fill us in on what exactly? What the hell's going on?"

Emily starts laying out the whole situation in our realm. The shake-ups with the werewolf packs and their territories, the witches popping up like weeds, and the fresh crop of rules, especially in sin havens like Karma.

Erik finally chimes in, his tone cool as steel, "We were just informed of this ourselves—it was only a matter of time before all things supernatural revealed themselves."

Lucian runs his fingers through his golden blonde hair, his brow furrowing in frustration. "Yeah—it makes perfect sense why my club has taken a dive—the money I've lost, the drop in clientele."

Lucian was in the middle of grilling his club partner over the drop in crowd numbers. His partner was trying to trace every change that had occurred during our five-year absence. These new asinine laws were clamping down on any real fun, scaring regulars away. And to top off this crap fest, the witches are stirring up a whole heap of trouble, making everyone edgy as hell.

"There's something else," Emily says, and our heads snap up in unison like we're on puppet strings. "Get this—Azrael, Mister Tall-Dark-and-Drink-Your-Blood, crowned himself king of the fang parade because the vamp council vanished. Now he's sitting pretty on his self-made throne. No one's throwing shade or challenging him. He's practically BFFs with the witchy cliques." Her voice tightens, and it's clear the supernatural political climate just got more interesting—or dangerous.

It figures. Once the real dangers are gone, trust Azrael to snatch control. This gets me thinking—what happened to the council? Were they really taken out?

"Where's he hiding out?" I press Emily, "Same shithole?"

Emily tosses out the info like she's dealing cards, "Yes. And as far as I know, not even the big shots in suits are giving him side-eye. The guy waltzes onto live TV, feeds everyone some grade-A bullshit about 'protection' and 'mortals need not fear,' and—bam! He's got new laws popping up. It's like he's preaching the vampire's Ten Commandments, and everyone's nodding along. Guess the fangs and charisma combo does wonders. The whole thing is so damn theatrical—you half expect him to take a bow and disappear in a puff of smoke." Emily rolls her eyes, skeptical with every word.

"Okay, now that we're all caught up on the latest episode of 'Vampire Dickwad Azrael and the Shitshow That Is the New World Order,'" Lucian chimes in with his usual snark. He looks knowingly at me, his eyebrows practically waggling off his face. "Don't keep the lady waiting. Show her what you've got, and I don't mean the 'impressive' equipment you're packing below the belt."

DANICA

83

I can't help but roll my eyes at Lucian's crude attempt at humor. Seriously, does everything have to be a dirty joke with this guy? But I'd be lying if I said I wasn't curious about what Rhyland has up his sleeve.

Rhyland reaches into his pocket, his expression uncharacteristically serious as he pulls out a small velvet pouch. "Adrian was holding this when Erik disposed of his body," he says, his voice low and grave.

Clutching the item, a strangled sound threatens to escape as I grapple with the tidal wave of realization. The black stone, nestled within the confines of a silver ring, holds a presence as chilling as it is significant—Azrael's ring. Adrian made a last-ditch effort to arm us with an advantage, perhaps even a parting gift swiped before his untimely end. Adrian paid the ultimate price, and it wasn't for nothing; his final act, a testament to his desire to aid us, now rests heavily in my grasp.

The question dangles in the air with confusion. "How?"

The word barely leaves my lips, but it carries the full weight of everything unfolding in front of me. The stone, its tie to Azrael's power—none of it makes sense yet, and the implications spiral through my mind like smoke I can't grab hold of. I'm grasping for answers in the dark, and the dark isn't giving anything back.

There's some major supernatural sleight of hand at play, and it's not the kind that comes with a handbook. "I mean, how did Adrian get this off him?"

"How indeed," Erik agrees beside me.

Lucian lifts his shoulders in a shrug. "Beats me, but I've got a sneaking suspicion that Mr. Tall, Dark, and Douchey might have a plan B—something to keep his batteries charged, if you know what I mean."

Lucian leans back, resting his arms on the back of the seat. "I mean, think about it. We were out of the picture for, what, three years?"

"Five," I correct him.

Lucian looks frazzled for a second, then continues. "Right, five. According to the timeline of terror. Who knows what kind of freaky rituals or unholy alliances he could've cooked up during that time? For all we know, he could be siphoning power from some ancient, eldritch horror."

Rhyland nods, his face serious. "Could be. We've been off the grid for quite a stretch; loads can go down in that time. Even more so when dealing with a sly bastard like Azrael."

I shudder at the thought of Azrael allying with an even greater evil. As much as I hate to admit it, Lucian might be onto something.

So, if we've managed to disarm Azrael of his shadow whips and shadow demons by stealing the Soul Stone, it stands to reason that he's been left significantly weakened. This was his primary weapon.

Without it, he's like a snake without venom, a lion without claws. He's still dangerous, cunning, ruthless—but he's lost his edge, that terrifying aura of power that made him seem almost invincible.

It's like what happened when I took Amara's stone—one second she was this un-stoppable force with compulsion at her fingertips, and the next she's just... a bitch. Still dangerous, sure, but not the untouchable nightmare she'd been before.

"So, what you're saying is that Azrael might have some new secret weapon or power source we don't know about?" I ask, my brow furrowed in concern.

Emily, always the one with a quick answer, barely pauses. "Witches," she declares, as if unveiling the climax of a murder mystery she's solved in her head ages ago.

I shake my head, the fog of confusion pounding at my temples. "Witches—How? What do you mean?"

I press on, unwilling to let the topic drop. How could witches imbue Azrael with formidable power? This is my first real introduction to the supernatural's chessboard of witchcraft, and I'm desperately trying to catch up with the rules of this arcane game.

"Witches hold immense power, Little Huntress." Erik's silver eyes lock onto mine, his tone carrying the weight of someone who's seen centuries of it firsthand. "Especially when—"

"Yeah, yeah, Professor Fang." Emily tosses her rainbow-streaked blonde locks back and cuts him off with a cocked eyebrow, claiming the floor without an ounce of apology.

"Okay, strap in because shit's about to get Hogwarts-level weird." She holds up a finger. "These spooky bitches have their own little clubs, right? And each one comes with its own brand of freaky-deeky powers."

Emily rattles off the witchy roster like she's reading a supernatural lineup card. There are the illusionists—bitches who can make you question your own eyesight with their shadow tricks. Then there's the coven that treats ghosts like personal interns, running errands from beyond the grave. Can't forget the pyromaniacs who get off on setting shit ablaze. And the emotional terrorists who can have you sobbing into your pillow with a single look, weaponizing fear and misery like it's a fine art. The flesh-warpers take body horror to a whole new level—think plastic surgery by way of a nightmare. And the seers? They're the ones pulling strings from behind the curtain, watching your every move before you even make it.

Emily pauses, sucking in a breath, her expression caught somewhere between genuine awe and her signature sarcasm.

"All these covens with their tricks—rituals, blood magic, pacts with the devil, and hocus-pocus potion brews—are out in the open now. It's like Salem said, 'Fuck it, full speed ahead.' But here's the part that's got everyone talking—rumor has it something big is coming. Some kind of massive spell that's going to shake everything to its core."

Erik grunts—the kind of sound that says he's either heard this a thousand times over or he's just categorically done with witches as a whole.

Emily raises another shot glass in a mock toast, a smirk pulling wide across her face. "Welcome to the supernatural shit show of the twenty-first century, ladies and gents. Ain't it a blast?"

I sit here, mouth slightly open, gobsmacked from the sheer avalanche of information she just unloaded on us like it was nothing. A beat of stunned silence passes before I find my voice again.

"Okay, hold up." I blink, shaking myself out of it. "How in the *hell* do you know all of this?"

Because I'm somewhere between genuinely impressed and mildly terrified that my best friend has a PhD in witchy Wikipedia that I knew absolutely nothing about.

"Look, it's simple," Emily huffs, smirk firmly in place. "I've got this friend, Sable. The girl is absolutely *unhinged* for all this magical shit. Like, obsessed. She's been dying to buddy up with one of these witchy covens since forever. There's a whole mess of them out there—way more than I can keep track of, and frankly, I've got better things to do with my brain cells. But if there's even a *whisper* about where and when this ritual throwdown is happening, Sable's the one who'll know. That girl's got her ear to every supernatural grapevine and her nose buried in every spellbook from here to the Cascades." She pauses, taking a drink. "I'll get it out of her."

Lucian leans back, leveling Emily with an appreciative look, that signature shit-eating grin tugging at his mouth. "Has anyone ever told you that you are *spectacularly* terrifying? Like, seriously—no fangs, no supernatural upgrades, and yet you're out here hoarding secrets like a doomsday prepper hoards canned beans. I gotta say, I'm a *little* turned on and a *lot* impressed."

Emily's face twists like she just swallowed something rancid, her nose scrunching up as she looks Lucian up and down with pure, undiluted revulsion.

"*Ew.* Dial it back, Fang Boy." She shakes off the visible cringe and straightens up. "*Anyway*—When the world decides to go full Jumanji on your ass, you make it your goddamn business to know what's lurking in the dark. Knowledge is power, or whatever fortune cookie bullshit they slap on motivational posters. So yeah, I've been stockpiling every scrap of witchy and werewolf trivia I can get my hands on." Her expression sharpens, all humor draining.

Rhyland locks onto Emily with intensity. "And this shitstorm the covens are brewing—it's got to be tied to dragging Moretemis into our realm. The Shadow demon. That's got to be the endgame."

Erik's voice cuts through. "A barrier of that magnitude demands an extraordinary expenditure of energy." His tone is clinical, measured. "It would require a sacrifice—one drawn from a being of considerable power."

"*What?*" The word punches out of me before I can stop it.

Emily holds up a hand, a slow grin creeping across her face like she's savoring every second of being the most informed person in the room. "Chill out. If there's so much as a whisper about where and when this thing is happening, Sable will sniff it out. That girl is practically a bloodhound for this shit." She taps her temple. "I'll get us what we need."

DANICA

84

The decision was unanimous—a hard pass on prematurely rolling out the welcome mat for good ol' Morty—inviting that shadow demon to the party? That's like throwing gasoline on a bonfire. Nope, we're hunkering down to ride out this ritual rodeo, sorting the sinister from the sorcery before he gets wind of the shenanigans brewing in our backyard.

Because let's face it, playing with dark magic is one thing; dealing with an ancient shadow-lover with a penchant for soul-snacking is on a whole other level of 'nope.' We've got our hands full untangling this witchy web, and the last thing we need is him crashing the soiree, turning our tactical retreat into a full-blown sprint for our lives. So it's locking shields and sharpening wits until I can check off my stone-grabbing to-do list—with or without the confetti.

After four days of hitting dead ends, we've scored a jackpot of intel. Thanks to Emily and Sable's sleuth skills, we've snagged a juicy snippet of the witchy world's best-kept secret—a location. And the kicker? These witches are shopping for none other than a vampire for their grand sacrificial shindig.

Oh, but the plot thickens—they're not on the prowl for your garden-variety night-walker. Nope, these spellcasters want the crème de la crème—a vampire with a pedigree, someone dancing the eternal moonlit waltz for centuries, maybe even millennia—the kind of ancient blood that doesn't just whisper history; it roars it.

Well, game on. It's time to crash their party and rewrite the guest list.

Over the last few days, Rhyland and I have dissected and pondered pressing issues, including the mysterious Soul-Tie situation. Rhyland assures me that the mating bond we solidified is essentially the same—our souls are already knotted together. I figured it might be wiser to seek an expert on this matter. He's on board with the idea, so we tabled the discussion for another time.

Lucian and Erik took a field trip to the Obsidian Enclave—the supernatural equivalent of an ancient library—snatching up textbooks on Aquaria and the other realms. All in hopes that I'll have a solid reference to whip up a portal when the clock's ticking down to showtime. The elusive Book of Shadows was the only book they couldn't get their hands on.

I studied my ass off with Rhyland and Sable. Thank the gods, they can both read Latin because Google Translate was not going to cut it for this one.

Aquaria is a realm straight out of a supernatural Atlantis. Ruled by Queen Undine, this watery paradise is a mosaic of vibrant coral reefs, bioluminescent caves, and mystical creatures that would make Ariel's jaw drop. The Merfolk, Selkies, Pirates, Sirens, and Krakens call this place home, each adding their unique flavor to the magical melting pot.

We've made my place—or Emily's place now—our HQ. Emily's in the guest room to give Rhyland and me some couple's bubble space while Lucian and Erik are bunking at the club. Our daily pow-wows have turned into a routine blood drive with me as the star donor for Erik and Lucian; it's second nature now that I have the proper equipment, ensuring they are well-sunscreened.

"So, the ritual is being held at Thornewood Castle," Sable tells us over the kitchen island.

Despite the grave news, Sable's petite punk-rock vibe—bubblegum pink hair, edgy nose ring, and vampy black nails and eyeliner—almost makes the apocalypse look fashionable. Her big brown eyes, delivering the end-of-days itinerary, seem too doe-like for their dark message.

"Where is that exactly?" I ask.

Emily slides me a steaming mug with caramel macchiato creamer—my personal brand of morning salvation. The sweet and rich scent blissfully assaults my senses. I take a generous sip, letting the liquid gold work its caffeinated magic.

Rhyland wraps his arms around my waist, nestling his chin on my shoulder as he joins the conversation.

"Lakewood, Washington. The castle is a historic English Tudor Gothic mansion, complete with a labyrinth of catacombs and an ancient chapel. It's been off the grid for ages. Word on the street is that it's the witches' covert gathering spot for their most sacred rituals. There are even whispers about a hidden chamber where some dimensional rift was cracked open, leaving a permanent scar between realms. That could explain the heavy arcane vibes. Crazy stuff, right?"

As Sable's fingers dance across her laptop, she summons an image—a chilling view of Thornewood Castle. There it stands, a brooding titan on the edge of a silent, obsidian lake swathed in fog. The place is all menacing spires and shadow-laden archways, with wild ivy scaling its ancient stones like nature's siege. Built by some rich hermit with a passion for the Dark Ages, the castle's been left to ghosts; at least, that's what the town claims.

"Not creepy at all," I say, rolling my eyes. "Do they have a vampire yet? Or a date for this ritual?"

"Not that I've heard. Though whispers claim their big move will coincide with the full moon's rise this Saturday night. We're on a tight timeline—the stars and planets will be aligned perfectly for their purposes by the next lunar peak."

"Good," Emily chimes in, a wicked grin spreading across her face. "Sounds like it's high time we crashed this witchy kegger." Her gaze slides slyly toward Rhyland. "Pose as tribute?"

"No. Absolutely not." The words fly out before I can stop them, my gaze cutting between Emily and Rhyland. "If my hunch is right and Azrael is wrapped up in this, walking in there would blow everything wide open—and I am not putting you anywhere near that man." My eyes land firmly on Rhyland. "Not a chance."

"Then who can we use as a decoy?" she muses, tapping a finger against her lips. "We need someone who can sell it, strut in there, and fool these mystical Mofos long enough for us to get a leg up. Someone not afraid to dance with the devil—or, in this case, a coven full of them."

"Me." The voice cuts in from behind us: our heads whip around, and Lucian saunters in with a smirk plastered on his too-handsome face.

Rhyland stands rigid behind me, the air around him thick with concern for his brother. "You think you've got the chops to pull this off, pretty boy?" he teases with forced levity.

"Already in the works, big guy," Lucian announces with a shit-eating grin that practically screams 'I'm the man.' "What, you think I've been twiddling my thumbs and braiding my ball hair? Hell no! I've been getting all up close and personal with one of these witchy bitches." He snatches my coffee, taking a swig before making a face like he just licked a hobo's armpit. "Gah! What is this, motor oil? Where was I? Oh yeah, the witch. She's putty in my hands, thanks to my mad mind-control skills. Just call me Jedi."

Lucian drops a bombshell. He's been using his supernatural charm to snake his way into the coven's confidence. Somehow, this sly vampire has managed to weave a compulsion spell without the witches being the wiser.

"How?" I blurt out, with enough skepticism to drown a small village. "How, when your mind tricks don't work on supernaturals?"

Ever the insufferable know-it-all, Lucian leans in like he's about to reveal the meaning of life. "Witches get their power from rituals, spells, and incantations. You picking up what I'm putting down, or do I need to break out the sock puppets and crayons?"

I resist the urge to smack him upside the head, settling for a glare that could set him on fire. "Yes, Lucian, I understand witchcraft. But that still doesn't explain how you compelled one of them. Last I checked, your vampire voodoo only works on mortals."

Emily folds her arms, a mix of impatience and anticipation written on her face.

Lucian lets out a long-suffering sigh. "Here's the thing. Witches might have fancy-schmancy powers, but at the end of the day, they're still human. Sure, they can shoot fireballs out of their asses and turn people into toads, but their brains? Totally susceptible to a little mental manipulation, if you know what I mean."

Sable rolls her eyes, and Rhyland hums in agreement behind me.

I blink, struggling to process this new information. "So, you're telling me you can waltz up to any witch, do your 'these are not the droids you're looking for' shtick, and they'll just... obey?"

Lucian grins—wide, wolfish, and dripping with the kind of self-satisfaction that makes you want to smack him. "Well, not *exactly*. It takes a little more finesse than just waltzing in and asking nicely. I had to do some digging—figure out which witch was the weak link in their cute little coven." He shrugs like it was the easiest thing in the world. "Turns out, one of them has a teeny-tiny crush on yours truly." He presses a hand to his chest, feigning humility for exactly zero seconds. "And honestly? Can't blame her. I mean—" He motions to himself with both hands. "*Look* at me."

I roll my eyes so hard I'm sure I strain a muscle. "Yes, Lucian, you're a regular Adonis. Can we focus, please? So you compelled this witch... then what? What did you learn?"

"Everything about this coven and their weaknesses. I also compelled *Sabrina* to convince the coven not to allow Azrael at the ritual, as it would 'interfere with the magic.'" Lucian explains, casually strolling over to my fridge and helping himself to my leftover Chinese food.

He takes a bite of my General Tso's chicken, talking with his mouth full. "And she's certain the coven will accept me as their offering after I filled them with the notion that I am the ancient of all vampires... Mwahaha!" He laughs like a discount Dracula, complete with a cheesy accent and dramatic cape flourish.

Emily snorts so hard she nearly launches coffee out of her nose, one hand slapping the counter to steady herself. "Oh my *God*," she wheezes, eyes watering. "You are absolutely *delusional,* and I am here for it."

"See? She thinks I'm hilarious." Lucian jabs his fork into another piece of my chicken without a shred of remorse, chewing like he owns the place.

I stare at him, torn between being genuinely impressed and wanting to shove that self-satisfied grin down his throat."Okay, first of all, that's my food, you *ass*. Secondly, how did you convince them you're some ancient vampire? You're not exactly radiating wisdom and gravitas here."

Lucian grins, chicken stuck in his teeth. "Oh, ye of little faith. It's called acting. I just channeled my inner Bela Lugosi, threw in some 'thees' and 'thous,' and bam! Instant elder vampire cred. These witches may be powerful, but they're not the sharpest stakes in the coffin."

I pinch the bridge of my nose, feeling a headache coming on. "Okay, ignoring the fact that you just butchered that metaphor worse than a blind lumberjack, are you seriously telling me that your entire plan hinges on you playing dress-up and hoping the covens are too dumb to notice?"

He shrugs, licking his fingers. "Hey, don't knock it till you've tried it, Princess. Sometimes, the simplest plans are the best. Besides, it's not like we have a lot of options. It's either this, or we sit around while Azrael turns the world into his personal blood buffet."

I hate to admit it, but he's got a point. We're not exactly swimming in alternatives here. If Lucian's managed to infiltrate the coven, we might stand a chance of stopping Azrael before it's too late.

"Fine," I sigh, resigned to our fate resting in the hands of a vampire with the maturity level of a horny teenager. "But if this blows up in our faces, I'm kicking your ass. And you owe me new Chinese food."

Lucian smiles. "Wouldn't have it any other way, sweet cheeks. Now, if you'll excuse me, I have a ritual to crash and an evil vampire overlord to dethrone. Wish me luck!"

DANICA

85

After days of strategizing and dealing with all this witchy nonsense, Emily, bless her well-meaning soul, thought it was the perfect moment for a girls' night. But when I say girls' night, I really mean a night out with my crew of fanged hotties. Emily, in her nostalgia, chose the Playful Pint—probably for old times' sake—even though the place hasn't quite had the same vibe since John's brutal murder.

It's still hard to believe he's gone. John was more than just my boss; he was a true friend. I miss his fatherly advice and how he always looked out for me. At least his son stepped up to keep the Pint going in his memory, even if it meant putting some new "strict conditions" for vampires in place.

But no matter, Emily assured me Mark was working tonight and would happily invite my sharp-toothed posse inside. Crisis averted.

I'm hopping out of the shower, ready to slip into something more "I'm the savior of the Seven Realms, bow before me" and less "I heart fuzzy bunny slippers" when Rhyland barges into my room with that sexy smirk plastered across his face.

"Got a present for you, baby," he purrs, his voice a low, seductive rumble.

Oh, I do love surprises. But Rhyland's predatory look tells me this won't be a bouquet of roses or a teddy bear kind of gift.

"Oh? What is it?" I ask, trying to play it cool even as my heart does a giddy little mambo in my chest.

In a flash, he's on me, strong hands gripping my wrists, the smooth glide of black rope against my skin as he binds me. A gasp escapes my lips as he bends me over the bed, my ass in the air, my hands secure and tied to the headboard.

"Rhyland, what the *actual* fuck?" I snap, yanking at the ropes, digging into my wrists. My voice comes out somewhere between pissed off and incredulous. "Is this your idea of a joke? Because I'm not laughing, you overgrown Nordic Neanderthal!"

Rhyland just laughs—low, deep, the kind of sound that rumbles through his chest and has no business sounding that good. "Oh, this isn't a joke, baby," he drawls, voice dropping into that sinful register that makes my spine tingle even when I want to strangle him. "This is payback. Pure and simple."

I glare at him over my shoulder, trying to ignore the way my body responds to the dominance in his tone. "Payback? For what, exactly?" I play dumb.

He leans down, his lips brushing the shell of my ear. "For being a goddamn cock-tease, kära," he murmurs, voice low and dangerous. "Walking around in those tiny fucking shorts, grinding on me like a bitch in heat. And let's not forget your little shower performance—" his breath fans hot against my skin, "then leaving me high and dry for the past week. Ring any bells?"

I can't help the smirk that tugs at my lips. "Oh, that? That was just a bit of fun."

He growls—low, feral, the kind of sound that has no right sending a bolt of heat straight through my center. "Well, now it's *my* turn," he promises, his hand coming down on my ass in a sharp slap that makes me yelp. "And trust me, baby, you're gonna fucking love it."

I bite my lip, suppressing a moan. Damn him, but his dominance, the raw power emanating from him—it's intoxicating. "Maybe I just like seeing you squirm," I taunt, my voice breathy.

Another hard slap lands on my ass, the sting delicious, drawing a moan from my throat. "Keep up the sass, baby," he warns, his hand soothing the heated flesh. "We'll see how bratty you are when I'm done with you."

I try to kick, to twist free, but he's an immovable force, pinning me down, spreading my thighs with his knee. "Don't you fucking move," he commands, his voice a harsh rasp.

A whimper escapes me, my body trembling with anticipation. I'm caught, at his mercy, and god help me; I want whatever he's got planned. "What are you going to do to me?" I breathe, my pussy clenching.

I can feel his smile against my skin, wicked and full of dark promise. "Oh, Angel, the things I am going to do to you..."

Then, the sneaky bastard reaches around, holding some object in his hand. "What's that?" I ask, my curiosity piqued despite myself.

It's a red silicone rosebud toy with a flat top that resembles petals and a tiny hole in the center.

"It's called the Rose. A vibrator with suction," he explains, his voice rough with desire. "Now, let's see what kind of magic it can work, shall we?"

"Where the hell did you get that?" I look over my shoulder and raise an eyebrow, impressed.

"I have my ways when it involves this tight little ass of yours," he growls. "Now hush, baby, and let me work."

Rhyland sinks his teeth into my neck, a possessive bite that marks me as his. I moan, the sharp sting of pain only heightening my arousal. His tongue soothes the bite mark, leaving wet, hot trails down my spine until he reaches my ass, claiming me again with another possessive bite.

He positions the toy over my clit while his tongue teases my ass. The vibrator comes to life; its gentle suction and vibrations send shockwaves through my body. I buck and gasp, my breath coming in short, sharp pants. "Oh, God!"

The toy's suction and vibration send me into a frenzy, moaning and groaning with pleasure.

He continues his assault, swirling his tongue and flicking that tight ring of muscle, driving me mad. My orgasm builds, an exquisite coil of tension hovering just out of reach.

And then, the bastard stops.

"Not so fast, Angel," he murmurs, his desire thick and rough.

I growl, my need building to a fever pitch. "Goddammit, Rhyland! Don't do this to me!"

He chuckles, the vibrations tingling my sensitive skin. "I seem to recall telling you to watch that filthy mouth. Do you want me to punish it, too?"

I clamp my jaw shut, refusing to give him the satisfaction of a response. "I need you to relax for me, baby," he says, his voice a low rumble.

I feel a warm, slippery liquid being rubbed into my ass, and I gasp. "What are you doing?"

"You'll see, baby. Just relax."

The feeling of his fingers working the lubricant into my ass is both invasive and arousing. I squirm and writhe as he probes deeper, anticipation building.

Rhyland's hand locks onto my hip—unyielding, possessive—maneuvering me back onto my knees with a slow, deliberate authority that makes it crystal clear there is no negotiating, his fingers never once losing their rhythm as they work my ass with maddening precision. It's a wordless command that short-circuits every coherent thought in my head and sends heat scorching straight down my spine.

"You like that?" Rhyland purrs. "You like being at my mercy, feeling my fingers prepping this gorgeous ass while you're aching to explode."

I moan, my breath catching in my throat as he continues his magic. My body winds tighter, coiled like a spring, ready to unleash.

He adds a third finger, stretching me wide, and I gasp. It's overwhelming, my body trembling on the brink.

"You want me to fuck this tight little ass?" Rhyland murmurs, his breath a scorching whisper against the shell of my ear. "You want me to make you come so hard you'll see stars."

I can't deny it. My body is aching for it. Every nerve ending in my body is lit up, screaming *yes*. But I know what this is—his way of staking his claim, of reminding me exactly who's running the show.

"Please," I beg, my voice a mere whisper. "Please, Rhyland. Fuck me."

"You are one filthy, naughty girl, and you're all mine, Dani. Never forget that." But instead of feeling offended, a rush of desire so strong takes my breath away.

Then something cool and smooth presses against my ass. I tense up and try to pull away, but Rhyland's grip is too strong.

"Relax," he commands, his voice low and rough.

"What..." I swallow hard, my voice barely a whisper. "W-what is that?"

The words come out shaky, caught somewhere between breathless anticipation and a flicker of uncertainty.

Rhyland ignores my question and continues to push whatever it is deeper into my ass. I feel my muscles clenching and relaxing as he moves it in and out, the sensation both painful and pleasurable. To my surprise, I feel my body responding, my hips bucking to meet the intrusion.

It's obvious he's inserting a butt plug in my ass.

Rhyland starts to massage my clit with the toy again. "Fuck, look at how wet you are, dirty girl." His praises turn me on more, and I moan and throw my head back. My arms are numb, but I'm too turned on to care.

"There we go, just a little more, Angel," he encourages. I feel him slide the object in further, almost too much to bear.

"Fuck, oh God," I pant, my body quivering with pleasure. That damn clit massager is going to send me skyrocketing, especially now that my ass is filled.

With the object fully seated in my ass, Rhyland sets the toy aside and swiftly undoes the ropes binding my wrists. I go to growl at him, but it comes out as a whine.

I wince as the blood rushes back into my arms, my fingers tingling with pins and needles.

Rhyland scoops me up and carries me to the bathroom, setting me on the counter. It's uncomfortable sitting with this object, but I manage.

Rhyland cleans the lube off me with a warm rag and then tells me to get dressed.

"Wait, what? That's it?" I ask incredulously.

"Yup. We have dinner and drinks planned—and you better keep that plug in your ass. I expect to see it still there later."

I stare after him in disbelief as he leaves the bathroom.

Stepping into the Playful Pint is like taking a trip down memory lane, with a touch of "Oh shit, remember that?" But hey, I am not about to let the past ruin my night, and neither is Emily. She is on a mission to ensure we have a blast, and who am I to argue?

With the impending witch raid looming, this is our chance to let loose and forget about the stress. It is time to trade in our battle gear for some cocktails and laughter.

"Girl, you better drink up. I am not drinking alone tonight," Emily demands, pushing a colorful concoction my way.

I happily oblige, downing my third cocktail. But as I shift in my seat, I'm reminded of Rhyland's "gift" still occupying its place. The damn object is making its presence known, and I have to bite my lip to keep from yelping.

Why did I agree? Well, apparently, I have a thing for Rhyland's twisted brand of punishment. The man knows how to push my buttons in all the right ways, and I can't get enough.

Who else would willingly park their ass on a barstool with a foreign object shoved up *said ass*, acting like everything is perfectly normal? *This girl.* I must be a special breed of fucked up to get off on Rhyland's sick, twisted games, but what can I say? The heart—and my needy-ass pussy—want what they want.

So here I sit, nursing my fourth drink, secretly dripping and turned on by my Viking's little power trip. It's going to be a long night, but at least I've got Emily and the crew to keep me from completely losing my shit.

Cheers to good friends, strong drinks, and kinky vampires who keep us on our toes! Let the night of debauchery begin!

RHYLAND

86

Sitting at the table, watching Dani squirm, I can't help but grin like a sadistic bastard. It's taking every ounce of my self-control not to drag her back to our room and fuck her senseless, but I'm enjoying this little game too much to end it just yet.

Lucian, ever the nosy little shit, leans over and asks, "What's got you smiling like the cat that ate the canary, Rhy-Rhy? You finally pull that stick out of your ass and discover the joys of a good prostate massage?"

We've been here for about an hour now, relaxing and enjoying the peace. No battles, no strategizing, no planning, no looking over our shoulders—just some fucking fun for a night.

"Fuck off, Lucian," I retort, not wanting to reveal my little secret. "My ass is none of your business."

Erik is lounging next to Lucian, sipping on his bourbon—his go-to drink—and watching the bar with his keen eyes, as always. The man never truly relaxes, but I can't blame him. It's in our nature to be on guard.

"Aww, come on, don't be like that!" Lucian whines, pouting like a petulant child. "You know I live vicariously through your sordid sexcapades. Throw a brother a bone here, would ya?"

Earlier, I went back to Lucian's little den of debauchery and grabbed the few choice items for Dani's "punishment" tonight. Let's just say I've got plans to make her squirm in more ways than one.

"I know you raided my fuck dungeon, you sneaky bastard," Lucian says, waggling his eyebrows suggestively. "Find anything you like? The nipple clamps, perhaps? Or maybe the vibrating butt plug? Oh, oh! Tell me you grabbed the edible body paint. That shit's delicious."

I shrug, not bothering to confirm or deny his accusations. He knows me too well.

"Hey, mi sex toy es su sex toy, am I right?" Lucian grins, slapping me on the back. "What's mine is yours, bro. Just make sure you sanitize anything you stick up your ass. I don't want your booty cooties all over my precious collection."

I roll my eyes, fighting back a smirk. "Lucian, *Christ,* if you don't shut the fuck up—"

"You'll what? Spank me?" He laughs, throwing his head back. "Please, Rhy-Rhy. We both know I'd enjoy that way too much."

Despite myself, a laugh slips out. Lucian might be the most insufferable bastard on the planet, but the son of a bitch has a gift for cracking me up.

Even if ninety percent of what comes out of his mouth would make a truck stop hooker clutch her pearl.

Dani and Emily make their way over to the table, Dani clearly buzzed and walking extra carefully. She slowly sits down on the bench next to me, knowing full well she's trying not to push the object in further. I can't help but smile at her struggle, my cock twitching at the thought of what I have in store for her later.

Leaning over, I whisper in her ear, "Having trouble, Angel?"

She glares at me, but I can see the desire burning in her eyes. "You're an asshole, you know that?"

"Yeah, but you love it," I grin, my hand sliding under the table to rest on her thigh, giving it a possessive squeeze.

She's wearing this sexy little number, a simple black dress that clings to her curves. It's short, barely skimming her thighs, and sexy as hell, just like her.

I let my gaze roam over her body, taking in every delicious inch. The way the fabric hugs her hips, the tantalizing glimpse of cleavage, those long, toned legs that seem to go on for miles—it's enough to make a man lose his fucking mind.

Dani knows exactly what she's doing, the little minx. She's playing with fire, and I'm more than ready to burn. My cock throbs in my jeans, hard as steel and aching for her touch.

"You look good enough to eat, baby," I rumble, my voice a low, predatory purr. "Good thing I'm fucking starving."

Dani shifts in her seat, biting her lip to stifle a moan. I can tell she's getting more and more turned on by the second, and it's taking all my willpower not to say fuck it and take her right here on this table.

But I'm not done with her yet. Not by a long shot. Tonight, I'm going to push her to her limits and watch her come undone in the most delicious ways possible.

So, for now, I'll sit back, enjoy my drink, and watch my sexy little mate squirm, knowing that later, I'll have her screaming my name as I fuck her into oblivion.

After a couple more rounds of drinks during their intense conversation about the *new world order,* I whip out the remote from my pocket and press the button. Dani nearly jumps out of her seat, slamming her hands on the table. "Jesus fucking *Christ!*" she screams.

The vibrator in her ass goes off, causing her to let out a low moan of pleasure mixed with frustration. I can't help but smirk at her as she shoots me a look that says she will make me pay for this little stunt later. Her caramel-gold eyes are filled with lust and anger, and it's all I can do to keep from laughing out loud. The confident and feisty scientist is putty in my hands, and I fucking love it.

Emily's quick on the draw, the concern etching her features as she leans in, "What the hell is wrong with you? Are you okay?" Her words tumble out fast and sharp,

Dani shifts uncomfortably in her seat, the vibrator still buzzing inside her. She tries to maintain her composure, but it's clear she's struggling. "Uh, y-yeah. I'm good. I just need to use the ladies' room for a sec," she says, attempting to keep a straight face.

Emily cuts in, "I'll go with you."

Dani practically leaps out of her seat, hands flailing as she tries to wave off Emily's offer. "No! I mean, no thanks. It's fine. Really. You stay here and keep the guys company," she says, trying to sound casual. But her voice is strained, and her movements are jerky, giving away just how much she's affected by the toy I've activated. Dani may be confident and feisty, but even she can't completely hide how much the vibrator is affecting her.

I can only manage a twisted, wicked-ass grin as I watch Dani saunter off to the ladies' room.

"You fucking bastard, I swear I'm going to gut you!" I can't help but chuckle at Dani's fiery resolve piping up through our mental connection.

"You dirty bird," Lucian says with a smirk.

I quickly switch off the vibrator, "Just give us a minute," I say before pushing away from the table and stalking Dani toward the restrooms. "I'll be right back."

"Keep your fucking thoughts to yourself," I grumble in Lucian's head through our mental connection, letting him know I mean business—my hand already reaching for the restroom door.

The second I'm through the door, I slam it shut and throw the lock, scanning the dimly lit space. Dani is braced against the counter, white-knuckling the edges, staring at her reflection as her chest heaves in ragged, uneven breaths. She's barely holding it together.

Without hesitation, I blur swiftly behind her, gripping her hair and pulling up her short dress, and exposing her smooth and toned ass. "Need some help, baby?" I ask her, a hint of playfulness in my voice.

"You bast—" Dani starts, fighting back against my grip on her hair.

"Uh-uh, Angel, what did I tell you about that mouth?" I remind her as I tighten my hold on her hair, pulling her head back to expose her neck. "I want to hear those sweet little moans and gasps coming from those lips, not those feisty little curses."

"Rhyland, *please.* Take away this ache," she pleads, her voice low and needy. Her gold eyes are melted pools, swirling with desire.

I can't fucking wait any longer. Been tortured this past week, and I'm done fucking waiting. Quickly unzipping my pants, I let my cock spring free, ready to give her exactly what she needs. "I know, baby," I say, gripping her hips and pulling her back against me. "Are you ready for this cock? Ready for me to fuck you hard and make you scream?"

"God...*yes*. Please..." she begs, her voice a breathless plea for me to take her. I smirk at the sound, knowing she is ready for what I have in store.

With a gruff and dominant tone, I swiftly spin her around, lift her up, and slam her sexy ass on the counter. She moans like the filthy girl I've turned her into—insatiable and craving only my touch. Gripping her hair firmly at the base of her neck, I demand, "First, you're going to drink." I swiftly pull out a knife from my pocket and make a small incision on my neck.

I want her out of her mind for this.

Dani whimpers against me, her legs locking around my waist as I crush her to my chest. She doesn't waste a second—her soft lips find my neck, latching on. I groan low, the sensation of her drinking me in pushing me to the edge. "Fuck," I growl, ripping her panties aside and sinking into her with one hard thrust.

I snatch the remote and click it back on, and the instant response has her clenching around me, her body bowing into mine as she gives in completely. She drinks from my neck in deep, greedy pulls, moaning against my skin in a way that nearly undoes me. I fist her hair and tilt her head back, forcing her gaze to meet mine—those eyes wild, glazed, my blood stoking the fire in her even higher.

"Feel good, Angel?" I grunt, watching her body shudder and squirm beneath me. "I'm not stopping until you're begging me to."

Every thrust unravels her a little more, turning her into a trembling, desperate mess underneath me—exactly where I want her.

DANICA

87

I'm on the verge of exploding, and Rhyland is turning me into a wild, insatiable slut. With that vibrating plug in my ass and his thick, throbbing cock slamming into me, I can't resist the delicious blend of agony and ecstasy.

Fuck it, I'll take all the pain for this kind of pleasure any day.

His blood strikes my senses like lightning. Each drop is a cascade of spice and cinnamon that dances through my veins, igniting an intense, unquenchable desire. The sensation is different—it buzzes with electricity, starkly contrasting our previous encounter's slow, simmering heat.

"Tell me, baby..." he growls, his voice filled with possession. "You like having all your holes filled—Say it. Say you fucking love this."

"I-I love it," I moan. "I fucking love it."

And I do. Oh my god, I do. Rhyland has me so worked up that I'm teetering on the edge of oblivion.

"Yeah, you fucking do," he grunts, shifting the angle of his thrusts to hit the spot that sends me over the edge.

My pussy tightens around him at his filthy words—on the edge of orgasm. "Don't you come—not until I say," he commands, pumping into me with brutal force.

"Rhyland..." My brain can barely form his name as my body shakes from the pleasure overload. "Rhy..." I gasp, my voice hoarse with need. The vibrating plug nestled inside me sends delicious shivers through my body, each pulse matching the relentless pounding of his massive cock.

Tears of pleasure stream down my face, my makeup likely a mess, but I couldn't care less. "Please..." I beg.

Who knew double penetration would be this fucking mind-blowing? The combination of sensations has me on the edge of oblivion, teetering on the precipice of the most intense orgasm I've ever experienced.

His fingers close around my neck, choking off my oxygen supply, while the other hand tugs viciously at my tangled locks. I'm immobilized and gasping for air, but dying here with Rhyland fucking me senseless? Sign me up any day.

"Yeah—You want to come, baby?" Rhyland's primal desires surge as he takes control.

"Yes! Fuck—please." I choke out under his tight grip, unable to hold back. My vision starts to go white; the pleasure is too much.

"I should make you wait; I should make you burn like you made me burn," he growls.

Pinned against him, I surrender to the relentless pounding of his cock. It's erotic surrender at its finest, and I wait with bated breath for his next command.

Every thrust of his hips against mine sparks an eruption of pleasure so intense it borders on pain. That sweet, familiar pressure builds—the need to pee, a sign of the tsunami-like orgasm that's about to detonate within me. The kind of release he fucking lives for.

"I want your tight pussy drowning me." His thrusts become faster and harder, his hips a blur as he slams into me. "Now, be my dirty girl, baby. Make a fucking mess all over me."

I can barely process his filthy words, my body too consumed by the eruption that's coming. "Rhyland... oh fuck..."

One...two more powerful thrusts, and my body detonates like a bombshell. "FUCK!" I cry out, my voice is hoarse, as the orgasm tears through, spinning the room out of control. "Rhyland..." I don't even recognize my voice. My body convulses, my release drenching both of us, a warm gush that paints the floor and soaks him.

Rhyland silences my screams with his hand, his eyes burning into mine. He doesn't miss a beat, his cock still pounding into me through the aftershocks of my climax. "There it is, what I've been *waiting* for," Rhyland purrs, with satisfaction. "That's it, baby, just like that. At my mercy and completely wrecked. You're all fucking mine."

His words are a drug to me, pushing me higher as I ride the waves of my orgasm. He owns me, body and soul, in this moment.

His teeth sink into the tender flesh of my neck, a sharp bite that blends pain and pleasure, sending me spiraling back into the abyss. "Fuck!" I cry out, my voice a plea for mercy as he thrusts deeper, claiming every inch of me. "Don't stop... please... again..."

The room echoes with our grunts and moans, our bodies a tangle of sweat and ecstasy. This is how we fuck—wild, untamed, and utterly consumed by one another.

Rhyland wrenches me off the counter, and the next thing I know, I'm bent over the nearby bench. "Oh, you think I'm finished with you, huh? Not even close, baby. I told you, you will be begging for mercy."

I'm panting, my breath coming in hot, shallow gasps as Rhyland yanks the plug from my ass. He looms over me, his eyes dark with hunger, then jerks my head back, devouring my mouth with his. Our tongues clash in a savage dance, a prelude to the raw, animalistic fucking we both crave. A strangled moan tears from my throat—a sound only he can wring from me.

He pulls away, his lips curved in a devilish smirk. "Beg me to wreck this tight ass of yours, Dani. You know you wanna feel me there." His voice, a gritty rasp, betrays his own pent-up desires.

I can barely string two words together. Every nerve ending in my body is on fire, buzzing with a desperate, aching need that won't quit. It's like someone lit a fuse inside me and the whole damn thing is burning straight down to my center, white-hot and merciless.

His deep, raspy voice whispers in my ear, the sound sending pleasurable shivers down my spine. "You're my filthy little temptress, Angel. Admit it, you get off on being a dirty, cock-hungry slut for me." His grip on my hair tightens, a delicious pain as he pulls my head back, forcing me to look up at him.

"I want to see your pretty eyes, baby," he growls, his breath hot on my skin. "Look at me while I fuck you senseless. I want to watch you fall apart around my cock."

My pussy is soaked, throbbing—a testament to how much I want this. And when he pushes into my tight channel, there's no need for lube. The friction is exquisite agony as he stretches me, forcing me to accommodate his massive size.

"Holy *shit*, Rhyland," I breathe, my eyes widening as the fullness of his girth washes over me. "Your cock... It's too much." I bite my lip, a whimper escaping as I struggle to adjust to his size.

He senses my momentary hesitation, and his challenge is swift. "Can't take it, baby? Can't handle my big cock tearing you open?"

Oh, but I can. With an urgent growl, I push back harder, meeting his thrusts with matching ferocity. I want all of him, every thick, veined inch buried deep. My muscles strain, embracing his cock like a silk glove.

"Christ, baby," he grunts, his hips snapping forward, driving himself deeper. "So fucking tight. Your ass is gonna milk my cock until there's nothing left."

I grind against him, my desire hotter than the sun, dripping like honey down my legs. I push back harder, riding the wave of pleasure, letting any lingering pain wash away in the tide of ecstasy.

With a slight adjustment, Rhyland finds a new angle, his leg propped for better leverage. He thrusts deep, hitting every sweet spot, every nerve ending, making me feel utterly possessed by him.

"FUCK!" I scream as he slams deeper, harder, each punishing thrust branding me from the inside out. The obscene sound of skin against skin echoes off the walls, a relentless rhythm that matches the feral hammering of my heart.

The sounds escaping my throat are animalistic and unchecked. I'm stripped down to pure instinct, words a lost cause, but the whimpers and moans spilling from my lips say everything that needs to be said.

It's dirty, it's raw, it's punishing, and I love every fucking second of it.

"Play with that sweet little pussy for me, baby," Rhyland grunts, his voice heavy with his own need. "Rub that clit while I pound your tight ass."

My fingers instinctively obey, finding my clit, teasing and circling it as his thrusts become rougher, more desperate.

"Harder," I demand, my voice hoarse and wanting. "I want to feel you, all of you. Want to be sore tomorrow, knowing it was you."

"Fuck, you're so needy," Rhyland grunts, his voice edged with satisfaction as he obliges my demand, thrusting with relentless force. My body explodes with blinding pleasure, orgasm after orgasm rocking my world, my cries echoing off the walls.

He lets go, too, his pleasure building to a peak before he curses, his body rigid as he spills himself into me, marking me as his. There's nothing sexier than a man who loses control, who knows what he wants, and takes it.

In the aftermath, he pulls me tight against him, his lips skimming my neck, tasting the salt of my sweat. We're breathless, our hearts pounding erratically, our bodies quaking in the aftershocks. "You drive me out of my fucking mind," I whisper, my voice soft and sated.

A smirk plays on his lips as he nuzzles my neck. "Good. That's exactly where I aim to keep you, baby. Right at the edge, begging for more."

S ashaying back to the table, I find Emily standing at attention, her face a cocktail of worry and nosiness. "You good, girl?" Her eyes give me a once-over like she's searching for clues.

My ass is sore in all the right ways, giving my walk a distinct "just got royally fucked" swagger— like I just hopped off a mechanical bull. The knowing looks from everyone at the table confirm that my post-sex glow is on full display: tousled hair, smudged lipstick... the whole "thoroughly ravished" package.

I flash Em a cheeky grin. "Oh, I'm peachy. Just needed a little... private chit-chat." I throw her a wink that says, "Get ready for the most scandalous shit, babe." She's gonna have a field day when I spill the tea on this steamy sesh.

Let's just say Rhyland's given her enough ammo to tease me 'til the cows come home. That man knows how to leave an impression in more ways than one!

Lucian, never one to miss an opportunity for a smart-ass comment, "Can you guys ever go anywhere without acting like horny teenagers? Seriously, it's like watching a fucking National Geographic special on the mating habits of the sexually frustrated."

He leans back in his chair, a shit-eating grin plastered across his face. "I mean, don't get me wrong, I'm all for a good ol' fashioned bathroom bang sesh. But you two? You're like rabbits on Viagra. It's almost impressive, in a slightly disturbing way."

Rhyland shoots him a lazy glare, not quite angry but clearly growing annoyed.

"Alright, alright!" Lucian holds up his hands, his grin never leaving his face. "I can take a hint. I'll just be over here, basking in the afterglow of your sexual exploits. Don't mind me."

He winks at me, blowing an exaggerated kiss, and I can't help but laugh. Insufferable pain in the ass though he may be, Lucian certainly knows how to keep things interesting.

Never a dull moment with this crew, that's for damn sure.

RHYLAND

88

My fingers drum on the steering wheel, my eyes fixed on the dark road ahead. Three days of non-stop strategizing and planning, and here we are, heading straight into the lion's den—Thornewood Castle. What a fitting name for a place crawling with witches.

I glance up at the night sky, the full moon looming ominously. It's like the universe is setting the stage for some seriously spooky shit. Could the atmosphere be any more on the nose? All we're missing is some fog and a few ominous raven caws.

I sigh, shaking my head. But aside from the atmosphere, we've got a solid plan. We discovered their weakness: once those witches link up during their ritual, they're all connected. Kill one, and the whole lot of them go down like a supernatural domino effect.

Dani and Erik are in the back seat of Lucian's SUV, with Lucian riding shotgun beside me. Emily and Sable follow close behind in her car.

I grip the steering wheel tightly, my knuckles white as we fly southbound toward our destination. The tension in the car is palpable, an undercurrent of anxiety and determination. We're heading into the unknown, and every second counts.

The only wild card is the numbers. We still don't know how many will attend this shindig.

I tighten my grip on the wheel, my jaw clenched with determination. But it doesn't matter. However many there are, we'll take them down. We've come too far to back out now.

As we make our way through the dark, winding streets, I can't help but do a double-take at Lucian's getup. Seated next to me, he's decked out in a medieval ensemble, complete with a billowing cloak, a doublet that looks like it's been through the wars, and a pair of tights that leave absolutely nothing to the imagination.

Lucian rubs his hands together like a cartoon villain who just discovered the destroy button, that unhinged grin splitting his face wide open. "Oh, I am *so* hard for this right now." He practically vibrates with excitement. "Is it a bunch of mystical hocus pocus bullshit? Absolutely. Do I care? Not even a little. Crashing a witch party?" He presses a hand to his chest. "This is better than Christmas. This is *better* than Christmas *and* my birthday combined. Let's go ruin some shit."

I shoot him a sharp look, my patience wearing thin. "For fuck's sake, Lucian, this isn't a game. We're about to walk into a damn snake pit, and you're treating it like a joke."

He holds his hands up, eyes wide with feigned innocence. "Whoa there, big guy. Dial back the alpha male rage, will ya? I know this is serious business, but lighten up a little. We're about to fuck up some witches and save the world. I want to have some fun!"

I grit my teeth, my jaw clenching so hard I'm surprised my molars don't crack. "Lucian, I swear to god, if you don't start taking this seriously, I will personally shove a stake so far up your ass you'll be coughing up splinters for a week."

He clutches his chest, staggering back dramatically. "Oh, be still my beating heart! I love it when you talk dirty to me, Rhy. But seriously, I get it. This is life-or-death shit. I'm just trying to lighten the mood. Besides, I've tangled with scarier bitches than these discount Charmed rejects. I ain't afraid of no ghost... or witch, or whatever."

I take a deep breath to calm myself. As much as I hate to admit it, the bastard has a point. We can't afford to let our emotions get the best of us, not when the stakes are this high.

"Fine," I growl. "But if you fuck this up, if you put any of us in danger because you couldn't keep your damn mouth shut, I will personally rip your fucking head off and use it as a footstool. Are we clear?"

Lucian mimes, zipping his lips, a mischievous glint still dancing in his eyes. "Crystal, boss man. I'll be on my best behavior, scout's honor."

I snort, shaking my head in disbelief. "You were never a fucking scout, you asshole. But I'll hold you to that.

"And what is this shit you are wearing? You're trying to blend in, not headline at the Renaissance Fair. You and your goddamn peacocking," I grumble, my eyes narrowing in a mix of disbelief and exasperation.

Lucian strikes a pose, one hand on his hip and the other clutching at his cloak like he's about to take flight. "Excuse you, but I'll have you know this is authentic 15th-century garb. If I'm going to sacrifice myself for this coven, I need to look the part. And let's be real, they wouldn't expect anything less."

Erik chimes in from the backseat, raising an eyebrow. "If we get caught because of your fashion choices, I'm leaving you behind."

Lucian gasps, clutching at his chest. "Et tu, Erik? I thought we were brothers, man. Brothers don't let brothers get left behind enemy lines, especially not when they're rocking a look like this."

"Boys, boys." Dani's voice cuts through the tension, a mix of amusement and exasperation. "Do I need to put you two in timeout?

I glance at her in the rearview mirror to see her sitting there, arms folded, golden eyes on me, eyebrow arched, looking like a sexy schoolteacher about to lay down the law.

"Little Huntress, this is par for the course with these two. It's like watching a never-ending pissing contest, only with more dick jokes," Erik deadpans, his face as expressionless as ever.

Lucian clutches his pearls, his eyes wide with mock indignation. "Excuse me? I'll have you know my dick jokes are top-notch, fuck you very much! And I don't always fight with Rhyland!" He pauses, considering. "Only, like, 99.9% of the time. But who's counting?"

I pinch the bridge of my nose, wondering how the hell we're supposed to save the world when I can't even get through a conversation without wanting to throttle someone. "Lucian, I swear to god, if you don't shut your damn mouth, I'll..."

Dani squeezes in between the front seats, her hands held up in a placating gesture. "Whoa there, cowboys. Let's save the measuring contest for after we've dealt with the apocalypse, mmkay?"

I take a deep breath, trying to rein in my frustration. "Fine. But I still think we're walking into a fucking shitshow. And if anything happens to you, Dani..."

She fixes me with a look that could make a lesser man piss himself. "I appreciate the concern, babe, but I'm a big girl. We've faced worse than a bunch of witches with a hard-on for world domination."

Lucian nods sagely, stroking his chin like a discount Gandalf. "Truth, sister. Our little ass-kicker here could probably take on all these bitches and Azrael with one hand tied behind her back. And with the dream team assembled? Pfft, it'll be like taking candy from a baby. An evil, all-powerful baby, but still."

I look around at my dysfunctional little family, feeling a grudging sense of pride and affection beneath the layers of snark and posturing. "Alright—let's keep our heads in this and not get killed."

Lucian rubs his hands together gleefully, a maniacal grin spreading across his face. "Fuck yeah, that's the spirit! Time to go all Leeroy Jenkins on their magical asses. LEEEEROOOOYYY JENKIIIINS!"

"Baby, remind me again why we keep him around?" I grumble, even as a reluctant smile tugs at the corner of my mouth.

Dani snorts, slipping her hand into mine. "Honestly? I have absolutely no idea." She glances at Lucian with a look that's equal parts fondness and bewilderment. "I think it's like a stray cat situation—we made the mistake of feeding him once, and now we're stuck with him forever."

We ditch the ride a good stretch from the castle, Lucian's SUV blending into the dense forest surrounding us. Lucian, ever the drama queen, insisted on hopping in with Emily and Sable, claiming he needed to make a "grand entrance." I couldn't help but roll my eyes.

Emily and Sable play along, driving Lucian up the long, winding driveway to the castle gates. They know just as well as I do that they're in for front-row seats to the impending clusterfuck.

I glance over at Dani and Erik, sharing a silent understanding. This is it. Time to face whatever the hell awaits us inside that castle.

We quietly move through the forest, waiting for Emily to signal Dani.

I pull Dani close, my arms wrapping around her like a shield, and tilt her chin up so those honey-gold eyes are locked on mine. "Listen up, Angel. When we step into those tunnels, you stick to me like glue, got it? I don't want these witches getting even a hint of your scent. They could fuck you up seven shades of sideways with a few hocus pocus words, and I'll be damned if I let that happen."

Dani bobs her head. "Guessing you've had a few rounds with the abracadabra crowd?"

"Both of us have," Erik says before I can respond. "They're ancient, their powers formidable. But evading them shouldn't pose a significant challenge if we deal with the diluted descendants Sable and Emily mentioned."

A memory rips through my head—Erik and I dismantling an entire clan, knee-deep in blood and black magic, locked in a vicious fight against a coven of witches. We've tangled with these spell-casting bitches before. We know exactly what kind of twisted shit they're capable of.

"You got the plan locked down?" I press, praying to whatever gods are listening that this insanity works. If Sable's intel is solid, Lucian's going to be under some voodoo mindfuck, so it's on us to pull this off without a single hiccup.

"Yup." Dani exhales a heavy sigh, tension lining the air. "Let's just cross our fingers and pray to whatever's listening that this Hail Mary plays out."

I fix Dani with a stern look. "Under no circumstances are you to get involved, you hear me? Not unless it's absolutely necessary, and there's no other choice. I mean it, Dani. These witches are no joke, and I'll be damned if I let you get caught in the crossfire of their twisted magic. Promise me you'll stay out of it unless there's no other way."

"I promise."

DANICA

89

The catacombs? More like a damp, dreary dungeon. Each step echoes like a drumbeat, reminding me that this place is as lively as a graveyard. I coax my little ball of light closer, and it dutifully floats ahead, a tiny hero fending off the darkness.

I'm clad back in my well-worn leathers, the supple material molding to my curves like a lover's caress. The familiar weight comforts me, and a sense of power and purpose settles over me.

My fingers dance over the hilts of my daggers, the blades gleaming in the dim light like predators' eyes. These deadly little beauties are more than just weapons. They're an extension of myself, a part of me.

Beside me, Rhyland and Erik are a mirror image, their leathers hugging their muscular frames. Erik's hand rests on the hilt of his sword, the blade name of which I recently learned: *Gravewarden*. Fitting.

The walls are covered in moss, and nature's attempt at interior decorating has gone wrong. The air is thick with the smell of decay as if centuries of stagnation have thrown a musty party. And let's not forget the subtle hint of something metallic, like a forgotten penny in a puddle.

Emily's text arrives, sending a tingle down my spine.

> It's go time, bitch! 100 witches.

The witches' chanting grows louder with each step, their ancient words bouncing off the stone walls.

A hundred witches? Great.

Their voices swell, a magical medley oozing from the rocks. I can practically taste the magic in the air, and it's not a flavor I'd recommend.

As we approach the undercroft, flickering candlelight beckons us closer. And there, in the center of it all, lies Lucian, sprawled on an altar. The witches form a circle around him, but wait—where's the rest of the coven? I count maybe half of what Emily mentioned. Something's not adding up.

We duck behind some columns, holding our breath like we're playing the world's most intense game of hide-and-seek. We're about twenty paces away, close enough to smell the magic but far enough to avoid being turned into toads. Erik and Rhyland are like ninja statues behind me, so quiet I'm half-tempted to check for a pulse.

"There's only half the witches here," I shoot into Rhyland's mind, my thoughts like a bullhorn in a library.

Rhyland nods. *"We stick to the plan,"* he whispers. His eyes then lock with Erik's, relaying the same message telepathically.

The chamber is straight out of a medieval fantasy, complete with flickering candles casting eerie shadows. And there, in the center, stands the High Witch, looking like she raided Morticia Addams' closet.

Her hair is so black it could be mistaken for a void, and her skin is pale enough to make a ghost look tan. Her icy blue eyes could freeze a lesser witch in their tracks. Her hands are decked out in rings that look like they were forged in the fires of Mount Doom.

When the High Witch speaks, her voice slices through the noise like a blade drawn clean from its sheath. "Sisters of the night, gather 'round," she commands, and I swear her words carry a gravitational pull—something ancient and magnetic that tugs at the very air. "The hour of convergence is upon us."

Dramatic much?

The coven circles the altar, which looks like it was ripped from a heavy metal album cover, complete with silver skulls and symbols. The witches join hands, forming a tight link.

The High Witch raises her arms, kicking her voice into high gear. *"Feremous, avanteen, liricoul..."* The words fill the air, and I feel the ancient power vibrating in my bones.

The coven joins in, their voices blending like a supernatural choir. *"Aetherus spiricor, noctarum revelous!"* The air hums with their chanting, and the candles flare up like they're trying to high-five the heavens.

Here we go.

The chanting swells like a dark tidal wave, and I can't help but glance at Lucian in the center of the ritual circle. He's the picture of serenity, but his eyes sparkle with mischief. He looks like the perfect sacrifice, a helpless lamb among the witches' gathered power.

I sneak a peek at Rhyland, his presence as solid as the column he's lurking behind, his steel-blue eyes laser-focused on the unfolding scene. Despite the carvings and gloom providing our cover, the anticipation between us is so thick you can choke on it.

The witches' voices rise and fall like a hypnotic metronome. "*Nocturna ligatu, umbra secorum,*" they chant, their words bouncing off the stone walls like verbal ping-pong balls.

Lucian goes limp under their spell, eyes closed, dead to the world.

"This better fucking work," I mutter.

"Corpus et anima, entwine in our divine chorus!" the High Witch's voice booms, rising above the collective chanting. Her fingers twitch like she's directing an orchestra of shadows.

Lucian's role is risky, but it's crucial. The witches, focused on their spell, are oblivious to the ruse. They think their power is peaking, the sacrifice moment near, unaware they're about to be sacrificed.

Every word they utter makes their fates more tangled. "Bind as one, heart and soul, life and essence, to be undone by ourselves."

Rhyland gives a subtle hand signal. Timing is everything. We're waiting for the witches to reach maximum connection, their Achilles' heel.

The High Witch steps back, her chant blending into the others. *"Seraphim corentei!"* her voice thunders, signaling the ritual's grand finale.

The electric charge of anticipation hangs heavy as Rhyland unfurls from his concealment, his gaze locked on the High Witch. He's a coiled serpent, ready to strike.

And then, he moves.

It's a blur, a shadow of motion that defies the eyes. Rhyland is a streak, a specter haunting the edge of vision, his speed redefining quickness. There's no sound, just the whisper of displaced air.

For those who blink, it's a moment lost. The High Witch's incantations command the air a second before facing her downfall. Her eyes, flickering with power, widen briefly in realization.

Rhyland's hand strikes with lethal precision, his fingers locking around the witch's throat before she can draw another breath. A sickening crack splits the air—quick, clean, like a branch snapping under frost—and the High Witch crumples, lifeless.

The circle breaks. The witches around her, moments ago, linked in arcane solidarity, collapse. They fall like marionettes deprived of purpose, lifeless on the cold stone.

The hum of magic dies instantly—snuffed out like a candle pinched between wet fingers. The silence that rushes in is suffocating, heavy enough to press against my chest. Even the flickering flames seem to shrink back in fear. The magic that once filled the air dissipates, leaving shadows and the chill of the grave.

Erik begins his task of decapitating the witches, methodically slicing off their heads with *Gravewarden.*

Eww.

Lucian comes to, sitting up quickly and looking around. It takes him a minute to shake off the effects.

"Shit, yeah! I knew you wouldn't let me down, you big, sexy hunk of man-meat," Lucian crows, grinning. Before Rhyland can react, he's lunging toward him, lips puckered up.

Rhyland reacts with lightning speed, catching Lucian by the shoulders and holding him at arm's length.

"Whoa—Keep it in your pants. I don't need your herpes on my face," Rhyland growls.

Lucian gasps, clutching at his heart. "But Rhy-Rhy, I thought we had something special! Don't tell me you're just using me for my body. I mean, I wouldn't blame you, but still. I have feelings, you know."

Rhyland snorts, shoving Lucian away. "Yeah, feelings in your pants, maybe. Now quit fucking around. We need to leave."

It worked. Against all odds, our plan worked. I'd do a victory dance, but this isn't the time or place for celebratory choreography.

We begin to make our way out of the catacombs, the echoes of our footsteps mingling with the silence through the tunnels. Suddenly, my phone buzzes in my pocket. I quickly pull it out, seeing Emily's name on the screen.

> More witches are heading that way. They know what happened. Move your asses!

Oh, fuck me. I quickly inform the guys, and Rhyland's face contorts into a mask of rage, his beautiful blue eyes darkening.

We quicken our pace through the tunnels. Suddenly, Rhyland sweeps me into his arms, and the world blurs as we race toward fresh air. Just as we burst out of the tunnels, we slam into an invisible wall.

In a split second, Rhyland, Lucian, and Erik fall to their knees, their screams tearing through the air. I tumble to the ground as Rhyland writhes beside me.

They clutch their heads, faces twisted in pain. I spot a young witch, her eyes glowing an otherworldly purple. She holds her hands out, lips moving in a rapid incantation as she incapacitates my guys with powerful magic.

Dread settles in my stomach.

"You will not escape after what you've done," the witch with dark hair and eyes spits, her voice dripping with venom. She looks at me like I'm a stain on her favorite pointy hat.

Their collective gaze is heavy and oppressive, trying to bore holes into my soul. The air crackles with rage, and I almost see sparks flying from their linked hands.

My powerful vampires are reduced to helpless puppets, their brains scrambling. The witch's voice is a sinister melody slicing through the air and into their souls.

I stand frozen, my mind racing. This wasn't part of the plan. We were supposed to hold the cards, not the other way around. But here we are, caught in a web of our own making.

"Stop," I command, my voice ringing out with a force I didn't know I possessed.

The purple-eyed witch ignores me, her focus on Rhyland and his brothers as they thrash on the ground, blood pouring from their ears. The sight of their agony sends a surge of panic through my veins.

"Dani!" Emily shouts, her voice cutting through the chaos, but I can't see her. My vision narrows, my world shrinking to the three figures writhing on the ground and the witch who holds their lives in her grasp.

And then, something inside me snaps. I feel hot, angry power charging within me like a building storm. It's wild and untamed, a force of nature demanding release—a power I've been honing to control for weeks—I'm about to detonate a human-shaped bomb filled with magic.

"Big mistake," I growl.

My hands ignite, white-hot flames engulfing my fingers. The heat is so intense it should be painful, but all I feel is a surge of raw power. A scream rips from somewhere deep inside me—guttural, unhinged—reverberating off every surface as I hurl my power outward in a blinding, devastating wave.

White fire surrounds me, a blazing inferno that consumes everything. The screams of burning witches fill the air, a cacophony of agony.

The purple-eyed witch's concentration shatters, her hold on Rhyland and his brothers breaking as the flames engulf her. Her screams join the others, a symphony of suffering.

I stand at the center of the maelstrom, a pillar of light and fury. The witches fall like dominoes, their charred bodies hitting the ground.

And then, it's over. The flames die out, leaving nothing but the acrid stench of burnt flesh and eerie silence. I stand there, chest heaving, hands still glowing.

Holy shit. Did I just...? I can't finish the thought. I look at Rhyland and his brothers, their eyes wide with awe. I've just unleashed a force I never knew I had, a power that saved their lives but ended many others.

The last time, it was just a blast of power. This time, I unleashed a ring of white-hot fire. The difference is staggering, and I can still feel the heat lingering on my skin.

I look around at the devastation, the charred bodies of the witches scattered like discarded dolls. The air is thick with the stench of burnt flesh and dark magic gone awry. It's a scene from a horror movie, and I'm the monster at the center of it all.

But even as the horror settles in, I can't deny the protectiveness that still courses through me. These witches were going to kill Rhyland and his brothers, and I did what I had to do to save them. I'd do it again in a heartbeat.

Rhyland pulls me to his chest, his arms wrapping around me like a lifeline. "Thank you, Angel," he whispers. I can feel the steady thrum of his heartbeat, a reassuring rhythm amid the chaos.

Lucian and Erik drag themselves upright, hands still pressed to their heads, blood trickling from their ears in thin ribbons. The pain is gone—I can see that much—but the hollow, distant look in their eyes tells me the echo of what they endured isn't fading anytime soon.

Suddenly, Sable comes running from the castle. She stops, eyes widening in horror. Then, she drops to her knees, a broken sob tearing from her throat.

I watch as she kneels before a witch, possibly a friend, hands covering her face as she weeps. The sound of her sorrow is like a knife to my heart.

"No...Emily!" Sable's anguished cry pierces the air, her voice raw with grief.

My mind misfires, the sound of my best friend's name falling from Sable's lips like a blow. Rhyland stiffens against me, his body mirroring the icy numbness spreading through me.

"No..." The word falls from my lips, a broken whisper.

I tear away from Rhyland, my feet carrying me toward Sable. I drop to the ground beside her, the impact sending shockwaves through my knees, but the physical pain is nothing compared to the agony in my heart.

There, lying before me, is Emily. Half of her body is burnt, the once-vibrant skin now charred and lifeless. She lies still, no breath passing through her lips.

"No, no, no...EMILY!" I scream, my voice raw and broken, as I gather her into my arms, cradling her against my chest. Sobs wrack my body, tears pouring down my face as I stare at the lifeless form of my best friend.

I can't breathe, can't think, can't do anything but rock back and forth, holding Emily's body as if I can will life back into her. This can't be happening. This can't be real. But the weight of her in my arms, the stillness of her once-lively form, is a truth I can't escape.

This is my fault. The power I unleashed to save the ones I love has taken the life of someone I never imagined living without. I couldn't control the magic burst from me like a supernova, and Emily paid the price.

Guilt and grief war within me, threatening to tear me apart. How can I ever forgive myself for this? How can I look at my reflection again, knowing that this power is responsible for the death of my best friend?

I bury my face in Emily's hair, tears soaking the once-vibrant strands. "I'm sorry," I whisper. "I'm so sorry, Emily. I never meant for this to happen. I never meant to hurt you."

But my words are meaningless, hollow apologies that can't bring her back or undo the devastation. I've lost her, lost a piece of myself. And as I kneel here, holding the lifeless body of my best friend, I know that nothing will ever be the same again.

DANICA

90

O r does it have to be?

The Atherite stone. It failed with Adrain—I can use it to bring Emily back. But how does this damn thing work?

"Seraphina!" I scream, my voice tearing through the air like a wounded animal. "Help me, goddammit!"

Silence—deafening, soul-crushing silence. Rhyland crumples to his knees behind me, his heart shattering in tandem with mine, our souls bound by an unbreakable thread of love and agony.

His arms reach for me, but I flinch away, my words a broken whisper. "No. I need to bring her back."

Rhyland's hands fall to his sides, understanding etched in the lines of his face. I lower Emily to the grass with trembling fingers, my hands resting on her motionless chest. I close my eyes, diving deep within myself, grasping for the power that pulses through my veins like molten gold, the essence of Atheria.

It surges through me, a searing warmth that starts at my fingertips and rushes through my body like wildfire. It pours into Emily, a blinding light that seeps into her very pores.

Sweat drips down my face, my brow furrowed in concentration, my jaw clenched so tight I feel my teeth might shatter. The energy courses through me, a raging river of light and life, a bridge between worlds, between life and death.

Sable's gasp shatters the air, her eyes wide with awe and disbelief as she watches the impossible unfold before her. Emily's burns fade, knitting together the charred flesh, replaced by smooth, unblemished skin. The flush of life returns to her cheeks, breathing life into her still lungs. And then, a gasp, a shuddering intake of breath that seems to still the very world. Emily's eyes fly open, wild and alive, darting around in confusion and wonder until they lock with mine.

A smile breaks through my tears, a profound joy that steals my breath. I crush her to me, our tears mingling, our hearts beating.

I did it.

It worked.

Rhyland exhales, his hand clutching his chest as the ache that mirrored mine slowly fades, replaced by a warmth that spreads through him like the first rays of dawn.

"I'm so sorry—don't ever leave me again," I whisper fiercely into Emily's ear. "I can't lose you, not like that, not ever."

She gives a firm nod against my shoulder, the weight of her head a solid reassurance. "Next time, control your damn fire, pyro!" she quips, but her voice betrays the depth of her feelings, thick and rich with emotion. "I'm here, Dani, and I'm not going anywhere."

"Damn right, you're not," I laugh through my tears, pulling back to look at her. "I didn't just pull off the most epic resurrection in history for you to bail on me now."

Emily snorts, a grin spreading across her face. "Please, like I'd ever miss out on the chance to give you shit for the rest of your life. You're stuck with me, bitch."

"Wouldn't have it any other way, asshole," I retort, my heart lighter than it's been in ages.

Rhyland shakes his head, a smile tugging at his lips. "You two are something else, you know that?"

"You love it," I smirk, pulling him in for a kiss that sets my soul on fire.

The illusion of safety shatters as slow, taunting clapping fills the air. "Well, well, well... Bravo! Aren't you all just the perfect little team?" Azrael's voice oozes into the moment like venom, its contempt permeating the air, causing my flesh to crawl with disgust. His words dripped with scorn and derision.

He's got another coven of witches behind him, at least a dozen strong.

We rise as one; an instinct and unity bind us. I shove Emily behind me, a shield against the oncoming storm. Rhyland, protective as ever, moves me further behind him, assuming the frontline role.

The sight that greets us stops me cold—a full coven convergence, witches flanking Azrael on every side like a wall of dark magic made flesh. His sharp, calculating gaze finds mine; his words are laced with venom. "You know, I really despise it when insignificant pests like you stick your noses where they don't belong. And what have you done here?

Not very polite at all," he scolds, his gaze boring into me like a drill. "Especially you, Doctor Pierce," he clicks his tongue, his tone oozes with false disappointment as if addressing a misbehaving toddler. "Slaughtering all these witches like cattle. My, my, whatever happened to that bleeding heart of yours?"

Rhyland's response cuts through the air like a blade, each word dripping with lethal contempt for Azrael's hubris. "Fuck off, Azrael," he snarls, the growl in his voice a clear threat. His hand sweeps across the area, signaling a clear ultimatum to all the witches watching. "Unless you're itching for a repeat of the last witch bloodbath."

Azrael's face contorts into a mask of feigned distress, his voice laced with sarcasm, "Ah, yes, this little stunt of yours has certainly created quite the inconvenience for me. You see, Dani, you and your merry band of do-gooders just slaughtered over half of my precious witches. Now I'm left with a pitifully inadequate number to carry out my grand ritual."

Screw him.

"That was the plan, asshole." Lucian fires back.

Just then, my crown buzzes, the vibrations shooting down my spine like an electric current. It's like having a swarm of bees trapped inside my skull, their incessant humming drowning out everything else. I try to shake it off, to focus on the clusterfuck of a situation we're in, but it's like trying to think through a layer of thick, suffocating fog.

Azrael and Rhyland are going at it like two alpha dogs fighting over a juicy bone, their voices rising and falling in a symphony of testosterone-fueled bullshit.

I catch snippets of their conversation, something about needing a powerful vampire to complete the ritual, but it's like trying to piece together a puzzle with half the pieces missing and the other half covered in glue. My head is so fogged with this incessant humming that I can barely string two thoughts together, let alone make sense of their macho posturing.

The pain in my head is excruciating, like someone's taken a jackhammer to my skull. I press my fingers to my temples, trying desperately to massage away the pressure, but it's like trying to stop a tidal wave with a paper towel. The humming in my crown pulses in time with the agony, a twisted symphony of torment that threatens to split my head in two.

Is this some mystical migraine from what I did? A cosmic punishment for playing god?

My knees buckle beneath me, and I crumple to the ground, my body curling in on itself like a dying leaf. The conversation around me grinds to a halt, all eyes turning to me in a mix of concern and confusion.

"What is it? What's happening?" Rhyland's voice is laced with panic as he drops to his knees beside me, his arms wrapping around me like a shield. I can feel his desperation, his need to understand, to fix whatever's broken inside me.

But before I can form a response, all hell breaks loose. The witches, those manipulative bitches, seize their moment, their magic wrapping around Rhyland and his brothers like invisible strings. They jerk and twitch like marionettes, their bodies no longer their own as they're forced to march behind Azrael, leaving me alone and writhing on the ground.

Necromancy.

"Baby, I—I can't fight them..." Rhyland's voice cuts through my thoughts, blending his pain and mine. *"Fight, Angel..."* he implores, a desperate whisper urging me to keep battling the darkness that threatens to engulf us all.

"Dani!" Emily shouts somewhere in the distance. I want her safe.

"Emily, GO!" That's all I can manage as I claw at my crown, my fingers scrabbling against the unyielding metal as I try to rip it from my head. But it's fused to me, the humming intensifying with every desperate tug, threatening to shatter my bones.

Through the haze of pain and the chaos that surrounds me, I catch a glimpse of Sable pulling Emily away, back toward the road. It's like a moment of clarity amidst the madness, a brief respite from the agony tearing me apart.

Good, stay alive, Emily. The thought flickers through my mind like a candle in the darkness, a desperate plea for the safety of my best friend. She's been through enough, seen enough, and the last thing I want is for her to be caught in the crossfire of this fucked-up battle.

"It's not working!" one of the witches shouts, her voice shrill with frustration.

"Don't you dare stop now! It will work; it must work!" Azrael shrieks, his voice cracking with a frenzied, unhinged desperation that borders on madness. "Just offer it over, Dani, and we can stop the pain."

And then I see her, a blonde witch with eyes that glow an eerie green. She's young, too young to be caught up in this shitstorm, but her face is set with a grim determination as she reaches for my crown, her fingers crackling with arcane energy as she continues her chanting.

I try to fight her off, to summon even a spark of my power, but it's like trying to light a match in a hurricane. The pain is all-consuming, a white-hot agony that obliterates everything else.

"FIGHT!" Rhyland's voice in my head—urging me not to give up.

I'm helpless, a pawn in a game I never asked to play, and as the witch's hands close around my crown, I feel a scream tear from my throat, a sound of pure, unadulterated anguish.

Is this how it ends? Am I destined to be another casualty in this war between gods and monsters? The thought fills me with a rage so potent it takes my breath away.

No. Fuck that. I am Danica fucking Pierce, Savior of the Seven Realms, and I will not go down without a fight. I summon every ounce of strength I have left, every shred of defiance, and with a roar that shakes the very foundations of the earth, I surge to my feet, my body moving on pure instinct.

The blonde witch stumbles back, her green eyes wide with shock and fear as I lunge for her, my hands closing around her wrists like vices. I can feel the crackle of her magic against my skin, the searing heat of it, but I push through the pain, my power rising to meet hers like a tidal wave.

"You picked the wrong bitch to mess with," I snarl, my voice barely recognizable through the rage that consumes me. "I am the fucking savior of the realms, and some two-bit witch with a god complex will not take me down."

I can feel the crown on my head, the metal pulsing with a power that matches the rhythm of my heartbeat. I focus on that connection. I feel a surge of energy unlike anything I've ever known.

It's wild and untamed, a force of nature that courses through my veins like molten lava. I channel it into my hands, into the grip I have on the witch's wrists, and I watch as her eyes widen in terror, her mouth opening in a silent scream.

"Release them," I command, my voice echoing with a power that seems to come from somewhere beyond myself. "Release Rhyland and his brothers, or I swear to every *god* in every realm, I will burn you *all* alive from the inside out."

Azrael holds his position, eyes locked onto me, scrutinizing every detail as if assessing a worthy adversary. "You're quite the slippery little eel, aren't you? No matter what obstacles I throw in your path, you somehow manage to wriggle your way through."

He's buying his time; he knows he can't lose any more witches and is unsure how to proceed.

The witch's face contorts in agony, her skin blistering and peeling as my power sears. I can feel her resistance, her desperate attempt to cling to her control, but it's like trying to hold back the tide with a sandcastle.

"By all means, darling, set them free," Azrael orders, his voice deadly with condescension and a hint of amusement.

She relents with a final, agonized shriek, her magic dissipating like smoke on the wind. Rhyland and his brothers stumble forward, their bodies once again their own, and I feel a rush of relief so intense it nearly brings me to my knees.

But I don't have time to savor the victory. The other witches and Azrael are not finished, their faces twisted with rage and hatred, and I know this fight is far from over.

I release the blonde witch, letting her crumple to the ground, and I turn to face the rest of them, my body draining with a power that feels as ancient as the realms themselves.

"So, what's it going to be, Doc? What brilliant scheme have you concocted this time?" Azrael taunts, his voice oozing with derision. Each word is a stinging barb designed to inflict maximum pain and humiliation.

And then he strikes. Azrael moves with such blinding speed that I completely miss it.

DANICA

91

Azrael's fangs pierce the delicate skin of my neck, searing agony spreading like wildfire through my veins. A scream tears from my throat as I claw at his head, desperate to wrench him off. Suddenly, he's gone, launched across the yard in a blur.

Rhyland's roar shakes the air, his body swelling with fury. His eyes blaze with the promise of retribution, fixed on Azrael's form. The tension crackles between them, a force threatening to ignite an all-out war.

"A-ha-ha! Oh, yes, the sheer potency coursing through your veins is absolutely intoxicating. Mmm..." Azrael's tongue drags across his lips in a grotesque display of hunger, my blood painting his face. His eyes glitter with obsessive fervor as he fixes me with a predatory stare. "Make no mistake, my sweet, delectable morsel. In the end, you will belong to me, body and soul," he says matter-of-factly, his voice a low, possessive growl that sends icy dread slithering down my spine.

Rhyland's barely leashed rage is a tangible force, his entire being vibrating intensely. His eyes, usually a mesmerizing ocean blue, now burn with an icy hate that could freeze hell itself. Every muscle in his body is coiled, ready to unleash a devastating attack. It's as if reality itself is straining to contain the maelstrom of emotions within him. The only thing keeping him from erupting into violence is a fraying thread of self-control.

Rhyland stands before me like an immovable wall, shielding me. "You listen to me, you sick fuck! You will never lay a goddamn finger on her again!"

Pain sears my neck. I clutch at the wound, feeling blood pour out, hot and sticky. Rhyland doesn't budge; his body is a fortress between me and the monster who dared to violate me.

"I will fucking destroy you, Azrael," Rhyland snarls. "When I'm through with you, you'll be begging for death. But know this: she will never belong to you. Not now, not ever."

The coven stands ready, their eyes gleaming with anticipation. The air around them shimmers with dark energy, sending ripples of unease through the atmosphere. They are a formidable sight, a united front of malevolent intent waiting to unleash their arcane power.

My head throbs with a vengeance, the pain pulsing behind my eyes. My vision swims, the world around me blurring into a kaleidoscope of colors and shapes.

I'm losing blood rapidly, and Rhyland can't budge to offer me his. My vision goes black at the edges, and panic starts to creep in. I need to stay conscious.

"Oh, Dani, Dani, Dani. You've been a naughty girl, haven't you? Taking something that doesn't belong to you," Azrael croons. "But fret not, my dear. I fully intend to reclaim what is rightfully mine."

The Soul Stone. The key to everything and the one thing that could turn the tide of this entire war. It remains tucked away, locked in a safe back at my apartment.

No way in hell would I bring that damn thing here. It bleeds malice like an open wound—a corrupting poison I refused to unleash on an already volatile situation.

The Soul Stone's power is a beast better left caged, its secrets locked down tight. Sure, it could tip the scales in our favor, but the cost of losing control over it isn't a gamble I'm willing to take. For now, it stays buried, its true potential left sleeping.

I still remember when we brought the pieces together—Amara's and Azrael's. They fused seamlessly as if they were always meant to be one.

Now it's ours—a weapon of unimaginable power, a tool that could reshape the realms.

It's almost pitiful how Azrael cowers behind his coven of witches, a frightened child clinging to his mother's skirts. The once-mighty Lord of Shadows, reduced to a mere puppet master, pulling the strings of his magical minions to cling to power.

He tries to maintain his veneer of arrogance, but I see the cracks, the fear lurking in his eyes.

Through the haze, I feel Rhyland's arms around me, his strength keeping me upright. Lucian and Erik take up positions beside us, a united front against the brewing storm.

But even with their support, I can barely stand. My knees tremble, threatening to give out. Without Rhyland's solid presence, I'd be a heap of flesh on the ground. My eyes feel raw and burning; keeping them open is an exercise in pure willpower.

That witch bitch, with her glowing green eyes and her fucking magic, did something to me. Drained me like a battery, leaving me hollow and weak.

Rhyland senses it, too. He pushes me behind him, a human shield against the horrors looming before us. "Hang on, Angel," he murmurs, his voice a lifeline.

But Azrael knows. He sees the slump of my shoulders, the pallor of my skin. I'm a sitting duck, ripe for the taking.

"Well, well, well, the mighty Viking vamp-warrior himself," Azrael cackles, his eyes sparkling with sadistic delight. "Do you really think you stand a chance against me now that your precious little secret weapon has been drained dry?"

I want to scream, to rage against the injustice. I hate that he can see my weakness. Rhyland's strong, a force to be reckoned with, but can he stand against Azrael and his coven?

Bless his stubborn Viking heart; he isn't backing down. He steps forward, his body a wall of muscle and fury. "Don't push me, Azrael," he snarls. "Or I'll unleash my wrath, as you know and have seen."

Rhyland's newfound power—lightning—hangs in the air like a crackle of energy that sets my nerves on edge.

For a moment, I see a flicker of fear in Azrael's eyes, a chink in his smug armor. But it's gone as quickly as it came. "Ah, yes," he drawls, smoothing his hair. "I had been curious about that peculiar ability and how a vampire like you inherited such a potent gift."

He gestures to the witches that flank him like rabid dogs. "You know, once you embarked on your little quest, leaving me to roam free, it dawned on me that there are many ways to flay a feline."

I feel my strength waning, my body growing heavier. It's like I'm being dragged into the earth. I sway on my feet, my vision darkening, and then I'm lifted, cradled in Erik's strong arms.

"Rest, Little Huntress," he murmurs, soothing my frayed nerves. "I got you."

Even as I sink into his embrace, I can't tear my eyes away from the scene unfolding. Azrael's voice cuts through the haze like a knife. Malicious.

"You see, Moretemis needs to be brought into one realm to complete his destiny. And it just so happens that we," he gestures to his witches, a smirk playing on his lips, "can do just that."

"Not now that you've lost most of your hocus pocus, you pathetic fuck," Lucian quips from somewhere above me. "Seriously, have you seen yourself lately? You look like a reject from a Harry Potter cosplay convention. And don't even get me started on your witch squad. I've seen more intimidating Girl Scouts."

But Azrael merely wags his finger, prowling back and forth. "Ah, how astute, Golden Boy. But alas, there's one crucial component I require." His gaze snaps to Rhyland, hunger lurking in his eyes. "And that, my dear Viking, is you."

Lucian's voice cuts through the fog in my mind, urgent. *"Dani, if you can hear me, open the portal now. We need to get out before these magical asshats turn us into newts!"*

A portal? He wants me to open a portal. But how? I'm so weak, so drained. I can barely keep my eyes open.

"He's going to take Rhyland as a sacrifice. If you don't want to lose your man, dig into whatever is left and get us out of here," Lucian urges, his voice uncharacteristically serious.

Sacrifice. The word echoes in my mind. They want to use Rhyland as a sacrifice to bring Moretemis into our world.

"So, here's the deal, Rhyland. You come quietly, and I'll allow Dani to walk away unscathed—for now," Azrael proposes, with false magnanimity. His eyes glint with calculation.

His words hit me like a gut punch. The thought of losing him, of watching him die in some twisted ritual, is enough to make my blood run cold.

No. Not on my watch.

I grit my teeth, summoning every ounce of strength. It's like trying to spark a flame in a tornado, but I refuse to give up. I focus on the power that flickers deep within me, the embers of the inferno that once raged through my veins.

I picture my apartment at first, but out of nowhere, a wave of nausea strikes me, making me feel as though I'm adrift at sea, unsteady and disoriented. Vertigo sweeps over me, similar to the sensation of being on a swaying boat.

I can feel the portal manifest, a swirling vortex of light and energy, and I pour everything I have into making it real. My body screams in protest, every nerve ending on fire, but I push through the pain, through the exhaustion.

This is the only way. I have to believe in it and make it tangible—the vortex shimmers, solidifying as I channel every last drop of strength into it.

And then—by some goddamn miracle—it's there. A shimmering doorway to freedom tears open before us. Azrael screams behind us, but the thunderous roar of the portal swallows his voice whole.

Rhyland's roar shakes the air—a sound born of fury so deep it vibrates in my bones. A wall of telekinetic force explodes outward from him, slamming into Azrael and his coven like a wrecking ball.

The blast launches them off their feet, bodies ragdolling through the air in a violent tangle of limbs before crashing into the ground with bone-jarring force.

Erik races us toward the portal, his arms locked around me. Lucian's desperate shouts for Rhyland ring in my ears.

I glimpse Lucian's face, his eyes blowing wide with horror, and then he's nothing but a streak of motion, hurtling toward Rhyland. Erik pivots, and my heart seizes in my chest as I see Azrael locked onto Rhyland, the two of them grappling like wolves. Rhyland's fists hammer down, his body a coil of unbridled wrath fighting to throw Azrael off.

Time slows as I watch, helpless in Erik's embrace. I'm running on pure adrenaline now.

My heart pounds in my chest as I watch him. The fear of losing him, my focus narrowing to Rhyland, and the distance between us.

"Rhyland!" I scream, reaching out for him.

Lucian crashes into Azrael, sending him flying off Rhyland. A witch who survived Rhyland's blast slowly rises, chanting faint words, but sends icy fear down my spine. Rhyland surges to his feet, racing toward Lucian.

"Rhyland, GO!" Lucian bellows, his head snapping sideways as a fist connects with his jaw. "Get her out of here!" The words rip from his throat like a battle cry—absolute, final, leaving no room for debate.

Azrael struggles to get free, but Lucian holds him in an unyielding grip.

I can see the sorrow in Rhyland's eyes, the agony of having to choose. He turns and runs toward me, his movements seeming to slow as if he's moving through molasses, each step an eternity.

The portal gutters and shudders, its edges dissolving as my power drains away. Azrael's roar tears through the chaos, tangling with Lucian's agonized screams until I can't separate one from the other. The witch bears down on us, her dark magic rolling forward like a black tide—suffocating, crushing the breath from my lungs as she unleashes everything she has on Lucian and Rhyland.

"NO! No... no!" The words claw their way out of me, shredded and desperate. We can't leave them behind. We *can't.*

Rhyland writhes on the ground, his hands clutching his head, his face contorted in agony. Lucian, too, is caught in the same torment, his body convulsing in the distance.

"Rhyland!" I scream his name, my voice cracking with desperation.

I reach deep within myself, grasping for that burning ember in my soul, searching for something, *anything*, to fight back. With a surge of determination, I hurl my light at the witch. She stumbles, her hold on Rhyland and Lucian momentarily broken. Rhyland, seizing the opportunity, stands fast and begins to make his way toward me.

But Lucian is still trapped in Azrael's grip, locked in a vicious fight with no end in sight.

Erik turns and starts heading to the portal.

"Erik, stop!" I plead, my voice a desperate cry amidst the chaos. But my words are lost, swallowed by the deafening din of clashing bodies and shattering magic.

Why aren't they helping him?

We can't leave.

Erik's voice is iron wrapped in velvet, every syllable final. "I can't, Little Huntress... I apologize. Your well-being is my priority."

Panic rises in my throat, a bitter taste on my tongue. The portal shudders, threatening to collapse at any moment.

Lucian's screams echo in my ears, each one a dagger to my heart. I'm helpless, unable to do anything. The situation spirals out of control, a dizzying whirlwind of chaos and terror.

The distance between us grows, a chasm threatening to swallow me.

"LUCIAN!!" His name rips out of me—a guttural, wrecked scream that shreds my vocal cords. "LUCIAN!!"

But it's too late. Erik steps through the portal, Rhyland's fingertips brushing mine as the doorway collapses with a deafening crack, sealing us from the horrors we've left behind.

We tumble onto a hard, unyielding surface, the impact driving the breath from my lungs in a painful whoosh. The tang of salt fills my nostrils. Wind howls and waves slam against wood, the sounds crashing together in my ears until I can't tell them apart. I blink hard, my vision tilting and swaying as the world comes into focus—a tangle of ropes and barrels, towering masts and billowing sails reaching toward a sky so blue it doesn't look real.

A low moan escapes my lips as I struggle to rise, my body protesting with every movement. But before I can find my feet, the cold kiss of steel against my throat freezes me in place, sending a bolt of pure terror through my veins.

"Aye—What do we have here?"

THANK YOU

Hey You, Yes You—The Amazing Reader Who Just Finished Book Two!

First off, high-fives, hugs, and a whole parade in your honor, because you? You're the real MVP here. Give yourself a round of applause for sticking with Dani and Rhyland through another chapter of their pulse-pounding, realm-hopping escapades.

Thank you from the bottom of my caffeine-fueled heart for diving back into the whirlwind world of the Crown of the Seven Realm series. Your support means the world to me and quite possibly to all seven realms (they're still counting votes on that one). These characters and their stories are my babies; you've just helped them grow.

Now, take a breath, grab a snack, and pat yourself on the back because you've survived the twists, turns, and cliffhangers (oh, the cliffhangers!). Your dedication to following our fearless (and sometimes fearsome) lovebirds on their journey is more appreciated than you know.

But hold onto your hats—or crowns—because this roller coaster isn't done yet. Get ready for Book Three, **DARK TIDES** which is available now, and it's packed with more realm-hopping shenanigans that'll test the limits of our fearless heroes.

With all my thanks and anticipation,

Your Favorite Portal-Pushing Author,

A.L. Hampton

THE SEVEN REALMS

 1. Atheria. The Realm of Light and Creation. It is a realm of divine beauty and purity where celestial beings and creatures of light reside. It is a place of harmony and enlightenment, where the power of creation flows freely, shaping the fabric of existence.

 2. Aquaria. The Realm of Water. Aquaria is a vast world with vibrant marine life and mystical creatures, such as Merfolk, Skelkies, and Pirates. It is a realm of serenity and fluidity where the ebb and flow of tides hold great power.

 3. Luminara—The fae reigns supreme in the realm of Luminara, a world filled with enchanting beauty and mystical wonders. Luminara is a realm of ethereal forests, shimmering lakes, and glowing meadows, where the natural world is interwoven with magic and wonder.

 4. Mortalis—The Mortal Realm, where humanity resides with immortals and explores the boundaries of their existence. It has diverse landscapes, bustling cities, and uncharted territories. Humans navigate their everyday lives in Mortalis, unaware of the existence of other realms.

 5. Pyrothos—The Realm of Fire. Pyrothos is a land of perpetual flames and scorching heat, where volcanic landscapes and fiery mountains dominate. It is a realm of passion and intensity, where the essence of fire fuels the powers of its inhabitants. Pyrothos is home to powerful fire elementals, fire-breathing creatures, and ancient fire temples.

 6. Unbra—The Realm of Shadows. A world consumed by eternal darkness, where pure evil lurks, and creatures of nightmarish origins dwell. It is a realm shrouded in mystery and treachery, harboring ancient secrets and maleficent forces.

 7. Zephyria—Realm of Sky and Air— Zephyria is breathtaking, with endless skies and gentle breezes. No one knows what this realm is besides vast expanses of open air, where the wind guides the movement of everything.

Also By A.L. Hampton

ACKNOWLEDGEMENTS

This book? It wouldn't even be a thing without some truly amazing people.

To my rockstar beta readers, Kerry Taylor, Talia Harris, and Samantha Parisi: You dived into those early drafts, gave me feedback gold, and kept me going when the writing got tough. You're the real MVPs.

A massive shoutout to my awesome ARC readers: Seriously, I couldn't have done this without my squad. Your belief in my wild storytelling keeps my creative engine running. Thank you for making this dream a fab reality.

To my special friends and massive indie author champions, Enola Henderson and Emily Davis: Your unwavering support and determination to promote my work? Absolute game-changer.

To my fam and friends: Thanks for putting up with my obsessed writer moments and endless book talk. Special thanks to my husband—your cheerleading is everything.

To the fantasy community and my fellow Indie authors: You guys rock. Thanks for the inspiration and the warm welcome.

And last but never least, to my fabulous readers: Your love for the Crown of the Seven Realm Series is the icing on the cake. Thank you for every read, comment, and bit of excitement. You make it all worth it.

ABOUT THE AUTHOR

Hi there! I'm A.L. Hampton, and like so many of you, I've been completely obsessed with books for as long as I can remember. There's nothing quite like getting completely lost in a story—you know that feeling when you look up and realize hours have passed? That's my happy place.

I'm absolutely head-over-heels for fantasy, urban fantasy, romantasy, and anything dark and paranormal. And yes, I'm totally here for the spice! After years of devouring every book I could get my hands on in these genres, I found myself thinking, "What if I combined all my favorite elements into one series?" That's how the Crown of the Seven Realms Series was born. I'm a total sucker for witty banter and characters that feel like real people—flawed, funny, and fierce. When I'm not busy torturing my characters, you'll find me gaming, or exploring the gorgeous Pacific Northwest with my patient husband and two spoiled dogs.

My background is a bit all over the place—I have an A.A. in Criminal Justice, a B.S. in Psychology, and an M.Ed. in Education. Turns out, studying human behavior comes in pretty handy when you're trying to write believable characters and relationships!

As a debut author, I'm beyond excited to share these stories with fellow book lovers.

Welcome to my world!
-A.L. Hampton

STAY UP TO DATE WITH UPCOMING BOOKS
AND FOLLOW ME ON MY SOCIALS
AUTHORALHAMPTON.COM

www.ingramcontent.com/pod-product-compliance
Lightning Source LLC
Chambersburg PA
CBHW070703010826
48975CB00015B/2723